Mona picks up one jar and turns it over.

Like the others, this one is smoked, but there are places that are a bit clearer. The contents look like a bunch of small grapes hanging from the jar's lid, but they're oddly yellowish, and they jiggle strangely. They keep jiggling even when she stops turning the jar over. It takes her a minute to realize they are turning, and on each grape is a dark spot that seems queerly reflective, and each grape turns until the side with the spot is facing her...

Almost as if it is an eye, Mona thinks. As if there's a bunch of tiny eyes hanging from the inside of the jar, and they are all staring at her.

She gasps and nearly falls back, but a pair of hands helps steady her.

"Goodness, dear, whatever is the matter?" asks Mrs. Benjamin's voice.

Mona jumps back the other way, for what she's found in the tea racks makes her just as frightened of Mrs. Benjamin as she is of the thing in her hand. Then she looks around at the tea racks, and sees that all the strange jars are gone: she sees no smoked beakers with labels in an alien language, nor does she see any teas that resemble bizarre scientific experiments. Even the jar in her hand has changed: it does not contain eyes, but jasmine blossoms...

By Robert Jackson Bennett

Mr. Shivers

The Company Man

The Troupe

American Elsewhere

American Elsewhere

ROBERT JACKSON BENNETT

orbit

www.orbitbooks.net

Orbit
Hachette Book Group
237 Park Avenue, New York, NY 10017
HachetteBookGroup.com

First Edition: February 2013

Orbit is an imprint of Hachette Book Group, Inc. The Orbit name and logo are trademarks of Little, Brown Book Group Limited.

The Hachette Speakers Bureau provides a wide range of authors for speaking events. To find out more, go to www.hachettespeakersbureau.com or call (866) 376-6591.

The publisher is not responsible for websites (or their content) that are not owned by the publisher.

The characters and events in this book are fictitious. Any similarity to real persons, living or dead, is coincidental and not intended by the author.

Library of Congress Cataloging-in-Publication Data
American elsewhere / Robert Jackson Bennett.—1st ed.
      p. cm.
   ISBN 978-0-316-20020-2
   1. Ex-police officers—Fiction. 2. Inheritance and succession—Fiction. 3. Home—Psychological aspects—Fiction. 4. Family secrets—Fiction. 5. New Mexico—Fiction. I. Title.
   PS3602.E66455A83 2012
   813'.6—dc23
                                   2012016166

10 9 8 7 6 5 4 3 2

RRD-C

Printed in the United States of America

"Men always forget that human happiness is a disposition of mind and not a condition of circumstances."

—John Locke

PAY ATTENTION

CHAPTER ONE

Even though it is a fairly cool night, Norris is sweating abundantly. The sweat leaks out of his temples and the top of his skull and runs down his cheeks to pool around his collarbones. He feels little trickles weaving down his arms to soak into the elbows and wrists of his shirt. The entire car now has a saline reek, like a locker room.

Norris is sitting in the driver's seat with the car running, and for the past twenty minutes he's been debating whether leaving the car running was a good idea or not. He's made several mental charts of pros and cons and probabilities, and overall he thinks it was a good idea: the odds that someone will notice the sound of a car idling on this neighborhood lane, and check it out and sense something suspicious, feel fairly low; whereas the odds of him fumbling with the ignition or the clutch if he needs to start the car quickly seem very, very high right now. He is so convinced of his own impending clumsiness that he hasn't even dared to take his hands off the steering wheel. He is gripping it so hard and his palms are so sweaty that he doesn't know if he could remove them if he tried. *Suction*, he thinks. *I'm stuck here forever, no matter who notices what.*

He's not sure why he's so worried about being noticed. No one lives in the neighboring houses. Though it is not posted anywhere—in any visual manner, that is—this part of town is not open to the public. There is only one resident on this street.

Norris leans forward in his seat to reexamine the house. He is parked right before its front walk. Behind the car is a small, neat gravel driveway that breaks off from the paved road and curves down the slope to a massive garage. The house itself is very, very big, but its size is mostly hidden behind the Englemann spruces; one can make out only hints of pristine white wooden siding, sprawling lantana, perfectly draped windows, and clean red-brick walls. And there, at the end of the front walk, is a modest, inviting front door with a coat of bright red paint and a cheery bronze handle.

It is a flawless house, really, a dream house. It is a dream house not only in the sense that anyone would dream of living there; rather, it is so perfect that a house like this could exist only in a dream.

Norris checks his watch. It has been four minutes by now. The wind runs through the pines, and the sound of thousands of whispering needles makes him shiver. Otherwise, it is quiet. But it is always quiet near homes like this, and it is always ill-advised to venture out at night in Wink. Everyone knows that. Things could happen.

He sits up: there are noises coming from the garage. Voices. He grips the steering wheel a little harder.

Two dark figures in ski masks emerge from the garage dragging something bulky between them. Norris stares at them in dismay as they begin making their way up to the car. When they finally get close enough, he rolls down the passenger-side window and whispers, "What happened? Where's Mitchell?"

"Shut up!" one of them says.

"Where is he? Did you leave him in there?"

"Will you shut up and open the trunk?"

Norris starts to, but he is distracted by what they are carrying. It appears to be a short man wearing a blue sweater and khakis, but his hands and feet are tightly bound, and a burlap sack has been pulled down over his face. Yet despite all this the man is speaking very, very quickly, almost chanting: "...Cannot succeed, *will not* succeed, such a vain hope that I personally cannot *imagine*, do you understand, I cannot *imagine* it. You do not have the *authorities*, the *privileges*, and without those this is but sand brushing over my neck, do you understand, no more than reeds dancing in violent waters..."

"Open the fucking trunk already!" says one of the men.

Norris, startled, reaches over and pulls the trunk lever. The trunk pops open and the two drag the hooded man back, stuff him in, and slam it shut. Then they scramble back around and jump in the backseat.

"Where's Mitchell?" asks Norris again. "What happened to him?"

"Fucking drive!" shouts one of the men.

Norris glances at the house again. There is movement in all the windows now—could those be dark figures pacing back and forth in the halls? Pale faces peeping out the windows? And some of the front lights are on, ones Norris could have sworn were dark just a second ago. He tears his eyes away, puts the car in first, and guns it.

They rip through the neighborhood lanes until they reach the main roads. The two men remove their ski masks. Zimmerman is older and bald with a graying beard, his cheeks bulging with the promise of pendulous jowls in later life. Out of the three of them he's by far the most experienced in this kind of thing, so it's extra unnerving to see how obviously terrified he is. The other, Dee, is an athletic young man with blond, perfectly parted hair, the sort of hair found only in Boy Scout advertisements. Dee either doesn't understand what's going on or is so dazed by everything that he can hardly shut his mouth.

"Jesus," says Zimmerman. "Jesus. Jesus fucking Christ."

"What happened?" asks Norris again. "Where's Mitchell? Is he all right?"

"No. No, Mitchell isn't all right."

"Well, what happened?"

There is a long silence. Then Dee says, "He fell."

"He what? He fell? Fell into what?"

The two are quiet again. Zimmerman says, "There was a room. And...it just seemed to keep going. And Mitchell fell in."

"And when he fell," says Dee, "he just didn't *stop*... he just kept *falling* into the room..."

"What do you mean?" asks Norris.

"What makes you think we understand what we saw in there?" asks Zimmerman angrily.

Norris turns back to the road, abashed. He points the car north toward the dark mesa that hangs over the town. Sometimes there is a thud or a shout from the trunk behind them. They all try to ignore it.

"He knew we were coming," says Dee.

"Shut up," says Zimmerman.

"That's why he'd prepared those rooms for us," says Dee. "He knew. Bolan *said* it'd be a surprise. How could he have known?"

"Shut up!"

"Why?" asks Dee.

"Because I'm willing to bet that that thing in the trunk can hear us!"

"So?"

"So what if this doesn't go right? What if he gets away? You just gave him one name. What more do you want to give him?"

There is a heavy silence. Norris asks, "How about some music?"

"Good idea," says Zimmerman.

Norris hits the tuner. Immediately Buddy Holly begins crooning "That'll Be The Day" from the car's blown-out speakers, and they all fall silent.

As they climb the mountain road they leave the town behind. The grid of streetlights shrinks until it is a spiderweb beaded with morning dew, stretched across the feet of the mesa. The town sits in the center of a dark fan of vegetation running down the mountain slopes, fed by the little river that winds through the center of the city. It is the only dependable source of water for miles around the mesa, a rarity in this part of New Mexico.

A painted sign swims up out of the darkness ahead, marking the northern border of the town. It has a row of white lights at the bottom, making it glow in the night. It shows a smiling man and woman sitting on a picnic blanket. They are a wholesome, white-bread sort, he square-jawed and squinty, she pale and delicate with cherry-red lips. They are looking out on a marvelous vista of crimson mesas at sunset, and at the top of one mesa is a very small bronze-colored antenna, one that would obviously be much larger if you were close. The clouds in the pink skies seem to swirl around the antenna, and there is something beyond the antenna and the clouds, something the man and the woman are meant to be looking at, but the two rightmost panels of the sign have been torn off, leaving raw wood exposed where there should be some inspiring vision. Yet some vandal has tried to complete the picture with a bit of chalk, though what the vandal has drawn is difficult to determine: it is an outline of a figure standing on the mountains, or where the mountains would be, a giant, titan-size body that would fill up the sky. The figure is generally human but somewhat deformed: its back is too hunched, and its arms are too ill-defined, though that may be an indication of the limits of the artist.

At the bottom of the sign is a line of white words: YOU ARE NOW LEAVING WINK—*BUT WHY?*

Why indeed, wonders Norris. How he wishes it were not so.

Up in the high mountains the air is unusually thin. It makes the night sky seem very blue and the stars appear very, very close. To Norris they seem closer tonight than normal, and the peak ahead seems unusually tall as well. The road unfurls from its top and comes bouncing down the hills like a silver ribbon. Blue lightning plays in the clouds around other peaks in the distance. Norris shifts uncomfortably. It feels as if the farther they get from town, with its hard little grid of streets and its yellow phosphorous lights, the more unreal the world becomes.

There is a burst of static from the radio, and "That'll Be The Day" twists until the music is gone and there is only a tinny voice madly chanting: "This is futile, futile. You nudge at boundaries of which you are only half-aware, trade in influences you are blind to. Stop this and let me go and I will forgive you, all will be forgiven, and it will be as if this never happened, never happened…"

"Fucking Christ!" says Zimmerman. "He's gotten into the fucking radio!"

"Turn it off!" cries Dee.

Norris slaps the tuner again and the chanting stops. They drive on in quiet for a bit.

"God," says Dee. "Have either of you ever done anything like this before?"

"I didn't know it could be done," says Norris.

"Let's just keep our heads," says Zimmerman. "We've gotten this far. If we follow through, we'll all be taken care of."

"Except for Mitchell," says Dee.

"We'll all be fine," says Zimmerman sternly.

"Why is this our job, anyways?" asks Dee. "This isn't our concern. This is B—"—he rethinks his word choice—"this is the *boss's* concern."

"It's our concern too," says Zimmerman.

"How?"

"What if he said no? What if he told them no, he wasn't going to have anyone do it?"

"Then he'd be in the hot spot, and not us," says Norris.

"Oh, and you think they don't know who works for him? Wouldn't that make us a concern, too? And wouldn't you say we all know a little too much?"

There's a moment of silence. "*I* don't know much," says Dee sullenly.

"They wouldn't take that risk. We're all in this together. They tell the boss what to do, and he tells us. And we do it. Even if there are"—he glances out the window at the dark landscape below—"casualties."

"How do we even know it will work?" asks Norris.

Zimmerman reaches below his seat and picks up a small wooden box. It has been sealed shut with several pieces of tape, both horizontally and vertically, and tied with heavy string. It is clear that whoever prepared the box intended it never be opened unless absolutely necessary.

"It'll work," says Zimmerman, but his voice shakes and grows hoarse.

The car keeps climbing, weaving along the little road that dances atop the peaks. Soon the road begins to run parallel to the river in the valley below, and they finally converge where the water tumbles from a rocky outcropping on the cliff side, a discharge of recent rains. The fan of vegetation comes to a point there; above that the soil is too rocky for anything except the hardiest pines.

"There," says Zimmerman. He points to the foot of the waterfall.

Norris pulls over to the shoulder and turns the flashers on. "Damn it, Norris, don't turn those on!" says Zimmerman.

"Sorry," says Norris, and turns them back off.

All three of them get out of the car and gather around the trunk. They exchange a glance, and open it.

"...Nothing possible for you to do, nothing conceivable, so I cannot understand what you are planning. Can a fish fight the sky? Can a worm battle the ocean? What can you even dream of accomplishing?"

"He doesn't shut up," says Zimmerman. "Come on." Norris reaches in and heaves their cargo up by the shoulders, and Dee takes his bound feet. Zimmerman turns on a flashlight and leads the way, holding the wooden box in a gloved hand. They carry their captive to where the road ends and begin to navigate down the rocky slope to the waterfall.

The falls lie just beyond an old chain-link fence that staggers across the hills. A rusty tin sign hangs from one post by a corner. Its words are barely legible, though what can be read is printed in a chipper, space-age font that went out of style decades ago: PROPERTY OF COBURN NATIONAL LABORATORY AND OBSERVATORY—NO TRESPASSING! The three men ignore it, and crouch as they carry their ranting burden through one of the gaping holes in the fence.

Norris looks up. This far from the city lights the stars seem even closer than before. It makes him uncomfortable, or perhaps it is the ionized taste that seems to hover in the air around the top of the mesa. It is a Wrong place. Not the Wrongest, God knows that's so, but still deeply Wrong.

Dee eyes the surrounding cedars and ponderosa pines nervously. "I don't see it," he says over the babbling of the hooded man.

"Don't worry about that," says Zimmerman. "It'll come when it's called. Just set him down beside the falls."

They do so, gently laying their captive down on the rock. Zimmerman nods at them to back away, and he reaches out and pulls off the burlap sack.

A kindly, plump face looks up at them from underneath a messy mop of gray hair. His eyes are green and crinkled at the edges, and his cheekbones have a happy red tint. It is the face of a bureaucrat, an English teacher, a counselor, a man used to the shuffling and filing of papers. Yet there is a hardness to his eyes that unnerves Norris, as if there is something swimming in their depths that does not belong there.

"There is nothing you can do to me," the man says. "It is not allowed. I cannot understand what you are attempting, but it is useless."

"Get back a little bit," says Zimmerman to his two companions. "Now." Dee and Norris take a few steps back, still watching.

"Have you gone mad?" asks their captive. "Is that it? Guns and knives and ropes are mere ephemera here, chaff on the wind. Why would you disturb our waters? Why would you deny yourself peace?"

"Shut up," says Zimmerman. He kneels, takes out a small penknife, and begins to cut at the tape and the string on the small wooden box.

"Have you not heard a word I said?" asks their captive. "Can you not listen to me for one moment? Do you not even understand what it is you do?"

The box is now open. Zimmerman stares at its contents, swallows, and places the penknife aside. "Understanding isn't my job," he says hoarsely. Then he picks up the box with both gloved hands, moving gingerly so as not to disturb what is within, and brings it over to where their captive lies.

"You cannot kill me," says the bound man. "You cannot touch me. You cannot even harm me."

Zimmerman licks his lips and swallows again. "You're right," he says. "*We* can't." And he tips the contents of the box over onto the bound man.

Something very small and white and oval comes tumbling out. At first it looks like an egg, but as it rolls across the man's chest and comes to a stop before his face it becomes clear that it is not. Its surface is rough like sandpaper, and it has two large, hollow eyes, a short, snarling snout with two sharp incisors, and many smaller, more delicate teeth behind those. It is a tiny rodent skull, lacking its jawbone, and this gives it the queer impression of being frozen mid-scream.

The bound man stares at the tiny skull on his chest. For the first time his serene confidence breaks: he blinks, confused, and looks up at his captors. "W-what is this?" he asks weakly. "What have you done?"

Zimmerman does not answer. He turns and says, "Come on! Now!" Then all three of them sprint over the rocky slopes to the chain-link fence, arms pinwheeling when they misstep.

"What have you done to me?" calls the bound man after them, but he gets no answer.

When they reach the fence they pull open one of the holes and help each other through. "Is that it?" asks Norris. "Is it done?"

Before Zimmerman can answer a yellow light flares to life in the trees beside the waterfall. The three men look back, and each is forced to squint even though the source of the light remains hidden. The light seems to shiver strangely, as if the beam is interrupted by many dancing moths, and the way the light filters through the glade gives it the look of a leaning rib cage.

In between two of the tallest pines is what looks like a man, standing erect, hands stiff at its sides. Norris cannot remember its being there before; it is as if this newcomer has appeared out of nowhere, and with its appearance there is a new scent to the air, an odor of shit and rotting straw and putrefaction. Norris's eyes water at the barest whiff of it. The figure stares down at the bound man, but its head appears strange: sprouting from the top of its skull are two long, thin ears, or possibly horns. It does not move or speak; it does not seem to even breathe. It simply stands there, watching the bound man from the edge of the pines, and due to the bright light from behind it is impossible to discern anything more.

"Oh my God," whispers Dee. "Is that it?"

Zimmerman turns away. "Don't look at it!" he says. "Come on, run!"

As they climb back up to the road the voice of the bound man cuts through the sound of the waterfall: "What? N-no! No, not you! I didn't do anything to you! I never did anything to you, I didn't!"

"Jesus," says Norris. He moves to look back.

"Don't!" says Zimmerman. "Don't attract its attention! Just get up to the car!"

When they vault over the highway barrier the shouts from the waterfall turn into screams. The light in the trees begins to shudder, as if more and more moths are coming to flit around its source. From this height the three men could look down and see what is happening there at the foot of the waterfall, but they keep their eyes averted, staring into the starlit asphalt or the lightning in the clouds.

They climb into the car and sit in silence as the screams persist. They are screams of unspeakable agony, yet they do not seem to end. The driver hits the tuner on the radio again. It's Buddy Holly again, but this time he's singing "Love Is Strange."

"Must be playing a marathon or something," says Dee softly.

Norris clears his throat and says, "Yeah." He turns the volume up until the song overpowers the shrieks from the valley below.

Dee is right: it is a marathon, and next comes "Valley of Tears," and after that is "I'm Changing All Those Changes." The screams continue while the men listen to the radio, swallowing and sweating and sometimes clasping their heads. The scent of sweaty terror in the car intensifies.

Then the unearthly light beside the road dies. The men look at each other. Norris turns the radio down, and they find the screams have stopped.

As the last of that septic yellow light drains out of the pines, dozens more lights appear farther up the mesa. They are common office lights, the lights of many structures standing on the mesa. It's as if they all share a common power source that's just been turned back on.

"Well, I'll be damned," says Zimmerman. "He was right. The lab's up and running again."

There is a moment of shocked silence as the three men stare at the lights on the mesa. "Should we call Bolan?" asks Norris.

Zimmerman takes out a cell phone, then rethinks. "Let's get the body first," he says.

"Is it safe?" asks Dee.

"It'll be done by now," says Zimmerman, but he does not sound totally sure.

At first they do not move. Then Zimmerman opens his car door.

After a moment of reluctance, the other two follow suit. They walk to the side of the road and stare down at the waterfall, which is now dark. There is no sign of anything unusual having transpired on the rocks. There is only the spatter of the waterfall, the hiss of the pines, and the pinkish light of the moon.

Finally they climb back over the barrier and begin the awkward journey down. As they descend, Norris takes one last glance up at the lights on the top of the mesa. "I wonder who it's bringing here," he says softly.

There is an angry shush from Zimmerman, as if the trees themselves could hear, and the men continue into the darkness in silence.

CHAPTER TWO

Mona Bright's been to some pretty piss-poor funerals in her day, but she has to admit that this one takes the cake. It even beats her cousin's funeral in Kentucky, when the grave was hand-dug in a tiny church graveyard. That was a pretty medieval affair, she knows, but at least then the gravediggers were all family members, and they treated the ceremony with a little dignity. Here in this miserable potter's field in the middle of nowhere, there is no one to attend but her and the grave-digger, a local contractor with a backhoe who currently has his rattling old vehicle parked just beside the open grave. He hasn't even turned it off, he just has it idling. He sits on the footstep and when he isn't wiping his face clean of sweat he is eye-fucking her something fierce. Already she can see him formulating any number of lines he hopes might magically translate this sordid little afternoon into a quick fuck in whichever motel is closest.

She asks him what his next job is. He is surprised, and thinks and says, "Well, they got a parking lot they need leveled off in Bayton."

Christ, she thinks. Gravedigging at two, parking lot at three. What an interesting little county her father chose to die in.

"You got anyone else coming?" he ventures.

"Doubt it."

"Well. You want to go ahead and get on with the show?"

"There isn't a minister coming or anything?"

"I believe you have to schedule him."

"So it isn't an automatic civil service or whatever?" she asks, and laughs morosely. "I thought this was God's country."

"Not for free, it isn't," says the gravedigger.

Where they are is Montana City, Texas, which is a joke of a name: it can only be called a city in that it has two traffic lights. One is broken, but they don't count that against it. Mona had the option of transferring her father up to Big Spring, which is bigger in the sense that a gnat is bigger than a flea, but she doesn't see why she should foot a dime more than she has to to plant her father, Earl Bright III, deep in this godforsaken soil. After all, he was a horrific skinflint, and it feels appropriate to stick him in a stretch of earth just as begrudging and hostile as he was in life.

The gravedigger climbs into his backhoe. "You want to say something?"

She thinks about it, and shakes her head. "It's all been said."

He shrugs, revs the engine, and starts it forward. Mona watches impassively behind her silvered sunglasses as the crumbly clay earth tumbles down to embrace the pine coffin below.

Ashes to ashes, dust to dust, yadda yadda yadda.

Earl, of course, had not been foresighted enough to write a will, so all of his belongings enter the complicated and cryptic world of probate. Or at least it would be complicated anywhere else, but here the judge plans to go elk hunting in a week, so they cut down the time before the heirship proceeding accordingly, because honestly, who cares.

On the appointed hour, Mona dutifully appears at the local probate court, a low-ceilinged place filled with the reek of burned coffee. It looks as if it moonlights as a VFW hall. There's a moment of confusion when the officials see Mona, for though Earl was as white as snow, Mona's looks are all her mother's, so she is quite Mexican. But Mona was prepared for this—she has to be, in Texas—and the appropriate forms and badges of identification mostly quell the questions. Then they get down to business.

Of a sort. The judge is present, but he's got his feet up on the table and is utterly absorbed in his newspaper. Mona doesn't mind. The easier this is, the better, because she's looking for something specific, a treasure Earl would have never parted with even in his most extreme old age: his 1969 cherry-red Dodge Charger, the pride and joy he spent most of his life on, and which Mona was forbidden from ever driving. As a teenager she often dreamed of sitting in its leather seats and feeling the motor burst to life with the push of the pedal, the vibrations of the pistons dancing up the steering shaft and into her arms. Once, on a hot summer evening when she was sixteen, she tried to steal it for the night. She hadn't even gotten it out of the garage before he caught her. Even today, the resulting scar has not healed.

So it is a very bitter grin that blossoms on her face when the gray-faced little court officer informs her that yes, that vehicle is still licensed to Mr. Bright, and as the deceased never indicated who it should go to she can claim it if she is willing. "By God, I am willing, sir," she says. "I am damn willing."

"All right," he says, and makes a note. "And what about his other properties?"

This comes as a surprise. Judging by his living conditions, her father had been scratching out a miserable and penniless life in this tiny town. "What other properties did he have?" she asks.

Oh, a fair few, the officer tells her. The car, for instance, is located at a storage unit with several of his other belongings, and these are hers if she wishes. She shrugs and says, why not. There's a small sum of cash, which she takes. There are also a few parcels of land he still owns, the officer says. These Mona turns down: she is well aware that her father has sold any land worth selling and has been living off the proceeds; the rest is unsellable scrub. The officer nods and tells her that just leaves the matter of the house.

"No sir, I do not want that flea-infested shack he was living in," she tells him.

"Well, that's good, because he didn't own that," he says. "That he was renting. This would be a house left to him in"—he checks the paper—"New Mexico."

"It's what? In New Mexico? I never heard of him owning a house out there."

The officer turns the document around to show her. "Looks like he didn't, originally," he says. "It was left to him, but went unclaimed. In his case, it was left to him by one...Laura Gutierrez Alvarez?"

At that, Mona is almost struck dumb. Though the clerk is nattering on about New Mexico law and uniform probate law, Mona can hardly hear a word of it.

Momma, she thinks? Momma had a house? Momma had a house in *New Mexico*?

Then, slowly, her shock turns to rage. She cannot believe that the old bastard never told her that. For years she peppered him with questions about her mother, whom she barely remembers save for a few childhood images of a thin, trembling woman who wept constantly and stared out of windows, yet never went outdoors. Mona never knew that her mother had once had a life beyond their tiny West Texas home; yet here, recorded in the fading ink of an ancient typewriter, a paper tells her of a paper that tells her of a deed in her mother's name, which in turn tells her of another life far from here, a life before Earl, and Mona's own birth, and all the bitter years they spent together as her father roughnecked across the country.

"What else can you tell me about it?" she asks.

"Well...not much. There's nothing else in the original will, which is pretty basic. I suppose your father never acted on it."

"Never? He just sat on it?"

"Seems that way. The will itself has an expiration date of"—he checks—"thirty years."

Something about this troubles Mona. "Thirty years from Earl's death?"

"Erm, no," says the official. He checks the papers. "This would be thirty years from the date of your mother's death."

Mona closes her eyes, and thinks—*fuck*.

"What?" says the official. "Something wrong?"

"Yeah," says Mona. "That means it expires in"—she does some math in her head—"eleven days."

"Oh." The official whistles lowly. "Well. Better get a wiggle on, I suppose."

Mona gives him a prime *no shit* glare, then squints to read the home's address:

1929 LARCHMONT

WINK, NM 87207

Mona frowns.

Wink? she thinks. Where the fuck is Wink?

The question stays on her mind as she drives into Big Spring to track down her father's storage unit. It even pushes out all thoughts of the Charger. She has never felt there was much to know about her father—and what else was there besides the bitter silences, the smell of cordite, and the Silver Bullet tallboy clutched in one hairy fist?—yet now she is given to wonder. If all this is true, if her mother really did leave him a house in a distant town, then he must have known at least a little about it—right? You don't just inherit a house and then stick all knowledge of it away and forget about it, do you?

It strikes her as she pulls into the storage center that if anyone would ever do such a thing, it would be her daddy. He was just the type.

The storage center attendant is initially suspicious of her. Not just because she's asking to open someone else's unit, and has to produce a lot of documents and fumble with a lot of keys to prove her case, but also because that particular unit hasn't been opened in over two years. Finally he gives in—though Mona suspects his objection was mostly fueled by a reluctance to get out of his chair rather than some professional honor—and he leads her through the maze of boxes and metal doors to one of the larger storage units at the far back.

"Is he dead for reals?" asks the attendant.

"He is for reals dead," says Mona. "I've seen him."

"If that's the case, you got a week to clear all this out, just so's you know," he says, and he unlocks the unit and sends the door rattling up.

Mona's eyes spring wide. The court officer described the storage unit as having "several" of his belongings, and she also recalls the term "a fair few" being used. But what confronts her in the storage unit is such an imposing pile of tottering shit that she is almost faint with the idea of sorting it. It'll take her twelve days at least to get a quarter of the way through it.

She gets a hefty Maglite from the storage clerk and a dolly to wheel some of this stuff away. She is thankful to have driven her old truck here, as it will definitely come in handy. But it does not take long for her to spot a shape on the side of the unit, something long, with sleek angles, draped in a thick tarp. She spies a tire peeking from underneath one fold, and her heart leaps.

It takes her more than a half an hour to get all the boxes off it, but soon the powerful form of the Charger emerges from the beige clutter. When she has enough cleared she rips the tarp off, and a cloud of dust rushes up and balloons out to fill the unit and most of the pathway outside. It is so thick it cakes her sunglasses. She waits for it to settle before she removes them, leaving flesh-colored holes in her now-dusty face.

She blinks. The Charger stands before her. She has not seen this car in fifteen years, and yet it has not aged a day. It is as if it has just fallen out of a memory. Not even the dust can taint its vibrant red color, which seems to fill the unit with a merry glow.

She moves to touch it, wishing to confirm that this moment is indeed happening, when her toe catches one of the cardboard boxes and sends her tumbling over. She falls so fast she does not even have time to cry out or try to stop herself, and the cement floor flies up and cracks her on the forehead.

It is a solid hit, and for a moment she sees nothing but green bubbles of light bursting in a sea of black. Then one light begins to grow steadier, and she hears the Maglite clattering on the floor nearby. Forms calcify in the darkness, blank gray faces all stacked in a column, and on one of the faces is a word: LAURA.

She realizes she is lying on the dusty floor with her cheek on the cement and her feet up on a crushed box. The Maglite is caught in the tarp and shooting a spotlight on one box in a tower of them. But it is the box below it, the one with the word LAURA written on it in Sharpie, that Mona is most interested in. That, and the state of her head.

She sits up and touches her brow. There is a leak of blood forming there, and her fingers shine wetly. "Fuck," she says, and looks around for something to stanch it. Seeing nothing useful, she tears off a corner of dust-covered newspaper and slaps it to her head. It sticks.

She has entirely forgotten the Charger behind her. She removes the boxes on top of the LAURA one, and pulls the lid off.

She blinks again. Her head is beginning to pound and everything feels woozy. It is hard to see into the box in the dark. She grabs the Maglite and shines it in.

It's all papers, like the rest of the storage unit. But these are not papers she thinks her daddy would ever normally have. They are too official, too...technical. She sees the initials CNLO in a lot of the corners, next to some kind of corporate logo, and some of them are copies of graph paper with a lot of numbers and equations on them.

Then Mona spies something at the edge of the box. It is a glossy corner of a photo, she is sure. She pulls it out and examines it.

It is a photo of four women on a back porch, seated around a wrought-iron table. They are all well dressed and holding up cocktails and laughing at the camera, which, judging by the hazy shadows and soft colors, was some kind of old Polaroid. Behind the women is an impressive vista: there are tall pines mere yards away, and behind those is a wall of immense pink crags, striated with dusky crimson.

Mona does not know three of the women. But the fourth she recognizes, though never in her life did she see that face in a look of such happiness. For Mona that face was always fearful and sad, the eyes constantly probing the room as if expecting to spy some invisible intruder. But the person in the picture is definitely her mother, decades younger than when Mona knew her, perhaps lives younger, free of years of illness and sour marriage.

Mona turns the picture over. On the back, written in loopy blue ballpoint, are the words: MOUNTAINS ARE PINK—TIME TO DRINK!

She turns it back over and examines the faces. The idea of her mother, a trembling creature who needed dark, empty rooms more than life itself, having a casual cocktail with friends is beyond bewildering.

Mona digs farther into the box. There are more photos, evidently from the same roll of film, documenting the same afternoon party. They are all taken around the same house, and at first she thinks that the house is made out of stone or mud before remembering that they have adobe houses out there, don't they? She catches only corners and stray walls of the place, but in one photo where her mother, clad in a tight, appealing blue dress, hugs a new arrival on the front walk, Mona manages to see part of the front.

She holds the picture closer. There is a number on the wall beside the front door. She squints, and though the light in the unit is bad and the camera renders everything fuzzy, she believes it reads 1929.

"Nineteen twenty-nine Larchmont," Mona mutters. She flips back through the photos, taking in the people, the view, but especially her mother and the big house she apparently owned far away from here in some beautiful country, surrounded by happy friends.

Mona's house, now—if she can get to Wink in time. She has not really realized it until this moment, but now that she has a picture of the thing rather than some vague, ancient papers, she understands what it is she's walked into. Though she has never laid eyes on this house or even known it existed before, it could belong to her. To Mona, who has had a bad couple of years and has been migrating and renting a lot—and once, in Corpus Christi, even living out of her goddamn truck and bathing in a gas station restroom—the idea is absolutely crazy.

There is a knock at the door of the unit. The storage center attendant looks in warily. "Everything okay in here? Thought I heard a shout."

Mona looks up at him, and he withdraws a little to see this short, dark-haired, dust-covered woman glaring at him with a shred of newspaper and a trickle of blood on her forehead. Mona does not know it, but the shred of newspaper blares *AUTHORITIES APPALLED*.

"Doing good," she says, and her voice is raspy from the dust. She nods at the Charger. "Where can I get some gas and a mechanic for that?"

It takes most of the day to take care of Earl Bright's last possessions. A lot of it she'll leave for the attendant to trash. Most of the papers are about land purchases, as her father apparently tried to elbow into the speculation racket, with poor results. There are a shocking number of bowling trophies, none of them for first place. There are also some photos. Most of them are of him and his family. These Mona throws away. The pictures of him, Mona, and her momma she keeps, at least for today: she promises herself she'll toss them too, in the morning.

She manages to sell her old truck for 250 dollars, and in her frank opinion the buyer overpaid, though she definitely does not say so. The Charger takes minimal work at the mechanic's to get it running like a charm. God can damn her father for a whole host of things, but he was handy with a car. The only sticking point is the tires: naturally, a mechanic's in Big Spring doesn't have the stock to service a classic car like this, and Mona's not interested in waiting around, so after grilling the mechanic rather mercilessly she purchases a set that should be "serviceable" until she can find a place that can get her something real. She's pretty sure that will eliminate most of the small pile of cash she's just inherited, but feels certain it will be worth it. When the mechanic's done, she loads her meager possessions into the car, and she moves the most important ones last: her Glock 19, its holster, and a box of rounds.

By the time the sun sets Mona is richer than she's been in years. Not only does she have over a thousand dollars, she now owns a flashy car, a box of her mother's papers and photos, and a goddamn house in New Mexico.

She sits in the driver's seat and does some thinking.

Eleven days left. Maybe fewer. She'll have to seriously book it.

That night at the motel she orders takeout from a barbecue joint and sits on the bed eating and reading her mother's things. Lots of them—most of them—she doesn't understand. They look like data reports from some old computer system—the kind, she imagines, whose screen is rendered in black with dark green letters. There are reams and reams and reams of data, and sometimes there are words but she doesn't understand a damn lick of it—"cosmic bruising" gets tossed around a lot, as well as "aphasic," and there's a lot of talk about "binary states," which Mona doesn't get. There are also some other papers, interoffice memos, all of which originate from the same laboratory: CNLO, Coburn National Laboratory and Observatory, whose name is always paired with the same corporate logo, an atomic model of an element (hydrogen, Mona guesses) encased in a drop of water, or possibly a ray of light.

And it appears her mother was once employed there, probably as some sort of engineer. She sees "Alvarez" on several of the memos, even "Dr. Alvarez." Mona's been getting surprised all day, but this surprises her most of all: she cannot imagine her mother having a PhD in anything, especially advanced stuff like this.

She looks at a few old family photos from her father's belongings. The one she lingers on the most was taken in front of their old cinder-block house. The house is as small and white and drab as she remembers, drenched in sun and dust. Mona, Earl, and her mother stand before the front door, smiling a little, a snapshot taken on the way to church. Mona cannot imagine who took the picture—maybe a neighbor?—but even in this moment, early in their family's history, Mona thinks she can detect some brittleness in her mother's eyes, something ready to break.

Mona can still remember the last time she saw her mother. Alive, that is. It took place right there, on that step in the photo. She remembers the hot, red day when her mother ventured out onto that front step—her first time outside in months—and called to Mona, playing in the yard, hardly seven years old. Her mother was wearing a teal bathrobe and her hair was wet, and Mona remembers how embarrassed she was when the wind rose and the bottom of her mother's bathrobe lifted up and Mona saw coarse pubic hair and realized her mother was nude under that robe, just naked as a jaybird. Her mother called to her to come, and when Mona obeyed her mother knelt and whispered into Mona's ear that she loved her, she loved her more than anything, but she couldn't stay here, and she was so sorry. She couldn't stay because she was not from here, not really, she was from somewhere else, and she had to go back now. Mona, terrified, asked where it was, and was it close and could she visit, and her mother whispered that no, no, it was far, far away, but she said not to worry, everything would be fine; one day she would come and get her little girl and everything would be fine. Then her mother said to stay in the yard, to just stay there until the ambulance came and took care of everything, and with one last profession of love she kissed Mona and walked back inside.

Mona's last memory of her mother is of her walking down the long, dark hallway, teetering uneasily on pale, skinny legs, her hands mindlessly probing her ears. After that, though Mona was not there to see it (having minded her mother), Laura Bright wrapped her head in two towels, climbed into the bathtub, shut the curtain, put her husband's shotgun to her chin, and painted the aquamarine tiles of the shower with the wet, simple matter that composed her mind and soul.

Judging from her mother's preparations, she had evidently tried to make a clean job of it, but the grout kept a pink stain that never went away, no matter how her father scrubbed. Mona hated the house after that, and she was thankful when her father moved to a new job. And to this day Mona has never forgotten the way her mother looked when she apologized to her on that front step: she looked more sensible and saner than she had in many years. It was not until later, when Mona became a cop, that she learned how unusual it was for a woman to kill herself with a firearm, especially one as devastating as a shotgun. To this day, it still bothers her.

She keeps forgetting that in eleven days it will have been thirty years ago. Even though all of her adult life has occurred after that moment, it still feels as if it happened only yesterday, like Mona is still waiting on the front lawn, waiting for her mother to tell her to come back inside.

She remembers almost nothing of her mother apart from that moment and brief snatches of other memories that amount to nothing. Yet in this dingy motel room, with the sounds of *Jeopardy!* bleeding through the bedroom wall, Mona is confronted with the fact that her mother was much more than that sad, confused woman. How she got to West Texas and into Earl Bright's life is something Mona cannot imagine.

Yet it is something Mona decides she will find out. She will go to this town in New Mexico and find out what her mother was doing there and what turned her into the weeping wreck of a human being Mona knew. And after all, Mona has no reason to stay in Texas: she's had a rocky couple of years since her divorce, and though after her resignation the Houston PD made it obvious they'd welcome her back, she does not feel like being a cop anymore. She has become comfortable with drifting, with the endless chain of cheap motel rooms and the scents of diesel gas and watery beer. God only knows how many W2s she's filled out for a month's or two months' wages. She has been all over Texas and Louisiana and, in one rock-bottom fit, Oklahoma, and though she has seen many miles she is now unsure if she's actually found anything during her sojourn. Certainly never a house, or a car, or the ghost of her mother's history.

Mona shoves the papers aside and starts trimming and filing her toenails (she has always taken very good care of her feet), and she watches the curtains change color with the neon lights outside.

She wonders how she will get there. She wonders what Wink is like, and why she's never heard of it before. And she wonders if she will find any more to the stranger she has just unearthed in this little cardboard box.

CHAPTER THREE

On the outskirts of Wink, nestled in the western side of the mesa so it is shielded from the worst of the midday sun, there is a narrow, wandering canyon that is curiously treeless and silent. It is almost hidden within a thick thatch of pinyon pines, yet none of them has managed to penetrate this canyon despite having successfully invaded far harsher regions. It is mostly invisible to the town itself, but if the inhabitants wished, it would be an easy thing to climb down to the forest and hike their way over. Yet despite the canyon's scenic appeal and accessibility, none of the residents of Wink ever enters. At least, not without an invitation.

Because this is where Mr. First resides, and Mr. First values his privacy.

It is early morning, and pink hues are just beginning to seep into the dark sky above, blanching out the stars. A flock of sparrows suddenly takes flight from the forest in a rush, and they wheel about before settling on the opposite side of Wink. A family of white-tailed deer also flees the mesa's shadow, springing through the pines as if startled by a hunter, yet there is none. Even a pack of coyotes hurries away, an anomaly if ever there was one, as they'd normally be asleep by now.

Soon a heavy silence pervades the forest. There is no sound but the wind in the pines. For Mr. First is waking, and most creatures around the mesa know it's wise to make themselves scarce at such times.

This occurrence is unusual, and Mr. First realizes this, for it is not his time to wake. He observes that it is morning, not evening, and more so he has set a very rigorous schedule for himself, and if he's gauged the current date correctly he is well short of his appointed time. He should still be slumbering here, hidden from the raw, new world in the many rocky folds of the canyon. It is very curious.

Something must have awoken him, he decides. This is concerning, for few are the things that can awake Mr. First. So, in a series of slow, complicated movements, he unfurls himself and begins to examine his surroundings: he tastes the air, the moisture, the sandy canyon floor, and many other things besides.

It is this ability for perception (along with his seniority) that differentiates Mr. First from his many siblings. For example, while his family is unique in a variety of ways, only he is able to perceive the shape and shift of time itself: he can glimpse ahead and make out the rough, tumbling shape of things to come, like looking down into the sea and discerning a swell of silver and identifying it as a school of fish—and, if he concentrates very, very hard, he might even be able to make out the form of things that could have happened (or even *should* have happened) but did not.

Now, trembling and quaking in the cool morning air, Mr. First realizes this is what awoke him: the shape of the future has just violently shifted. A multitude of possibilities were eliminated, and everything has just been forced onto a single track. He exercises his talent for perception, and peers ahead at the blurry shape of future events, and sees...

He stops almost immediately. If Mr. First had eyes to widen, they would be quite wide right now.

He thinks about what he has just seen, and two thoughts enter his mind:

One is that someone has been murdered. This is unprecedented, and rightly so: such a thing should be impossible here. Yet merely by glancing at the next few hours, he can see it is true.

The second is far more confusing, far more ominous, and totally perplexing to Mr. First. Yet he knows what he saw, and though it was as vague and shadowed as all glimpses of things yet to come, it is clear as day to him:

She is coming.

Mr. First hunches down in his canyon, withdrawing utterly until there is nothing to distract him. He begins thinking, very hard and very fast, which is difficult for him, for his thoughts usually proceed with the pace and implacability of tectonic shifts.

Things are changing. They are changing here, in a place that should not ever, ever change. Even he, eldest of his siblings (give or take), could never have anticipated this.

Should I tell them? he asks himself. He extends his attention to the tiny town threaded through the valley before the mesa. They are all still asleep, for the most part.

No, he decides: they will know soon enough, and besides, it would make no difference.

But his own preparations will have to change, he knows. They'll have to be sped up, for one. That is all he can do. And soon he will have visitors, and he will have to get ready for them.

He sighs a little. He was quite enjoying it here. They all were. But such things happen, he supposes.

CHAPTER FOUR

Anyone who wants to rhapsodize about the beauty of nature should drive from Texas to New Mexico, Mona thinks. There is about a hundred-mile stretch of nothing, genuinely nothing, no crops or buildings of any kind, though of course it's hard for her to tell how big it is because it all looks the same. It is just flat, gray, sunbaked scrub, flatter than any land Mona's seen before. She's pretty sure that if she were to pull over and stand on the hood of her car she'd be able to see for miles in every direction. There are barbed-wire fences everywhere, but Mona can't figure out for the life of her what they're fencing out.

I-40 just keeps going. It has almost no intersections, and it passes through no towns. This is an empty country, untamed simply because there is nothing here to tame.

Except, Mona learns, the wind. It is when she first enters the hills that she sees the wind turbines, and she's so surprised she nearly drives the Charger off the road. They are so unexpected, these shining white machines standing on the ragged mountaintops. She knew they had built wind farms out here, but she hasn't returned to West Texas in over fifteen years, so she has never seen one. The turbines seem limitless, dotting the farthest hilltops. It is an alien sight.

Mona sees there is a gap in the fence beside one of the turbines, and she decides now is a pretty good time to take a break. She pulls over and grabs her maps and her lunch—a bean burrito that's been warming in the sunlight on the passenger seat—and she hops out and starts up the hill to where the turbine stands. It is probably trespassing, but she doubts there is anyone around to object. She can't remember the last time she saw another car.

The turbine is farther away than she thought, for she underestimated its size. It seems like the biggest thing she's ever seen, though it can't be, she thinks. It is about five stories tall, and she's seen buildings much larger than that, yet this seems bigger, somehow. When she gets close she finds it makes a hum so deep and loud it makes her sinuses vibrate. It is a terrifying and strange contraption, rotating so slowly under the blindingly blue sky. But it's also the only source of shade around here, so Mona sits down in its shadow and unpacks her burrito and opens up her maps.

She looks them over, and thinks.

It took three days to figure out where, approximately, Wink is. Three wasted, frustrated, furious days, for as it turned out, Mona wasn't the only person who'd never heard of it: no mapmaker, including Rand McNally and the goddamn Department of Transportation, had heard of it, either. The DOT kept referring her to the state level, which in turn referred her to national, and so on and so forth. She spent nearly a whole day finding every highway map she could and scouring it for the town, but her search was fruitless. She even called the tax appraisal district for the county, hoping to check the property tax rolls, but the county had no record of it.

Mona then tried another route: she had several official documents saying she now owned the house, so presumably the offices and institutions that had issued them should be able to tell her where it was, right? But she was wrong: all anyone had was the address. The rest of the information about the house—like where it was—was conspicuously absent. Mona argued that clearly the house was real, so the town had to be real as well, and real things generally show up on maps, but the clerk on the phone responded that no, actually, they did not know if the house was real, they could only confirm that her *inheriting* the house was real; the rest, the clerk primly said, might be either an error or a fraud, and the way she told Mona this made it plain she now considered her suspect. Mona then said a lot of things she'd never say in church, and the clerk hung up on her.

She was so angry that it took her a long while to calm down and figure out a solution. While Wink now seemed unfindable, there was something else she realized she could search for: Coburn National Laboratory and Observatory, whose logo was emblazoned on the corner of almost every paper of her mother's. This idea came to her on the way to Amarillo, since she'd decided to start moving in the general direction of New Mexico to avoid wasting any more time. When she arrived she swung by the public library to see what she could find on it.

Again, what she found was negligible, but it was at least more than what she'd found on Wink. Coburn National Laboratory and Observatory was referenced in seven places, all of them old scientific magazines from the sixties and seventies. The one with the most detail was the oldest, from 1968, a sort of profile on the lead scientist done by *Lightfirst Magazine*, which itself went out of business in 1973.

The article featured a large picture of an elderly but robust man smiling and standing in front of a magnificent mountain panorama. Though it was rendered in black and white and the photo had turned a dull yellow from age, Mona could tell the region was astonishingly beautiful. The man was dressed a little like an explorer, with big boots and a vest with many pockets, one of those adventurer-intellectuals who seem inspired by the previous century. There was a lot of construction going on behind him at the foot of one of the biggest mountains. The caption read:

Dr. Richard Coburn, standing before the future site of Coburn National Laboratory and Observatory at the base of the Abertura Mesa.

Abertura Mesa, thought Mona. She wrote that down, then scanned the rest of the article for something usable. It was mostly an interview with Dr. Coburn (rendered, bizarrely, in transcript—she guessed this

just appealed to those of the scientific persuasion), centering on physics stuff, which frankly bored her to tears, so she couldn't make heads
or tails of it. The interviewer mostly fawned over Dr. Coburn, who
must have been some big-shot physicist back in the day, and though he
was enthusiastic he didn't seem eager to talk details. She zeroed in on
one section in particular:

LFM: So what expectations do you have for the project? If your
  recent publications are anything to go by, they must be very
  high.

RICHARD COBURN: Well, really, I think it's only healthy to enter
  into any new endeavor with the highest of expectations. I
  mean, you want to make yourself work, naturally, and you
  won't work if you don't think you can accomplish anything. I
  sort of become an enemy of myself, in a way. I'm a bit embarrassed to admit it, but I tend to assume I'm failing all the time.
  There is so much more I can be doing at any moment. Perhaps it's unhealthy, I'm not sure.

LFM: What more do you think you can be doing, then?

RICHARD COBURN: I'm sorry, I don't believe I understand the
  question.

LFM: What I mean is, you say you're going into this expecting great
  accomplishments. What would those accomplishments be?

RICHARD COBURN: Well, unfortunately, since our funding is
  largely through government avenues, there's not much I can
  say about our plans. You know, it's the kind of thing that has
  all sorts of clearance levels and such. It's all a bit irritating,
  honestly. There is so much I'd like to talk about, yet I can't.
  But I will say that this just might be—and I do not think I am
  overestimating myself, here—the first really genuine American foray into the quantum realm. And with each new thing
  we learn, the possibilities become more and more amazing.
  We've assembled a great team here, and though we're all
  pretty much camping in the desert for now, I expect that'll
  change soon.

LFM: They have you camping out there? In tents?

RICHARD COBURN: Oh, no, they have temporary housing set up. It's fairly comfortable. I believe there are some plans to make something more permanent, but I'm only peripherally involved in those. It should be very pleasant, I think. They're allowing us some say in the aesthetics. But I honestly cannot wait to get started. We will be examining the way the world works at the smallest level possible, and I can't overstate how important this research will be. Things we've assumed, things we've taken for granted for hundreds if not thousands of years are being brought into question. It really is quite startling. I'd be unnerved by the whole thing, really, if I didn't love the research so much.

Mona had expected government funding—it was a national lab, after all—but this sounded distinctly more...secret. As if whatever they'd been doing out there required housing and domesticities that were very much off the books, like a federal enclave.

Which might explain why there was absolutely nothing to be found about Wink. Having once been a reservist, Mona was dimly aware of how the government operates in situations like this: first they build the facilities, then they construct the residential area for its staff. Maybe Wink was a federal town built to house the staff of CNLO, which would explain why it never showed up on any maps, and why so many state and federal institutions had no record of it.

And this was what her mother had been wrapped up in? She'd been a government research scientist? The more Mona learned about her mother's past, the more bizarre it all seemed.

As she copied the article, she realized it all put her in a hell of a spot: she'd been entrusted a house, but it just might be in a fucking federal enclave. How could that have happened? What would she have to do, climb a barbed-wire fence to get to it? Was any of this *legal*? Mona had no experience with federal law on this scale. And she still hadn't found anything definite about the exact location of the town. All she had was the name of the mesa that might or might not be nearby.

But after checking another map, she found that at least the mesa was real—the Abertura Mesa, just on the north tip of the Jemez Mountains, to the northwest of Santa Fe and Los Alamos. It looked fairly accessible, as well.

That just left one question—was she willing to drive all the way out there to see if either Coburn National Laboratory and Observatory or Wink was around?

She looked up and saw her reflection in the library window. Ever since finding the old photos of her mother, Mona had been reminded of how similar they looked: Mona was a little shorter, and her skin a little browner, but besides that they were almost the same.

It had been so powerfully strange to see her mother happy. Not just happy: effervescently happy, *incandescently* happy. As Mona stared at her reflection in the library window, she tried to remember if she'd ever seen her mother in such a state. What had she possessed in Wink that made her so happy?

Then Mona tried to remember the last time she herself had felt that way.

She could. But it was a long time ago, and she'd never wanted to remember it. To forget, to shut down entirely, had always been the better option.

Though Mona did want the house, she realized she would go to Wink even if she missed the deadline. It would be worth it if she could catch just a glimpse of that smiling woman in the photos.

And maybe Mona could find what her mother had found in Wink, as well.

She stacked up all the papers and stood up. *Maybe it's still there*, she thought as she walked out. *It's got to still be there.*

So now here Mona is, squatting on a hilltop beside a huge, humming wind turbine on the Texas border with not a soul around for miles. She looks over her maps for the hundredth time. Most of them she's notated by hand (Mona was far too poor for a GPS for a long while, and even though she now has the funds her practicality scoffs at the very idea), since many don't acknowledge the Abertura Mesa at all, and none of them make any reference to Wink, of course. It is a queer thing to be traveling in such a manner. It's like sailing without a rudder. Sometimes she thinks she is making her own maps so she can figure out how to get back from wherever she's going.

She sets the maps down, finishes her lunch, and stares off into the west. The sky is huge and bright, yet it is rent in a thousand places by the slowly swirling blades of the turbines. With the sun at the right angle they make a million dancing shadows on the barren hills. She takes a breath, lets it out, and wonders if she really wants to get back in the Charger.

She doesn't want to think of this as a second chance. Because Mona Bright has never really believed she ever got a first one. Not really.

A powerful ache begins seeping into her stomach.

Don't think about that. Pick it up and put it away.

She opens the door to the Charger, puts it in gear, and continues on her way west.

Eight days. She can make it in eight days.

CHAPTER FIVE

Slowly, the country changes.

It happens in the distance, initially. The horizon begins to crumple; then shadows form on it like thunderstorms in a cloud line. Soon the shadows gain a red tint, and Mona sees that they are mountains. Beside her the earth changes from colorless gray barrens to orange steppes rendered fuzzy and indistinct by the clusters of chamisa. The little feathery plant clings to everything out here, making Mona feel like she has glaucoma: it is as if someone has painted pale green and yellow brushstrokes over a bright orange canvas.

It is much cooler in the high countries than anywhere else Mona has been recently. She rolls the windows down and lets the cool afternoon air come rushing in around her, and she smiles as she points the Charger up another slope. It is not hard to believe that this is the land that birthed the nuclear age: anything feels possible out here. There is even something electric in the air, though that may just be the sky: if God painted the sky piece by piece then He surely finished this country last, for here the sky is so fresh and new it almost hurts to look at it.

Mona is enjoying herself so much that she almost forgets to start checking the road signs. When she finally does she sees that she is much closer to her general target than she expected. She begins to pull over at little stops to ask if the people there have ever heard of Wink.

At first, not many have. They stare at her uncertainly, and after they say no they ask if she wants something else, as if she should buy a gallon of gas or a soda just out of politeness. But Mona has neither money nor politeness to spare, and she hops back in her car and speeds along to the next stop.

Yet then the name produces a reaction: they stare at her, puzzled, but direct her down the road (this instruction is needless—there is only one road) and tell her to keep an eye out for a well-paved road leading north.

One woman tells her, "Odd that you're going there. Can't remember the last time someone went there. Come to think of it, can't remember the last time someone came from there, either."

If Mona's lucky, she'll make it before nightfall. Then she'll have a whole week to try to get the house. She hopes that will be enough.

Mona finds the paved road very easily. It is impossible to miss, so smooth and unbroken and black. It is easily the nicest road she's seen in a while. It winds down the mountain slope into fuller and taller pines, away from the rocky heights of the plateaus. It becomes rather shocking how far the road keeps going down; she wonders if this town, if it's still around, exists at the bottom of a hole in the ground. But then there is a break in the trees, and she sees it is not quite a hole but rather a steep, narrow valley.

When the road reaches the bottom of the valley it curls around itself, toward the mesa. A large, painted sign stands on the right-hand side of the turn. Mona slows to a stop to look at it.

The sign must mark the southern entrance to Wink, she thinks. It is large and colorful, and depicts two men and a woman standing at the mouth of a valley, staring at a sun-dappled mesa before them. All of them, Mona notes, are exceedingly white. The men have their hands on their hips (very authoritative), while the woman has her hands clasped together below her breasts. The men have smooth, parted hair, virtually the same except that one's is blond and the other's is brown, as if they're different versions of the same doll. They wear khakis and plaid shirts with the sleeves rolled up, as if there's work to do and darn it, they plan to do it. The woman has long, curly blond locks and a bright white-and-red sundress. They look like the kind of adults all children expect to be when they grow up.

But it is what they are gazing at that Mona finds odd. There is something on top of the mesa at the end of the valley. It looks like a tiny bronze antenna, like the kind that used to sit on top of the world in the old RKO Pictures logo. It is such an antiquated addition to the picture, yet there is something else strange about it. Are there streaks in the sky all pointing to the antenna? They look almost like very faint bolts of lightning.

At the bottom, the sign reads: WELCOME TO WINK—WHERE THE SKY TOUCHES THE EARTH! Below that, in much smaller writing: POP.: 1,243.

Mona realizes that the valley looks familiar. She gets out of her car, steps back, and looks around.

After a while she realizes it is *this* valley, and the mesa in the sign is the one just ahead of her, yet the trees have grown so tall that they obscure nearly everything below it. She can see no antenna on it. Perhaps there are buildings, but it is hard to see from so far away...

She finds the sign puts a bad taste in her mouth. She climbs back into the Charger and starts off down the road again, happy to leave it behind.

A twist of dark road, a leaning fence, the grasping brush of a soft pine branch. On and on and on the road goes... Mona feels sure she's driven the length of the whole valley, but there's always more, as if the landscape is unfolding as she travels.

Then she spots something pink out of the corner of her eye, something bulbous and smooth gliding through the air. She can see it only through the gaps in the trees. There is writing on one side, though she can see just two letters: WI.

She sees it is not flying, but standing on a tall, round post. A water tower, she thinks. But she didn't see any tower before, and she definitely should have...

As she ponders this a splash of red comes swooping out from

between the pines: a stop sign. Startled, she comes to an abrupt stop, and discovers she has arrived.

She's at an intersection, but it's completely different from those of the rough country roads she's been traveling: on her left is a small white wooden house with green trim, and on her right is another house, this one of adobe, the walls and corners smooth and brown like a sculpted chocolate cake. Each one expands back into the uneven terrain, disappearing behind thick beds of flowers. The change is so sudden that for a moment Mona sits and stares around, confused.

She realizes she has entered the street grid of Wink. She sees small shops ahead, and telephone wires, and tall pines in the parks. And yet there is no one on the streets that she can see, nor is there any sound at all besides the wind.

This is the town on the federal enclave? she wonders. She saw no signs warding trespassers away, or border guards; the only thing that hindered her arrival was the downward incline of the road.

She starts off into the streets. It is nearly evening, and the first thing she plans to do is ask someone where a motel is. She'll tackle the issue of her mother's house in the morning. So long as she presents her identification to the right people tomorrow, the house should be hers.

But she finds no one to ask. As she roves through the street grid (each block is nearly perfect—if she took out a protractor and measured the corners, she is sure they would be at an even ninety degrees) she does not spot a single soul. Every street and every shop and every home is deserted. There aren't even any cars parked in the lots.

This is why Wink wasn't on any maps, she thinks. *No one fucking lives here anymore.* It is just her luck to inherit a house in a ghost town.

But it can't be abandoned, not really, she decides. It is too well maintained for that: the neon lights of the diner, though unlit, look functional; the cafés all have (somewhat) fresh coats of paint; and as the sun sets the streetlamps all flicker on, bathing the streets in a white, phosphorescent glow, and none of the bulbs are out.

But though it is deserted, the town is quaintly beautiful. Many of the shops and buildings have a faint Googie influence to them, which contrasts hugely with the New Mexican stylings: standing beside a smooth, earthy adobe home might be a metal porthole window and an angular, upswept roof, or an amalgam of glass and steel and neon. Both the diner and the café have parabola-shaped signs done in soft, Easter-egg blue. It feels inappropriate to be cruising these streets in the Charger. What she needs is an Eldorado with tail fins and rocket-ship taillights. Or, she thinks as she passes a round-walled adobe house with pine corbels, maybe a horse-drawn wagon. It is a strangely schizophrenic place, but not unwelcoming.

She tries to imagine her mother living here. Maybe she went to that diner, bought flowers from this shop on the corner, walked her dog down that sidewalk. *Jesus*, Mona thinks—*could she have had a dog?* For some reason, this fairly irrelevant possibility confounds her.

Then Mona turns one corner, and she sees the street ahead is lined with parked cars. They are not, as she expected, vintage cars, but Chevy trucks and the like. She speeds up a little, wondering if this could be something, and as she does a wrought-iron railing emerges from the bushes along the sidewalk, and at the next corner is a white wooden church with a tall steeple.

When she pulls up alongside the fence she finally sees what is on the other side, and she slams on the brakes in surprise. The tires squeal a little as she comes to a halt.

Just on the other side of the wrought-iron fence is a huge crowd of people, hundreds of them.

When her tires squeal they all jump, turn, and look at her.

Mona looks back, and sees they are all wearing black, or at least dark gray, and some of the women's faces are veiled.

The yard with the wrought-iron fence, she realizes, is a graveyard. And at the center of the crowd is a lacquered casket hanging over an open grave.

Wink is not deserted: everyone is attending a funeral. Which Mona has just interrupted, in her rumbling muscle car with squealing tires.

"Ah, shit," says Mona.

For a moment she has no idea what to do. Then, haltingly, she waves. Most of the people do nothing. Then a small boy, about seven, smiles and waves back.

An older man in a black suit says something to the woman beside him, and walks to the iron fence. Mona rolls down the passenger window, and he asks, "Can I help you?"

Mona clears her throat. "I-is there a motel around here?"

The man stares blankly at her. But not, she feels, in shock or reproach: it is as if his face can make no other expression. Then, without taking his eyes off her, he raises one arm and points down the road ahead. "On the left," he says, slowly but clearly.

"Thanks," says Mona. "I'm real sorry for interrupting everything."

The man does not respond. He stays stock-still for a couple of seconds. Then he lowers his arm. The rest of the crowd keeps watching her.

"Sorry," she says again. "Real sorry." She rolls up the window and drives away, but when she looks in the rearview mirror they are all still watching her.

There are probably worse first impressions, but right now Mona cannot think of any. She's come from one awkward, unhappy funeral to another. She wonders what they will think when they hear she's inherited a house in town.

Her face is still bright red when she finds the motel, a low, long, dark building at the edge of town. The motel sign reads PONDEROSA ACRES in orange neon, and below that, in smaller red letters, is the word VACANCY. It looks a little like a cabin, with walls made of—or made to look like they're made of—huge pine logs. There are no lights on in any of the rooms except the office.

She gets out and scans the parking lot. There are no other cars here, not even any on the street.

She walks into the office with her bag over her shoulder. The office is surprisingly spacious, with green marble floors and wood-paneled walls. It smells of beeswax and dust and popcorn. There is only one light in the room, a yellow ceiling lamp that casts a spotlight on a small desk in the corner, littered with papers. In the corner she can just make out an old yellow sofa. Keys glint on the wall behind the desk, and somewhere a handheld radio tinnily plays "Your Cheatin' Heart." Besides that corner, the office is oppressively dark. She can barely make out a dead palm in a pot before the desk. Its curling brown leaves are still scattered on the floor. On the wall is an old calendar turned to the wrong month; it is brown with age and unmarked, the tool of someone who has had nothing to do for a long, long time.

The office appears to be empty. "Damn it," she says, and wonders where she will go now.

"Can I help you?" asks a deep, soft voice.

Mona turns around, looking for the speaker. The room is so dark that it takes her eyes a moment to adjust. Then she sees there is a card table in the corner of the room beside the door, and seated at it is an old man with a board of Chinese checkers in front of him. He is bald and gray-bearded, and his pock-marked skin is so dark that initially his gray beard appears to simply float in the darkness. In one of his hands is a Styrofoam cup of steaming coffee. He wears a gray zip-up sweater, red-and-black-striped pants, and alligator shoes, and he watches her over a pair of half-moon spectacles with calm, reserved eyes.

"Oh," she says. "I'm sorry, sir, I didn't see you there."

The old man sips his coffee but says nothing, as if to mean—*Obviously.*

"I'd like to rent a room, please, sir. Just for tonight."

The old man looks away, thinking. After nearly a full thirty seconds of meditation, with nothing but Hank Williams to break the silence, he says: "Here?"

"What?"

"You want to get a room here?"

"What? Yes. Yeah, I want to get a room here."

The old man grunts, stands up, and goes to the keys on the wall. There are about twenty hanging there on the corkboard. He surveys them very carefully, as if searching a bookshelf for the appropriate tome, and with a quiet *aha!* he selects one from the bottom corner of the board. What marks this key as different from any of the others,

Mona cannot tell. Then he lifts it to his lips and blows. A significant cloud of dust flies up from the key to dance around the ceiling lamp.

"Been a while since you guys had customers?" asks Mona.

"It has been a very long while," says the old man. He smiles and holds the key out to her.

Mona reaches for it. "How much?"

"How much?" He pulls the key back, confused. "For what?"

"For...the room?"

"Oh," says the old man, a little irritated, as if this were a needless formality he'd forgotten. He lowers the key, grunts again, puts his cup of coffee down, and begins to sort through the papers on his desk. As he does, he notices the dead plant on the floor. He stops and leans forward, examining it. Then he looks up at Mona and sternly says, "My plant has died."

"I'm...real sorry to hear that."

"It was a very old plant."

He seems to be waiting for her to say something. She ventures, "Oh?"

"Yes. I had it for nearly a year. It was my favorite plant, because of this."

"Well. That's understandable."

The old man just looks at her.

She adds, "You get attached to things if they're around long enough."

He keeps staring at her. Mona is beginning to feel quite disturbed. She wonders if he is senile, but there is more to it than that: it feels very unsafe in this big, dark office, where only one corner is lit and tangible, and the rest is hidden from her. For some reason she gets the sense that they are not alone. When the old man returns to his papers, Mona checks the corners—still nothing. Maybe it's just a weird feeling she got from seeing that funeral.

"I am not sure what to do with it now," he says grudgingly. "I liked the plant very much. But I suppose these things happen." He sniffs, and produces a tiny note card from the mountain of old papers on his desk. This he consults carefully, as if it is the ace in his poker hand, and pronounces, "Twenty dollars."

"For a night?"

"It seems so," says the old man solemnly, and he places the card back on the desk.

"So...you don't know how much your own rooms are?"

"There are several rooms, with several prices. I forget them. And we have not had any visitors in some time."

Mona, glancing at the piles of paper and dust, can completely believe that. "Mind if I ask how you stay open, then?"

He thinks about it. "I suppose you could say," he concludes, "that there is no shortage of goodwill around here."

For some reason, Mona feels he is telling the truth. But this does not exactly comfort her. "Just curious—is this the only motel in town?"

Again, he ponders her question. "If there is another motel, I am unaware of it."

"I guess that's an honest answer." She reaches into her bag, takes out a twenty, and hands it to him. He takes the bill and clutches it tight in his hand, as a child would, and looks hard at her again. "Have you ever been here before?" he asks.

"Here? In Wink?"

"Yes. In Wink."

"No. This is my first time."

"Hm. Allow me to show you to your room, then." He picks up the key, the twenty-dollar bill still clutched in his hand, and walks out the office door.

As she follows, Mona glances behind the desk. She sees no gun, no weapon, nothing suspicious. But she does not feel entirely satisfied. It is as if there's a tiny wound in her mouth she can't quit playing with. Something is wrong with this.

On the way out, she looks at the Chinese checkers board. There is something different about it now. She cannot say why—after all, it is dark, and she didn't get a good look at the board—but she is sure the checkers have been rearranged, as if someone has just made a complicated play. But perhaps the old man just jostled the table when he stood up.

He leads her down the row of motel-room doors. Night has fallen very quickly. The sky was bright blue, then streaked with pink, but now it is a soft and dusky purple cut short by the dark mesa surging into the heavens. The air has chilled considerably with the onset of evening, and Mona wishes she'd brought some winter wear.

"What is your name?" the old man asks.

"Mona."

"I am Parson, Mona. It is very nice to meet you."

"Likewise."

"It's good that you are staying the night here." He gestures into the dark trees that crawl up the slopes. "The area around Wink can be a little treacherous, especially at night. I would not advise going out at night, especially outside of downtown. People get lost very easily."

"I can imagine," says Mona, remembering the steep hills and sudden precipices. "Can I ask you something?"

He stops to consider it, as if this is a very serious proposition. "I suppose so," he says finally.

"I tried to find this place on a lot of maps before I came, but—"

"Really?" he says. "Why?"

"Well... I don't really want to get into it too much now, since nothing's settled yet... but I inherited a house here, supposedly."

Parson stares off into the distance. "Did you," he says softly. "Which house would that be, if I might ask?"

"It's on Larchmont, or so they tell me."

"I see. You know, I believe I know the residence in question. It is abandoned. But it is in fairly good shape. And you say you inherited it?"

"That's what all these papers say."

"How curious..." says Parson. "I cannot remember the last time someone new moved here. You will be quite the oddity, if so."

"That's kind of what I wanted to ask about. You might not have anyone moving here because no one knows this town's here. It's not on any map. Is there some reason for that? Something to do with the lab on the mountain?"

"Lab?" asks Parson, puzzled.

"Yeah. Coburn National Lab. And, uh, Observatory."

"Oh," he says, and smiles. "Goodness. If you're looking for a job there, I'm afraid you're about thirty years late."

"What do you mean?"

"Coburn was shut down years ago. End of the seventies, if I recall. I'm not sure why, exactly. I think they just never produced what they said they would. Lost funding. Wink was originally built around it, you know."

"Yeah, I figured."

"Did you?" he says. "Well. When it was shut down, it just left us all here. Where were we going to go? I suppose they took us off most maps to keep the place undisturbed. No spies sniffing around the lab, or some such. But now that we are forgotten, they never remembered to put us back on. To be honest, I like the peace and quiet. Even if it is bad for business."

"Can I ask you something else?"

"You have done so already—I see nothing barring you from doing so again."

"Did you ever know a Laura Alvarez here?"

"Here in Wink?"

"Yeah. She would have left about thirty years ago or so. She worked at the lab up on the mountain. I'm trying to find out more about her. She's—she was my mom."

"Hm," he says. "I am afraid I cannot help you. I am not the most social of people. I remember very few names."

"Even in a town this small, you don't know?"

"Small?" he says. "Is it so small?" He looks up, examines the room numbers, and selects one. "Ah. Here we are. Our bridal suite." He smiles at her, but does not open the room.

"Thanks," she says.

"We do not really have a bridal suite," he says. "It was a joke."

"Okay," she says.

He unlocks and opens the door and shows her in. The carpet is brown shag, and the lamps on the walls are made out of deer horns. The bedspread is done in a colored diamond pattern that Mona identifies as Native American, and it looks comfortable enough.

"The TV," says Parson firmly, "does not work."

"Okay."

"I will help you move in," he says, and begins to walk back to her car.

"That's okay," she says. "I have all my things in my bag."

He stops and peers at her bag. "Oh," he says, both irritated and disappointed. "All right, then."

"Is there a good place to eat around here?" she asks.

"There is the diner, but it is likely closed for the funeral."

"Oh. Yeah, I saw. Who died, the mayor or something?"

"Someone important," he says. But he adds, "Ostensibly."

"And you didn't go to the funeral?"

He gives her a cryptic look, face suddenly closed. "I do not go to funerals. It would not befit my station. Luckily for you, I do offer a complimentary breakfast. I may provide it now, if you wish, rather than in the morning."

"I'd be much obliged."

"Excellent," he says. "I will return shortly." Then he turns and shuffles back across the parking lot.

Mona has had a lot of weird encounters in her life, but she feels like this one has just made top seed. But before she can think on it more, there is a flicker of light in the sky. Startled, she looks and sees that blue clouds have gathered around the mountains behind the mesa. They are small but violent: each one flickers with lightning every thirty seconds or so, which makes the mountains look like they're crowned with a tangle of blue neon lights. It is a powerfully unearthly sight to see this island of chaos in an otherwise peaceful night sky.

It is then that she sees the moon is up, but there is something strange about it. It takes her a few moments to put her finger on it.

"It's pink," she says out loud. "Why is the moon so pink?"

Parson's voice comes from behind her. "It always is, here."

She looks and sees the old man has sneaked up on her. He's carrying an aluminum tray with an egg sandwich and sausage that look like they came out of a vending machine. To her amusement, the meal is paired with a Corona and a Pop-Tart.

"Bon appétit," says Parson.

CHAPTER SIX

Every night it is the same, Bolan thinks. Every night the truckers spill into the Roadhouse, reeking of cheap tobacco and old sweat, sleep-deprived and claustrophobic and half-blind from the sight of endless highways. Every night they order the same drinks and demand the same songs and shriek the same half-intelligible catcalls. There is always some lout who gets too hopped up on whichever substance is available that night and has to get hauled out and spanked in the parking lot. (And just three months ago Zimmerman and Dee laid one man out and left him breathing under a timber truck, yet in the morning they found him frigid and pale and still, one eye dark with blood and his fingers at many angles; the boys admitted they'd been overzealous, and the man still sleeps somewhere out in the woods under the stones and pine needles, and sometimes Bolan wonders who else is out there with him.) Then, finally, the truckers approach the downstairs girls in stages, and they'll spend the rest of their evening in the back rooms, coaxing favors out of the girls, or the girls coaxing money out of them. Sometime around three or four they will come stumbling out of their wretched fog and wander out to the parking lot to sleep in the cabs of their trucks. And then, just before dawn, once she's made all the totals and rechecked the registers, Mallory will stalk upstairs to Bolan's office, and tell him what the night's take is.

It's almost always good. Often it's very, very good.

And every night, Bolan thinks as he stares out his office window, there is lightning on the mountains, and the bulbous red-pink moon. It does not matter what phase the moon is in, nor does it matter what the weather is like. These are the things that compose Bolan's world: the red-pink moon, the Roadhouse, and the blue lightning on the mount.

Well. Maybe not *just* those things, Bolan thinks, perhaps a little bitterly. There will always be the little favors he has to do for the people in charge. But without those, where would he be? Certainly not here, listening to David Dord, occupant of the absolute bottom rung at the Roadhouse, except maybe for the downstairs girls. Or some of them, at least. A couple of the whores are pretty canny, more so than Dord.

Bolan turns back to him. "What do you mean, you think it went *well?*" he asks over the thumping music from downstairs. "How does a funeral go well? How would you deem one a success, Dave?"

"Well, I don't know," says Dave. "You stick the fucking guy in the ground and hopefully he stays there. Then the preacher says all the appropriate whatnot and you're done. That's how I judge it."

Bolan blinks slowly. "That's a very low bar, Dave," he says. He wishes the Roadhouse were not doing such good business tonight: this is a conversation he's been dreading all day, and he wants to hear every bit as clearly as he can. "Think, Dave," he says. "Think real hard for me. Did anyone say anything? Did anyone do anything at all? Anything out of the ordinary? I'm just curious here, Dave. Enlighten me."

David Dord, who in his funeral garb looks like a child wearing Daddy's suit, simply shrugs and shakes his head. "Tom, it was a funeral. It wasn't a hot spot for talking. No one was particularly eager to discuss their affairs or any such fucking thing."

"As far as you saw it."

"Yes, as far as I saw it."

Bolan slowly blinks again. He is already regretting sending Dord. If he could have he would've sent Zimmerman, who is in charge of security at the Roadhouse, and is always very dependable. But after their little job up on the mesa, Bolan knew Zimmerman would be far too hot to send to the funeral. He's given Zimmerman the next two weeks off, and hopefully the man is spending his time somewhere indoors and quiet, maybe with one of the house girls, which might make everything a lot less quiet. The other two—Norris and Dee—Bolan is keeping close to the Roadhouse. They're both young and, like a lot of the help Bolan seems to get, quite stupid, and the other night was their first real trial. Bolan needs to know if they're going to crack. So far Dee seems steady, which does not surprise him: the boy has coasted by on looks and muscle for so long that his mind is too underdeveloped to realize how dangerous their job on the mesa really was. But Norris, well...he isn't so sure. The kid is definitely messed up. Bolan doesn't think he should've sent him along at all now, not even as the driver.

But he can't really blame Norris. Zimmerman told Bolan what happened to Mitchell in that place. The room that just didn't *stop*... and even though Norris never actually went inside, Bolan is aware of how disturbing those kinds of places can be. There are places in Wink you just don't go.

But all this means he had no one better to send to the funeral than Dord. Dord is not a man Bolan would trust with buttering a piece of toast. He hates looking into Dord's soft, pasty face and seeing those dull little eyes peeping back at him. He wishes now that he had sent Mallory. Mallory would've done a good job, and come back with simply piles of information. But because she is so good, Bolan has Mallory off doing another little errand tonight, one he is even more nervous about than the funeral.

He checks his watch. It should not be long now.

"So it all went quietly," says Bolan.

"Yes."

"And nobody mentioned anything of note."

"Note?"

"Nothing about, oh, foul play."

"No," says Dord.

Bolan smiles at him coldly. "That seems pretty unlikely, Dave."

"Why? I thought you said things went well up there."

"They went well. Well enough, I guess. But they know what's up." He swivels in his chair to stare out the window again. It is a black night with a strong wind, and he can see the ponderosas waving in the blue luminescence of the parking lot lights. "They know something's wrong. They just don't know if they can do anything about it."

"And they can't, right?"

Bolan stares out the window for a moment longer, watching the dancing trees. Bolan is the sort of person who has looked like he's in his late fifties for the past thirty years. He has no hair on his head except for his eyebrows and a small, snow-white goatee, and his eyes are puffy and hooded. His face does not emote particularly well: the best expression it makes is one of cynical disappointment, as if he's expected this sour turn of events and it has confirmed his worst suspicions about the world. Luckily for Bolan—or perhaps unluckily—this is the exact expression he needs to make most of the time.

From downstairs there is the sound of breaking glass, and a whoop. Bolan absently says, "Go downstairs and help Norris. It sounds like we've got a real crowd on our hands."

"Fucking truckers," says Dord, standing up.

"Yes. Fucking truckers." He does not watch as Dord leaves. He just hears the sudden burst of music as his office door opens, then closes. He's tried to soundproof his office as much as possible, for although he runs a roadhouse, he cannot stand country, specifically Nashville country. But it always finds its way in somehow.

He opens a drawer in the side of his desk. In the drawer are his two most important fallbacks: a loaded .357 Magnum, and fourteen bright pink bottles of Pepto-Bismol. With a soft grunt, Bolan plucks out one bottle, strips the cap of its protective plastic, and cracks it open. He throws away the cup that came taped to the top—the suggested dose became insufficient about a year ago—and opens up another drawer, this one containing highball glasses and paper napkins. He takes one glass and fills it to the brim with the thick, pink fluid, and then, without a moment of hesitation, he downs the entire thing. He sighs a little as he sets the glass down, its sides now coated with milky pink residue. Perhaps this will mollify the ocean of acid currently swirling around his esophagus, or perhaps not. Bolan then picks up the now-empty bottle of Pepto, gauges the distance between the desk and the trash can beside the liquor cabinet, leans back in his chair, and shoots. The bottle twirls through the air and bounces off the lip of the can to fall clattering to the floor. Bolan lets out another irritated grunt and stands to walk over to it.

As he stands he glances out the window again, and stops. The ponderosas are still dancing outside, and the parking lot is still mostly empty.

Will they call tonight? he wonders. They would have to. Too much has happened for them not to drop in. But then, they might not. They have been getting harder to predict and understand recently. Which is saying something, for them.

Bolan is not actually a resident of Wink, nor is the Roadhouse part of the town. His proximity to it is entirely coincidental: Bolan was told ten years ago that this highway route would soon be open to more trucking, and so would be a prime spot for a roadhouse, but the people who told him this were quite wrong: all the traffic to Santa Fe chose a very different route, one that bypassed him entirely. Bolan, desperate, wondered then if any of the nearby towns could possibly sustain the Roadhouse, yet all of them were too far away. Except, of course, for Wink.

For the first few years of his time at the Roadhouse, Bolan was not sure that Wink still existed. He had been told about it by several locals—something about government work decades ago—but he never met anyone from Wink, and he sure as hell didn't sell anything to them. The signposts to Wink never even seemed to lead anywhere. But one morning as he was cruising through the mountains, wondering what to do with his crumbling business, he looked down and spotted the prettiest little town square he'd ever seen, nestled at the bottom of the valley.

It stunned him. He'd had no idea it was there. It took several hours to find the way down. Perhaps, he wondered, this was why he never saw anyone from Wink—it was too hard to decipher the goddamn roads in or out. But as he drove along the town's streets, marveling at this quaint little burg he'd been living right next door to for God knew how long, he began to get a different idea.

Wink seemed to be a singularly pleasant place. The sunlight felt different here, and the trees were so big and the sidewalks so pristine and white...he actually parked his car and watched a group of boys play baseball. Bolan had no memory of something so blissfully pleasant as that short little game of three innings, but he wished he did.

Maybe no one left Wink because you'd be crazy to leave. It certainly wasn't a boomtown by any stretch of the imagination, but everyone here seemed so content.

He eventually noticed a few suspicious glances coming his way, mostly from parents. He realized what an odd figure he must cut, sitting in his bright red Camaro, watching the children play. Some residents, coming in from some errands, actually stopped on their lawns to look at him. No one said anything, but the message was clear: *We'll tolerate you for now, but that doesn't mean you're welcome here.*

Small towns, Bolan thought. *Always so damn hostile to outsiders.* He started the car, pulled away, and watched in the rearview mirror as the town disappeared in the hills. It'd seemed an interesting discovery, but a useless one—none of those people seemed like the kind to visit the Roadhouse.

Yet one day, about three years ago, he had a visitor from Wink. And the damnedest thing about it is, he cannot now remember what this visitor looked like. Bolan remembers the bright light shining down from his office lamps, and there was a man with a briefcase in the chair in front of his desk...and Bolan thinks he remembers a blue-gray suit, and a panama hat, yet the way the light struck the hat made the face below nothing but shadow...

But what the man told him he remembers very well.

Bolan eyed this strange, indistinct figure, sitting up ramrod-straight in his office chair, and he cocked an eyebrow when the man said, *I am told you are a man in dire straits.*

Well, fuck whoever told you that, then, Bolan told him.

A moment of silence. Yet Bolan did not get the impression the man was either intimidated or offended. *We have a business opportunity for you,* he said.

And Bolan said, Oh? And what kind of opportunity would that be?

And the man said, *Please lower your blinds.*

My blinds?

Yes. The blinds on the window behind your desk. Then I will show you.

And when he did this the man opened his briefcase, and there inside, packed tightly as one would pack socks and underwear, were plastic bags containing a very bright, clean white powder. *We have a business opportunity for you,* the man said again.

And Bolan listened.

Even today, Bolan is not sure where the heroin comes from. Presumably they have someone somewhere, probably Mexico, he guesses, because God knows what's up with the border these days. But Bolan, who already did a small amount of dealing when the visitor from Wink made his offer, has now managed to build a fairly respectable little kingdom up here in the mountains, and gotten quite rich. It is mostly a ferrying industry: he is not an outlet, but a warehouse. He is also not entirely sure how this happened, or why the visitor from Wink put it all in motion. What the hell did Wink, a tiny town out in the middle of nowhere, have to do with the drug trade?

Bolan does not know. But though he is indisputably the ruler of his little kingdom, he knows there is a bigger kingdom out there, one of which he's but a part. He is not sure who its king is, or even if there is one; he just knows that he makes fortunes only on the whims of someone else, and that he, like Dord and Norris and Zimmerman and Mitchell (who, he has to remind himself, is now Out of Service), takes orders and follows them without question. Now it is no longer a question of their turning off the tap on him; now he wonders what they would do if he refused.

Bolan is not stupid. He does not bite the hand that feeds him. But he has looked closely at the hand, and what he saw deeply disturbed him.

There is a reason Bolan has never gone back to Wink after that first visit. He would not even go there if you held a gun to his head. He knows what's there now.

He walks to the trash can, picks up the bottle of Pepto, and throws it away. As he returns to his desk he sees there is something on the corner: a soft pink blob of fluid. It must have been flung off the bottle when he made his shot. He wipes at it with a finger. It does not come off, but smears.

A knock at the door. "Come in," he says.

The door opens, and in walks Mallory. To his amusement, she has on a floral sundress that is yards longer than anything she usually wears. This wardrobe choice is not incidental, of course: in Wink her normal garb would attract a lot of eyes and clucking tongues, and entirely too much attention.

Mallory scowls at him. "What are you smiling at?"

"The head of the PTA, I think," he says.

"Fuck you." She walks to the liquor cabinet, a heavy canvas satchel swinging from her shoulder, and pours an absolute vat of scotch. Mimicking Bolan's own feat with the Pepto, she downs it without even blinking. Mallory is a marvelously talented woman, Bolan knows that, yet she has always been a virtuoso drinker. Back when the Roadhouse was first founded, she was its original downstairs girl, taking the boys riding high off their payday to the basement for a half hour's indulgence. After the visitor from Wink, the establishment gained customers and they hired more girls, and she became the downstairs manager, tending to all the needs and issues the girls inevitably had. And to manage it efficiently, Bolan knew, you had to have a sharp eye for human weakness, and the ruthlessness and shrewdness to act on it. As such, Mallory has assumed the unspoken role of number two at the Roadhouse.

She pours herself another, but before she can drink Bolan walks to her and gently takes the glass. "How'd it go?" he asks.

"I got it, didn't I?" She raises and lowers the shoulder with the satchel.

Bolan watches her carefully.

"I did," she says. "It went fine."

"Who did you use?"

"A junkie," she says.

"Who?" Bolan insists.

"A girl named Bonnie," says Mallory. "You don't know her."

"The same girl you used last time?"

"Yes. But I don't know if we can use her again."

Bolan cocks an eyebrow. "And why is that?"

"She's all screwed up, Tom," says Mallory. She takes the scotch back and downs it, throat clicking, and grits her teeth as it settles. "And not just because she's a goddamn junkie. She knows what we're having her do is fucking weird. She just doesn't know how."

Bolan gives a faint, unpleasant laugh. "I'm not surprised," he says. He takes the satchel off her shoulder and walks back to his desk, where he unzips it.

Inside the satchel is a polished wooden box, about the size of a cigar box. It has not been taped and tied shut; these precautions are not yet necessary. But he still feels extremely anxious holding it.

"She says she's being followed," says Mallory.

Bolan looks up. "By who?"

"She doesn't know. She doesn't actually *see* anyone, she says. But she knows it's there."

"It?"

"That's what she said."

Bolan purses his lips, then sits down on the floor behind his desk. Underneath the desk on the left-hand side is a thick metal safe. "Is that all she said?"

He hears the clink of the scotch bottle against the lip of the glass, then another click as her throat forces the scotch down. "Christ, no.

She was babbling. But she says when we send her to go get…that thing, that someone watches her. She feels something *there*, Tom, in that place underground. It watches her come in, and it watches her take that thing, and it watches her leave. But she says when she leaves, it follows her, and it keeps watching her."

Bolan twists the dial back and forth and opens the safe. Supposedly, the salesman said, this thing is so dense and impenetrable you could store uranium in it and sleep next to it and go cancer-free for years. What Bolan is about to store there is not radioactive—at least, he doesn't think it is—but he would still prefer more protection if he could get it. But if this safe were any denser it would probably break through the damn floor.

He sets the little box in his lap. Before he undoes the clasp, he asks, "Do you believe her?"

"Believe her? Are you kidding? Of course I don't believe her, she's out of her gourd."

He smiles a little. He expected that answer. Mallory is not the type to suspend her disbelief for anything. Which is a pity, because Bolan probably knows more about what is going on in Wink than anyone else, and he knows not to scoff at stories like that. So many of them turn out to be true.

He carefully undoes the bronze clasp on the box, takes a little breath, and opens it up.

Sitting inside on a cushioned interior of dark green velvet is a tiny skull. To most people it would appear grotesque but unremarkable, simply a fleshless, bleached rodent skull like that of a rat or mouse. Bolan knows it is actually a rabbit skull. Or it *appears* to be a rabbit skull. He's studied their messages, and though they did not state outright what they needed him to get—and what he in turn had someone else get for him—he can read between the lines as well as anyone.

It only *looks* like a skull. Bolan knows it is really much more than that.

He closes the box, rehooks the clasp, and places the box in the safe and shuts it. Then he sighs a little. It is getting so goddamn hard not to bite the hand that feeds him these days.

When he stands back up he sees Mallory is looking into the mirror behind the liquor cabinet shelves. She appears a little rattled, which is odd: Bolan has seen Mallory take care of stabbings and ODs without even blinking an eye, so the idea that anything could upset her is new to him.

"What is it?" he asks.

"Hm? Oh. Nothing. I was just thinking about something she said."

"The junkie?"

"Yeah. She wanted to come with me. Back to here, if you can believe it. But not for a hit or anything like that. She doesn't like being alone at night anymore. She says her dreams have changed."

"How so?"

"She says she dreams about the same thing every night now," Mallory says faintly, still staring at herself in the mirror. "She dreams about a man, standing in her bedroom. He's very tall, dressed in a dirty blue canvas suit. And he's got little wooden rabbit heads sewn all along his suit. And his *head*...she said she doesn't know if it's a helmet, or a mask, like an Indian mask or something, but it's all wooden too, all painted up like a rabbit head, with two pointy ears. He just stands there, and though she can't see his eyes she's sure he's watching her. Can you believe that, Tom?"

Bolan is silent. Again he remembers what Zimmerman told him: there was a light in the trees, and then a man was there, watching them. And they could see nothing about him except two points on his head, like horns or maybe ears...

He watches Mallory carefully. He told the boys a little bit about what they were doing on the mesa—not much, but enough—but Mallory is now coming very close to a truth Bolan would prefer to keep hidden.

"Come here," he says to her, and gestures. She walks over to the desk.

"Sit," he says, and she does so, curious.

"Let me tell you what we're going to do here, Mallory," he says. "This is some delicate work. And you've handled it delicately. But we're going to need to be even more delicate from here on out."

"What does *delicate* mean?"

Bolan opens a drawer on his desk, reaches in, and produces a small plastic baggie containing a white powder. He places it on the edge of the desk before her.

"You offering me a bump?" Mallory asks, entertained.

Bolan smiles humorlessly and shakes his head. "No. No, I am not. That shit is not pure, Mal. It is quite the *opposite* of pure. If you were to partake of that, why, you'd be pale and stiff within an hour. Do you see?"

Mallory glances at the baggie again. "No."

"Well, let me explain. Sometime soon—not now, but soon—you're going to go back to that girl of yours..."

"Bonnie."

"Right. Bonnie. You're going to go back to her and make her run that route in the tunnels again."

"She's not going to want to do that, Tom," says Mallory. "She's shook up as it is."

"Well, that's tough, because you're going to make her. She's not going to have a choice. Not the way her good friend Mallory sells it."

Mallory is quiet for a bit. "And how is she going to sell it?"

He smiles again. "Mallory's going to say that she's carrying some seriously quality shit, and she'd be all too happy to pass it along if Bonnie does this one little favor again for her," says Bolan. "For us."

For a while there is silence, broken only by the whoops from downstairs.

Mallory looks back at the little white baggie. "And where does that enter into it?" she asks.

Bolan stares at her balefully with his hooded, puffy eyes. "Are you fucking stupid, Mal?" he asks. "Don't tell me you're fucking stupid.

Because I know you, and I know you're not fucking stupid. You're a very smart girl. That's why I keep you around, right?"

"I'm not...I can't do something like that."

"But you can, and you will. You're going to do it, Mal. It's going to happen. That girl has too many stories rolling around in her head. She did some real choice work for us, sure, but things are getting too hot to just leave her walking around." He nods at the baggie. "This is the easy way. We don't want to do it the hard way. I know the hard way, Mal, and it's hard on everyone."

Mallory looks from the baggie to Bolan, and her eyes gain a steely glint. "Who's saying to do this? Is it you? Or is it them?"

Bolan stares back impassively. "It doesn't matter."

"It does matter."

"No, it doesn't. Because it's going to happen, one way or another, so who gives the order is irrelevant."

Mallory loses a little color, but the steely glint grows. Bolan is amused and surprised by this reaction: Mal's never personally killed anyone, sure, but he knows she's seen people die. What does it matter, he thinks, whose hand does the actual act?

"Who's it for?" she asks.

"Who's what for?"

"The skulls. I know who the last one was for. They just buried him today, for God's sakes. So who is this one meant for?" Her eyes thin. "And, if you're making me run her again, the next?"

Bolan, who has been perfectly still throughout this, grows even stiller. Then he stands up, walks around his desk, and sits down in the chair beside her. He watches her with his hooded eyes, disappointed. Because they are not discussing a murder: this is business, and Mal is inconveniencing him.

He takes a breath, the air whistling through his nostrils, and lets it out. Then he snatches out with his thick boxer's hands and grabs Mallory's head by the temples. Mallory cries out and tries to push back, but Bolan is extremely strong, and this is a dance he knows too well.

He pulls her close, close enough that his breath washes over her face. "Are you going to fucking do it?" he asks. "Huh? You had better, girl, you had fucking better. Because though I need you, and I *do* need you, you got an easy job here. I ain't asking you to put a bullet in her or cut her any, but I could and I'd expect you to do it. I'm just asking you to give her a dose. And you're going to give her a dose, Mal. Because like I said, the hard way is hard on everyone, but it'll be especially hard on you."

Mallory groans and screams and struggles against him, but Bolan knows no one can hear over the noise from downstairs. "What do you say?" he breathes. "What do you say, Mal? What do you fucking say?"

Then he stops. She stops moving as well.

A small white light has just lit up on his desk. Both of them freeze and look. Then they look back at one another, wondering what to do next.

Bolan's mouth twists. He shoves her away and stands up. "Stay right there," he says.

Mallory laughs and looks up at him, grinning. "They whistle and you come running, is that it?"

Bolan makes a move to hit her, and she flinches and raises an arm. But he lowers his hand and adjusts his collar. "Stay right fucking there," he says again, and he goes to his closet door and opens it.

Behind it is a low, dark hallway with foam-soundproofed walls. There is only one light, a bare bulb hanging by a wire from the ceiling at the very end. This bulb is always on. Bolan has to change it every two weeks.

Below the light is a very curious contraption. It stands on a small iron pedestal, and is protected by a tall glass dome. It has a wide, round, heavy base, and a bronze frame, and many small gears and wheels laid against one another. The biggest wheel holds a large roll of white tape, and the machine is clacking and clicking away merrily, writing something out on the tape. Once, decades ago, the machine was used to print out the prices of stocks, recording the falling and rising of fortunes and making a small pile of financial data on the ground. But Bolan knows that what it is printing now is definitely not stock prices.

He shuts the door carefully behind him and locks it. This side of the door has been soundproofed as well. He cannot afford to have anyone listening to the conversations he has in here.

He takes a breath and walks to the stock ticker. It has just printed out a very small message, composed in neat, staggered writing. He picks it up (trying hard not to notice his trembling hands) and reads:

WHO   THE
        WAS   GIRL

"What?" Bolan asks. He does not direct this to the stock ticker, but to the air just above it. "What girl? Which girl do you mean?" He wonders if they mean Bonnie, or Mallory, or maybe even some other girl they used for…whatever. Bolan has so many plates spinning on so many poles, sometimes it's hard for him to keep them straight.

And then, despite all the soundproofing, and no one being nearby that Bolan can see, a response ticks out. As it always does.

THE   AT   FUNERAL   THE   CAR
    GIRL   THE   IN   RED

"I don't know what you're talking about," says Bolan. "I had a man at the funeral. He didn't see…" He pauses. Then he sighs, shuts his eyes, and pinches the bridge of his nose. *Fucking Dord!* he thinks, but he dares not say this out loud. *Fucking dumbshit fucking Dord! Didn't see or hear anything, did you?*

Bolan swallows. "You may be right," he says. "I apologize for missing this. What would you like me to do?"

The stock ticker comes to life again. It prints out:

FIND   WHO   IS
OUT   SHE

"I will," says Bolan. "I promise I will. I'll find out right away and let you know. Is that all you want me to do?"

The stock ticker does not answer. It is not dead, he knows, but dormant. Sometime, maybe soon, it will come to life again.

He tears off the tape, takes out a lighter, and sets it alight. Then he drops it on the floor and watches it wither into ash before stamping it out. The floor is black and ashen there. It has been for years. How many secret orders has he taken here? he thinks. How many cryptic little messages has he burned at this spot? Sometimes they are so simple: pick up a box there, mail it here; have someone put a line of paint on this window; threaten this man, and mention this woman; or, perhaps, go trawling through the sewers of Wink looking for a dark, tiny passageway that ends in a round chamber, and in this chamber will be a pile of many, many little skulls, and you must bring one skull to this person at this place, but you must be so, so careful not to touch it...

And now this. There is someone new in Wink, something that has not happened in years, and Bolan missed it.

He charges back down out of the hall and storms into his office. Mallory is at the liquor cabinet again, hair fixed and dress arranged as if nothing has happened: she is a creature used to abuse, both the giving and receiving of it.

"Bad news?" she asks.

"Go and get Dord," Bolan snarls.

"Why?"

Bolan marches over to her, takes the glass out of her hand, and flings it against the wall. It shatters, leaving a dark stain spreading on the crimson wallpaper. "Go and get fucking Dord," he says. "Or so help me God you will be drinking out of a fucking straw, you hear me?"

"Fine," Mallory says mildly, and—with an intentionally slow, graceful pace—walks out the door and down the stairs.

Bolan stands in his office for a moment, fists clenched. Then he looks back down the hall at the stock ticker. He half expects it to move, printing out some other harrowing little request. But it does not, and thankfully remains silent. He shuts the closet door, locks it, and leans up against it as if there were something behind it fighting to get out. Then he lets out a breath.

The stock ticker was installed in his office not long after he made his agreement with the visitor from Wink. There was no explanation offered: the installation crew, all blank-faced little men in gray jumpsuits, just handed him an envelope with his name on it before walking into the Roadhouse and going to work. Inside was a card that read:

PAY ATTENTION.

And for the past three years it has ticked out orders for him now and again, and each time he obeyed his fortunes improved. Only once did he dare get curious: he examined the cord running to the ticker and followed it throughout the Roadhouse, through the walls and across the ceilings and down the stairs (and how did the installation men do that in an hour? Had they been, he wondered, secretly entering the Roadhouse during closed hours and laying yet more line?) until it went outside, snaking into the lot behind in a small tin pipe... where it finally ended in the woods, the end of the pipe unsealed and open. When Bolan found this, he stared at it. The pipe went nowhere? How could that be? But his confusion increased when he knelt and peered into the pipe, and saw the end of the fraying wire exposed, unconnected to anything at all.

The night after he followed the pipe into the woods, the stock ticker printed out a single command, and this time it was familiar:

PAY
ATTENTION.

Now, whenever the ticker springs to life, Bolan's heart almost stops. He does not know how it receives any signal, but, like so many things in his new endeavors, he does not really want to know.

But sometimes they send someone along to make sure he gets the message. And tonight, as Bolan waits for Dord to come lumbering up the stairs to explain why he missed the arrival of this new girl in the red car, he wonders again if they will come.

He walks to the window, but does not look out. He shuts his eyes, hoping to see nothing. Then he opens them.

There, standing in the center of the blue spotlight of the farthest parking lot lamp, someone looks back at him. The figure is so far away that it is tiny... but Bolan is sure he can make out a blue-gray suit, and a white panama hat, and below that a face lost in shadow...

The white hat inclines slightly, then rises up again: a nod. Then its owner steps back into the darkness, and is gone.

CHAPTER SEVEN

Mona's night at the Ponderosa Acres did not go well. She found no restful sleep in a place where the air felt so stale and undisturbed, and though she knew there were no other boarders she never felt alone. And sometime around one thirty she awoke—or she *thinks* she awoke, because the whole thing might have been a dream—with the strong conviction that something was wrong, and she went to the window and saw someone standing in the parking lot perfectly still with his hands at his sides, his face and front darkened by the yellow streetlight behind him. Though Mona felt a great unease at the sight of this person, she was not sure if he saw her or not; he might not have been looking at the motel at all. He made her think of an escapee from a mental institution, wandering aimlessly and wondering what to do with all this freedom in a strange new world. She must not have been terribly disturbed by this, she thinks as she fumbles through her morning routine in the motel room, if she went back to bed after.

Once she gets herself cleaned up she goes to see Parson. The morning sky is blindingly blue, and the air is crisp and cold. She finds it hard to reconcile this sky with the one last night, dark and wreathed with blue lightning and burdened with the pink moon.

When she enters the front office she sees that the darkness from last night was concealing absolutely nothing: the office is completely empty save for the card table and the desk. It feels like an awful waste of space. Parson is sitting at the table playing Chinese checkers as if he's never left the spot. He is too involved in his game to look at her when she enters: he purses his lips judiciously, scratches a temple, and begins to make a move before suddenly rethinking, his hand darting back as if the checkers were poison. He shakes his head, silently scolding himself for considering such a poor choice.

"Do you often play checkers by yourself?" Mona asks.

He looks up, surprised. "By myself?" he asks. Then he smiles and laughs, as if this is a grand joke. "Ah, I see. By myself...very good."

Mona chooses to change the subject. "Any idea how the probate courts work around here?"

Parson sets his coffee aside to think. "I am not sure about probate courts. There is only one court, though, and only one court officer—Mrs. Benjamin."

"There's only one officer? How does that work?"

"Very well, apparently," says Parson. "There is not exactly much to do in the courts here. I believe it is overstaffed with just one person, really."

"And where is this Mrs. Benjamin?"

"In the courthouse. Her office occupies the majority of the basement. You need only find a set of stairs there—any stairs will do—and go down them. Inevitably, you will find her."

"Where's the courthouse at?" Mona asks, slipping on her sunglasses.

"It's in the center of the park, which is in the center of the town. Go inward. If you find yourself on the border of town—and it would not take very long—then you have missed it."

"You can't give me any street directions?"

"I could," says Parson, "but they would not be as good."

"Fine," says Mona, and thanks him.

"Are you hungry?" asks Parson earnestly, as if her allowing herself to be hungry would be an abominable crime. "I can spare you another complimentary breakfast, if so, even though you have already eaten yours."

As Mona has kicked the habit of morning beers, she politely declines. "When's checkout time?"

Parson appears to debate getting up and going to his desk and rifling through his cards and papers again, but instead he just shrugs. "Whenever you check out, I suppose."

"Is it okay if I leave my stuff here until I figure out how long I'll be staying? I don't expect that they'll let me have the house too easy."

But Parson has glanced at his board of checkers again and spied some brilliant move hidden among the pattern of marbles. With an impatient wave he returns to the game and the unoccupied seat across from him, and does not notice when Mona leaves.

As Mona drives across Wink all the sprinklers start to come on, not instantly, but in a slow, graceful procession, like water jets in a huge fountain, starting at the corner of one block and moving down to the next. In the morning light the streams of water take on a white glow, and when they begin waving back and forth, each one a little more delayed than the last, Mona feels like she's watching a synchronized-swimming performance. It isn't until she's near the end of the block that she realizes the idea of watering a lawn here is strange: they're in the high desert mountains, with barren scrub less than half a mile away. It feels impossible that she should find so many soft, verdant lawns lining the streets, and Mona glances up at the mountains and the mesa to confirm they're still there.

All around her the town is coming to life. An old woman wobbles out on her porch with a watering can to fuss with a splendid bougainvillea that appears to need no attention at all. Fathers climb into their sedans and trucks and—rarely—their luxury cars and slowly cruise out onto the cement streets. Eventually Mona realizes she does not think of them as just men: they are all *fathers*, they have to be, for why else would they wear such bland but imposing suits and plaid shirts, and choose such stolid, unassuming hairstyles? For God's sake, one of them is even smoking a pipe.

On one street a clutch of aproned mothers herd their children out onto their driveways and into cars, each child swinging a tiny tin lunchbox. Mona slows a little as she passes them. Though she wants to ignore it, the perfection of the scene is powerfully striking.

No, she thinks. *Not today. I won't go there today.*

She speeds up.

She passes the diner, whose enormous, curving neon sign says CHLOE'S. It's evidently a hot spot, with parking spaces rapidly disappearing even as Mona watches. But what she finds most curious about it is what is happening in the back alley. She slows again to watch: there are two women there, each in pale pink waitress uniforms with their hair up and little white caps nestled in the exact center. One is much older and more mature, holding herself with the posture of a confident, seasoned veteran. She stands to the side and watches the other, a girl not even out of her teens. The girl is walking down the alley in a measured stride with a waiting tray balanced in one hand. The veteran watches keenly and barks out an order, and the girl makes an abrupt turn and paces from one side of the alley to the other. On the tray, Mona sees, are five pie pans, but they do not contain pies, but marbles. One pan shifts a little bit—just a centimeter to the left or so—and the marbles clatter around in the pan. The girl blanches but recovers, ferrying the tray of marbles back across the alley with a grim face and more care than a surgeon. *Practice*, Mona thinks, and she smiles as she passes them.

Mona has not yet considered living here in Wink. She's inherited a house but not a life, and she has determinedly avoided having a life for several years, choosing instead barren roads and empty motel rooms. Yet now, somewhere in one of the closets in the back of her mind, she imagines what it would be like to live in this tiny town, where carrying pies is a serious, studied art and the sprinklers put on a balletic performance every morning.

She warms to the idea. The world has been so big to her for the past years that it is very inviting to imagine it so small.

No wonder her mother was happy here. Though the town is odd, it seems it would be difficult to be *un*happy here. It is like a place Mona dreamed about once, but she can't remember when or what exactly she dreamed about. There is something to these clean streets and swaying pines that sends a stir of echoes fluttering up in her mind.

Her tour of the town is not entirely peaceful, she notices. Everywhere she goes, people watch her. She can't blame them: she cannot imagine anything more out of place than the Charger, with its bright red paint and guttering engine, not to mention its driver, who is looking back at them from behind silvered glasses and years of careful cynicism. But they are not just surprised, nor are they mistrustful: it is as if they are waiting for something, like this bright red muscle car and its strange driver are just a loose end someone will soon take care of.

The park at the center of town is quite large, constructed in a perfect circle with the clean white stone courthouse in one half. But it is the structure in the other half that attracts Mona's attention: at first she thinks it is just a huge white ball the size of a small building, but as she pulls into the courthouse parking lot she sees its curves are actually angled, formed of tiny triangles. It looks like a smaller version of that enormous, spherical structure she always glimpsed in the ads for Walt Disney World as a kid. There is no sign indicating why this space-age-looking sculpture sits in this picturesque little park. It is as if it's rolled here from down out of the mountains, and no one's bothered to move it.

Mona immediately stops when she walks through the front doors of the courthouse, for the interior is in such extreme contrast to the exterior that it takes her brain a moment to process it. On the outside it is a happy little white building, yet its interior, or at least its lobby, is musty and dim. She takes off her sunglasses, but it makes no difference: the floors are a dark, sick yellow marble, and the walls are neglected imitation wood. Somewhere an air-conditioning unit clunks asthmatically, and there is a dusty breeze rippling through the close air.

An obese security guard at the front desk looks up from his book when she enters. She watches as his eyes perform a motion very familiar to her: they widen a little, then leap down to her feet and slowly trail up her body, taking in every detail. It is disappointingly predictable, a ritual that must be completed before she can begin a conversation with nearly any man (and the occasional woman). With his eyes still fixed on her, the guard mindlessly turns a page in his book—*The Secret Joys of Lake Champlain*—but says nothing.

"I'm here to see Mrs. Benjamin," says Mona.

The guard continues staring at her with his little eyes. Then he nods his head. Mona is not sure what this gesture means, but she walks ahead into the dark hallway. She glances back and sees the guard is leaning forward in his seat, head craned out to stare at her. Even while he is in this position one of his hands turns another page in his book, though his attention is nowhere near the text.

The hall ends in a series of strange decorations. First is a large, colorful mural that is familiar to Mona, though she can't say where she saw it: it shows a green atomic model of an element encased in a ray of gold light. Beside this optimistic sight is a display case with many taxidermied specimens of local fauna. The little songbirds are fixed in the same position as the hawks—wings raised up and head ducked forward, a raptor beginning its dive-bomb—as if the taxidermist knew only one pose for birds. Next to the display case is a door with a framed picture hanging from the exact center. Its frame is curling and gilded, like something in a museum, though it needs dusting. Under the glass is a piece of parchment with a single word written on it in careful calligraphy. It reads STAIRS.

Mona looks back again. The guard is still in the same pose, leaning forward and watching her with unabashed fascination. She hears a little *flit* and though she cannot see she knows he's turned another page. Then she opens the door and starts down the stairs.

When Mona reaches the bottom it's so dark it takes her eyes a moment to adjust. It looks almost like a forest, many trunks with spindly branches at the top and a thin white light filtering through from above...

It is not a forest, she sees: she is looking at dozens and dozens of immense wooden filing cabinets all along the walls. Piled on the tops of the cabinets are mounted heads, mostly deer, lying on their backs with their horns rising up in spiked tangles. There are so many horns that they look almost like tree branches, and now that her eyes have adjusted she sees that there are many types of horns, some the traditional twelve-point, some curling rams' horns, so there must be many species.

Mona walks forward into the labyrinth of filing cabinets. As she moves she finds there is another scent in the air, buried below the aroma of old paper and formaldehyde, something like rotten pine. She rounds a corner and sees there is a big wooden table ahead, and unlike the rest of the furniture in this place it has a surface that is clear, except for four things: a box labeled OUT, a box labeled IN (both empty), a small desk light, and a cup of tea sitting on a saucer. Hanging from the front of the desk is a sign so similar to the one on the stairway door she's sure it was made by the same person. This one reads M. BENJAMIN!

Mona walks to the front of the desk. The tea stinks horribly: it is a thick, muddy, piney concoction that has left a dark brown residue on the sides of the cup. It does not look like something the human digestive system could make any sense of.

"Hello?" she calls.

There is a flurry of noise from among the cabinets behind the desk. "Hello?" says a voice, surprised. Then a woman emerges from some hidden passageway in the back. Though she is quite elderly, seventy at least, she is still enormous, over six feet tall, with wide shoulders and big hands. Yet she is dressed in the most matronly way possible: her hair is an immense, gray-blond cloud, and her dress suffers from an abundance of purple fabric and gray polka dots. A string of thick pearls rings her skinny neck. She blinks quickly as she totters out of the shadows to the desk. "Oh," she says when she sees Mona. "Hello." With a long, soft grunt, she sits down, face politely puzzled.

"I'm here about a house, ma'am," Mona says.

"Which house?" asks the woman, and she fixes a set of spectacles to her nose.

"Uh, this one on Larchmont here. I inherited it."

"Inherited it?" asks the woman. "Oh. And…are you a current resident?"

"No, ma'am, I'm not, but I have all the paperwork here, or at least, you know, a hell of a lot of it," says Mona. She produces her folder with all the documentation and begins to hand the pages out to the woman, who is presumably Mrs. Benjamin.

Mona expects her to begin sorting through them officiously, like any world-weary bureaucrat, but Mrs. Benjamin simply holds one paper—the copy of the will—and stares helplessly at the rest of the pile. "Oh," she says. Then, hopefully, "Are you sure?"

"Pardon?"

"Are you sure you inherited a house here? I must admit, it's not very common. Most properties bequeathed are usually bequeathed to people already living here."

"I'm just going by what the paper says," says Mona. "I had a couple of courts say it was all legit back in Texas, and I'd hate to have come all this way for nothing. I understand the will expires in less than a week, too."

"I see," says Mrs. Benjamin. Finally she begins to pick through the paperwork. "And you would be Mrs. Bright?"

"Miss. Yes."

Mona expects her to ask for identification, but she says, "Wait. I remember you…weren't you in the red car yesterday? At the funeral?"

"Uh, yes. That was me."

"Ah," says Mrs. Benjamin. "You were the source of a bit of gossip, my dear."

"Sorry."

"Oh, these things happen," says Mrs. Benjamin carelessly. "Honestly, it helped lighten the mood a little."

"Who passed away, if I might ask?"

"Mr. Weringer." She looks at Mona like this should mean something. When Mona does not react, she asks, "Did you know him?"

"I just got in last night, ma'am."

"I see. Well, he was...a very well-respected member of the town. We've been all in a tizzy ever since."

"How'd he die?"

But Mrs. Benjamin has turned her attention to the papers, squinting at the faint, staggered writing. "I don't recall any Brights ever living here..."

"The original owner was Laura Alvarez."

"I do not recall any Alvarezes, either," she says, with an inflection that implies—*and I would*. A thought strikes her, and she peers up at Mona and asks, "Can you please step back a little?"

"I'm sorry?"

"Can you step back? Into the light? So I can see you better."

Mona obliges her, and Mrs. Benjamin peers at her through her tiny spectacles. Through their lenses the old woman's eyes appear very far back in her head, like they are too small for their sockets, and she looks at Mona as if searching for something in her face, some familiarity or flaw that would tell her far more about Mona than any crumbling old paperwork.

"Are you really sure about this, my dear?" she asks finally. "You don't seem like someone who should be here...perhaps you ought to go home."

"Excuse me?" says Mona, indignant.

"I see," says Mrs. Benjamin mildly. "Well. If you are sure, then you are sure. Your paperwork seems to all be in order. It shouldn't be an issue. Let me check a few things." She stands, smiles at Mona, and hobbles off into the cabinets.

"I am so sorry for my rudeness," says Mrs. Benjamin's voice from the back. "You surprised me. We have not had any new arrivals here for years. I should've introduced myself—my name is Mrs. Benjamin."

"Yeah, I kind of figured," says Mona. "You do all the court work here?"

"I do. There's not a lot of activity. So I mostly do crosswords, but please don't tell anyone." She laughs. Mona suspects it's a well-worn joke she enjoys trotting out.

"You seem to, uh...have quite a few deer heads in here."

"Oh, yes. Storage, you see. They used to have them all throughout the courthouse. I am not sure why, but dead things were the primary decoration in Wink for many years. Now I'm stuck with them down here. But they do make me feel a little less lonely on slow days."

Mona glances into the frozen amber stare of one ratty old buck's head. She has no idea how anyone could take comfort from such a thing.

There is the sound of old, creaky drawers being pulled. "Larchmont...I believe I know the house, actually," says Mrs. Benjamin. "It is abandoned."

"I've heard."

"For a while it wasn't. After its initial abandonment, possession was ceded to the town. Someone scooped it up and it was rented out to a family who lived there for a short time."

"But you don't have *any* record of a previous owner?"

"My records go back to 1978, and indicate it was abandoned," says Mrs. Benjamin. "But then my predecessor was *not* the most organized of people. It was swiftly abandoned again, though."

"Why?"

"Oh. There was a mishap."

"What, is it haunted or something?"

A goose cry of laughter sounds from the cabinets. "Haunted?" says Mrs. Benjamin, delighted. "Oh, no, no. It was one of the buildings struck by lightning. Hit the little girl, who was bathing in the tub at the time."

"My God," says Mona. "Was she all right?"

"No," says Mrs. Benjamin primly. She hobbles back out of the cabinet passageways. "Here we are. This will only take a moment for me to get everything filled out and filed. I have the number of the locksmith. You should be able to move into the house this afternoon, if you'd like."

"That fast? I thought there'd be more of a turnaround time."

"Well, I suppose there normally would be, as it needs to be

approved by various officials of several different agencies...but luckily for you, these are all me. And I approve. Isn't that nice of me?" She takes out a tackle box full of rubber stamps and begins applying them to Mona's paperwork with a surprising ferocity.

"What happened to the house after it got struck by lightning? Is it all right?"

"Oh, it's fine," says Mrs. Benjamin. "Unlike some of the others. But it was never rented out again after, I know that. It was eventually abandoned again."

"Pardon me, but did you say other buildings were hit by lightning?"

"Yes."

"Like...in the same *storm*?"

Mrs. Benjamin looks up at her. "Oh, has no one told you about the lightning storm yet?"

"I just got in last night," she says again.

"It was a historic event for the town," says Mrs. Benjamin, with the relish of a gossip revisiting an old tragedy. "Many buildings were struck and burned down. Some pessimistic people believe we never recovered. I don't agree with that, but it certainly was something. Why, it hit one of the trees in the park and split it in half. It even hit the dome, but, well, the dome being the dome, no damage was done."

"Is that that...ball thing out front?"

"Yes, in the park. It is a"—she thinks—"a *geodesic* dome. A model of what they thought future architecture would look like. They constructed it long ago, back when the town was first built, I think. They were dead wrong, of course." Mrs. Benjamin takes a breath. "My God, I've just about used up all the air in here, haven't I? And heaven knows there wasn't much to start with." She glances at Mona, sensing an audience, and asks, "Are you interested in the town's history much, dear?"

At first Mona wants to say no, she isn't. Small-town history is the same all over. Yet this is not just any town: this is her mother's hometown. She feels an unexpected duty to hear more of this place, to give its history context and color in her head, and perhaps doing so would color in a bit of her mother, too. She might even learn why her mother was here, and why she left. "You know what, I think I'd enjoy that," she says.

"Excellent. You must come around tomorrow and have lunch with me and the rest of the girls. It'll serve as a good greeting from all of us. Now, don't get the wrong impression—they are not all old hens like me. Some of them are sprightly young things, like yourself. And I assure you, I keep my house in much better order than I do my office. I'll be curious to hear what you think of my tea."

Mona glances down at the cup of stinking brown swill. She is speechless at the idea of drinking it.

"Do you know what the secret ingredient is?" asks Mrs. Benjamin, and her eyes grow wide and her voice a little soft. Somewhere a clunking air conditioner gets louder, building to a moan.

"No," says Mona.

"It's resin," says Mrs. Benjamin. "The blood or pitch of a pine. You find it while walking in the woods, usually. All the trees will be hale and hearty, but then you'll see one that will have a ragged wound, or some unsightly bulge. The tree will look a little bent, perhaps, or its leaves will have an orange tint to them. That is because the tree is *dying*, you see. It is bleeding out. The bulges are what I prefer, their resin is white or yellow and is quite viscous. It looks almost like butter. It gives such a good taste to the tea. Of course, it is pretty solid stuff. They use it to make torches, after all. You have to dissolve it in a little bit of wood alcohol...it's the only way to get it down." She smiles, and Mona sees her teeth are small and amber-brown, just like the eyes of the goats and deer around her, and they glisten queerly in the faint light of the basement. "Perhaps I'll make you some. It makes the rest of the day go so much better."

"I guess I can see that," says Mona, who suddenly wants nothing more than to get away from this strange place filled with cabinets and dead things and the perfume of wood alcohol and pitch.

"Well, I won't hold you up," she says. "I am sure you want to see the house. Run along, and I'll look forward to hearing all about it later."

"All right," says Mona. She begins backing away, papers clutched tightly in her hands.

"Good day," says Mrs. Benjamin, and she laughs quietly, as if enjoying some private joke, and she returns to her work, muttering and humming to herself in several clashing octaves.

CHAPTER EIGHT

The careful striae of small towns. Invisible boundaries, reflecting pay grade, church attendance, model of home. Blue-collar neighborhoods with open garages packed to bursting; houses deeply set in wooded copses, accessible only by winding driveways—the upper crust, surely; then packed, denuded, Puritanical homes, white and harsh and cauterized. The value of the cars (all American) fluctuates wildly from street to street. Crowds of children at play burst out of hedges, then disappear like flocks of pigeons wheeling over cityscapes. In all yards and at all corners, people wave constantly, at everything and everyone, hello hello and how d'ye do, and how d'ye do again.

And there, just on the corner ahead, below a big, leaning spruce, is a low adobe home she's seen before, though last time it was rendered in the yellow hues and dusky shadows of instant film taken decades ago.

Mona pulls up in front of her mother's house. The sense of déjà vu is overpowering. She sits in the car for a while, just staring at it. She knows she has never been here, but she can't help but feel as if she has, as if Earl and Laura once swung by this house on a summer vacation when Mona was still terribly young, and she now has only echoes of the memory.

Once, she knows, a woman in a tight blue dress greeted her friends on that front walk, and then they had a pleasant afternoon in the backyard, with cocktails and gossip and, maybe later in the evening, a little too much candor. Perhaps she or a friend commented,

"Mountains are pink—time to drink!" and laughed and thoughtlessly scrawled it on the back of a photo and forgot about it, leaving it to be tossed in with some meaningless papers from work and travel hundreds of miles to the bleak oil flats of West Texas.

It all feels so impossible. It was one thing to learn via papers and photos that her mother had once been happy and whole, but it is quite another to actually see the real, definite place where she lived her life.

Mona feels like the victim of a crime. It is *wrong* for her mother to have been someone else once. It is not *just* that Mona was stuck with the frail, decaying husk she became.

But finally she climbs out, legs wobbling and eyes watering, and she sits down on the front step like a latchkey kid and waits for the locksmith to come.

She gets enough control over herself to take stock of the house while she waits. Parson was right—the house is in very good shape. There isn't a weed in the yard, the grass is watered, and unless she's wrong the house even has a new layer of adobe.

When the locksmith comes she asks him about it. "It was probably your neighbors," he says. "I'm sure they didn't go in, they just kept the place tidy."

"Well, that's kind of them. Do you know which neighbor? I'd like to thank them. I'm willing to bet this adobe stuff isn't cheap." She looks at the neighboring houses. There are no visible cars, and all the garages are shut. There's only one old man, who sits in his front yard in a lawn chair and watches her with open curiosity.

Mona memorizes his address and makes note of his shoes and his watch. *Stop it*, she thinks. *He's just an old man. And you, Miss Bright, are not a fucking cop anymore.*

"Oh, no," says the locksmith. "We just take care of things here. Or someone does." He looks at the red Charger, and she can see he recognizes it from the funeral. He begins to look a little worried. "You're new here, right?"

She nods.

He hesitates, as though he is about to say something against his better judgment. "You know not to go out at night, right?"

"I think I was told the mountains can be dangerous...is that it?"

"Sort of," he says, discomfited.

"Is there a curfew?"

"No, nothing official like that. It's kind of a rule. It's probably okay here, where it's so close to downtown. But I wouldn't go too far. People get lost real easy. It's hard to see where you're going in the night." He looks across the street and at the tall pines behind the houses, as if he's already making sure everything around him is safe, even though it is hardly mid-afternoon. He's so eager to leave he gets all the locks changed within a half hour and even undercharges her. He practically sprints to his truck. Mona watches him go, and then opens the front door to her house.

The interior has been done in what Mona thinks of as a ranch style, or maybe a lodge or cabin style, with lots of knotty natural-wood surfaces. The rooms are low and wide with cedar or ponderosa crossbeams, Mona can't tell which. There isn't a stick of furniture in here, except in one corner, where there's a single wooden chair and, interestingly enough, an aquamarine rotary phone that's plugged into the wall. She walks to it and sees it is covered in ages' worth of dust. She grimaces and picks up the receiver, her hand immediately smearing with gray, and holds it close to her ear. To her surprise, there's a dial tone.

She hangs it up and walks throughout the house, wiping her hand on her shorts. There is a wide foyer that ends in a set of rustic wooden stairs leading to a second-floor balcony. She can see light spots on the wooden floor where furniture stood for years on end. The same faint patches appear in spots on the wall where pictures once hung. It's like she's in a room of reverse shadows.

She walks through the hallway to the living room and kitchen in the back. Everything is done in Mid-Century Modern, with butcher-block countertops and huge, bulky sinks. The oven has only one dial, and she's pretty sure that if she uses the microwave, which is the size of a couch, she'll be sterile for the rest of her life.

So this was Momma's kitchen, she thinks. Mona herself hasn't had a real one in years. But she chose that, of course, preferring wandering purgatory over a real life, so burned was she by her last attempt. She is not sure she wants to try again here. Thinking about it makes her stomach hurt.

She walks through a set of French doors to the backyard. Unlike the front, it hasn't been maintained at all. There's no grass on the ground, but dull orange gravel, and ivy has taken over, strangling what might have once been a small tree and bowing down the back of the fence. Beyond the fence are pink crags striped with crimson. Mona tilts her head, thinking. They're the same crags she saw in the background of the photo of afternoon cocktails, unchanged after decades.

There is a lump of ivy in the center of the yard. She walks to it and takes one huge vine and pulls. Whatever it's attached to is heavy as hell, but there's a squawk of iron on stone. She plants a foot on the lump, wraps the twist of ivy around her wrist, and tugs.

A significant strip tears away. Below it is a rust-covered wrought-iron table. The very iron table her mother and her friends sat around for cocktail hour, she thinks.

The sense of déjà vu increases. She turns around and looks at the back of the house, which is just as picturesque as the front, despite the messy backyard. Some of the clay hanging pots have even been left behind, though now of course they are empty. Once, though, they were probably bursting with geranium blooms or drapes of ice plants. She feels an intense happiness when she imagines this.

This house, though it is empty, feels perfect in some way. It's all anyone could ever want. This is a place to raise children, to live a life. This is the kind of house you dream of living in as a kid.

But she glances to the side and sees the neighboring homes, and she thinks that the same could be said of them, and the ones across the street. There is something strangely perfect about this part of town. It is like she's walking through old photographs or home movies, images layered with longing and nostalgia. Even if they are hollow or overgrown with ivy on the inside.

She walks back inside and resumes her tour. She has no idea what her mother did with all this room, nor can she imagine how she afforded such a big place. She must have been a pretty big wheel at Coburn, whatever it was they did there. Upstairs are smaller rooms, ones probably used as kids' rooms by the family that rented this house in the interim. Which means that somewhere around here would be...

She opens one small door at the end of a hallway and is greeted by a tiny bathroom with one wooden wall of a much lighter color than the other four. It's newer, she guesses, and unvarnished. Up against the wall is a white bathtub, and running down the center of it in a thin, long V is a stain of deep black with faint, spidery edges, and she notices the linoleum around the tub is bubbled and curling, like it's been cooked.

This is where the lightning struck. It must've split the wall like an ax and come shrieking down on anyone who was in the tub. Much of the bathroom is still smoky and charred. The faucet is even fused shut, and its knobs droop a little, like a Dali painting.

Mona steps out of the room and shuts the door. She is relieved to have the sight hidden from her, for the ruined bathroom feels very out of place with the rest of the house. It's as if it belonged to another house entirely, one dark and broken and empty, not at all part of this happy, rustic place.

Suddenly there is the peal of a high-pitched bell, and Mona gasps and jumps. She leans up against the wall to catch her breath as the bell rings again. She wonders if it could be the doorbell, but it is not.

She walks downstairs to the aquamarine phone sitting in the corner beside the wooden chair, the one that looks like it's been sitting there for years, and stares as it rings again and again. Finally she answers it.

"Hello?"

There is the hiss of static, as if the call is coming from a very long way away. But there is no voice in it, no greeting back.

"Hello?" she says again.

Still nothing. But somewhere in the static she hears something: someone is breathing, lowly and slowly.

"Hello?" she says. "I can hear you. Did you get the wrong number?"

She expects the caller to hang up, but he or she does not. There is just the breathing, the whine of the static rising and falling like a theremin.

"I think there's something wrong with the phones, whoever this is," she says. "You can't hear a damn thing I say, can you?"

No answer.

"I'm hanging up now," she says. "Goodbye."

She drops the receiver onto the cradle and stares at it. She almost expects the phone to start ringing again, but it does not.

Mona will be damned if she's come all this way and done so much work just to sleep on a wooden floor, so she cruises around for a department store to put together something resembling livable conditions. She finds Macey's, a sort of general store, though like so many shops here at first it seems totally abandoned. She isn't worried, however: she knows many stores in small towns keep wildly irregular hours, often opening whenever the owners feel.

It is not abandoned. She is walking by the lines of mannequins in dresses when she hears the sound of someone weeping. Curious, she turns around and sees the door to a back room is open, and seated within are two women with their faces in their hands. She can see a pair of feet wearing men's shoes just before them, like someone is standing or leaning against the front of a desk. She can hear a man's voice talking quietly, as if giving comfort or condolences. Then the feet shift, and a small, bald head wearing Coke-bottle glasses pokes past the side of the door frame. The man looks at her and says, "With you in a minute."

He wraps up the discussion with the two crying women pretty quick. It is a little bizarre to see them having such an emotional moment in what appears to be no more than a closet. The two women shuffle out, still dabbing at their eyes, and the storekeeper follows.

He is an elderly gnome of a man, dressed in a button-up white shirt, red bow tie, and suspenders. He smiles wearily at Mona as he approaches, and says, "Sorry about that. They were a bit distraught."

"What was wrong? If it's not too rude to ask."

"Oh, nothing. Well. Not nothing. We had someone pass away just recently, you see."

"Oh, right," says Mona. "The funeral. I'm sorry, I should have known."

"Yes," he says. He looks Mona over and smiles. "I suppose you'd be the new arrival in town."

Mona coughs. "That's right. I'm Mona."

"And I'm Mr. Macey," he says, and shakes her hand. "I must say, no one ever told me you were so pretty. Were I but a younger man... I'm sure I'd make a pest of myself. I might still, you know." He smiles crookedly. Mona is not offended: she can tell he is the sort to innocently flirt with every woman, regardless of age or beauty. He might have been waiting to get old just so he could have such a freedom. "What can I do for you, Miss...?"

"You can just call me Mona," she says. "I'm looking for a mattress and a set of sheets."

"Ah. Moving in, are we?" He gestures and leads her through the aisles. It is a rather schizophrenic store: shelves of cheap novelty gags segue into imitation jewelry, which stands beside a case of knockoff watches and sunglasses.

"Maybe. I inherited a house around here. I guess I'll be bedding down there for a while. I just went to see the lady at the courthouse about it, in fact."

"Mrs. Benjamin," he says, and groans a little. "I can't imagine what sort of impression she made. Don't worry, we're not all as batty as that around here. Did she offer you any tea?"

"Uh..."

"Do *not* drink any," he tells her, and laughs. "You'll be drunker than a boiled owl for hours, and hacking up pine gum for days. There's always been a nutty herbalist-holistic tendency in New Mexico. People trying to cure your cold with sprigs of rosemary, that kind of thing. Mrs. Benjamin is the worst offender, mostly because all her cures have more in common with backwoods cocktails than they do with medicine."

He sells her a mattress and a set of sheets at 15 percent off—a "greeting discount" on which he refuses to budge—as well as some toiletries. She gets the impression he's a canny negotiator, and the way he carries himself has a certain casual power to it. As she's checking out, a young man comes rushing into the store, presumably to speak to Mr. Macey. But Macey simply looks at the young man, all the cheer and goodwill blinking out of his eyes, and shakes his head—*Not now.* Embarrassed, the young man bows himself out and waits outside, hands behind his back.

"Any way else I can help you?" he asks her when they finish.

"Maybe. I'm looking for information on someone who might have lived here—Laura Alvarez, my mother."

Mr. Macey screws up his face to think about it. "Alvarez...hm. I don't know. I don't *think* I've ever heard of anyone by that name."

"Were you here thirty years ago, or so?"

"Of course," he says.

"Well, she would have lived here about that time. Or moved away from here. She worked on the lab on the mountain."

"Ah," says Macey. "That might explain it. The dealings of the lab were—how shall I put this—not for the minds of mortals like me. I never knew what they did, and their personnel changed quite frequently."

"Kind of a black hat operation?"

He chuckles a little. "I suppose."

"There're no offices in town that would have kept track of that information?"

"If there ever were, I never knew of them."

"Well...if you could ask around, I sure would appreciate it. Sorry to grill you, but...she was my mother. I just want to know a little more about her."

"I understand. Don't you worry about it, then. I'll try and find something out. Is there anything else I can get you?"

"Not unless you got a steak behind your counter."

"Hungry, eh? Tell you what. Head on down to Chloe's—you know where Chloe's is, right? Okay, good. Head on down there and tell them I sent you." He winks. "Another greeting discount, let's say."

"You don't have to do that."

"I absolutely do. We don't get many newcomers here, as I'm sure you've heard a million times over by now. We need to do them right." His smile fades a little bit. "I hope you like it here for however long you stay. Most do. Though we have our fair share of trouble."

"Would it have something to do with the funeral yesterday?"

Mr. Macey's smile thins a bit, and his eyes grow a little sad. "Oh, well," he says. "I certainly hope not. It was an old friend of mine who died, you see."

"Who was it, if you don't mind my asking? I keep hearing about the funeral, but never about the deceased."

"His name was Norman Weringer. He was probably the most-liked man in Wink. He and I would spend hours walking the countryside around here, talking and—sometimes—arguing. He made arguments a treat, Norman. I suppose that might be why I liked him so much."

"I'm sorry to hear he died."

"I am, too. Even now. I always felt he'd outlive us. Yet here we are." He purses his lips and stares out the window. "I almost feel like doing something about it myself."

Mona isn't sure what to say to that. She knows too damn well what happens when people start self-policing. But there is a cold, quiet rage to Mr. Macey's face that makes her reluctant to press the point. She is new in town, and it might be the light in this store—for it is very dim in here—but she almost thinks she sees something fluttering in the backs of his eyes.

He takes a little breath and smiles again. "Now. Would you like me to get one of my boys to move this to your house?"

Moving all this stuff into the house tires her out pretty quick, so Mona is more than eager to take Mr. Macey's suggestion and head to the diner, which is still as hopping as it was this morning.

Just before she walks in, though, Mona counts the vehicles outside. She's not sure why—something's just buzzing in the back of her head, telling her to keep an eye out. So she counts each car and truck and memorizes the first letter or number of each license plate before she feels satisfied enough to go in.

Chloe's turns out to be a bright, clean, well-lit eatery with wide, curving tables and snug booths. It is filled with the aroma of bacon and pancakes, and the hiss of the griddle makes the jukebox (which is playing some Perry Como number) sound like it's coming through an ancient radio. Pies and cakes, each as lavishly prepared as a bridal gown, gracefully orbit one another on the dessert stands on the countertop, which is beaded with spotlights from the pendant lamps dangling above. Mona is a little disappointed to find it is not an all-night diner; she feels this would be the perfect place for restless night owls to come and contemplate their loneliness over a cup of coffee. That is, if Wink had any night owls.

When Mona enters she stands at the door for a moment and watches the waitresses take orders from the customers. None of them, she notices, are writing anything down. Some of them aren't even taking orders: people walk in and sit down, and a plate of hash browns and biscuits—or a plate of steak and eggs, or just a cup of coffee—is placed in front of them with no more than a happy greeting and an inquiry about the state of the family. They are all regulars, Mona realizes. Everyone knows everybody here, and what they want.

Everyone except her. She can already feel the confused glances darting her way. They silently ask—*Who is this?* And then there is a turn, a realization when they all say—*Oh, the girl from the funeral in the flashy car . . .*

Mona is too hungry to care. She sits down at the counter and looks at the menu, which is made of old and coffee-stained paper. The murmur of confusion dies, but she can still feel a few lingering stares.

A waitress arrives, a girl Mona finds faintly familiar. She is a delicate, dark-haired thing with a neck so skinny Mona can hardly believe it's holding up her head. Her eyes are huge and brown, with a certain glimmer of anxiety. "Can I help you, ma'am?" she asks.

Mona glances at her name tag. It reads GRACIE. "Sure," says Mona. "But I was told to say that, uh, Mr. Macey sent me . . ."

"Oh, Macey," says Gracie. She smiles briefly, but it feels like a formality: Mona gets the sense that Macey is one of those people everyone has to pretend to like, whether they really do or not. "Sure, we can take care of you, then. What'll you have?"

"What's the house specialty?"

"Specialty?" asks Gracie. "Well, ma'am, our pancakes and coffee are pretty talked about."

"Oh, please don't call me *ma'am*. It just about kills me every time."

This brings about a small smile. "All right."

"I think I may need something a little more substantial than pancakes, but I would love to try a cup of your coffee. What else you got?"

Gracie looks Mona over. She seems to come to some decision, and says, "I'd recommend the biscuits and gravy, if you haven't had much all day."

"Hm. You know, I don't mean to pry, but I think...I think I might have seen you today. Were you in the alley this morning, showing off your balance?"

"What? Oh." Gracie smiles, embarrassed, and turns a brilliant shade of red. "Yes. Yeah, that was me."

"I don't think I've seen Marines go through training like that. You must be made of tough stuff."

She grins sheepishly. "Miss Chloe takes her customer service seriously."

"Well, it has definitely paid off. Tell Miss Chloe I'll have the biscuits and gravy and a cup of coffee, if you could." She folds up the menu and hands it to Gracie, who gives her a bit of a puzzled smile before heading to the back to relay her order. Within the blink of an eye, another waitress—this one giving her no more than a small smile and a "Here you are, shug"—has slipped her a ponderous mug of steaming coffee, along with some cream and sugar. Mona takes a sip, and she can immediately understand why it's talked about: it is rich and strong and faintly chocolatey, so good it induces a sigh of satisfaction.

For a moment she does no more than look around the diner, and as she does the clank of plates and the mumbled greetings and the scrape of silverware all align until it feels as if she's in the center of some warm, cozy nirvana. Everyone here has been ordering the same thing since forever, and asking the same questions about the family and receiving the same funny little answers, and they'll all keep doing it, over and over again, and that's just fine with Mona. She's almost disappointed when Gracie arrives with her food, which breaks the spell.

"What's in this coffee?" Mona asks her. "It's like…chocolatey and piney, or something."

"It's probably the pinyon nuts you're tasting. We mix them into the grounds. It's sort of a New Mexican specialty."

"Well, it should be a specialty in a hell of a lot more places."

"You're new in town, aren't you?" asks Gracie.

"Yes," says Mona, who already knows what's coming next.

"Not to be rude, but I think I heard about you. Are you the—"

"The lady from the funeral," says Mona. "I am. Word travels fast."

"It doesn't have to travel far, here. Why are you visiting, if you don't mind my asking? We don't get much through traffic."

"Well, I'm not sure if it's a visit." Again, she has to explain about the house. She's going to have to incorporate this explanation into all her introductions around here.

"Oh," says Gracie. "I'm so sorry to hear about your dad."

"Really?" says Mona. "I wasn't."

Gracie smartly sidesteps this subject. "So your dad lived here?"

"My mother. A long, long time ago, I guess. I don't think she was born here, but I guess it was her hometown. I don't know. You wouldn't happen to have known much about any Alvarezes? I'd expect not, since you're so young." Gracie shakes her head, but Mona gets an idea. "Say—you wouldn't happen to know where the hall of records is around here, would you? I'd like to try and find out more about her."

"I know where it *was*," says Gracie. "Though it burned down before I was born. It was one of the buildings that got struck by lightning in the storm. They never got around to rebuilding it. It's just a vacant lot next to the gas station."

"I heard about that storm," says Mona. "It sounds like it was a disaster."

"I guess we think of it that way. There's a memorial to the people who died in it just down the block, where the city park begins," says Gracie. "It's a tree that was struck. About half of it is still there. They lacquered it so it stays the way it is and doesn't rot."

"I just might have to see that."

"It's that way," Gracie says, and points out the front windows.

As Mona looks, she sees she's being watched: there is a man in the corner booth in a blue-gray coat and a white panama hat. He looks a little like a Native American, with angular, tough features and long, straight black hair. Despite the meal steaming in front of him, he is sitting with his hands in the pockets of his coat, and he stays totally still. If he cares that Mona has spotted him, he doesn't show it: his dark black eyes just stare right back at her.

"Is that so," says Mona softly. Then she thanks Gracie and begins to eat her meal, though she's a little less hungry now.

When she is done Mona pays and leaves, looking to the side as she walks out. The Native American is no longer there, but his plate remains, the food untouched, though it's stopped steaming. Once outside she looks up and down the sidewalk but does not see him.

She counts the vehicles again. They're all there. She wonders if he somehow set off her little mental alarm, or if it was something else.

She walks up the street to the park with the huge white geodesic ball. She finds the memorial opposite the courthouse. It is a tall, splintered tooth of dark, gleaming wood, and it sits crooked in the lush green grass, about thirty feet tall. She sees there is a dark blush that starts at the top and curls down around the old bark. It looks almost like modern art.

She walks up to it and reads the plaque at the bottom:

IN MEMORIAM

IN LOVING MEMORY OF THOSE TAKEN FROM US

ON JULY 17TH 1983

WE LEAVE THIS TREE AS A TESTAMENT TO OUR LOSS

It doesn't feel right to Mona to leave this tree as a memorial, really. This is not a pleasant memento at all. Wouldn't they want something more inspiring, more hopeful? And...

She stops. Thinks. Then she reads the date again.

July seventeenth, she thinks. Nineteen eighty-three...she knows that date. Of course she knows that date. How could she forget?

"My God," she says out loud. "Oh, my God. That's the day Momma died."

CHAPTER NINE

Around nine o'clock every evening Joseph Gradling gets the itch, and this night is no exception. Naturally, as a sixteen-year-old, Joseph is vaguely aware that the itch is a common malediction among his age group: nearly every young boy at Wink High has it in some way or another, though it manifests at different times and they take care of it in different ways. He has heard, for example, of Bolan's Roadhouse on the outskirts of town, where some of the more adventurous boys have gone to spend money on something alternately described as blissful or repellent. And for the less daring there are smut magazines you can buy at certain stores in town, which quickly attain the value of cigarettes in prison among the student population, and are pored over with the enthusiastic disbelief of Old World peasants reading of foreign lands.

But Joseph is convinced he's found the best possible way in town: Gracie Zuela, who, for some reason, seems to hold some affection for him, or perhaps even like him. This revelation came to him quite slowly, as he could not believe it for the longest time. But one day, with his hands trembling and heart fluttering, he made some vague, stuttering proclamations to her about his feelings (to his embarrassment, he kept returning to the subject of her "niceness" because she was "so nice"), and, in a development that still confuses him to this day, she smiled and stood on her toes and whispered a time and a place into his ear.

That was the first time they met in the woods outside her home. There have been a few others after that. And with each visit, Joseph has grown aware that Gracie is scratching a deeper itch than the one that originally made him seek relief. There is something to their nocturnal visits, something fleeting and wonderful, that draws him back to this place. He is not sure what it is. But though the itch might be managed, he is now more distracted than ever, yet he is perfectly content with this.

Tonight, Joseph waits in their usual place in the woods, nursing a bottle of gas station champagne and a fearfully powerful erection. He's brought two bottles, one strawberry-flavored the way she likes it, and he's about a third of the way through his so he's feeling a little puzzled by everything. He is puzzled by the way the very trees appear agitated, like a herd of deer that has just caught scent of a wolf. But he is also puzzled by the moon. Tonight it looks slightly pinker than usual.

It is at times like these that Joseph tries to forget why he has no competition for the affections of Gracie Zuela: her house is just on the edge of a No-Go Zone, as his parents have termed them. These are the places no one ever visits, not even during the day. This Zone in particular is the woods on the northwestern side of town, just beside the mesa, and is said to be one of the worst places; but no one has found all of the No-Go places, or if anyone has, they haven't told anyone about it. And who would ever go looking? The idea is unthinkable.

But Joseph knows that Gracie's family has an arrangement, so this place is actually quite safe. Though others might fear to come, he knows he can walk here without worry. Or at least without much worry. No one is entirely worry-free when out and about in Wink at night. Everyone knows it's best to stay indoors. But he checks his watch again and drinks more champagne.

Finally there is a soft footfall behind him. "You came," says a quiet voice.

He turns and sees Gracie standing behind him. She has always moved very quietly, though recently she seems to be getting quieter and quieter. One day, he thinks, her footfalls will make no sound at all. "Of course I did." He holds the bottle of strawberry champagne out to her, but she shakes her head. "No?" he asks.

"No," she says.

"You're sure?"

"I'm sure."

Gracie is a slight, skinny creature, with toothpick arms and a stooped posture, but it is obvious she will one day be a great beauty. There is a placid sadness to her deep, dark eyes, as if she is pained by some phantom wound but does not know what to do about it. She stands in the pine needles with her shoulders slouched and her slight body turned away. Her arms are crossed and Joseph's heartbeat quickens as he sees her fingers curled around her bicep: Gracie is a creature of fine, delicate features, and for some reason the sight of her hands and neck makes something fragile and trembling in him unfurl its wrinkled butterfly wings and take flight.

"So you snuck out okay?" he asks, coming closer.

"Snuck out?"

"Yeah. They didn't notice you?"

She looks at him, curious. "Joseph," she says, "my parents know I'm out. Don't you know what tonight is?"

And at that, his blood runs cold. Joseph looks around at the trees and the cliffs and the queerly colored moonlight, and he realizes he has made a terrible mistake. "It can't be," he said. "Not again. Not so soon."

"It's been a month," she says.

"It hasn't felt like it."

"No," she admits. "It hasn't."

She holds a hand out for him to take, and, to his shame, he hesitates. He covers it up by fumbling with the bottles, and when he does take her hand it is ice-cold.

"I'm sorry," he says. "I'll leave if you want."

"Don't leave," she said. "You can't come with me. Not past the woods, anyway. But I don't want you to leave."

They walk through the woods hand in hand, with the grapefruit moon shining down on them. Up ahead the trees thin out and the rocky side of the mesa begins. In the moonlight the cliffs are white and gray, miles and miles of beautiful desolation. Were the sun up they would be pink and blood-red, but tonight under the clear skies they are like bone.

"Is it bad that I'm here?" he asks.

"It…might be," she says. "I don't know. Things are difficult right now. Everyone is upset."

"What is it? Is it why you left the diner early?" Gracie is currently in training at Chloe's, and her early absence would normally not be tolerated. Something serious must have happened to excuse her.

"Yes. A little." She falls silent, and bites her lip.

"Is it something to do with…what it wants?" he asks.

"It's a he, Joseph. We've talked about that."

"Or that's what it says it is," says Joseph sullenly. He wishes now that he had not come. On other nights Gracie is free and fresh and beautiful; he thinks of how he holds her in his arms, her black hair gleaming on the pine needles, her laughter and breath on his neck. But tonight she is a frightened, shy little thing, disappointed with everything that's ever happened to her.

"It's Mr. Weringer," she says.

"Yeah. I figured. Everyone is worried about it," says Joseph. "I didn't even think something like that could happen. Did you go to the funeral?"

She nods. "But it's not that. They don't think he just died, Joseph… they think he was murdered."

Joseph is shocked. He almost stops walking altogether. The idea of Mr. Weringer being murdered is even more unbelievable than him dying. "Who told you that?"

She nods ahead to the gray-and-white canyons. "Mr. First, of course."

His face darkens. "I thought you only saw Mr. First once a month."

"I visit him, yes, but sometimes he comes to me."

"And he visited you last night?"

She reluctantly nods.

"In your bedroom?" he asks.

She does not answer.

"Did he visit you in your bedroom, Gracie?"

"Yes," she says, and there is an edge to her voice. "Are you really interested in this?"

"No," he says.

"You are. We always talk about this. I'm so sick and tired of talking about this. I wish we could talk about anything else."

"It's just…I don't like you keeping things from me."

"But you knew I would. Right from the start of this, I told you I would have to."

Joseph can think of no answer. It is true that she warned him about this. At first he laughed it off, thinking it was a small price to pay in comparison to the rewards he'd get out of it. But with each visit the subject grows heavier and heavier, and it feels like every conversation they have circles it but never truly touches upon it.

But perhaps the problem is that he is getting older, and with each day he grows aware that the entire town is doing the same thing—treading carefully around many anxious, unspoken truths—and this perplexes and saddens him in a way he cannot articulate.

"I'll tell you," she says. "It doesn't matter. I was lying on my bed. About to go to sleep. But then I heard his sounds. It sounds like flutes, when he's coming. And the doors to my balcony opened, and he came in and sat in the corner and talked to me. We just talked, Joseph. He's very troubled."

Joseph, of course, now realizes she was right: he did not need to hear this. He wants to rip his hand free and maybe even push her down. Yet he also wants to pull her close and hold her. It does not feel right, to have her telling him this. It is not right to have to share her. He takes another swig of champagne.

"Everyone in town is upset," she says. "You can feel it, can't you? Even you can. Everything is stiff and cold…no one is sure what's going on, though they won't admit it. No one is telling anyone anything."

"But Mr. First tells you."

"Yes."

"Is that all he ever does when he visits?" Joseph asks. "Does he just talk to you?"

"Sometimes he just looks. But mostly we talk, yes."

"About what?"

She is silent for a while. "I won't give you that, Joseph. I give you a lot of things, but I won't give you that."

"Why not?"

"Because it isn't mine to give."

"Then what is yours to give?" he asks, and he stops her.

"Jesus," she says. "I don't know why I meet you here. You just keep getting angrier and angrier." She pulls her hand free and begins to walk toward the edge of the trees without him.

Joseph watches for a moment, then runs to catch up. "You keep looking paler. Every month. It's something he's doing to you, isn't it?"

She stops with her back to him. He can tell he has wounded her with this remark, and he half-wishes he could take it back. But he also feels he has a right to be angry. She deserves to hurt just as he does.

"There are some things that are just not for us to know, Joseph," she says. Her voice trembles. "For me, for you, for everyone. You just have to accept that, okay?"

Joseph swallows hard. Perhaps it is the champagne, but he suddenly feels very ill, his mouth and throat suffused with a putrid sweetness. The world blurs, and he realizes he is tearing up.

To his shame, Gracie sees his tears. "Here," she says. "Come here." She takes one of his arms and pulls him into an embrace. Silently they hold each other on the edge of the woods. Beyond them a small, curiously treeless canyon winds through the rocks. To the north the dark swell of the mesa blocks out the clouds. "I wish you'd just stop coming here," she says softly. "It's tearing you up."

"It'd be worse if I didn't."

"When you first started coming, I thought it was just for the fun. The play. Nothing more." Again, skirting the issue at hand.

"It was at first. But it isn't, anymore."

"I know. It's worse that way." One delicate hand probes along the waistband of his pants until it finds the button. Her fingers deftly open it; she has gotten much better at this as the weeks have gone by.

Joseph pulls away a little. "I don't want to."

"But I do," she says. She looks up at him. "Let me give you that at least. Okay?"

As she works at another button, Joseph fills with self-loathing and rage. He has been coming to these woods to see her for over two months now, and though he knows he has it better than most other boys at school, not once has he had sex with her. She will not even allow his fingers to enter her. That last, most precious privilege is held only by what is waiting in the canyon below, and he hates it and he hates himself for being drawn back here again and again.

She stops as a voice rings out through the woods: "Gracie?"

They both jump. Joseph whirls about, and his heart nearly stops when he sees who is standing across the clearing: it is Mr. Macey, from the general store. Yet he is not at all his normal flirty self: he stands stone-still with his white shirt glowing in the pink moonlight. His face is cold and inscrutable, his eyes lost behind his glasses. He is clearly quite displeased.

"Ah," he says, "and it's…Joseph, isn't it?"

Joseph almost feels sick. If there is one person he would never, ever have wanted to find them here, it would be Mr. Macey.

"You're not supposed to be here, Joseph," Macey says in a very soft, calm voice, and though he is a ways away his words resonate through the clearing. "What happens here does not concern you. You're interfering in another's business."

"I'm not…not interfering with her business," he says, though he sounds as terrified as he feels.

Mr. Macey does not respond: he simply stares at him. He is completely different from how he is in the day; it is as if something distant and unknowable is wearing his body.

"You're not supposed to be here, either," says Gracie, much more authoritatively than Joseph. "You're interfering just as much as Joseph."

Mr. Macey slowly turns his head to look at her. His expression does not change. Then he walks across the clearing and stands beside them to stare into the mouth of the little canyon below. "Is he awake?" he asks.

"That's none of your business," says Gracie.

"He should be soon, correct? Tonight is your night, after all."

"How would you know?"

"Weringer told me of your arrangement."

"Our arrangement has nothing to do with you. Or Weringer."

He turns to look at her. He studies her for a long while. "You know what has happened."

"I know Weringer died, but so does everyone."

"You know more than that."

Gracie does not respond, but she looks slightly nervous.

"You know he was killed," says Macey.

"I never said so."

"But you do. I can see it in you. How did you know? This was deduced just recently. Unless *he* told you. But we have not told him yet." His eyes swivel in his head to stare out at the canyon. It is an unnervingly reptilian motion, and Joseph feels a bit sick to see it. He does not want to be here at all, does not want to hear any private discussions of the powerful elite in Wink. "So he knew before we did."

"He had nothing to do with it," says Gracie, nervous.

Mr. Macey does not answer.

"You know he sees things his own ways," she says.

"Yes," says Macey. "And this is why I wish to speak to him. Does he know about the new arrival in Wink? That woman in the red car?"

"I don't know."

"Is she connected to what has happened?"

"I said I don't know."

He looks back out at the canyon. "Is he awake?" he asks again.

Gracie bites her lip, but gives in. "He will be. Soon."

"How soon?"

From somewhere down in the canyon there is the sound of soft, atonal pipes, almost like flutes. They make no melody; it is as if the piping is done at random, or perhaps by someone mad.

"Ah," says Macey. "Then I will go and see him."

"You aren't invited," says Gracie.

"These are extenuating circumstances."

"But you *aren't invited*. These are the rules. And this is *my* arrangement. There's never an exception. Isn't that what Mr. Weringer said?"

Macey pauses, frowning. Joseph can see he's trying very hard to think of a way around the rules that have governed life in Wink for so long.

Then Macey appears to have an idea. He looks up at Joseph, and something flutters in the back of Mr. Macey's eyes, and he begins speaking low and quickly in a monotone voice: "Joseph Gradling. Born March fourteenth, 1997. Parents Eileen and Mark. Episcopalian. Good math student. Bad English student. Sometimes at night you sit up in your bed and stare out the window when you know you shouldn't. Sometimes when you go back to sleep you dream of a green field with a black tower, and at the top of the tower is a blue fire. Someone is standing beside that fire. But you do not know who it is, and you cannot see."

"Enough," says Gracie.

"You do not like it here in Wink. You are brazen, condescending. You like to talk and ask questions. You do not like minding your own affairs. You like crossing boundaries, doing what you shouldn't, knowing what you shouldn't."

"Stop," says Gracie.

"I know you, Joseph Gradling. When you slipped out of your bedroom window tonight you had to lift your hips up, up just a little, for as you slid over the window ledge you felt your penis twitch as it filled with blood, hugely and wonderfully stiff, and you feared it would be pinched between your belt buckle and your belly—"

"Stop!"

"—And you wanted it to be *in rare form* tonight, didn't you, Joseph, isn't that what you thought as you walked across the forest to this place, this place where you should not be, and though you came here for her and her slender hands and heady musk you also came here because you love knowing something you shouldn't and breaking every rule you can, didn't you Joseph, Joseph Gradling—"

"Fine!" says Gracie. "Stop! I'll take you down! Just leave him alone!"

Mr. Macey's babbling ceases instantly. He stares at Joseph a moment longer before shifting his gaze to Gracie. "So you are inviting me?"

"I am," she says bitterly.

"Good," he says.

Despite Macey's agreement, Joseph is trembling and white, horrified to hear all of his deepest, strangest thoughts and feelings chanted out in a mad rush. Gracie watches him, troubled, but Macey interrupts before she can comfort him.

"There's no time to waste. I must see him now."

She sighs. "All right. Follow me, then."

With one last glance at Joseph, she leads Mr. Macey out of the trees and down into the mouth of the tiny canyon. She looks so little and alone; she seems to grow paler as they enter the moonlight, until her hair and skin gain a faint sheen. Then they pass behind one outcropping, and they are gone.

Joseph stands at the edge of the woods and does not move. He looks out at the mesas and canyons and feels as if he is on a shore bordering a violent, white-watered sea, and Gracie has just jumped down into their depths to drown. He wants nothing more than to go after her, but he knows this would be a terrible mistake, for both of them. There are things you cannot do in Wink, and to upset someone's arrangement is one of them.

Joseph does not walk back to the road, but along the edge of the woods. He is not sure why; perhaps the woods allow him to indulge his melancholy a little longer. Again, he hears the sound of soft fluting from down in the canyon. He stops; his perspective has changed enough that he can see down the slope to what is happening below.

He would not even admit this to himself, but this is the true reason he stayed: he wants to see, he *must* see. And perhaps if he claims it was an accident, or only glances at it out of the side of his eye, then all will be forgiven if he is caught.

He stands still, not turning his head, and strains to see everything happening in the corner of his vision. He can see the white snarls of the cliffs, and the smooth white streak of the little canyon floor. There is movement on the canyon floor, though it is difficult to make out: he can see two small figures almost lost in the shadow of the cliffs, staring down the canyon. But Joseph cannot see what they are looking at.

Something has fallen in the canyon. He can see where it's made an impact on the canyon floor, the sand and dust rising up in little clouds. Yet he never saw anything fall; he sees only where it struck the ground. Then something else falls, now closer to the people in the canyon, and again he misses it. He suddenly feels very worried for the people in the canyon, for what is falling seems very large.

Twice more the things strike the ground, closer and closer, though each time Joseph cannot see any rocks falling through the air or any other object. It's as if the ground itself is shifting away, but only in select spots and in a straight path leading up to the figures in the canyon. He wonders what could possibly cause such a thing.

The fluting echoes in the rocks again. Then moonlight begins to show between one little figure's feet and the ground, increasing inch by inch, and to his shock Joseph realizes the person is levitating, lifting several feet straight up in the air...

Or, he wonders, is the person being picked up?

And then he begins to wonder if the puffs of dust he saw in the canyon were footfalls, the pounding footsteps of something invisible to the eye, and if it is lifting up the little person in the valley in a slow, loving embrace, perhaps to touch its cheek to hers and cradle her in its arms, while the other figure in the canyon puts his hands on his hips and watches, disapproving of this naked show of affection...

Joseph falls to his knees and begins to retch, yet even as he does he keeps two things in mind: the first is that he must stay completely silent, for to alert the thing in the canyon would have consequences too awful to imagine; the second is that if what he was seeing was correct, and those *were* footfalls, then their owner must be vast enough to fill the canyon.

The next thing Joseph knows he is running, sprinting through the pine woods and stumbling through the undergrowth. Finally he vaults over the roadside barrier and tumbles to the ground next to the asphalt. Then he sits there, hugging his knees, and he begins to weep.

WELL HELLO
THERE NEIGHBOR

CHAPTER TEN

Mona's been walking for what feels like an hour, up and down hills of many intimidating gradients, but she hasn't broken a sweat yet. There's something to the morning air here—it's cool, but not chilly. It seems to wriggle into every crevice of your body, waking it up and reminding it it's alive. She comes to a hill and looks out at a small vista—the road loops down to encircle a small adobe bungalow, where an ash tree slowly waltzes in the wind.

She keeps thinking of that word. *Alive*: that's how everything feels. It's like she's gotten a really good sleep, even though she definitely didn't last night, not in that huge, empty house.

Mona hasn't made much progress on her mother—though the people here are gregarious and eager, they are also totally useless on that front—so this morning she's turned her attentions to the town itself. It's small, so she knows she should be nearing the end of the town soon, but it never comes: there is always another twist to the road, or another hill behind a hill, or an immense tree hiding a path she didn't see before. The town goes farther and farther, tunneling inward. It is a very disparate feeling, as if Wink is not one place, but a place made of many smaller places, little bubbles accessible only by one entry point each.

She looks ahead and sees a small knoll that is half covered with bobbing wildflowers. It's a curiously uneven sight—the flowers are restricted to the sunward side, so the knoll looks a little like someone with a half-shaved head. The flowers are so dense and so brightly colored that Mona immediately thinks that were she a little girl, she'd love to go rolling down the hillside among them, petals of bright yellow streaking by as the blue sky whirled around her.

Since Mona is not a little girl, she opts to go walking in them instead, rounding the hill and looking up at the sight above her. On the other side of the hill is a little trickling brook that has carved a small green scar in the landscape. It seems a bit out of place—Mona saw no sign of a brook on the other side of the hill—but, curious, she follows the brook down to where it winds through the trees.

She keeps following the brook, ducking under branches when they're too big to push aside, and suddenly there is the flutter of sunlight…

Mona looks out, and gasps. She's standing on the lip of a rocky cliff, and below her is a fifty-foot drop into the valley. Vertigo beats on her senses, telling her she'll step forward anytime, and go plummeting down…

"Maryanne, hon, I told you I wanted to be *alone* today," drawls a voice nearby.

Mona wrestles her eyes away from the drop and looks right along the cliff. There is a little clearing not more than twenty feet away, grassy and shaded by a tall spruce, and in the middle of the clearing is a woman sunning herself on a deck chair. There's a second unoccupied deck chair beside it, along with a small table, on top of which is an aluminum shaker sweating with condensation.

Mona relaxes, steps away from the edge, and walks to the woman. She is tall and lean, and she wears very short white shorts and a blue halter top, and a pair of pink cat's-eye sunglasses with rhinestones. In between her thighs is a half-empty martini glass.

"Sorry?" says Mona.

The woman raises a finger to tug down one lens of her sunglasses. An eye of lapis lazuli peeks from behind it. "You are not Maryanne."

"Nope," says Mona.

"Who are you? I don't know you. Wait. Wait, are you the…"

"Yes," says Mona. "I am. Didn't mean to disturb you, I was just following the creek down here."

"Ah. Well, you've stumbled onto my secret hiding spot. So. You're the new girl in town. You certainly are making yourself known. Not that that's a bad thing. What's your name?"

"Mona."

"Mona. That's a good name. Not used very often anymore. Suppose people think it's too...gloomy." She licks her lips. Mona gets the impression that the martini between her legs is not her first. "Mona. Moan. See?"

"I see."

The woman sits up. She's definitely of A Certain Age—her tan is interrupted by liver spots flowering on her wrists and the backs of her hands, and her cat's-eye sunglasses can't conceal the wrinkles at the corners of her eyes. "I'm Carmen, Mona. It's a pleasure to meet you. How are you doing on this fine morning?"

"Good enough, I guess."

"I'm going to have to guess that no one here's exactly thrown you a welcome party yet?"

"A welcome party?"

"Sure. Welcoming you to the town."

"Well. I wouldn't want to bad-mouth anyone, but...kind of."

"You're not bad-mouthing anyone." She sighs and sits back. "I'm not surprised."

"I imagine the funeral sort of put a damper on that."

"Oh, I suppose it did. But even more so, though we like fun here, we just don't like to make a show of it. Hence the, ehm." She slurps noisily at her martini and waves at the surrounding trees. "Why don't you sit down?"

"I didn't really want to intrude."

"Oh, you're not intruding. I'm just being neighborly."

"But I thought you said you wanted to be alone?"

"That was because I thought you were my daughter. I've been helping her and her kids—she's married with her own kids, you see—and I insisted on having a few moments of my own. I mean, they can take care of their own shit for a few hours, can't they?"

"I guess?"

"Of course they can. And Hector—Hector, that's my husband—he could weigh in and actually *do* something occasionally, too. It's good to let them be on their own. Sink-or-swim kind of thing. Now sit. You look like you've been working yourself half to death. Here." Carmen fetches a martini glass from underneath her chair and pours something cool and clear. "I would like to state that this *isn't* something I do often. I don't just hang out here in the woods drinkin' all morning. Life does not permit. But, you know, I sure would if I could. I can't think of a better use for a morning." She hands the drink out to Mona.

"Uh, I'm not really a gin person."

"You'll be this kind of gin person. I promise."

Mona sips, not wishing to be impolite. But the drink is cool and biting and refreshing, like a dash of cold rain on a hot afternoon. "Huh," says Mona.

"I told you it was good," says Carmen. "Where you from, Mona?"

"Texas."

"Where in Texas?"

"All over."

"All over? That's a big all over."

"I didn't quite have a permanent address, I guess you could say."

"I see," says Carmen. "Then what brings you to Wink?"

Mona recites her usual explanation.

"Goodness," says Carmen. She appears honestly affected by Mona's story. "It sounds like you've had quite a time."

"You could say that."

"Well. Why don't you lie back and enjoy the morning with me? Sounds like you've earned it."

"Oh, I couldn't possibly—"

"I'm willing to bet you possibly could. Do you have anything else to do today?"

Actually, Mona does. She'd meant to ask Mr. Parson more about

Coburn today, and to see if she could get him to make a damn bit of sense. But she says, "Nothing that couldn't happen later, I suppose."

"That's the spirit. Relax. We get to relax so rarely. Give it a shot."

Mona lies back. Relaxing isn't something she does easily, but she finds it easy here: the sun is warm but tempered by the overhanging tree, and the chuckle of the nearby brook makes her worries melt away.

"So what do you think so far, Mona?" asks Carmen. There's a soft *slurp* as she sucks at her own drink.

"I think I could get used to this shit."

Carmen laughs. "I believe you, but I meant about Wink."

"Oh. Well. It's... it's damn nice."

"Yes, it is, isn't it. I guess we get too used to it. Acclimated. Take it for granted. But then a morning like this happens, and you remember."

"It feels... a little different at night."

"Hm," says Carmen, but she does not comment further.

"New Mexico is a damn pretty state. I wish I'd come here sooner."

"You know, I've been here all my life, but I can't imagine any place more pleasant than this. Well. I'd be lying if I said you didn't have to *look*. Like this place here. Sometimes you have to work for your bit of peace. But it's there. And I know what you're thinking—you're thinking, what the hell would a housewife know about work?"

"I actually wouldn't think that at all, ma'am," says Mona.

"Oh, really? Pardon my forwardness, but I didn't quite see you as the family type."

"Tried it once."

"Didn't take?"

"Something like that."

"Ah," says Carmen. She turns her black-glassed eyes to the sky. "Well, if anyone gives you any shit about that, you can tell them to go to hell for me. If they haven't been there, they can't talk."

Mona tries to smile gratefully at this bracing advice. "So is this part of your property?"

"Kinda," says Carmen. "Our house is back toward downtown

more. This is just mine, really. I asked Hector for it. For my little bit of sun I could lay out in—though I did ask for a little bit of shade, occasionally—and he went and got all that arranged. That's kind of how things work for us. A lot of favor-corralling, I guess you could say. I've no doubt you'll figure it all out, if you hang around long enough."

Mona looks around at the glen. Maybe it's the gin, but it's hard to have a troubling thought here. Yet there's also something vaguely hermetic about this place, as if the trees have sealed them in and this tiny glen and its stunning vista are totally detached from Wink.

"Will you be hanging around?" asks Carmen.

"Sorry?"

"Around Wink. You've got a house, you said, but are you thinking to stay?"

"I don't know," says Mona. "Maybe. I guess the real estate market might not be exactly hopping here, if I want to sell the house."

Carmen gives a husky laugh and finishes her drink. "You'd be surprised, m'dear."

"I have to ask—you wouldn't happen to have known my mother, would you?"

"Sorry, hon. I didn't. Or if I did, I don't remember, which ain't out of the question. My memory isn't what it used to be. But if you ever need anything—advice, or a drink—I'm always available. Or I'll make myself available, even if I'm not."

"I appreciate that."

"Well, you seem like someone who's seen a lot. It's like I said, peace flourishes here, if you ask for it. I hope you'll find some here."

Mona considers it as she finishes her martini. As she does, there's a snort from Carmen, followed by a second one that never quite stops until it's a snore. Mona sits up and looks in the shaker, and is not surprised to see it is totally empty.

She gets up and follows the brook back up to the street, walking until she emerges in a greenbelt where three small girls play hide-and-seek, giggling and shrieking as they dash among the trees, and she turns toward home, thinking of peace.

*   *   *

So far Mona hasn't had a single good night in Wink. She tries to sleep, but it does not come easily. Often she awakens to roam the house's empty hallways. The windows cast queer shapes on the faded wooden floor, and in some places the air takes on a hot, electrical scent, like the smell in a room with too many copiers and printers going at once.

Mona thinks herself a practical person, so she knows the world abounds in coincidences that can really fuck with your head if you invest too much in them, and she tries to tell herself the shared date—of her mother's suicide and the lightning storm—is one of them. Tragedies happen every day, and it doesn't mean anything if two coincide. Yet each time she remembers that black, lacquered shard of wood leaning crookedly in the park, she is troubled.

When sleep finally takes her it is blessed and hard, a dreamless black slumber that will leave her covered in pink wrinkles from the sheets when she wakes. Yet eventually—it is hard to say when—she begins hearing voices in her sleep.

"...And she just came in the other night, she says," says one voice. It sounds like it belongs to a very old woman who is standing just nearby.

"She says so because she did. I was there," says another. This voice is masculine, firm and deep. "I was the first she came to."

"To you? Was this your doing?"

"Her coming to me was purely coincidental. I had no hand in it. I had no idea she was coming at all."

Mona does not open her eyes. She is sure she is dreaming, but she does not want to open her eyes in the dream, because then she might do the same in real life and wake up and ruin her sleep. So she lies on the mattress with her face in the sheets and her eyes tightly shut, listening to the two voices talk.

"And do you think it is all coincidence?" says the old woman's voice. "I would like to believe so, I must say. Then we could rest easy."

"Something this important...I cannot help but think otherwise."

"Why do you think her arrival is important?"

"She comes right after a death. A new face, after an old one is lost. It is too soon for me to feel comfortable about it."

"Ah," says the old woman's voice. "So you think..."

"Exactly. She is not here by accident. She was brought here. This is someone's doing, but I am not yet sure whose."

Mona has no idea what they're talking about, but she's slowly becoming aware that the air on the back of her neck is nothing like that of the air-conditioning in the house. It is far too cold and dry. It feels like a wind out of a barren desert, one that has never known moisture in all its life. And she feels she has heard those voices before...

She begins to lift her head a little. She is not going to *look*, she is certain of that, because this is still just a dream. She's just going to crack her eyes a little, and maybe something will just trickle in.

She cracks her eyelids. And something does indeed trickle in.

Mona is on her mattress, but she is not in her house: the mattress lies on a field of black stone, like volcanic basalt, its surface cracked into nearly perfect little hexagons. There is a red light shining down on the black stone field, and Mona keeps lifting her head until she spies a familiar sight: the red-pink moon, as fat as a happy tick, and just below it is the blue flicker of cloud lightning.

This is some dream, she thinks.

"Do you believe she has any involvement?" asks the voice of the old woman.

"I do not think she knows a thing," says the man's voice. "She is mostly confused, and sad. She is a broken thing."

"So she poses no threat."

"I did not say *that*. With so much recent madness, how are we to be sure what is a threat and what is not?"

"Hm. I believe I may wish to confirm for myself," says the woman's voice.

"I do not think it'd be wise to attempt anything dangerous now."

"Oh, it wouldn't be dangerous. At least, not for us..."

Mona is now sure these voices are familiar. Did she not once hear one of them offer her breakfast, and the other one offer her tea? Confused, she lifts her head higher and begins to roll over.

She sees there are two statues, one standing directly on either side of her, enormous ones done in odd shapes: one looks like a single queerly organic column, the other resembles a mammoth, headless bull with many limbs. They seem taller than the Statue of Liberty and the Sphinx, respectively, and appear to be made of the same black stone as the sunless wasteland. Both statues tower just above her, as if they were strolling by (if such things could stroll) and found her lying here and are investigating together. Yet the moon is just behind them, so she cannot see more of them as they look down on her...

"Wait," says the man's voice. "Is she looking at us?"

"Can she *see* us?"

"How can she—"

Then there is a flicker of movement, lightning-fast. It takes Mona's brain a few moments to translate what it just saw, and though she cannot believe it her brain keeps on insisting it was real.

The statue that looked like a bull waved a limb. Which statues should not be able to do, she says to herself. If it really did wave a limb, then it could not be a statue at all, but...

Suddenly Mona is falling, plummeting away from the black wasteland and into darkness. She falls until she strikes her mattress—which is odd, because she is certain she was just lying on it—and she jerks awake with a gasp and looks around.

She is lying in the corner of the master bedroom of her new house. Though she could have sworn that just now she was not alone, she looks at all the dark corners and sees no one at all. The room, though spacious, is empty.

Then the braying, shrill peal of a bell splits the silence. Mona's whole musculature flexes in surprise, causing a stab of pain in her belly and arm. Then the bell rings again, and she realizes it's the aquamarine phone sitting in the dusty corner of her living room.

She goes to it and watches it ring four more times. Whoever it is, he or she isn't giving up.

Mona expects it to be the same jerk who called earlier. So she picks it up and barks, "Who the fuck is this?"

There's an "Ah" of surprise on the other end, followed by an "Uh..."

"Yeah?" says Mona. "Go on. Talk."

Silence.

Then: "You need to go home."

"What?" says Mona. "What the hell do you mean?"

"You need to go home, Miss Bright." The speaker is talking through what sounds like a sock pressed against the phone, but this cannot disguise the fact that the speaker is obviously very young.

"I am at home," says Mona.

"No. The home you came from. You need to leave this town."

"Okay, or—you could just mind your own fucking business."

"They're *watching* you," says the voice. There is a note of genuine terror in it. "They're talking about you."

"Who?"

"All of them. Don't you know what they *are*?"

"'What'?" says Mona. "What do you mean, 'what'?"

"Go as soon as you can," says the voice. "If they'll let you." Then there is a click, and the line goes dead.

Mona looks at the receiver, thinking, then slowly puts it down.

She knows that voice. She's sure of it.

She is back in bed, just on the verge of slumber, when it comes to her: didn't she hear that voice recommend the biscuits and gravy to her once? But then she returns to sleep, and the thought is gone, and forgotten.

Mrs. Benjamin's luncheon is held in her backyard. It is a cool seventy-two degrees outside, and her cottonwood trees have been carefully pruned so that they form a light canopy that shields the yard from the noon sun. Her gardens are nothing short of astonishing: huge clumps of flowering vines sprawl along its iron fence, and blades of sprouting bulbs droop along the pink granite borders. It looks like something out of *Southern Living*, and, unfortunately for Mona, the same goes for the rest of the attendees: everyone here is wearing a sundress with matching jewelry, heeled sandals, and sleek sunglasses. Mona, who was raised in the oil flats with nothing but an unsociable ex–Army

Ranger for company, has always felt profoundly insecure about her lack of femininity, and she feels incredibly out of place here, where she just can't compete with this level of estrogen. It doesn't help that she is quite short, dresses like she is planning for a hike, and is obviously Latina, unlike everyone else here.

Yet it is odd: the question of race never pokes its head above the waves. This is unusual for Mona, who has been all over Texas and worked in some of the whitest communities out there and has witnessed a vast array of reactions to her race. Since Wink is about 98 percent white, she expects at least *something*, especially from these socialites: maybe they would ask her, somewhat tentatively, where she was from, or clumsily inquire if she was bilingual (to which the answer is a sort of *no*—the only Spanish Mona knows is what she picked up on the force in Houston, which is limited to commands, threats, and thoroughly indecent questions). But these questions never come. In fact, now that she thinks about it, no one in Wink has ever said *anything* about her race: both it and her general appearance have gone mostly without comment or reaction. It feels as if the citizens of Wink have gotten used to people different from them.

Still, her insecurity intensifies as the luncheon goes along. These are a type of woman Mona has never encountered: they drink cocktails at noon and smoke cigarettes in slender little holders, and they discuss almost nothing but housekeeping and the states of their husbands and children. Perhaps they are what Carmen was fifteen years ago. They seem a cheery, bubbly lot, with their hair perfectly coiffed and their eyes bright and smiling behind their sunglasses, and they greet Mona with an enthusiasm she finds downright intimidating. None of them seem to be employed. The mortgage rate around here must be great for everyone to live so well on a single income. She manages to briefly redirect the course of conversation to her reason for being in Wink, and pop in a few questions about her mother—but of course they, like everyone else so far, know nothing: they laugh at their own ignorance, and bounce gaily to the next subject. Though Mona feels contempt for them—so privileged, so sheltered—she also cannot help but wish to be one of them.

For the most part they are all too happy to do the talking for her, but when they finally ask her a direct question it's one Mona's been dreading all along:

"So, Mona, any plans to settle down?" asks one, who Mona thinks is named Barbara. "I know you're young, but don't wait too long."

The statement puts a bad taste in Mona's mouth, but she still tries to smile. "I'm not that young," she says. "I'm almost forty."

"What!" cries Barbara. "Almost forty! You don't look a day over twenty-seven! What *is* your secret? You *have* to tell me. I'll bend your arm if you don't." The other women nod. Some even look insulted to hear her true age.

It is not a new response to Mona, who has watched friends grow gray and lined while she stays the same, more or less. She knows she's lucky, but she's never figured out why. Her mother and father looked well *over* their ages, but then one drank himself to sleep every night and the other was schizophrenic, so that doesn't mean much.

"Just genes, I guess. I can't say it's clean living."

"Well, it's high time someone snatches you up," says another, a platinum blonde who might be named Alice. "I notice there's no ring on that finger..."

Mona tries to smile again, but it comes out as a grimace. "Well. There was, once."

Discomfort flutters through them, the first time on this sunny afternoon. "You mean you were engaged, and it was...called off?"

"No," says Mona. "I was married. But we divorced," she says, before they ask if her husband died, which is probably a more pleasant alternative to them.

"Ah," says Barbara. Some of the women grow very still. The others are exchanging glances. After a few beats of silence, the subject is forcefully changed and the flow of conversation resumes burbling cheerily along, though now far fewer questions are directed to Mona.

Yet Mrs. Benjamin does not react at all to this news. In fact, she hasn't done much all throughout the luncheon besides pass food around and watch Mona. Mona begins to find it very unsettling, for every time she looks up, Mrs. Benjamin is watching her with a small smile.

*   *   *

It's not until the luncheon's over and everyone is leaving that Mrs. Benjamin speaks to her: "If you could please stay behind, dear, I would appreciate it. I feel like we have a little to discuss."

Mona obliges, loitering on her porch while Mrs. Benjamin sees the other guests out. When she returns, the small, clever smile is back on her face. "Did you enjoy yourself?"

"It was certainly..." She trails off, wondering how to finish.

"Awful?" suggests Mrs. Benjamin.

Mona is not sure what to say, but Mrs. Benjamin just laughs. "Oh, don't look so concerned, my girl. Anyone with sense can see they're a bunch of empty-headed fools. That's why I didn't give them any of the *good* tea." She winks.

"Then why did you have them over at all?" asks Mona, irritated.

"Oh, just to spite them, I suppose," says Mrs. Benjamin vaguely. "Stir up trouble. They can't stand one another's company, you see. I have to get my amusement somehow."

"And you brought me in to stir up more trouble?"

"No. I wanted to see how you'd handle them."

Mona stops. Takes a breath. She then says, "Ma'am, I admit I do not understand the intricacies of your social spheres here, and to be honest I really do not wish to. But one thing that I really, really do not want for you to do is involve me in them for what seems to be no damn reason at all. And, believe me, you do not want that either, though you will have to trust me on that."

"Oh, please hold on. I didn't intend to be cruel. I just wanted to see how you'd be fitting in here."

"Well, I will guess that I will fit in quite shittily, but that's my problem and none of yours. Now...you got me here under the pretense of answering a few questions about the town, and my mother," says Mona. "Can I ask you those questions?"

"Oh, certainly," says Mrs. Benjamin, miffed. "Fire away, dear."

They sit down on the porch and she tells Mrs. Benjamin about how she inherited the house, and her very strange trip here. When she finishes her story Mrs. Benjamin stays quiet for a long, long time. "Hmm," she says finally. "Well. I'll say again that I have no memory of a Laura Alvarez living or working in Wink."

"I've got photos of her living in my house," says Mona.

"From when?" asks Mrs. Benjamin.

"I don't know exactly...I guess sometime in the seventies."

"Hmm," says Mrs. Benjamin. "My memory goes back far, but... not *all* the way back. So I could be wrong. She could have lived here before I ever came."

"I also have documents from Coburn saying she worked there," says Mona. "Is there any remnant of their operation still in the area that I can go to? Any government agency? I just need to find *something* about her."

"Coburn..." says Mrs. Benjamin, a little contemptuous. "That damn lab. Who knows what their papers say? I wouldn't trust anything I heard about up there. All of their facilities were located up on the mesa, and those were gutted and abandoned when the lab was shut down."

Mona makes a mental note of this. Because she intends to go up to that mountain, and damn soon. "What was it they did up there?" she asked. "I read they did government research, and something about... quantum states."

Mrs. Benjamin stares off into the distance for a while. "They did nothing that was worth doing," she says finally. "They should have put more effort into commercial prospects. *Usable* ideas. Rather than conceptual research. It did not end well."

"Because they never came up with anything," says Mona.

"Hm?" says Mrs. Benjamin. "Who told you that?"

"Mr. Parson. He's the man who runs the—"

"I know Mr. Parson," says Mrs. Benjamin. "We're well acquainted. And Coburn, well...they only ever did one thing." She thinks for a moment. Then she asks, "Here—would you like to see a magic trick?"

"A what?"

"A magic trick. The party bored me stiff, dear, so a trick should be entertaining. Come inside. I'll show you."

"I thought you said you were going to help me," says Mona as she follows Mrs. Benjamin into her house.

"I am," says Mrs. Benjamin. "Just indulge me, please."

She sits Mona down on the couch while she wanders off to the back. The inside of Mrs. Benjamin's house is much less attractive than the exterior: everything is done in awful flowery wallpaper, except the living room, which has a bright red pattern depicting a foxhunt. There are also several stuffed owls, which Mona assumes were brought home from work. Somewhere there must be a room full of clocks, for she can hear a constant chorus of ticking. Everything smells of bad potpourri.

"Here we are," trills Mrs. Benjamin as she returns. She sets a wooden case down on the coffee table in front of Mona, and stops. Her smile vanishes, and she looks up at Mona with a dark expression. She opens the case. Inside is a silver hand mirror. "An ancient swami gave me these mirrors," she says in a theatrically hushed tone. At first Mona is confused, for she can see only one mirror, but then she looks again and sees there are actually two, stacked on top of each other. "They came from far away, in the Orient."

"They did?" asks Mona.

Mrs. Benjamin's solemn demeanor breaks. "Of course not, silly girl," she says. "It's all part of the trick." She resumes glowering. "He gave them to me, and told me they were entrusted with ancient…" Her expression wavers. "Wait, I already said 'ancient,' didn't I? Oh, forget this part…let's get to the fun stuff." She takes out the mirrors and hands them to Mona. "Here. Take them."

"I have to hold them?"

"Yes, obviously," and Mrs. Benjamin sounds genuinely impatient now. "Take them. Hurry up."

Mona takes one mirror in each hand. They are surprisingly light, and almost paper-thin. She expected something gaudy and decadent— this is a magic trick, after all—but these mirrors have almost no ornamentation. They are silver surfaces and silver handles, and nothing more.

"The mirrors are actually halves of one," says Mrs. Benjamin. "Like one mirror was split down the middle, shaved in two. The thing is, when the mirror was split, it never noticed. It still thinks it's whole, even though it's not. But this confusion has given it some interesting consequences. Let me tell you how the mirror trick works.

"First, hold one mirror in front of you at an angle so it reflects an object nearby. Say, this ashtray." She points to a horrible brass tchotchke on the coffee table. "Then slide the other mirror behind this one, so they touch and are whole."

Mona stays still, waiting for more. "Well, go on," says Mrs. Benjamin. "Hurry up."

"Oh," says Mona. "You want me to...oh, okay." She angles the first mirror so that it is reflecting the ashtray. "Is this okay?"

"So long as you see the ashtray, it's fine," says Mrs. Benjamin. "Now place the other mirror behind it."

Mona does so, sliding the second mirror behind the one reflecting the ashtray. They seem to click into place, as if magnetized.

"Now...concentrate," says Mrs. Benjamin softly. "You must look at the reflection of the ashtray in the mirror, and do not look away. Stare at it, and concentrate on it. Remember what it looks like, and hold that image in your mind." She is grim and serious again, but now Mona thinks it is not part of the act. The sickly-sweet smell of potpourri becomes intense and heady, and Mona feels a little ill. "Are you concentrating?" asks Mrs. Benjamin.

"Yeah," says Mona. She is staring very hard at the mirror. It has no frame, she notices, nor is there any flaw or scratch on its surface. It gets hard to remember she is looking at a reflection. The mirror is so smooth that it is like a window, or perhaps a little bubble of light floating in her lap, and inside the bubble is a picture of an ashtray...

"Good," says Mrs. Benjamin. "Now, just keep staring at the reflection on the top mirror. Keep concentrating on it. And as you do, I want you to slowly, slowly pull the other mirror out from underneath it. Don't just yank it. Do you understand?"

"I guess."

"Don't guess. Do you understand or not?"

"I do."

"Then do it, please."

This is the weirdest magic trick Mona's ever taken part in, but she decides to keep indulging the old lady. She keeps staring at the reflection of the ashtray, and begins to pull the mirrors apart. There is a *click*, like she's just severed the magnetic attraction between them, and everything…changes.

It is impossible to say how things change. It is as if every object in the room is now a false version of itself, a cheap, manufactured copy of the real thing. The stink of potpourri gets so strong that the air seems to shimmer with it. But out of the corner of her eye Mona thinks she can see *light* seeping through objects she knows to be opaque: she can see the sunlight through the roof, through the chandelier, and even through the floor, as if it is all made of ice. And underneath that light are a thousand shadows…

"Concentrate," says Mrs. Benjamin softly.

Mona remembers the task at hand, and she keeps staring at the reflection of the ashtray in the top mirror.

And as the second mirror slowly emerges from underneath the first, she sees that the ashtray is there, too: the exact same ashtray is reflected in that second mirror. Even though she's moved the second mirror enough that it's not pointing toward the ashtray, or even toward the coffee table, but toward the dining room.

It's not a reflection, she thinks, irrationally. *The ashtray is trapped in the mirrors…*

Mona tries to keep concentrating. And it is then that she begins to see that something very strange is happening.

For starters, the tchotchke ashtray is still sitting on the coffee table. She can see that. It's also being reflected in the first mirror, which is totally fine, as the first mirror is pointing at it. But the ashtray is *also* being reflected in the second mirror, which makes no sense, as the second mirror is not facing toward the ashtray at all. And while this is troubling in its own right, what really gets to Mona is that the second mirror is showing the ashtray above the dining room table, ten feet away to her right, yet she can see the ashtray itself sitting on the coffee table right in front of her.

But is it her imagination, or can she see something floating in the dining room out of the corner of her eye, just above the table, perhaps right where the second mirror is suggesting the ashtray should be?

That's not possible, she thinks, because a) How can an object defy gravity? and b) How can an object occupy two different spaces *at the same time*? For she can see the ashtray sitting on the coffee table just before her, yet it is also in both of the mirrors, and unless she's gone mad it's also floating very slowly out of the dining room at the same rate at which she's moving the second mirror. It's as if since the ashtray is reflected in both mirrors, the world is working to accommodate them and ensure that what is being reflected is actually there, even though it shouldn't be.

"Good," says Mrs. Benjamin's voice somewhere. "Very good…"

Mona is trying to work all this out when she sees there is something slight and insubstantial about the ashtray on the table. It too has turned a little translucent, and she can see light filtering through it. And then the ashtray begins to *shudder*, like a strobe light, and it starts to disappear…

Mona gasps. "No!" cries Mrs. Benjamin, but it is too late. Whatever was floating out of the dining room plummets to the ground, then vanishes without a sound. Immediately things revert back to how they were: there is only one ashtray, sitting on the coffee table, and the rest of the house is opaque and hard and real again.

"What was that?" asks Mona. She hastily puts the mirrors back in their case. "What the hell kind of magic trick was that?"

But Mrs. Benjamin seems even more disturbed than Mona. Her face is gray as she stares at the ashtray on the table. Finally she clears her throat and says, "Perhaps I was wrong, my girl. Perhaps you do belong here in Wink after all."

"What do you mean?" asks Mona.

Before Mrs. Benjamin can answer there is a knock at the front door. Both of them jump a little, and Mrs. Benjamin stares at the door, not comprehending. "Oh," she says when the knock sounds again. "I suppose I ought to answer that…" She stands up and hobbles to the door.

As she does, Mona looks back down at the mirrors in the case.

There does not seem to be anything strange or extraordinary about them now; they are merely two small mirrors, each reflecting the ceiling. But still she shivers a little.

She hears the door open. Mrs. Benjamin says, "Oh," again, though this time she sounds far less pleased.

"Hello, Myrtle," says a man's voice softly. "I—"

"Oh, hello, Eustace," says Mrs. Benjamin, quickly and loudly. "Please do come in. I have company." She stands aside, and Mona sees it is the little old man who sold her her mattress, Mr. Macey. But he is not flirty or wry this time, but terribly grave.

"Company?" he asks.

"Yes," says Mrs. Benjamin. She ushers him inside. "This is Miss Bright. She's new in town. Miss Bright, this is Eustace Macey. He works at the general store."

"We've met," says Mona.

"Oh, I'm so glad. What brings you here, Eustace? I was just showing Miss Bright a little magic trick of mine."

"I came to discuss something with you," says Mr. Macey. He does not even look at Mona. "Alone."

"Would it be possible to discuss this later, Eustace?"

"No," he says. "No, it wouldn't, Myrtle."

Mrs. Benjamin eyes him angrily and looks back at Mona. "Are you sure, Eustace?" she asks, her voice brimming with false politeness.

He nods.

"It can't wait at all?"

He shakes his head, expression unchanging. Mrs. Benjamin is smiling so hard Mona is worried her cheeks will crack. "Fine," she says through gritted teeth. "Mona, could you please excuse us for a moment? I know . . . weren't you interested in getting some of my tea?"

Mona was most fucking certainly *not* interested in getting any of Mrs. Benjamin's tea, but the old woman is in such a fearsome mood that she doesn't object.

"Excellent!" says Mrs. Benjamin. "My tea rack is in the kitchen. Feel free to help yourself to anything you'd like."

Mona thanks her and withdraws to the kitchen as Mrs. Benjamin and Mr. Macey begin bickering in hushed tones. She wonders if she's just been made privy to a lovers' tiff (an idea that disgusts her) before she remembers the awkward way Mrs. Benjamin greeted Mr. Macey at the door, as if she wanted to stop him from talking as fast as possible. She wonders why this could be until she comes to Mrs. Benjamin's tea rack, which, she discovers, is not a tea rack but a tea *vault*, an entire room with walls covered in shelves of little tins and vials and glass containers. Each has been carefully labeled: she sees one section of rooibos tea (of the lemon-and-honeybush variety), then several containers of oolong, white, and green tea leaves (each label paired with a Latin name for a different type of camellia, which Mona guesses is in the tea), then several pots of something called "brick tea," and then there's a section whose labels are all in Asian-looking writing.

It's the section after this one that really catches her eye. These are the glass vials and beakers with old, yellowed labels, and what they contain is not tea leaves, or tea pearls, or anything so orthodox. These are teas Mrs. Benjamin seems to have made herself, and they have a distinctly fungal look to them. In one vial Mona can see thick yellow globs of pine pitch, and there is something green and loose sprouting from the top. Its label reads OLD PINEFEVER. Mona guesses this is what Mrs. Benjamin was drinking the other day.

There are many more. In one stoppered flask are half a dozen pink, fleshy roots suspended in something that looks a lot like Lucite. This is labeled ASTER'S CURL. In another a mass of white moss floats in greenish fluid, and this is labeled MAMMON'S TEARS. There is an Erlenmeyer flask with a powdery, cloudy fungus growing on the bottom that is paired with the name AL BHEEZRA'S REMORSE. And then there are three vials whose contents look like herbs ground up with white or yellow soap crystals. These are labeled AGONY, then WRATH, and finally GUILT.

Mona reads these a second time. *She names her teas after emotions?* she thinks. But a small part of her, one that has to be a little bit nuts, says, *Or maybe she makes teas out of emotions.*

Unbelievably, the tea racks get weirder. (And the farther Mona goes into the closet the darker it feels, though there is plenty of light.)

The names become utterly unpronounceable: EL-ABYHEELTH AI'AIN, HYUIN TA'AL, and CHYZCHURA DAM-UUAL are just a few. What they contain is difficult to make out: the jars appear smoked, like someone left them in a barbecue pit. After this, the labels use an alphabet Mona has never seen before. She can't imagine the country that uses this alphabet, either: it is such a harsh series of slashes and strokes, and so many of the letters stand at strange angles to one another, like they are not meant to be read left to right, but up and down, or right to left...

Where the hell did she get these from? Mona wonders. Did she make all these herself? Around *here*?

Mona picks up one jar and turns it over. Like the others, this one is smoked, but there are places that are a bit clearer. The contents look like a bunch of small grapes hanging from the jar's lid, but they're oddly yellowish, and they jiggle strangely. They keep jiggling even when she stops turning the jar over. It takes her a minute to realize they are turning, and on each grape is a dark spot that seems queerly reflective, and each grape turns until the side with the spot is facing her...

Almost as if it is an eye, Mona thinks. As if there's a bunch of tiny eyes hanging from the inside of the jar, and they are all staring at her.

She gasps and nearly falls back, but a pair of hands helps steady her.

"Goodness, dear, whatever is the matter?" asks Mrs. Benjamin's voice.

Mona jumps back the other way, for what she's found in the tea racks makes her just as frightened of Mrs. Benjamin as she is of the thing in her hand. Then she looks around at the tea racks, and sees that all the strange jars are gone: she sees no smoked beakers with labels in an alien language, nor does she see any teas that resemble bizarre scientific experiments. Even the jar in her hand has changed: it does not contain eyes, but jasmine blossoms.

She looks back at Mrs. Benjamin, and there does not seem to be anything that frightening about her, either. She's just a worried old lady standing at the door to the tea closet.

"Did I startle you?" she asks.

"I...I think I need to sit down," says Mona.

"Did you lose your balance?" asks Mrs. Benjamin. She helps Mona to a chair. "It happens to me all the time. One moment everything is crystal-clear, the next the world is wheeling around me. One of the defects of this old body of mine, I suppose."

She gives Mona a glass of water. Mona drinks it quickly while glancing back at the tea closet. She is half convinced that at any moment it might change into that room of disturbing specimens again, yet nothing happens.

"Did Mr. Macey leave already?" she asks.

"Yes," says Mrs. Benjamin. "He just stopped by to tell me some news. Or what he thought was news. It's not news if you already know it, is it?"

"What was the news?"

"Oh," says Mrs. Benjamin vaguely. "You know us old ones. We do enjoy getting into little competitions and skirmishes. Fighting over rose blooms and dead tree limbs and pets and such. And whenever someone hears of a new crime, they rush all over town telling everyone. Even if it is rather petty, once you look at it with some perspective. I suppose we have to find a way to distract ourselves."

"Is he going to be all right?" Mona asks.

"Oh, he'll be fine," says Mrs. Benjamin. "He'll be fine, I'm sure. We'll all be fine." And she turns to stare out the window at the forest and the mesa beyond, but there is something in her eye that makes Mona think she's trying to convince herself as much as Mona.

"Something the matter?" Mona asks.

"Why?" asks Mrs. Benjamin. "Do you think there's something wrong?"

The answer to this is a resounding *yes*, of course. Mona feels that magic trick with the mirrors did something to her, like it broke something inside her (with the same little *click* as that of the two mirrors sliding apart), or perhaps it reached in and opened all the windows in her head. Perhaps that's why she had that strange moment back in the tea closet.

Or maybe it's something worse, she thinks. Her mother was mentally touched, to say the least. But Laura was fine originally, so she must have broken down all at once, at a later age...say around forty. And aren't these things inherited, Mona thinks?

"I think I need to go home," she says.

"Oh, you don't look well, dear," says Mrs. Benjamin. "Are you sure you're good to drive?"

"I'm fine," Mona says quietly, and she thanks Mrs. Benjamin and walks outside and climbs into the Charger. But she does not start it just yet. Instead she just looks at herself in the mirror, examining her eyes, as if she might be able to see a change in them that would tell her if she's gone as mad as she feels.

CHAPTER ELEVEN

When the sun crests the peaks and the afternoon rays come spilling through the valley, Wink slowly fills with the overpowering aroma of pine. It comes from the forest, of course: the sun is literally roasting the sap while it's still in the trees' limbs. The outer neighborhoods get the most of it, naturally, and while they claim they love the scent some privately admit that they'd enjoy something else for a change, honestly, even a paper mill would do.

Helen Thurgreen is one of the few who is perfectly fine admitting such a thing in public. While most residents prefer to keep their dissatisfactions quiet, Helen spends most of her time out in her yard, where the smell is nothing short of overpowering, so she feels she has every right to complain. And she *has* to spend so much time out in the yard, because somehow her house has become quite the thoroughfare, with thoughtless passersby wracking havoc on nearly every single one of her rose beds.

She almost curses to herself as she lugs a spade, a rake, and a hoe from the garage. Someone really should have mentioned how popular this route was when they moved in, she thinks. They might have not even bought the place. But people don't mention much here.

As she gives one final heave and tears the rake free from a tangle of garden hose, she staggers back and happens to spot what should be the thick, magnificent blooms of a Nacogdoches Rose (a rare transplant); however, three of the most promising buds have been broken off, and dangle dead and browning from the rose's branches. No doubt it was done by some traveler who carelessly plowed through the poor thing.

"Son of a bitch!" she says. She will have to fix it, she supposes. There are so many things she needs to fix. But nothing compares to the state of the backyard, which is what's sent her out on this hot afternoon, rummaging through her garage for spades and rakes.

"Is something wrong?" asks a voice.

She looks over her shoulder and sees something unusual in Wink: a total stranger. But then she thinks, and realizes she recognizes this short, striking young woman with the black hair and dark skin: it's the new girl from down the street, the one who came roaring into town in that ridiculous car and ruined the funeral. Helen had imagined her being a fat, loud creature, but the girl on the sidewalk is fairly becoming, or at least she would be if she cared about her outfit (Helen has never thought much of cutoffs) and her hair (which Helen finds a bit dykey).

"Oh, hello," she says to the girl. "No, no. Everything's fine. Just... swearing at the flowers."

"Oh," says the girl. "I don't believe we met, ma'am. I moved down the street, I'm Mona." She aggressively sticks out her hand.

"Helen." She shakes off one dirty gardener's glove and shakes the girl's hand.

"Doing some yard work today?" Mona asks.

"Yes," says Helen, who wishes the girl would go away.

But she doesn't. She looks around at the front beds and says, "Well, you can't have much to do. These look gorgeous enough already."

Helen smiles thinly. The girl obviously does not know what she's talking about, and cannot see the numerous damages. "Well, it's not for these," says Helen. "The backyard's a bit of a mess."

"I see. Sorry to ask, but would you mind if I ask you a question, ma'am? Us being kind of neighbors and all."

"I suppose not."

"Have you lived in this house long?" Mona asks.

"Oh, God," says Helen, laughing wearily. "Too long."

"Would you have happened to have lived here when a Laura Alvarez lived at the house I'm in now?" She points down the street as if Helen can't tell where she lives by the absurd red thing parked outside. "That one?"

Helen thinks. "No," she says finally. "I'm afraid I can't recall. I doubt it, though."

"She would have worked up at the lab on the mountain. Coburn."

Helen frowns at her mistrustfully and glances around. "I don't know anything about that."

"You don't? Wasn't the town built around it?"

"I don't know anything about that," she says again. "Coburn was gone long ago."

"Do you know how long?"

Helen, growing impatient, shakes her head. "No. I don't."

"Oh," Mona says. She looks at the spade in Helen's hand, then up at the gate to the backyard, which is hanging open. Helen cannot help herself: she slowly moves to block the girl's view.

"Well," says the girl, "thanks anyways. If you think of anything, I'd really appreciate it." She waves and walks back down the street, hands in her pockets.

"Ta ta," says Helen. She watches the girl go, happy that the conversation ended there. There are a few subjects you never discuss, and Coburn is one of them, even though its logo—the hydrogen atom encased in light—discreetly adorns nearly every municipal structure in Wink, if you know where to look. Often you will see it tucked away in the corner of a building's foundation, or engraved on the very, very bottom of a light post; but then you must forget you ever saw it, which of course is no issue in Wink, where knowing how to forget what you've seen is like knowing how to blink. And there are much, much harder things to forget than a little logo.

Helen hauls the yard tools around back. She was not lying to the girl: the backyard is in a bit of a mess. But it's not the lilies, which need to be thinned, nor is it the morning glory, which is taking over; it's the enormous sunken hole right in the center of the backyard, nearly five feet across. It's a very curiously shaped hole, really: it has a large roundish section in the middle, and four rather odd protrusions stick out of its edges, with three bendy ones on one side of the circle and a large square one sticking out of the opposite side. It would be difficult for anyone to imagine what could ever make such a bizarre shape. It could be a sinkhole, one might think, but the rest of the ground is very firm. And it could have been done by flooding or standing water, but these possibilities are ruled out, for those forces take time and this hole appeared overnight.

Helen throws down her tools and begins hastily filling in the hole. Her husband Darrel, who, as always, is mostly worthless, comes out to watch, but does not offer any help.

"It's huge," he says softly after a while.

Helen nods sourly as she works at the hole.

"It came right into the yard," he says.

"Isn't that obvious?" says Helen.

"They're not supposed to come in here," he says. "*They* stay out in the woods. And we stay *away* from the woods. Those are the rules."

"Do you think," asks Helen between spadefuls, "that I am an idiot? Do you really think I don't know that?"

"Which one do you think it was?" he asks. "We can report him, if we like. We should report it anyway. If there's anyone left to report it to... I guess Macey will have to do."

For a moment Helen stops digging, and looks up. Though the fence around their yard is tall, from here she can see over the top and down into the valley. After years of living in this house, she can see why their yard is such a popular thoroughfare: it's the lowest and most accessible point between the wooded slopes and the rest of the town. Anything out in the woods would naturally wander this way when trying to get to Wink. And what's out in the woods, Helen thinks, has never really understood the concept of private property very well.

At the bottom of the mesa is one barren, treeless canyon that her eye lingers on for a long while. *Of course it had to be that one*, she thinks. *It couldn't have been one of the little ones. It had to be the biggest. That is just my luck.*

How I hate this house.

She turns around to face her husband. "No," she says. "We are not reporting this. Not about *him*, anyway. Now are you just going to stand there? Or are you actually going to do anything?"

"My back's hurt," he says, defensively.

"Oh, it's always your back." She returns to filling in the hole. "Or your knee. Or your ankle."

"I have joint problems," he says. "It's genetic."

Helen scoffs.

After a while, Darrel says, "It came right up and stood in the yard. Why would it ever do that, I wonder?"

"I expect it was doing what everyone else is doing," says Helen.

"And what's that?"

She lays the spade aside and starts smoothing over the dirt with the rake. Soon she'll have to lay sod out, and keep it soaked, but in time it should all be patched up, and no one will have any reason to think anything strange has happened here at all.

Helen says, "Coming to get a look at the new girl."

CHAPTER TWELVE

It's a bad night, Joseph can tell. He can tell by how the trees begin to devour the sun, and the way the stars stab through the soft blue sky and shine down just a little too brightly. It's in the way the wind rubs its back on the pines, and they bend a little more than they should. It's even in the way his family's chandelier lights the dinner table: the light is flat and lifeless, like it's cast from a neon light filled with the powdery remains of trapped insects. It makes the food look like gruel and gives skin the look of parchment.

On nights like this, his family knows, you get your day done as fast as you can, and then you go to bed. It's not enough to just stay indoors. You don't even want to be *awake*. Being awake attracts attention, which you definitely don't want.

But awake is exactly what Joseph is, as he lies in his bed and stares at the ceiling. He tries to ignore the shadows dancing across the blinds in his bedroom window. He tries not to think of Gracie, and her cool touch and saddened eyes. She seems so much sadder these days, and since Mr. Macey caught them he hasn't dared contact her. And he tries not to think of what could be happening out there, among the buttes and bluffs around Wink, or in its darkened streets and alleys, or in the playground at the elementary school. Tonight is most definitely a bad night. One of the worst in a while.

He freezes, and sits up in bed a little. Was it his imagination, or was there a tap at his window? He soon realizes it wasn't his imagination, because there's another tap, this one much louder. Then a soft pitter-pat as something rains against his window, like sand...

He stands up and walks to his window, but does not open his blinds. They glow slightly from the streetlight outside. He sees something dark fly up and strike the glass on the other side, and there's another tap.

Someone's throwing things at the glass, he thinks. Or are they being tossed by the wind?

Joseph reaches toward the blinds, but hesitates. He has never heard of someone's window being tampered with at night...that's not how things are supposed to go. But what if it's known that he's awake? What if this is how his crime is addressed? Maybe this is how it happens...

But Joseph throws caution to the wind, and he takes one slat of the blinds and lifts it up ever so slightly. A blade of light pokes through, and he squints to see through it.

His window is on the ground floor, and he can see the edge of the forest just beyond his house. There's a figure standing just beside the trunk of one tree: a white hand is resting against its bark and is barely caught by the luminescence of the streetlight.

The hand rises and gestures to him, telling him to come out, and his heart nearly stops. He should never have looked through the blinds, he thinks. This was all a huge mistake...

The figure seems to grow frustrated at his lack of response. It gestures again, and Joseph is just about to shut the blinds when the hand's owner steps out into the light.

It is Gracie. She is dressed in black, except for a checked skirt. Her skin is paler than usual. She looks almost bloodless in the streetlight. She gestures to him again.

This worries Joseph: they shouldn't be seeing one another after Macey caught them, and it's definitely not a night to be going out. He glances around at the trees, then pulls his blinds up and opens his window.

"What are you doing?" he hisses as Gracie approaches. "Go back home, Gracie! It's dangerous out!"

"Not for me, it isn't," she says. There is something soft and hollow in her voice. "Come out with me. I need to talk to you."

"What? Are you insane? I can't come out in this!"

"You can if I'm with you," says Gracie. "Come out, Joseph. You won't be harmed."

"Mr. Macey caught us, though. We can't risk it."

"Mr. Macey's what I want to talk to you about."

He looks at the trees bending in the wind. They bend so much he's sure they'll break. "They're angry," he says softly.

"They aren't angry," she says. "They're scared. Scared and confused. Come out with me."

Joseph looks into her eyes. There is something new there, something that shouldn't be. It's as if there's a flaw in their color that's appeared overnight. "All right," he says.

He puts on some slippers and climbs out the window to her. She holds out a hand for him, then leads him away into the woods.

The woods are cold and strange in the night. The way the wind runs through them makes it sound as if they are filled with voices. Sometimes he and Gracie pass through a glade and it looks like no place on earth: the stones are black and shiny, and boulders with queer angles lean drunkenly against the night sky. Joseph smells the air and realizes it has that electric, ionized scent to it, and he understands she is leading him through No-Go Zones, one after the other. But these are ones he has never seen before, ones no one in town might even know exist. He is almost faint with fear at the idea of it.

"Where are you taking me, Gracie?" he asks.

"To the lake, to talk," she says. "In quiet. There are too many eyes here in the woods. Too many eyes in town, too, too many ears listening to everything and everyone."

"And the lake will be safe?"

"Safer. Yes."

"Why?"

"Because no one wants to be near the lake," she says simply.

The woods go on and on. Joseph never knew they were so big. But then, he has never really ventured into them before. As a young boy he always wanted to, for what child would turn down an untamed kingdom just beyond his doorstep? But it was drilled into him from the start that his life, like everyone's in Wink, was to be anchored to the streets and sidewalks and well-lit areas, places of sunlight and fresh breeze. The other places, the places in the forest and those hidden in the canyons, well... those just weren't theirs to have.

Gracie holds up a hand, and they stop. She places a finger to her lips. Then she looks up and scans the pines above them. Joseph looks with her, but sees nothing. It feels like they've been looking forever when they hear a sound coming from the treetops.

It's an awful sound, one that makes Joseph's teeth hurt, like someone's taken a swarm of some particularly vicious cousin of the cicada, tossed them all in a bag, and given the bag a shake, pissing them off. And yet Joseph feels there are words in that buzz. The thing in the trees is calling out a message, like a warning—*This territory is mine. Stay off.*

Gracie motions to him to stoop down low, and they begin to creep around the area the sound came from. As they pass through one glen Joseph looks up through the branches, and he sees something at the top of a tree, near the trunk. It is dark, but he thinks he sees the silhouette of a man, balanced perfectly on a high branch like a rooster on top of a barn. In the starlight Joseph thinks he can make out the edge of the man's face, and while he can discern a nose and a mouth, he cannot see any ears, or eyes... as he looks closer, the dark figure shifts a little on the branch, settles back its shoulders, and it lifts its head, and as it does the horrible buzz fills the forest again.

Joseph feels his heart ratchet up its rate until he can feel his pulse in his eyes. The shadowy figure in the tree trembles as the buzz dies to a close, and he can see the thing begin looking around from the top of the tree, searching for intruders...

Gracie takes Joseph by the shoulder. "Come on," she whispers. "Hurry."

"I thought you said nothing in the woods would hurt you," Joseph whispers back.

"I think so, but I don't want to test that."

They slip around the thing in the tree and come to a path down to the lake. The path is very steep, but Gracie seems to have no issue seeing in the dark, and with her to guide him Joseph has no problem. Soon the trees draw back and the lake emerges: it is not really a lake, but more of a pond, fed by an underground spring. It is long and thin, a gash in the mountain's side. The waters are so still they are like a mirror, a puddle of stars among the rocks. On the far side is the elderly Miss Tucker's house. He notes that she is awake, apparently without concern: all of her lights are on, and he can see her moving in the windows. But then, he has heard she has an arrangement, just like Gracie.

Gracie sits down on a stone shelf beside the lake, and Joseph joins her. "What is it?" he asks.

Gracie just stares at the pink moon in the skies. Then, "You know I love you, don't you?"

Joseph is startled by the question. He is not sure what to say. He has never even considered the question. He longs for her, needs her, yes, but that's quite a bit different from love.

"I hope you do," she says. "You are the only good thing in my life, Joseph. The only normal thing. The only thing that reminds me that I'm a person. My parents don't, not anymore. Everything changed after they made my arrangement. And Mr. First... God. Sometimes I fool myself into thinking he's... it's..."

She falls quiet. Joseph watches apprehensively, not sure what to do. "What is it?" he asks. "What's wrong?"

"Someone needs to know," she says. "And I want to take care of you." She steels herself. "You remember the last time you came to see me? When I went to go see Mr. First, and Mr. Macey caught us?"

"Yes," says Joseph, who honestly wishes he could forget it.

"They let me stay when they talked. I guess they didn't think I could hear them, or understand them. It's not... normal when *they* talk among themselves. They don't talk like people."

"I don't know if I want to know this, Gracie," Joseph says. "I know

too much already. I know I used to laugh about things like that, but…
but ever since Macey found us…"

"Macey doesn't care," she says.

"He doesn't?"

"No. He has bigger things to worry about. He's been walking out
into the countryside, every night. I've seen him."

"Why?"

"He's been talking. Letting everyone know the news. Gossiping, I
guess."

"To who?"

"There are many of them that look like us, Joseph," she says.
"More than you think, probably. That's what they'd all do, if they
could—look like us. But some can't. Like Mr. First. And others. And
they can't stay in town. They have to find their own way wherever
they can."

She looks into the waters. Joseph follows her gaze, staring into the
starlit lake. It takes him a moment to realize he can see beyond its surface: there are rocks down there, spectral and silvery, and some plant
life, like moss or reeds. But some of the plants do not look like reeds.
They're too fleshy, too pale. And they all seem connected to something, like there's a big tangle of them down in the lake.

A minnow, no more than a dart of black in the water, comes swimming by one of the fleshy reeds. The flow of the reed changes—from
sine to cosine, thinks Joseph, who's a bit of a math geek—as if it's resisting the current of the water, which a reed definitely should not do. But
then the reed snaps out, silent and snakelike, and he sees a flash of
tiny, shining needle teeth, and the minnow is gone…

"Wh-what's that?" Joseph stammers. "What's down there?"

"It's why there's no one near the lake," says Gracie. "But it won't
bother us. I've talked to Miss Tucker about it." She bows her head. "I
listened to them speak, Mr. Macey and Mr. First. They talked like old
friends. Which I guess they are. But Mr. Macey…he was terrified. I'd
never seen that before."

"Everyone seems nervous, after Mr. Weringer died," says Joseph.

"And that's what's strange. No one's ever said it—no one ever *says* anything, of course—but they can't *die*, can they? It's not…allowed. There are *rules*."

Joseph nods.

"You're afraid of them, aren't you?" Gracie says.

"Shouldn't I be?"

"Some, maybe. They're not *bad*. They're just lost. But for the longest time, I thought they weren't afraid of anything." She looks back at him. "But I was wrong, Joseph. They are afraid of someone. And they're afraid of that person just as much as we're afraid of them."

"What are you talking about?"

"Mr. Macey came back to Mr. First again," she says. "He said he'd learned who killed Weringer. Or he *thought* he'd learned who. He said a word then—I couldn't understand it—and Mr. First went all quiet. And after that, Mr. First was so dismayed he could barely talk, to me or Mr. Macey. I didn't know who it was they were talking about, but it's someone new, and the…I guess the *rules* don't apply to them. Whoever this person is, they're allowed to hurt things, to kill them. I don't know why they haven't before now, but that's what they're doing. Or what they did, to Mr. Weringer."

Joseph huddles close to Gracie on the stone shelf. His intentions are far from amorous: he is terrified, terrified of the thing in the water and those strange glens in the woods, and now she's telling him about someone even *worse*, someone that inspires fear in things he thought couldn't even understand fear. Yet Gracie is still and calm, a stable rock on this dark, swirling mountain, so he clings to her.

"Why are you telling me this?" he asks.

"Because I don't want to see you hurt," she says. "Things are changing in Wink. Things *never* change in Wink, but that's what's happening now. I want to make sure you'll be safe."

"Would you run away with me, Gracie?"

"Run away?" She is quiet. "I've never thought about it…I don't know if…I don't know if I'll be able to get away."

"But I'd want you to come with me."

"Oh, for God's sake, Joseph, are you *listening*? This is much, much more important than you or me."

Joseph draws back a little, stung.

"You don't understand how bad this is," says Gracie. "I might be one of the only people who knows what's going on, thanks to Mr. First. He's given me certain . . . authorities, though I'm not sure he knows it."

Joseph looks at her out of the side of his eye. She is staring into the dark waters with queerly lifeless eyes. "Is that why you seem so different?" he asks.

She shuts her eyes. "It gets worse at night. In the day I feel all right, but at night . . . things change." She swallows. "I'm in one place . . . and then, if I'm not looking, I'm suddenly someplace very different. Somewhere with red stars, and many mountains . . ."

There is a ripple in the water, then another. At first Joseph is nervous, eyes searching for those fleshy tendrils in the water, but then he realizes Gracie is crying, her tears falling into the pond. It is a disturbing sight, for she cries without moving her face at all: her eyes are wide and calm, with tears simply welling up at the rims to leak down her face.

Joseph embraces her and holds her close. "It's all right," he says.

"It's not," she says. "It isn't and it won't be. Not for me."

"We'll make it all right."

"How?"

"I don't know. We'll do what we can, I guess. We can't do anything more than that." But though Joseph's words are comforting, he is disturbed. He's held her as she's cried before, but not like this, arms limp and eyes wide open as she talks into his lap in a monotone voice.

There is the sound of singing from the other side of the lake. Miss Tucker has hobbled out of her cabin and is standing on the dock with a lantern, singing a tuneless little reel. There is a splash from the center of the lake, a bit of froth stirred up—perhaps by the wind, perhaps by something else—and he sees the old woman stoop and hold something just above the waters. Perhaps a fish? A hunk of meat? He isn't sure. There is another splash, and a moan from somewhere near the dock, and she stands back up and wipes her hand on her dress. But now her hand is empty, and she is smiling out at the waters with the fondness of a trainer observing the antics of a well-behaved pet.

"What I would give," says Gracie, "for an arrangement as simple as that."

CHAPTER THIRTEEN

Mona discovers that her house's attic is stuffed full of boxes, and over the next few days she sorts through them all, trying to see if their contents can tell her more about her mother. Many of them seem to be from the family who lived here before, but every once in a while she comes across a document or artifact of her mother's that urges her on. And as she works and lives her life in this town, she begins to understand Wink a little more, or she thinks she does.

Wink is a sunny place, but you never have to go far to find a welcoming porch, or the shade of a pine, or a cool shelf of rock. There you can sit and watch the midday sun turn honeyish and dusky, and soon the streets will echo with the sound of children and the clatter of bike wheels, and people will begin venturing out to knock on neighbors' doors with pitchers of iced tea or lemonade or martini in their hands.

Wink is a place where no vehicle ever seems to go faster than thirty miles an hour. The cars drip and slide through the neighborhood lanes with the gentle pace of raindrops weaving down window glass. There just isn't any need for a rush; nothing is far away, and no problem would ever require you to hurry. If you're late, everyone will understand.

And all the cars in Wink are American. Maybe it's because it'd be tough to get them serviced here if they were anything else, but the residents all take a special pride in it, regardless.

Everyone freely walks across everyone else's lawn, and sometimes people even hop a fence; in Wink, this is totally understandable, because what's mine is yours, my good fella, and maybe I wanted you to swing on by so you could see how my roses are doing, or to have an Old Fashioned and a game of pool.

Wink is a place of evening baseball and dazzling sunsets and the cheery hiss of dance music through an idling car's radio. It is a porch place, a place of folding chairs and electric fans and crystal glassware, and pitchers and pitchers of carefully prepared beverages. It is a place of homegrown tomatoes and crawling ivy and roses heavy and drooping with blooms. People get dressed up to go to the diner in Wink: it's where all the official meets and greets are held, where everyone goes to hear the news, where you take your folks out when you want to treat them to a good time and a good piece of meat.

Wink is a quiet place, a laughing place, a place where you can throw down a towel anywhere you want and stare up at the pale blue sky and no one will bat an eye, because it's always early summer in Wink, and such things are meant to be enjoyed.

Every second is a forever in Wink. Every day is a cool afternoon waiting to happen. And every life is one lived quietly, with your feet up and your sun-dappled lawn before you as you watch the world happily drift by.

Sometimes Mona feels she has come back to a home she never knew she had. But each time she begins to feel this way, she finds herself watching the children.

Of all Wink's pleasant wonders, it is the mothers and the children Mona studies the most. She watches them as they walk down the sidewalks, holding hands; she watches the children playing in the parks, the mothers lounging on picnic blankets, occasionally intervening in some spat; she watches the children sit on the porches as their mothers read them stories from their rockers before returning inside when it's dark. A single window fills with golden light, the bedtime rituals are completed, and then it winks out.

Night-night.

As Mona watches, the old pain in her arm and stomach returns.

Did Momma have that with me? Mona wonders. *Did I? Could I have ever had such a thing?*

Put it away. Push it all away.

You are empty. Empty.

Mona asks, and asks, and asks. But she gets no answers. At first she suspects the entire town is hiding something from her. But after a while, she begins to believe them: they really don't remember her mother's time here. Was her mother here in secret? Did she live under another name? Was it something to do with Coburn? They cannot say.

Despite this, Mona's first weeks in Wink are some of the most pleasurable ones she's ever had. The afternoons are so beautiful they almost hurt. She has never wanted to shed her life and start anew as much as she does here. She almost wants to give up finding out more about her mother. But then she finds the cans of film in the attic.

It's real film, motion picture film, spools and spools of ghostly amber images. She has to find an old-school projector to view it, but this isn't hard to find in Wink, where the stores keep plenty of old appliances. She has to go through a tutorial to figure out how to feed the film through the projector (a marvelously complicated process), but when she figures it out she returns home, shuts all the curtains and doors, feeds the film in, and turns the projector on.

There's a whir, and a blob of dancing colored light appears on the living room wall. She fiddles with the knobs to get it to resolve into distinct shapes, and soon faces and hands emerge from the colorful fog.

What the camera is projecting is a room. This room, in fact, this very living room in this house, and it's not empty, but full of people. It's some kind of holiday party, one set during the summer—on the Fourth of July, probably, judging by the red-white-and-blue cake—and everyone in attendance is about the same age, around thirty or so. The men all wear open-throated shirts with blue or brown sports coats, and the women wear incredibly bright dresses, so bright they look like Christmas ornaments. The air is thick with smoke, everyone has a glass of punch, and they all laugh as they walk in and out of the French doors in the back. Some of them wave to the camera, or squint irritably when the cameraman turns its blazing light on them. There is no sound, so the images are accompanied only by the rattle and whir of the projector.

One man calls across the porch to the backyard. Mona can see a woman turn and say something, but she's far away and out of focus. The man (to Mona he looks like a professional golfer) says something again, louder, and the woman shouts a response so loudly she practically bends double. Mona feels certain she's just witnessed the "What?... *WHAT?*" exchange that has to happen once at nearly every big party. The golfer, giving up, waves to the woman, and she comes trotting in, moving very gracefully in such huge high heels.

It is Mona's mother, Laura Alvarez herself, wearing an amazing red dress, and she is undoubtedly the life of the party. A silent cheer goes up among all the attendees when she strides through the French doors, and she laughs, embarrassed but gleeful, her fingers fluttering to her chest to calm her heart. And as she laughs, something in Mona breaks, and she begins crying as the ghost of her mother smiles at her from the wall.

This is all just not fair. It's wrong—no, it's just fucking *rude*—for Mona to see her mother living a happy life among all these happy people. The blurry woman laughing on her wall has no idea that just ahead of her lie years of madness spent in dark rooms, and somewhere in one of those rooms will be a child who can't understand why every sight seems to make her mother weep.

Suddenly Mona hates them all. She hates her pleasant neighbors in Wink, she hates the sound of the kids laughing as they fool around on the baseball field, she hates the cheery neon lights and the waves of hello, and she hates the painted people on the town's sign who stare at the antenna on the mesa with eyes full of hope. She hates them all for having a happiness that is denied to her, because they don't *know*, do they? They don't know what the world is like outside Wink. Those people in the film don't know that their dreams will come to nothing. They don't know how things really are, how they will be.

But Mona knows. She knows too well.

Mona's last name wasn't always Bright. Once, only a few years ago—though it feels like a lifetime now—when she was on her fourth year with the Houston PD, she happened to meet a state trooper named Dale Loudon, a brick wall of a man who had large, sad eyes and a soft, slow way of speaking that charmed Mona's hardened (or so she thought) heart. Dale liked old movies, mowing his grass, and making fly-fishing lures, though he was a terrible fly-fisherman himself. He was kind, he was attentive, he was, more or less, thoughtful; in other words, he was everything Mona had missed out on so far in her life. And the fact that he had a dick like a plantain certainly didn't hurt his case.

They got married when Mona was thirty-two, and she was, to her suspicious disbelief, quite happy. The quiet, dull domesticity Dale offered appealed to her, resonated with her. She had never known you could live like that, so relaxed, just simply *there*. There was something perfect about the Sunday mornings when they would lie in bed lazing away the day. It was like some kind of wonderful exotic drug—but then, it would be, because never in her life had Mona ever had a home like that. A *real* home.

She was pregnant four months into the marriage. It was not something either of them had intended, yet she couldn't ever call it an accident. Because Mona was, despite all logic, quite thrilled at the news, which was not something one would expect. Honestly, no one could ever hear the question "Would you like for your body to play host to a whole person, and, upon painful extraction of that person, would you allow every waking and even unwaking moment of the next years or decades of your life to bend at the whims of a tiny, tyrannical, larval human, to the complete devastation of your financial and social life?" and respond in the positive. Let alone Mona Bright, she of the fierce right hook, cold grimace (which she picked up from her father), and deadeye shot (for Mona had been far and away the best shot in her graduating class—something else she had learned from her father).

But Mona did. When she saw the tiny pink plus sign on the white stick, something inside her opened up, unfolded its limbs, and stretched its palms toward sunlight. She could not articulate it, but it felt like she now had a chance to make things *right*, even though she was never entirely sure what had been wrong. (Besides, a tiny voice always reminded her, absolutely everything.)

She soon found herself buying all sorts of ridiculous shit for the nursery: carpets and drapes and a crib and bedding (all vetted by the most scrupulous baby magazines, which suddenly seemed terribly wise) and onesies and hats that would only ever be worn about twice before the little thing's head grew too big. Most of these items were a gender-neutral yellow, because Mona could never get her head around this binary blue/pink bullshit. She also refused to learn the baby's gender, because that would just ruin all the damn fun, wouldn't it?

Dale bought her similarly ridiculous maternity shit. Slippers. Body pillows. A foot massager for her swollen ankles. He even bought her a pink maternity dress. A *pink* one, because, bless his heart, Dale could never get his own head around Mona's problems with the blue/pink situation. But the thing was, Mona had *worn* it. Even though it made her look like a deflating balloon or a piece of goddamn chewing gum, she'd worn it. And she hadn't cared. The second she saw the tiny dancing shrimp-person displayed on the screens at the ob-gyn, none of that niggling stuff could ever bother her again.

If anything bothered her, it was the whole family process—and there *was* a process. She began to think about the phrase *start a family* more and more: it was like *start a car*, suggesting that there was a pre-assembled apparatus and you could just hop in and hit a switch and off you would go. Or as if there were a cheap-suited huckster who, once you had a ring on your finger and a mortgage sucking off dollars from your bank account, could fix you up with the right kind of family and you could drive it off the lot to*day*. It was a creeping feeling she had when reading the magazines, as if they were saying, "This is how one births and rears a child," and they'd brook no other suggestion. You had to look *exactly* like the picture in the magazine, otherwise you were doing it wrong.

And none of that seemed right to her. She didn't want this to be a product, a commodity, something that had to look like what was advertised on the fucking *box*. This was her one chance to give love she'd never gotten herself, and she didn't want it to be turned into something she was being fucking *sold*, just buying the Motherhood Experience, one internet purchase at a time.

Her life and her child were the only things she'd ever really had. And she made herself promise never to forget that.

It was eight months into the pregnancy when it happened. Eight months of nausea, of swollen feet and fingers, of nosebleeds and blurred vision and exhaustion; eight months of little wiggles and shimmers down in her belly, the poke and prod of tiny limbs; eight months of black-and-white photos of the slumbering stowaway growing inside her; eight months of mounds and mounds of impossibly tiny clothing. And then when she was on her way back from the grocery store she passed through an intersection with the blessing of two green lights, and yet just as she trundled through she caught a blur of red in the corner of her vision—just the tiniest blur, like the flit of a hummingbird's wing. Then she felt her head snap back and her arms go limp, and in that moment her world shattered.

The entire earth seemed to buckle up and throw her car several feet to the right. She blacked out briefly. When she came to, with screams and tinkling glass and the hiss of machinery in her ears, she looked through what was left of her driver's-side window and saw the crumpled front of a red Ford F-150, its windshield sporting a frost-rimmed, gaping hole on the right side, created when the driver—unbuckled, drunken—had been ejected through the windshield like a man shot out of a cannon, his face pushed back through his brain as he dove through the glass.

And all she could think was—*Where did that come from? Where did that come from?*

Then the ambulance and the parade of lights, some red and blue, some cold white. So many white flashing lights, light after light after light, and pokes all along her side as they put pins in the bones of her left arm...and then there was Dale, seated beside her bed with his big hands clasped before him, his face the color of a currant and his eyes dripping tears, and he said, honey, honey, she didn't make it.

And Mona said, Who? Who didn't make it?

And Dale said, Our little girl. She died. He killed our little girl.

And as Mona understood who this *she* was and realization dawned in her sputtering, bruised brain, some little shelf under her heart collapsed and she caved inward, crumbling to pieces and falling down the big, dark mine shaft that occupied the space where her daughter had once peacefully slept.

Dale kept talking, but it didn't matter. Mona was walking through the hallways of her mind, turning off lights, shutting off switches, locking doors, shutting everything down, down, down, until all that was left was the barest fundamentals.

Shut down. Turn it all off.

Make yourself empty, and drift.

After the funeral Dale held her hand and said she'd be all right. He said they'd get through this. He was wrong on both counts.

She wished so badly to have known her at least a little before she lost her. Much in the same way, Mona knows, that she wished to have known her mother before she excused herself from this world.

Why is it, she thought, *that people always leave us just before we know them?*

After her marriage fell apart, her old lieutenant came by to pay her his respects and offer her her old position. But Mona turned it down. The person who had worked that job was gone, just as the happy creature of lazy Sunday mornings was gone. Now she could tolerate nothing but endless highways and miles of ugly country and the constant shuffle of motels, a beery, dreary life of mundane odd jobs and faceless, wordless lovers. And somewhere in the midst of all that miserable wandering she looked at herself in the mirror and saw a glimpse of the trembling, mad woman who had once told her to stay in the yard until the ambulances were gone, just before she lay down in the bathtub and stuck her chin on the barrel of a twelve-gauge.

Mona considered doing the same. Perhaps, she thought, it was a kind of family duty, carrying on in her mother's footsteps.

Yet almost as the thought crossed her mind she got a letter notifying her that her father, Earl Bright III, had sloughed off his mortal coil to transcend this earth and touch the heavens, and so on and so forth, and waiting in the bleary wreckage of his life was a confusing invitation to come visit this little slice of paradise in the shadow of Mesa Abertura.

Now Mona is here, sifting through the remains of another person's life, yet this life was over long before she died. How and why this happened, why some germ of madness infected her mother's brain, remains a mystery to Mona. And though she hates herself for it, she feels nothing but anger at the woman projected on the wall. She hates that Laura Alvarez and the rest of this town has a joy that has always eluded her. She hates that this place is perfect forever, whereas she has only a dream of something that now feels as if it might never have happened, a dream of two people, mother and child, who never truly were.

Mona isn't really paying attention to the movie anymore; she's just staring through the morass of flickering blue faces as she imagines her own failings. Yet then her anger goes cold and something in her brain, the tiny cop part that still scrutinizes everything she sees, speaks up and says—*Did I just see...?*

She sits up, watching the film. The cameraman is following her mother through a dense thicket of people, all of whom are waving to the camera. Mona waits, but she doesn't see it again, so she has to go through the laborious task of rewinding the film.

She starts it again and sits before the glowing wall, waiting, watching. The cameraman turns a corner and begins wading through the throng, Mona's mother sometimes stopping to wave him forward. People keep turning to look at the camera and its blinding light as it passes, and then one huge, pale face comes swooping out of the crowd like a wayward moon...

"What the fuck?" breathes Mona.

She rewinds it again, and watches it once more. The empty room seems even bigger than before, and she shivers a bit, feeling cold and vulnerable. For projected on her wall, just very briefly, was the smiling face of none other than Mrs. Benjamin, the very woman who not more than a few days ago claimed she did not remember Mona's mother at all. She's standing in the crowd to the side, listening to conversation with a polite smile, and as the camera passes by, her eyes flick over, irritated—*Who brought that damn thing?*—before her polite smile returns and the camera moves on.

"She lied," says Mona aloud. "Why did she lie?"

But even more concerning, Mrs. Benjamin does not appear thirty years younger in the film. She looks the exact same age as she did the other day, around seventy. Yet this film has to have been taken more than thirty years ago. Right?

CHAPTER FOURTEEN

There is only so much nothing a man can take, Norris learns, before he has to do something. It's only been three weeks since Bolan sent them to do that job on the mountain, yet it feels like an eternity, each hour stretched to a day by Norris's screaming paranoia. But so far nothing has happened, and Norris has made sure to do nothing as well. This, of course, is part of Bolan's orders: don't do a damn thing, he told him. Buy groceries. Watch television. Read, cook, whatever. Just don't talk to me or anyone else, and don't step a single fucking toe out of line, you hear?

Norris is only too happy to oblige. He's one of the few Roadhouse employees to actually live in Wink. This is not, of course, coincidence—Bolan decided (or was told) a year ago that he'd need people actually in Wink, rather than on the periphery like the Roadhouse. Zimmerman and Norris got stuck with the job, which only occasionally seems like a bad one—Wink *is* a terribly nice place to live—though the job does come with a lot of rules. Some of which make it a little difficult on a man like Norris.

He tries to be good during this cautious period. He buys groceries, and cooks, and watches television. He cleans his house and mows his yard and just tries to be a generally agreeable neighbor. And everyone just smiles and waves to him, as if there's nothing wrong.

And there isn't, Norris says to himself. Nothing is wrong at all. They certainly didn't kill the town's eldest, most respected resident up on the mesa nearly a month ago. Why, it's just insane to consider. No, it's just old Norris here, going about his normal, respectable business.

But then it happens: he's at Mr. Macey's checking out (his bag contains only tuna, bread, and mustard, for though he attempted cooking as Bolan said, it was an unmitigated disaster) when his eye scans the magazines at the counter. Most of them are the usual forgettable fare (but the magazines in Wink, though all slightly bland, are ones Norris has never seen elsewhere, like *Southern Housekeeper and Gardener*, *Our Day Today*, and *Southwestern Steppes Outdoorsman*). Yet one, a fitness magazine Norris has never seen before, features a cover that leaps to his eye: a young man in a white T-shirt and acid-washed jeans leans against the hood of a Corvette, staring into the sunset. He is thin and bronzed and his oiled hair features a wandering forelock, an enticing thread of hair that curls across his smooth brow. And there is something about him—the way his hips are thrust forward, maybe, proffered to the viewer, or the way he seems both aware of the beauty of the sunset and totally indifferent to it—that puts a cold fire dancing down Norris's bones.

He freezes up. Bolan *said* to be good, after all. And the urge that has charged every molecule in Norris's body is most certainly *not* good. Yet Norris cannot help himself. He swallows, picks up the magazine with trembling hands, and places it in his bag as he checks out.

Even though he pays for the magazine honestly, he feels as if he's stolen the damn thing. He tucks his bag under his arm and hunches over as he walks out. Yet as he leaves, he sees he is being watched: he looks up to see an old, lined face staring at him from the yellowed office windows near the exit. It is Mr. Macey, the shop's owner, and though he is often genial and pleasant, now his face is fixed in a look of terrible fury.

Norris runs out the door, and even hides behind a parked truck, watching the store's door and waiting for Macey to follow. Yet he never comes. Norris slinks away, feeling guilty and jittery and nauseous.

For the rest of the day he goes through his normal routine. He eats his tuna sandwiches and watches *Howdy Doody* on the TV. He plays darts on his porch and has to turn down an offer from his neighbor to join in. When night falls he returns inside.

Sometimes Norris must remind himself that he is not on friendly territory. Somewhere in the woods there is a border, and what is on one side of the border is not the same as what is on the other. The Roadhouse, he knows, just barely rides that invisible line. Most people can cross the line, if they wish—but most don't, fearing what would happen if they tried. Yet *They* can't, at all. Norris knows that, and thanks God for it. But since Norris is in here with Them, on the inside of the border, he has to be mindful about himself.

He turns on all the lights in the house, for to turn them off would look suspicious. He makes sure all his chores are done, all the dishes put away and the laundry neatly folded and sorted, and as he finishes up he picks up a stack of books very nonchalantly—*Just carrying these books around, no problem here*—and begins placing them on random shelves. About halfway through, he comes to the fitness magazine he bought at the store, and he grunts as if to say—*How did this get here?* And he absentmindedly leaves it on a shelf in the linen closet of the bathroom, making sure it appears as though he just set it down on whichever surface was available.

Then he decides to go through the cleaning supplies under his sink. And again, he finds something that should not be there: a bottle of baby oil. He shakes his head, *tsk*ing and bemoaning his poor organizational skills, and again returns to the bathroom. Yet rather than putting the baby oil away, he enters the linen closet with it, and shuts the door behind him.

In Wink, it is always smart to live your life as if you're being watched. Because so frequently, you are.

Norris blindly reaches out and picks up a waiting flashlight from one of the closet shelves. He turns it on, grabs the magazine, stoops, and crawls below the biggest shelf at the bottom of the closet. There, curled up in the fetal position, his breath trembling and his fingers quivering, he begins to page through the magazine, his eyes devouring every image.

Wink has strict rules, and though one of its rules is never to discuss what the rules are, there are certain things that just don't happen. No one gets divorced in Wink, for example. Premarital sex is deeply frowned upon, and pregnancy out of wedlock is beyond scandalous. Yet there are things even worse than these.

Norris is not sure why, but he's always found it easier to fall in love with men than women. He's just more comfortable around them. And he knows it is wrong—it *is* wrong—yet he cannot stop himself. He cannot stop the bolt of energy that sometimes comes rushing out of his heart. He has never really acted on it: though sometimes he might desperately wish for physical contact (the brush of knuckles on the back of his hand, perhaps) he cannot allow it. His one moment of perfection, his guilty, trembling moment of joy, occurs once a month in the cramped dark of his linen closet, lit only by a flashlight and perfumed with the puerile aroma of baby oil. It is the only time he feels happy and whole, and each time it is followed by unspeakable self-hate. What a fool he is to follow such passions, and what a coward he is to do so in such a craven way.

He is just about to unbuckle his pants when he hears a crash from his kitchen. He sits up so fast he knocks his head on the shelf above him. A single thought cracks through his mind like a caroming bullet:

He's been found out. They know what he is.

He sits in the closet for a moment, listening, but he hears no other noise. Then, slowly, he emerges from the closet, making sure to leave the baby oil and the fitness magazine hidden below piles of bedsheets. He looks down his hallway but sees nothing there. He grabs the only weapon he can find—an old brass candlestick—and, feeling like a cartoon out of *Clue*, he stalks down the hall.

He finds his French press has fallen off the top of the stove and shattered on the kitchen floor. He can't imagine how this could have happened, yet it seems innocent enough. He sighs, relieved, puts the candlestick on the kitchen counter, and stoops to pick up the glass.

It's as he's on his hands and knees, brushing shards into a paper towel, that he hears the hiss. And it's just sheer coincidence that he looks up and sees the severed tube resting against the wall behind his stove. And isn't the air at the mouth of the severed tube awful shimmery? And what is that smell in the air...

Norris's eyes shoot wide and he stands up and bolts out of his house, stumbling out the back door to his porch. He jumps his fence and peers back through a crack, watching his house for any sign of movement.

He isn't sure how they got in, but someone's broken into this house and cut his gas lines, he's sure. Just the tiniest spark could have set the whole thing off. But why would someone do that? Is it because of what he was about to do? Was it a message?

A cloud drifts over the moon, and Norris absently glances up at it. He does a double take, and freezes as he realizes he's just broken another cardinal rule of Wink: he's outside his property at night.

And he has committed worse crimes than what he was about to do in the linen closet, hasn't he? Isn't it possible that what they really wanted to do was flush him out of his house, to the dark, where he'd be vulnerable?

As he realizes this, a soft, twinkling light creeps across the fence and around him. Its source is behind him, and he *knows* he should not look at it, yet he turns.

Down the hill is the start of the forest, and there are lights in the trees, lights like will-o'-wisps, slowly orbiting a few of the trunks. Some lights are a pale blue, others a soft pink. They are so beautiful and enchanting that Norris cannot help himself: he walks down the hill to them, wishing to touch them and hold them.

Yet somehow they elude him. They always seem a few more feet away, circling the next few trees over rather than the ones he'd thought, and soon he's deep within the forest, wandering under the dark, whispering pines.

He enters a wide, grassy glade. The will-o'-wisp lights go out, and Norris stands there, confused.

Then someone enters on the opposite side of the glade.

It is difficult to see in this faint light, but he thinks he can see a small, elderly figure in white shirtsleeves and a red bow tie, yet the face is dark. Just as he begins to think the person is familiar, the image flickers like the flame of a candle, and as it does the moon seems to dim too, and the glade grows deeply dark, so dark Norris cannot even see what is in front of him.

"Hello?" he calls, and he walks forward, arms outstretched, trying to find the man on the other side of the glade.

He thinks he is close when he hears breathing. Relieved, he turns toward it, but as he grows near he finds it no longer sounds like normal breathing. The air is passing through too many passageways, he thinks, and some of them seem to rattle, as if they are filled with mucus...

He stops. Something is standing just beside him underneath the tree, and it is not a little old man. He can just see it out of the corner of his eye, and he glimpses something low and broad and chitinous, and what tops it is not a head but a mass that appears somehow nasal to him, a sphenoidal lump riddled with gaping conchae and sinuses, yet clutched under the upper shelf of two of these cavities are two pieces of anatomy he recognizes:

Eyes. Very human, very clear eyes, with pupils and corneas, watching him.

He opens his mouth to scream, but it never gets out. The thing falls on him and he feels hard and rigid limbs grasp his back and pull him to it, and something fleshy and many-headed (like a sea anemone, he thinks, even as he struggles against it) wraps itself around his mouth, pries his lips open, and begins to worm its way into his throat...

Then things go dark.

Norris awakes with the dawn. He groans and rolls over and cracks an eye. He's lying on his gravel driveway with what feels like most of its pebbles digging into his back. But that isn't the most painful thing: the worst of it is his skin, for it feels like a million mosquitoes have been feasting on him while he slept. He sits up, scratching and expecting to see many frog-belly-white lumps lining his arms and hands.

He stops. For what is on his skin—or, rather, *underneath* it—is not mosquito bites at all.

Norris is covered with what looks like some horrific fungal infection, bands of virulent black stretching across his arms and hands and belly. It's not on his skin but *below* it, and the skin itself is pebbled and moist.

But this is not the worst thing, nor is it the thing that will send him running down the street, screaming. For though the infection is horrendous, the most unnerving thing is that its many splintered webs and rings are not distributed randomly about his body. Quite the contrary: their arrangement obviously resembles *letters*. And what those letters spell is the same thing, written over and over again:

GET OUT

CHAPTER FIFTEEN

Wink is not perfect. Its residents are well aware of that. But then, they say, no place is perfect. There's always a few mild irritants you have to put up with, no matter where you go. So Wink is really no different, is it?

No, they say. It really isn't.

For when night falls and the blue lightning blooms in the sky, things change.

It is something in the very air. Suddenly the Googie architecture and the pleasant white wooden cottages no longer look so spotless. Streetlights seem dimmer, and the neon signs appear to have more dead insects clogging their tubing than they did during the day. People stop waving. In fact, they hunch over and hurry back inside with their eyes downcast.

It is very regular to have strange experiences at night in Wink. For example, in Wink it is common to wake up with the powerful feeling that someone is standing in your front or backyard. It is never known to you whether this stranger has come to your house in particular, or if he or she is watching you and your family; the stranger is simply there, shadowy and still. What is most exceptional about this is that all of it is conveyed only in *feeling*, an irrational conviction like that of a dream. Most people in Wink do not even look out their windows when this occurs, mostly because they know doing so would prove the conviction true—for there *is* a stranger on your lawn, dark and faceless and still—and moreover, seeing that stranger has its own consequences.

There are houses in Wink where no one ever sees anyone going in or out, yet the lawn is clean and the trees are trimmed and the beds are full and blooming. And sometimes at night, if you were to look—and of course you wouldn't—you might see pale faces peeping out of the darkened windows.

In the evening in Wink, it is normal for a man to take the trash out to the back alley, and as he places the bag in the trash can he will suddenly hear the sound of someone speaking to him from nearby. He will look and see that the speaker stands behind the tall wooden fence of the house behind his, and he will be unable to discern anything besides the shadow of the speaker's figure and the light from his neighbor's windows filtering through the pickets. What the speaker is whispering to him is unknown, for it will be in a language he has never heard before and could never mimic. The man will say nothing back—it is *crucial* he say nothing back—and he will walk away slowly, return to his home, and not mention it to his wife or family. In the morning, there will be no sign of anyone's having been behind the fence at all.

In the morning in Wink, people frequently find that someone has gone through their garbage or left footprints all over their lawn. On discovering this they will set everything to rights, replacing the garbage or smoothing over the grass, and they will not complain or discuss it with anyone.

There are very few pets in Wink. The few pets people own are decidedly indoor pets. The outdoor, wandering pets are unpopular, for they have a tendency to never come home in the morning.

On the outskirts of Wink, where the trees end and the canyons begin, people often hear fluting and cries from down the slopes, and, on very clear nights, one can see flickering lights of a thin, unnerving yellow, and many dark figures standing upright and still on the stones.

They are trying to remember. They are trying to remember their home, where they came from. And they are trying to remind themselves that now, this is home, here in Wink.

The residents of Wink know about all these things, to the extent that they wish to. They tolerate them as one would a rainy season, or some pestering raccoons. Because, after all, no neighborhood is perfect. There will always be a few problems, at least. And besides, people can make arrangements, if they want.

CHAPTER SIXTEEN

It is nearly two o'clock in the morning, and Tom Bolan is ass-over-head, military-grade, wearing-more-booze-than-he's-ingesting drunk. He's sitting on the floor of his shadowy little corridor with the stock ticker, and for the past two hours his lone companion has been a 750-milliliter bottle of Bushmills (what Bolan thinks of as a "polite-size bottle of booze"), and it's been a pretty good companion as far as Bolan's concerned, for he's said a great deal of controversial things and the bottle hasn't vocally dissented yet.

He'll pay for this in the morning, and it won't just be the hangover: his indigestion will be nothing short of mutinous. But he doesn't care. It has been a goddamn difficult couple of days.

No man of his—not Dee, Norris, Zimmerman, or any of the few others—can get within a mile of Wink without something going wrong, and not stepped-in-dogshit wrong but nearly-crushed-by-a-falling-piano wrong. Dee's tires got slashed while he was in a corner store, and someone left an ice pick stabbed in the cushion of the driver's seat of his car; Zimmerman's safe house had an electrical fire (while he was out, thank God) and it ate through his apartment and the ones on either side; and Norris...Jesus. Words can't begin to describe it. It was one thing to have him running in, sobbing and covered in fungal, spindly words, but when they started to crack and ooze...

Bolan knows it's all a message. In the case of Norris, a bit too literally. Someone knows who the triggermen were, and wants them to skip town. He knows he's lucky they didn't just kill anyone or... whatever it is they do to people.

Bolan's taken this personally. His crew was never supposed to be at risk. Bolan isn't the world's greatest boss, that he knows, but he's not going to sit idly by while his boys get circled by sharks.

But he's also never confronted the people in Wink on anything, ever. *And isn't it time*, he thinks, *to stop calling them people?* But Bolan doesn't really have a name for what they are... He thinks of the man in the panama hat not as a person but as an index finger poked up into this place from deeper waters, and perhaps the finger has a smiley face drawn on its pad, and it's wearing silly little people-clothing, so it *looks* like a person but really... really it's connected to a lot more down below, an extremity of something vast.

Which explains all the Dutch courage currently bubbling away in Bolan's gut.

The stock ticker comes to life at the end of the hallway. Bolan sits up, then lurches to his feet as the bronzed contraption spits out a little tongue of paper:

WHO   THE
IS   GIRL

"The girl?" says Bolan. "You're seriously asking about the girl? My boys are under fire, and you're still on about that goddamn *girl*? We did everything you said, and you told us we'd be *protected*. We wouldn't come to any harm. Where's your goddamn protection now?"

There is a pause. He feels like the stock ticker is a little taken aback by his response. He has never smarted off to them before.

Finally it begins writing again:

DID   DELIVER   NEXT
YOU   THE   TOTEM

"The skull?" says Bolan. "Yeah, we dropped the thing off earlier tonight."

It writes:

THEN   HAVE   TO   ABOUT
     YOU   NOTHING   WORRY

"How do you fucking think?"

In response, the ticker spits out one word:

TERRIFIED

Bolan eyes the slip of paper blearily. "You think that'll frighten them off?"

The stock ticker does not answer, as if to say—*Clearly.* Bolan isn't sure how an inanimate object can appear snooty, but somehow the stock ticker pulls it off.

When it begins printing again, it's a familiar question:

WHO   THE
          IS   GIRL

He sighs. "Her name's Mona Bright. Word is she inherited a house in Wink. How the fuck something like that happened is beyond me. She hasn't done much more than move into the place, which I don't know anything about. No one's lived there for, like, thirty fucking years or some such. She's asking questions, but none of them are dangerous. Mostly she asks about her mother, who apparently worked at Coburn when the place was still ticking, but no one's heard of her. She must've left Wink before"—he pauses, aware that he's touching on a very sensitive subject—"everything happened."

He expects a quick response, but none comes.

He glances around the hallway awkwardly. "Hello?" he asks.

He wonders if he's offended them. They definitely don't like that he knows where they came from, or at least *when* they came. But then the stock ticker begins typing again:

HER
MOTHER

Bolan stares at it drunkenly. "What?"
It writes:

YOU   SURE   SAID   MOTHER
ARE   SHE   HER

He remembers that the damn thing can't punctuate. It must've meant: "Her mother?" "Yeah," he says. "She's talked to a couple of people in town about it. That broad at the courthouse, the one you hate, for one. I don't know if she's found anything."

Another long, long pause. Then:

YOU   POSITIVE
ARE

Bolan isn't sure if he feels more confused or irritated. They've never asked so many questions before. "Yes," he says. "Yes, I'm sure. I've had four people verify it. Though my boys almost got scalped finding it out. Is there anything you want us to do about it?"

There is another pause, this one the longest yet. He can tell they're thinking very hard, wherever they are. He feels a little satisfied by that. It's nice to see them confused.

Then it begins ticking again:

DO
NOTHING

"That's it?" says Bolan. "You want me to just sit tight? You can't even tell me what'll go down tomorrow?"

The response from the ticker is almost as short and sweet as the last one. It reads:

ABSOLUTE
CHAOS

CHAPTER SEVENTEEN

That night, Mona sleeps. It is, again, good sleep, hard and black and solid. And just as before, Mona dreams.

She dreams she is standing on the front walk to her mother's house. It is night, and the trees dance in the wind. She can see there is a light on in the front window, and under the light is a mattress, and someone, a black-haired girl (a black just like her own hair), is sleeping there on her side with her face turned away from the window.

Mona walks up to the front door and places her hand on the knob. Then she looks back.

There are people in the street. They are watching her as if they expect something from her. They look a little like some people she's seen around Wink, just acquaintances she's met—there is Franklin the cook from Chloe's, and Mrs. O'Cleary, who works part-time as the mail lady, and so on—yet their faces are obviously masks, masks made of papier-mâché with hard, ragged angles. Their eyes are dark and empty, their mouths twisted into queer frowns. Behind them, beyond the light of the streetlamp, are other figures watching her, but though she cannot see much of them in the darkness they do not look much like people. Some are low and many-armed. Others are tall and spindly as if they are made of glass. And somewhere behind them all is a fluting sound, like a broken pipe organ.

Mona turns back, and opens the door.

It does not open onto the foyer. Rather, it opens onto a single long, dark hallway. Shaded lamps on the wall cast little pools of yellow light. Mona can see there is something at the end of the hallway, maybe a light, but she can't tell what it is.

She glances back at the paper-faced people. They stare back at her, expressionless. She turns away again and walks down the hallway.

The hall seems to go on forever. At some point the floors and ceiling begin shuddering, as if there is an earthquake nearby. Puffs of dust twirl down from the ceiling, and somewhere there is a low rumble.

At the other end of the hallway is a mirror. Not just a mirror—a bathroom. She sees the drooping, Daliesque faucets and realizes it's the upstairs bathroom, the one that got struck by lightning. Mona can see herself approaching in the mirror...yet is it her? As she walks by one lamp it looks almost like her mother, smiling at her...

She comes before the mirror and gazes into it. The rumbling increases, and the walls shimmer.

Then her reflection smiles at her, raises a hand, and waves.

Mona looks at it for a moment, then waves back.

Her reflection raises a finger—*Watch*. Then it reaches up to the light in the ceiling and plucks at it. The light goes out in the mirror, and suddenly there's a tiny pearl of luminescence in her reflection's hand, like she's stolen the light out of the bulb.

Mona glances up at the lightbulb on her side of the mirror. The light is still on, un-stolen.

Her reflection holds up the pearl of light, showing it to Mona. Then she opens her mouth wide, and she lifts the pearl up and places it far back in her throat, past her tongue, and when she does her eyes and nose light up and Mona sees that her reflection is utterly hollow, and where she once had eyes she has ribbed, cavernous sockets, like those of a jack-o'-lantern. Her reflection keeps shoving the light down her throat, farther and farther, and then she tilts her head forward and stares at Mona with those empty eye sockets, a hollow puppet-person with barely any skin...

Then Mona hears the screaming, and she wakes up.

She's in her bedroom, on her mattress. The wind is whipping about the house, and every window is filled with rustling trees, and at first Mona thinks she imagined the screams. But then a fresh peal rings out from upstairs, the high-pitched shriek of a terrified child, and Mona leaps out of bed.

She's halfway up the stairs when she realizes she has her gun in her hand. Old habits die hard, she guesses, but she doesn't have time to think about that because the person upstairs is screaming again. Mona wheels about when she reaches the second floor and homes in on the source.

She stops. The door to the lightning-struck bathroom is shut, but the light is on inside. She can see it through the cracks around and underneath the door. And someone on the other side is screaming.

She lowers her gun and slowly walks to the door. She places one hand on the knob, and remembers the image of her hollow reflection with carven-pumpkin eyes…

She braces herself, turns the knob, and throws the door open.

At first she can see nothing but smoke, but then a great gust of wind blows through the room and clears it out, and Mona sees there is someone in her tub, a child-size person looking away from her with its head bowed. But it is not a child, not anymore, for its scalp is black and smoking and its fingers are withered and Mona can see bone where its flesh has been burned away from its jaw. It hears Mona open the door and it turns to her and she sees it is a little girl, or it was once, but she sees its eyes have been burned out of its skull, leaving just gaping, blackened sockets, and it opens its mouth (its tongue singed and scarred) and takes a rattling breath and shrieks again, a cry of horrific pain and fear.

Initially Mona is too terrified to see anything more than the girl. But the little cop voice in her brain asks—*Where did the wind come from?*

And Mona lifts her eyes from the burned thing in the tub, and she sees that the wall is gone.

What is on the other side of the wall is the most awesome and horrifying sight she has ever witnessed.

It is a storm, but a storm like no other. Blue bashes of light erupt in the swirling dark clouds, and fires rage throughout Wink. One storm cloud shudders with lightning, and then the lightning slowly—not quickly, but slowly and gracefully—descends to touch the ground, like a soundless, blue-white finger of pure energy. And where it touches, flames sprout up and a pillar of smoke comes barreling up to join the dark sky.

So many buildings burn. There is so much smoke and so many dark clouds. Yet Mona feels there's something else wrong, something larger, yet more subtle.

It takes her a bit to realize there's been a change in the landscape on the horizon: the mesa is wrong. It's not a mesa at all anymore, but a mountain. It no longer ends in a wide, flat top, but keeps ascending to a towering point. She can see the silhouette of it even from here, through the smoke and the fire and the clouds. It's as if someone sneaked in and delivered a mountaintop while no one was watching.

The mountaintop trembles. What new catastrophe is this, Mona wonders? Is it an earthquake? Or an avalanche? Yet then the entire top shifts to one side, and while any glancing familiarity with physics would make one think the whole thing should come tumbling down now, it doesn't. The mountaintop shifts back, swaying slightly, almost like a tree...

Then Mona spots some protrusions on the edge of the mountaintop. They are familiar. From this angle they appear to rise out of the slope and withdraw in an almost organic, reactive motion. And when she sees them, Mona's mouth falls open.

Her mind staggers to understand it. It can't be. That *can't* have happened. Yet she knows what she saw. There was no mistaking the silhouette that rose up from the mountainside, then fell.

Fingers. Fingers from an enormous hand.

Mona stares at the fires and the mountain, dumbfounded. Then the girl in the tub howls again, jarring her from her fixation. "Jesus Christ," Mona says, and she turns and bounds back downstairs to the phone, because she knows the limits of her first aid skills and that charred child is well beyond them.

The aquamarine phone is in the corner, as always, and she snatches it up and dials 911 on the rotary. There's popping on the line, like the phone is trying to find a connection. Then it begins ringing, but no one answers.

"Come on, *come on*," says Mona. She glances around fretfully.

Then she stops and lifts her head.

She listens.

There are no more screams, and the wind has died. Everything is silent.

The phone keeps ringing. She hangs up before anyone can answer. Then she walks to the window and looks out.

There are no fires, no blasts of lightning, no pillars of smoke. The night is calm and peaceful.

She stares out the window for a while, stupefied. Then she tilts her head, listening. She hasn't heard a scream since she picked up the phone.

She walks to the foot of the stairs and looks up. She can see no lights on upstairs.

Her gun is still in her hand. She lifts it and places her finger just above the trigger. Then she begins silently moving upstairs.

The second floor is totally dark. She can hear no noise at all from any of the rooms. She slowly walks over to the bathroom. The door is shut, but didn't she leave it open when she left? And there is no light on behind the door that she can see.

She puts her hand on the knob and, for the second time, thinks. Then she turns it and slowly pushes the door open.

She can see nothing, for the room is utterly dark. She waits a bit, then reaches out with one hand and turns on the light.

The bathroom is empty, and though the tub is still scorched the wall is whole and there is no smoke. She feels faint at the sight, and she totters forward and feels the wall with one hand. It is solid and firm.

Mona looks at her hand and tries again. The wall is still solid. Then she squats and feels the bottom of the tub. The porcelain is cold: it has not been used in hours at least.

Mona's squat turns into a sit as she falls backward onto the floor of the bathroom. She sets the gun down on the floor with a *clunk*. She just sits there, unsure what to do next.

Finally she stands, gun in her hand, and walks downstairs and out the front door. She walks to the middle of the street and stares north. The mesa is there, and it's definitely a mesa again, ending in a plateau.

She shakes her head. "No, goddamn it," she says. "No. I am not crazy, *no*."

She sprints across the street, flings open the door of the Charger, leaps in, and starts her up. And then Mona, defying every bit of advice everyone in Wink has given her, goes speeding off into the night.

CHAPTER EIGHTEEN

Comes he walking windy-ways, wandering under spruces and through canyons and across shadowy glens, hands in his pockets and head bowed as if all the weight of the world lies teetering on his slumped shoulders. Which it is, in a way, and this is a change of pace for Mr. Macey, he who is so often the delight of Cockler Street, always there sweeping off his store's front steps and waiting to favor passersby with a wink or a smile or a piece of bawdy flattery. The very idea of merry old Macey ever falling into a gloomy spell is preposterous, inconceivable, for Macey is indomitable, unchanging. Were the town ever washed away in a freak flood Macey would remain, still ready with a snippet of gossip or an idle joke. Yet here he is, making a lonely crossing through the desolate countryside, the pink moon lazily swimming through the purple skies above him, and though Macey may tell himself his midnight perambulations serve some deeper, more secret purpose, he cannot deny that partially they serve to relieve his mind of its many burdens.

As he winds around a staggered cliff side he glimpses a flash of lightning over his shoulder. He stops and watches the blue luminescence bloom in the clouds above the mesa, strobing the mountains, the pines, the red rocky flats beyond that seem

(so much like home)

queerly threatening recently. The lightning is soundless, but his ears imagine quiet thunder rolling across the countryside. It will gather at the mesa (it always gathers at the mesa) and disperse, trailing north and east to fade to nothing.

Then he cocks his head. His eyes go searching, curious, tracing over every line of dark on the mountain. He saw something, he's sure of it, not the brilliant blue of lightning, no, but a flat box of dull white light, like a window. But what could lie yonder on the mesa save the remains of the lab, with its twisted tunnels and blackened antennae (all sticking up from the ground like barbecue spits)? And he is sure there is nothing else there,

(except the door)

nothing at all, for they would know about it, wouldn't they?

He looks. Waits. Sees nothing. Then continues home.

His manner of walking is counterclockwise and peripheral, approaching the town always from the side, crossing empty playgrounds and parks and isolated intersections. It is good to move through the forbidden places, the halfway patches. He's spent too much time in the havens at the center of Wink, far too much time puttering around his store and among his neighbors. Here at the edges, in the cracks and at the crossroads, stepping from shadow to shadow in the river of darkness that runs through the heart of Wink, he feels much more at home.

As he walks under one tree a harsh buzz sounds out from above. He stops, peers up. Though the tree is dark he can see the form of a man standing at the top, balanced perfectly on a single branch. The buzz increases, wheedling and reedy, as if telling him to clear off. It is not a sound any human could ever make.

Macey watches for a moment, but grows impatient. He has no time for such mannered gestures. "Oh, shut up," he snaps.

The thing in the tree falls silent. Mr. Macey glares at it a moment longer, then continues on.

Mr. Macey can go anywhere he likes in Wink, anytime,

and no one knows more about the town than he does. Except, perhaps, for Mr. Weringer. But Mr. Weringer is dead, dead as a doornail, dead as dead can be. Whatever that means.

And what does it mean, he wonders as he walks? What could it ever mean? Macey does not know. What a foreign concept it is: to die, to cough up what you are as if it is no more than mucus pooled at the back of your throat, and perish. Where is his friend now? What has happened to him? Where has he gone? Still he wonders.

It is this death—and the answers about it he so desperately desires—that has sent Macey on these midnight errands, visiting the hidden residents of Wink and telling them his news and thoughts: have you heard and what did you do, who knew before you and how and why, why? Why did they know, why did they not know, what has happened, what is happening? Do you know? Does anyone know?

No. They do not. They, like Macey, like the town, are now alone.

He misses Weringer as one would miss a limb. Weringer was always the stabilizing force in town, the rudder steering their little ship across dark, unsteady seas. It was his idea to use the names of the town's residents. "And are we not residents of the town?" he said to them. "Are we not these people now? I feel that we are. We are part of a community. And so we should be named accordingly."

Part of a community...Macey badly wishes this were the case.

For now the unthinkable has happened: one of them has *died*. No, more than that—he has been *murdered*. How can such a thing occur? Do the seas sometimes float away into the sky? Do the planets crash into one another in their orbits? Can one hold the stars in the palm of one's hand?

No, no. And so they cannot die.

But Macey has a few ideas about how this happened. He knows those men at the truck stop had something to do with it, such weaselly little things with small eyes and cautious movements. He can smell it on them, a heady, reeking perfume of guilt and malice. It's as if they went rolling in it, like dogs. Macey's scared a few out of town, and oh how he's enjoyed doing that, especially the last one. He's never toyed with the natives like some of the others do, but how fun it was to rouse one of the slumbering ones to join him in his little jest. And that was all he wanted

(kill them)

to do, really. Just a joke.

Yet how often has he said they should blockade the Roadhouse entirely, even detain its employees? It is a threat, a taint to their peaceful way of life. Especially since they started bringing in that drug, the heroin. But it was Weringer who always talked him out of it. "Let them be," he would say. "They're little people making little fortunes off of little vices. They're no concern of ours. And were we to do anything about them, I'm certain it would attract attention, and that we do not need." How ironic that those he defended should be the very ones who took his life.

And that is the crux of it, the howling, snarling, silly old crux of it. How could *men*—and poor, stupid, foolish ones at that—ever manage to kill one of *them*? Hasn't it been said from the start, even decreed, that they are not to die? That they could never harm another or perish

(oh Mother where are you)

so long as they waited here?

Of course, the answer came from the very last person Macey wanted it to. Nearly all the hidden residents of Wink reacted the same way to the news: they trembled, quaked, asked many questions themselves, before finally admitting they knew nothing, and begging Macey to please let them know once an answer was found.

(Yet how troubling were those he visited who did not answer his call, those caves and canyons and old dry wells he came to and spoke into, and remained silent though he expected them to emerge—with the sound of rustling scales, or the burbling of deep waters underground—and turn their attention to his being and join him in parley? He now wonders—were they gone? Had they fled? Or were they too terrified by what had happened to even poke their heads out of their makeshift domiciles?)

And Macey expected old Parson to cower like the rest or perhaps he *wanted* him to, for Macey has never liked old Parson, so contemptuous of everything they try to accomplish in Wink.

But to his chagrin, Parson did none of those things. Instead he went still, thought, and said, *It's true that none of us is allowed to kill any other. Or, rather, we promised so before we came here. But did we all make that promise, Macey?*

Macey said, *Of course we did. We wouldn't have been allowed to come if we didn't. We would have been left behind. So every one of us did.*

And Parson said, *But what if there was someone in Wink who . . . what is the word . . . stowed away with us when we came? Someone who's been living here in secret, or who's unable to get out of wherever it is they are?*

Macey said, *That can't be. There's no one else besides us. There's always been us, only us, and no one else.*

Parson said, *But that's not so. There was another. Before all of us. Even me and Mr. First. Wasn't there?*

Mr. Macey was confused at first. What jabbering was this? Silly old fruit, the loneliness and isolation has gotten to him.

But then he realized what the old man was getting at, and as the thought trickled into his brain he turned white as a sheet. And Macey said, *No . . . no, you've got to be wrong.*

Parson only shrugged.

Macey said, *You have to be wrong. It can't be here. It just can't be.*

Parson said, *Many things that couldn't be have happened recently. But if it is here, wouldn't it have a very good reason to want to hurt us? And I don't think She would have ever extracted a promise from it. I doubt She even knew it came with us. That is, if I'm right. It is only one possibility.*

Yet the idea resonates in some dark, awful corner of Mr. Macey's heart. It would confirm so many of his worst suspicions that it must be true. What can one do against such a

(woodwose, wayward and wild)

thing? They would be helpless. Such a being is beyond comprehension, even for them, and they comprehend a great deal.

Macey looks up as he walks, and is a bit surprised to see what he has come to.

A sprawling Mid-Century Modern mansion is laid out against the hillside before him. It is done in the style of a Case Study House, with broad, overhanging flat roofs, floor-to-ceiling windows, and a sparkling blue pool dangling over the mountain slope. Though the house is currently dark, he can see white globe lamps hanging from the ribbed steel roofing, and white womb chairs lined up against an elegant Japanese wall screen. It is a house that has absolutely no business being in Wink; it is more suited to Palm Springs or the Palisades than a sleepy little town in northern New Mexico.

And Macey says, with a slight sigh, "Home again, home again, jiggity-jig."

He pulls a set of keys from his pocket, takes a winding path through the perfectly manicured cypress trees (each paired with its own spotlight), walks up to the front door, unlocks it, and enters his home.

The entry hall is white, white, terribly white. White marble walls, white marble floors, and what few unwhite spots there are (tables, pictures) are simple black. This is because Macey does not care to see color when he comes home; he is unused to the sensation, and it aggravates him so.

Yet there is color, he realizes. There is a splash of color at his feet, screamingly bright. They are the colors called *pink* and *yellow*, and once Macey gets past this irritation he realizes he is staring at a gift-wrapped present sitting in the center of his entry hall. It also features an extremely large pink bow, and attached to this is a white tag. Upon examination, he finds it reads BE THERE SOON!—M

Macey scratches his head. This, like the sudden intrusion of color, is a new experience for him: he has never received a present before. He wonders what to do with it. Though his familiarity with this process is limited, he knows there is really only one thing you do with a present: open it.

So he does. He lifts off the top, and inside are heaps and heaps of pink tissue paper. He prods his way through the top layer yet finds no gift inside, so he reaches in, arm up to the elbow in pink paper, and he wonders: why would the present not fit its box? Or (and even he knows this is absurd) does the box contain nothing but pink tissue paper?

Yet then his fingers brush against something small and dry and rough, some item nestled among all the tissue paper. He jerks back, and as he does he cannot help but notice all the lights in the house flickered a bit just now, almost exactly when his fingers touched that hidden little...whatever it is.

Curious, Macey starts pawing through the paper, digging past its layers until he grasps the hard little object. He rips it out, stuck in its own ball of paper, and begins to peel away each pink sheath.

And as he does, the form of the object becomes clear (and the lights flicker more and more and more) until finally the last layer is gone and his disbelief is confirmed:

He holds in his hands a small rabbit skull, its eyes empty and its teeth like little pearls. He turns it over in his hands,

(and does he feel a door opening somewhere in the house, invisible and tiny, a perforation in the skin of the world through which black aether comes rushing?)

examining it and thinking what a bizarre little gift this is, but his examination is interrupted.

There is a clicking sound in his hallway. He looks up, searching for its source, and he tracks it to the little (black, of course) table at the end of the hall. There is a plate of decorative black marble balls on it, and they are all clacking against one another as if someone is shaking the plate.

And then something happens that even Macey finds strange: slowly, one by one, the marble balls lift from the plate and begin floating into the air.

Macey stares at this, astonished, his eyes beginning to hurt from the flickering lights. He turns and looks at the window at the end of the hall. He can see the reflection of the living room there, and he sees that all his belongings in that room are floating, too: the womb chairs dangle in nothing as if hanging from invisible string, the copies of *Southwestern Steppes Outdoorsman* drift by with pages fluttering.

Then he feels it, a sensation he has not felt in a long, long time.

The world is bending. Something from elsewhere—something from the other side—is making its way through.

Macey rises, and walks to his open front door.

There is a man standing on the front walk.

(you know this man)

His figure is pale and somewhat translucent, as if his image were rendered in the blue flame of a dying candle, but Macey can see two long horns or maybe ears rising up from the sides of his skull...

(Brother Brother do you see me)

Macey stares at him, and whispers, "No, no. It can't be you, it *can't* be."

Yet the figure remains, watching him impassively. Macey does not wait: he throws the door shut, locks it, and sprints down the hallway.

All around him his possessions are leaving the ground to hang in the air. The floor and walls shake as if the mountain were threatening to cut the house loose and send it sliding down into the valley. And each room begins to flood with an awful smell, a scent of horrific rot and hay and shit...

"No, no!" screams Macey. "Not you, not here! I didn't do anything to you! Leave me alone, please!"

He hits the stairwell, grabs the post, swings himself around, and leaps down the black marble steps, knees protesting with each bound. The lights in the floor above him are dying out, leaving each room dark, and he feels he can hear something rushing through the house after him, moving with the sound of a thousand dead leaves striking pavement...

The floor below is no different. The filament of each bulb sputters, and everything—chairs, tables, lamps—hangs suspended in the air. Macey dodges these obstacles and throws himself toward a large black door tucked away under the stairs. He opens it, falls through, and slams it behind him.

The other side is dark. Macey, breathing hard, fumbles for the switches on the wall beside him. When his fingers finally find them he slaps them all on, and the room fills with light.

The room is huge, nearly two hundred feet on each side, and the ceiling is lined with bright fluorescent lamps. Ordinarily this room would be the garage, filled with expensive, fancy cars that would suit the taste of the house's owner. But Mr. Macey's garage is totally empty, nothing but blank gray surfaces on all sides except the ceiling.

This room has one advantage, however: none of its doors have ever been unlocked or used except the one Mr. Macey has just run through. It is completely barricaded off.

How could it be here, he wonders? Such a thing is impossible. Yet then he thinks of the

(invitation)

skull in the box . . . and he begins to realize that there are many more machinations operating within Wink than he ever suspected, and he has just stumbled into one.

He puts his ear to the door. He cannot hear anything on the other side, nor can he see any hint of flickering lights through the crack at the bottom. He wonders what this could mean . . . yet just as he does the lights above flicker, just a little, and he begins to smell a horrible odor pervading the room, the smell of an untended barn, stables and coops of livestock lying dead and rotting in the hay . . .

"No," he whispers.

He sits up and looks around. And he sees he is not alone.

There is a man standing in the exact center of the garage. He is very tall, and he stands motionless with his arms stiff at his sides. He wears a filthy blue canvas suit, streaked with mud in a thousand places, and sewn into the surface of this suit are dozens and dozens of tiny wooden rabbit heads, all with huge, staring eyes and long, tapered ears. On his face he wears a wooden helmet—or perhaps it is a tribal mask—whose crude, chiseled features suggest the blank, terrified face of a rabbit, complete with curving, badly carved ears. Where its eyes should be are two long rectangular holes. Somewhere behind these, presumably, are the eyes of the mask's wearer, yet only darkness can be seen.

Mr. Macey falls to his knees. "No," he whispers. "No, no."

The figure does not move, yet when the lights flicker out and come back on he is suddenly closer, just yards away.

"You can't be here," says Macey. He hugs his chest and wilts before the intruder. "You can't have followed us. You can't have been here all along…"

The lights flicker again and the figure in the rabbit suit is closer, standing only a few feet in front of Mr. Macey. He stares up into that blank wooden face, and those dark, rectangular eyes, and he sees…

(a cracked plain, red stars, and a huge black pyramid rising from the horizon, and all around it are thousands of broken, ancient columns, a place where a people once worshipped things that departed long ago)

(a scar-pocked hill, at the top of which is a twisted white tree, and from the tree's branches are many swollen, putrid fruits, un-plucked and untended for centuries)

(endless darkness, stars flickering through the ether, and then empty, sunless cities made of black stone, each leaning, warped structure abandoned eons ago)

(falling, falling through the black, forever)

(a mesa, sharp and hard against the starlit sky, and clouds gather around its tip and lightning begins to leap from cumulus to cumulus, staircases of light waiting to be lowered to the ground)

And though the figure does not speak, Mr. Macey knows what it is trying to say, and he thinks he sees eyes behind the mask now. They are wild and mad, filled with an incomprehensible fury. The figure's hands, fingers thick and scarred and filthy, are bunched into fists. And slowly, bending at the waist, the figure leans down to him.

Mr. Macey begins screaming. And the last thought that enters his mind is: he was right. Parson was right. The wildling is in Wink. It has been in Wink all along.

CHAPTER NINETEEN

Mona is driving so fast she's about halfway across town before she realizes she has no idea where she's going. Is she leaving Wink, she wonders? Though that would make sense, the thought never crossed her mind. She jumped in the car with no intention other than just to get *away*, to get the hell out of the house. And possibly just away from the crawling, nauseating feeling that she's going as batshit crazy as her mother did. Because that would make sense, wouldn't it? She remembers her mother staring out of windows, describing things that weren't there: old buildings, thousands of caves, cities in the ice...the similarities are so exact it makes Mona feel physically ill.

She needs to talk to someone about what she saw, to articulate it aloud and pick it apart, and let them weigh in on whether or not she's exactly as nuts as she feels. But she doesn't have a single friend in this town. She only talked to Carmen for ten minutes, and this seems out of her league. And she certainly doesn't trust Mrs. Benjamin, because somewhere in Mona's furious thoughts is the suspicion that that crazy bitch's mirror trick is the cause of all this: it *opened* something in her head, or maybe a lot of somethings, and now she feels like she's seeing double all the time. There is the peaceful little town of Wink, but behind that is something much stranger, like one piece of wallpaper pasted over another, yet she can see both at once.

But evidently there *is* someone she can go to, for she looks up as if waking from a dream and finds that not only is the car stopped, but it's parked before the manager's office of the Ponderosa Acres.

A shadow splits the golden stream of light pouring through the door, and the form of Parson comes shuffling into view.

He looks at her. Her fingers are still clutching the wheel. He scratches his chin and gives a deep, amused "Hm."

"Help," says Mona softly.

He looks over his spectacles at her. "I beg your pardon?"

Mona manages to let go of the wheel, open the car door, and hobble out. "You've . . . you've got to help me."

"Help you what?"

Mona wonders how she can possibly phrase this. "I really don't know. I'm . . . I think something's really wrong with me, Mr. Parson."

"How so?"

She thinks for a long time, feeling ashamed of what she's about to admit to. "I know it sounds crazy, but I'm . . . seeing things."

He raises his eyebrows and waits for more.

"I'm seeing two things at once. Seeing people and places here, and something *else*. I . . . I saw the goddamn lightning storm from thirty years ago, through my own wall."

"Did you?" He does not sound alarmed at all, but quite intrigued. "Well. I am unused to having so many people come to me for advice. But I admit, it is not unpleasant. Please come in," he says, extending a hand to the door.

She enters, and his office is almost the same as before, though now "Only the Lonely" is playing on the radio. He turns to face his card table—a game of Chinese checkers is again in progress—and says, "Will you please excuse us?"

Mona looks at him, then the table. It is totally empty. She is not sure whom he could be addressing, but he shuts the door as if whoever it was has just left.

He gets her a cup of coffee and gestures to the card table. She sits at one chair, he at the other. Her chair is unpleasantly warm, as if someone was just sitting in it. And of course someone was, she reminds herself: Parson was just sitting here. Wasn't he?

"Now," he says, and he takes a long, messy slurp of coffee, "why don't you tell me what happened?"

And she does. She tells him about the dreams she's been having, and Mrs. Benjamin's mirror trick, and the tea closet, and the horrifying glimpse of the lightning storm she's heard so much about. "I mean, is it possible I imagined it?" she asks. "I got told about the storm so many times, maybe I just thought up what it'd look like and then... hallucinated it."

"Hm," Parson says slowly. "No. I doubt that."

"You do?" she says, relieved. "Then what could it have been? How could I see something like that?"

Parson is still for a long, long time. He looks at Mona, and though she once suspected he was senile she now feels a terrible intelligence in that gaze, like he is trying to silently communicate many things to her. "You know by now that Wink is... *different*. Correct?"

She wonders what that means, but says, "I... think so."

"There are some things I can discuss about it, Miss Bright, and some things I cannot. I am not permitted to, I should say. But, since you have experienced this firsthand... I do not feel I would be giving you information you are not already privy to." He takes another contemplative sip of coffee. "You probably will not believe it, I expect."

"I might."

"We shall see," he says, indifferent. "In my time here, I have found that there are places in Wink where things do not precisely *work* right. Not like pipes or plumbing or electricity. Specifically, *time* no longer works right."

"Time?"

"Yes. Please forgive me, I am not familiar with all of the terminology, so... here. Imagine time as a clock, with many gears and wheels—an easy enough metaphor, I imagine—but some gears have some damage or imperfection in them that causes them to sometimes catch, and skip back several notches, and run again. Do you see?"

"I certainly fucking don't."

"What I am saying," he says, "is that what you experienced was not, I feel, a hallucination, or a symptom of some madness within your"—he thinks for a while, searching for the word—"*brain*, but rather you were witness to this occasional skipping of the gears. The time where you were was damaged, so you saw something that had happened already. It is common enough, I expect, though understandably you were quite perturbed."

The wind rises outside the motel. It sounds unusually sharp, and even Parson appears a bit disturbed by it.

"How can time be damaged?" asks Mona. "You can't hurt *time*, like it's some ... like it's a fucking engine or something."

Parson raises an eyebrow—*And you would know this how?*

"Wink is goddamn weird, but it can't be ... you can't have something like that happen. Things like that aren't real."

"I said I did not think you would believe it," he says mildly. "It is always possible for time to be nonlinear. Some perceive time to be in a straight line—others perceive it as having many different branches, like those of a tree, leading to could-have-beens and might-have-beens and should-have-beens and so on. The idea of seeing the past is not an extraordinary one."

"Are you really saying I saw the *past*?"

"A few seconds of it. Unfortunately for you, the past in that place was quite troubled. I think if you saw the past of someplace else—say, some park or closet—you would have hardly noticed anything at all. You would have simply experienced some feeling of wrongness, like there was a change in light, before things reverted to normal. The past, for you people, is often not very different from the present, beyond some superficial differences."

Mona remembers the way the town was lit up with flaming houses, and how the lightning slowly snaked down to brush the earth ... "So *that* was the thunderstorm?"

Parson shrugs. "You saw it. I did not."

Yet Mona knows she saw something worse than the burning town, and the charred girl in the tub. "Do you know ... if, when the storm came, there was something on the mesa? Something standing there, like a person would? But ... bigger? Much, much bigger?"

Parson gives her a very closed look and shrugs again.

"You don't know?"

His face grows grave. "I cannot say."

"You can't say, or you don't know?"

Parson frowns and sips his coffee, but does not look her in the eye.

"So how does something like time get damaged?"

Now Parson looks positively anxious. Outside the wind keeps rising, and there is a burst of static on the radio. "I am not permitted to say," he says.

"What do you mean? Why not?"

"I am sorry. But it is not...allowed," he says, and when he sees Mona's irritated glare, he adds, "I cannot. There are *rules*."

"What the hell do you mean? Whose fucking rules?"

He blinks slowly and exhales, as if he is suffering from a tremendous migraine. Mona notices sweat beginning to shine on his forehead. "I am sorry, Miss Bright. But I am not permitted to say much more than what I have. It would be indecent for me to say more upon this matter."

He gives her a pained look, and Mona begins to wonder if discussing this subject is physically *hurting* him, like every word he says wounds him in some hidden manner. Just telling her that he can't tell her appears to be making him sick.

"Can you tell me about Benjamin's mirror trick?" she asks. "Is that what did this to me?"

Parson looks relieved to have changed the subject. "Ah. Well. I doubt it," he says. "The mirror trick was precisely that—a trick, or a small and largely meaningless show."

"But it changed something in me."

"It did not *change* anything, I believe. It simply made you aware of something that was already there."

"And what is it that's there?"

"You have spent several weeks here. Long enough to know that this place is not normal, by your standards. But do you ever feel, Miss Bright, a sense of kinship with this town? A sense of familiarity, like you have walked these streets before? Or, rather, have you felt throughout your life a quiet type of pain, a nostalgia for a place to which you've never been? I think I see such a thing in you. Am I wrong?"

Mona feels a warmth in her palm, and realizes she is trembling and has spilled coffee on her hand. She places the coffee cup on the card table. "Yes."

"Yes. I feared it was that way when you first came. We do not have new arrivals in Wink, Miss Bright. Unless, that is, they are *supposed* to be here. And how you came to this place is extraordinarily troubling to me."

"Why?"

Parson opens his mouth to answer, but then the motel is absolutely blasted by wind. Tree branches and whirling leaves strike the sides of the building, and the windows flex and quiver in their frames. There is another burst of static on the radio, long and loud, and it might be Mona's imagination but it almost sounds like there is a voice trying to speak through all the white noise.

Parson looks around, stands up, and murmurs, "Oh, dear."

"What is it?"

He walks outside, and as soon as he is beyond the doors his clothing balloons up and whips about from the gales. "Oh, dear, dear. They are quite upset."

"Who?" asks Mona. "What's going on?"

He looks up, appearing to consult the stars and the moon, and he cocks his head and listens. "There's been another murder."

"A *what*?"

She stands and joins him at the door, but he quickly says, "*Do not* come outside, Miss Bright. It is very dangerous out here right now."

"What the hell are you talking about? What was that about a murder?"

"Someone else has been killed," he says. He holds up a hand, asking for silence, and listens more. "It is Mr. Macey."

"Macey? The old man from the store? You're saying he's been *killed*?"

"Yes," says Parson.

"How do you know?"

He looks around as if he can read something in the quivering pines or hear it in the wind. "I know." He gives a deeply disappointed sigh. "I am coming back inside."

Mona stands aside as he comes back in to sit at the card table. He looks quite shaken. "This will not be good," he says. "Not at all. *Another* death..."

"Who was the first?" asks Mona, but she already knows the answer. "Mr. Weringer? It was him, wasn't it? The guy whose funeral I interrupted?"

Parson nods.

"But I was told it wasn't foul play."

"You should know by now that what people say in Wink is often not very truthful," Parson says.

She laughs bitterly. "No shit. So what's going to happen now?"

Parson stares into his game of checkers, looking from bead to bead. Finally he raises his head and studies Mona, and she doesn't care at all for the look in his eye. "You seem like someone used to death. Am I wrong?"

"I don't know what the hell you mean by that."

He picks up one of the beads and turns it over and over in his palm. "I mean, you have seen violent death before, and dealt with it."

"I was a cop for a little while, if that's what you're asking."

"I suppose it is." He smiles. It is not a pleasant sight, for his face seems unused to the expression. "Miss Bright, I am going to help you. You want answers, and I think I know how I can give them to you. But you, in turn, must also help me."

"How am I supposed to do that?"

"It is simple," Parson says. "All you have to do is solve a murder."

Parson lets her sleep on the office couch that night, for it is too danger-ous outside to return home. How it is dangerous, he does not tell her—he cannot.

He sits behind his desk as she sleeps, listening to the radio. He likes the radio. It is a very soothing experience, he finds, to hear the voices of the dead past in his ear like they're still alive and fine. Two moments in time brushing against one another.

He looks at the woman asleep on his couch, rolled up in an old white blanket and face buried in the cushion, and he wonders what she truly is. For he knows she is more than just a rather pretty woman with a sad past, as she first seemed: he is beginning to suspect that what he is looking at is something like a bomb, waiting for the spark to set it off.

Parson stands and examines the board of keys on his wall again. He looks for a long, long time before finding the right one, which is last in line behind a long row of them in the corner. The key is unlike most of the others: it is long, its metal is dark, and it has one thick, awkward tooth at the end.

He walks to one section of the paneled wall in his office. He looks back at Mona and confirms she is asleep. Then he feels the wall, fingers probing its nooks and crannies, until he finds one hole whose existence would not appear coincidental to a casual glance.

He inserts the key in the hole and turns it. There is a *clunk* from somewhere in the wall, and one section of the paneling pops out a little. Parson works his fingers into its edge and pulls it open.

It is a small, narrow door, one that could not comfortably allow a taller person to pass. On the other side is a wooden staircase, and Parson peers down it, inspecting its wooden steps, for they have not been used in some time and he is not sure they're still sound.

He begins down the staircase, which is dark and unlit. After the first turn he begins feeling the wall for a switch, and on finding it he hits it. A string of caged lights along the ceiling flicker on, leading him down the rickety passageway, and he continues until he finally comes to the motel basement.

The basement is lit by a single old halogen work lamp dangling from the ceiling. Besides this, the basement is almost entirely empty, its cracked cement floor totally bare.

But it is not completely empty. In the center of the basement, directly under the work lamp, is what appears to be a large, rough-hewn cube of dark, stained metal. It is nearly four feet tall and wide on all sides. Its edges are somewhat notched and its sides a little scratched, and it's missing one corner, but besides that it is whole and unharmed. Yet despite its simplicity, one cannot help but get the feeling that there is something more to the metal cube; perhaps it is how it manages to attract the eye, no matter where you look: you could stare at your shoes as hard as you like, yet eventually you would find your gaze slowly, inexorably lifting to rest on the cube sitting in the light of the work lamp. Or maybe it's the way the very air seems cooler the closer you get to the cube, eventually growing so cold that, if you were to approach it, you'd feel sure you were about to freeze over. Or maybe, if you were particularly observant, it would be the cracks in the cement floor that would disturb you, for a quick study would show that all the cracks radiate outward from the cube, as if it has been slowly pushing down on the slab of cement with greater and greater pressure.

Parson does not enter the basement. He stays on the stairway, on the very bottom step. He is not willing to venture any closer.

He looks at it for a long time, reflecting on how little it has changed since he first stored it here.

He says, "This is your doing, isn't it."

If he expects a response from the cube, it does not come.

"You brought her here," he says. "I don't know how you did it from so far away, but you pulled her here."

Still the cube does nothing: it simply sits in the center of the room, gleaming darkly in the light of the lamp.

"Why?" he asks. "What are you doing? What do you need her for?"

No response. But is Parson mistaken, or is the work lamp moving a little bit, as if the cube is pulling it closer and closer?

"Answer me," he says. "*Answer* me. I deserve that. I deserve one answer, at least."

The work lamp keeps getting closer and closer, its cord stretched to the breaking point, until finally it can take it no longer and with a snap the lamp breaks free and flies to the cube like a bullet from a gun. The light goes out, and there is a *clang* and the sound of glass shattering from somewhere in the darkness. Then nothing.

Parson gazes into the darkness. "Fine," he says bitterly. "Have it your way." And he stomps back upstairs to his office.

WE ARE NOT HAVING THIS CONVERSATION

CHAPTER TWENTY

Okay, so.

Mona knows now, or at least generally feels, that she isn't insane. She is not hallucinating, nor is she schizophrenic, nor is any of this a result of years of profound and bitter depression, depression she thought she was escaping when she came to Wink. No, she now feels that this madness is being done by *Wink itself*, as if the little town is toxic or soporific in some way and she's slowly being drugged or poisoned just by being here. Why this town has such an effect on her, she isn't sure; but she knows now that it's not some genetic defect in her brain that may one day send an impulse to her hand telling it to please pick up that loaded Remington in the closet, lift it to her temple, and await the hot kiss of cordite-perfumed lead. Which is a pretty big relief.

But if she's not crazy, she thinks as she drives the Charger through town with evening rushing on above her, then why is she still here? And, more importantly, why is she suddenly so cavalier about committing very prosecutable breaking and entering on behalf of a semi-lucid old man who runs an empty motel on the outskirts of this town? Because, she reminds herself as she parks her car on the side of the road next to a steep cliff, that's exactly what she's about to do.

She gets out and peers down the cliff and sees the home nestled in the pines below. It is a huge, sprawling mansion, and though she cannot see much of it from here she can tell it's one of those houses in Wink that's absolutely perfect, a house that should exist only in the backgrounds of fashion magazines and Rockwell paintings.

It's getting quite dark out by now, and she checks her equipment one last time. She's wearing her black boots, a pair of dark jeans, and a dark coat she borrowed from Parson. Around one shoulder is a black, compact backpack that contains a set of improvised lockpicks (and Mona, having worked quite a few burglaries in her time as a cop, knows these are frequently all that's necessary), a small flashlight, a utility knife, and a pair of gloves. Tucked in the back, as usual, is her Glock, but she hopes to Christ she's not going to need it. Mona has never shot anyone, and she doesn't want her first time to occur when she's doing something ridiculously, ridiculously illegal.

"I do not expect for there to be anyone there, or anyone watching," Parson told her back at the motel. "The death happened weeks ago, and I expect all eyes will be on Macey's residence, since his passing is so much more recent. So getting in and out of Weringer's house should be no issue."

"The way you say that makes me think there's problems some-where else," Mona said.

"You are correct," Parson said. "It's what's *inside* the house that may be an obstacle for you."

"I thought you said Weringer was just an old man who lived by himself?"

Parson squirmed uncomfortably, and Mona knew they were skirt-ing one of the many subjects he couldn't discuss directly. "There are very few 'justs' in Wink," he said. "Let me simply say that what you encounter in the house, even if Weringer no longer lives there, will probably be unlike many things you have ever seen before."

"I really do not like being sent into anything blind," she said to him. "If I wind up hurting someone doing this, I will be fucking mad."

But it's what he said just after this that really got to her, Mona thinks as she begins sliding down the slope, grasping rocks and roots to slow her descent. For Parson just smiled, and said, "If it is any consolation, if you find anything within the house I doubt you would be able to hurt it at all."

She comes to the base of the cliff and squats there, listening. She can hear no one nearby, nor can she see anyone. The fence of Weringer's backyard starts just ahead. It's made (of course) of perfect white pickets, but the advantage to this is that they have significant gaps between them, so she can see quite a bit of the house and the yard on the other side. The house is utterly dark and still, the yard totally disorganized but with plenty of cover.

Mona sighs a little, and, mentally kicking herself every step of the way, runs up and hops the fence.

She feels as if she's just broken some solemn rule when she crests the top of the fence and lands on the ground on the other side. She looks around at the dark, quiet yard. It is overgrown with leafy brush, and an unpruned cottonwood leans drunkenly toward the house as if about to impart an impolite secret. She remembers what Parson said:

"What you are looking for is something that will not belong there at all. It will be a key, but not just any key: it will be a large, technical-looking key, like a key for some rare and extremely dangerous piece of equipment. Which it is, in a way. It will be unusually long and have many, many teeth, and its head will be striped yellow and black. And I expect that, if it is still there, Weringer will have attempted to hide it very, very well."

"And what is this key to?" Mona asked.

"A place," said Parson. "A place that has answers for you, and me."

Answers for you and me, Mona thinks as she makes her way to the back door. She kneels and produces her lockpicks, and grasps the knob as she examines the lock. It's as she reaches for the right pick that she twists the knob a little bit, and is surprised to find it gives.

She twists the knob all the way and gives the door a little push. It falls open.

Well, she thinks, *that makes things a lot easier.*

She slips inside and shuts the door behind her. She turns on her flashlight and sees she's in the kitchen, and it's done in that nauseating sort of faux French country that requires lots of rustic chicken decorations. A genuine Kit-Cat Klock hangs on one wall, tail at an angle, eyes suspiciously at one side. Mona's about to start forward when she hears something: there's a song being played somewhere in the house.

She calms herself, and prowls forward through the rooms, all of which are a little shabby but quaint. The song is coming from an ancient-looking record player, which, defying all logic, is playing twenty seconds of "How Much Is That Doggie in the Window?" over and over again. Mona flashes the room with her light, sees no one, and approaches.

Immediately she spots the signs of a struggle. She can see where the couch has been moved, its clawed feet out of place with the years-old indentations in the green shag carpet. She's guessing someone bumped it, and bumped the record player in the process, which is why it's stuck on repeat. It must have been playing this section of song for weeks, over and over again. Mona debates turning it off, but if there *is* someone else here (and there *won't* be, she tells herself, but if there *is*) then whoever it is, they'll definitely know they're not alone if the music stops. So as much as it sets her teeth on edge, she lets it keep playing.

She begins searching for this key of Weringer's. She's not sure why Parson talked up the interior of this house so much, because to Mona it's just another old-man house, and she's been in plenty of those, mostly when the neighbors called the police because they hadn't seen Mr. So-and-So in a while and could they please send someone out to check on him. And often she did find him, sometimes in the bedroom but often in the bathroom, which Mona began to think of as a genuine death trap for the elderly after she found her third limp, starving octogenarian curled around the toilet with a broken leg or hip or skull. Having toured the homes of the elderly in the worst, most bizarre way possible, she doesn't find anything all that extraordinary about this one, beyond its size: the old photos, trophies, stuffed fish and animal heads, and Tiffany crystal lamps are all de rigueur, in Mona's experience.

But that doesn't mean finding this key is easy. She checks all the places she'd expect it to be—desks, mattresses, sofas, drawers, wall safes (of which there are none, but she pushes aside each hanging picture to make sure)—but she doesn't find a damn thing. As far as she can tell, there are no deceptive security measures in this old man's house. Unless he's got a hollowed-out book somewhere, but being as he owned tons of musty old tomes Mona wants to eliminate all other possibilities first before she starts flipping through his collection.

She checks, then rechecks, then re-rechecks all the rooms, starting with the first floor and moving to the second, and it's on what has to be the fourth round that she notices something she missed. She's walking from the library to the bedroom, and she glances to the side and sees that the hallway she previously thought led to the bathroom does not: now it appears to keep going, and never arrives at a bathroom at all, and whereas before it was only about ten feet long now it is nearly a hundred, and dark and lined with many doors.

She isn't disturbed by this, initially. Mona's very observant, but she knows she's capable of making mistakes, even big ones like missing a whole hallway. Yet as she starts to explore this hallway she realizes two things:

1) She can remember *exactly* where the bathroom door was, yet now there's no sign of any bathroom at all, and 2) She can't shake the feeling that this hallway is actually quite a bit longer than the whole house.

She goes to one door and opens it and shines her flashlight in. Inside is yet another library, except it is much, much bigger than the last one, and one whole wall is an enormous crystal window. The room is lit with pink-white moonlight traced with intricate designs from the glass, and there is a brass telescope set before the window, pointing off at one dark corner of the sky. *An observatory*, she thinks, though she notices there's some artwork in here, too: sculptures made of black stone sit on top of the bookcases. Initially she thinks they're just abstract art, a collection designed around a single theme (amoebic or microcellular life, she thinks), but she cannot help but feel that the sculptor was not sculpting from sheer inspiration: there is a familiarity and intelligence to the sculptures, as if the artist worked with subjects, which is bizarre, as Mona cannot imagine any organism with so many unnecessary tails or fins. Either way, she doesn't think anyone would hide a key in here.

She continues on down the hallway and opens the next door. The room within is dark, and she shines her flashlight in and sees it is a large storage room with many rolls of fancy fabric stacked along the walls. She unrolls one partially and sees that it's a tapestry, like the medieval kind, but she doesn't think there was ever a medieval tapestry like this: it is done in what appears to be different shades of black, if such a thing could even be possible. It's sort of like a Magic Eye poster, because when she stares at it long enough she begins to see the hints of an image. After a moment she realizes it's a large city laid out under a black sky. The structures are strange, however: there is almost something aquatic to their design, resembling a mass of growth from a coral reef more than any city Mona's seen before. She checks out a few more tapestries (the one of the tree with the unsightly white fruit is especially disturbing to her) before continuing to the next room.

This room appears to be devoted to beer-brewing, or at least *something*-brewing, and if she's right then Weringer must've been thinking about opening his own goddamn brewery, as this is no small-time operation: there are kegs and barrels and coils of tubing arranged across many shelves, and there's a dripping sound coming from every direction. She considers looking through this room, but the stench from the barrels is so noxious she can't bring herself to get past the threshold, and she happily shuts the door.

She goes to the next room and places her hand on the door, but freezes. The flashlight almost falls from her hand, and she stops breathing.

For some reason all the hair on her head and arms has just stood up, and she's broken out in goose bumps. Her hand is clutching the knob so tightly it is beginning to hurt. She can see the white forms of her knucklebones poking through her skin. Though she does not know how, she is sure that there is something very wrong on the other side of this door.

Breathing hard, she stares at the knob in her hand, which is plain and unexceptional, just like the door. She leans forward and puts one ear to the door and listens.

She can hear something, very faintly, and it does not take her long to realize what it is.

Screaming, tinny and faint, like through an old radio. There is someone screaming on the other side of the door.

Mona takes a deep breath and opens it.

Immediately the screaming halts. The room is dark, and she takes out her flashlight and shines it about. It reveals a room almost exactly like the observatory from before, with the notable exception that there is a very large desk in the center, and when her flashlight beam crawls over the top she sees there is someone sitting behind it.

She jumps, and the person looks up. It is an old man, his face white and luminous in the beam of the flashlight. He stares at her, startled, and says, "Who are you? What are you doing here?"

Mona nearly falls over from shock. She gasps for a moment and says, "I'm sorry, I...I thought there was no one home."

The old man looks at her keenly. He has a messy mop of gray hair, and his cheeks are red and happy. Yet there is something insubstantial about this man—and, indeed, about the entire room—that makes Mona feel like her flashlight is shining through him.

"Who are you?" she asks.

"I am Mr. Weringer," he says. Then he smiles, the light glinting off his spectacles. The immediate switch from suspicious to pleasant is unnerving. "Please come in."

Mona hesitates. "I thought you were dead," she says. "I saw your funeral."

The old man does not respond. He just keeps smiling at her from behind his desk. Then he says, again, "Please come in."

"Who are you?" Mona asks for the second time.

The old man keeps smiling the exact same smile, but he tilts his head from one side to the other, a queerly avian gesture. Again: "Please come in."

"Why don't you come here?"

The smile, wide and innocent, does not twitch a bit. The old man tilts his head back the other way and blinks.

Then Mona feels it again: that same feeling she had in

Mrs. Benjamin's house with the mirrors, and when she saw the storm through the wall in her mother's house. She sees two things at once: one is the library with the smiling old man behind the desk, and the second is...

A chasm. A deep, endless chasm, enormous and dark, and she is staring directly down into it, as if all dimensions are twisted beyond the threshold of that door and were she to pass through it she would begin falling, not down or up or to the side but just *falling*, falling forever. She realizes she can hear the faint screaming again, and she squints and can just make out a figure lost in the chasm, plummeting through all that empty black. It is a man, she thinks, writhing and tumbling as he falls, and she believes he has been falling for a long, long time.

Then the sight flickers, and she sees Weringer sitting behind his desk again, smiling that idiotic smile of his.

It's a trap, she realizes: the man behind the desk is just an image, like a projection.

"Please come in," says the old man kindly again.

Mona swallows. She is sweating very hard, powerfully aware of how close she came to utter annihilation just now. "No," she says, voice trembling. "No, thanks."

"Please come i—"

She slams the door shut and steps back, still breathing hard.

"Jesus fucking Christ," she says, and she almost sits down on the floor.

She was wrong, she realizes. Weringer actually does have some security measures set up in this house. They're just of a kind she's never seen before.

Even though Mona has just encountered something totally inexplicable, just as Parson said she would, the calm, cool-eyed part of her brain goes on thinking, and she listens to it, grateful for any morsel of sanity.

He was expecting intruders, it says. He knew someone was going to come for him. In fact, she's willing to bet the man falling into that chasm was one of them. It just wasn't enough to save Weringer's life.

This is all a lot worse and a lot bigger than she realized.

"Let's get this fucking key and get out of here," she says quietly, and she steels herself and continues down the hallway.

She ignores the doors on either side. These are just storage and entertainment rooms, she thinks, or probably more traps. She wants to see what's at the very end of this hallway, if it does have an end.

And getting to the end proves surprisingly difficult. It is impossible to describe, but though the floor appears level and flat, she feels the hallway twisting around her as she moves. Her eyes and inner ear report a standard hallway with an even floor, but some instinctive part of her brain believes she's walking up a steep hill. At another part she feels as if the hallway is tilting to the side, and she almost has to lean on the doors and walls to move forward, yet everything tells her it's still totally flat, a normal hallway.

It's as if some invisible dimension of the hallway, one she'd never normally notice, is twisting more and more the farther she walks into it. It's like the chasm she saw in that room: the physics are completely fucked, as if space here can be manipulated like clay.

The walls themselves begin to change. They are not white wood anymore: now they are made of dry-stacked stone. Mona isn't sure if it's a modern look or a primitive one. The doors, however, remain the same boring white ones with brass doorknobs.

She begins to wonder where the hallway is taking her. She starts thinking it's going someplace that's not in Weringer's house. Maybe someplace that's not even in Wink.

Eventually the hallway sorts itself out, deciding that it liked it when the floor was down and the walls were on the sides, and it feels like she's on firm ground again. Panting, she shines her light ahead and sees a golden twinkle: it is the knob of a door standing at the very end of the hallway.

"Finally," she says, and she walks to it and places her hand on the doorknob. She waits. There is no thrill of fear, no burst of goose bumps. Whatever intuition helped her avoid falling into the trap before, it is silent now.

She opens the door and shines her light in. She is both surprised and a little disappointed by what she finds, for it is a rather plain, boring bedroom, with pink-beige walls and ghastly frilly lamps. But she suspects that this one is the master bedroom, the sleeping place of Weringer himself, and if he cared about this key as much as Parson suggested then it's likely he kept it somewhere in here.

She walks into the room, shining the flashlight around. It is like the rest of the house outside of this one queer hallway: a little drab and dull, a place for a quiet elderly man to putter around harmlessly. There is the arrhythmic ticking of an ancient clock from the wall. The bedspread is pale blue, the window above it layered in pink, frothy drapes, an odd touch for an old man.

Yet as she approaches the bed, it seems to get farther and farther away. The entire room seems to be getting bigger with each step she takes. The boring, empty walls fall back, and soon the sound of the clock is echoing off huge stone walls…

Stone walls? thinks Mona.

Then it happens again, and she sees double: she is standing in a small, dull bedroom in one way, but in another, she is standing within a huge cavern of black stone, one with stalagmites like church columns that glitter in the light of her flashlight. There are low, guttering fires burning in the many atria of the cavern, but they seem to cast no light. But there at the center of the cavern she can see a huge, blank stone shelf, one nearly the size of a football field, with many indentations in its surface from friction, as if something very big and very heavy has been laid down here again and again.

This is where he slept, says a little voice in Mona's head.

She agrees, though she feels she has to correct it: *Not a* he. *An* it.

She walks toward the stone shelf. The spot from her flashlight is a tiny dot dancing in the gloom. She feels an immense pressure on her thoughts, as if the enormity of this place and what dwelt within it is so great her sanity cannot bear it, and surely she will snap…

Yet she does not. The vision releases her, and the room begins to resolve itself—or perhaps she is *forcing* it to resolve itself—and soon she is inside the boring old master bedroom again, standing just before the bed.

She knows this isn't quite true. She knows, on some wordless level, that this room exists in two locations, as if one reality is hidden within another like a Russian nesting doll, or perhaps if you advance in one direction then reality itself expands inward (or perhaps outward) in an almost—what is the word—*fractal* manner.

She is not sure how, but she wills herself to stay within the bedroom and avoid the huge stone cavern. *Just like swimming in a pool*, she thinks, *and staying out of the deep end*. She walks to the nightstand and goes through its drawers. There is a copy of *Southern Housekeeper and Gardener* in one drawer, along with a box of Kleenex, but there is no key. Then she kneels and looks under the bed. There is nothing underneath it, but a thought hits her, and she lifts up the bedspread and reaches underneath the mattress and feels around.

Her fingers brush something long and thin and hard. Her heart leaps, and she thrusts her arm in, grabs the object, and pulls it out.

It is a key, just as Parson described. It is nearly six inches long with nearly two dozen impossibly complicated teeth, and its head is fat and striped diagonally in yellow and black. It appears scuffed and very old, yet she can feel the indentations of writing on the key's head. She holds it up to the flashlight to try to read it.

She can make out a logo of some kind on the key, an atom encased in a smooth ray of light.

A place that has answers for you, and me.

"Goddamn it," Mona says, and she turns the key over. Written on the other side is COBURN NATIONAL LABORATORY AND OBSERVATORY.

CHAPTER TWENTY-ONE

It's Tuesday night, so Mrs. Benjamin starts off on her weekly tour of her backyard, swinging her compost pail, which is redolent of the tea and coffee she consumes by the gallon. She totters out, hits the flood-lights, and is about to sprinkle a cupful around the base of her yucca when she notices a figure standing in the corner of her yard, beyond the reach of the light.

Whereas most people in Wink would immediately retreat back inside, eyes averted, Mrs. Benjamin does nothing of the sort. She straightens up, looking directly at the intruder, and crosses her arms.

"Well?" she says. "What are you waiting for? Come into the light at least, and let me have a look at you."

The figure steps forward slowly, feet rustling in the grass. When it enters the light she sees it is a tall, thin, waxy-skinned young man in a brown suit two sizes too big for him. His eyes are large and eager, and he stands with his hands clasped at his waist and watches Mrs. Benjamin with a faint smile.

"Hm," says Mrs. Benjamin. "I assume you're here for a reason?"

"Meeting," says the young man softly. His eyes gleam wetly, as if he is so pleased to have delivered his message that he is on the verge of tears.

"What's that?" she says. "Meeting?"

He nods.

"Oh, I can already tell you're one of the young ones," she says. "You can't just walk into someone's yard in the dead of night and say *meeting* and assume they know what you mean. What meeting? What are you talking about?"

"Mr. Macey's," says the young man. "It's tonight. They would like you to come."

"Mr. Macey is dead, dear thing. Did you not know?"

He nods, still smiling, eyes still shining.

"Then what do I care about his meeting?"

"You're the next eldest, after Macey," explains the young man.

Her mouth drops open as she realizes his meaning. "Oh, no," she says. "You want *me* to lead his meeting?"

He nods.

"I couldn't possibly...I've always said I supported you all, whatever it is you chose to do, but I did *not* want to get involved. Why don't you go and get Parson? He's older than me."

"Parson does not want to get involved, like you," says the young man. "But he also does not support us. That he has made clear."

She groans and sets the compost tin down on the windowsill. "He always has been adept at making his most unpopular opinions clear, yes. I suppose I would be very rude to turn you all down, wouldn't I?"

The young man does not respond.

"Fine," says Mrs. Benjamin. "I can get some better shoes, at least, can't I? You're not about to make an old woman go running off in the night in some wicker sandals, are you?"

The young man shrugs, his face still placid and eager.

"Thank you," says Mrs. Benjamin acidly. "You're a corker for conversation, by the way."

Once she's changed footwear the young man offers her an elbow and leads her out into the streets of Wink, waiting as she slowly and uncertainly mounts each curb. "I can't imagine what they're going to say," she says. "I mean, I doubt if they know anything more now than they did before. If Mr. Weringer didn't see it coming—whatever it was—and Mr. Macey didn't either, then what chance do they have? I expect it's all a formality, really. We have to do *something*, so we might as well get together and admit we don't know what to do."

If this means anything to the young man, he does not show it. He simply guides Mrs. Benjamin through the shadowy streets with a serenity usually seen only in lobotomy patients.

She peers at him. "I don't recognize you," she says. "What's your name, child?"

"Murphy," he says.

"Would that be a first or last name?"

For the first time his expression changes, his smile fading and his brow creasing in puzzlement.

"You don't know, do you?" asks Mrs. Benjamin. "I suppose it doesn't matter. What's your *real* name, child?"

"Murphy," he says again, confused.

"No. Your *old* name."

He stops. She turns to look at him, expectant. He stares at her, eyes huge, and then from somewhere on his person—perhaps at the neck, near the base of his skull—there comes a reedy, whining, buzzing noise, filled with many harsh clicks. Though his mouth does not move at all, the sound rises to a painful crescendo, then abruptly halts.

"Ah," says Mrs. Benjamin. "Well, I'm sorry, I don't know you. But we do have such a large and illustrious family, don't we."

They continue down the street to Macey's store on the corner. The young man opens the door and leads her through the maze of coatracks and shelves. The store is mostly dark, but some track lighting is on along the wall, catching the silhouettes of many mannequins that stand on display like dancers frozen in mid-step.

"How is this done, exactly?" asks Mrs. Benjamin.

The young man crooks a finger but says nothing, and with an irritated sigh she follows on.

He takes her to one of the dressing rooms, pulls aside the red velvet curtain, and gestures in. A pendant light is on at the top, bathing the tiny room in dim light. Frowning, she steps into the dressing room. He closes the curtain behind her and waits on the other side.

There is a chair placed before the angled mirrors. "Ah," she says. "I see we still stick to the same tools."

She sits down and waits. Nothing happens.

"Is there anything I need to do?" she asks.

A muffled, almost erotic sigh comes from the other side of the velvet curtain: "Light switch."

Mrs. Benjamin looks around. There is indeed a light switch on the wall. She leans out, her old bones creaking, and hits it.

One light goes out in the dressing room, and another comes on. It is a yellowish, filmy light, one that has the strange effect of seeming to seep into every crack and corner of the room, like spilled oil. And it also seems to seep into the mirror, for its surface has changed: it is as if it is a two-way mirror, but behind the mirror is another set of mirrors, and behind each of these is yet another set, and they are all reflecting one another. It would be a powerfully confusing sight for any casual onlooker, like an endless reflection of many other rooms, dozens and dozens of them, a jumble of shards of light from many disparate places.

And in each shard of light, there is a face. Sometimes it is very well lit—such as the face of what looks like an eager housewife, skin like alabaster and red hair perfectly coiffed, sitting in her kitchen at home—but frequently the faces are shadowy and veiled, their owners sitting in secret rooms or dark corners.

Some are even vaguer. They do not quite look like faces at all. There is a suggestion of movement in their dark reflections, like a school of fish flitting through a black sea, but it is impossible to distinguish any normal human features in them.

"Mrs. Benjamin," says the housewife, and though she is in the mirror her voice resonates softly throughout the dressing room, coming from everywhere and nowhere. It is cool and low and earnest, as if she is used to calming upset children. "It's so good of you to come."

"Yes, it is," says Mrs. Benjamin. "Though I can't imagine why you wanted me to come. There's nothing for me to say."

"It's a matter of propriety," says one of the shadowy faces. It appears to be that of a ten-year-old boy. A pink Band-Aid is stuck to one brow, and he peers at her with a queerly solemn expression for a child.

"Oh, propriety," says Mrs. Benjamin. "We're always so concerned with propriety. Even in total madness, we still stick to our hierarchies and chains of command."

"We have to," says the housewife, a bit sternly. "We must. Especially in times of such distress. Are you not distressed, Mrs. Benjamin, by what's happened?"

The contempt in Mrs. Benjamin's face decreases very slightly. "I am. Of course I am."

"Everyone is," says another of the shadowy faces. This one looks like a rather handsome man with cleanly parted hair. He could almost be a model. "But you should be, especially."

"Why's that?"

"You're the next eldest, are you not?" asks the housewife. "First Weringer, and then after him came Macey..."

"Mr. First and Parson are both older than either of them," says Mrs. Benjamin sharply. "And last I checked, they're both fine."

There's an awkward pause. Some of the faces glance around, as if seeing all the reflections in their own mirrors.

"Mr. Parson is," says the housewife. "He remains in his motel, like always. But as for Mr. First...well, that's why this meeting was called."

For the first time, Mrs. Benjamin looks worried. "Why? Has something happened to him? I haven't heard anything. And we would all know if he were hurt, wouldn't we?"

"We can't confirm," says the model. "Because we can't find him. We went to his dwelling place, but...he has changed it. The canyon does not lead to him anymore."

"Then where does it lead?" asks Mrs. Benjamin.

"It twists and twists, but never goes anywhere," says a shadowy face. "It is like a maze. He may be within, but if so we cannot contact him."

"It's a security measure, then," says Mrs. Benjamin. "He's worried like all the rest of us. I can't blame him. But what do you expect me to do about it?"

Another awkward pause. The model glances about, as if he's searching through all the faces in his own mirror. He says, "Haven't you noticed, Mrs. Benjamin, that the turnout for this meeting appears a little...low?"

Mrs. Benjamin frowns and searches through the many reflections in the mirror. "I see all of us who live in town..." Her eye touches on a few of the vaguer reflections, those that do not resemble human faces in any way. A few of them buzz to her, and the twitches of motion increase. "But where are the children? Where are the young sleepers from the hills and forests? I only see a few here."

"That is what we're worried about," says the housewife. "When Mr. Macey went to speak to everyone, he found many of the young ones were *gone*, Mrs. Benjamin. He thinks—*thought*, I should say—that maybe they did not answer him. But we don't believe so. We looked again, and found nothing. We think they've *left*. They've gone some-where else. Without telling us. But where, we don't know."

"Could they be in danger?" asked Mrs. Benjamin. "What hap-pened to Macey and Weringer cannot have happened to them as well, because we'd all know..."

"We searched their homes," says the housewife. "The canyons, the caves, the glens. There was no sign of a struggle."

"And they can certainly fend for themselves," says the model.

"We don't know what happened to them," says the young boy. "We hoped you would."

"I don't speak to them any more than I speak to any of you. I've no idea. What about the natives of Wink?"

"The people of Wink, of course, know nothing," says the young boy.

"But one native was the last to have contact with those who dwell in the mountains," says the model. "Mr. Macey talked one of the young ones into *attacking* the native. It placed its kiss upon him, set its many eyes dancing in his skin. We believe it was Macey's idea of frightening the native off. Macey was convinced this man had somehow injured Weringer. But how, he did not say. He kept his counsel to himself in his last days."

"Perhaps that was wise," says Mrs. Benjamin. She picks something green and pink out from between her incisors, flicks it away. "Perhaps I ought to do the same. Yes, I think so. Everyone who tries to help you people winds up dying, one way or another. It's the only intelligent thing to do. So, I will choose to excuse myself now." With a grunt she begins to get to her feet.

"But you can't!" says the young boy.

"And why not?" asks Mrs. Benjamin.

"Because if you don't find those in the mountains, who will?" he cries.

Mrs. Benjamin pauses. All the faces are watching her. She sits back down. "This is why you wanted me here, isn't it?" she asks. "You want me to find all our missing brethren." Her face curdles at the revelation. "For God's sake, you come calling on an old woman in the dead of night for this…I can't go running around the countryside, willy-nilly."

"You are famous for your strength," says the housewife.

"I am an old woman, thank you," Mrs. Benjamin says angrily. "And that's not the point! I don't know what happened any more than you do. I can't help."

"But you must know something," says another of the shadowy faces. "You are older and more powerful than any of us. You have talents that we do not."

"Oh, goodness," sighs Mrs. Benjamin. "I haven't used any of them in years."

"I am sure you can remember," says the housewife.

"But I don't want to. For so long I didn't need to. I was *happy* where I was."

"So were we all," says the housewife.

"We were happy being people," says the model.

"Happy being small," says one of the shadowy faces.

"Happy being happy," says the young boy.

"And we can lose all that, if we don't correct things," says the housewife. "We must fix this, Mrs. Benjamin. We need your assistance."

Mrs. Benjamin eyes each one of them. It is clear, though nearly all of them appear over thirty, that each and every one is in essence a child. Sometimes she forgets that.

She grumbles a little, and shifts forward in her chair. "Well," she says. "I suppose I can see what I can do."

"You agree, then?" asks the model.

"Yes, yes, I agree. I'm not going to lead your damn meetings, but I will try and find where the youngest ones have gone."

"We are so grateful for your help," says the housewife.

"Save it until I get some results," snaps Mrs. Benjamin. "What I find might be very unpleasant. I expect it will be, honestly, considering everything that's been going on."

All the faces in the mirror grow a little sober at that.

Mrs. Benjamin sits up and coughs politely. "Now," she says. "I am going to need someone to bring me coffee while I go to work. A lot of it. So which of you is it going to be?"

CHAPTER TWENTY-TWO

Getting out of the house proves to be one hell of a lot easier than getting in, and Mona is quite relieved to hop back over the fence and climb up the brambly hillside. She's got the key in her backpack, and she can feel it bumping around awkwardly in there. She's wrapped it up in her gloves, since she was afraid that one of its delicate teeth might get bent, rendering it unable to open...well, whatever it's supposed to open.

She can't help but feel that the key is hot, like it's going to burn a hole in her gloves and her backpack and go sliding down the hillside. The item is forbidden, like the subject of Coburn itself. Like so many topics in Wink, she can tell that the lab on the mesa is always in the background of everything, present but unmentionable. The entire town was built around it, for God's sake. Though it is distant and dark, she feels it is the heart of this town.

Coburn did something, she thinks as she starts the Charger and begins heading back to the motel. And she cannot help but suspect that whatever happened on the mesa has something to do with what she just saw in that house.

And what did she see in that house? She has no idea.

When she was in elementary school in her podunk town in Texas, one of her classmates, Nola Beth, experienced a sharp drop in grades around the second grade. They quickly figured out that Nola's vision had steadily become worse and worse: she just couldn't see the black-board. One day Nola came into school wearing a set of incredibly thick glasses, and though they did no favors to her appearance, Nola was ecstatic: she could see all kinds of things now, things she'd never known were even *there*. She'd had no idea trees were so pretty, she said. She could see every single leaf waving in the wind now.

For some reason, this terrified young Mona. It wasn't that Nola's vision had changed: it was that her vision had changed *without her even knowing it*. There were all kinds of things happening around her that she'd never known about, that she was blind to. Though her experi-ence of the world had seemed whole and certain to her, in truth it had been marred, filled with blind spots, and she'd had no idea.

That same terror comes burbling up in Mona now. She wonders, *What am I blind to? Is there more to the world that I could never see before? And why can I see it now?*

But all these thoughts go flying out her head when she hears the bang and the Charger starts weaving out of control.

Mona immediately knows she's got a flat, which would normally not trouble her, but this time she's going about fifty along a mountain road with a two-hundred-foot drop on her right. She can feel panic rising up inside her, but she mentally slaps herself and swallows it. She gently pushes down on the brake and turns the wheel so the car puts pressure on the remaining three tires and comes sliding to a stop.

She does an internal check. She is not hurt, and though all the items in the car have moved about a foot, none of them seem dam-aged. Then she reviews the last ten seconds . . .

Did she see a sparkle in the road, just before the wheel popped?

She grabs her flashlight and the Glock, steps out of the car, and locks it. She shines the flashlight ahead up the road, sees nothing, then shines it behind.

There's a sparkle again. She walks to it—it is farther away than she thought—and stoops down.

They're tire spikes. Homemade ones, welded together out of wood nails. They look a little like big, crude jacks from a ball-and-jacks game.

Mona doesn't say a word. She just takes out the Glock, makes sure there's a round in the chamber and the safety's off, and shines the flashlight around. She sees nothing but red stone cliffs and the odd juniper. But she remembers that it's not wise to be out in Wink at night.

She turns out the light and stays there, not moving. If someone put down the tire spikes, then it's likely that person was waiting for someone—possibly her—to come by and hit them. Which means she's probably not alone out here, so she doesn't need a light telling anyone where she is.

She silently moves to the side of the road and hunches there, waiting. She waits for nearly a half hour. She debates abandoning the car and heading back to the motel on foot, but she remembers the multiple warnings she's received about going out at night in Wink, and after seeing what she saw in that house she now thinks those warnings weren't idle. Eventually she decides that the smartest thing to do is get to the car, get the tire changed, and get the hell out of here.

She creeps back to the car, turns it on in case she needs to jump in it quick, and goes about the business of jacking up the car and putting the doughnut on. If she weren't so confident in her ability to change a tire quickly she wouldn't be so cavalier; but since this is a dance she did about a million times in her previous career, she doesn't panic and her pulse doesn't rise a single beat, and soon she's got the last lug nut tightened.

It's then that she hears the footsteps. Wooden-soled shoes, walking down the road behind her at a slow, steady, almost thoughtful pace.

She rises, steps behind the car, and turns both the flashlight and the gun in the direction of the footsteps. "Whoever that is, come out slowly," she says.

The cadence of the footsteps doesn't change one iota. After a few more steps there's a pause, then a tinkle of metal—brushing the tire spikes out of the way, she guesses—and then the footsteps resume.

A pale figure enters the beam of her flashlight, walking in the middle of the road. She sees it is a man dressed in a blue-gray suit and a white panama hat: the Native American from Chloe's, she realizes, the man who was watching her. He still has his hands in his pockets, and he stares at her with coal-black eyes as he approaches, his two-tone shoes clacking against the asphalt.

"Stop," she says. "Hands where I can see them."

The man pays no attention, but just keeps walking toward her.

"Stop, goddamn it," she says. "I am armed."

He keeps walking, but finally halts when he's within about ten feet of her car. He looks at her, then at the doughnut, then at the torn, ruined tire, and then back at the road behind him. "Looks like you had some trouble," he says. His voice is quiet and calm and a little high-pitched. It's also a little mush-mouthed. *He talks like a deaf person*, Mona thinks. "I thought I heard something."

"Please get your hands where I can see them, sir," says Mona angrily.

"Tire problems are common on these roads."

"Hands," says Mona again. "*Hands.*"

He smiles and takes his hands out of his pockets. They're empty. "Hands. Hands," he says, echoing her as if it's a joke he's still getting. "I came to help you."

"You can help by leaving."

"Are you often so brusque with those who try and help you?"

"No, but I'm often brusque when I hit some fucking tire spikes and nearly wrap my car around a tree."

"Tire spikes?" he says. He looks back down the road. "Is that what those were?"

"Yes," says Mona. "And to be honest, sir, I find it highly coincidental that you happen upon me right after I nearly drive off the fucking road."

He smiles at her, his eyes glittering in the ruby-red glow of her taillights.

"What are you looking at?" she asks, disconcerted.

"We've met before," he says.

"No, we haven't."

"We have. I know the curve of your face and the light in your eyes. I know you. And you know me."

"I fucking don't. I'd remember you."

His eyes thin, but his smile doesn't leave. "Perhaps not...perhaps you were described to me by someone, long ago...I never thought I'd meet you here, wandering these roads. These dark roads. They go a lot of places, the roads. You find a lot of things, if you keep walking."

"Then please keep walking."

"What are you doing out here?" he asks softly.

"Go away," says Mona. "Just turn around, walk, and go away. It ain't hard."

"What's your name?" he asks. "Where are you from? You're not from here. So where?"

"Turn around. And walk."

"You were in his house, weren't you?"

Mona swallows but does not answer.

"Yes," he says. "Once I knew a woman who was brave and strong and beautiful. We lost her to the horizon. She went a-walking and I saw her only once after that, one sad little moment. For then she died. She died for you. For me. For us. For everyone."

Mona tries to ignore how her flashlight beam is trembling a little.

"I want to bring her back," he says. "And I think you do too."

"Get the fuck out of here," Mona says.

He leans forward a little. "She whispers to me, from deep in the earth," he says. "Wrapped around the mountain's spine. Do not lose hope. She is not gone. She is only sleeping. She is waiting for you. She's been waiting for you from the beginning."

"You have me mistaken for someone else," says Mona. "Now get the hell out of here, or I will shoot, and it will fucking hurt."

"I can show you," he says. He extends a hand. "Take my hand."

"Mister, did you not just hear what I said? I am going to fuck you up like no tomorrow if you don't get moving."

"You can't hurt me," he says. "Nothing can hurt me. I've died so many times. Gone walking through so many starlit fields. I lie rotting in so many barrens, even now. Nothing can hurt me."

"Then you won't mind me putting a round in your knee," says Mona. She points the Glock at his leg.

"I can show you," he says again, voice still soft and even.

Mona's grip tightens on the Glock.

"I can show you so much," he says. The man takes a step forward, eyes shining strangely.

And in the split second before he takes a second step, Mona swears she sees something in his eyes—or maybe *behind* his eyes—squirming, many little tendrils flicking about in the pools before his brain.

She's so horrified by this that she almost doesn't notice the gun go off. Even though she is transfixed by what she sees, Mona's aim is as straight and true as ever: the flesh above the man's knee, just where the quadriceps tendon connects to his kneecap, completely erupts. The man grunts slightly (and Mona can't help but notice that it's not a grunt of pain, but of surprise, as if the man is saying to himself, *Well now that's inconvenient*) and falls forward to the ground.

Yet he does not fall completely. He supports himself with the other knee, steadies himself, and then lunges forward and grasps her right wrist.

There is the crash of lightning, and the world fills with blue, and she hears his voice say, "I can show you."

She stands on the road, but the world is gray and thin and flimsy, as if made of fog and mist. There is a dark form beside her holding her hand, but she has no attention for it: her eye is immediately drawn to the countryside around her.

She can see the pale shapes of trees and shrubs and hills, but in places the countryside is pockmarked and filled with a bright blue light, as if massive spotlights are hidden in the hills. All of them are pointed straight up, shining directly into the sky, piercing the clouds and rising into the dark heavens.

Or, she wonders, is something above the clouds shining down *onto these spots? And do they coincide with another vision she had? Did she not once see coils of lightning streaming down to brush these very places?*

But as she stares at these glowing spots in the countryside, her eye eventually falls upon the faint form of the town in the valley. She can see through it, past it, underneath it, and when she realizes this she sees that the earth below the town and even under the mesa is not solid...

There is something underneath the town. Something buried there, sleeping, waiting. It is broken into a million pieces, it feels like. And though it is shattered, she can feel it turn its attention to her, dreaming of her, this lost, broken woman standing on the hillside...

And it recognizes her.

She begins screaming, and she writhes and rips her hand back and squeezes it...

There is a crash, and Mona is released. She realizes she has her eyes shut, and she opens them and sees she is still standing on the road, but the world is no longer gray and misty.

Then she smells gunpowder, and she realizes she has just fired the Glock again.

She looks around. The man is kneeling before her, face fixed in a look of complete surprise.

"Oh," he says, and he falls back until he is sitting on the road.

There is blood pouring from his chest. She can see the tiny rent in his shirtfront with blood spurting out of it, and she slowly, stupidly realizes that she has put it there.

"Oh, fuck," says Mona.

The man touches his wound and looks at the blood as if he has never seen such a thing.

"Oh, oh fuck," says Mona again.

He sits in the middle of the road, still staring at his chest in shock. He looks around himself, contemplating his situation, as if he's just tripped and he's wondering who saw.

"Just...just sit there," says Mona. She sticks the gun back in her pants and cautiously approaches him. "Just don't move, you'll make it worse. Lie down, and just..."

The Indian appears to come to some decision. He reaches into his coat and produces something dark and glimmering. It takes her a moment to see it's a snub-nosed .38.

Mona doesn't even pause to think. She dives to the right, behind the Charger, pulls the Glock back out, and points it at him again. "Don't!" she says. "Don't you fucking dare!"

But the man does not point the gun at her. He examines it, as if trying to remember how such a contraption works, before lifting it and sticking it under his chin.

"No!" cries Mona.

She stands up, but it is too late: the gun goes off. Streamers of red come bursting out of the top of the man's skull like fireworks, and he topples back.

"Fucking Christ!" screams Mona. She rushes to him, but she can see he's already far beyond help. His body is totally limp, the asphalt already covered in a spreading sea of blood.

Mona stops and stares, wondering what to do now. She has never shot someone before now, and though she has seen people die it was never in such a horrific manner.

But the man's body is not completely still. His ruptured head is twitching from side to side. And somehow Mona does not think his neck is jerking it back and forth: instead, she thinks the source of the motion is coming from *inside* his skull, as if something within is beating against its walls.

There is a squelching sound, and she thinks she can see something sprouting from the gaping wound at the top of his head, tiny gossamer tendrils wriggling out as if trying to taste the air, and as the thing struggles the flow of blood triples...

"What the *fuck*," says Mona softly.

Then with a tiny, reedy cry, the wriggling stops, and the little tendrils appear to foam up (exactly like baking soda and vinegar) and dissolve. The dead man lies still in the middle of the road, gun still in his hand. Mona stares at him, not sure what to do.

There is a flash of lightning from out over the town, the bolt rushing down to strike to ground, and a clap of thunder. Mona turns to look. The cloud lightning above the mesa is roiling as always, but that strike was much closer, and unlike the normal lightning it produced a thunderclap...

She does not need to think about it more. She dashes around to the driver's side of the Charger, jumps in, and peels out.

CHAPTER TWENTY-THREE

When Mona comes rushing into the office at the Ponderosa Acres, Parson looks up from his desk—his expression stuck between amusement and irritation, as always—and asks, "I take it your visit was a success?"

Mona wonders what to say. Something shudders and curls in her stomach. She runs to his trash can, grabs it, and vomits into it prolifically.

Parson looks on, mildly perplexed. "Or perhaps not?" he asks.

"Things got fucked," gasps Mona.

"They got what?"

"Fucked," she says again, angry. "Things went fucking nuts on the way back here!"

"In a matter that concerns the key?"

"No, it does *not* concern the key. I don't *think*. Hell, I don't know."

"Then you have it?"

She glares at him, streams of spittle still hanging from her lips. She wipes them off with a forearm, rummages around in her backpack, and takes out her glove with the key wrapped inside. She looks at it, then up at Parson. So far, he's given her very little reason to trust him.

He seems to sense this. "*I* am not going to do anything with this key," he says.

"That's not really a comfort, Mr. Parson."

"I will not even take it from you. This key is more for *you* than for me, Miss Bright. I only wish to see it, and verify what it is."

She throws it to him, and he does not react at all, as if he's never caught anything before in his life: the glove bounces off his shoulder and lands on his desk. He looks at it, confused.

"There's your fucking key," she says.

He opens up the glove, looks within, and smiles. "Good. Very good."

"No. No good at all," says Mona.

"Why not?"

"Some crazy fuck attacked me on the road," she says. "And I shot him. Well...I actually shot him a couple of times. But then he took out his own gun and, and..." She mimes holding a gun to her chin and pulling the trigger, and makes a childish *pkchoom* noise. "Blew his own fucking brains out, right then and there, like it was nothing."

"This man...shot himself?"

"Yes!" says Mona. "Are you not fucking hearing me?"

"But why did he attack you?"

"I don't know! He just did! He was, like...lying in wait for me. He'd set up some tire spikes, I'm almost sure of it, and I blew a tire and had to change it and that's when he came at me."

"He...came at you?"

"He tried to grab me." She pauses. "Well. He actually did grab me. And when he did, I saw..."

Parson is sitting forward. He asks, "You saw something?"

"I saw underneath the town. There's something there, something broken and laid out all over and under this valley. And it saw me, and I felt like...like it *knew* me."

Parson is quiet for a long, long time. "And you saw this when this man grabbed you? As if he was showing it to you?"

"I guess."

"What did he look like?"

Mona describes him, but Parson shakes his head and says, "He does not sound familiar...I have never seen such a man in Wink. This is troubling."

"More troubling than him blowing his brains out?" she asks.

He bobs his head from side to side, as if to say that they are roughly equal in his mind.

"What's going to happen?"

"To you?" asks Parson. He thinks about it. "Well. If he is dead, he was no one of note."

"Are you *serious*?"

"Yes. I can tell when someone...*important* has died. As I did with Weringer, and Macey. And if his body is there, I expect someone will come to collect it in the night. Such things happen frequently with items left out. Even corpses, I assume, though I have never witnessed such a thing."

Mona tries to ignore the sea of crazy shit he just said, and focuses on one thing in particular: "What do you mean, *if* he is dead? The top of his goddamn head was gone!"

Parson looks at her stony-faced. He shrugs.

"You can't tell me, huh?" she says. "It isn't allowed?"

Parson does nothing. He is hardly even breathing.

"And I guess you can't tell me about the thing that tried to crawl out of his fucking gourd, can you?" says Mona. "The thing that foamed up like a...like a fucking science fair project when it touched asphalt? Or what I saw in that house?"

Parson clears his throat. "We should discuss what you are going to do with this key." He pats the glove on the table.

"No," says Mona.

He raises an eyebrow. "No?"

She coughs, hawks, and spits a lump into the trash can. Then she takes a Kleenex and blows each nostril thoroughly. "No," she says. "I'm not doing a fucking thing, Mr. Parson. Not until you start telling me what the hell is going on."

"I have told you about this," says Parson calmly. "There are some things I am not allowed to discuss, or do."

"I honestly don't care," says Mona. "I just endured some serious shit for you. I say we play fair and spread it around. This is a two-way street, Mr. Parson. Get fucking driving."

"I do not understand your metaphor," he says.

"What I am saying," says Mona, and she hauls herself up and sits in the chair before his desk, "is you tell me something worth knowing. For starters, why the hell would I care about this key, anyway, let alone why would you?"

"It is a key to a door."

"That's specific."

"I *think* it is the key to a door."

"You don't even know?"

"I have never...been there. And I do not know exactly what is inside the door. But I think...I think it is important."

"This sounds like the worst setup I could imagine. I'm not just going to go out and open this mystery door of yours because you ask politely."

"It is important to me," Parson says quietly. "And it will be important to you."

"Mr. Parson, you might not understand the meaning of this, but whatever you had me do tonight, it involved something apparently worth dying over. Because I'm fairly sure that spook in the hat offed himself to make sure he couldn't talk. That's a lot of devotion right there. I was a cop for seven years, and I never saw *anyone* do that. Usually folks are all about self-preservation. So whatever it is you have me doing, people are willing to die for it, and if they're willing to die they're almost certainly willing to kill. Now, don't try and tell me you don't know anything about this. And don't send me out to some fucking mystery door without giving me the details, Mr. Parson. Don't you even try to tell me to do that. I'm shocked I have to tell you this, but that dog won't hunt."

Parson contemplates this. He looks a little weary, as if this is a task he's been dreading for a long time. He swallows, takes a breath, and says, "Are you quite sure about this?"

"After what I've seen tonight, I am damn sure, Mr. Parson."

He nods and swallows again. "All right, then. I admit, I have thought about how best to do this," he says. "Here is what is going to happen. Listen carefully. And you must trust me."

"Well, I don't really cotton to the idea of you telling me how to run this sho—"

"You *must* trust me."

She gives him a glare, but gestures to go on.

"I am going to tell you more about what you need to do with this key." He thinks. "And after that, I will do several things that make no sense to you. They might even seem to be quite silly. Is this acceptable?"

"What part of your crazy fucking head thinks that's a fair shake?"

He takes another breath. "The things I will be doing will be done for *no reason*," he says forcefully. "They will make *no sense whatsoever*. Neither to you, or to me. They have *no bearing on what we are discussing at all*. Do you understand?"

Mona looks him over. She worked with criminal informants only a couple of times as a cop, but in those times she became quite aware that double-talk and insinuation are the natural grammar of C.I.'s. Now, listening to Parson describe his plans, she perceives that he is using those same techniques, albeit in the most ridiculous way possible: he cannot even admit that what he is saying could be important, so he must claim that it is wholly unrelated. It's as if he's trying to trick himself into talking.

"Okay," she says.

"All right," he says again. He looks a little relieved, but he's sweating prolifically, like his feet are being held over a flame. "You know about Coburn. You know that it is situated on top of the mesa."

"I also know it's gone."

"Nothing is ever truly gone in Wink," he says. "Everything tends to come back, even if it does not wish to. In the case of the lab, it is still there, though it is empty . . . but if you should visit it and look at it the right way, I think it might prove otherwise. If not, I am sure there are records within that might help you. But the main door to Coburn is gone."

"What do you mean, gone?" she asks.

"I mean it is buried under several feet of caved-in rock."

"How the hell did that happen?"

"Please do not interrupt," he says. "You need to listen, not speak."

"Jesus."

"That door is gone, but there are many other doors that lead to Coburn. There is one door in particular we can consider."

"And where can I find this door?"

He shuts his eyes, as if envisioning it. Sweat is pooling in the wrinkles around his cheeks. "There is a road that leads out of Wink," he says hoarsely. "It climbs high, high up, up to the mesa. It is the only road that does so. Take this road, but as you travel you must look at the fencing alongside it. There will be a stretch that is black and mangled as if it has been burned. At one point there will be a break in the fencing. It will look like there is nothing exceptional beyond this gap— more rocks, more scrub, more wilderness—but it is lying to you. It is the start of another road. Follow it, carefully. It winds around the mesa, through rocks and trees and gullies, and...and some things I cannot describe. Keep going. Eventually, you should find a door where none belongs. That is the door to Coburn. The *back* door."

"And am I going to find the same things in Coburn as I did in Weringer's house?" asks Mona.

"I have never been to Coburn, so I cannot say," Parson tells her. "I honestly have no idea what is waiting for you there. But if any place holds answers, it lies atop that mesa."

"Why haven't you looked yourself?"

He smiles sourly at her.

"Ah," she says. "It's not permitted, is it. It seems you're not allowed to do much, Mr. Parson. I bet you chafe something awful."

He shrugs. Mona looks at him for a long time. His speech appears to have horribly strained him. "It sounds to me," says Mona, "like this is mighty dangerous."

His brow declines in the slightest of nods.

"And you seem to know a lot about it," she says. "So why don't you come with me, so I don't get my dumb ass killed?"

Parson is still as a stone.

"Why not, Mr. Parson? Why don't you and I hop in the car and take a road trip?"

"I cannot," he whispers.

"I know you're not permitted and all, but I'm the one who's going to have my goddamned life at stake, so the least you can do is come with me. You're trying to help in your own way, but to be frank it don't seem like much help to me right now, and I really, *really* don't care to be your errand girl, Mr. Parson."

"I have already done too much...," he says. It's like his stomach is paining him horribly. "I cannot tell one of *you* what is there. I cannot help you. I cannot"—he grunts a little, as if something in his gut has just turned over—"directly help you to know what you do not know."

"What's happening to you? What's wrong?"

He looks at her pleadingly. "Please...please, stop."

Mona goes quiet. She definitely does not like how he called her "one of *you*," as if she were a foreigner. "What did they do up there, Mr. Parson?" she asks softly. "What happened on that mountain?"

Parson, panting, takes a sip of coffee and turns up his handheld radio. The Sons of the Pioneers are playing now, crooning "Blue Shadows on the Trail." When he turns back around Mona sees his eyes are brimming with tears, though his expression is not sad or anguished in any way. He wipes the tears away, sits down, and takes another breath.

"I've made a gift for you," he says.

"Oh?"

"Yes," he says. He takes out a small stack of note cards. "I have written down some of my favorite words and their definitions." He holds them out to her, and his hands are trembling. "Please look at them. Later."

Bewildered, Mona takes them and glances at the top card. It reads:

CAT

(noun)

A small domesticated carnivore, Felis domestica *or*
F. catus, *bred in a number of fun, fuzzy varieties.*

"The fuck?" she says.

"Please keep them somewhere safe," he says. "They are very important to me. Allow no one to see them. And I mean *no one*."

"Are you serious?"

"Very."

"All right...I guess I'll do that." She puts them in her pocket.

"Thank you." He sits back, head cocked as he listens to the radio. "Would you like to hear a story?"

"What kind of story?"

"A fairy story. A parable."

She shrugs.

"It is about many things. It's about family. About travel. About home. I think you'll find it very interesting. It's one I think about a lot, every day." He stares at her gimlet-eyed, and for the first time Mona thinks she can see genuine terror in that gaze; it is the sort of look given by people about to march to the scaffold, not old men about to relate fairy stories in broken-down motels.

"Are you ready?" he asks.

She shrugs again.

He clears his throat, takes a deep breath, and begins to speak.

Once upon a time, in a place far, far away from here, there was a big, leafy tree with many big, strong branches. The tree reached up very high in the sky. In the morning its leaves touched the bottom of the sun, and at night they touched the bottoms of the stars. And in between the two biggest branches at the very, very top of the tree was a big, happy bird making a nest.

"Oh, how happy I shall be when I have children!" said the bird. She worked on the nest and worked on it, and when she thought it was ready she laid a single egg in its middle. It was a very large egg, and she sat on it, and sat on it, and when it finally hatched...

Out came her first baby bird.

But the mother bird was not happy with this baby bird. For though it was large—very, very large, in fact—it was not pretty, or intelligent, or graceful; it was an ugly, ungainly, cruel thing. This was because the mother bird was unused to making children, and she realized she needed practice. This was but the first sketch before the real work could begin.

"I am sorry," said the mother bird to the baby bird, "but I cannot keep you." And one night as the baby bird slept she kicked it out of the nest, and it tumbled down through the branches of the tree, and out of sight.

Such is nature.

But the mother bird had learned a great deal in laying this egg, so she tried again. And this time she laid not one egg, but **five** of them. And these baby birds were far finer and more beautiful than the first one, and each had its own talent.

The first baby bird to hatch was gifted with perception, and could see things far, far away, even things hidden to most eyes.

The second baby bird possessed great wisdom, and could spot folly and truth where others could not.

The third possessed great hope, and all who came near him felt sure their futures were bright and rosy.

The fourth was shrewd and practical, and could think up cunning plans and clever plots while other birds were dumbfounded.

And the fifth baby bird was incredibly strong and fearsome, and could overcome any foe or obstacle.

The mother bird was so encouraged by this that she laid many eggs and hatched many baby birds besides these, but all of them were far younger than the first five, and did not know much of the wider world.

Yet soon there were so many birds in the tree that it began to bow down with their weight. The bigger the little birds got, the more it bent, and someday—probably soon—the tree would break apart under their weight. The mother bird realized she would have to find somewhere else for them all to live.

So one day she told her younglings, "Stay here, and wait for me. Each of you should obey the next eldest while I am gone, and you should never harm one another or anything else besides. If you do this, you shall not perish or come to any harm, and you will see me again." And the baby birds all agreed, and they wept as their mother flew away.

They waited and waited for her, worrying day and night. Then one evening a terrible storm broke open in the skies, and it seemed as if the tree would break in the wind. But then they saw a speck on the horizon: it was the mother bird, and though she was returning to them she looked weary and tired and faint.

When she landed the trunk of the tree began to creak, and crack, and groan. They knew it would not be much longer.

"Climb on my back, all of you," the mother bird said to them. "Those that can, carry the unhatched eggs with you."

"But where are we going?" asked the baby birds.

"To someplace safe and quiet, far away from here," she said.

All of them crowded upon the mother bird's back, and with one great leap, she took off to the skies. This huge leap was the last straw for the tree: with a great **snap!** it fell apart, branch by branch.

All the baby birds watched as their home was destroyed. Yet as the second-eldest bird watched, he noticed something. Was there another bird following them, winging its way through the rain? It could not be, for how could there ever be a bird so large, so ungainly, so ugly, and so cruel-looking?

Yet then they entered the night sky, and all was dark, and the baby birds were fearful.

"Will it be long, Mother?" they asked her as she carried them through the darkness.

"No," she said. "It will not be long." But her voice was no more than a whisper, and her breath rattled in her chest with each beat of her wings.

Soon they saw their new home: it was not a tree, but a huge old mountain. She swooped down to its peak, yet her landing was not graceful: she struck the ground with a terrible force, and collapsed, yet all the baby birds were saved.

They all climbed off and looked at their mother. She was gray and weak, falling apart just as the tree was. The flight had destroyed her.

"She will die," said the first baby bird, who could perceive much.

"She is dying now," said the second baby bird, who was wise.

"It is true," she whispered to them. "I am dying."

All the little birds wailed to hear this.

And she told them, for the second time: "Stay here, and wait for me. Each of you should obey the next eldest while I am gone, and you should never harm one another or anything else besides. If you do this, you shall not perish or come to any harm, and you will see me again."

And then she died: her feathers were blown away by the wind until there was nothing left.

"She will come back some day," said the third baby bird, who had hope.

"Why should you believe such a thing?" said the fourth, who was practical. "She is gone, gone forever."

"How dare you say such a thing after we have just lost her?" asked the fifth baby bird angrily. And she, who was hugely strong, picked up the fourth and threatened to throw him down and dash him apart on the mountain.

"Do not do it!" said the third. "She forbade us from violence! And besides, we must find a home here." And he led them down the mountain, except the eldest two stayed behind.

"I wonder," said the second-eldest bird, "what sort of place these children shall make. I doubt if it will be much good."

But the eldest bird was quiet, and looked to the sky. He could perceive many things, and what he saw in those moments no one could guess. Finally he said, "I know what kind of place."

"What kind?"

"It does not matter."

"Why not?" asked his brother.

And the eldest little bird said, "Because she **will** come back one day, regardless of what they do. And when she does, they will see she

But there Parson stops. He looks around as if he's just heard something disconcerting outside and is listening to see if he can hear it again.

"What is it?" Mona asks.

Parson opens his mouth, but he never answers. All the features of his face, which is usually so blank and reserved, suddenly snap open: his eyes shoot wide, his lips stretch back into a horrible grimace, and his eyebrows leap inches up his forehead. He shoves himself back in his chair, veins bulging, and a wet gagging sound comes from somewhere in his throat.

"Mr. Parson?" says Mona.

He begins shaking, his cheeks quivering and his hands clutched around the armrests of his chair. He sticks his legs out so hard and so straight that he shoves off the desk and knocks himself out of his seat.

Mona jumps up and begins to rush around the desk. "Mr. Parson!"

Parson lies on his back on the floor behind his desk, knees and wrists strangely bent. He rubs the knuckle of one hand against his breast; the fingers of the other mindlessly search the inside of his thigh, next to his crotch. His back and neck are almost completely bowed up: he is balancing on the very top of his head (his wide, oddly purplish mouth open to the ceiling) and the base of his buttocks. He coughs, and a dark cloud of urine blossoms across his khaki slacks.

"Oh, Christ," says Mona. She recognizes this as a seizure, and for a moment she considers sticking a pen in his mouth or something before recalling a snippet of a first aid class that said the whole swallowing-your-tongue thing was horseshit and the best thing to do is make sure people seizing can't hurt themselves. So she grabs his chair and pushes it away, a well-timed move, as Parson soon starts thrashing from side to side.

Finally he goes limp and falls to the floor, his eyes shut and his head on one side, facing the wall. Mona can see he's breathing—just barely—and she stoops and feels his pulse. It's regular, or at least regular enough.

Mona gently takes him by the chin and moves his head so she can see his face. He appears uninjured, for the most part. "What the hell was that?" she murmurs. She wonders what to do. There's no hospital for miles, and she isn't aware of any doctor in Wink.

She's about to check his fingers to see if any are broken when, with absolutely no warning, an immense pain stabs through her shoulder. Then gravity stops working for her, and she starts flying over the desk.

It's true that, in moments of extreme stress, things appear to slow down, like putting your finger on a revolving record or running a roll of film at the wrong speed. As Mona flies over Parson's desk, every-thing slows down just enough for the cold, quiet cop part of her brain to contemplate what's happening to her and dissect all her sensations one by one. Because as crazy as this night has been for her, it's still not the sort of crazy where people suddenly start flying, especially not with such great speed and alarmingly terrible coordination.

The first thing Mona thinks is: *My shoulder sure does hurt. Why is that?*

The second thing she thinks is: *Where's my gun?* After a moment of mental searching, she identifies the cold lump against her pelvic bone as the Glock. It doesn't seem to be budging yet, which is surprising as right now Mona appears to be upside down.

Which, naturally, makes her think a third thing: *How the fuck did I get upside down?*

And as the world tumbles over and over again for Mona, she realizes that, among all the dusky honey colors and darkness of Parson's office, there is a large splotch of purple fabric with white polka dots at his desk, something Mona definitely didn't notice before. The pattern is familiar to her, she thinks...

But she forgets all this when she collides with Parson's sofa at such a high speed that the frame completely cracks underneath her. Mona's world fills with dust and unwashed pillow covers and the smell of old coffee. She feels her arms and legs flailing around as she tries to get her bearings, which is extremely difficult as the blood in her head is still swirling around like a whirlpool. When things slowly begin to resolve themselves around her, she blinks hard and starts to make out the form of someone standing over Parson, shoulders heaving with deep, angry breaths...

"What did you do to him?" demands Mrs. Benjamin. Her fists are clenched and her face is white with rage.

Mona doesn't bother to answer. She remembers the Glock was digging into her pelvis, realizes it's now lodged up under her back, and without a second's thought she's already reaching for it. Her fingers find the mouth of the Glock, and she whips the gun around while twirling it up in the air like a baton until its handle neatly falls into her waiting palm. She doesn't think she could do that trick again even if she practiced.

Mona brings her other arm up to support the butt of the gun, but this is shockingly hard: not only is her head spinning and her neck aching with whiplash, her left shoulder is in incredible pain, and when she glances to see the cause of this she finds four red welts appearing on her upper arm.

They sort of look like finger marks, but small ones.

As Mona draws a bead on Mrs. Benjamin's face, she tries to ignore the madly amused part of her mind that wonders if this quaint elderly woman just hurled her across the room with the speed and force of a driver being ejected from a rally car mid-lap.

"Stop right there," says Mona. Her words are slurred.

"What have you done to him?" demands Mrs. Benjamin again.

"Stay where you are, goddamn it," says Mona.

Mrs. Benjamin kneels to look at Parson.

"And don't you fucking touch him!" Mona yells.

Mrs. Benjamin reaches out to touch Parson's face. So Mona decides that now is a diplomatic moment to fire a warning shot.

Every ounce of her training screams against this. Popping off a round is a last resort, for a pistol firing live ammunition is not exactly a surgical, precise tool: bullets have a nasty tendency to ricochet, burst, or punch through walls. But Mona's done a lot of things for the first time tonight—commit armed robbery, shoot a guy, etc.—so she decides, shit, why not add to the list.

She points the Glock at the handheld radio above both Mrs. Benjamin and Parson, takes a breath, and pulls the trigger.

The gesture achieves its intended effect: the gunfire cracks through the office, and immediately the radio shatters and slams against the office wall. Little pieces of plastic go flying, and Mrs. Benjamin's hand stops in midair. She slowly turns to look at Mona, face fixed in an expression of utter outrage, as if Mona has just spilled coffee all over her carpet or shown up in casual clothes to a formal-only affair.

"What do you think you are doing?" she demands in a quiet voice.

"Stand up," Mona says. She puts the sights back on Mrs. Benjamin. "And get away from him."

Mrs. Benjamin glowers at her. The radio is still trying to work: one speaker dangles from it by a rainbow of wires, and the Sons of the Pioneers are just finishing up their song in a sputtering, stuttering chorus.

"Lady," says Mona, "I don't miss twice."

Mrs. Benjamin slowly stands and steps away from Parson. She glares at Mona before asking, "What are you doing here?"

"I'd ask the same of you."

She sniffs. "I merely came to discuss a personal matter."

"So did I."

"And *your* discussion resulted in *this*?" scoffs Mrs. Benjamin. "I doubt it."

"I don't have the damnedest idea what did that," says Mona.

Mrs. Benjamin appears a little troubled to hear this. "What did he say to you?"

"If you think I'm going to tell you, you're out of your damn mind."

"Why?" asks Mrs. Benjamin, affronted.

"Well, for starters, you just"—she pauses, not wanting to give voice to the ridiculous idea that she was *thrown*—"attacked me."

"I did not *attack* you, my dear," says Mrs. Benjamin, who appears very calm for someone who has a gun in their face. "I merely removed your person to a safer distance."

"Yeah," says Mona. "At about forty miles an hour. How the hell *you* did that, I don't know. But worse..."

"Worse what?"

"You did something to me," Mona says quietly. "You did something to my head."

"Your head?" Then Mrs. Benjamin appears to realize, and she laughs, delighted. "Oh, do you mean the *mirrors*, my dear?"

"Yeah," says Mona. "And I don't find it that goddamn funny."

"But the mirrors aren't anything!" she says. "Or at least *those* ones aren't. Are you really so troubled by them? The mirrors were, well... just sort of a test. And you passed. Doesn't that make you feel good, my dear?"

"It does not," says Mona. "That *did* something to me. I'm sure of it. I keep...I keep seeing things I *don't want to see*."

The humor drains out of Mrs. Benjamin's face. The yellow light of Parson's lamp catches every wrinkle in her face, and her eyes appear to glint from very far back in her head. Mona wonders, not for the first time, exactly how old this woman is supposed to be. "Then you are seeing things that are there," she says. "*Really* there. And the mirrors couldn't make you do that, Mona Bright. Whatever change allows you to see what you're seeing happened long, long ago, I'd imagine."

Mona lowers the gun, but only slightly. "What the fuck are you people," she asks softly.

Mrs. Benjamin smiles and laughs a little. Her mouth is filled with mounds of pink gums topped with tiny dots of dirty brown teeth. She stops laughing, but does not stop smiling. "What happened to him?" she asks. "Tell me. Now."

"We were just talking."

"Talking about what?"

"Crazy shit. I don't know. Some story."

"A story? His or yours?"

"His. He told me some story about a bird carrying its babies."

"What?" says Mrs. Benjamin. "Babies?" Mona is a little pleased to see she looks just about as confused as Mona felt.

"He told me a story about a bird carrying its babies to safety," she says, feeling ridiculous. "Then he just...wigged out."

Mrs. Benjamin turns this over. She gasps a little, and says, "Oh." Then she sighs sadly, looks at Parson on the ground, and shakes her head. "Oh. Oh, I see now. You wanted to tell her," she says to him. "But that isn't meant to be told, old thing."

"What do you mean?"

"There are some things we are not allowed to discuss, dear," says Mrs. Benjamin.

"He told me that. Like, a million goddamn times."

"Well. He tried to bend the rules. But those rules aren't the kind you bend. So he paid the price."

Now Mona lowers the gun all the way. "That happened to him... because of the *story* he told me?" It seems inconceivable—it's like she's saying he did the mental equivalent of crossing an invisible electric fence.

Mrs. Benjamin stoops down, picks up Parson in both arms, and begins walking toward the couch. "Get off," she snaps at Mona, and Mona is already moving before she realizes the weight of a grown man doesn't appear to strain Mrs. Benjamin at all.

She watches as Mrs. Benjamin lays him out on the couch cushions. "What's going to happen to him?"

"I don't know," says Mrs. Benjamin. "I have never witnessed anyone attempt to tell someone something *not* meant to be discussed. There are *rules*, you see."

"I don't. Will he die?"

Mrs. Benjamin laughs. "Oh," she says. "Aren't you so sweet." Then she peers at Mona, and all her good humor is gone again. "What I wonder is, why would he tell you such a thing? It's not for you to know, dear. It's very bad for us. We're sensitive about such things, you see."

"I don't know what you mean," Mona says. "I don't know what the hell he meant by anything he said, either. None of it made sense to me."

Mrs. Benjamin surveys Mona for a long time. "He meant for you to do something, didn't he. He trusted you. I can't imagine why, but he did. He had—he *has*—intentions. It's likely he even knew this would happen to him, I suppose." She looks back at Parson, who lies unconscious on the couch with his mouth open. "You do know, my dear," she says absentmindedly, "that I could kill you, if I wished? I could tear your head from your neck, or gut you with my bare fingers. It's allowed, you see. You're not from here."

"I'd drop you before you moved," says Mona, who begins backing away slowly.

"Hm," says Mrs. Benjamin. "No. I doubt it. I very much doubt it." She frowns. "But I won't. He was doing something. He knew something. Maybe something I don't. Parson's always been quite damnably good at knowing things. So I'll let you be. For now." She picks Parson back up. Once more he seems to weigh no more than a feather to her. Without a word, she begins walking toward the open door.

"Where are you taking him?" asks Mona.

"To my home, where it's safer," says Mrs. Benjamin over her shoulder.

"Why's it safe there but not here?"

"Because *I'll* be there, silly," says Mrs. Benjamin. "But maybe nowhere's safe anymore. If I were you, dear—and I'm not, but if I were—I would stay inside for the rest of the night. I know you probably have something important to do, but I assure you, it can wait until morning. Who knows what's out here with us? Even I can't say." And she totters across the parking lot with the limp body in her arms until she passes out of the light of the neon sign, and disappears.

CHAPTER TWENTY-FOUR

A bump for David Dord isn't a bump for your average cocaine user, if such a thing could even be said to exist. He does not sniff at a tiny dot of coke balanced on the rim of a novelty spoon, or haltingly insufflate a fragile line running along the edge of a bowie knife. No, Dord prefers his cocaine to be administered in heaps, hillocks, veritable mountains, tumbling, tumbling piles and pyramids and pylons of cocaine. He wants each bump to be so significant that he has trouble actually getting it into his nostril, like a man wrestling a big sandwich into his mouth. He wants it to inadvertently coat his upper lip and maybe his chin and cheeks; he wants there to be *accidents*, damn it, needless, wasteful accidents, immense avalanches of cocaine lost en route between the bag and his sinus lining. For David Dord does not use or abuse cocaine (and the difference between the two when they refer to an illegal, highly addictive drug is mystifying to Dord); no, he applies it *liberally* and *generously*, not only to his mucous membranes and from there the tangle of tissues that form his nervous system, but also to his face, neck, shoulders, arms, fingers, and, if he's entertaining someone, maybe even his junk.

This is because Dord holds to one rule and one rule only: *If you've got it, flaunt it.* And you had better motherfucking believe Dord has it. Dord has it big-time. He's been sitting on a pile of gold ever since things started picking up at the Roadhouse. Ever since they got that visitor from Wink, in fact.

"You're getting it all over the goddamn seats," says Zimmerman. He glances at Dord disapprovingly as he pilots his Chevy truck around another M. C. Escher–like bend in the road.

"So?" says Dord. He takes another pinch from the bag (which never leaves his vest pocket), places it in the general vicinity of his nose, and takes a big waft. He can feel that peculiar banana perfume start broiling away in the bottom front of his brain. Soon it will suffuse each lobe and tickle his spine, making everything dance and jitter to an engaging rhythm.

"You do know that we're doing some pretty fucking high-pressure shit here, right, Dave?" asks Zimmerman.

"I been made aware."

"So it probably isn't too advisable to be coked to the gills for this, is what I'm saying."

"I know what you're saying. I'd generally argue in the opposite direction, though."

"And why is that?"

Dord stares into the highway ahead of them. The headlights make pools of light on the asphalt. Sometimes it feels as if they are chasing the pools rather than following the road, like they are about to leap up off the earth and dive into that glittering stream of tarred rock and white streaks. "You been in to see Norris lately?" asks Dord.

Zimmerman shifts uncomfortably in the driver's seat. "No."

"Well. That's why."

"Norris is why you're getting fucked up?"

"Sort of, sure." Dord takes a massive pinch of coke—costing upwards of seventy bucks, he'd guess—and rubs it on his teeth. Then he laughs, amused by his own decadence. He's worked for dealers and movers before, but never on this level. Bolan is the prime conduit of a variety of interesting substances for most of the American Southwest, and apparently he's able to fund this little venture solely through the goodwill of the man from Wink, that spooky fuck in the panama hat.

Or at least the revenue his heroin brings in. But as things have heated up in Wink (and especially since Norris staggered into the Roadhouse, shrieking like a banshee with his skin cracked like parched earth and oozing something yellow), Bolan's cared less and less about keeping an eye on his product, which has allowed several people—well, only Dord, really—to go about self-applying that product with a zeal usually only seen in infants eating pudding.

They give you an inch, you take a fucking hemisphere, Dord thinks. Because after all, this shit ain't lasting. He knows that whatever's happening in Wink, things won't stay put for long. Bolan and his crew are holding on to the wolf's ears with their goddamn fingernails, though Dord seems the only one to have cheerfully accepted this.

"What road was it again?" asks Zimmerman.

Dord pulls out a shred of paper and squints at it. He has to shut one eye to get the words to stop hopping around. "Copper Valley."

"Fuck," says Zimmerman. "That's right over near Weringer's."

"So?"

"So I don't much care for revisiting that place."

"Why? Ain't he dead? You're the guy who did him in, I thought."

"Something like that."

"Is that not the case? Did you fib to the big man?"

"Shut the fuck up, Dord."

Dord chuckles, rolls down the window, and sticks his head out into the night. The lights of the town turn to brilliant streaks along the cliffs.

"Don't do that!" hisses Zimmerman.

"Why not?" asks Dord.

"It'll attract attention," says Zimmerman. He grabs Dord and hauls him inside. "Roll it up."

"Aw, come on."

"Roll it up, damn it."

Groaning, Dord obeys. "You're no fun, you know that, Mike?"

Zimmerman eyes the side of the road. "You don't come to Wink often, do you, Dave?"

"I come a tolerable amount."

Zimmerman laughs. "Horseshit, you do."

"I do. I swear I do."

"What'd Bolan last send you out here for, then?"

Dord crosses his arms sulkily and mutters something.

"What's that?" asks Zimmerman.

"Box," says Dord.

"Box? Box what?"

"Had to deliver a box," says Dord angrily.

Zimmerman caws laughter. "A box? He had you deliver a box? And when was this, a year ago? More?"

"It was a goddamn important box, I'll have you know."

Zimmerman is so tickled by this that he starts pounding the steering wheel.

"Fuck you, Mike," says Dord. "It ain't funny. He just…he just don't appreciate my talents."

"I guess he should have you test the coke," says Zimmerman. He looks Dord over. "Though I guess he wouldn't want to have you bathing in it. What the fuck, Dord, you try and take it in by osmosis?"

"This is a lifestyle choice, Mike," says Dord.

"And what lifestyle would you be choosing, exactly?"

"I'm living it. Living the dream. I'm living like a fucking rock star, Mike, one hundred percent. Fucking Def Leppard, that kind of shit. You ever lived like that, Mike?"

"No," says Zimmerman.

"You're missing out, then. You ought to give it a shot." Dord ruminates on this for a moment. "You ever hear about how Def Leppard, like, at this one party at a hotel, they got this chick to put a baby tiger shark up her cooter?"

"Did you really just say the word *cooter*, Dave?" asks Zimmerman.

"Chick had nine orgasms," says Dord. "Nine fucking orgasms. Can you believe it? Nine."

"I heard you the first time."

"Well. That's some crazy shit right there. I can dig that shit, though. Living loud's the only way to live, I say."

Zimmerman gives a noncommittal grunt as they drive by the town library. It's a white limestone, space-age-looking structure that looks like it could take off and zip through the stratosphere at any moment. It stays lit up at night, which makes it a vaguely disconcerting sight in the darkness. Dord can just make out someone standing motionless in the window, and he turns to see, wondering who'd be at the library in the middle of the night.

"Don't look," says Zimmerman softly.

"Why not?"

"Just don't, all right? People don't live loud around here, Dave. Take that as a word of advice."

"Fuck that."

Zimmerman sighs and points the truck into the hills.

They come to the spot after about twenty minutes. Zimmerman's been cruising at five or ten miles an hour, murmuring to Dord to keep his eyes open, when they spot the glitter of something lying in the road. He immediately brakes and throws the car in park. Then he hops out and flicks on a flashlight.

"Looky," he says, and points it at the road.

A string of tire spikes runs across the asphalt. There's a big gap in the middle, and some thick tire tracks just beyond.

"They got something," says Zimmerman. He follows the tire tracks with his flashlight, but the beam fades before it can find the end.

"What the fuck are these?" says Dord. "Why'd anyone put these out here?"

But Zimmerman just laughs, grabs a tarp from the back of the truck, and motions Dord on.

They walk for about thirty yards before Zimmerman comes to a halt. He mutters a swear, dismayed. "Wish I'd brought some overalls," he says, and he flashes something in the middle of the road.

At first the only thing Dord's eyes can track is the color purple, and he's convinced there's just a big purple slug lying in the middle of the road, because that's exactly what it looks like. But as they approach and his eyes adjust, he sees it's not purple, or at least it wasn't originally: once the thing was blue, a very pale shade of blue, but since it is now soaked in red the two colors have mixed to form a bizarrely vibrant purple.

The thing is a man. A man in a pale blue suit. But it's like someone popped a firework out of the back of his head, covering his body in bright red blood.

"Holy shit," says Dord. "Is that guy dead?"

"I sure hope so," says Zimmerman. He unrolls the tarp and lays it down next to the body. "Come on, help me roll this out."

"Wait. Wait, I thought we were just gonna go pick something up."

"We are. What did you think we were going to pick up? You thought this was another one of your high-pressure box jobs, Dave?"

"Well I thought someone would've mentioned if it was a goddamn dead body! Why didn't they get Dee to do it?"

"Dee is off doing something else important," says Zimmerman. Then he scratches his head. "Shit. I forgot something. Look around for a gun."

"Where? On the ground?"

"No, in the goddamn trees," says Zimmerman. "*Yes*, on the ground. Jesus Christ…"

They both stoop and squint as Zimmerman flashes the beam around the road. Finally there's a glint of metal below the dead man's arm.

"There it is," says Zimmerman. "Grab it, will you."

Dord is wishing he weren't quite so high right now, and with trembling hands he grabs the dead man's wrist and lifts his arm (and who would have ever thought a man's arm would be so *heavy*) and reaches underneath. When he touches the gun he screams and whips his hand back.

"Quiet, damn it!" says Zimmerman. "What's the problem?"

"It's covered in blood! And it's cold!"

"Oh, for Christ's sake," says Zimmerman. "Will you sack up and grab the thing?"

Wincing, Dord eases the bloody gun out from underneath the body. He holds it away from himself with two fingers, as one would a smelly sock. "What…what do I do with it?"

Zimmerman rolls the body onto the tarp with the practiced movements of a veteran. "Stick it in your pocket or something."

"What! I ain't doing that! That's fucked up, Mike."

"Dord, you are either sticking it in your pocket or I am going to stick it somewhere that'll make you bowlegged for quite a while, all right?"

Dord swallows a cry as he slides the gun in his pocket and the cold wetness soaks through to his thigh. Then he stops. "Wait a minute. So, did I just get...like, DNA evidence all over myself?"

Zimmerman laughs hoarsely as he starts wrapping the body up, rolling it tight like a particularly gruesome cigar. "Don't worry about it. No one's going to come looking for this guy."

"Why not?" Dord sees there's something lying in the middle of the road, about ten feet away from the body. It's a white panama hat, though its top is blown out and it's spattered with blood.

Dord remembers something and peers at the body being folded up in the tarp. His jittering eyes trace over the once-Easter-egg-blue suit and the white tie...

"Wait a minute!" says Dord. "This is that creepy motherfucker of Bolan's!"

"Is that a fact," says Zimmerman. "Please grab this creepy mother-fucker's legs."

"What happened? Who shot him, Mike?"

"Just grab his goddamn legs, Dave."

Dord is too surprised by this realization to argue. He picks up the body (which, like the arm, is really just *shockingly* heavy) and helps Bolan drag it to the truck. "So are we out of business? This guy was the one footing the bills, right?"

But Zimmerman just laughs again, which doesn't calm Dord at all. But it's not like much would right now, short of a couple of Vicodin and a shot of bourbon, which is his usual post-party concoction.

They toss the body in the back of the truck. There's an odd tinkling sound when it lands. Zimmerman looks it over with the flashlight. "Aw, damn," he says. "We forgot about the tire spikes...Jesus, they're all stuck in his back."

"I ain't looking," Dord says quickly.

"I'm not asking you to. Ah, well. It's not like he's going to complain. Come on, let's get hopping."

Zimmerman has to pull a three-point U-turn to get going back the way they came. He lights a cigarette, and his craggy, weathered features are reflected in the truck's window, making it seem some flickering specter is floating outside.

"And Bolan knew just where that guy was gonna be?" asks Dord.

"Kind of," says Zimmerman.

"How? Did we shoot him? This was a play of ours, wasn't it?"

Zimmerman gives Dord a pitying look. "Dave, do you have any idea how things work around here?"

"Yeah. Well. Kind of. Kind of, I guess."

Zimmerman clucks and shakes his head as he makes an abrupt turn. They wind away from the town and the mountains, out into some of the flatter countryside surrounding Wink. The headlights catch stray chamisa sprawling into the road and make them look like bursting fireworks.

"They work the same way here as everywhere, once you think about it," says Zimmerman. "Because you might think the chain stops at Bolan, but it doesn't. Bolan's got his superiors, too."

"The guy from Wink," says Dord. He glances over his shoulder. "The guy in the back of the truck."

"Maybe," says Zimmerman. "Bolan's got . . . let's say, a phone. He's got a phone that rings every once in a while, and when he answers it a voice on the other end tells him what to do. But I guarantee you—I just *guarantee* you—that that voice on the other end's got someone of his own telling him what to do. Maybe they don't call him, maybe they have meetings or send letters, who knows. And above *that* guy, there's someone else. There's always someone else. A man tells a man tells a man."

Dord's brain feels like it's bubbling away as he tries to absorb what Zimmerman's telling him. Everything is crackling: there is dust striking the car, pebbles pinging off the undercarriage, the tarp in the back keeps wrinkling as the dead body (*oh my God we have a dead body in the back of the truck*) shifts around with each turn. The chamisa leaves blue streaks on his eyes and the country outside the window looks positively lunar, and as Zimmerman's voice chants in his ear he wonders if the truck will just lift off and go sailing through the stars.

"But here's the thing—none of them *really* know what's going on," says Zimmerman. "They think they do. They really, really want to believe that. But they don't. All they've got to go on is the say-so of the guy above them. And sure, somewhere way, way up the ladder, there's a top. A guy at the top of the chain, talking down at everyone. Everyone passing his word along, like gossip. And his word is like the word of God, I guess."

"Why?" asks Dord.

"Why? Well. I guess because everyone on the ladder has agreed to it. Because it's easier that way. Because they want to believe the person above them. And they don't want to know what they're not supposed to know. And so this guy riding high on the chain gets to say how things are and how they aren't, what's to be known and what isn't, and that's a lot easier than everyone else doing it for themselves."

Dord turns this over. "I think that's bullshit."

"Oh?" asks Zimmerman.

"It ain't so organized. I'm at the Roadhouse all the damn time, and all I ever see is everyone running around batshit crazy. There ain't no chain."

"Well. Things have been a bit chaotic of late."

"Chaotic? That don't hardly begin to describe it."

"I don't describe it at all," says Zimmerman. "Not my job."

The truck coasts on through the darkness. Then it slows and Zimmerman turns onto a rocky dirt road. Dord can barely make out something ahead: a ravine, it looks like, a big one.

"So where's your place on the chain?" asks Dord.

"Low. Not as low as you, Dord, but low."

"And what are you gonna do when the chain falls apart?"

The truck pulls to a stop. Zimmerman shrugs, throws it in park, and gets out. "I don't know. Find another chain, I guess. Come on. You're helping me carry our passenger down."

They each grab a flashlight and walk to the back of the truck. "I'll let you get his feet," says Zimmerman. "It's easier. Watch for the tire spikes, though."

Dord puts the flashlight in his armpit, grimaces, and grabs the pair of ankles sticking out of the tarp. The man's socks are bloody and his two-tone shoes now sport a third tone. Zimmerman clambers in, grabs the other end of the tarp, and pushes their burden out.

It is a long and dangerous route down to the ravine. Dord, who is backing, takes extra care with each step. He is convinced that the wrong step would snap his ankle and send him tumbling down the ravine, so he ignores Zimmerman's chiding ("You're moving slower than fucking Christmas!") and backs down baby step by baby step.

He cannot imagine any punishment more hellish than this. He swears to God, as he so often does in the throes of his addiction, that this is the last fucking time he's getting high, because every fucking time he gets high something goes absolutely bugshit, and then the next thing he knows he's carrying a dead body down an uneven precipice in the middle of the night, and fuck me, is that something cold and wet running down my arm, oh Christ almighty I hope I'm imagining that...

Finally Zimmerman says, "Okay. Stop." He maneuvers to the edge of the ravine and looks out. The bottom is dark, yet he does not point his flashlight down. "All right. We're gonna throw him over. You ready?"

"Sure," gasps Dord.

"Okay. Count of three. One. Two..."

With each count they swing the dead body back and forth, each time moving longer and faster. Then on the final count they let him go, and he's moving so fast and he's so heavy that Dord almost sails into the ravine with him. Zimmerman has to reach out and snatch him by the wrist to keep him on the path. "Careful," he says calmly in Dord's ear, like this is a routine occurrence for him.

There is a thud at the bottom of the ravine. But there is no sprinkling of rocks, nor any dust rising up from the darkness. And that thud did not sound right: there was a wetness to it, one that shouldn't be heard at all out in the desert.

"Did something break?" asks Dord. "In him, I mean."

"Don't know, don't care," says Zimmerman. "Give me the gun. The one you picked up at the road."

Dord hands him the bloody pistol, happy to be free of it. Zimmerman shines his light around the path until he finds a large, flat red rock just off to the side. Brown stains lie across its face in streaks. Zimmerman walks to the rock, places the gun in its exact middle, and turns it so it's facing the path, as if he wants anyone who comes down to the ravine to see this gun on this stained rock.

"All right," says Zimmerman. "Back to the truck."

Dord looks back at the dark ravine. "Ain't we gonna look to see if he's hid right?"

"He's hid fine. And we were told *not* to look."

"What? Why?"

Zimmerman gives him an angry look. "Dord…this is just one of those things, okay? One of those things we talked about. Let's just go."

"I'm so goddamn sick of that, Mike," says Dord. "I'm sick of being told what I can and can't do. We're being led around by the nose here."

"Dord…"

"Come on, we just hid a fucking body for these folks, and we can't even check to see if the work's done right? It's our asses on the line if he's found out here. I got a fucking pocketful of DNA evidence here."

Zimmerman does not answer. He just watches Dord with anxious eyes, and says, "Listen. I'm going to walk back up to the truck. And I'm not going to look anywhere but ahead of me. I suggest you do the same. You do, and you'll be fine." Then he turns and trudges back up the path, head bowed and eyes averted.

"Oh, for fuck's sake," says Dord. He struggles for a moment, wondering what to do. For though Dord has a talent for belligerence, he likes Zimmerman and he doesn't want to disbelieve or disappoint him. He seems to be the only sane voice in Dord's life at the moment.

Yet his curiosity is too much. He wants to know. He *has* to know. He has to find out what they don't want him to see, especially when it's just a few feet below him.

"Just to check," he mutters. Then he turns and shines his light down into the ravine.

At first he sees nothing but rock. This concerns him. He even starts to wonder if the body has disappeared. Then the light falls upon a two-tone shoe in a pale blue pants leg, and he inwardly sighs in relief. It's way down at the bottom, where no one would ever think to look, and it'd take a rock climber to safely get down there.

He is about to leave when he stops. Didn't they have the body wrapped tight in a tarp? If so, how could he see the leg? When he carried it down the only thing that stuck out was the man's feet. And those shoes were quite bloody, yet the one he just saw was not…

Dord turns and flashes the light back down. He finds the two-tone shoe and shines the light on the rest of the body.

The tarp is gone. *Did it unroll?* he wonders. But something else is different… the man's suit is not bloody anymore. It's dusty and dirty, but not bloody. Dord can see the blue color from here. And he still has his white panama hat on… yet Dord is sure they left that behind in the road.

Then the light falls upon the bundle of red hair spilling out from under the hat, and he sees that the man's fingernails are painted bright red, and he realizes this is not a man at all.

It's a woman. A dead one, but a woman all the same. Yet she is dressed in the exact same clothing as the man from Wink.

"What the fuck?" breathes Dord. He realizes he is sweating, and has to blink the drops out of his eyes. Then, trembling, he shines the light out a little farther.

The dead woman is not alone. Far from it. The bottom of the ravine is littered with dozens of corpses, all of them dressed in pale blue suits, two-tone shoes, and the odd white panama hat. They have been killed in a number of ways—throats or wrists slashed, or, judging by the bruises around some of their necks, some were hanged—but by far the most predominant method is a single bullet wound to the head, just like the man Dord and Zimmerman scraped off the road not more than a half an hour ago. Dord can see their man in the tarp now: he has landed in something dark and gray-black and glistening, yet Dord thinks he can see the shape of a hand or a curled foot among that rotting mass, and through all the yammering and howling in his mind Dord wonders exactly how long this has been going on.

Most of them are men. They vary in size: short, tall, fat, skinny. A few of the bodies are women. But it's not until the beam of light falls upon a small boy, no older than eleven, dressed in a small pale blue suit and cute two-tone shoes, that Dord begins screaming, especially when he sees the neat little hole drilled right between the boy's eyes, which stare up at him from the bottom of the ravine with hollow, rotted sockets.

The next thing Dord knows he's sprinting up the path to Zimmerman's truck. Because as it turns out, Zimmerman was right: he did not want to know. He did not ever, ever want to know.

CHAPTER TWENTY-FIVE

It's easy, Mona thinks, to understand why so many prophets found gods while wandering out in the desert. Because there cannot be any place on earth as strange and empty as a desert. Merely passing through it warps your thoughts: your perceptions of how the world works are broken down with each empty mile until civilization feels like a dream. And though any barren wilderness falls well short of achieving anything close to infinity, the sight of so many leaning red cliffs and so much empty horizon manages to inch the mind closer to understanding what infinity *is*.

For as Mona powers the Charger up the road to the mesa, she realizes she has never felt so small in her life. It's as if the world has been upended, and she is clinging to the point of a copper-red stalactite hanging from the roof of an endless cave, and below her are oceans and oceans of that cloudless, electric-blue sky, and were she to slip and drive off the road she would surely go plummeting into it, falling into that endless, flat blue, and though she might plead and beg for the fatal kiss of hard earth she would never, ever receive it. She would just keep falling.

She's been eyeing the chain-link fence running alongside the road. She passes yet another sign about Wink, this one a half-ruined thing asking her why she would ever wish to leave, though Mona could think of a few million reasons. She slows down when the fence's silver glimmer turn to snarls of black. She pulls over and sees that there is indeed a gap in the fence, and it's quite large, nearly twenty feet across.

"This must be the place," she says. Then she frowns, thinking of the doughnut tire. It can't hold up on uneven terrain, and it'd be impossible to get a good tire for the Charger out here. And besides, she doesn't trust a damn soul in this town anymore.

She decides this will have to be done on foot, as she feared. She'll drive the Charger in just far enough for it to be hidden from the road, because while she hasn't seen anyone else along the highway, she's not willing to take the chance. So, wincing each time she hears a rock or branch snap under the tires, she slowly, slowly steers the Charger through the gap in the fence.

Mona parks it behind a fallen ponderosa pine, then gets out and scans the way ahead. She cannot see much of a road out here. She looks around, marking this spot, for though she's brought plenty of water the desert is large and it can't last forever if she gets lost.

She shoulders the pack she made for herself (using a pink child's backpack from the Ponderosa Acres's "lost and found" box, as her previous pack was too small for this expedition) and begins her trek to the mesa. It is not unbearably hot in such high deserts, but it is quite dry, and the wind seems to corrode her skin.

She crests one hill and stops. For a moment she thought she saw something in the landscape, but then it was gone...

She takes a step or two back and scans the countryside. Then things align just right, and she sees it.

There is a road, just as Parson said there would be. It is incredibly faint, like a whisper of a brushstroke on a painting, but it's there. She can see it winding across the rocky terrain, running over hills and ridges until it disappears behind the shadow of the mesa. It's like a seam in the skin of the earth itself, as if the desert was stitched together here.

It will be a long walk. But this, Mona has decided, is hostile territory. Parson can tell funny little riddles all day, but he doesn't know jack shit about infiltrating what essentially is enemy ground.

And that's what Mona's going to be doing. There are secrets at the mesa no one wants her to know. So she hikes the pink backpack up high on her shoulders, bows down low, and starts to jog across the desert.

*   *   *

She stops in the shadow of every tree and rock to survey the territory around her. She sees no movement. There is no wildlife, not even any birds. She is utterly alone here. Still she does not let her guard down. Sometimes as she runs she touches the butt of the Glock, reminding herself how close it is, and what she will need to do if she encounters any—she searches for the right term—*obstacles.*

Things feel more and more unreal as she runs. The sun does not seem to move: it is forever stuck at just a half hour after dawn. Its slanted light turns the shadows into a staggered calligraphy that loops across the red ground. Enormous cliffs somehow keep creeping up from out of nowhere, slowly emerging from behind what looked like a simple knoll, like she's being stalked by the mountains. And everything here is quiet, save for the wind. It is such a harsh change from the piney valley of Wink.

One peak rises, then slowly falls, as if she's wading through a red sea. But as this peak falls, she thinks she sees something behind it—something thin and gleaming white . . .

"The hell?" she says. She reaches into her backpack and takes out her binoculars. She glasses the hilltop behind the cliff and scans for what she saw.

It's hard to miss. There behind the cliff is a white column sticking straight up out of the ground. It contrasts brightly against the dull red of the terrain. And the column is too perfect, too unblemished, for her to think it's there naturally.

As she watches, a violet light on the top of the column blinks on, then off.

"No," she says. "Not naturally." She purses her lips and studies the area around the white column. She sees no one. She thinks for a moment, then takes out the Glock. Then she starts off toward the column. She's uneasy, because one thing Parson said has been bothering her:

It winds around the mesa, through rocks and trees and gullies, and . . . and some things I cannot describe.

It's the "things he cannot describe" part that gets to her. It was as if he thought she'd see things that were beyond his conception. And while she doesn't know Parson that well (and isn't sure she'll ever get the chance, now) she doesn't think there's much beyond him. Parson seems to be very good at knowing things, so if the things out here confound even him ...

She emerges from the shadow of the cliff and sees she is at the base of the hill with the white column. It's about twelve feet tall, standing perfectly perpendicular to the top of the hill. It looks like it's made of metal, yet she can't tell if it's painted white or if the metal just *is* white. She's not sure how long it's been out here—if it was part of the Coburn operation then the damn thing must be older than she is—but it shows no signs of wear and tear.

For some reason the sight of that tall, white column makes her hair stand on end. It is just too *perfect*. It's like the wind turbines she saw in West Texas, so strange and beautiful in an alien way, but even worse: the thing has no business being there, and yet there it is, blinking that violet light.

She considers what to do. She cannot say why she thinks it is dangerous, but she is sure of it. It is doing something in some intangible way, just as the wind turbines were turning and turning.

Against her better judgment, Mona decides to check it out. There is something strangely fascinating about the column, something hypnotic in the way its light keeps blinking on and off. So she starts off toward it, trying to ignore the sick sensation in her gut that suggests this is a damn stupid idea.

Though the column is not that tall it seems to tower over her as she approaches it. She feels a little sick; it's like the proportions of everything in this country are all thrown off. And there's something else wrong ... something about the shadows on the ground ...

Once she's about twenty feet away from it, she stops. There's an electrical taste in her mouth that she doesn't care for, like she's been sucking on a battery. She squats and studies the column. Its top is smooth and rounded, like it's a big white bullet sitting on the top of the hill. And though the light keeps blinking, she can see no bulb, not even a hole in its white casing. If it *is* a casing, that is.

She cocks her head so one ear is toward it. The column is humming, very softly, an electrical sound that seems to pulse a little bit. She smacks her lips. Maybe she's wrong, but she thinks the electrical taste in her mouth ebbs and flows with the pulse of the hum.

Mona brushes her hair out of her eyes and keeps studying it. She walks around it in a half-circle, trying to see if she can spot a seam or a bolt or a screw in its smooth white surface. She can't see any, but it's hard because her hair keeps getting in her face. The wind just doesn't let up out here.

Then the wind finally drops a bit, a lull in the breeze. Yet Mona's hair stays right where it is, right in front of her eyes.

She pushes it down and watches, confused, as it slowly rises back up.

She looks down at her arms and sees that every hair there is pointing straight at the column. Then she thinks, pinches a lock of her hair, and holds it taut in front of her face. She watches in amazement as the very tip of the lock slowly lifts to point toward the white column . . .

It's static electricity, she realizes. The damn thing must be giving off a crazy-strong static field for it to pull at her from here.

She looks around to see if the field is pulling on anything else, and as she does she sees what's wrong with the shadows on the ground: though the sun is in the east, behind her, all the shadows on the ground are pointed toward her. She walks a few feet back from the column, and sees that's not quite right: the shadows are actually all facing *away* from the column. It's like it's projecting a bright light, one her eyes can't see, but one that still casts shadows.

She's not getting anywhere near that fucking thing, she decides. If she does she's sure to die of cancer in a week or something. It was stupid of her to even get this close.

Mona decides she needs to forget about it. She turns around and starts back to the road. The mesa isn't too far ahead now. Less than an hour's walk, probably, and the more distance she puts between her and that thing—whatever it is, and whatever it does—the better.

She walks at a brisk pace, eager to get away from the white column, but when she's about thirty feet past it her nose and eyes start watering. She pauses to sneeze, then continues, but it gets even worse. It's as if she's having an allergic reaction: every lining and every tissue in her skull has just swollen up like a balloon. Coughing, she staggers back down the hill and sits down on a stone to recover.

The attack fades. Mona rubs at her throat, wondering what the hell that was. She's never had an allergic reaction to anything in her life. What could have caused it now?

She takes a sip of water, then stands and makes for the road again. But right at about the same spot on the hill, her eyes burn and she starts sneezing over and over again, awful, painful sneezes that make her throat burn.

"Fuck!" gasps Mona. She falls to her hands and knees and crawls back down the hillside. Again, once she's moved several feet the attack fades.

She contemplates her situation as she catches her breath. She glances up at the white column, which is still implacably blinking its weird purple light. The more she looks at it, the more she doesn't trust it.

"You're doing this, aren't you, you son of a bitch," she says to it.

The column just keeps blinking. Mona glares at it, then looks back toward the mesa.

It doesn't want me to get over there, she thinks. It's a very stupid thing to think, she knows that, but she also feels certain that it's right. Someone put this thing here as a deterrent. Maybe they didn't want anyone getting to this side of the mesa. And if they were able to make a piece of machinery affect people in such a way...well. What else is around the mesa? It makes Mona wonder if she really wants to go farther.

"Hell yes, I do," she says angrily. She stands, glances at the white column, and grasps the pink straps of her backpack so it's pulled tight against her back. Then she bends low, flexes her knees, and breaks off at a dead sprint.

At first she thinks she's made it. She's going so damn fast that it feels like she's already passed that invisible line. But then the attack hits her like a freight train, a lightning bolt, a ten-ton weight hurtling down out of the sky, and suddenly she's stumbling forward like a drunk, sneezing uncontrollably, her vision blurring and her cheeks wet with tears.

Goddamn it, no, she thinks. *No, I am not going to be beat by some fucking white stick on a hill.*

She digs in her heels and starts trotting forward again.

About six steps out there's a loud, sharp *pop*, like a lightbulb burning out, and Mona collapses, sure the thing just fried her like a Tesla coil. But the attack immediately stops. The burning sensation recedes from her eyes, nose, and throat, and she sits up, taking deep, slow breaths. She sees that her skin is red and blotchy, like she's just been swimming in bleach. Hopefully that will go away soon.

She must have pushed through whatever barrier the thing maintains. She looks back at the white column. "Fucker," she says, and she's about to get back up when she does a double take.

There's a hill about two or three hundred yards past the column, and she could swear she just saw another violet light on that one, too.

She reaches into her backpack, takes out her binoculars, and looks.

She's not wrong: there is a second column standing on that distant hill. And unless the binoculars are lying to her, there's a third column, just barely a hair of white, standing on a hill far beyond that one. The three of them all form a line extending from just before the mesa and partway around the valley, silently blinking their purple lights in unison.

"Like a fence," says Mona. She puts down her binoculars and looks at the column closest to her. "Like an electric fence, or a wall."

This begs the question: what is it meant to be fencing out?

She turns this question over, and looks back down the slopes to the small green valley below. She can see a few roofs from here, and the black, charred memorial tree in the park.

Maybe the columns aren't meant to fence anything out. Maybe they're meant to fence something in.

Mona stands and starts walking back toward the mesa. Things no longer feel quite so distorted to her. Though the desert is still a striking place, it is not so surreal or disorienting. She wonders if the white columns project more than just an invisible barrier. Perhaps they are regulating something, like a water filter in an aquarium, and though she can't see the effects of that regulation she can sense it somewhere in the back of her head.

She is almost sure of one thing, though: whoever put the columns there didn't do it with people in mind. Otherwise she's positive she wouldn't have been able to get through. They must be meant for something else.

Maybe there's a reason people never leave or come to Wink, she thinks. This troubles her deeply. Because she did not experience any barrier when she first entered this valley. That means that either there are no columns and no barrier on the other side—which she thinks unlikely—or she was *allowed* in. As if she'd been expected.

She absently glances up as she considers this disturbing thought, but stops dead in her tracks. She stares at the sky, then shields her eyes with her hand to better see.

"No way," she says. "No fucking way."

Five minutes ago, the pale face of the morning moon was its usual dusky pink. That was on the other side of the white columns, she remembers, inside whatever field it is those machines are putting out.

On this side, sure, the moon is still in the same place, hanging just above the tip of the mesa. But it's returned to its normal white color. There's not a trace of pink in it.

CHAPTER TWENTY-SIX

Dee Johannes may not know what the hell he is doing, but he is determined to look good while doing it. As he sets out on his curious errand, which is the first of two for today, he's sporting his freshly-ironed Larry Mahan paisley pearl-snap shirt, a pair of extra-starched Wrangler retro jeans that he's got hiked up real high so they don't sag around his ass, and of course his ostrich-skin Luccheses, which he buffed and polished to a fine shine last night. He's been polishing them every night since he came to work at the Roadhouse, because goddamn is there a lot of dust out here in the desert, and you can't even walk to your car without your boots turning a pale gray. He's not sure how all the cowboys stay so good-looking in the movies when the country is so openly hostile to sartorial maintenance. There isn't even a dry cleaner for miles.

Of course, these items are just accessories to the real centerpieces of his look: the nickel-plated Desert Eagle riding in the front of his belt, and the Mossberg 4x4 bolt-action .30-06 hunting rifle slung over his shoulder. The Eagle he got off of a man he and Zimmerman pummeled half to death in the parking lot of the Roadhouse last winter; the Mossberg was a meticulously researched online purchase that he had to get shipped to a post office one town over for him to pick up. He has, of course, polished both of these before beginning on this outing, and he's very pleased with how they gleam in the dawn sun.

Though Dee has a lot of possessions, many of them deeply treasured—his HDTV, his Bowflex, and his Ford F-150 King Ranch pickup, for example—none of them is closer to his heart than the Mossberg. For the Mossberg, in Dee's mind, is the definitive, undeniable emblem of manhood, his holy token of vigor and virility; he is convinced that merely holding the Mossberg bestows upon him a sort of animal, savage charisma, like just touching its walnut stock (with matte blue finish) to his shoulder (which he has done sometimes in front of his full-length mirror, occasionally shirtless and occasionally a little more) causes him to exude a primal musk that will send nearby men packing and will cause any women who happen to look upon him to be filled with an almost evangelical, foaming-at-the-mouth arousal.

Dee's experiments with using his firearm as an aphrodisiac have yielded, sadly, pretty mixed results, since a) There isn't a place nearby with available women where he can just casually walk around with an enormous, high-caliber hunting rifle, and b) Most of the good-looking girls are at the Roadhouse, where you don't need the Mossberg to get laid, but around fifty to a hundred dollars or a couple of ounces of blow. And besides, Dee's already had all of them anyways. (Also, Bolan gets mad as hell when Dee brings the Mossberg into the bar. He says it upsets the room.) This is not to say, though, that Dee has not considered using the Mossberg in some sort of kinky role-playing game with one of the downstairs girls at the Roadhouse, perhaps slowly strutting into the room, wearing nothing but oil, his cowboy hat, and a pair of aviators, with the Mossberg jutting out proudly from his hands like he's stalking a beast in the jungle, and the girl would be on the bed cooing in pleased surprise as he enters her chamber, or whatever it is she's supposed to do. He almost went through with it once, but all the girls there are gossips and he knows if word got out he'd never live it down. So unfortunately the Mossberg remains relegated to a mere prop in Dee's fantasies, and though most people would find the idea of a naked man standing in front of a bathroom mirror with a hunting rifle in one hand and his lubed, erect dick in the other to be pretty sad, for Dee Johannes it's actually getting to be a little routine.

Dee tries to forget these fantasies as he strides to his truck with the rifle slung over his shoulder. In the light of day they seem a little silly. Before he climbs into his truck, he reaches into his pocket to check the list Bolan gave him. There are two locations written on it:

> *313 Madison—creek behind it in the backyard*
> *The lab—not sure*

"Aw, goddamn," says Dee. He sighs, pushes his hat back, and scratches his head. There is no place he hates more than the lab. He wishes he'd read the list before accepting this duty from Bolan. But it would have gone to him anyways. Dee is the only one strong enough and with a powerful-enough truck to transport the items he's been sent to procure.

But it's okay. He likes riding his truck all over this rugged country. And though he is aware that the denizens of Wink are dangerous—as was proven when he accompanied Zimmerman, Norris, and Mitchell to that house not too long ago—Dee is confident there's nothing in Wink he can't handle. The logic that results in this conclusion can be kind of fuzzy in places, but essentially it boils down to the fact that if a man has a large enough vehicle and a large enough gun, there isn't much he can't do.

Granted, Dee hasn't actually ever shot anyone with the Mossberg. He also has not ever actually hunted with the Mossberg. He did shoot several trees and targets with it when he first got it in the mail, but this tends to make the gun pretty dirty, and Dee finds cleaning it incredibly tedious. So since then it's been mostly dry-firing for Dee, which can't be *that* different from the real thing because the fundamentals remain the same: you are still pointing your gun at a target, still pulling the trigger, etc. And dry-firing has yielded another nice bonus: he's hardly gone through any of the expensive ammunition he bought with the rifle, so there are still boxes and boxes of it sitting on the floor of his truck cab.

When Dee pulls up to 313 Madison—a small, neat adobe home on the outskirts of Wink—he is still riding high on swagger. He considers walking up to the front door with the Mossberg slung over his back, but remembers that Zimmerman always says that's overkill. (Zimmerman, like Bolan, considers the Mossberg to be both totally absurd and superfluous.) He reluctantly yields to his mental Zimmerman, and leaves the Mossberg sitting on the floor of his cab. But he does lift up his shirt and make sure the Desert Eagle is still in the right spot.

As he walks up the front steps, the swagger returns. He raps on the frame of the screen door with a feeling of genuine authority, and pastes a big smile across his face when he hears the footsteps coming to the door.

The dead bolt slowly turns. Then there's a snap, and the door opens just enough for one small, watery, terrified eye to stare out at him.

"Morning, uh—" Dee cannot confirm the gender of the person on the other side of the door. He struggles before saying, "Morning! I was wondering if it'd be possible for me to check the creek out behind your house? My wallet fell in it last night—got up to some high jinks, I'm afraid—and it got plumb washed away. Won't be a moment, and I'm terribly sorry to intrude."

The watery eye continues staring at him. Then it bobs up and down in what might be a nod, and the door slams shut. There's another snap as the dead bolt slides home again.

"Sheesh," says Dee. "So much for hospitality." He hops off the front porch and heads to his pickup. He looks back at the house. After confirming that there's no one in the windows, he discreetly takes a small spade and a tough piece of canvas from the bed of his truck and hotfoots it around back.

Christ, he thinks. Everyone in this burg has gone nuts after what they did on the mesa. It was just one guy, too. Seems like Bolan has Zimmerman kill a guy every other month, and no one freaks out about it, or at least not like this. But then, the people Zimmerman kills are usually people everyone expects to die: druggies, lowlifes, small-time enforcers, etc.

He remembers what he's come here for as he approaches the creek. He realizes now that his story about the wallet was a dumb one: the creek is completely dry. That doesn't matter, though, not now. He hops down into the creek bed, takes off his sunglasses, and looks around.

Here's the hard part: Dee never has any idea where his quarry could be. Conceivably, it could be anywhere. It's in the fucking ground, after all, and there's plenty of ground around here. And it can vary in size...

He shuts his eyes, counts to ten, and opens them. Nothing. He shuts them again, counts to twenty, opens them, and sees...

There is the very subtle suggestion of an unnatural bend in one part of the creek. Like the running waters get pulled to one side, rubbing up against the earth. If you didn't know to look for it, you'd never see it; but once you did, you wouldn't be able to stop seeing it.

Dee walks to the bend in the creek, reaches into a pocket, and takes out a nickel. (He prefers nickels because not only do they have more copper than pennies, they're also easier to see.) He holds it out straight in front of him between two fingers, and lets it drop.

Theoretically, it should fall straight to the ground. But it doesn't: about halfway down it swoops away from Dee, just very slightly, as if the wind is pushing it. But there isn't any wind in the creek bed.

He steps back, shuts one eye, holds his arm out, and sticks up his thumb like an artist taking stock of a painting. He estimates the direction in which the nickel was headed, and lines it up with the wall of the creek bed.

"Bingo," he says, and starts to hack away at the creek bed wall with the spade.

It doesn't take long until he hears a high-pitched, metallic *ping* as his spade bites into the earth. He wriggles the blade of the spade back and forth, spilling more earth onto the ground. Then the wall of the creek bed gives and something small tumbles out.

The object is small, but the *thud* it makes when it hits the creek bed is not. It strikes the ground so hard Dee feels it in the soles of his feet.

He winces. He is not looking forward to getting this son of a bitch back to the truck.

He kneels and brushes the soil off the object. Underneath the pile of earth is a small block of what looks like a very dark, worn metal. It's not more than four inches wide on any side, yet there is something about this block—perhaps the way it pulls your gaze, even if you're not looking anywhere near it—that would give any onlooker the impression of profound heaviness. Perhaps you would even begin to wonder if this small cube of metal has resulted in the odd slope in the neighboring yards, which all appear to funnel toward this point, once you really think about it.

Because Dee spends most of his nonwork, non-fucking time getting his pump on with his Bowflex and free weights, he's the only one in Bolan's crew who's in the sort of physical condition to carry this little item. (Maybe. Or maybe they just want to give him the shit jobs, he thinks.) He starts by laying the sheet of tough canvas out next to the cube. Then he pulls a pair of thick gloves out of his pocket and puts them on. These gloves were a little tough to get out here: they're made for handling blocks of dry ice, because the cube of metal is very cold. He can see condensation forming on it even now. He's seen others lose layers and layers of skin to the damn things before, so he's cautious.

Dee squats, sets his legs (because you always lift with your legs, not your back), and starts to tip the little block over. It's always surprisingly hard: this is not a material that ever wants to move. And the size of the cube is never an indication of the weight: there was one that was hardly bigger than a quarter that was a *huge* pain in the ass to move.

Dee successfully gets the block tipped over onto the heavy canvas. He looks around at the creek bed and finds the shallowest spot. Then he folds the canvas patch up over the cube, knots it in his hands, and starts dragging it over.

He was right: it is a goddamn headache to get this thing out of the creek. It digs a four-inch trench as Dee hauls it, and it tears the shit out of the creek walls and the grass up top once he finally gets it over. Every time, he waits for an ache to blossom in his loins, because he's sure this work will give him a hernia someday, but so far he's been golden, and hopefully today won't be the day.

It takes him the better part of twenty minutes to move the cube fifty yards. The worst part—which is *always* the worst part—is when he has to pick it up in a dead squat and place it in the truck bed. He asked

Bolan to get him one of those hydraulic lifts—maybe the kind for getting handicapped people on buses, or something—but his boss's response was not positive, to say the least.

He wipes the sweat from his eyes when he slams the truck bed door shut. He cracks open a bottle of water and pounds about half of it. Then he glances north, to where the mesa is.

He sighs and leans on the side of his truck. The lab is big. It's always bigger than you think it is. And he's covered in sweat, and—he checks very quickly—his boots are already dusty again.

He checks the list again. "Not sure, huh?" he says. "This'll take all day..."

He might as well get started now. Bolan's boss—that spook in the hat—hates waiting. Dee has never spoken to this man, or even seen him; he's just heard reports about him. And apparently Dee's cube-collecting project is one issue the spook has a lot of problems with. Dee is told that in certain communications with Bolan and Zimmerman, the spook describes one cube in particular that he's been looking for for a long time, the mother of all of these damn things, one a couple feet high and a couple feet wide. Dee goes white at the idea of having to pick up such a thing, and is frankly quite happy that they have not found it yet.

He hopes that's not what's waiting for him up on the mesa. He'd rather dig a hundred of the bastards out of a creek bed than deal with that.

It's a long drive up to the mesa. He enjoys it less than he thought he would. This part of the country always feels very peculiar, like it's *stretched*. It's so peculiar, in fact, that Dee almost swears he saw a red muscle car parked behind a pine somewhere out in the desert. But that's stupid. Even for Dee, that's stupid.

CHAPTER TWENTY-SEVEN

The door is made of dull metal and is striped like a yellow jacket. The neon-yellow bands run diagonally from its top right corner to its bottom left. There are old yellow block letters spray-painted at the top that read WARNING, but what they are supposed to be warning you about is not made clear. On the whole it is not a large door: it is about seven feet tall and three feet wide, and it's set about a foot into the rock side of the mesa, by means of a construction method with which Mona is not familiar.

(And she thinks—Coburn is *in* the mesa? Like *inside* of it? Is the entire mesa hollow? She remembers an article she read about that particle accelerator thing in Europe, CERN or whatever—wasn't it completely underground? Perhaps Coburn isn't all that different— underground, yet also raised into the air.)

She is surprised by the size of the door. She expected it to be a loading door, but it's obviously meant just for people. She wonders why.

But what is most surprising is that the door stands open about an inch or two. It has a huge, clunky doorknob, one of those kinds you usually see in really old public restrooms, but it is not engaged: someone forced the door ajar, probably by kicking at it, judging by the way the metal frame has bent. From the pile of dust built up at the bottom, it seems it's been this way for some time.

The thing that Mona doesn't like is the way the door was kicked open. Because, judging from the way the lock and frame are bent, whoever did it was kicking from the inside.

She reaches into her pocket and takes out the key Parson sent her to get. Since the lock is broken, it would appear the key is unnecessary. But then, Parson never explicitly said the key was for this door. She just assumed that was what he meant.

She examines the key and the lock. The lock is pretty basic; the key, however, remains an intimidating four-inch piece of industrial technology with about two dozen teeth.

No. No, this key is meant for something else. Something much more important.

"Shit," says Mona.

She rubs the back of her neck. She doesn't like this at all. This is worse than Weringer's house. Even Parson, who is often so dismissive of the oddities happening around town, holds Coburn in some kind of reverence.

His words echo in her head until she feels she's about to have a panic attack. She wishes now, more than anything, that she understood him more. She wishes she could grasp the meaning behind his little parable, which seems to have been so crucial that it drove him into a coma. And she is beginning to wish that she'd chosen to just beat it and leave town, leave this little clutch of shifting shadows and veiled words behind and find a new life somewhere else.

But another part of Mona knows that a new life isn't coming. She's used up all her wishes, all her fresh starts, and this is the last place to find anything that could remake her. And when she remembers the film she watched back in her mother's house—the smoke-filled room, the glamorous, cheery woman striding in from the patio—she knows that there are secrets behind this door she simply must understand. Because unless she's wrong, somewhere behind this surreal, forbidding door is the history of her mother, or at least a part of it. But that's more than Mona's ever had in her life.

She remembers Parson gave her one other clue, one she hasn't had the time to look at yet. She sits down in the shadow of a large rock, reaches into her pocket, and pulls out his note cards.

She looks at the "Cat" card to see if she's missed any hidden code, but if so a closer look doesn't help. It appears to just be an innocuous and rather vapid definition of the word, like one a grade-schooler would make for a project.

She looks at the next card. She is not at all surprised to see that it is:

DOG
(noun)
A small domesticated carnivore, Canis familiaris, *noted for its loyalty and servitude. Its puppies are a lot of fun!*

"What the *fuck*," says Mona, shaking her head. She starts flipping through them. They are all fairly insipid and utterly useless. There is a card for "Octopus" (*the mother dies after laying her eggs, which is quite sad*), for "Sunshine" (*it's what makes plants green!*), and for "Home" (*where your family and friends are, and where everything makes sense*). She looks at the definition for "Home" for a while. Maybe he's coding something into the first letter of each word? But when Mona actually takes the time to test this idea the letters spell nothing but gibberish.

Frustrated, she starts flipping through the cards. There must be over thirty of the damn things. But then she comes across a card that is markedly different from all the others:

PANDIMENSIONAL
(adjective)
1. The quality of existing in several different aspects of reality at once, rather than just one
2. The ability to operate or move across the same

Mona stares at the note card, and again says, "What the fuck?"
She flips through the remainder of the stack, but finds no other

card like it. She is certain that this card was the purpose of Parson's entire charade. But what it means is beyond her.

Yet then she remembers that moment back in Weringer's house, when one room felt nested inside another, yet occupied the same place. And when she focused, she could stay in one room, and avoid that huge stone cavern with the enormous fires...

Mona thinks for a moment, then stands and throws the door open.

Behind it is a long set of cement stairs leading up. They are dark and she cannot see where they go. So she takes out her flashlight, flicks it on, and starts up.

The staircase is completely black, and though she can see fluorescent lights hanging at each landing she can find no switch for them. Mona's been climbing for about an hour, but the stairs seem to go on forever. She looks over the metal railing once and shines her light down and sees an endless blocked spiral of gray yawning below. She can't even see the bottom anymore.

She remembers that Coburn is supposedly located at the top of the mesa, and she started at the very, very bottom, and she groans. Her legs are already aching and she's almost out of breath, but she's willing to bet she's not a quarter of the way up.

She keeps climbing with nothing but her flashlight to guide her. The railings and the stair corners cast jigsaw-puzzle shadows on the walls. Occasionally she'll shine it up the stairwell to see if she's finally getting close to something, but there is always darkness and more stairs above.

The only sounds Mona hears throughout all of this are the stomping of her feet and her labored breath. Her calf muscles feel as if they're about to snap, like guitar strings stretched too tightly.

Then she hears a third sound.

She stops and listens, and realizes she's right. But it's one she never expected here:

Someone is singing.

It's only because the stairwell is so quiet that Mona can hear it. But it's definitely there. Someone very far above her, maybe a woman, is singing.

She stares up at the darkness. She can see no lights up there, nor can she hear the sound of anyone moving. Yet as she listens, she hears saxophones and trumpets joining the singer. It's like there's a Big Band performance happening up there.

Very, very slowly, Mona takes out the Glock. She points the flashlight down at the ground to lessen the chances that someone above will spot it. Then she starts climbing the stairs again, moving slowly and softly with her eyes trained on the next flight of stairs above her.

The singing gets louder as Mona climbs. Eventually she recognizes the song: to her total confusion, it's "I Saw Mommy Kissing Santa Claus."

Then more sounds join it. There's the sound of laughter, the mutter of conversation, glasses tinkling. But that shouldn't be right at all… she thought Coburn was abandoned.

Somewhere above a voice shouts, *"Charlie? Charlie! Come on! Get in here!"*

It's a party, she thinks. *They're throwing a fucking party up there*. She can't even begin to understand it.

After a few more flights of stairs Mona thinks she can discern a very faint light cast on the wall at the top. She stops and turns off her flashlight and waits for her eyes to adjust to the darkness. She isn't wrong: a very dim blade of light is cast across a wall on one of the topmost landings. She isn't willing to shine her light up there and give away her position, but she'd bet now that she's reached the very top of the staircase.

She slows her ascent to a crawl. As she rounds the landing opposite the light, she sees there is a thin, glowing line at the top of the staircase, and it marches around the wall to form a rectangle.

It's a door. There's a door at the top of the staircase, and someone is throwing a party just behind it.

Mona stares at it, breathing hard. Every inch of her shirt is sticking to her skin. There are many, many voices now, so whatever party it is, it must be a big one. She starts to approach the door, but she brings the Glock up just a little, just in case.

She hears shouting from the other side again. Someone cries, "Cheers, everyone! Look at me. Hey! Fucking look at me! All right, good. Finally. Now, come on, everyone, to the New Year, am I right?"

"And on Uncle Sam's dime, too," says a second voice, a woman.

"Fuck Sam's dime," says a third. "The DOD ain't footing this bill. We paid for this out of our goddamn pockets."

"Then we better get our money's worth!" shouts the first voice, and there's a round of cheers and laughing.

It's a New Year's Eve party, thinks Mona, *but it's July, isn't it?* What the hell could be going on?

She's right next to the door now. Barging in on a party with a gun drawn really isn't her style, to say the least. But whatever her style is, it's been woefully inadequate the last couple of days. She supposes it's time to adapt.

She decides she's going to take a peek. She grasps the knob, and slowly applies pressure. It is not locked. She swallows and keeps turning the knob, tensing with each twitch of the bolt.

Finally it will turn no farther. She positions herself at the opening and begins to ease the door open.

"Say," says a voice on the other side, and it sounds mere feet away, "what kind of gin is this, anyways?"

The door is almost open a crack. Mona puts her eye to it, tries to steady her hand, and keeps easing the door open.

Then, abruptly, the light on the other side of the door dies, and the music and voices cease entirely. The stairway fills with total, impenetrable darkness.

Mona is so shocked she almost falls over. She stands in the dark, wondering what happened. Did the people on the other side know she was about to peep in on them? But surely they couldn't have reacted *that* quickly? There is no light of any kind anymore, and no sound. It's as if they simply stopped existing.

She pushes the door open all the way, and though she can't see it, she's very aware that she might be standing in front of a hallway with a bunch of people staring right at her. She tries to remind herself that the people in the hallway can't see her either...or at least they shouldn't be able to.

She raises her gun to point directly ahead. Then she lifts the flashlight, places it over the wrist holding the gun, and turns it on.

What is before her is indeed a hallway, but it looks as if it hasn't seen people in years. The ceiling panels have fallen in and the Pergo paneling is blooming with corrosion. She can see several doors to what look like offices—because this does not look like a lab hallway to her, but an ordinary office hallway—but they are all open and she can see no movement within them.

She fights the urge to call, "Hello?" and begins to stalk down the hallway, gun wheeling to cover each angle of approach. It is an awkward and clumsy dance in this decrepit, musky hallway. Each office is littered with rotting yellow paper. Yet nothing appears to have been disturbed. No one has been here in decades.

The place looks like it was built in the sixties and never updated: all the desks are streamlined, Mid-Century Modern affairs, and they're surrounded by chairs resembling tulips and eggs. The lamps are skeletal, geometric contraptions, like things pried off Sputnik and plugged into the wall, yet the lamps in the ceiling are rounded, organic sculptures of glass and chrome (now rusted) that look inspired by undersea life. The sheer silence of the place is intimidating. This is not a place where a party was being thrown not more than five minutes ago.

Finally Mona gives in to her worst instincts: "Anyone home?" she asks aloud, softly.

There is no answer. She continues on with quiet footsteps.

So this was where her mother worked, she thinks as she wanders the halls, even though no one in Wink can remember it. Again, it feels impossible to reconcile what she's found here with the woman she knew. This was once a sleek, stylish place to work, even if it was out in the desert. It would have been a haven for thinkers and researchers, a magnet for the most ambitious professors and scientists and graduate students out there. People with beards and glasses and chalk—shit, Mona doesn't know. This isn't her scene, no matter what decade.

She tries to imagine what it was like when it was first built—hell, when *Wink* was first built. She imagines it bustling with intellectuals, each one trying to think up a way to make the nation stronger, to push the very limits of what humanity could do. It must have seemed like such a tremendous hope to everyone. For the first time, she can understand the compulsion of the men and women who first built the town in the valley. They thought they were making something. Maybe something like a utopia.

Yet what did they do here? What did the occupants of all these modish offices work to accomplish? And what did Laura Bright, *née* Alvarez, once do in this place? If she was ever here at all, that is.

The woman who worked here, thinks Mona, would have been such a wonderful mother. Smart, cultured...what happened to her? Why was she not the inspiring figure Mona now imagines her to have been?

And somewhere inside Mona is a tiny voice that says, *Maybe one of us is always supposed to die, the mother or the daughter...maybe that's just the way we're made. We're weak, breakable. Maybe it was right that I never had the chance...*

"Shut up," whispers Mona. "Shut *up*."

The voice quiets, and she continues on.

Mona comes to the reception area. Somehow it remains untouched by the decay. The walls are rounded and white, the front desk shaped like a teardrop, done in pale wood paneling. On one of the flatter spots of the wall there's a huge starburst clock that, to her concern, is still ticking.

It has been maintained, obviously, so someone's been here. Someone might still be here. But she still isn't sure what happened to the party she heard.

There's a bright, happy mural painted on the wall behind the desk, depicting a mountain landscape. It does not take Mona long to recognize the splinter of piney green running through the feet of the striking red peaks. She can even see the pink balloon of Wink's water tower situated on the far side of the valley. She eventually sees that Mesa Abertura—the mesa she's currently inside of—is also shown in the mural. Yet she sees that its top is bedecked with immense white orbs and cups, like sculpted white icing on a red cake. They're telescopes and satellite dishes, she realizes, but she sure as hell hasn't seen any of those on the mesa in her time here. They must have been totally removed. But that would have taken a lot of work, even more than getting the damn things up here.

For a fleeting second, she remembers glimpsing something huge and dark perched on the mesa, swaying back and forth against a black sky bursting with lightning...

She shudders and moves on. She walks around the receptionist's desk and starts down the main hall, which is where things start to look a little more like a lab.

The carpet turns to cement. Then the doors turn into huge slabs of metal with tiny, thick windows set in the exact centers, and they feature some fearfully complicated locks.

She takes out Weringer's key again, and thinks. Then she tries fitting it into one of the locks.

The key fits, but she can't turn it. So it's not the key for this lock. But at least she's in the right neighborhood now. This key must fit one of the lab doors.

She moves on.

She comes across one door that doesn't lead to a lab at all, but to some kind of electrical closet. Circuits and panels crawl across the wall in a rusty tangle. Against one wall is a box of dictionaries. Yet up against the circuit wall is a huge electric generator that doesn't look as if it had been made more than two years ago. It's a new addition for sure.

Someone has definitely been in here. But somehow she doesn't think they had anything to do with the party. Whoever was drinking and carousing didn't sound like the generator-toting sort.

She squats and examines the generator. She pops the cap to the fuel tank and shines her light in. It's full. Then she looks at all the cables running to the circuits in the wall, and, though her electrical knowledge is rudimentary at best, everything seems hooked up to the right place in order to run a fair amount of the building. Probably not whatever the hell is behind those metal doors, but maybe the lights.

She considers her choices. Again, if she turns on the generator, she could be alerting people that she's here. Yet at the same time, Mona really, really doesn't want to be stumbling around in the dark in this place, with so many dark corners occupied by who the fuck knows what, so she shrugs, shuts the cap, grabs the rip cord, and starts her up.

It takes minimal effort to get the thing going. The lights outside flicker, then fully come on. She walks back out and looks around.

With the lights on the place is not quite so intimidating. It is antiseptic and cold, yes, but it's not the dour cenotaph she was trawling through before.

She keeps walking down the hall, trying her key in all the locks. None of them gives. One door's little glass window is broken, and she stands on her tiptoes and peers inside. It's like an airlock from the sci-fi movies in there. She starts to wonder if she needs to be wearing a lead shield over her torso as she walks around in here, because though Mona has absolutely no desire for children anymore, she still doesn't fancy the idea of her uterus bubbling away like a teapot.

Some of the laboratories have windows that allow her to see in. There are huge old electrical conduits on the walls and floors, and she can see places around them where enormous pieces of equipment once stood. It's like her mother's house, with the ghostly inverse shadows on the walls and floors telling her of belongings long gone.

She absently glances in each window as she walks from door to door, trying her key. It's the same thing, as far as she can see: a dimly lit, empty room with severed electrical cords dangling from the ceiling or snaking out of the walls. They must have had a hell of a power bill at this place. But this was a government-funded lab, so they must—

She freezes where she stands. "What the *hell*?" she says aloud. She turns back and peers in one lab window.

This lab is empty like all the others. But for a moment she could have sworn that it was different. It's like it *changed* when she turned away, just for an instant.

She thought she saw the lights were on, glowing much cleaner and whiter than the fluorescent ones out in the hall. But there was also something new in the room: a huge, cone-like device sitting in the middle of the floor with an unbelievable amount of wiring leading to it. And though her brain refuses to consider this suggestion, she is *sure* she caught a fleeting glimpse of two men standing around the cone-like device, dressed in gray suits and skinny black ties and horn-rimmed glasses, discussing something that seemed to be slightly irritating to them, as if it were just a casual workday.

But now the room is empty, just like the others: the lights are gray and weak, and there are no people inside. There are no men inside, and no cone-like device sitting on the floor, either, but she can definitely see where one *was*: there is a circular indentation in the blank concrete, like the device was sitting there for years and years, years and years ago.

Is it possible, she wonders, to see the imprint that lives have left on a place, just like how she sees the shapes of departed machines on the floors and walls of each tiny room?

As she wonders for the hundredth time what happened in this place, her toe catches something on the ground and it almost sends her sprawling. She curses, mentally thanks God her finger was nowhere near the Glock's trigger, and looks back at what tripped her.

There is an enormous crack in the paved floor. It stretches across the hallway and crawls up the walls and even across the ceiling. The hallway beyond the crack is askew, in fact: the floor ahead is one to three inches higher on the left side and correspondingly lower on the right. It's like a miniature tectonic rift. The crack she tripped on isn't the only one, either: it appears to be the papa crack, with many baby spiderweb cracks radiating outward down the hallway, but only in one direction, away from her.

The sight gives Mona vertigo. Whatever caused this (and whatever it was, it must have been *huge*) has also screwed with the electrical systems, because the fluorescent lights in the ceiling tend to flutter more the farther away they are from the crack. She gets that same queer unease as when she first found the lightning-struck bathroom in her mother's house: it is as if some horrible accident has warped this place, like it no longer belongs in the building at all.

Wary, she continues down the hallway, staggering a little due to the uneven floor. She studies the cracks in the wall, worried that this whole place might cave in. As she does, she sees that there are immense cables running along the ceiling, some of them so heavy they have to be bolted directly into the concrete. Most of them branch off into the various lab rooms, but one of them, the biggest, goes straight ahead before passing through the wall above the largest, darkest door in the entire hallway.

Mona looks at the door, then down at the key in her hand. She's about to try it when she hears footsteps coming down the hallway behind her.

She turns and points the gun toward the mouth of the hall. The footsteps, like those of the Native American in the panama hat, suggest wooden-soled shoes. She moves up against the wall and steadies her aim.

He followed me here, she thinks. *I don't know how he survived, but he followed me here.*

Yet though the footsteps keep getting louder, no one comes. She can see no movement below the fluttering fluorescent lights at all. The footsteps get loud enough for her to think that the walker is only a dozen feet in front of her, but she sees nothing. Then she hears a few other sounds—the shuffling of papers, and a grunt—and the footsteps come to a stop.

Mona doesn't move. Her ears are telling her that this person is just fifteen feet or fewer in front of her. But she can't see a damn thing. Just feet and feet of blank gray concrete, lit by the strobing neon lights.

She hears more papers turning. Then a quiet "Hmm," and the sound of a match being struck.

Mona feels sweat trickling down her temples. She can see no flame, nor any change in light, nor can she smell or see any smoke. Yet she can hear the faint crackling of a tiny fire in the hallway.

What the fuck is going on? she wonders.

She hears a series of throaty clicks—like someone puffing at a pipe?—and then the footsteps resume, though they're much slower, and they sound like they're walking to the side of the hall rather than down it.

Then, though she sees absolutely no doors move at all, she hears one open, the lock clanking and the hinges making a slow screech. Her eyes jump from door to door, confirming that they are all still shut.

A voice rings out: "Paul, have you seen these numbers? They're ridiculous!" Then the sound of a door slamming, and silence.

She stares at the empty hallway. It was always empty, of course—or at least it *looked* that way—but now her ears are also telling her it's deserted. Still, she doesn't dare move for the next five minutes. Her legs start to tremble, since they're already exhausted from the climb up here, but she forces them to stay taut, keeping the Glock trained on the center of the hallway.

Nothing happens. The invisible mystery man must have found Paul, whoever he is, and must now be discussing his ridiculous numbers.

First the party, then the men standing around that machine in the lab, now this.

Is this place—her brain almost refuses to process such a ridiculous idea—*haunted*? Or maybe she's just going insane again...

Then she remembers the last time she thought she was going insane, and seeing things that weren't there. She hears Parson's voice in her head: *The time where you were was damaged, so you saw something that had happened already.*

Is this the same thing? she wonders. Is time broken here, and she's catching stray seconds from long, long ago?

She lowers the gun. It would make sense, wouldn't it? Perhaps a man did once actually walk down this hall, light his pipe, and enter a room and ask a question. Maybe they did throw a New Year's Eve party here, decades and decades ago; and at some point two engineers probably stood in one of the laboratories scratching their heads, teasing out the problem before them.

And perhaps, if time is indeed broken here, those events could echo down through the years to be witnessed by Mona herself. Maybe she is seeing ghosts, but they're ghosts of moments and seconds rather than people. The past is still happening here in some unseen way. Her path just happens to convene with those taken by the people who worked here long, long ago.

She is not comforted by the idea, but she feels it's the right one. The things she's glimpsed and heard have not responded to her or acknowledged her in any way. They're just doing what they did decades ago, over and over again. She finds the thought a little horrifying.

Something cold calcifies in her belly. What if one of the little moments that gets replayed before her happens to feature none other than Laura Alvarez herself? What if she catches some ghostly imprint of her mother, going about her daily duties? Mona is both disturbed by and attracted to this thought: it would be practically the same as seeing her on film, but it would feel a little more *real*, wouldn't it? And she could finally see what she was like, here at work, before marrying Earl...

She returns to the door. It is substantially thicker than the others, and its metal is a bit darker. She wonders if it's made of lead; the others appeared to be steel. She is not eager to walk into a room that's still hot, and it would be, wouldn't it, because doesn't radioactivity take centuries to die out? That was what they taught her in school. They have to stick radioactive waste in some giant round canister, like a poisoned, malicious Easter Egg, and drop it down a mine shaft out in the desert. It suddenly feels as if all of America's nasty secrets could be found out here among the rock and sand, buried in the wilderness, forgotten.

She grips Weringer's key a little tighter. The dozens of little teeth bite into her fingers. She braces herself and slides the key in the lock.

The lock gives with the slightest amount of force, and the door, though it must weigh hundreds of pounds, silently falls open, smoothly gliding through the air.

Mona walks to the threshold, and looks in.

It is a wide, low room with a ceiling, walls, and floor all made of the same metal as the door. The room is rounded, with no distinguishable corners. It is completely bare except for the large apparatus hanging in the center, lit by the beams from tiny spotlights in the ceiling.

It is a mirror. But it is a mirror unlike any Mona has ever seen before.

The mirror portion is a wide, gleaming, silvery circle with a diameter of about ten feet. It hangs from the ceiling by a long, triple-jointed arm that looks like it would allow for rotation in many directions. The mirror is mounted on a thick copperish-looking plate, which is fed by dozens of thick wires that wind down the arm. A variety of machinery and equipment hangs off the arm as well: wires and tubing and chambers and pressure plates. Surrounding the apparatus are numerous steel frames stacked with old analog devices (to Mona they look like VCRs), but she does not get the impression that they are part of it: they sport microphones, lenses, electronic readouts. No, these devices, whatever they are, were meant to monitor the mirror and record it.

And if you record things, Mona thinks, *then you have to keep your recordings somewhere...*

She hesitates, again worrying that the room is radioactive. She holds a flat palm out, which she knows is stupid because you can't feel radiation on your bare skin. As she expected, she feels nothing. Still, she is reluctant.

She notices that the mirror apparatus is not whole. A second arm branches off the main one, and it looks as if it held a mirror once, yet the mirror is gone, as if it's been unscrewed or ripped off. She wonders where it went

(Would you like to see a magic trick?)

and who has it. From the look of things, the door to this room hadn't been opened in a while.

Mona realizes she is breathing quite hard. She stuffs the Glock in the back of her pants (she no longer trusts her shaking hands), shuts her eyes, and steps into the room.

Though her eyes are shut, Mona is sure she can feel things change. It is the same as in Weringer's house: though she cannot say why, she is positive that, though this room may appear to be connected to the rest of Coburn via that long, cracked hallway, she is now somewhere *else*. She is no longer on the mesa, she feels: she is no longer in New Mexico, no longer in America. Perhaps she is no longer on Earth.

She opens her eyes.

The room looks the same. And when she looks behind, she can still see the long, cracked hallway with the quaking lights. And yet she is sure this room is separate from everything, floating freely in . . . what? Nothing? Is it floating in nothing, like a space capsule?

She looks at the mirror. It seems far larger now that she is near it. She slowly walks around to get a better look. The arm is bent so the mirror's face is pointed slightly upward, facing the ceiling, which Mona finds a bit curious for a mirror to be doing. But it is a beautiful thing, really. There is something about the way the light glances off its surface, as if when the spotlights' rays touch it they turn to silver liquid and go skating around it in a shimmering orbit before sliding off the side.

She walks until she can see herself in the bottom half of the mirror. It does not distort her at all, but reflects her as any mirror would do. What was this thing meant for, she wonders? Is it really a mirror, or is its reflective surface just a byproduct of whatever alloy the plate is coated in? She leans in until her nose is almost touching its surface.

She stares into her eyes. For some reason she is suddenly sure that the woman in the mirror is staring back at her, not as a reflection but as a thing with its own agency. She keeps staring at herself, wondering if perhaps she is seeing a Mona that never was . . .

And then things *click*.

It happens purely in her head. And, just as when she first entered this room, she feels things change, almost imperceptibly. She looks around, but she sees no visible shift. The hallway is still outside, the lights are still fluttering, and the mirror...

She gasps and jumps back. Her own reflection does the same, of course. But for a moment, Mona was sure that her reflection was not there. What she saw was not the ceiling of this lead room, or any little spotlights, but a wide, endless black sky with many red and white stars.

And the woman standing in front of the mirror was not Mona. But she recognized her. Mona's seen her only once before, projected onto an old white wall in fuzzy ochre tones, laughing as everyone at her party clapped for her.

Then she hears the footsteps again.

Mona looks out at the hallway. Unlike the last time, she can see movement at the end. She quietly steps to the side, hiding behind the huge door, and takes out the Glock.

The footsteps come closer, heading directly for the room. They slow a little bit, and she hears the walker stop just at the threshold of the door.

"Hello?" says a man's voice. But it is a very curious voice, Mona thinks. Not only is it not very threatening, it is also faint and crackly, like it is coming out of an old radio catching a signal from a broadcast far, far away.

The person walks forward, toward the mirror. And when he clears the door, Mona sees it is not a man at all.

It *looks* like a man, just a little, but it is like a black-and-white image of a man from an old, broken television, one overlaid with fuzzy lines and bursts of static, and in some places he is even transparent. He is wearing a ragged tweed coat and a stained pair of slacks, and his shoes are scuffed and beaten and his collar is torn. His salt-and-pepper hair is curly and thick. Though she can see him only from behind, he looks very much like an absentminded professor who has been lost in the wilderness for a long, long time.

He looks around, staring at the room. Finally he glances over his shoulder and sees Mona standing behind the door with a gun pointed at his head. "Oh, my goodness," he says in that odd, crackly voice. "*Laura?* My God, Laura, is that you?"

Mona's mouth drops open and she lowers the gun. Not just because this black-and-white static-man seems to know her mother, and has mistaken Mona for her: but also because, unbelievably, she recognizes him. She saw him once before, in an old book in a library, where she read an interview of his about his idealistic plans for his laboratory and the town it was going to have built around it.

"Laura, my dear, my dear, what happened to you?" asks Dr. Coburn. "Where have you been? What are you doing here?"

CHAPTER TWENTY-EIGHT

Whereas most of the other waitresses at Chloe's despise their jobs, secretly or openly, Gracie often cannot wait to come into work. She does not mind the scalding coffee, the heat radiating from the griddles and ovens, the uncomfortable wool skirt and the ridiculous, tiny hat; nor does she mind the balletic stride required to ferry however many pies (in Wink, pies are quite popular, and people usually order more than one piece) through all the aisles, which frequently resemble an obstacle course, with children's feet and stray boots standing in for tire runs; she does not mind that it is a demeaning job that demands a veneer of chipper friendliness, though behind each beaming smile every waitress is feverishly counting however many nickels and dimes Mr. So-and-So put down, and did he really just tip us with just change, good Christ, he really did, what does he expect us to do with that besides buy a newspaper?

Gracie doesn't care about any of this. Because when she puts on the pearly-pink uniform and sticks that rhinestone-covered name tag in her front pocket, people forget who she is. All they see is a waitress, and that's all they care about. That and when their food will get there.

At school and at home and nearly everywhere else, it's different. People know who Gracie Zuela is. She is Talked About. She is, after all, the girl who has been Tapped, Touched, Chosen. Though they don't know what she's been chosen for—God help them if they ever figure that out—they know she has Connections. They fear her as they would the child of a mafia don or a corrupt mayor, worrying her whims and attentions could result in dire consequences.

But the eponymous Chloe, owner of the diner, doesn't care about Gracie's relations at all. Her work ethic is so inflexible, so demanding, that she is blind to Gracie's background, and deaf to all the rumors that follow her around like so many muttering thunderclouds. Some people are aghast at this: Gracie's fellow waitresses, for example, exchange terrified looks when Chloe gives Gracie both barrels for whatever mistake she's just made, as if her recriminations could bring the whole roof down on their heads. These comments can't go *ignored*, they say; surely Gracie's—they stumble for the word—*benefactor* must intervene?

But nothing happens. Gracie always just nods meekly (she really cannot nod another way) and fixes her mistake. Chloe blows away the stray strand of blond hair that's always in her face, sighs, apologizes; then, as always, follows up that apology with another warning, though this one less severe than the last; Gracie nods again, and Chloe mutters, "All right, then," before moving on to more important affairs.

And everybody just stares. The sleeping dragon has just had its eye poked; surely there must be a column of blasting fire, and a terrible roar?

They just don't understand, thinks Gracie as she buses a table, mopping up coffee with a used napkin. They just don't understand how unimportant they are. How unimportant *I* am. And it is only at Chloe's that she feels as unimportant as she knows she really is. It's only here, except possibly in her times with Joseph, that she feels normal, whatever that means.

It has been a long while since Gracie's felt normal for any length of time. Perhaps she has never felt normal. After all, everything started when she was just an infant. She cannot remember her first visitations, and to this day she does not really know *why* she is visited, she over everyone else. Her own parents prefer not to discuss it. All they told her (and this was grudgingly given) was that one evening, mere weeks after she was born, they had just put her to bed and turned the baby monitor on, and both her mother and her father went to bed smiling as the speaker told them of the tiny creature across the hall snorting, grunting, and, frequently, farting; yet then, much later, they awoke to hear a voice in the room, murmuring softly in a language they could not understand or mimic, and at first they thought they had been Visited, and were terrified, before realizing the voice was coming through the baby monitor.

Gracie has never gotten her parents to admit what they did once they heard this voice. They will not tell her what actions they took when they realized their child was no longer alone in her room, that a stranger had come into their home and was standing over her and mumbling to himself in a low, awe-filled voice. Once her mother suggested, but did not explicitly say, that they went to look, and found the room empty except for Gracie; but her father has never corroborated this, and deep in her heart Gracie is convinced her parents did not do anything at all: she is sure they cowered in their bed in the dark, afraid to provoke those who secretly maintain Wink from basements and crawl spaces and attics and dark playgrounds.

She realizes, of course, that she is quite lucky that it was he who visited her, and not one of the others. And to this day he still likes to visit her in her room, and watch her sleep. She almost finds it comforting now.

The courtship, if it could be called such a thing, was both long and erratic. There would be a shifting of sand in a park sandbox, stirring under an invisible touch; or perhaps the sound of tall grasses being parted in a nearby field, as if some huge watcher was gingerly making its way near her; or small brass trinkets would appear on her windowsill, ones of a very exotic and peculiar make. And little Gracie would tell everyone that she had an invisible friend whom she went walking with in the woods, except he wasn't really invisible, because, after all, she could see him plain as day, and she had never seen anyone like him before, with a face like that, and so tall...

Even at that young age, Gracie noticed people turning away when she discussed her friend. They did not want to hear it. They did not want to know, to really know, what went on in their town. Eventually she learned to hold her tongue, but by then everyone knew who was visiting her, and she was permanently marked, and soon feared.

Now, standing in the diner, Gracie scribbles down another order for Chloe's banana bourbon pie (a town favorite). She works here because she likes how the people ignore her, and how Chloe doesn't care who she is; but that does not mean that she loves working for these people. Because over the past year Gracie has come to realize that there is a bright, vicious little coal of hate smoldering in her stomach, and it is a hate for these people, her neighbors and family and friends, all of whom are so happy to go on believing horrific, monstrous lies, all so they might claim a semblance of normality and peace. They have traded the happiness and well-being of their families, even themselves, all so they can have this quiet cup of coffee here, and their little white house, and a well-watered lawn, and a nice, gleaming car of their own.

It is not their own. Gracie knows that now. They do not own anything in Wink—their residence is only permitted. What control they think they have is all illusion. At any time one of Them could come walking into their houses, and they could do nothing about it.

Just like her. Just the way it happened to her.

She slashes at her order book with the pencil. Flakes of graphite trickle down the page.

God damn these silly people. Gracie doesn't care anymore. There's nothing to care about. She can't even summon the strength anymore.

Then she stops writing, looks up. Her eyes grow wide, and she almost gasps out loud.

"Something wrong, hon?" asks one of her customers.

"Oh, no," says Gracie. "No, no. I'm sorry. Please go on."

Yet there is something wrong: she feels a coldness in her stomach, near her loins. It is as if she's been penetrated by an icicle, and its chilled water is pooling in her abdomen. Her smile tautens, and she dutifully takes down the remainder of her customer's order before she wobbles to the back and leans against a wall.

Not here, not now. She doesn't need this here.

Though the patrons of Chloe's go about their business as they always have, to Gracie the walls tremble like skins on a beating drum, and slowly grow transparent. The walls and floor and ceiling become like gelled water, like she could pass through them with only the slightest effort if she wished. Sound begins to fall away from her, replaced by wind rushing through desert canyons, warbling, crying. The breath in her lungs is arctic; it feels as if her chest is frosting crystals with every second.

She is slipping over. She must stop it.

She shuts her eyes. Breathes deep. Holds it. Then she takes the web of her left palm in her right hand and pinches it, hard.

Gracie opens her eyes again. The rush and roil of Chloe's have returned: someone whoops and makes a comment about the quality of the pie; Chloe herself is totaling up a large party, nearly ten people, nodding along as every charge is listed.

Gracie takes a breath, relieved.

Something happened just now, she thinks. *Something triggered that.*

She glances nervously out the front windows and sees she's not done yet: for though the walls and noises of Chloe's are back, she can still see the evening sky outside, and it is dotted with red stars. And there is no mesa beyond the town; there are peaks, but they are black and curling and strange, rock formations of a kind not found in New Mexico.

Gracie blinks again, slowly. And when she opens her eyes, the mesa's back too.

She sighs again. The cold sensation in her loins is ebbing away. It's an unpleasant phenomenon, one that's been happening randomly for nearly three months now. She is being changed by her visitations, that is clear. At first she was not sure how, but the more she talks to him, the more they sit in the canyon and discuss his nature and origins, the more she realizes that in these moments she is crossing over.

She is becoming more like him. She is catching glimpses of where They are from.

There is a gust of wind out in the street, so strong and loud that all the customers look up. They hear a clattering outside, like someone's just thrown an enormous deck of cards up in the air to let them fall on the ground.

"What was that?" someone asks.

"Something got blowed over."

People stand up and trickle outside to see. Initially Gracie has no intention of following them, but then she remembers the cold feeling in her stomach, and wonders if its being followed by the wind is just a coincidence...

Heart sinking, she walks out of the diner to join the crowd. There are letters in the street, big black ones. They've been blown off the marquee signs of the restaurants and stores along the sidewalk, leaving patchy messages of gibberish behind. Someone comments that this is damn curious, which casts a pall over the crowd as they begin to suspect that this was not accidental.

Gracie carefully scans the signs, looking from one to the next. Then she walks a few steps down the street and turns around and starts walking backward, and then things just...

Line up.

The letters ME and ET remain on the garden shop sign. Then, on the mechanic's, she can still see M E and after that T ON, and just behind that sign she can see the barber shop's sign, which has a single lonely I, and looking down the street she can see a G on one sign, and then an H T.

"Oh, brother," says Gracie, and she pinches the bridge of her nose.

He always does use such awkward methods of conversation. She keeps asking him to try just sending her a letter every once in a while. But he never listens. He's never been very good at listening.

CHAPTER TWENTY-NINE

It is night, oh holy blessed mother of God, it is night, and with night comes all the nighttime things, all the tremors and whispers, all the burning veins and teary cheeks, all the minutes (or hours, maybe months) of misery stretched out in the unblinking stare of the sodium lights. Oh, thinks Bonnie, oh my dear, oh it is night, actually night, forever night. I thought it would not come this time.

Each morning Bonnie rises and says well that's over, that's finally over, night is over and it will never come again. For how could night persist in the pink broiling sky of the dawn? With a sky like that, why, night cannot exist at all. There cannot be night anywhere, not with that up there.

Bonnie knows, of course, that this is stupid, and that's the worst part of it, because she's aware, she is just so fucking aware, that some crucial part of her brain has corroded and now she cannot keep the sky where it is supposed to be, nor can she keep the ground where it is supposed to be (the walls, thankfully, seem pretty stable—they generally stay where they are), and so often she forgets where she is. She sort of knows—she knows the squalid cinder-block apartment with the burned-out tiki torches and the forever smell of rotting potatoes (and all the flies that come with them)—but ever since she first started doing the runs for dear old Mal she has felt that things are slipping. Things like day and night and the lengths of hours are undependable: they mix like yolk running out of a fried egg.

Or perhaps it is not the runs. Perhaps it is her dirty little habit, perhaps it is how she's just tapped the inside of her elbow with that magic wand, and it felt like someone took her by the nostrils and blew a billowing cloud of fairy dust up into her brain...

She isn't sure. Maybe it's a bit of both.

It is such a pity. She hates it so much it makes her want to weep.

Weep, weep. Weep, weep, weep for poor Bonnie.

There is a knock at the door, and poor Bonnie goes over and opens it and puts one eye (with a pupil like a pinpoint) to the crack, and she whispers, Who's there?

And a voice outside says, It's me, Mal, silly, open the door.

Bonnie does not want to let Mal in. The apartment is Bonnie's place, no one else's, so she opens the door a little more and awkwardly sidles out. Carefully shuts it behind her, locks it.

Jesus, says Mal, what have you done to yourself?

Nothing, says Bonnie.

Girl, look at me. Look at me, girl.

Bonnie pouts, but looks at her.

Jesus, says Mal. What happened to you. Have you bathed?

Bathed? Today?

Anytime. This morning. Last morning.

Bonnie just shrugs. Every morning is a restart to her, a total reboot. Today is yesterday and tomorrow, it doesn't matter.

Christ almighty, Bonnie, says Mal.

It's not that bad.

It's pretty bad.

I guess it is that bad, she says. She looks at Mal. I don't want to go tonight, she says.

Mal leans up against the wall of the apartment and rubs a twist of stray lipstick from her mouth. She eyes Bonnie sourly, and says, Oh really? Bonnie watches her. She takes in Mal's long, lean body, which so effortlessly fills her tight khaki pants and dark green blouse. Mal is everything Bonnie wishes she could be. Strong, smart, sexy. And not sexy in the pouty little-girl way, sexy in that freshly fucked kind of way, that I-just-had-it-and-I-don't-care-what-happens-now kind of way. She has that lofty, clever confidence about her that can only come from knowing that everyone in the room wants to fuck you. Bonnie wishes she knew what that was like.

I hate it, says Bonnie.

Mal says, What?

I hate it. I hate it so much.

Hate what?

The night. The night and where it lives. That's where I'm going again, aren't I? Where you're taking me.

Mal is silent.

Bonnie says, We're going to that place under the ground where the night lives. I know. It's okay. I just…I just hate it. I hate it so much, Mal.

The night doesn't live there, says Mal. It's just…oh never mind. Come on. Let's get you in the car.

I'm not coming. I won't, Mal. I hate it.

You are, says dear old Mal. You'll want to come.

Why?

She reaches into her pocket, grabs something, holds it out. Because I got a present, she says.

Bonnie looks at the bag. It is a lot, a whole, whole lot. Enough to keep her running for days and days. More than dear old Mal's ever given her before. Yet why, Bonnie wonders, is Mal's hand shaking as she holds the bag? Mal is not the type to shake.

It's so much, says Bonnie.

Yes, it is.

Why is it so much?

Why do you think?

Bonnie considers it. She asks, Because this is the last time?

Yeah, she says. Yeah, you're right, kid. This is the last time.

Oh, thank goodness. Thank, thank goodness.

Then you'll come?

Yes. Yes, I'll come.

Put your shoes on. Do you need help with your shoes?

Bonnie nods.

Oh Jesus, says Mal, and she sighs and sits and tries to force Bonnie's feet (toes black, nails yellow) into her Keds. Bonnie whimpers a little.

Stop it, says Mal.

I don't mean to, says Bonnie.

Yeah you do, says Mal.

I don't.

I don't even care anymore. I don't care. Come on.

Mal drives an old green Chevy Suburban that is as wide as a boat and it makes Bonnie scared because she's sure it'll tip over, yet somehow it never does. They drive north, straight north, because Bonnie lives on the southern side of Wink, which is not the "wrong side of the railroad tracks" because there are no railroad tracks in Wink, but if there were then Bonnie's neighborhood would be on the wrong side of them.

It is that kind of neighborhood. There are a lot of trailers.

Have you been dreaming more? asks Mal as she drives.

Bonnie shakes her head.

Well, that's good.

Bonnie shakes her head again.

It's not good?

No, says Bonnie.

Why not?

Not sleeping.

What? You're not sleeping anymore?

No. I don't like it.

That'll kill you, you know. You'll burn yourself up.

Bonnie doesn't answer. She stares out the car window. Rolls it down slowly.

You don't want to know why, do you? asks Bonnie.

You're right, says Mal. I don't want to know why.

I'll tell you.

I said I don't want to know why.

I'll tell you anyway. You put him in my head. You deserve to know.

Mal is silent. Though Bonnie slavishly adores Mal, she enjoys seeing her so disturbed. It is a power she has never had before.

Because when night comes, when I sleep, says Bonnie, there's another corner in my room. I can't see it, because I'm dreaming. But I know it's there. There's a fifth corner, suddenly out of nowhere, where it shouldn't be. It's like a door opens, and then there it is. And he's always there. Standing in the corner. He's got his back to me. I don't know why. But he's always there. And even though I can't see his face I can tell he's watching me. I don't think he needs eyes to watch me. I think where he's from no one needs eyes. They have other ways of seeing things.

You've said this before.

Have I?

Yeah. Mal asks, Where is he from?

I don't know. Somewhere far away. And underneath. Like when you flip over a board lying on the ground and there's all these bugs underneath. But it's not quite like that.

No?

No. It's more like you flip over a board and you see it's not the ground under there but a whole ocean, big and black, and there are things looking up at you from down there, watching you. They've been watching you all this time.

Jesus Christ. I hate talking to you when you're high.

I'm not high.

You are. You fucking are. Look at you.

Bonnie laughs. I'm higher than high, she says. She holds her hands out the window as if to embrace the sky. I'm higher than higher than higher than high, she says.

Shut up, says Mal. Now you're just being irritating.

Maybe, says Bonnie. She looks into the sky and drops her arms. You want to hear something funny? she asks.

I don't want to hear a goddamn thing after all the talking you've done.

I wonder whose sky that's in, she says, and she points up.

Mal ducks her head down to peer up through the windshield. What, she says, the moon?

Yeah.

What do you mean, whose sky it's in?

Bonnie stares at the moon. It is so huge, so pink, so smooth. She murmurs, I mean what I said. I just don't think that it's in ours. It must be in someone else's. Maybe it's their sky . . .

Shut up, says Mal.

Okay.

The Suburban goes straight into the heart of Wink, around the park with the dome and past the shops to a small dirt road that leads to a concrete ravine. Mal pulls the Suburban forward so that the headlights are pointing down into the ravine. Then she throws it in park and the two of them just sit there for a while, looking at the blank concrete, all lit up white in the brights. The ravine tapers away, ending in a wide, black drainage tunnel in the side of the hill.

They want two this time, says Mal.

Two?

Yes. Just put two in the box.

Hm, says Bonnie.

Silence.

Well, says Mal. You know how it works.

I know how it works.

Mal waits. She gets impatient. She reaches over and opens the glove compartment. Inside is a small glass lantern, like the kind miners used back in the nineteenth century, a pair of gloves, and a wooden box with a brass clasp.

She says, So are you going or are you going?

Bonnie stares into the black hole at the end of the ravine. She bends forward and starts rubbing the side of her head and rocking back and forth.

Jesus, Bonnie, says Mal.

Bonnie whimpers and looks away.

Get out of the goddamn car.

No.

Get out, damn you.

I need to cook up, says Bonnie.

What! Like hell you do. I let you cook again and you won't even be fucking walking. You'll fall asleep. You'll be dead.

I won't. I'll walk fine. I promise. Just let me cook up a little.

No. Get fucking going.

But it's mine anyway, you gave it to me, says Bonnie. She reaches for the bag on the dashboard.

Mal hits her so hard for a moment Bonnie thinks she's about to pass out. Bonnie leans up against the window of the car, the side of her head contracting, expanding, contracting, crunching like eggshells with each contortion. She blinks hard and looks around, gaping.

Mal says, Who the fuck do you think you are?

You hit me!

You're goddamn right I did. That isn't how this works, girl. You get what I need then you get what you need.

I want to go home, cries Bonnie.

You want to go back to that shit-ass apartment? Is that really what you want? Because you can rot in there if you like. I'm damn near tempted to drop you off back there.

And Bonnie wants to say no, no, that's not her home, not really. She almost tells her what she really wants, but she is so ashamed she can't even speak of it.

All right, she says.

Good, says Mal. She leans over and throws open the door of the Suburban. Go on, she says. Get.

Moving slowly like a beaten dog, Bonnie slides out of the passenger seat of the car and takes the lamp, the gloves, and the wooden box.

Wait, you got to let me light it, stupid, says Mal.

Bonnie holds the lantern out, and Mal strikes a match and sets its wick alight. Now go on, says Mal.

Bonnie says, This is it, right?

This is what?

The last time.

Mal looks at her for a while. Yeah, she says. Yeah, it's the last time.

Because I don't want to do this again, Mal. You don't know what it's like in there.

If you do it now, you won't ever have to know again, either.

No, says Bonnie. I'll always know. I can't go back. Not from that.

Then she turns and walks down the ravine and into the tunnel.

At first it is the same. A tunnel like any other, filled with the echoes of her footsteps and the wind being dragged across its mouth. It goes on and on and on, underneath the town and maybe even farther. The lantern's light is weak, turning the corrugated metal sides of the tunnel into a flexing, pulsing accordion with each step. They have to use naked flame because flashlights don't work where Bonnie's going. She's never been sure why but she's heard she is not the first person to try running the tunnels for Bolan and his people (whoever they are). Apparently there was someone they used before and he went in with a huge flashlight in his hand, like one of those mini-spotlights or something, but when he came to that one place (the threshold, the door, the hollow place) it went *POP* and just fucking *exploded*, exploded in his hand like it was a claymore mine, and he came running out screaming with blood pouring out of where his hand had been, and his side, even his face, and they tried to take care of him but then oops, so sorry, he up and died right there in the ravine, whimpering like a stuck pig.

He doesn't know it, but he got lucky. He never saw what was at the end of the tunnel.

Bonnie keeps walking. She wishes she were high right now. Well, she *is* high right now. But she wishes she were that special kind of high, which, sadly, is getting harder and harder to attain these days.

Bonnie's heard the phrase "chasing the dragon" before, but Bonnie's not chasing anything so exotic. What Bonnie wishes to see when she lays the needle to her bare skin, what she hopes to smell and hear and taste when the heroin floods her arm and comes rushing into that vast space behind her eyes, is, in this order:

1. The light from a flashlight filtering through yellow blankets, used to make a fort.
2. The sound of fish frying in an iron skillet.
3. Ankles, slender, bony, with feet in battered red heels.
4. A box of old batteries and buttons and chess pieces.
5. Sunset peeking through the limbs of the Arizona ash outside (its bottom half covered in truncated limbs, the result of serious pruning).
6. A hint of a teal flannel shirt, streaked in oil, perhaps glimpsed as a man working on the undercarriage of his truck in his garage wipes his brow (and the scent of sawdust, and gasoline, and old cigarettes, and the pleasant musk of cheap cologne, and everything is lit by old yellowed lightbulbs, which have not been changed in years). And, last but not least,
7. Bedtime stories.

Once she smelled him. Once when she was floating in fumes and all the world was wiped away she caught a stray whiff of his cologne, as if he'd just passed through her room and she'd only just missed him, and she wanted to run after him and say no, no, stop and pick me up and put me on your shoulders as you used to, but her arms and legs were leaden and she could not move, only moan and roll her eyes back and whimper in her sleep.

Even that misery was sweeter than never smelling him again. For more than anything in the world, Bonnie wants to go home. But she cannot. It is gone. It has amputated something from her, the incision reaching deep and dark. She now spends her days chasing ghosts, not dragons, and wandering down dark passageways, going places no one should ever want to go.

Weep for poor Bonnie.

Weep, weep.

I bet that's why they bring the heroin in here in the first place. So that they can get some of us hooked, get us to break the rules for them. Do things no one should ever want to do. Then you can get high again.

They tricked me.

I let myself be tricked.

I am dying. I am dying, dying.

It is then, at her most abysmal point of despair, that Bonnie comes to the changing place, the threshold, and she stops.

The changing place is never exactly in the same spot. Like most things in Wink (and Bonnie is only slightly aware that this is a terrible, terrible secret) it is not really where it is, or where it *says* it is. When she first made this run, when she first entered this dark maze to find their silly treasure, she had to walk for nearly three hours. But on the second it was only ten feet in. Like it was waiting for her.

She feels it in her brain first. Right in the middle of her forehead, the most terrible of migraines you could ever imagine. It's like her brain is being slowly pulled forward to put pressure on the front inside of her skull, threatening to worm out her skull and down her face like a maggot bursting from its egg sac.

She takes a step forward. Then another, and another.

She is passing through something hollow, some cyst or cavity or bubble floating in the darkness. She feels it in her bones.

Then it is like she is being ripped through a three-inch hole in a wall, inexorably pulled forward until she is a boneless, pulverized tube, her arms and shoulders and ribs sloughed away, and nothing will make it through but a baseball-sized fragment of brain and a tangle of nerve and maybe one eye dangling by a thread of tissue, and the last thing it'd report to her, the last signal it'd send to the sputtering, mangled ball of brain, would be the sight of the corrugated walls of this dark tunnel, flickering in the light of the lantern, her long journey into night abruptly (perhaps thankfully) halted.

This does not really happen. It just *feels* like it does. But then it is over, and she is done, and through.

Yet through what, and where she has gotten through to, Bonnie does not know. It is not where she was. The tunnel before is *not* the tunnel after. It is...somewhere else. Where things are different.

She keeps walking.

She is under Wink. Probably about under the courthouse, or the park. But just because she is underneath there does not mean she's not also somewhere else. After all, thinks Bonnie, you can have a different thing under a different thing.

My God I am so high, she thinks.

But that doesn't mean I'm wrong.

Sometimes there are cracks in the tunnel, and she can see light filtering in. Sometimes the light is gentle and pink. Other times it is harsh and silvery. Bonnie has never once put her eye to one of the cracks to see. She remembers the story about the flashlight—*POW*—and wonders what it'd look like if that happened to a human eye.

No. No, thanks.

She keeps walking. Just keep walking. Keep the lantern high and your eyes on the prize.

What lives down here, underneath Wink? What lives in Wink, above it, around it? Where is Wink, anyways? Where have we all gone? Which sky hangs over this town?

She is at the chamber. She stops at the doorway, small and round like that of a crypt, and looks in.

The chamber is big. It is bigger than big. So big she almost cannot conceive of it. *God* does not live in a place this big. Its gray, blank floor stretches for miles, oceans, hemispheres, and its black vaults stretch up and up and up and up until she thinks she can see

(a pink moon)
(many stars)
(a thousand twisting peaks)

She needs to stop.

Bonnie takes a breath. And focuses.

Or, she does *not* focus, because if she did she'd go fucking insane. To look at this place, to look upon it and perceive it, would be to destroy yourself. Bonnie secretly believes (and though she doesn't know it, she's absolutely right) that the heroin is her shield, that it inoculates her against the madness waiting here, puts an impenetrable film on her mind like a tarp protecting a boat against the rain. You cannot make someone mad if there is no mind there to make mad. So maybe Bonnie is one of the only people in Wink who can go here, and only then when she's absolutely fucking jazzing on H.

But while she is utterly dosed up when she comes here, she has come to understand two things about this place:

1. It is secretly a jail cell. (And Bonnie knows what is being jailed here.)
2. Though it is a jail cell, its occupant can be allowed out, though only briefly, and its exit (or invitation) must be arranged in a special way.

A very special way.

In the center of the vast gray floor is a pile of something. From this distance (though distance does not exist, not here) it looks like a pile of small stones, but Bonnie knows it is not.

She looks around, searching the edges of the room, at least what she can see of it.

It is empty. Or it appears that way. Bonnie knows better. And she knows she won't see it unless it lets her.

She begins the walk across the chamber. It takes a long, long time.

(Am I still here, she wonders? Is some part of me forever trapped in this place? When I go back to my room, and I am followed by the night, by the man in the corner? Or am I still here, torn in half, split down the middle, stuck in this room and wandering Wink all at once? Do I live up above while still trapped in here with it, him, the night?)

The pile gets closer. The closer it gets, the more she can make out the tiny, pebble-like teeth, and the long, desiccated snouts, and the gaping eye sockets...

They are not skulls, not really. They are a part of *it*, the thing that is jailed here. And if you take a piece of it out, and get someone to touch it...

(you must not touch it)

Gloves. Must remember gloves.

She sets the lantern down. She opens the wooden box. Then she carefully, carefully bends down, scoops up two tiny little skulls in a gloved hand, and lays them in the wooden box. She shuts it, clasps it, and sighs.

Done. Done, done. She grabs the lantern and begins to walk out.

It's always as she's leaving that it comes to her. She is not sure why. And she never *really* sees it. Like right now, she smells it first, an awful scent, decay and rot unknown, as if it is a noxious thunderhead bubbling down out of the sky.

And then it's *there*.

It looks like a man. A man in a blue canvas suit, standing off to the side of her, always in the corner of her vision no matter how she tries to directly look at it. But she cannot see much of it, or him, or whatever it is. Words fail to describe it. In this place it is always trembling, always quaking, a blue-gray ghost of a man standing in the shadows of this enormous room. There is no edge or line or section of its form that is not blurred. Yet she thinks she can see tall, thin ears on its head, and fists balled in rage.

It is the night, because before it all things are eclipsed.

It hates her coming here. It hates everything in the world. And it hates that it cannot hurt her.

Bonnie is weeping, tears running down her cheeks, but she keeps walking. It follows her like a hornet, dodging, buzzing, swooping through the corner of her vision.

She can make it. She's done this twice before.

You can't touch me. I'm not really here. I'm actually back at home, aren't I, sleeping cause I just cooked up, and...

And.

And.

Bonnie stops. Because the room just changed a little. And that's never happened before.

She notices a couple of things then. First is that she doesn't really feel that high anymore, which she can't understand. She dosed herself up goddamn good not more than an hour before Mal picked her up. And yet, and yet...

She remembers thinking when she dosed up that this shit was not all that good. It was, in fact, quite watery, just good old-fashioned aitch-two-fucking-oh, and she remembers thinking oh well goddamn it I got screwed now didn't I, I should have known better than to buy through anyone but Bolan.

Yet then she did get high. Maybe it was just gonna be for a little while.

But not long enough.

Because Bonnie is becoming aware that she is *becoming aware*. Usually when she's here she cannot see or understand anything. And that's good. You don't *want* to understand these things. You can't look at them. It's like looking at the sun.

But now she's coming down.

The room is changing. She is *seeing* it. It is showing itself to her. It is

(an immense black plain)
(stars red and white)
(surrounded by)
(so many)

(are they mountains)
(and then)

(a dead tree with rotting fruit)
(a city in the dark)

(and in the city is a lone wanderer)
(been waiting for so long)
(waiting)
(for me)

And then Bonnie sees it again, out of the corner of her eye.

Before—when the room looked like a room, and not (*this place*)—the thing that is jailed here looked like a man in a blue canvas suit with a strange head or skull or helmet. Yet now she understands she was see-ing only a *part* of it. It is like a diamond with many facets, and she was seeing only one.

Yet now she sees more. Maybe all of them. All at once.

She feels it behind her, just over her shoulder. And she thinks she sees something incredibly tall and incredibly thin, with long, thin ears, covered in coarse brown fur, standing under the red moonlight, and it is

Oh oh

Oh my god, my god, she thinks.

It has eyes, eyes like people

It can see me

Mallory never waits for Bonnie at the ravine because, quite frankly, the ravine creeps the ever-living shit out of her. She tried once, tried waiting on that poor girl all night, but she got the weird sensation that the tunnel at the end of that concrete river was an eye, and it was look-ing straight at her, and it gave her the heebie-jeebies. So instead she always pulls away and parks the 'Burban up the slope on an old gravel parking lot, where she sips from a hip flask and watches the stars and sometimes feels a little romantic, despite herself.

So it takes her a minute to hear the screaming. On account of her being so far away and all.

She sits up, listens for a moment.

"Bonnie," she says. "Aw, shit."

She doesn't bother to start the Suburban up. She just jumps out and starts running across the parking lot, and she kicks off her heels before she starts down the ravine.

It's stupid, because she knows Bonnie's pathetic, and she knows she's essentially been sent to kill her, or maybe just to let her die, though Mal can't really see the difference. But she still doesn't want Bonnie to die. Or she doesn't want her to be in pain, at least. And she sounds like she's in terrible pain.

To her relief, Mal sees that Bonnie is alive and whole, standing next to the entrance to the tunnel with her back to Mal. Beside her is the lantern and the little wooden box. Bonnie seems to be bowing over and over, like the way Orthodox Jews pray, just bowing quick little ducks forward while she screams her head off, though now that Mal's closer she notices she can hear a little *thuk thuk* each time Bonnie bows.

It isn't until she's about a dozen feet away that Mal sees the dark stain spreading on the edge of the tunnel.

Bonnie is howling hysterically. Her hands grip the corner of the tunnel and she is ripping herself forward and smashing her face into the corner, over and over again, each time making a wet little *thuk*, each time little fragments and flecks of something whirling off her face.

"It's everything!" screams Bonnie. "It's everything! It's everything in there!"

Mal watches, terrified. Gouts of blood are dripping off Bonnie's face. There are spatters trailing down the white cement. Mal gags and steps away.

And Bonnie hears her. She freezes, and whirls around drunkenly.

Her entire face has been split open. Her right eye socket is almost entirely gone, and Mal can see the whole of the orb, white and luminous against the little pool of red around it. Her nose is missing and there is a crack in its bridge that is incredibly black, so black you wouldn't believe it.

"It's everything, Mal!" shrieks Bonnie through ravaged lips and cracked teeth. "Everything in the world! In his eyes is everything in the world! I didn't want to see! I didn't want to see!" She howls again, clawing at her face, then turns around and grabs the corner of the tunnel again.

Before she knows it, Mallory is sprinting away. Somehow she has that fucking little wooden box in her hand, but she isn't sure why.

But she can still hear it, somewhere behind her.

Thuk thuk

Thuk thuk

CHAPTER THIRTY

Now, there are many odd situations that life has prepared Mona for. But she has no idea how to approach her current predicament, in which a man who seems to have stepped out of an old photo, or maybe an old filmstrip, is standing before her, addressing her as her mother. This is, to say the least, unexpected.

So all she can manage to say is, "What?"

The grainy, gray, washed-out image of Coburn cocks his head. "What?" he says.

Mona keeps staring at him. She manages, "Uhh..."

He grows a little frustrated, leaning forward eagerly. "Did you say something?"

Mona just looks back at him, confused, helpless.

"What are you doing here?" asks Coburn. "*How* did you get here? Were you caught in the storm as well?"

She sits up a little at that. "No," says Mona. "I wasn't in the storm... I actually think you have me confused with someone else, uh—sir."

Coburn frowns and peers at her. His image flickers like it's being received by mangled bunny ears on an old television, and Coburn shrinks, sputters, expands, before returning to his original state. Though the act is silent, Mona mentally accompanies it with the sound of hissing static.

"Jesus Christ," says Mona.

"This is quite odd," he says. "Your mouth is moving but...but no sound is coming out."

"Uh, I am afraid you're wrong there, too, sir. I think I'm even making an ech—"

"No, no," says Coburn. "No, nothing at all. And you do seem to be talking." He studies her. "Can you hear me, Laura?"

"Well, yes," says Mona. She is still too confused to broach the Laura topic.

He sighs, exasperated, rubs his forehead. "I just said I cannot hear you, so if you just said yes—and it looks like you did—I didn't hear it. Please nod or shake your head."

Mona, irritated, nods her head in an exaggerated fashion.

"So *you* can hear me, but I cannot hear you," says Coburn. "Interesting...I wonder why this is."

"Maybe you're deaf."

"I could be *deaf*, of course," he says, tapping his chin and looking away, "but I can still hear the wind...God, how I wish I could *stop* hearing the wind. I wish we had a pen and paper, but obviously there would be none in place like this."

He looks around, face baleful. She wonders if he's crazy. It's an odd thing for him to say (if this pale shadow of a person is a *him*, that is), because if he is really Dr. Richard Coburn, then he founded this laboratory, so he must have worked in it, and so he must know that there's plenty of paper back in the hall there. And she can't hear a damn bit of wind.

"You want paper?" asks Mona. "I can get you paper. Wouldn't be a minute."

But Coburn is not paying attention. He is grimly staring straight into the wall. "I wonder where you came from...everything is impassable, except the way I came. Perhaps through there?" He points at the wall. "Or perhaps up from that gully there?" He points down at the floor, where there is certainly no gully. He seems more and more like a maddened transient, albeit one rendered in flickering monochrome. "I doubt if you did," he says, "because that way is quite treacherous, unless you had some sort of way to pass lakes of acid. And it doesn't look like you do..."

"I don't know what the fuck you're talking about," says Mona. "There's no such thing here."

"We don't have much time here," he says, glancing up at the ceiling. "The moon is out, but it won't be for long. That's when things get dangerous," he says softly. Without warning, his image sputters and fades a little.

"Hello?" says Mona.

Coburn flickers back to existence in mid-sentence, as if he is totally unaware of the change. He is saying, "—ow are you *here* at all? I thought I was the only one who was transposed here. I haven't seen anyone from the staff since. And it has been"—he turns to consult something on the ground—"my God, over half a year since the storm."

Mona gets an idea. She holds up her hands to get his attention.

He glances up. "Mm? Yes?"

"You," she says, and points, "you stay," she holds her hands palm out, and mimes pushing on him, "right here," and she points down at the ground. She does it again, to make sure he catches on.

He watches her, blinking. "Ah. You want me to stay here? Well, fine, fine, though I can't imagine why. Where do you have to go?"

"Well, let's see," says Mona, and she slowly backs out of the room.

She's about a dozen feet away from the crackling image of Coburn when his mouth drops open. "My goodness," he says. He stares around himself. "Where...where did you go?" He turns completely around. "Laura? Laura? Are you still here?"

"What the fuck is going *on*," says Mona softly. She turns around and jogs down the hall to the administrative offices. She finds a yellowed, ancient notebook on one of the desks and a piece of colored chalk from one of the blackboards. Then she returns to the room with the mirror.

"Oh!" says Coburn. "And there you are again." He looks at what she's brought. "Wh—where did you get those? Those are...I know that stationery. That's from the lab. How did you get those?" He whirls around, staring at the walls. "Did some part of the building get transposed here, too? I've never seen any suggestion of it..."

Mona writes: "where do u think u are?" and turns it around to show him.

He reads it, and says, "Well, I'm right here. Why do you ask?"

Mona writes: "cause right now Im in ur lab."

"What!" says Coburn. "What do you mean?"

She pauses, frustrated, and points to the notebook—*I mean this, what I wrote.*

"You're in the lab?" he says. "You mean CNLO? Right *now*?"

Mona nods.

"Are you...you *sure*?"

She nods again.

He stares around her, his eyes taking in things totally invisible to Mona. "*How?*"

She shrugs, as if to say—*You're the fucking scientist.* Then she points to the first question: "where do u think u are?"

Coburn is so shaken that it takes him a moment to answer. "I suppose I don't know. It is a terrible place, where I am. The ground is glassy and black, there are lakes of bubbling fluid I dare not touch..I have lived off of terrible fruit that grows on strange trees in sodden fields. It is an abandoned place. But how can you be here if you are in the lab?"

Mona glances around. Naturally, she doesn't see anything that he describes: just the cold, dark metal walls of this room.

Coburn thinks. "Unless, of course, you are *not* here. And I am not really *there*, in the lab, with you, which, I presume, is what you're seeing. The lab, I mean."

She shakes her head.

"Am I wrong?" asks Coburn.

Mona writes: "no. u r right. agreeing. u look all black and white like an old tv show"

Coburn squints to read her answers. "I do?" he says, astonished, and he looks at his arms and hands. "How marvelous. I see no effects here. What *is* wrong with your writing, though? It's horrendous."

"Well, fucking forgive me," mutters Mona.

"Are you...let me guess." He looks over his shoulder, but evidently he can't see what he's looking for. "Are you in the room with the lens, Laura? Right now?"

Mona glances at the mirror. She supposes it could be a lens, though it's not transparent—at least, not in any way she can see. But she hasn't seen anything else that could be called a lens, so she nods.

"You are? How fantastic!" Even though Coburn sounds like he's in dire straits, he appears fairly delighted with what she's told him. He licks his lips and glances around, thinking very quickly. "Then it's true, I suppose. You know what this is, of course?"

Mona shrugs.

"You don't? Why, this is *bruising*, my girl. Just like we always discussed! I expect it can't be affecting a particularly wide area—not if you vanished only a few yards away. It must not extend that far past the lens. But I cannot imagine it'd be anything else. You and I would be quite pleased, my dear, if it hadn't had such awful consequences, wouldn't we?"

"Huh?" says Mona out loud.

"I wish I knew what I looked like right now. An image projected across realities…though it is projected poorly, if your suggestions are correct. I don't know why, but I can see you plain as day, though you are a bit colorless…I guess the bruising must be more severe on your end. Have you witnessed any other effects? Any other symptoms?"

"What?" asks Mona.

Coburn looks at her, perturbed. "Why do you look so confused? Laura, have you been injured? Is something wrong with you?"

Mona decides the jig is up, and writes: "not laura."

This just pisses him off. "What do you mean, you're not Laura? That's not…you look exactly like her. If you're not Laura, then who the hell are you?"

Mona glances at him warily, and writes: "her daughter."

When Coburn reads this it's as if all the air gets knocked out of him. He staggers back a little, then sits down on the ground. "What?" he says softly. "Her *daughter*?"

Mona nods.

"You're telling me the truth?"

Mona nods again. She sits down on the floor opposite him.

"You look a little different, I suppose...but I thought you'd—she—had changed. She vanished before it all happened, but...I thought she'd come back to help me. What happened to her?"

Mona wonders how to put this. Her own experiences with death have blunted any sensitivity to grief, so she mentally rummages through some greeting card expressions before giving up. She pulls a face, sighs, writes, "died," and shows it to him.

Coburn slumps forward in shock. "She died? In the storm?"

Mona shakes her head.

"Then...she died of natural causes, I hope." Mona diplomatically chooses not to correct him on this point. "But if you're her daughter, how...how are you so old? How old *are* you?"

Mona winces. This, she knows, is going to be a nasty surprise for this guy, who seems to have had quite a lot of those in the past couple of years, or months, or however time works for him. But she guesses these things have to be done like Band-Aid removal, quickly and ruthlessly.

She writes down her age and shows it to him.

He sits up, and his hands fly to his forehead. "What? You are *thirty-seven*?" There are pops of white at the edge of his image, and he briefly grows translucent. When he comes back, he is saying, "—irty-seven years *old*?"

Mona nods.

"But then...then how long ago was the storm? What *year* is it over there?"

She sighs, writes down the answer, and shows it to him.

He stares at it. His hands slowly drop. "No."

Mona nods.

"No. No, it's not possible."

She nods again, then shrugs with her palms up—*My sympathies, but what can I do?*

"No. It can't be, it just *can't*. I can't have been stuck over here for... for over *thirty years*! I just can't! I remember everything like it was yesterday!"

Mona watches him helplessly.

"Is everyone else dead, too? Did we lose everyone, everything?"

She shrugs.

"You mean you don't *know*?"

She writes, "dont know a damn thing sorry"

"But surely some of them have to be around, if you're at the lab?"

She writes: "abandoned"

"The lab? The lab is abandoned?"

She nods.

"Oh, my Lord," says Coburn. He slouches forward, face in his hands. "Then I'll...I'll never get back. How could this have happened? How could things have possibly gotten *worse* for me?"

To her discomfort, he begins sobbing. Mona is sure he's in some pretty trying circumstances, since apparently he's actually trapped somewhere horrific, but it still feels weird to see him, this shabby old man sitting on the floor, sobbing his eyes out. She wonders what to say, and decides grief counseling is not something that can be done via pen, paper, and a vocabulary that's been adversely affected by texting and the internet. So she just sits, and waits.

When his tears taper off, she writes: "what happened to u"

It takes him a while longer to gather himself. He stares into his lap, hollow-eyed, and says, "There was a...storm. A storm during one of our tests. I am not sure if it coincided with our tests, or if our tests...if perhaps our tests were the cause. But it was...it was apocalyptic. I cannot even describe it."

Mona, remembering her vision at the house, doesn't doubt it. She nods.

"You were—" His image suddenly grows fuzzy and his words hiss, as if his signal, being projected from wherever he is, is losing its strength. When he returns he's in a different pose, sitting up. It is an unnerving sight, changing abruptly from one position to the other. He finishes, "—at the time?"

Though she missed the majority of that, Mona takes a wild guess and shakes her head.

"Well," he says. "I suppose you wouldn't have been, would you. Did your mother ever"—a flicker of static—"—rk here, or do you have any, erm, theoretical physics background at all?"

"Sure don't," she says, and she shakes her head.

"I see. Well. I don't know how best to explain this, which makes me a bad scientist. It is fairly complicated stuff. I wish your mother had told you a little about it. She was crucial to its development." Another flutter of static.

"Bruising is also called universal collision signatures," he says. "It is, in layman's terms, when one univ—"—his image stutters, shrinks, returns—"—shes into another, like bumper cars. Because there is not just one universe. Think of it like bubb—"—his face freezes, while the rest of his body moves, hands gesticulating excitedly—"—face of water around a waterfall, all rubbing, bumping, popping into one another."

"Uh-huh," says Mona, who wishes he would stay still.

"This is what we were meant to examine here. Because if we could understand bruising, we could understand how the world works—how *all* worlds work—at the most fundament—"

He breaks up again, this time for a long, long time, more than a minute. Mona is sure he isn't coming back, and, panicking, writes, "BREAKING UP BREAKING UP" on her notepad.

When he comes back, he is saying, "—id you go again? Did you leave? It didn't look like you walked aw—"

He leans forward and reads her note card. Though he is black and white, she can see he pales a little. "Oh, no. Breaking up? Me? That must be why you faded out just then. Something's wrong. Whatever connection allows this, I guess it's"—his face blurs, solidifies—"—ill so much to explain, th—" His image begins strobing, one hand frozen, the other still in motion.

When he comes back, he is standing, his eyes alight, face fixed in mid-shout. "—ongest hall, west side! Do you hear? On the w—" He fills with static, rivers of bursting gray and white. When he returns, he is panicked, yelling, "—ear me? Plank! Plank! Six six two six! Do you hear me? Six six tw—"

Then he begins to fade out, a clearness starting in his center and moving to the edges until he is no more than a faint outline of a man in the air. Then he is gone, as if he had never been there.

Mona sits there, staring around, wondering what just happened. Then she feels it again.

Something *clicks*. It's some indefinable change in the room, but it's the same as when she was staring into the mirror (or the lens, as she reminds herself). But this time it's like something clicks out of place rather than, as she now feels happened before, clicking into it. She is reminded of those old phone operators in the fifties, taking a cord and plugging it into one jack, then unplugging it and plugging it into another. It's like the cord just got ripped out of here, the room, the lab, everything. But what could have caused that?

She looks at the lens. She is not sure why, but she is sure it has moved. Perhaps only minutely, but she's positive it's changed.

Is it a lens, she now wonders? Or is it an antenna, communicating with someplace very, very far away...

And perhaps when she was staring at it before, she somehow activated it, and it made some kind of connection to...wherever it is Coburn is, the poor bastard. She is not sure how she could do such a thing, yet she feels it's true.

She looks down at her notes. She did not realize it, but she was desperately scribbling down everything he said in his final moments. Scrawled at the bottom of the paper in pink slashes is:

SIX SIX TWO SIX

It was something he wanted her to know. Something important. Maybe a frequency? Or a code to something? She guesses she'll have to find out.

Mona sighs. "Well, shit."

It takes her a couple of hours of fruitless, frustrating, aimless searching to find it. Or she thinks it does. It's hard to tell time in here. What little power is coming out of the generator doesn't reach a lot of the offices, so it's just Mona and her flashlight, roving through the dim mess, scouring room after room of decaying, modernist clutter. Conference rooms. Stationery closets. Bathrooms with brown streaks on the walls, the remnants of ancient flooding.

Then, in the western part of Coburn (as, after all, the good doctor said something about the longest hallway on the west side), her beam falls across what looks like a white wall. She very nearly passes it by when she realizes there's a faint outline in it, like that of a box or a panel…

Or a door.

She walks to it and realizes she's right: there's a thick metal door here, painted the exact same color as the rest of the wall. She runs her hand along its edges, trying to find a handle or a button, but there is nothing.

She steps back and examines it. Curious, she kicks it. It's solid as all hell, but she's sure it's hollow on the other side.

There's a room there. Maybe this is what Coburn was directing her to. But how to get in? The door is heavy enough to be a vault door, which would explain the six-six-two-six combination he told her about, but she can't find any place to punch or enter it in.

Frustrated, she glances around. The door is innocuously placed behind a rather small, barren cubicle, probably that of a lower-end employee. She looks at the desk, which is fairly uninteresting: pencils, graph paper, a beat-up typewriter, some pictures on the wall. Then she looks at the pictures.

One is of the guy's family—wife, two kids, the wife sitting in a tire swing. She doesn't recognize any of them. Then her eye falls on another picture, but this one's a black-and-white photo of what looks like the stuffiest, most interminably boring man on earth. He's bald with a thick, droopy mustache, tiny spectacles, and dead, tired eyes.

There's an inscription at the bottom. It reads: MAX PLANCK.

Maybe Coburn wasn't saying *plank* at all. Then she remembers something from high school: Planck's constant. That's a thing, isn't it?

"Six-six-two-six," she murmurs. She thinks, then lifts the picture up off the wall.

Set in the wall behind it is a tiny brass combination lock, like one for a briefcase, with four little shining wheels with tiny numbers inscribed on them. Mona turns them until they read 6-6-2-6.

There's a soft *clunk* from behind her. She returns to the white door, and finds it's moved forward about a centimeter, enough to get her fingers around. She pulls it open.

On the other side is a surprisingly large room with walls covered in wooden cubbyholes. Inside are three old film projectors, about a dozen tape players and recorders, and an absurdly huge box of batteries. Hanging from the ceiling by small chains is a sign reading RECORDS.

"Huh," says Mona. She walks in and starts looking through the cubbies.

There are hundreds and hundreds of binders here. She flips through a few. They're all figures and transcripts of not only experiments, but discussions about experiments, and meetings about discussions about experiments, and on and on and on. She never had any idea that science involved so much *writing*. Everything in this lab must have been carefully recorded somewhere, somehow, from the figures that went into the studies, to those that came out of it, to the model, make, year, etc., of all the equipment involved (even the batteries, for God's sake, which apparently they made here specifically for the experiments).

Why lock all this up? Why should they be so secretive?

Well, they would have to be, she thinks, if what they were recording was incredibly, incredibly important, or expensive, or dangerous. And after talking to Coburn (or the picture of Coburn) she thinks that it might've been all three.

Mona looks at the film projectors. This would explain why her mother had so much film in her attic. She must've gotten a hookup at work.

She looks at the film canister labels. They all sound fairly boring or obscure, except for one, which bears the rather unprofessional label of SUCCESS!!! She pops the top off of the lid, and sees the film is intact.

She tests the wall socket, and finds that the generator is apparently putting power through to here. Since she's now a damn expert on loading projectors, she feeds the film in, turns the projector to face one of the blank walls of the records room, and starts her up.

As before, there's no audio. Just dingy, yellowed images fluttering across the wall. She fiddles with the lenses until they resolve.

The film shows the big, metal-walled room with the lens. Dr. Coburn is in front of the camera, standing so he's blocking the lens from view. He's dressed in a brown coat with elbow patches, and he sports a tremendous beard (very late-seventies, Mona thinks). He looks a little nervous, his eyes flicking about, his fingers rising up to adjust (and readjust, and re-readjust) his tie. Someone must say something to him from off camera, because he perks up, appears to say, *What? Oh!* and steps aside so that the camera has full view of the lens.

Only now there are two lenses: the second arm of the contraption, which looked so conspicuously empty, now has the missing mirror, or lens. A great deal of wires run down out of the top of the arm to somewhere off camera, probably behind whoever's filming.

Coburn is muttering quietly to someone, again off camera. He nods at them, eyebrows raised—*Are we ready?* He nods again, then clears his throat, smiles stiffly, and, after a pause, begins addressing the camera.

Of course, Mona hears none of it. She has to sit and wait for him to get through his whole spiel, which takes about five minutes. While Coburn talks, some assistants or scientists come in and hold up sheets of paper or boards with the date and time written on them, as well as a test number. Coburn, still stiff as starch, awkwardly gestures to them. Then he begins pointing back to the lenses.

Coburn reaches into his pocket and takes out a bright red ball, about the size of an orange. It's a croquet ball, Mona sees. Then, still talking, he takes out a knife and makes a long scratch down the side. He walks forward to the camera, holding the ball out (the operator has to hurry to adjust the focus) so that the viewer can see the scratch: it's shallow and made in the shape of an *S*. Then he walks back to the lens, and the camera zooms in and follows him (along with a boom mike that floats into view now and again).

There are two small metal tables on opposite ends of the round metal room, with the lenses in the middle. Coburn places the ball on the left table, square in the middle, where it's marked with a big *X* of black tape. He points to it, and talks to the camera a bit. Then he points across the room, and the camera whirls, eventually settling on the table on the right-hand side of the room. This table is empty, but also has a big *X* of tape. The camera zooms out and refocuses on Coburn. He talks at the camera a bit, and points at the lenses hanging from the ceiling. The camera zooms in to study them.

It appears that age did not touch the remaining lens at all. Its twin is the same: they are both perfect, maintaining a queer sheen even in the dingy light of the metal room.

The camera zooms back out. Coburn is advancing, gesturing to the room, then to his staff, who are still off camera. He looks excited, anxious, terrified as hell. He points off camera again, bows, and exits stage right. From the shadows Mona sees on the ground, it looks like all his people are leaving too. Then it's just the camera, still rolling, filming a wide angle that captures the table on the left with the croquet ball, the lenses in the middle, and the empty table on the right.

Mona sits forward. Obviously, it isn't safe for people to be in the room with whatever's about to happen.

She keeps staring at the room. Nothing happens. Then, slowly, the lenses rotate, so that one points at the table on the right, and the other points at the table on the left. A light on the base of the arm, near the ceiling, flicks on. There's a long, long pause, more than five minutes long, ten minutes long, more. Mona wonders what sort of SUCCESS!!! this could be.

And then it happens.

It takes her a minute, but she notices something's wrong with the curvature of the walls on the sides of the room. She can't tell which way they're curving now . . . is the right side of the room curving in, completing the circle as it should? Or is it somehow curving away? It's so bad her eyes begin to hurt. After a lot of blinking, she thinks she's got it figured out: when she looks at the left side of the room, she gets the uneasy sensation that she's actually seeing both it and the *right* side of the room at once; likewise, when she looks at the right side, she feels like she's also seeing the left side of the room. It's as if someone took two film negatives and laid them one on top of the other.

Then she notices something else odd. There is a shadow in the center of the empty table on the right. But it appears to be a shadow projected by nothing, hanging loose like the shadow from *Peter Pan*. It looks a little like the shadow of a ball...perhaps a croquet ball.

Then, slowly, like someone gradually increasing the light on a lamp, something faint and red begins to appear in the center of the table on the right.

Mona looks at the table on the left. The croquet ball is still there. But when she looks back at the table on the right, she sees something. It's not *exactly* a red croquet ball, but something a lot like it, like its ghost, if croquet balls could have ghosts.

It keeps growing brighter. And then there are two croquet balls, each sitting on its own table.

The light on the arm of the lenses flicks out. And when it does, the curving walls overlaid on one another vanish, along with the ball on the left-hand table. Which leaves only the croquet ball on the right-hand table, which doesn't seem to be going anywhere.

After a pause, Dr. Coburn bounds into view with a Geiger counter in hand. He remembers himself, and assumes the stately walk of an established academic. He walks to the right-hand table with the croquet ball and holds the Geiger counter over it; the camera wiggles a bit as whoever was running it reassumes his or her position, then it zooms in to show the readout on the Geiger counter: Mona doesn't know much about radiation, but judging by Dr. Coburn's face, and his cavalier attitude, the number must be very low.

Dr. Coburn picks up the ball and walks back to the camera. He holds it out again, and the camera focuses on its front.

Running along one side of the ball is a meandering, carven *S*.

"What the hell," breathes Mona.

Dr. Coburn, obviously pleased as punch, pops the ball back into his pocket. Hands folded before him, he addresses the camera with a few choice words. After remaining calm and respectable for a bit longer, he finally bursts out laughing. Two of the assistants (grad students, probably) come running in, one, the girl, to hug him, and the other, a pudgy, bearded man, to shake his hand. Then the camera operator walks around to adjust something below the camera's lens.

Mona gets only one glance at that face, which is serenely triumphant, the face of someone who's been holding winning cards for a long time and *knew* she'd take the pot but is still damn pleased to see it happen. And when she does, Mona can say only one word:

"Momma."

Then the screen goes dark.

Mona watches the film two more times. Then she starts to look at the records around her.

The reports don't make any sense to her, and since she has no intention of staying here all night she drops them and moves on.

The tapes, though…the tapes and the transcripts are worth something.

After about a half hour of gathering material, she starts playing a couple of the recordings and reading the files.

With a bit more arranging, they start to resemble a story.

WHERE THE SKY TOUCHES THE EARTH

TAPED REHEARSAL OF MEETING WITH CHAIR OF
AERONAUTIC DEFENSE SUBCOMMITTEE
AUGUST 4TH 1973, 10:30 AM ST
STAFF INVOLVED:
DR. RICHARD COBURN, PROJECT MANAGER
MICHAEL DERN, CHIEF OF STAFF

[*STATIC*]

RICHARD COBURN: —not even pertinent. I've never met this man, nor do I wish to. We have people for that, I thought. I'm sure I've seen some of them on the payroll at some point in time.

MICHAEL DERN: Yes, we've got people, but he's not coming to meet with people. He's coming to meet with you.

RICHARD COBURN: Oh, that's preposterous. Any...anyone else would be better. Why can't you do it? You're a perfectly sensible young man, more or less.

MICHAEL DERN: More or less?

RICHARD COBURN: Well, certainly. I mean, I don't know everything about you, but you seem...

[PAUSE]

MICHAEL DERN: Keep that charm flowing, and I'm sure our funding won't be touched.

RICHARD COBURN: Oh, but he can't really touch our funding. He's some junior senator, or something or other. There's that, I don't know, the overarching defense committee. *They* control our funding. They're the big boys we have to please.

MICHAEL DERN: And who do you think reports to them?

[PAUSE]

RICHARD COBURN: Are you serious?

MICHAEL DERN [CLEARS THROAT]: Why don't we get started?

RICHARD COBURN: Fine, but started *where*? I've never had to—to pitch myself to laymen before. Communication is not my strong suit, Michael. This is not the job for me.

MICHAEL DERN: Well, you're not going to be just pitching yourself. You'll be pitching all of us. Not to put any pressure on you, but a lot's riding on this. Hence my urgency. I wanted to make you flash cards, but—

RICHARD COBURN: I am not using flash cards. Don't be ridiculous.

MICHAEL DERN: Well. Then you'd better get started now. Start at the beginning. Like...what...what do you want to accomplish here?

RICHARD COBURN: Well, that is...hm. We set out to examine...well, originally we set out to examine the behavior of, of subatomic particles under conditions highly similar to, if not exactly similar to, those of cosmic bruising—

MICHAEL DERN: Okay.

RICHARD COBURN: —by which I mean multiuniversal breaches—though this term is under some scrutiny—whose signatures could only initially be registered by various frequencies of background radiation—

MICHAEL DERN: Yeah.

RICHARD COBURN: —and *certainly* have never been witnessed or measured in any location close to Earth. The reason being that, if there had in fact been multiuniversal contact, friction, bruising, or what have you, then there's a significant chance that the rules that reality usually observes could...I don't know why I'm telling you this. You know all this.

MICHAEL DERN: Yeah. Yes. But you're not telling me. You're telling him. And let me give you a word of advice.

RICHARD COBURN: Mm. Yes?

MICHAEL DERN: Don't tell him *that*.

RICHARD COBURN: What? Which part?

MICHAEL DERN: Any of it.

RICHARD COBURN: Why not?

MICHAEL DERN: Because to some junior congressman, or senator, or whatever from Illinois, that's going to sound like a bunch of abstract horseshit not worth spending money on. And that's what he's here to figure out. He's not here to be educated in the mysteries of the universe. He's here to figure out why this place, in the middle of a mountain, is worth the millions of dollars it's costing the American taxpayer. And he's gonna say that, too. He's gonna actually look you in the eye, and say the words, *costing the American taxpayer.* Those will be this guy's favorite words. I guarantee it. It's how he got elected, I'm sure. So we've got to give him his proverbial bang for his proverbial buck. Him and his taxpayer.

[SILENCE]

RICHARD COBURN: Oh, for God's sake, Michael. I, I told you I'd never be any good at this.

[CHAIR SCRAPING]

MICHAEL DERN: No. No! Come on, Dick, you are not getting up. You need to sit down and practice this! This is important!

RICHARD COBURN: There is no amount of practice I can do to make this go well, I am convinced of it.

MICHAEL DERN: Just...you know. Here. Do the whole Feynman thing. Explain it to a kid.

RICHARD COBURN: Feynman...my God, don't get me started on... and I enjoy the company of children even less than I do that of politicians, just so you know.

MICHAEL DERN: Well, I, I am fucking sorry. I am sorry you don't like politicians, or kids, or anyone without some amount of letters after their name. But this needs to get done.

RICHARD COBURN: Don't you cast me as an elitist! I'm not, it's just, it's hard to—to *talk* to people like that. We don't operate in the same sphere, so, so, so I...why are you looking at me like that? Don't look at me like that. Don't.

MICHAEL DERN: To a kid. Go on. Talk.

RICHARD COBURN [SIGHS]: Well. Let me see...it is...well, it is... *suggested* that there are other universes than ours. That's a pretty big thing to fit your head around, but it appears to be so. It's thought that there have always been these other universes, stretching back to the Big Bang, though we don't know exactly how many. And during the Big Bang, and especially the time directly, *directly* after, these various universes made a lot of contact with one another. They bumped and banged and scraped into one another. It has taken us some time to measure and quantify this theory, but we've found certain levels of background radiation near—

MICHAEL DERN: Drop that. And the names of the stars.

RICHARD COBURN: I hadn't even gotten there yet. How did you know I'd name them?

MICHAEL DERN: Just drop it. Stick to the basics, Dick.

RICHARD COBURN: You do know I'm your boss, don't you?

[SILENCE]

RICHARD COBURN: Fine. Well, the places where these universes bumped into one another did not fully heal, to use medical terminology. They *bruised*. And, since these places did not heal, the nature and behavior of these universes does not work ... quite right there. Like a football player tearing a tendon—it will heal, but it won't have the same range of flexibility, or it will twinge and pop sometimes. You know ... is this a good metaphor?

MICHAEL DERN: It's a fine metaphor.

RICHARD COBURN: I feel like athletics is very fertile ground for metaphors for politicians.

MICHAEL DERN: Athletics make great metaphors for politicians. Keep going. Tell him why this matters.

RICHARD COBURN [SIGHS]: Well. Well, if we can mimic these conditions—if we can create our own bruising, in other words, *without* having a whole universe crash into ours—then a whole host of possibilities opens up. Concepts like time, distance, tensile strength—

MICHAEL DERN: Tensile strength?

RICHARD COBURN: Yes. We did the tests with rope, remember?

MICHAEL DERN: It's awful specific.

RICHARD COBURN: How about just strength, then?

MICHAEL DERN: Sure.

RICHARD COBURN: All right. *Strength* and everything all becomes malleable, unpredictable. What we are chiefly interested in is ... travel.

MICHAEL DERN: What?

RICHARD COBURN: I am simplifying this for him.

MICHAEL DERN: Simplifying it into what? What do you mean?

RICHARD COBURN: I am referencing the neutrino signatures.

MICHAEL DERN: Ohhh. Oh. Say *transportation*, then.

RICHARD COBURN: Oh, that's good! I should have thought of that. Yes. *Transportation* is what we're concerned with. Because the primary consequence is a confusion of distance. Reality itself experiences aphasia—it forgets where certain things are, in other words. It's almost impossible to control, or at least it's *possibly* impossible, but we are attempting to see if it's possible to have one item traverse a distance—any distance—without actually *moving*.

MICHAEL DERN: Saying *possibly* a lot.

RICHARD COBURN: I know. I just thought that.

MICHAEL DERN: So how does the lens work?

RICHARD COBURN: Well...how much will he know about the lens?

MICHAEL DERN: He'll know it's over forty percent of our budget.

RICHARD COBURN: Hm. I see. Well, the lens was conceived to try and examine if our own day-to-day activities—at a subatomic level, of course—might hold some similarity with that of cosmic bruising. No reality is perfectly stable, in other words, just like no person—or, ah, football player—is perfectly healthy. But we quickly found that the lens had side effects. Not dangerous ones. At least, we don't think so.

MICHAEL DERN: I would *definitely* cut that.

RICHARD COBURN: Hm. Probably smart. Anyway, the side effects were that, if we examined a particle with the lens in a certain manner, then...it...well, the lens caused bruising itself. It seemed impossible at first, but, well, there you are. The closer we examine, the more the lens interferes, or disturbs, or interjects itself in such a way that it upsets things, like trying to look so close at someone that you actually knock them down.

MICHAEL DERN: You are doing great with the metaphors.

RICHARD COBURN: Oh? Should I stop?

MICHAEL DERN: No, no. Keep going. This is good, this is very good.

RICHARD COBURN: Well, I'm not sure where else to go. The lens causes what we are choosing to call *subatomic aphasia*. It interrupts our reality and elbows into a couple of others, a little, simulating bruising. Our reality forgets that that particle—or particles—is there. And in that moment, the thing it is examining is shoved—partially—into all those various other realities as well. So it could exist in a variety of states, places, et cetera. Even *times*, possibly, though of course that is quite hard to quantify. What we wanted to do was reduce the amount of possibilities until we had it in a binary state—that is, the particle is in two places at once, two *physical* places, I mean, within our reality. Or it seems to be. We're not quite sure. Then we would need to simply shut down one avenue, one possibility—again, this is all *so very* theoretical—and then ta-da, it's there. We'd like to be able to see if we can transport larger items, but, again, we're not sure. The most interesting thing about all this—

MICHAEL DERN: More interesting than practical application?

RICHARD COBURN: Incredibly more so, yes. The most interesting thing we've found from the lens is that it suggests our own experience of reality is myopic. It is a bit like...I don't know, like an ant crawling along a string stretched across a large room. The ant's experience is largely two-dimensional. It only cares about what's happening along the surface directly in front of it or behind it in a straight line. That's us. We're the ant. But the lens allows our perspective to expand outward. Our perspective gains more dimensions: there are things below us, above us, to our sides. There is an enormous, unexplored gulf of existence, of realities, all around us; we simply can't experience it because our perspective is a bit nailed down. You see?

MICHAEL DERN: Hm. Well...

RICHARD COBURN: What's wrong?

MICHAEL DERN: I...don't think this metaphor is a good one.

RICHARD COBURN: Why not?

MICHAEL DERN: Because he's gonna ask—what's in the corners?

RICHARD COBURN: The corners of what?

MICHAEL DERN: Of the room. There's this big huge room. Maybe there's something in the corners.

RICHARD COBURN: Well, we just don't know. That's the curious thing about it.

MICHAEL DERN: Ehh. I'd leave it out. These types of guys, they tend to fixate on stuff like this. It's the war mentality, I guess.

RICHARD COBURN: I can almost guarantee that there are no Soviets in the corners of this metaphorical room.

MICHAEL DERN: You know what I mean.

RICHARD COBURN: Well...well then, if it comes to that, I will just say to him that, that...that we just don't know. And...and that's why we need money, Mr. Senator. We need lots of it, all of it. In big bags. We need it to figure out what the fuck is going on.

MICHAEL DERN [LAUGHS]

RICHARD COBURN: Did you like that? It was rather good, wasn't it.

MICHAEL DERN: You say that and Laura will kill you.

RICHARD COBURN: I've no doubt.

[*STATIC*]

████████████████████████: So it's one hundred percent necessary that this is taped.

MICHAEL DERN: One hundred percent.

████████████████████████: Why? Who's going to listen to this?

MICHAEL DERN: Um. Not many people.

████████████████████████: How many is not many?

MICHAEL DERN: One?

████████████████████████: One? One person?

MICHAEL DERN: They get played, once. Then they get stored. Safely.

████████████████████████: Come on, Michael.

MICHAEL DERN: You're awful curious about this.

████████████████████████: Yes, I am awful curious about what happens to tapes made of me, of me talking. How would you like it? Wouldn't you be worried?

MICHAEL DERN: I have been taped so many times, I don't even notice anymore.

████████████████████████: But you do know what happens to the tapes.

MICHAEL DERN: Yes. The tapes get transcribed.

████████████████████████: Okay. Then what?

MICHAEL DERN: Mm. Probably shouldn't. But. Then the transcriptions get circulated to a committee—a really important committee— with your name removed.

██████████████████████: What? Why the hell would they do that?

MICHAEL DERN: Because there's always a chance that someone—I don't know who, but some asshole—could leak the interview.

██████████████████████: Ah. Because we do such [singing] top secret work.

MICHAEL DERN: Yeah. You do. You do, you know.

██████████████████████: Yeah. I know all about that.

MICHAEL DERN: Still, they want to hear, you know, thoughts, opinions, et cetera. They want to hear it out of your mouth. But not, you know, your mouth.

██████████████████████: Is your name redacted?

MICHAEL DERN: Nope.

██████████████████████: Well aren't you special.

MICHAEL DERN: My name is a matter of public record. So yeah. Yeah, I am special. Not as special as you, though, but ██████████████

██████████████████████: You sure know how to sweet-talk ████████████████

MICHAEL DERN: I do. So how's it going?

██████████████████████: That's it? Just how's it going?

MICHAEL DERN: We'll start there, sure.

██████████████████████: Seriously?

MICHAEL DERN: Seriously.

██████████████████████[LONG PAUSE]: Not good.

MICHAEL DERN: No?

██████████████████████: Yeah. Not good. And I'm saying that knowing full well that I could lose my job, and the job of everyone else here. It's not good.

MICHAEL DERN: What's so not good about it?

██████████████████████: The results we're getting. ██████████████ is excited about them, sure. His ██████████████████ but you've got to understand that…like, think of looking at a dark room. You see a flash on one side. Then you see it again on another. What's the guarantee that it's the same light? Isn't a much more practical explanation that it's just two different lights that appear similar?

MICHAEL DERN: You know I'm a physicist too, right?

███████████████████████: Yeah, but you went to Stanford, so.

MICHAEL DERN: Very cute. So you're saying you disbelieve ████████████ ████████████████ hypothesis about the photon tracking.

████████████████████████: What I will say is that I think we've made more progress exploring photon signatures than we ever have on cosmic bruising. If there's one great contribution we've made to science, it's that.

MICHAEL DERN: What do you feel is the problem?

████████████████████████: It's the math. Listen, I...I know this theory is popular. The multiverse theory, or what have you. Of course it is, it's dippy and crazy and fun. But the math isn't right. They can always adjust for whatever results they get. Nothing can get disproven. And if nothing can get disproven, nothing can get proven, Michael. And while I think ████████████████████████ is making progress in a lot of fields, they're not the ones we're supposed to be making progress in. We have not found any evidence that we are anywhere close to simulating suspended bruising. Nor have we found any evidence—hard evidence, mind—that the phenomena we're witnessing, if we could call them that, are a result of bruising. ████████████████████████████ which I know is just his absolute baby, is an impressive device that has led to remarkable breakthroughs in particle physics. None of which he was looking for.

MICHAEL DERN: None of which you were looking for either. You helped design it. A lot of this was your idea.

████████████████████████[PAUSE]: Yeah. Yeah. But. I mean, eventually you have to grow up, don't you?

MICHAEL DERN: How do you dispute the photon signature?

████████████████████: I dispute it because the two signatures— which appear to be the same, but, again, they can prove anything, because of how they're fiddling with the math—appeared an insignificant distance apart. I saw nothing suggesting transportation. It's not what we wanted to see.

MICHAEL DERN: What you wanted to see.

[redacted]: No. No, it's not what I wanted to see. I wanted to see something much larger. I don't know. I wanted to be talking nanometers, not Planck's lengths. Millimeters, even. Fuck, centimeters.

MICHAEL DERN: That's... extreme.

[redacted]: Well, we wanted extreme. What we were first shooting at—when we were using solid numbers, I mean—was something extreme. If we could honestly induce subatomic aphasia—really, really create our own bruising—then we would be seeing something extreme. Significant displacement. Indisputable duplication. I don't know. That's the thing. We just didn't know. And here we are. Now, I know [redacted] are all excited over this. But they have their own [redacted] club, and, you know, they all get together and titter over things. And yeah, it's not fun that I'm excluded from that group just because [redacted]. But I'm being impartial here. I really am. I don't think they're right. Even if they're using my math, my research. And the fucking competition...

MICHAEL DERN: You think it's harmful?

[redacted]: Are you stupid? Of course it's harmful! We've got all these people who do essentially the same thing, many of whom have been rivals for a damn long time, all cooped up in the desert spending their time inside a fucking mountain not getting the results they wanted. It's shark-infested waters here, Mike. Even if the sharks are wearing... what's that sweater that [redacted] wears?

MICHAEL DERN: Alpaca.

[redacted]: Yes. Fucking alpaca sweaters. Jesus Christ. You want us to lay aside our differences, sit down, create something great. Like they did at Los Alamos. But this isn't Los Alamos. There isn't a war going on, or at least not a real one. And we're not Oppenheimer, or Bohr, or Feynman, or any of the rest of them. Just a bunch of assholes in the desert gnawing their arms off.

MICHAEL DERN: And do you think they treat you differently? Even from the others?

██████████████████████: What, because I'm ██████████████████
or because I'm a good-looking ████████████████

[SILENCE]

██████████████████████: That's very tactful of you, Mike. To answer your question, yes, I think they treat me differently. I think I'm excluded from a lot. But it doesn't stop there. The town treats us differently.

MICHAEL DERN: You think the problems extend to Wink?

██████████████████████: Not these exact problems. And they're not overt problems. It's a... sense. A way they look at us.

MICHAEL DERN: Wink was built to support you all.

██████████████████████: And you don't think that pisses them off? Christ, I'd be disappointed. I mean, have you met us? They don't even have good television out here. They only broadcast shows from, like, fifteen years ago. The *Ozzie and Harriet* reruns... I'm surprised we don't have any suicides. But what's really bad about it is that we all know, somewhere in the back of our heads, that this is all supposed to be perfect. This place is supposed to be...

MICHAEL DERN: The future.

██████████████████████: Yeah. Yeah, the future. We give a little to the town. The streetlights. Power. Other little innovations. But they know, deep down, that it's not a real place. It's... invented. It's fake. Like Las Vegas, but worse. At least Vegas makes money.

MICHAEL DERN: What makes you think this facility doesn't make money?

██████████████████████: I guess that's a good point. We could be shoveling out patents and they'd never tell us. I guess ██████████ ████████ could have cooked up a whole lot of patents and they're just waiting to get out and... well. That would never happen, would it.

MICHAEL DERN: No. There are a lot of eyes on you all.

██████████████████████: You mean us all.

MICHAEL DERN: Right.

██████████████████████: For now, yeah. If we don't make more progress, I'm sure the eyes will look at something else. And the funding will go there too. Listen, I've said what I came to say. Anything more you want to ask me?

MICHAEL DERN: Relationships.

[SILENCE]

██████████████████████: Yeah?

MICHAEL DERN: Are you involved in any?

[SILENCE]

██████████████████████: No, Mike. No, I am not.

INVESTIGATION OF EQUIPMENT MALFUNCTION
DR. RICHARD COBURN
AUGUST 13TH, 1975

It is important to note when considering this case that the equipment involved (the Suspended Bruising Lens, or simply "lens") has so far functioned without issue, or noticeable issue, for the better part of half a decade. I have personally never witnessed any error with the equipment, and though our reports show what they show, I have some reason to doubt them, for reasons that will be made clear. But for the moment I would ask all of you to remember that thus far the lens has given no hint of genuine anomaly in its performance, or at least not one on this scale. In short, I believe my testimony below will lead you to believe, just as I do, that the issue is likely one of personnel, rather than an error in equipment, equipment maintenance, or data input. ▪▪

Some background:

Steven Helm is our chief lab assistant, and while previously his record was without blemish I must report that he has voiced some (unfounded, in my opinion) concerns regarding the lens with increasing frequency. These were never voiced to me directly, nor have they ever been reported on record with Michael Dern (COS), but his issues have filtered through to me mostly from Eric Bintly and Laura Alvarez, who are, as you no doubt know, our primary researchers on staff. I did note some curiosities in Mr. Helm's behavior, but I chalked it up to simple laziness or restlessness, which is, I feel, quite a reasonable assumption considering our location, our seclusion, and the high-pressure nature of this work.

The greatest symptom of Mr. Helm's suspicions was his reluctance to enter the testing chamber, which was of course quite an obstacle. Whenever someone needed him to enter the chamber, Mr. Helm was either not to be found or he would formulate some elaborate task that had fully engaged his time and efforts. Thus we, the project manager and primary researchers, would have to do his duties for him, which often consisted of adjustments, measurements, and other tasks that required little to no education. This went on for about a month before the incident. I suppose it is my fault that I allowed this behavior to continue; we have been working on this project together for so long, and have become so familiar with each other, that our strictures may have become a bit lax.

The second symptom is one I did not witness myself, for I was never present. (I assume the relevant testimonies are being presented to you independently—at least, I hope they are.) But on the rare occasions when Mr. Helm could be coerced to enter the chamber to do his work, he avoided the lens plates. Specifically, he avoided looking into their reflective surfaces. It was Dr. Bintly who first noticed this behavior, and he treated it with great levity (so I understand), making the usual comments one can expect about vanity, fixing one's hair, checking for food in one's teeth, etc., but Mr. Helm was not at all receptive to such humor, and I am told his reaction was quite rude, shocking both Dr. Bintly and Dr. Alvarez. Dr. Alvarez later confronted Mr. Helm about his comments, and Mr. Helm admitted he did not feel "all right, at all" around the lens. His reasons for this were vague and unclear, but if I may be honest I believe he thought that when he looked into the lens plates he imagined seeing something. I even believe he thinks he saw someone in the mirror who was not himself, i.e., a reflection of someone who was not there.

Naturally, this is quite ridiculous. I have requested to have Mr. Helm removed from my staff, as any responsible project leader would. But, since the mishap with the lens occurred before Mr. Helm's impending departure, you must understand that I have reasons to suspect him in what happened. I do not find it at all surprising that some minds cannot bear the burden of the tasks that have been laid upon our shoulders, especially considering the manner in which they were laid upon our shoulders. Though I am sure you know this, our lives are solitary and highly disciplined, receiving little return or reward day after day, and though we and the rest of the staff enjoy our time in the constructed village, it often feels as if civilization is worlds away. Which, I suppose, it is.

The next issue, and the one I feel is most unfortunate, concerns Dr. Bintly, whom I have always considered a very reliable and respectable scientist (I would not have him on my staff otherwise, but even by my standards he is most excellent), and thus I find his actions a cause for deep regret. While he has never voiced any concerns about the lens, or the nature of our work, despite its frustrating and often elusive nature, there were two events that I feel almost suggest a break with reality. I am very sympathetic to Dr. Bintly, and I understand that, again, our isolation and seclusion here, along with the nature of our work, will naturally have some pretty dire repercussions on the state of one's mental health (I myself am not above such maladies, and have even taken up meditation to remedy it, which I cannot recommend highly enough), but even so I cannot allow him to pass from suspicion.

The first event occurred over half a year ago (I cannot recall the date) on a very late evening spent in the chamber, going over some statistical models that were not behaving as we had forecasted. Mr. Helm was not present—it was only Dr. Bintly, Dr. Alvarez, and myself. Dr. Alvarez and I left Dr. Bintly alone for a brief period to perambulate about the offices while we reconsidered the nature of our problem, and we later returned with some possibly fertile ground (which proved quite fertile indeed, I am happy to say). But we heard Dr. Bintly talking quite agitatedly within the chamber. We looked in and found him flipping through the statistical models, angrily discussing their contents aloud, even castigating his imaginary audience for not knowing what he was talking about, when they (I do recall that he later referred to them as "they") knew quite well what he meant as they'd all been talking about it for the past four hours. Dr. Alvarez interjected from the door, and Dr. Bintly looked up, surprised, and asked how we'd gotten "over there" so quickly, and why we had changed clothes. Dr. Alvarez and I were quite confused by his comments, and reminded him that we'd only gone on a quick walk, and had not changed clothes at all, which caused Dr. Bintly to stare into the far side of the room with a puzzled look on his face as if expecting to see someone there. When no one appeared, he seemed quite disturbed, and he chose to retire for the evening, which we all agreed was the smart thing to do.

[black bars redacting text]

This situation was much more distressing. I had been meditating on the mesa top, as is part of my morning ritual, and I descended to find Dr. Bintly shouting at Dr. Alvarez with considerable alarm and volume. This attracted the attention of the other workers, who began to mutter and mill about as I suppose such people do. Yet when he saw me, coming down the stairs in my robe, he stared and almost fainted. We took him to the medical room straightaway.

Dr. Bintly was most reluctant to discuss the matter. Dr. Alvarez privately informed me that he had come running out of the chamber shouting that I, personally, was in trouble. So agitated was Dr. Bintly that he was unable to articulate the precise nature of my trouble, but I assure you I was not in any trouble, having been sitting atop the mesa doing breathing exercises at the time.

Eventually we were able to extract the truth from him, or the truth he was willing to give us. He claimed he'd been working on the lens data feeds when suddenly the chamber filled up with a great shouting. He was so astonished he leaped up and saw—and here I do pity him—me, Richard Coburn, standing in the chamber in ragged clothes, sporting a full beard, shouting the word *plank* over and over again. Then he claims I abruptly vanished.

But this does not compare to his later actions, which, if I took them at all seriously, would be quite upsetting for me. For it seems he had been hiding

[black bars redacting text]

It is quite sad to see that Dr. Bintly's mind has been so affected by our work. I have put through a request for transfer for him, and though I am dispirited by these developments I do not regret my actions. Moving him away from the facility—perhaps only for a time, as his contributions are so valuable—will aid his mental health enormously.

Dr. Alvarez, however, remains my most trusted and valuable colleague. I am aware she had issues with our work in the past (she is a little too devoted to details, I feel, and often misses the forest for the leaves) but these have been resolved and in recent months she has been more dedicated to our researches than ever. I say this because I am very aware that, since Dr. Alvarez is the one who was directly involved with the incident, the most suspicion will inevitably fall on her. But as she has no history of erratic behavior, unlike her other two colleagues, and since the nature of her involvement was so incidental (I presume you have seen the film), I cannot imagine that she had any intentional hand in what happened.

███

███
███
███

████████████████████████████████████

The facts are simple:

On Monday evening, Dr. Alvarez did a final check on the lens equipment. This is standard operating procedure for us, after which we always lock up the chamber.

Approximately four minutes into her check, she began to shut down the recording equipment.

Not long after that, the power flow to the lens abruptly spiked. This we know due to the electrical monitoring systems I insisted be installed (which we now all agree was quite wise). The duration of the spike was a little over forty seconds.

Three seconds into this spike, the lens plates rotated a full twenty-three degrees, clockwise. Then they stopped.

The spike persisted for another nine seconds. Then it ended.

And this, really, is all we know, which is not much. There is a lot of hoopla going on about the data outputs, and though what was recorded does suggest something very close to suspended bruising, ███████████████████████

██

██

█████████████████████████████████████ But we obviously cannot trust it because it occurred during what honestly seems to be either equipment malfunction (unlikely) or sabotage (in my opinion, much more likely).

There is also the position of the plates. While a reenactment of the incident does suggest that the plates rotated to point toward Dr. Alvarez's position in the chamber, I do not lend this development much credence. It does not stir any suspicion or concern in my mind. The position of the plates has so far proven coincidental to any success at suspended bruising.

What concerns me most—as it must also concern you—is ███████████

███

███

███

███

███

███

██████████

██

███

██████████

██

███

███

██

███████████

██

███

███

███████████████████████████████

██

███

███

███

███

███

███

███████████████

However, none of this can be proven to any satisfactory degree.

Dr. Alvarez remains an exceptional scientist—possibly, except for myself, the most exceptional one I have ever known—and she herself did not register anything out of the ordinary during her time in the chamber. Due to the nature of the lens, she did not even hear it rotate. And she did not notice anything during the time that, per the reports, suspended bruising was achieved.

Though there was some concern she had been exposed to ██████████████
██

█████████████ but totally ridiculous. I also have no reason to believe she was involved in the change in the lens.

To be frank, the behavior of the lens can only lead me to think it was the result of external control. I am not sure if either Dr. Bintly or Mr. Helm has the means of setting up this sort of control. But the sequence of events—power, rotation, data output—does not seem accidental. Someone, somehow, was controlling the lens.

I have requested your security teams examine and interrogate the facility staff in detail as a result. I am quite eager to hear what they will find.

██
██
██
██
██
██
████████████████████████████████████

INVESTIGATION INTO DISAPPEARANCE OF LAURA ALVAREZ
TAPED INTERVIEW c10.36-aB
CONDUCTED BY CHIEF OF STAFF MICHAEL DERN
SUBJECT: ERIC BINTLY
DECEMBER 14ᵀᴴ, 1975

MICHAEL DERN [CLEARS THROAT]: This interview is the first of the staff-conducted investigation into the disappearance of Laura Alvarez. It's, uh, important to note that, as of right now, this interview is not...officially sanctioned. Our instructions are still forthcoming. For now, we've been told to sit tight, but I figured that we...well, we needed to do something now, to prepare ahead of time, so no one got the idea that we were preparing statements.

ERIC BINTLY: So how do they know this isn't a prepared statement right now?

MICHAEL DERN: I think it's likely they'll understand we haven't had the time to prepare anything.

ERIC BINTLY: How do they know that? These aren't the most understanding guys in the world, am I wrong? Are we just promising them that we're making it right after she left?

MICHAEL DERN: You know you're on tape, right?

ERIC BINTLY: Yeah, yeah. But how do they even know when she left?

MICHAEL DERN: Eric, I'm going to level with you right now and say that...they have a lot more ways of keeping track of things out here than you'd expect.

ERIC BINTLY: Like what?

[SILENCE]

ERIC BINTLY: Cameras? Mikes?

[SILENCE]

ERIC BINTLY: Jesus Christ.

MICHAEL DERN: Let's just start from the top. Start from your return from your...

ERIC BINTLY: From my vacation?

MICHAEL DERN: Sure, let's call it that.

ERIC BINTLY: Well...it wasn't that long ago, but...things had obviously changed. We'd made huge advances. They had, I mean. I hadn't been there for it. They'd actually simulated bruising several—

MICHAEL DERN: No, Eric, what they want to know about is Laura. Tell them just about her. Just Laura.

ERIC BINTLY: Okay, okay. Let me think. Now...now, there were marked differences in how she, uh, acted since when I left and when I came back. I was only gone a couple of weeks. But I could tell... something was off. Something was wrong, I guess. She was... [PAUSE] Can I ask you something, Mike?

MICHAEL DERN: Me? Sure, I guess.

ERIC BINTLY: Did you...think I went crazy?

MICHAEL DERN: I'm sorry?

ERIC BINTLY: When they sent me away. Did you think I'd had a, a psychotic break? Because I don't. I wasn't sure at first, but now I am.

MICHAEL DERN: That's not really what we're asking about.

ERIC BINTLY: Yeah, but, see, it kind of is. You think Laura's disappearance is an aberration. You think it's unusual behavior. But I'm not so sure it is. Maybe it's something else.

MICHAEL DERN: So you think it's perfectly reasonable to just jump in your car, with no preparation at all, and leave, all the way out here in the desert?

ERIC BINTLY: I'm not saying it's reasonable. I'm saying...there might be other factors at play. Listen, Mike, I know that, on paper, I am a wildly untrustworthy witness. I am an untouchable, really. I'm here solely because Dick likes me, and I know it. But...that doesn't mean I'm wrong.

MICHAEL DERN: Wrong about what?

ERIC BINTLY: About the lens. About what it does.

MICHAEL DERN: I know what the lens does.

ERIC BINTLY: You know what it does on paper. But it does more than that.

MICHAEL DERN: For God's sakes. You sound like Steven.

ERIC BINTLY: And maybe we should have listened to Steven. I mean, he had problems with it well before all this happened. Before I... left. Before Laura.

MICHAEL DERN: Okay. Fine. Keep telling me about Laura. What was different about her?

ERIC BINTLY: Well, she used to be...to look quite...vivacious. There was an aliveness to her. You know? She used to run laps around the mesa like it was nothing. But when I saw her again, she looked unhealthy. She looked tired. Like something was being pulled out of her.

MICHAEL DERN: That was noted. We did two physicals, nothing showed up.

ERIC BINTLY: Right, and you attributed it to exhaustion. Which is a rational thing to do. But Dick was working just the same amount, right? And he didn't look that exhausted. And yeah, yeah, maybe it was all the meditation and the green tea. *Jasmine* green tea. But I don't think so.

MICHAEL DERN: So what was it?

ERIC BINTLY: I wasn't sure. I'm still not sure. But sometimes while I was talking to her, she'd suddenly look to the side, like she'd seen something, but nothing was there. Or she'd wince, like she'd just heard something loud or grating, right in her ear. It was like...me.

MICHAEL DERN: Like you?

ERIC BINTLY: Yeah. Like how I was. That was why you all thought I was crazy. Because I...saw things.

MICHAEL DERN: You said you saw the members of the research team in random places throughout the facility.

ERIC BINTLY: Yeah. I saw them. And we thought it was a hallucination. I did, too. But maybe not.

[SILENCE]

ERIC BINTLY: And maybe Laura was seeing and hearing things, too. Things that were actually there.

MICHAEL DERN: But things only she could see. Right. I'm gonna go ahead and remind you, one more time, that you are on tape.

ERIC BINTLY: I didn't just see staff, you know. There were some things I...I didn't tell you.

[SILENCE]

ERIC BINTLY: So that makes me wonder—what did Laura see?

MICHAEL DERN: Are you serious?

[SILENCE]

MICHAEL DERN: You saw this, and you didn't tell us?

[SILENCE]

MICHAEL DERN: It's really...it is *so* irresponsible that you were...that you withheld things from us, Eric. You were in danger, you should have told us *everything*.

ERIC BINTLY: I know. But I didn't want it to be real.

MICHAEL DERN: Want what to be real?

ERIC BINTLY: Well, it's like you said. I saw the lab crew, and I saw them in different places...but in different sets of clothing, at different *ages*. I didn't tell you *that*. Like, I saw you and Dick walking around, examining the facility, but you had hair, Mike, and I *swear* Dick had like half the wrinkles he has now. I saw Laura, and she looked about five years older, but she was filthy, dressed in a tank top and cargo shorts, and she was carrying around a fucking *gun*, for whatever reason. And I saw *myself*. When I didn't need glasses. Just doing whatever. Paperwork. Smoking. And once I saw...

MICHAEL DERN: Saw what?

[SILENCE]

MICHAEL DERN: Saw what, Eric?

ERIC BINTLY: I saw you. And Dick. And a lot of the other staff. Screaming. The walls were shaking. And the floor and ceiling were cracking. Lights going out. And someone said... "There's something up there."

[SILENCE]

MICHAEL DERN: What did he...do you mean?

ERIC BINTLY: I don't know. But...I thought he meant that there was something on top of the building. The mesa, I mean. I don't know.

[SILENCE]

MICHAEL DERN: Jesus Christ. Why didn't you say any of this?

ERIC BINTLY: Because I wanted to come back. Because I wanted to keep working. But now I know I shouldn't have. When I saw what Laura was doing...well, why tell you this. I'm sure you have it on film.

MICHAEL DERN: Have what?

ERIC BINTLY: What she was doing with the lens.

MICHAEL DERN: We don't...[PAPER RUSTLING] I don't, uh, think we have any recorded examples of any...uh, misbehavior with the lens.

ERIC BINTLY: You don't? At all?

MICHAEL DERN: No.

ERIC BINTLY: Well...I swear, she would just do it for an *hour* or something...

MICHAEL DERN: Do what?

ERIC BINTLY: Just...stare into them. She would just stare into the lens plates. With her nose about an inch away. Like she was transfixed. I caught her several times. That was when I really knew something was wrong.

MICHAEL DERN: I don't have any...God. I don't have that at all.

ERIC BINTLY: Then I guess she was screwing with the records.

MICHAEL DERN: She *couldn't.*

ERIC BINTLY: Well, she did, or someone did. I think I found her like that at least three times. And each time I caught her, there was something wrong with her *eyes.* It was like there was something else in there.

MICHAEL DERN: What do you mean?

ERIC BINTLY: I wasn't sure until I stopped her, on the day she left. The day she just jumped in her car and started driving east. Before that, I stopped her in the hall and asked what was wrong, because she looked troubled, and she stopped and looked at me and...it was like...it's impossible to describe. It's like there was someone else in there. In her head. Someone who wasn't Laura at all.

MICHAEL DERN: I'm going to just say, once more, with feeling, that you are on tape.

ERIC BINTLY: I know.

MICHAEL DERN: A tape that will be heard by important people.

ERIC BINTLY: I *know*. And I also know what I saw. I'm telling you, she didn't know me, Mike. Total lack of recognition. She wasn't sure who or maybe even *what* I was. And there was this shivering, or wriggling, all in her corneas, as if behind her eyes there was nothing but worms...

[SILENCE]

ERIC BINTLY: I let her go. I was so unnerved, I let her go. I shouldn't have done that.

[SILENCE]

MICHAEL DERN: No. You shouldn't have.

ERIC BINTLY: The lens does something, Mike. I'm sure of it. It pushes at the boundaries of things. I remember Dick once said the way it transports is like a kid throwing a ball up through one skylight so it comes down through another skylight a couple of walls away. And that just stuck in my head.

MICHAEL DERN: Why?

ERIC BINTLY: It was actually something you said before, about another metaphor of Dick's. The ant on the string in the room.

MICHAEL DERN: Oh. I think...yeah, the thing with—

ERIC BINTLY: The corners. What's in the corners?

MICHAEL DERN: Right.

ERIC BINTLY: Yeah, so...while his comparison with the skylights isn't correct—because that's *not* really how the lens works—it just makes me wonder if we are making holes somewhere, in some part of the world we can't measure or quantify, and if the holes are there, then...what else can come through?

MICHAEL DERN: You sound like—

ERIC BINTLY: I know. You said it already. Steven.

MICHAEL DERN: Did he—did he tell you everything, Eric? Because Steven told *me* everything. After all, he couldn't go to Dick, so he came to me. And it was fucking. Insane. It was fucking *insane*, Eric.

He said the, the lenses were windows, and there was someone on the other side of them. That's what he said, to me. He said there was someone on the other side, watching, and then—I swear I am not making this up, this is what he said—he corrected himself, and said, "or some*thing*." And he was dead fucking serious. Now, is this really something you want to get behind, Eric? Do you really want to discuss this, seriously, on tape, with me, and throw your career behind this sort of shit?

ERIC BINTLY: I don't know. I saw what I saw. There's no way around it.

MICHAEL DERN: Christ.

[SILENCE]

ERIC BINTLY: They'll have set up a perimeter, right? One of those search nets? APB, all that stuff?

MICHAEL DERN: I think so. I assume that's why no one's here to tell us what to do. They're all looking for her.

ERIC BINTLY: I ask because ... I think she made a lot of changes to the lens before she left.

MICHAEL DERN: What kind of changes?

ERIC BINTLY: I don't know. I'm not allowed to be around the lens that much since I got sent away. And besides ... I was never as good as she was.

MICHAEL DERN: You're sure? Sure she made changes?

ERIC BINTLY: Pretty sure.

MICHAEL DERN: Well ... fuck, man. Let's hope it wasn't anything important.

ERIC BINTLY: Dick will take care of it.

MICHAEL DERN: Yeah. Yeah. He'd fucking better. Jesus.

SOUNDTRACK TAPE TO JLB [FILM STOCK MISSING]
MAY 13ᵀᴴ 1983

[FOOTSTEPS, ECHOING]

UNKNOWN VOICE 1: Hurry! Come on!

UNKNOWN VOICE 2 (RICHARD COBURN?): I am hurrying! You should have warned me about this...

UNKNOWN VOICE 1: I did warn you! I told you two days ago it was happening.

POSSIBLY RICHARD COBURN: I don't even—

UNKNOWN VOICE 1: It wasn't just me. It doesn't matter now. Just come and look.

[BANGING, SQUEAKING, POSSIBLY HINGES]

UNKNOWN VOICE 1: Through here.

RICHARD COBURN: Is it really necessary we go all the way u—

UNKNOWN VOICE 1: Yes, it is! Come on. Up the ladder, you go first.

RICHARD COBURN: Oh, well, I...

[RUSTLING, BANGING]

[STATIC]

UNKNOWN VOICE 1: You're sure the lens is on?

RICHARD COBURN: Of course it is! The test is scheduled to continue for the next fifteen minutes, so we—

UNKNOWN VOICE 1: Good. Then it lines up perfectly. Let me just—

[RUSTLING]

UNKNOWN VOICE 1: Push!

[HINGES SQUEAKING]

RICHARD COBURN: My God, it's cold up here. I haven't...

[CRACKLING]

UNKNOWN VOICE 1: Do you see it?

[SOUND OF WIND]

UNKNOWN VOICE 1: Yeah. There—there it is.

[SILENCE]

RICHARD COBURN: My word.

UNKNOWN VOICE 1: Yeah. Jesus.

[SILENCE]

RICHARD COBURN: It's heat lightning.

UNKNOWN VOICE 1: No.

RICHARD COBURN: No?

UNKNOWN VOICE 1: No. I've seen heat lightning before, and *that* is not heat lightning.

RICHARD COBURN: Then what is it?

[SILENCE]

RICHARD COBURN: And you say every time we perform a test, then...

UNKNOWN VOICE 1: The lightning comes. Yeah. I don't even know how long it's been going on for. Paul just happened to notice it. It isn't on any meteorological forecasts.

RICHARD COBURN: It is so odd that it's silent.

UNKNOWN VOICE 1: I know.

[SILENCE]

UNKNOWN VOICE 1: So what do we do?

[SILENCE]

UNKNOWN VOICE: So what do we do?

[SILENCE]

[STATIC]

THE PEOPLE
FROM ELSEWHERE

CHAPTER THIRTY-ONE

Mona listens as the tape continues in silence. Every document she's read and every tape she's listened to has made her feel sicker and sicker, but it is not until this moment, as she listens to Coburn staring silently at the lightning-ridden sky, that she really begins to understand what happened here.

She punches the STOP button on the tape player. With a loud *pop*, the wheels stop turning.

She sits back. There's a knot in her stomach and it keeps getting pulled tighter. She has only pieces of what happened here, snatches of conversation and patches of reports, but she feels she is on the border of comprehending it. Yet it almost defies her. It is too huge, too strange, too impossible.

She remembers reading the word *pandimensional* and wondering what it had to do with anything. She remembers Mrs. Benjamin producing her two mirrors, murmuring (with a sneer) that Coburn never made anything actually worth making. She remembers Parson telling her about the little birds who flew to the top of a mountain from a dying world. And she remembers her mother whispering in her ear that she was not from here, she was from somewhere far, far away, and one day she would come back and take her little girl home . . .

There's another loud *pop*. Mona jumps. She peers at the tape player, puzzled. It isn't moving. But then, that pop sounded awfully metallic.

She sits back and sees over her shoulder that there's someone standing in the doorway, pointing something very large and very shiny at her, and she realizes the *pop* was not the tape player at all.

"Hey there, pretty lady," says a voice.

Without thinking, she tenses up.

"Ah-ah," says a voice. "You just hold on there. I would hate to do anything mean, you see. And what I got trained on your back does nothing but mean things."

Mona sees. She stays still.

"Hands," says the voice, relaxed. He sounds as if he's having just a ball of a time.

She raises her hands.

The barrel of the gun jerks up. "Now go on. Stand up."

Mona stands up. Then she turns her head to see who it is who's gotten the jump on her.

It is a young, chiseled-featured man wearing one of those not-really cowboy hats (because no real cowboy would be caught dead in that beaten straw thing), a pearl snap that is unsnapped past his sternum, and jeans so tight Mona is surprised he could get up the stairs to here. That is, if he *did* take the stairs. Despite these ridiculous ornamentations, he is quite attractive, and were this a year ago, when Mona idled her evenings away shithoused in dive bars, he would be the sort to receive from her a very, very forthright invitation to dance.

"Well, now," he says, and grins. It is a grin of perfect, thoughtless confidence. "What in the world is a cute thing like you doing in a place like this."

And that just does it. There is something in his cocksure smirk—perhaps its unearned, swaggering bravado—that makes Mona want to put a brick through it.

"Reading," says Mona.

"I don't really care," the man says. "It was one of them, eh. Rhetorical questions. You ain't supposed to be doing *any*thing in here. This ain't a place anyone's supposed to be in."

"Says who?"

"Says...says me. That's who." He looks around at the records room, uncertain. "Now...what the hell is this?"

He looks surprised—so he's been here a lot, but he's never seen this. "It is what it looks like, I guess," she says.

"How'd you find it?"

"By looking."

"Shit." He shakes his head, then nods his head down the hallway. "All right, then. Come on."

"Where are we going?"

"To wherever I say to go. I don't know how in the hell you got in here, but I know how you're getting out."

He steps to the side of the door and gestures with the gun. Mona, arms still raised, slowly walks out. But as she does, she eyes his piece. It's a Desert Eagle, the Humvee of pistols: ostentatious, impractical, ridiculous.

And he's holding it one-handed. She starts thinking.

He keeps the gun pointed at her while he enters the records room and picks up her backpack. "The shit?" he says, holding up the pink child's backpack. "What you got in here, Barbies?"

He starts digging through it. "Oh-ho." He holds up the Glock. "Goodness. This ain't no toy." He looks through the rest, smirking, and tosses the backpack over his shoulder. "Well, this is interesting. This is damn interesting," he says. "Now go on. Down the hallway."

They start walking. She listens hard, counting his footsteps. About four feet away, she thinks.

"So how'd you get in here?" he asks.

"I took the back door," she says.

"Oh, you did, did you?"

"Yes. And the stairs."

"The...stairs?" Mona can tell he's not sure if she's joking anymore. "What's your name?"

"Martha," she says, pulling a name out randomly.

"Like hell it is. You don't look no eighty years old, and that is a name for an eighty-year-old woman. What's your real name?"

"Martha," she says again. "What's yours?"

He laughs. "What the hell are you doing out here, Martha?"

"Reading."

He laughs again. "I'm going to enjoy you, I got to admit."

"Mister...what are you going to do to me?"

"Don't know. For now, we're just going to walk. Then I'm probably going to wind up taking you to meet some people."

"What kind of people?"

"The kind with questions. And those questions they got are the kind that get answered, if you see my meaning, Martha."

She is silent.

"You understand?" he asks.

"I understand."

"Good."

She angles her head to look at him over her shoulder. He lopes, strides, saunters. He is a perfectly relaxed creature, enjoying this game, ambling behind his captured quarry.

He hasn't done this before, she thinks. He doesn't know a damn bit about what he's doing. That doesn't mean she *has* to get ugly but, if she winds up having to, she's fairly confident she'll wind up on top.

She says, "Mister, I...I didn't know I was doing anything wrong."

Silence.

"I have a hundred dollars in my wallet. You can take it, if you just leave me be."

Of course, she has no such thing. She doesn't even have a wallet. But immediately she feels his hand invading her back pocket, and his fingertips encounter far more of her ass than is necessary for a wallet search. She flexes involuntarily, which makes him grip her buttock a little harder.

He removes his hand and laughs, delighted. "Bullshit. You ain't got no hundred dollars."

Mona is quiet.

"You got a lot, though. A whole lot."

She says nothing.

"And I'm in a pretty good mood today. A damn good mood. But it could get better. You know?"

She doesn't answer.

"Yeah. You know. You got a lot to give. And I'd let you go. If you were to give it. You see?"

She hears his footsteps getting closer behind her. She peers back over her shoulder a little, looking for the fish-lure silver of that ridiculous gun. He takes this for a positive signal, and moves a little bit closer.

Oh well, she thinks. *Might as well get ugly.*

There's a reason why, in real life, folks keep other folks at gunpoint from a distance of over four feet: primarily, if your guy jumps one way or another, you only have to move your aim a little bit to hit him. But if you're right up close and he jumps, you have to wheel around like an idiot to try to draw a bead.

So when Mona leaps back and to the left, she's out of the Desert Eagle's range of fire almost instantly. And, since he's holding this immensely heavy gun with just one hand, it only takes a firm grasp on his wrist and enough force down on the end of the barrel to pop it free from his grip, like a bar of soap in the shower.

For a moment they just stand there, Mona holding the gun by the barrel, the man staring at her blankly, wondering what just happened.

"Hey…" he says.

Which is when Mona pistol-whips him.

And maybe it's because she's still disturbed by what she discovered in this lab, or maybe it's because he just cupped her ass and suggested she fuck him for her freedom, but Mona puts a lot more weight into it than she normally would. The young man's cheek practically explodes. He staggers back against the wall, face bleeding freely, eyes wide. But there's something about hitting someone that makes you want to do it again, so Mona does. Six times more, in fact, each time about as hard as the last, and each time his Attractiveness Integer goes down a notch until he's nowhere near a 10.

When she's done she just stands there, breathing hard. It's dark, but his face looks caved in. She realizes she might have just killed him.

Then he moans. So he's still got a shot, unless she damaged his brain, but a lot of her work was on the more superficial parts of his face. *The world's loss*, she thinks.

She grabs her backpack, puts a boot in the middle of his back, and searches his pockets. She finds a set of keys, a wallet with a ton of money in it, and a piece of paper.

She reads it, squinting in the dark. It's directions of some kind, like he was sent to find something, and one of them tells him to check here.

So he was never meant to find her. That's good, she thinks. Then he must have come alone.

But they will be expecting him back, eventually. And since this is the last place on his list, it's likely it's the first place they'll look.

She stares back down the hallway. She wants to go back and grab as many of those old records as she can. Some piece of them, some rambling paragraph or static-smeared voice, must have a kernel of truth in it.

But she knows she can't risk it. She needs to leave, and soon.

She takes her boot off him and steps back a little. He is breathing, just barely. Mona has never killed anyone and she has no wish to start now, but abandoning him here might be a rough equivalent. Yet even she can see it's not particularly wise to try to lug an unconscious man down a mountain in the desert, especially one who now has plenty of reasons to kill her.

"You're on your own," she says. "Sorry."

She looks at his keys as she walks away. He seemed surprised to hear about a back door to this place. Which means he must have used another way in.

She walks until she feels a slight breeze on her face. She sees there's a little more light down one hallway than the others. She walks toward it, and finds there's a small, open door with a metal ladder inside, going up. Marked above it are the words EMERGENCY LADDER.

She starts climbing, the brilliant blue sky pouring in on her more and more with every rung. Then she heaves herself out.

The light is blinding after her hours in that shadowy place, but she's never been so happy to be out of the dark. She shuts her eyes, then cracks them and opens them wider and wider until she can see.

She's on the mesa top. She expected it to be a beautiful sight, but it's the exact opposite: the mesa is covered with twisted, blackened metal debris, shards of missing structures, exposed piping. Something big was here, she thinks, and she recalls the telescopes from the mural in the lab. But this does not look like the careful work of a government reclaiming its investment. Whatever was here was destroyed, decimated. It is a war zone.

She fights a wave of vertigo when she realizes how high she is. The brown ripples of hills and mountains stretch for miles in every direction. She walks to the edge and sees she can easily climb down, if she's careful. There's a glint of metal from just a few dozen yards ahead, and she can see a huge truck parked on a dirt road winding around the mesa. It must have been the cowboy's ride.

Then she stops. Thinks. And she turns around to examine the ruins on the mesa top once more.

Her perspective is a little better from here. She can see where the telescopes and the radio towers once stood. And perhaps Coburn himself once stood in this very place to watch the lightning in the sky.

But Mona's not interested in any of that. What she's interested in are the two huge, long depressions in the mesa's surface. They are more than a hundred feet long, oblong with undulating edges, forming awkward figure eights among all the devastation. They don't look natural, yet from the absence of piping or metal or concrete, they don't look man-made. But the damage to the mesa top radiates outward from them, as if it had been struck by two meteors...but meteors would have done a *lot* more damage to this place, and the two indentations in the mesa top would not match so perfectly.

They look, Mona thinks, a little like footprints. Big ones. As if something the size of the mountain itself once stood here, staring out at this dry, brown-red world, and the tiny town just below.

She remembers something from one of the tapes. She says it aloud, quietly: "There's something up there..."

She turns to leave as fast as she can.

The cowboy's truck is a battleship of a vehicle. Mona is about to hop in the cab when she recalls a time from her cop days when some foolish soul stole a truck with the owner's Rottweiler sleeping in the back, and was promptly mauled upon arrival at the chop shop. So, carefully, she walks to the edge of the truck bed and peers in.

It looks like the cowboy was preparing for a mining expedition. There are pickaxes, shovels, jackhammers, ropes, pulleys. There is a bundle at the end of the bed, something wrapped in canvas, presumably whatever the cowboy was mining.

Maybe it's gold, Mona thinks, for no reason.

Then she thinks: *What the fuck am I going to do with gold out here?*

She pulls the top of the canvas back. It is not gold, but two smallish cubes that look to be made out of old iron.

"Huh," says Mona, and she reaches out to pick up the smaller one.

She picks it up one-handed. It is not that heavy. But there is something odd about it. It does not feel like metal to her, but flesh. There is a give to it that is distinctly organic, and it sticks to her, like it doesn't want to be put down. Yet when she sets it back in the bed of the truck, it makes a metallic *clunk* sound.

It is when she takes her hand off of it that she suddenly smells something ionized and dusty, like a lightning strike out in the desert, and she imagines someone whispering softly in her ear…

She shudders. She needs to get the hell away from this place.

Mona throws the cab door open and looks in. Then she sees what's sitting on the floor of the passenger side.

Her jaw drops. "Oh, my God."

There are a few things you'd never guess about Mona from looking at her.

The first, as has been already mentioned, is her age. Mona is a good decade older than she appears to be, and on learning this people tend to instantly like her less. Partially it's because they are far more forgiving of her lifestyle if they think she's in her late twenties rather than late thirties, but mostly they're just upset she ages well and they usually don't.

The second thing is that Mona, who is an absolute tomboy in so many ways, is actually really good at crochet. She can make hats, scarves, mittens, potholders, and even coats of impressive quality and with many different and complicated patterns. She had to keep this a dead secret from her friends, especially those on the force, but she made quite a profitable side income selling her goods online.

And the third—which is probably the most surprising—is that Mona has probably received several times more expert rifle training than your average American soldier.

While her father roughnecked around West Texas, he and his daughter had little common ground until the day he took her deer hunting and she showed a remarkable aptitude with a gun. Part of it was just genetics, for Earl Bright himself had served in the 75th Ranger Regiment at the tail end of Vietnam, and had been a commendable marksman himself. Their hunting or training trips soon became the only oases in their acrimonious relationship, and Earl began taking her out to the country more and more, mostly just to get her to shut the hell up.

As a young girl Mona sucked up every bit of knowledge Earl Bright had to offer. She came to know the dance and wriggle of every type of round, the rifling twist rate of every rifle and the primer type of every commercially available cartridge, the difference between shooting with a hot barrel and a cold one. She came to intuit which parts of the landscape better serve the shot, and how to sit for hours at a time with her eye to a sight without allowing herself to cramp, how to ignore hunger for most of a day, how to keep her hands warm and functioning in the cold, and how to stalk through mesquite forests and huisache forests and pine forests.

Looking back, it is only fitting that Mona's childhood was not based around any sense of love, but the slow, bitter, patient task of killing. For a killing, as young Mona learned, does not start with the pull of a trigger and the bite of a bullet: a killing starts the instant your toe touches hunting ground and you begin circling what you've come there to fell.

So when Mona's eyes fall upon the marvelous piece of weaponry sitting up against the opposite truck door, it's a little like a Stradivarius falling into a violin prodigy's lap. To her this rifle is such a beautiful, powerful firearm that she almost cannot believe it. And when she grasps the stock and picks it up, a thousand muscle memories spring to life, kindling many long-dormant instincts and desires in her mind.

She can't imagine how much this thing must have cost. *Christ*, she thinks, and she smells its muzzle. It hasn't even been fired much. There are even boxes of rounds all over the floor.

She brings the butt up and peers through the optic. Then she wheels around and sights a tree below.

It has not been boresighted well: she immediately senses that the reticle is far too low for the distance to the tree. Were she to shoot now, the shot would be high. But she is overjoyed to have this realization come rushing into her head. It's like kissing or having sex for the first time in years: you remember where things are supposed to go, and how much they want to be there, and everything is so *impatient*.

She tosses her pink backpack in the cab and situates the rifle nearby. She wishes the cleaning tools were around, for she doesn't trust the state the cowboy left the rifle in, but it is still a gift.

She turns the truck on, the diesel engine guttering to a roar.

Maybe now, since things are going her way, she'll get some answers.

CHAPTER THIRTY-TWO

It is such a boring day for Megan Twohey, the most boring out of a boring couple of weeks. As she lies under a primrose jasmine, kicking at the cascade of leaves with her small bare feet, she reflects that all of this happened because of the funeral, which of course makes her wonder if this is her fault.

It shouldn't be, she thinks. She had never been to a funeral before. People die so rarely in Wink. When she first heard the news, she was so confused she asked her momma, "So what do we do now?"

"We pay our respects," said her momma. "We have to go and pay our respects, dear."

"How do we do that?"

"Well, we dress up, and we go see him get buried. We all go and hold hands and listen to the...the preacher speak. As a community."

"But I don't want to do that," said Megan.

"Well, that's too bad," said her momma. "You're going."

She wanted to ask her daddy what he thought. But her daddy stayed down in the basement, smoking cigarette after cigarette, and all they ever got out of him was a hoarse "Yes" or "No" or "Uh-huh" emanating from that thick blanket of smoke. She asked her momma once what he did down there, and her momma said, "Well, he..." and then she didn't say anything at all.

And since Megan had never been to a funeral, and since funerals are so stiff and uncomfortable, she behaved pretty poorly, taking off her shoes and picking at her toes, and though she didn't know it things got so bad that her momma got upset, like *crying* upset, and Megan's daddy leaned over, eyes glimmering and face cold, and he whispered something to her momma. Then her momma hauled Megan out to the parking lot where, for the first time in months, she pushed Megan over her knee and spanked her.

And this was not a spanking like any Megan had ever received before. This was no warning, no threatening tap. Two hits in, Megan realized her momma was really, genuinely trying to *hurt* her. And Megan got so scared she started crying too, and both of them just sat there in the car crying while those people put that box with the man in it in the ground.

"You can't do that," her momma said. "You can't do bad things in front of your neighbors. They all saw, all of them."

"I'm sorry! I didn't think it was bad."

"It was. It was so bad, Megan."

"I didn't know. I didn't, I promise."

"It doesn't matter," said her momma. She shook as she stared at the people standing around the hole in the ground. And then Megan realized her momma was scared, way more scared than she was, and she understood, a little, for there seemed to be so many unspoken rules to how adults lived their lives, always maintaining a constant image of prosperity and happiness. Megan felt sure she'd just shattered theirs for everyone, so went to see Lady Fish straightaway after, and that calmed her down a little.

But ever since, no one will come out to play. It is as if that day changed everyone. They stay inside, staring out the windows with wide, frightened eyes. It's like they're waiting for something. Only Megan gets let out to play, and that's because her momma sleeps all day now. And her daddy, of course, just stays down in the basement.

But there is no one to play with. Megan is alone. Even Lady Fish left, just up and vanished in the night.

She feels sure it is her fault. If she had not been bad in front of everyone, if they had not all been there to see, then perhaps everyone would still be happy together...

Megan sits up. Someone is walking her way through the brush. She peers through the branches and sees an old lady hiking across the hillside behind their house. Megan thinks she recognizes her, a little. Isn't she the lady from the courthouse, maybe? She isn't sure. Megan wonders if the old lady is coming for her, but she veers away down toward the woods at the bottom of the hill. Right away, Megan realizes where she's going.

Slowly, Megan creeps out of the jasmine's branches. She walks to the edge of the hill and sees the purple-and-white pattern of the lady's dress weaving through the pine trees.

She wasn't wrong. The old woman is going to where Lady Fish lived.

The thought first terrifies her, then intrigues her. She thought she was the only one who knew about it. But there's nothing down in the woods except that.

Megan wonders what to do. Should she tell her parents? She never told them about Lady Fish. But besides, what would she get out of her mother except a muttered plea for quiet, leaking out from underneath the pile of pillows on the bed? And her daddy...he wouldn't say anything.

Megan begins following the old woman's path down the hill. The soil grows very damp beyond the rocks at the bottom of the hill, and the trees ahead are very, very tall, unusually tall for this dry climate. A string of flat red rocks winds through the wet earth, and Megan has to hop from one to the other to get ahead, for just beyond the trees the ground just gets wetter and wetter, until it's almost like a marsh.

Megan had never seen a marsh before she found this place. She knows the marsh is there simply because Lady Fish wished it to be. And she is fairly sure no one else has found it, for no one ever goes into the woods. But she isn't sure why no one does. If people like Lady Fish live in the woods, wouldn't everyone want to go there?

But then she remembers one evening when Lady Fish, tall and shimmering and undulating, sang her a song about the other people in the woods, and how some slept and should not be woken, and some were quite upset to be there and should not be approached, and so on and so on...really, from the way Lady Fish described it, she was the only nice one in the forest.

And she *was* nice. On the days when her momma went down to the basement and came up cold and pale and stinking of cigarettes, Lady Fish was always there. She always had a few kind things to say. She was a wise, lovely person, Lady Fish.

Once Megan asked her why her momma and daddy seemed so unhappy sometimes. It was a question she had asked a few people, like teachers and the parents of friends, but they always grew awkward and coughed and changed the subject.

But Lady Fish didn't. She simply thought, and said (in her own special way of speaking), "Because they are pretending to be something that they aren't. We all are, child." And that was the perfect thing to say.

Megan misses her so much. How awful it was to come to her home, and call her name before the opening in the earth, and not hear the sucking of mud, the bubbling of water, and Lady Fish's low purr as she rose up to visit. Megan called her name again and again, but she did not come. It was then that Megan knew she was truly alone.

She stops behind a tree. She can see the old woman standing in front of Lady Fish's house. The opening in the ground is long and wide, like Lady Fish herself, and it turns away to coil underneath the hill. But though it is wet and stinking, the old woman hikes up her skirts and carefully descends.

Megan is shocked. She would have never dreamed of doing such a thing. Lady Fish's home was her own. It was not a place for visitors, not even Megan.

She walks to the edge and looks down. How often she observed the curves and crenellations of the muddy earth conforming to meet Lady Fish's long, swirling shape...

Then the old woman's face appears at the bottom of the tunnel. Her face and hands are filthy with mud. "Hello, there," she says.

Megan jumps. Then she draws back, slowly.

"Oh, don't be frightened, dear," says the old woman. She climbs out of the tunnel with remarkable agility. "I won't hurt you. I'm not here for you at all."

Megan still keeps her distance. The old woman smiles and sits down on the ground. "I think you're here for the same reason I am," she says.

Megan still does not trust her enough to answer.

"By which I mean, we share a common acquaintance." The old woman nods at the tunnel.

"Are you a friend of hers?" asks Megan.

"*Hers?*" asks the old woman, as if a little surprised to hear the term. "Oh. Well. I am actually, erm, her sister, if you must know."

"Her sister? No, you're not."

"I most certainly am, dear."

"But you don't look anything alike."

"That does not mean we are not sisters. It's why I've come looking for her." She looks back at the tunnel, concerned. "How long has she been gone?"

"Why?" asks Megan.

"Because I am worried about her." She pats the ground next to her. "Come sit by me. There's nothing to be troubled about."

Though initially reluctant, Megan does so. It is hard to mistrust a little old lady covered in mud.

"She was your friend, wasn't she?" the old woman asks.

Megan nods. "Was it wrong?"

"Was what wrong?"

"That we were friends," says Megan.

"Why would you ask that?"

"Because I do a lot of bad things," says Megan. "It's why everyone left. Why Lady Fish left."

"Lady Fish? Who do you mean by . . . ah. I see." The old lady considers it. "You think she left because of you? Well, I very much doubt that."

"You do?" asks Megan, hopefully.

"Yes," says the old woman. "You don't seem to be a very bad girl to me. And I think she had other reasons for leaving."

"Are you going to try and bring her back?"

"If she wishes to, I will try to make that happen."

"I hope you do," says Megan. "I miss her."

"You were very close, I take it."

Megan nods.

"When did she leave?"

"After the funeral."

"Mr. Weringer's funeral?" asks the old woman.

"I don't know his name."

"I see," says the old woman. "So it was very recent, then. Did she say anything to you before she left?"

Megan thinks as she stares down into the tunnel. And she remembers. It can be so hard sometimes to remember their conversations. It's like having spoken to someone in a dream.

"She said she was worried about me," she says. "She said...she never wanted anything to happen to me."

"Did she," says the old woman.

"But I wasn't sure why I would be in trouble. I hadn't done anything then. And I'm not in trouble, am I?"

"I have no reason to think so." The old woman goes silent, thinking. Then she looks around the edges of Lady Fish's house, examining the mud. "Hm."

"What is it?" asks Megan.

"Nothing, but...was anyone else here? Recently, I mean. Did anyone else come to see Lady Fish?"

Megan thinks. It seems like so long ago...but then she remembers one evening when she sneaked out of the house to see Lady Fish, because she had heard shouting from down in the basement, and her mother kept going down and coming up and going down, and the smell of cigarettes was so strong Megan just had to get out of the house, and she went straight to Lady Fish...but she saw someone was there.

"A man," says Megan. "A man came to see her."

"And who was this man?"

"I don't know."

"You don't?"

"No."

"Well, what did he look like?"

Megan thinks hard. "He was wearing a hat."

"A hat?"

"A white hat."

"A white hat...," says the old woman. "Hm. No, that doesn't mean anything to me. But perhaps it is something. Did you hear what they were discussing?"

"I could hear what he said. But I couldn't hear what Lady Fish was saying. You never can, unless she's talking to you."

"Really? She must be one of the very young ones, then. What did this man say?"

"He said he needed help. Help in bringing someone back, I think. And Lady Fish needed to come with him."

The old woman goes very still. She stares through the trees into the sunset, her face grave.

"I see," she says quietly. "That is very good to know, then. Very, very good." She stands up. "I must go now, my dear. You have been very helpful. For that I thank you."

"Will you find her?" asks Megan.

"I hope to."

"And she'll come back?"

"I'm afraid I don't know, my dear," the old woman says.

"But you have to know," says Megan. "How can you not know?" The loneliness that descends on her is blank and crushing. She sits down on the marshy ground and begins to cry.

The old woman, who previously seemed so grandmotherly, simply watches, her eyes small and inscrutable. It is then that Megan begins to feel, even through her sobs, that all of this person's actions and behaviors have been an affectation, like she was repeating lines from a memorized script that has worked well for her so far; and yet when confronted with something unwritten—like the sobbing of a small child—she has no idea what to do. She only stares, indifferent, unmoved.

"Understand," says the old woman, her voice wry and cold. "Understand, understand, understand. Understand that this is not a tragedy.

This is not a thing to be mourned. You should be relieved. What happened here was no more than glimpsing something from the side of your eye, but you did not fully witness it, you did not fully see, comprehend, know. If you had, well…what you saw and what you spoke to and what you think you possessed was an illusion, a mistranslation, a deception. Perhaps she deceived you, or she deceived herself, I cannot say. But I will say that you are a very lucky girl, not because you met Lady Fish, but because you met her and still exist. In a fashion."

"I don't understand," says Megan, sobbing.

"No," says the old woman. "And for that you should be very thankful." She turns and begins to walk farther into the forest.

"Where are you going?" asks Megan after her.

"To do the same thing many times over, I expect," says the old woman. "To knock upon many doors, and receive no answer. Do not follow me, girl. Where I go, you cannot come back from." And the old woman fades into the trees, and is gone.

Megan sits on the muddy ground, clutching her knees. Then, still sniffling, she stands up and walks to Lady Fish's home. She stares into it, trying to draw comfort from memories of her past meetings here. None comes.

She sits and slides down into the opening in the earth. The slick, dripping walls enclose her legs and shoulders. She keeps going down until she can no longer see open sky, and there she curls up into a ball and begins rocking back and forth, remembering better days when there was a voice in the darkness that told her everything was all right, and all the daily wounds life dealt her were far away, and nothing hurt.

CHAPTER THIRTY-THREE

Fucked, fucked, and more fucked, thinks Bolan. He cracks open another bottle of Pepto, the third tonight, and pounds it. *Triple-fucked*, he thinks. *Quintuple-fucked. Octuple-fucked.* More, perhaps, but his math skills are lacking.

Bolan sits on a column of boxes in the exact pose of Rodin's *Thinker*, staring out at the large basement below the Roadhouse. Every square foot is filled with large boxes, and inside each of these boxes are four shrink-wrapped sets of encyclopedias. To the average eye these would appear unremarkable, but within the fourth set in each box, in a hollowed-out space starting at *Uganda* and ending at *ultimatum*, is somewhere around seventy thousand dollars' worth of heroin. Where these encyclopedias go, Bolan isn't sure. But people pay a lot of money to make sure they get there.

He is trying to do three things right now. The first is to calculate exactly how much money is currently in his warehouse. This involves maneuvering around some astronomical numbers, but he is pretty sure he has about twenty million dollars' worth of heroin here at this moment, ten million dollars' worth of cocaine, and about twenty thousand dollars' worth of encyclopedias (which no one gives a shit about, of course).

The second thing he is trying to do is comprehend exactly where the encyclopedias and the heroin come from. The origin of the cocaine he knows, having arranged that deal himself with the funds generated from the heroin. But the heroin itself is a mystery. Before today he always believed (or perhaps *chose* to believe) that the man in the panama hat simply acted as a connection between Bolan and some foreign source. Yet after covertly sending out feelers into the networks of New Mexico, Bolan now knows that absolutely no heroin is being routed *to* the Roadhouse, especially not in any encyclopedias. It is only coming *from* the Roadhouse. Which means that these shipments he has Zimmerman pick up from many hidden caches in Wink are coming from somewhere local.

Perhaps Wink itself.

And that's odd. Because last Bolan checked, there were no enormous poppy fields around Wink.

The third thing Bolan is trying to do is keep himself from thinking about a nasty suspicion he has: that the heroin he is distributing across the Southwest, and also throughout Wink, serves a purpose beyond making a lot of fucking money. What that purpose would be escapes him.

But though Bolan doesn't remember a lot from his school days, one little factoid has come swimming up in his brain more and more: his history teacher once told them that Greek oracles had to ingest some very funny mushrooms to act as conduits for whichever god needed to speak. Bolan does not believe in a god or gods, but this bit of knowledge has somehow gotten stuck in his head: people might need a narcotic aid to navigate realms of the unknown.

And to his regret, Bolan knows there are a lot of unknown realms in Wink.

Is it possible that the only reason he is making millions of dollars off of heroin is that the man in the panama hat needs a select few citizens of Wink to be high?

The idea is stupid, ridiculous, laughable. Why would he need them to be high? What purpose could that serve? Well, they would need to be, reasons Bolan, if they had to go someplace the man in the panama hat could not go himself, and do something he could not do. But if he wants that, why not distribute the heroin himself?

Well, thinks Bolan, *because he's being watched too. He needs someone outside, someone distant.*

Yet even if all this is true—and every conclusion is one hell of a stretch—why provide a warehouse-load of illicit drugs? Why not give Bolan just enough to get the necessary people doped up? Why give Bolan millions of dollars' worth of product?

That one is a tough nut to crack. But Bolan thinks he knows.

They don't understand how people work. Not really. They couldn't present just a tempting offer: they had to make it unbelievable, something he absolutely could not pass up. Subtleties of any kind are lost on them.

And all of these mental arguments, which take several hours to sort out, lead to one question Bolan is absolutely terrified of:

If the people in Wink are able to make a fount of endless heroin out of nothing…what else can they do?

There is a tapping at the door, and Bolan jumps and nearly topples off the boxes. "Christ!" he says. "What?"

Dord is standing at the threshold. He is pale and twitching: one hand keeps tugging at his belt loops.

"Yeah?" Bolan asks.

"Got a call from Zimmerman," says Dord. "He found Dee."

"Yeah?"

"He was unconscious. Someone beat his face in."

"At the *lab*?"

Dord nods. Then he begins bobbing his head as if he's forgotten the conversation entirely and is listening to a song. He's obviously coked to the gills.

"Who the hell goes up to the lab except us?" asks Bolan. "Us and…" He gestures toward nothing with a nod. The man in the panama hat is such a presence in every conversation that he hardly needs to be acknowledged.

"Don't know," says Dord. "Zimmerman says Dee's up but he's not talking so good. Concussion, probably."

"Christ."

Bolan considers the conversation to be closed, but Dord keeps standing there.

"What?" asks Bolan.

"One more thing, boss," says Dord. "It's, uh—talking."

"What?"

"It's talking. Typing."

"What is?"

"That thing in your office. The light's on."

"What! You should have fucking said that first!" Bolan hops down off the column of boxes and sidles past Dord and makes his way upstairs.

He unlocks and enters the soundproof passageway. The stock ticker has printed out a long line of tape. It is the same word, over and over again, evidently repeated when Bolan did not answer:

MEETING   MEETING   MEETING
        MEETING   MEETING

"What's this?" says Bolan. "A meeting?"

A pause. Then:

YES

"A meeting between who?"

Another pause. Then the stock ticker types away:

BETWEEN   AND
                YOU   ME

Bolan pales. "You want us to meet? Then . . . well, come right up, I guess."

NOT   TONIGHT   GULCH   HIGHWAY
    HERE   AT   BY   CROSSROADS

He almost chokes. "What? You want me to come to *Wink*?"

The machine is still. Bolan imagines it to be a hunched predator contemplating its next move.

Then:

YES

MIDNIGHT

"But...I can't...I can't go there!"

The stock ticker is silent. It must not find that response to be worth an answer.

Then:

YOU   HAVE   LOOK
    WILL   TO   DOWN

Bolan stares at the tape. This has absolutely no meaning to him. "I don't understand," he says.

It barrels on without him:

YOU   WHERE   TAKE   NEXT
    KNOW   TO   THE   TOTEM

"Yes," says Bolan. "They're already on it. There might be a bit of a delay—my boy got his face caved in just today. But they'll be at the canyon soon."

The machine pauses for a long, long time. Longer than the machine has ever paused before. Bolan almost wonders if they've gotten pissed at him and given up.

But then it types:

I   NOT   THERE
    MAY   BE

"What? At the canyon?" Bolan realizes this is wrong. "Wait, you mean at the meeting? Then where will you be?"

Another extremely long pause.

The machine types:

DEAD

Bolan is utterly flabbergasted to read such a response. "What the fuck? Are you serious?"

It types:

AM   TO   SOMETHING
     ABOUT   ATTEMPT   DRASTIC

"Wait, like . . . more than what we've already done?"

It responds:

YES

"Well . . . then don't fucking do it!"

The machine types:

IF   AM   THERE   YOU   STILL   MET
    I   NOT   TONIGHT   WILL   BE

"By who?" asks Bolan.

The ticker is silent.

"By who?" he asks again. "What's going on? What are you about to do?"

But no matter how long he waits, he receives no answer.

CHAPTER THIRTY-FOUR

Evening is falling by the time Mona returns to Wink. She feels as if she is seeing it for the first time. She looks at the quaint adobe homes and the little cottages with sky-blue siding, the old men at the drugstore and the children playing tag at the greenbelt. The streetlamps are pristine, the grass moist, the trees thick and tall. A place of quiet days and quieter evenings.

And yet.

A man stands on the sidewalk, perfectly still, with his hands at his sides. He wears a charmingly cheap suit that is a few sizes too large for him. He stares at the sky with his head cocked as if he is listening to something only he can hear, and when she passes him in the huge truck he looks at her and smiles wistfully. She keeps watching him in the rearview mirror: he returns to staring at the powder-blue sky, a wide smile on his face.

Is he one of them? Are any of the people she sees?

A young woman stands in a gravel alley between two homes. A frail thing with skinny wrists. She holds an empty tin can in her hands and she turns it over again and again, feeling its metal sides, and as she does she twirls about in a slow shuffle, as if dancing with it.

What does she feel when she touches this mundane little trinket? Mona wonders. What do they see when they look at the world?

An old man stands in the window of the hardware store, staring out with eyes rimmed blue-black. His hands are spattered with what looks like ink, maybe black paint. He holds a bowl and a fork, and he dips the fork down into the bowl and brings up a steaming pile of mashed potatoes. He opens his mouth hugely, far wider than he should, and paints his tongue with the forkful, unblinking, not swallowing. As his hands rise the black ink runs down his forearms in rivulets to stain his shirtsleeves.

He is one. There is no doubt.

How many are there? They seem to be everywhere, when you look: stragglers occupying drab little between-places in the town, ditches and empty parking lots and alleys behind shops. The interstitial parts of a city no one ever thinks about. These places, perhaps, are where these dazed wanderers go to collect their thoughts, to be themselves.

To be themselves, thinks Mona. *Whatever they are, behind their eyes.*

And when they are done, will they return home, cheery smiles on their faces, ready to put food on the table? To cut the grass or play a game of cards or share a pipe? To gossip and scratch off yet another day in their peaceful, small-town lives? Is that it?

What do they do? What do such people do? Why are they here?

She circles the block twice, easing through the alleys, counting all the cars and memorizing the license plates. She sees no one watching, no shift of a curtain or movement in any of the cars, and she certainly sees no one tailing her—road traffic here is so sparse it'd be almost impossible to stay hidden.

When she's as satisfied as she can get, she parks down the street from Mrs. Benjamin's house and watches it.

Once she had lunch there, only a few days ago. Yet now she wonders what lives in that house, or pretends to live there, and what it does when no one's watching.

She takes out the Glock and wipes sweat from her brow. She does not want to do this. Yet she must know.

She gets out of the truck and walks to the front door, barely bothering to hide the gun in her hand. She goes to the window and peers in. The house is dark, but she is not sure that means anything.

She goes to the door, and is not surprised to find it is unlocked. After all—why would such a thing ever need to lock the doors?

She walks in. The dark color of the floor and walls makes the house even darker. It is still every inch an old woman's house, stuffed with ticking clocks and piles of mail and forgettable trinkets. She hears nothing. It seems the owner is not at home.

Mona stalks through the house, gun drawn, eyes hunting for any movement. She turns left and follows a short hallway to the bedroom. And there she sees him.

He is lying on the bed with his fingers threaded together on his chest, peaceful as the dead. Yet she can see he is not dead, not quite: his chest rises and falls, slowly.

He looks the same, like your average old man. Perhaps a little caustic. Someone who has spent too much of his life indoors.

She sits down in the overstuffed chair beside Parson. She looks into his face and wonders what is behind it. It is not, she thinks, an eccentric old man who's spent his waning years running a motel. Any more than the owner of this house is a doddering old bureaucrat.

She raises the gun a little, but does not point it at him. The clocks seem to tick louder and louder. She wonders what it would be like to break their ponderous ticking and spill his skull across these yellowed sheets.

Would it be such a bad thing? Would it be wrong? Would it even do anything?

There is a voice from the door: "No. No, it would do nothing."

Mona very nearly pulls the trigger. She looks up and sees Mrs. Benjamin is standing at the door, and though she watches Mona coolly, indifferently, her dress is muddy, torn, and tattered. Streaks of blood show through the rents in the blotchy purple fabric.

"You stay right there," says Mona.

"I am," says Mrs. Benjamin. "I would wish no violence on him."

They stare at each other for a moment. In the hall the clocks tick and tock endlessly.

"Why wouldn't it?" asks Mona.

Mrs. Benjamin cocks an eyebrow, uncomprehending.

"Why wouldn't it hurt him?" she explains.

Mrs. Benjamin is silent.

"You aren't permitted to say," says Mona.

"No," says Mrs. Benjamin. "We are not."

"*We*," says Mona. "How many?"

Mrs. Benjamin still does not answer. The clocks tick on and on.

"Tell me," says Mona. "Tell me or I'll pull this trigger and blow his fucking brains out."

"Did I not just say it would do nothing?"

"Are you telling me the bullet in the chamber of this gun wouldn't punch through to his brain and turn it to soup? I've seen it before. Oh Lord, I've seen it before. It makes a mess, Mrs. Benjamin. You'd be doing laundry for days."

Mrs. Benjamin purses her lips.

"Yeah," says Mona. "I don't quite know what you all are, but I know you aren't bulletproof. How many?"

"If you know so much, why don't you guess?"

Mona can feel sweat running down her arms. She glances at Parson, then back at Mrs. Benjamin. "Can't be the whole town. Not everyone. Most of them are people, real people. But you all are... from somewhere else."

Mrs. Benjamin raises her head and thins her eyes, an inscrutable gesture that neither affirms nor denies it.

"I've been up on the mesa," says Mona.

"Have you," says Mrs. Benjamin. "*He* sent you there, didn't he?"

"Yeah. He wanted me to know. And now I do. I saw the records there. I know your mirror trick now."

She expected that to get some reaction from her, but Mrs. Benjamin does nothing. Then Mona realizes—how could she have expected such a thing to react in any normal way?

"It makes things soft, doesn't it?" asks Mona. "*Bruised.* It makes the boundaries of things...permeable. And when that happens, things can come through. Things like you, and him."

Mrs. Benjamin is stone-faced, dead-eyed, totally dormant. Mona gets the feeling that certain muscles are going slack in her face that no normal person could relax. The hairs rise up on Mona's arms as she begins to understand that Mrs. Benjamin's physical form is but a puppet in a very real way, and she's no longer bothering to maintain her appearance.

"What are you?" asks Mona softly. "Don't tell me you can't say."

"I cannot," says Mrs. Benjamin.

"Don't tell me you're not fucking permitted."

"The issue is not so much that," says Mrs. Benjamin.

"Then what is it?"

"Such things cannot be explained."

"Why not?"

"How does one tell a fish it swims in an ocean? How would one tell it of currents, of skies, of mountains? How could you make it understand?"

"Tell me anyway. I'm a quick study."

"I cannot."

"Do it."

"I cannot. It would kill you."

There is a rattling gasp in the room. Mona tenses up, but does not take her eyes off Mrs. Benjamin. Then she glances to the side and sees Parson's eyes fluttering. He frowns, shifts on the bed, and opens his eyes. He does not look at the gun, but stares straight ahead.

"She is not like the others," he says in a croaking voice.

Mrs. Benjamin and Mona do not move. The clocks keep ticking, on and on.

"That does not mean she can understand," says Mrs. Benjamin.

"We can try to show her," says Parson.

"What do you mean?" asks Mrs. Benjamin.

"The hell are you talking about?" asks Mona.

He does not answer either of them.

"Do you mean...take her *there*?" asks Mrs. Benjamin.

"Yes," says Parson. "And see what she can see."

"Take who where?" asks Mona.

"It would destroy her. She cannot go to such places mindfully. She is not like us."

"Mm. No," he says. He turns his head to look at Mona, totally ignoring the gun in his face. "She is not bound to this place, like we are. But neither is she truly free. She is drawn here against her will. She is different."

"Different enough?" asks Mrs. Benjamin.

Parson does not answer. He just stares at Mona.

Mrs. Benjamin sighs. "Do you really want to see, dear?"

"See what?" asks Mona.

"What we are. What we are underneath it all."

"What we are on the other side," says Parson.

"What we were in the beginning," says Mrs. Benjamin.

"Do you want to see?"

"Do you wish us to take you there?"

"To the halfway spot, not here, not there?"

"Where we reside?"

Mona is trembling. They speak so fast it is hard to keep up. "What the hell are you all talking about? If you're gonna try something, hurry up and do it. But I am handy with a gun."

"We have no reason to harm you," says Mrs. Benjamin.

"But what I know—"

"You know what you know," says Parson, "because I led you to it."

Mona sees the truth in this, but she still is not comfortable with what they are suggesting. "I thought it wasn't permitted," she says.

"You know enough," says Parson. "We would not be showing you something new."

"Nothing you do not suspect," says Mrs. Benjamin.

Mona pauses, uncertain. But she cannot turn away, not now.

"All right," she says.

Mrs. Benjamin and Parson glance at one another, faces slack and dead, eyes watery and small.

"Please put down the gun," says Parson. "Please."

Mona hesitates, but lowers it.

"Good," says Parson. "Now."

For a moment nothing happens, and Mona thinks they have just tricked her. Yet the two do not pounce on her, but stay stock-still.

The clocks stop ticking in the hallway. Everything in the room is silent: all the background noise, the susurrus of sounds from the forest and streets, has died. Then the walls begin to tremble and shudder, like they are drum skins being fiercely beaten by hammers, and with each blow they become more and more transparent until finally Mona can see out of them, glimpsing red stars and a huge pink moon and a gray, lunar terrain...

And then she sees

(no no)
(please no)

(endless canyons)
(glittering flats)

(and there beside her, swaying)

(a column, a stalk)
(tall, tall, infinitely tall)
(rigid and chitinous and dripping)
(hollow, honey-chambered)
(countless sinews and polyps)

(and in each chamber)
(a tiny black eye)

(like a fungus, she thinks, a huge, dripping fungus)
(roots like the root of a tooth)
(worming down into the heart of the world)

(and there beside it she sees)

(bulky and broad, shoulders spanning miles)
(thousands of powerful limbs)
(clutch the ground)

(a tiny, malformed skull)
(hundreds of spider eyes)
(like black marbles, glittering)

(she feels herself shake)
(it is too much)

(too)
(much)

Mona awakes gripping the carpet so hard she feels certain she's broken her left ring finger. She is facedown on the ground. Every muscle in her body is tense to the point of snapping. She can't even remember how to breathe. Then she gasps and goes limp.

"She's alive," she hears Mrs. Benjamin say, with some amount of surprise.

"Did I not tell you?" asks Parson.

"But is she whole?"

Mona just lies there blinking for a moment, telling her body to remember how to draw air. She feels fluid running down her face and she realizes she is weeping.

In some sensible part of her malfunctioning brain, she is beginning to understand that all information, from numbers to colors to sensations to words, is really just a means of establishing perspective: we know what green is only because we have blue to compare it to, just as we can understand three because we can match it up with two and see there is one more. The approximate qualities, behavior, and pattern of any witnessable occurrence are determined only by how it is like and unlike its neighbors; we know a thing only to the degree that we know what it is next to.

And what Mona just experienced for that one awful, endless, titubant moment neighbors nothing at all. She has nothing to compare it to. All of her many frames of reference, which were so carefully, thoughtlessly constructed during all of her life, and which she always assumed to be as solid and undeniable as the very earth, have been proven to be tottering, fragile little popsicle-stick structures, vulnerable to a breeze or a shift in the carpet.

Her faculties struggle under the weight of this revelation. It is too much. Her mind wishes to throw its hands up and quit.

But she will not let it: she rallies, coughs, and says, "What...what the fuck?"

"Apparently so," says Parson.

She rolls over and sees the two of them standing over her, their figures indistinct in the dark room. Immediately she shoves herself away and looks for the gun, but it is nowhere to be found. She crawls to the corner and grabs a lamp and threatens to throw it. She's too shaken to realize how ridiculous she looks.

"Do you see now?" asks Mrs. Benjamin. "Do you see what we are?"

"What you are?" asks Mona. "Those...that...that's what you *are*?"

They are silent, two shapeless shadows slouching in the center of the dark room. Slowly, the clocks in the hallway resume their ticking. The two of them shift a little bit, and evening light spills in, lighting a bit of their faces.

Mona can see their eyes. There is something behind them, something wriggling, squirming.

"Yes," says Mrs. Benjamin.

"We are not from here, Mona Bright," says Parson.

"Nor are we *here*, not entirely," says Mrs. Benjamin.

"Just a bit of us is," says Parson. "As the tip of an iceberg pokes past the ocean's surface, yet the rest of it lies below."

"Hidden."

"You cannot grasp it, cannot comprehend its size, its breadth. Just as you—or most of your kind, at least—cannot see us."

"Jesus," says Mona. "What...what are you all? Monsters?"

"Monsters?" asks Mrs. Benjamin. "We have been thought such before."

"And we have also been thought of as gods," says Parson.

"In the places we took."

"The worlds we conquered."

"In the other place."

"Elsewhere from this."

"Our family is vast, Mona Bright," says Mrs. Benjamin. "And we are most esteemed. You cannot imagine what we have conquered, what we have controlled, there in the aspects of reality you and your kind still have not touched."

"Imagine a building, tall and narrow, many floors, many stairs," says Parson. "Many, many tiny rooms, many places stacked on one another. In some spots they overlap, but in most they are whole, contained, hermetic. Walls stiff and unyielding. Most people in the building would only live on one floor, one level. One plane. Yet imagine if someone could live in several at the same time, occupying many places, many floors, rising up through the whole of the building and moving through it all at once, just as sea creatures move through many meters of the sea, vertically, horizontally."

"Pandimensional," Mona says.

"Yes," says Parson.

"We are from a place underneath this one," says Mrs. Benjamin.

"Behind it."

"Beside it."

"Above it, around it."

"Everywhere," says Mrs. Benjamin.

"Then why the hell are you here?" asks Mona.

They pause and glance at each other. Their eyes seem to move independently of their slack faces.

"We were forced to leave," says Mrs. Benjamin.

"Yes. And come here," says Parson.

"We are ... emigrants."

"Refugees, you could say."

"And this place is our haven."

"To an extent," corrects Parson, sounding suddenly bitter.

"Christ," says Mona. "This is what you were trying to tell me with your little fable, wasn't it ... your story about the birds in the trees."

Parson nods.

She laughs madly. "But you don't look like any fucking birds I know. Not how you really are, I mean. In that...that place." She stops laughing as she remembers a line from Parson's story: *Then one evening a terrible storm broke open in the skies...*

And it all begins to make sense.

"And you didn't just fly here, did you," she says. "You didn't crawl out of the mirror, or the lab. And you didn't just pop into existence."

"No," says Parson.

"The change happened to the whole town," says Mona. "To everyone. Everything. You came here in the storm. That was what it was. But it wasn't really a storm, or *just* a storm."

"No," says Parson.

"It was bruising," says Mona. "Bruising *miles* wide. It was just a bunch of doors opening everywhere, all at once. Wasn't it?"

"In a way," says Mrs. Benjamin. She stares at the ceiling. "The whole sky opened up," she says. "And then we came."

And she begins to speak.

CHAPTER THIRTY-FIVE

The evening was cool, dry, and quiet, like all evenings in Wink. Mrs. Benjamin had passed the day as she passed nearly all of them, whiling the hours away in bored tedium at her desk, kept afloat only by the rumors people dropped by, each one spawning hours of gleeful conjecture. For despite her bureaucratic title in the small government town, Mrs. Benjamin's true role, the only one that mattered, was that of town gossip.

And despite the fact that almost nothing happened in Wink—for the lab on the mountain had made no discoveries, nor had it attracted any worthwhile attention in years—Mrs. Benjamin still ran a thriving trade. Her chief strength was fashion, for she and she alone was the unspoken authority on what was and was not acceptable these days. And these days were quite deplorable, really: she could not bear to see men sport such ridiculous sideburns and gaudy glasses, and it was wise not to even get her started on the women, in their absurd, ragged pants and low-cut tops and untamed hair.

For years Mrs. Benjamin had been doing her damnedest to keep all of that out. It was mainly her efforts that had protected Wink from the encroaching decades: they'd made it to 1983 without showing any sign of having moved past 1969, and she intended to make that last until she was in the ground. Then those children could do as they please, but perhaps—just perhaps—they'd feel a twinge of regret for disobeying Mrs. Benjamin's silent strictures. Because, after all, Mrs. Benjamin was undeniably right.

As the sky grew darker, she sat on her porch and surveyed the street, sipping her tea and waiting for someone to stroll by so she could plumb them for information.

But she was not wholly interested in her duties: she kept glancing toward the mesa, idly wondering if the lightning would be there again.

It had been there every night for the past month or so. No one was quite sure what it was. Was it heat lightning? It made no sound, but still . . . no one had ever seen heat lightning like that. Perhaps it was something to do with the lab . . . No one knew.

There was a spark in the skies. Mrs. Benjamin, pleased, sat up and hauled her rocking chair around to face the horizon.

They'd had parties when it first started, picnics on the baseball field as they watched the show in the sky. It was like their own version of the Northern Lights. Though they did not understand it, they were glad to have it.

But this night the lightning was curiously brighter than normal. The sight was so queer Mrs. Benjamin simply stared at it, transfixed. Sometimes it looked like the lightning in the sky backlit something, some form in the clouds. In her more fanciful moments, she imagined there was a giant in the sky, huge and dark, looking out at the town from its vantage point in the sky.

There was another flicker, but this one was different: it was closer. She frowned, and watched as the heart of another cloud burst with lightning, this one closer still.

That was odd. The lightning usually stayed directly over the mesa. But as she watched, the flickers in the sky marched across the clouds as if jumping across links in a chain, bit by bit, until they came almost to hover over the town.

Mrs. Benjamin stood and walked to the center of her yard, looking up. She heard squeaking, and saw young Eddie Jacobs riding his old bicycle down the sidewalk. The squeaking slowed as he came to a stop, looking up, openmouthed. He got off and let his bike fall to the ground. Then, wordlessly, the two of them wandered over to stand next to one another and stare at the sky.

Then the lightning died. The two of them blinked and looked around.

"That was funny," said Eddie.

"It was, wasn't it," said Mrs. Benjamin.

Yet then a soft breeze filled her yard, and she frowned, for she smelled something quite odd . . .

Was it ozone?

One of the clouds built to a point. Its innards flickering mutinously. Then it blazed bright, and a rope of lightning stabbed down into the rooftops.

She had only a moment to register the sight before the blast hit her. It was like an artillery shell had just gone off, a tremendous eruption that sent her staggering back.

She fell onto the grass. The wind raged around her, pulling at her hair and her dress. Her eyes wheeled about until she saw another bolt of lightning shoot down into Wink, and another, and another, each one followed by the screaming, earth-shattering crashes.

When she regained herself, she heard the wailing of air-raid sirens as some long-dormant disaster system rattled awake. Then she saw a faraway tree lit by dancing red light, and gasped.

"Fire," she said, though she was almost deaf to her own voice. "Eddie—run home. Get on your bike and run home and get your parents!"

Eddie leaped onto his bike and pedaled away. Mrs. Benjamin managed to stand back up and started to rush off toward the fire, not certain what she would do if she got there. More bolts of lightning came shooting down, decimating houses, shops, trees. A florist's shop mere yards away burst apart as one of the arcs of lightning brushed it, sending waves of dust dancing across the street. People rushed out of their homes, looking about wildly, holding hands.

She could hear screams. Some sounded like women and men. Others, children.

"My God!" cried Mrs. Benjamin. "My God, my God!"

She was near a corner when one of the bolts of lightning struck the middle of the street just around the bend. It almost knocked her over again, and she had to hold on to a lamppost to stay up. When she recovered, she saw red-and-orange light flickering on the houses across the road. The middle of the street just around the corner must have been on fire.

Yet there was a shadow projected onto the houses by the flames. She was not sure if she was imagining things, but if the shadow was right, something huge and many-limbed was standing in the street, just out of view around the corner. She stared at the shadow, watching its arms heave as whatever it was took huge, gasping breaths, like some kind of enraged animal, and though the whole town was roaring with thunder and fire she thought she could hear deep, rattling gasps...

She walked closer to the corner, wondering if she really wanted to look down that street, and see... but then she heard an awful noise from just around the corner, like a thousand cicadas beginning to whine, and she knew she had to run, run as fast as she could.

Because there'd been something inside that lightning bolt. Something had come down from the sky with it. And Mrs. Benjamin did not know what it was, but she did not want to see it, or for it to see her.

She saw Mr. Macey running in her direction. "Myrtle!" he shouted. "Myrtle, for Christ's sake, don't go that way! Everything's on fire back there!"

"But you can't go that way, either!" she said, pointing at the corner. "There's . . . something there!"

"What?" he cried. "What's there? What do you mean?"

"I don't know! But there's something in the lightning bolts! Something's coming down with them!"

"Have you lost your fucking mind?" he screamed. This made her pause, for never in her life had she ever heard Eustace Macey use such a word. "We've got to move!"

"But Eustace, please! You can't—"

She stopped. Though the air was thick with smoke and brilliant light, she saw through it, just briefly, and glimpsed the mesa just a few miles out of town.

The top of the mesa was on fire. All the dishes and satellites and telescopes there were in ruins. But the fire on the mesa lit something above it . . . something massive and dark, swaying back and forth . . . and she thought she saw **eyes**, *yellow and luminous like huge lamps . . .*

"There's something on the mesa!" she screamed, and she pointed.

"What?" said Macey, and he turned to look.

But as he did, Mrs. Benjamin smelled that awful ozone smell again. And then the whole world went bright.

She was aware of a wave of heat, followed by a blast of pressure that lifted her up off the ground and sent her tumbling back. When she came to a stop she thought she had her eyes closed and fought to open them, only to find she was actually blind. Everything around her was dark, and all she could see were bubbles of green and blue swelling and fading.

Then she began to see light. Images calcified around her. Everything nearby was on fire. There was a huge circle of absolute black on the sidewalk, scorched from the lightning. And there, in the center, was Mr. Macey, standing perfectly still as if struck by an odd thought.

She struggled to her feet, sure he would collapse at any moment. She could hear herself saying his name. Then she grabbed him by the shoulder and turned him around.

His eyes and his mouth were wide and he was trembling, arms stiff and neck stretched to its limit.

She cried out his name and shook him, telling him to please snap out of it.

Then fire spilled out into the street around them, and bright light filled his face. And she looked into his eyes, and saw.

It was as if his eyes were windows, and there behind them was something squirming, something with many tentacles and a long, flowing, flowery body, and his mouth opened wider and wider and she began to hear an awful, reedy whine...

It was like the sound from that shadow in the street. But it came not from his mouth, but from the base of his skull, near his neck...

And when he looked at her she saw nothing in his eyes that was Eustace Macey, nothing of the small-town shop owner she'd spoken to nearly every day of her life. The lightning had emptied him out, and filled him up with something else.

She turned and began to run down the street, shrieking. Everything was smoke and fire and deafening crashes. She saw neighbors she knew and loved screaming and running through the blazes—there, Mr. Cunningham, his daughter thrown over one shoulder, and there Mrs. Rochester, holding one black, wounded hand in her armpit...

The town was unrecognizable. She ran without knowing where she was going, just running in the hope that somewhere this would end, somewhere the devastation would stop.

Then the cloud of smoke parted before her again, and she saw the mesa once more.

She stopped. Choked. And fell to her knees.

She saw enormous shoulders bathed in lightning. Long, sinewy limbs, a faceless, slumping head wreathed in clouds. And the thing on the mesa pointed, and when it did another bolt of lightning fell shrieking to crash into the earth.

It shifted on the mesa, and pointed again. And she could have sworn it pointed at her.

She looked up. There was a bright, glimmering breach in the clouds above her. The clouds fluttered with light, and the breach glowed furiously bright, and then...

Light. Heat. And fire all around.

She stood totally frozen. There was something warm behind her eyes, something soft that tickled her sinuses.

Then all the world turned white.

*   *   *

Mona waits for Mrs. Benjamin to finish her story, yet nothing comes.

"I don't get it," she says. "So...are you saying you died?"

Mrs. Benjamin looks at her, and even though her face is slack Mona thinks she can see scorn in it. "Miss Bright," she says, "to whom do you really think you are speaking?"

Mona thinks about it for a moment, confused. Then she realizes, and for a moment she stops breathing.

She stares into Mrs. Benjamin's eyes. There's a fluttering in her corneas, a squirming as if each of her eyes is the shell of a snail, inside of which is something flexing and undulating, feeling the boundaries of its casing.

She begins to understand. "You're...you're not Mrs. Benjamin, are you."

Mrs. Benjamin smiles a little.

"And you're not Parson," says Mona. "But they were both people before, weren't they? Real people with real lives, and you just...came and took them over."

"In a way. As we said, we are here in only the slightest sense," says Mrs. Benjamin.

"What are you...in there?" says Mona, horrified.

"It is not *us*," says Parson, gesturing to his head. "You have seen *us* already."

"And it very nearly killed you," says Mrs. Benjamin, who sounds a little pleased by that.

"This thing inside this vessel is more like a *device*. Like a walkie-talkie, one could say."

"It is our link to the other side," says Mrs. Benjamin. "The story I just related to you is, I suppose, the last memory of whoever or whatever occupied this vessel before me."

"Whoever occupied...so you *killed* her?" says Mona. "You killed the real Mrs. Benjamin when you...crawled into her skull?" She is horrified and disgusted by the idea, but also by the realization that all the times she has spoken to these people (and who knows who else in

Wink) she has really been addressing the frothy, fleshy masses in their skulls that tweak their nerves like the strings of marionettes and report everything they see to those *things* in that gray, red-starred abyss...

"I did not have a choice," says Mrs. Benjamin. "I agreed to come to this place. I chose to accept safety. I did not know what I was coming to, or how."

"None of us did," says Parson. "We did not come here. We were *brought* here."

"Brought by who?" asks Mona.

The two of them do not speak, but turn to look at one another. Then there's a series of sounds in the air a bit like someone blowing a dog whistle: while her ears cannot detect the noises, they can tell *something* is going on. And from the way Parson and Mrs. Benjamin are staring into each other's eyes, Mona thinks that those things in their heads are choosing to discuss something at a frequency she can't hear. It is a disturbing thought: has the air in Wink been full of silent, invisible communication this whole time, and she was simply unable to perceive it?

Parson clears his throat. "What we are about to tell you," he says, "is the most dangerous secret we know."

"It is the only secret, really," says Mrs. Benjamin. "It is the secret of *us*. Of everything."

"Were anyone to find out that we told you—"

"Any of our *kin*."

"Yes," says Parson, "then the consequences would be...unimaginable."

Mona asks, "You won't go into a coma this time?"

"No," says Parson. "On that occasion, I broke a rule. But there is no rule made for this, because that which made the rules never believed we would ever do what we are about to do."

"Which is what?"

"Tell you who brought us here."

Parson blinks slowly. He looks back at Mrs. Benjamin, and she nods, urging him on.

"We were brought here, Miss Bright"—he shuts his eyes sadly—"by Mother."

*   *   *

Mona stares at them. "Are you *serious*?" she says after a while. "By your *mother*? Then that part of your bird story was *true*?"

The two of them do not respond; they just stare at the ground, shocked, as if they have just committed an abominable betrayal.

Mona shakes her head. It is hard to believe that such things (she remembers the fungal stalk, and the bulky, heaving thing from before, and shivers) could even have a mother. Then she remembers her own vision of the storm, and how she glimpsed that huge, dark figure on the mesa top...

"She actually came here, didn't she," says Mona. "Your mother... your mother actually came here, and pulled you through. That was... *her* on the mountain."

The two of them do not answer.

"Jesus... that thing was your *mother*?" asks Mona.

"Yes," says Mrs. Benjamin. "She pulled us through, scattered us across the valley like seeds. And how we have grown..."

Parson says, "But when Mother brought us here, it was on Her terms. We were confined by Her rules. Rules about what we can and cannot do, what we can and cannot say. Some of us—the eldest, particularly—were too large to come here in whole, and were forced to live through devices housed within the people of this town, and thus be safe and hidden. Others, either because they were too young, or—in the case of one—too old, manifested fully."

"These, naturally, stay concealed through their own designs," says Mrs. Benjamin.

"Mother was powerful," says Parson. "She made us. She was the architect of our lives. She wished us to be perfect. And we tried so hard to be..." A slightly angry note creeps into his voice. "It was through Her designs that we came here. She dwarfed us in all ways. She was vast, vast, incredibly vast... even we do not know Her reaches."

"Then what happened to her?" asks Mona.

"The effort of bringing us here, of saving us, destroyed Her,"

Mrs. Benjamin says. "She was here for one moment...and then She was gone."

"But Mother is never truly gone," says Parson. "She cannot die. Death cannot touch Her. Age cannot wound Her. She cannot die. She may sleep, or wait, but never die."

"Then what happened to Her?" asks Mona.

"We do not know," says Mrs. Benjamin. "We were told to wait here, and each should obey their elders, and we should never, ever harm one another...and that She would come back."

"And we have been waiting ever since," says Parson. "Waiting for Mother to come back."

"It has been a long time," says Mrs. Benjamin. "So long. It wears more on some than others. They get restless."

"What would happen if that...that *thing* came back?" asks Mona.

Parson and Mrs. Benjamin are silent. Then they slowly turn to look at each other, and back.

"Then we would be brought through entirely," says Parson.

"The lines between your world and ours," says Mrs. Benjamin, "blur to almost nothing in this place. Wink is neither here nor there. Some parts are more your world—and others are more *ours*. It is in these parts that we are *hidden*. Our true beings, our true selves, are sealed up in little inaccessible pockets, floating on the borders of our world. We stay anchored," she says, and brushes the side of her head, "through *these*, the sleepers in our skulls. We are safe, but we are trapped. We are trapped in this physical location, and we are trapped in these bodies, which we are forced to use to preserve us, just as sea turtles hide their eggs in the sand."

"But if Mother returns, then we would no longer be stuck halfway," says Parson. "And we would no longer be confined to this place."

"Our world would be pulled through to yours," says Mrs. Benjamin. "The very skies would change. We would be free."

Mona's head begins swimming as she realizes what they mean. (*And how*, she thinks stupidly, *do they know about sea turtles?*) She still does not really understand what she saw on the other side, with those red stars and glittering, volcanic fields, but to imagine such things coming through to here, able to do as they please...

"Why are you telling me this?" asks Mona.

They do not answer.

"You wanted me to understand," says Mona. "You sent me up to the lab so I'd understand enough for you to tell me the rest, to get around your Mother's rules. You want me to *do* something about this. But why? Isn't that what you want to happen? Don't you *want* to be freed?"

"Us?" says Parson. "No. No, we do not wish for that to happen."

"Why, though?" asks Mona.

Mrs. Benjamin asks, "How well did you love your parents, Miss Bright?"

"I only had the one," says Mona. "And I wasn't too fond of him."

"So why should we be any different?"

Mona stares at her as she realizes what she means. Of all the things she's heard, somehow this is the most bewildering. "So...this is all some kind of...fucking teenage *rebellion*?"

"You make it sound so trite," says Parson. "You went past the borders of this place to get to Coburn. So you must have seen the barrier."

Mona thinks, and recalls. "I saw white columns that didn't want to let me pass..."

"Yes. *She* put them there. We cannot pass them. We are trapped here, at Her choosing. We live by Her rules, and Her rules alone."

"We did not know another way of living," says Mrs. Benjamin. "Until we came here. But part of growing up is being forced to be on your own."

"And we have been on our own these past thirty years," says Mr. Parson. "And some of us have grown up."

"What do you mean?" asks Mona.

The two of them hesitate. There is genuine insecurity in their faces (which Mona realizes is remarkable—do the things in their heads actually *feel*?), like they are about to divulge an embarrassing secret.

"When we came here to this place, and took on these lives...something happened that Mother did not expect, or intend," says Parson. "We were not sure what to do with the people living here. We did not even know where we were. But then some of us began to examine our surroundings. And...adapt."

"They watched your television," said Mrs. Benjamin. "And read your books. They lived in your houses, looked at your pictures. They learned to talk like you. To look like you. To act like you. And they began to think that here they could have something they had never possessed before. They could find something here they'd never even dreamed of. In this small, quiet place, filled with so many small, quiet people, they could be something they had never been."

"What?" says Mona.

Parson's face contorts into one of utter disgust. He turns to Mona, and when he speaks his contempt is almost overwhelming: "They believed they could be happy."

CHAPTER THIRTY-SIX

Listen:

Down the street from Mrs. Benjamin's house are Mr. and Mrs. Elm, who live in a very nice bungalow with an impeccably groomed garden of irises. Their grass is trim; their gutters are clean of leaves; and their drapes are of a subtle off-white that works wonderfully with the robin's-egg blue of the window trim. But the indisputable pride and joy of the Elm household is hidden from the street, and hardly ever seen: for in their garage, almost concealed by a leaning stack of oil cans and dented old Dagmar bumpers, is a lime-green 1966 Cadillac Eldorado.

It looks exactly as it did when it was driven off the lot, and this is solely due to the tireless efforts of Mr. Elm. At this moment he lies on the garage floor under the car, drizzled in oil and grease, working away on the beast's marvelous undercarriage. Mrs. Elm stands at the garage door, smiling and holding a pitcher of lemonade.

The lemonade is quite watered down, for the ice has all melted. This is because Mrs. Elm has been standing at the garage door, smiling as she watches her husband work, for four straight days.

"It's a beautiful car, Harry," she says.

Harry does not answer. He is busy. He is always busy on the car. Sometimes he is busy only for a few hours—eight or nine at most. But sometimes it gets bad, and he needs to be busy, really quite very busy, and on those occasions he works underneath the car for so long his body develops bedsores and bruises and pooling blood, and when he emerges (or attempts to emerge) his joints are so atrophied and stiff they sound like machine guns going off, and it takes him the better part of an hour just to stand up.

And she waits on him. Of course she does. She is his wife, and this is what a wife does. She waits on her husband, helps him, serves him. She knows this. She's seen it. She knows what she must be.

Mr. Elm eats nothing during these sessions: the only thing he consumes is can after can of warm Schlitz beer, which he drinks, every time, in one long, foamy draught. He does not move to urinate: his pants and shirt and entire back become soaked with cold urine, which he lies in for so long his crotch and back turn a raw, brilliant red.

There is a mound of empty beer cans just beside the car. Mrs. Elm knows she should go to the store to get more, but this is such a busy time that she can't get out of the house. She must be there to attend to her husband. So she stands in the doorway, smiling, proffering ignored lemonade, listening to her husband pound and twist and tinker with the guts of the Eldorado.

"It's a beautiful car, Harry," she says.

It *is* a beautiful car. It is a remarkably beautiful car. But at times Mrs. Elm feels a little troubled: she is fairly certain that sometimes— not all the time, but *some*times—they should *drive* it somewhere.

But they have never driven the Eldorado. It has never been out of the garage. This is because the car is undrivable.

Under the hood or in the undercarriage of the car, soldered or hammered or screwed or even taped into place, are:

A rotary phone.
Most of a ceiling fan's motor.
Six curling irons.
Two waffle irons.
Thirteen hundred and seventy-four iron nails.
One television tube.
Nine feet of garden hose.
Two neon lights.
Two feet and seven inches of PVC pipe.

The majority of a lawn mower blade.

The door of an ancient microwave.

A combined thirty-eight feet of electrical tape.

One pint of roofing tar.

The tracks of a sliding glass door.

And, last but not least, one Scrabble piece. (An *S*.)

What you would not find underneath the hood of the Eldorado is anything resembling a functioning engine, transmission, radiator, alternator, air filter, or even battery. Mrs. Elm knows her husband needs to work on the car—a car like this requires maintenance, and the husband is the person who does that—but though she would never say it out loud, she secretly believes Mr. Elm does not know what he is maintaining, nor how to maintain it.

"It's a beautiful car, Harry," says Mrs. Elm.

And it is. She loves it. She loves the car. How could she not? It is beautiful.

But sometimes she gets tired of standing there and waiting on her husband and their car. Her kneecaps begin to *itch*, right around the tops where they connect to her muscles, and the itch just grows and grows until it's an outright burn, like her patellae are floating in little pools of lava. Her bra, which is a brutal, industrial contraption, begins to eat into her skin, leaving a dense tangle of red welts over her back and shoulders. But this does not compare to her feet, which are pressed into three-inch, red patent-leather heels. Once, not that long ago, she glanced down to see that the color appeared to be leaking off the shoes, pooling on the tile floor and running down the grout lines like a curiously crimson irrigation network. It was blood, of course: she had stood there until her feet bled. The blood has hardened to become a flaky grid of brown, but she knows that since this fix-it session is so bad it's likely she will bleed again, probably soon.

An image, always still, always melting. Oh, what a pain it is to wear these bodies.

Why is the work never done? Why must we work so hard to maintain these trappings that only harm us?

But these are bad thoughts, she knows. Because they are living a good life. They just need to work a little harder to make sure everything is all right. And they have a beautiful car.

Such a beautiful car.

Listen, there is more:

Mr. Trimley is old and alone, but he has his diversions. Specifically, his model trains, which occupy nearly every waking moment of his life and most of the eighteen hundred square feet of his adobe home. His trains are his *hobby*, he tells himself, just a *hobby*, yet sometimes he wonders if it is all right for a hobby to grow so extensive that he throws out his bed, stove, tables, chairs, all in the cause of allowing more room for his many trains.

No, he thinks. That's silly. He is an old man, and old men are allowed their eccentricities.

One day, Mr. Trimley thinks, he might have enough trains. But he is not sure when—for there is always an anxious, gnawing hunger inside him, telling him that this is all not *quite* right, and he needs to adjust things just a *little* more...

It often takes a lot of adjustment. He has somewhere in the range of 950 model trains, all running on electrical tracks from four to four hundred feet long...and perhaps longer. Mr. Trimley knows that it is a good thing to be a man, just a simple old man living in his simple house, but he does not feel it is wrong to *help* things a little, all in the name of his trains, of course. After all, if he *can* alter things to make his trains more impressive, then he *should*, correct?

Yes. Of course. And Mr. Trimley can alter quite a bit.

Some of his trains, when they enter a little plastic tunnel or trundle under a miniature wooden bridge, take a very, very long time to come out on the other side. The most extreme example is the Northern Line, which comes back to his house only every three days or so, usually at around nine in the morning. And when it returns, the Northern Line is frequently bedecked with snow, and reeking of sulfur.

Mr. Trimley has laid a lot of track for his trains. It's just that some of the tracks go places outside his home, or to places invisible to the naked eye. But that's just a detail, really—after all, this is just his quaint hobby. Isn't it?

Listen:

The Dawes children are merry children, playing fun games in their big sandbox in the backyard. It is just slightly unusual that they come out and play at odd hours—often well after midnight—and that, in their happier moments, they sometimes have the tendency to levitate.

But the neighbors do not mind. No, they do not mind. They are not allowed to mind.

Listen:

No one goes in or out of the Crayes house—you can only tell it is the Crayes house by the name on the mailbox out front. But during certain nights, often around nine o'clock, you can hear Big Band music blaring through the windows, and if you watch the drapes (and you would never do such a thing) you would see the form of someone very, very small dancing a curiously stiff dance...

Listen:

Mrs. Huwell tends to her garden every morning and every night. What she plants there, no one is entirely sure: no one ever sees anything grow, or ever sees a single blade or stem poke up through the soil. Yet on windy nights, if the neighbors listen closely, they can hear leaves rustling in the wind, as if on the other side of the fence is a lush, dense jungle of a garden, though there is nothing to be seen; and in spring, when it is cool and wet, sometimes a soft green glow filters through the fence boards...

Listen:

Mrs. Greer throws a garden party once a year, and she invites the same list of guests every time. This party lasts only forty minutes: the guests will walk down the sidewalk in single file, enter without saying a word at ten p.m. sharp, and walk straight to her backyard. There they will stand in rows, staring up at the night sky in silence. Mrs. Greer (who is a widow, sadly, but really no one can ever remember her having a husband) will stand on the side of the porch and tend to her grill, where she will cook upward of forty hamburgers. When they are ready (she cooks all her hamburgers to well, well done), Mrs. Greer will arrange them on paper plates, and the guests will come by and pick them up, and hold the plates in one hand throughout the night. They will not eat them: at the end of the night, they will throw them away.

At ten thirty p.m., on this specific evening, the skies will clear and all the guests will have a view of a dark corner of the night sky, and at this time the corner of the sky will be very, very clear to them.

They will stare at this corner of the sky, and will not move.

If you were to be nearby at that moment, and if you listened, you would hear a noise like hundreds of crickets cheeping softly in the same rhythm; and there would be a somewhat sad, desperate note to their cheeping, as if the crickets were mourning something, remembering something incredible they'd one possessed, but had lost. If you could name it you would say it was a sound of aching, overwhelming nostalgia, a terrible desire to return to a place you are never even sure you've ever visited.

Then the song will end, the sky will cloud up once more, and the guests will turn to one another, each with one hand raised with its fingers extended, and they will touch one another's fingertips, index finger to index finger and thumb to thumb. As they touch, they will stare into one another's eyes as if swearing to some silent oath; then they will nod, turn to the next person, raise their hands, and do it once more.

At ten forty p.m., all of Mrs. Greer's guests will line up in single file once more, thread out the door, and return to their homes.

And as always, Mrs. Greer will sit down in front of the grill. The flames will bathe her face; her hair will grow brittle and withered in the heat; her skin, deprived of moisture, will tighten as if it is the skin on a drum.

She will stare at the fire, and she will think—*This is a good life. A very good life. But what is missing? What do we lack? Why do I not feel whole?*

But listen, just once more:

At this very moment, not far from the Elms, Margaret Baugh is standing in her backyard. And unlike many of her neighbors in Wink, Margaret is not from Elsewhere; she is a native, born and raised here, as human as human can be.

She stands in her backyard, and she weeps.

She is not sure why she is weeping. Tonight she will have one of the few joys she can get these days. But still, she weeps.

She supposes that part of the problem might be her dinner: that night she tried to cook something a little less conventional than normal: salmorejo, a Spanish tomato soup she found in a recipe book. But her husband Dale Baugh is frequently quite vocal about having meat with his meals: this is an American house, is it not, so should he be denied beef with his dinner? So Margaret stressed to good old Dale that he could have ham in this soup if he wished, as it was traditionally made with ham, and that was all right, wasn't it? And so Dale went to the refrigerator, took out an entire packet of ham lunch meat, chopped it up into huge, silver dollar–sized chunks, and dumped it into his bowl. Then he took out a whole sleeve of crackers, just the *whole sleeve*, crumbled them up, threw them in, and mixed it up until the soup had turned into a pink-whitish paste with thick chunks of cold pork at the bottom.

And, looking her in the eye the whole time, he ate it. He choked down that thick pink slop, silently recriminating her for forcing him to eat such a thing.

For some reason that hurt Margaret more than anything else Dale has done recently. It reached into her and crushed some fragile part of her. Could she not at least end the day well? Was that so much to ask?

It probably was. Things have not been very good with Dale in a long while. Perhaps since they got married: Dale was not exactly a catch, but at the time he was kind enough, and he owned a mechanic's shop, and Margaret, who had always been very bad at talking to men, was happy to receive the attention and the security his favor offered.

She wishes now she had thought about that more. About that choice, and about herself. She wishes she'd realized why she was so bad at talking to men, and why she preferred the company of her few close girlfriends; she wishes she'd realized that, throughout her friend-ships with other women, she was often trying to peripherally approach some silent, forbidden subject, hoping to tempt both herself and her friend into a revelation so illicit she could not even admit to herself she was doing so. It was not until her wedding night, with all the awk-ward, sweaty fumblings, some of which were pleasant but quite a few of which just hurt, that she realized what she'd done, and regretted it and hated herself for it.

In Wink, boys like girls and girls like boys, and no one ever, ever gets divorced. That was part of the rules. When They first came, all those arrangements were made: *We offer you a good life, a wholesome life, and all you must do is live it.* And to so many in Wink the life They offered seemed good, and wholesome, and safe, and they agreed. And per-haps some of them are happy.

But here Margaret is, weeping in the backyard. Yet unlike some in Wink, she knows exactly what is missing. She will get a little taste of it tonight, enough to keep her going for a while.

A light goes on in the top room of the house next door. Margaret stops weeping, and looks. The light goes out, then comes back on again. Then it goes out.

Her heart trembles at the signal. She sniffs and wipes her tears away. Then she stands on her tiptoes, looks around over her fence for any watchers (*But would I even see them if they were there?*), and walks to the fence that runs between her house and the house next door.

She stands beside the fence—exactly in front of one fence board with a large hole in it—and she waits.

She has been waiting for this moment all month.

She hears the back door of the house next door open and close. Feet crunch through the grass. The person comes to stand just on the opposite side of the fence from Margaret, and Margaret longs to look through the cracks, but she cannot bring herself to.

A woman's finger extends through a hole. It is not an unusual fin-ger: it is longish, with dark red nail polish, and it has a few freckles on the last knuckle. But new tears spring to Margaret's eyes at the very sight of it, like she is a pilgrim finally reaching her shrine.

Her hands quake, but she manages to extend her own finger and curl it around the one poking through the fence. The finger curls as well, embracing Margaret's, and the two squeeze each other tight, so tight it hurts.

She is so, so lucky that she happens to live next to Helena. And she is so lucky that she happened to look up one fall evening nearly two years ago when she was raking leaves, and see the wife of her next-door neighbor watching her with a strange, distant look in her eye: a look of longing, of quiet grief, and of awe. It took her a moment to understand this look.

Helena, her next-door neighbor of nine years, thought she was beautiful. It was likely she'd thought Margaret was beautiful for a long time.

Margaret turned away and pretended she had seen nothing. But she kept that moment close to her heart, as if that one look were a burning ember that could keep her warm no matter what happened.

They pursued their relationship without ever admitting they were doing so. They spoke in glances, in nods, in tiny, insignificant gestures invisible to the rest of the community: a certain audaciousness in Christmas decorations, a sudden predilection for listening to Bach on the radio outside at night, and, most importantly, a tendency to go to their fence one night once a month, poke a finger through the fence, and revel in one brief, glorious minute of touch, genuine touch. They do not dare more. They have not even *spoken* to one another, not honestly: to do so would be to risk the punishment that awaits anyone who breaks one of the rules in Wink. And everyone, especially natives like Helena and Margaret, is bound to them; and while no one knows what the punishment for breaking the rules is, everyone knows they don't want to find out.

After their minute is done, they release one another. It is like coming down off a thundering, blinding high, like trying to regain your legs after a moment of paralyzing sexual ecstasy: they must return to this muddy world they briefly circled above, like albatrosses dancing on the breeze, and soil themselves for one more month, one more agonizing month.

They smooth down their skirts and return to their homes. Margaret sits down on the couch beside Dale, who is watching *Bye Bye Birdie* for the fortieth time. But as Margaret watches Dick Van Dyke dance around, begging Janet Leigh to put on a happy face, something within her starts to crumple.

She begins to weep again. She is not sure why. She got her moment, didn't she? Shouldn't that be enough?

Dale coughs and asks if she thought to buy bourbon this week, and did she buy that expensive stuff again, because he really can't taste the difference between the expensive stuff and the normal stuff, so she bought the normal stuff, right? Didn't she? Didn't she?

Margaret says, "Yes." And she stands and goes to the pantry to fetch it.

CHAPTER THIRTY-SEVEN

"So...they want to be *people*?" Mona asks.

"That is their wish," says Parson. "Some are more successful than others. They have turned their prison into a paradise, though a misguided one. They kept the people here, and said to them, *We can provide a wholesome life here, if only you agree to live it, and to live it on our terms.* And the people here, to my surprise, agreed."

"They *did*?" says Mona. "They're here by *choice*?"

"Yes," says Parson. "You must understand, Mona, that my brothers and sisters came here and fell in love with a dream. *Your* dream. A dream of your country, your people. A quiet, small life...I do not know if the dream was ever real or not, but it is yours. I believe it appeals to your people just as much as it does mine."

"Everyone gets their four-bedroom house, their shiny car, a place of their *own*," says Mrs. Benjamin. "The grass is green even though it should not even grow. Everyone here is happy."

"Until recently," says Parson. "Until Weringer."

"He was one of you?" asks Mona.

"He was the leader of this place," says Mrs. Benjamin. "In a way. Much of Wink was his idea. He was the one who suggested we take the names of the vessels we inhabited, and live their lives as if they'd never died. It was amusing, for a while."

"It was never amusing," says Parson. "It was foolish. To pretend to be something you are not will always end poorly."

"There we disagree," says Mrs. Benjamin. "I do not consider it to be as grave as you. It is a triviality, a diversion."

"And yet here we are," says Parson. "With members of our family dead. When we were told they could never die at all."

The subject of family brings one question bobbing to the top of Mona's mind. "So...what does any of this have to do with my mother?" she asks.

"What?" asks Parson.

"My mother. How is she involved with this at all?"

"She isn't," says Mrs. Benjamin. "Like I told you, I don't think she was ever here, or if she was, she wasn't involved."

"She was," says Mona. "I'm sure of it."

Despite Mrs. Benjamin's otherworldly origins, she has obviously picked up a few human affectations, for at this she scoffs quite noisily.

"She was here," says Mona, "when Coburn was first operating. And before she left, she did something to that fucking mirror up on the mesa. She changed something in it. Something to bring you all here, I think."

Parson scratches his chin. Mrs. Benjamin starts sneaking glances at him, gauging his confusion to see when she can be honest about her own.

"We were never told of such a thing," says Parson. "I have not ever heard of any previous contact with this place at all."

"Why would she do that?" asks Mrs. Benjamin.

"I think the mirror did something to her too," says Mona. "The records said she would just stare into it for hours. I think that's why she went...mad. She wasn't schizophrenic. She saw something in it. And maybe something saw her. Maybe one of you."

"If this is true," says Parson, "then it was kept secret from me."

"And me," says Mrs. Benjamin. "I always thought it was all Mother's doing. But a woman? A human woman? How could she—" Mrs. Benjamin freezes, but does not stop exhaling, turning her last word into to a sustained, croaky *eeeeeeee*. Her wide eyes swivel in their sockets quickly enough to be revolting.

"What is it?" asks Parson.

She lets the *eeeeeee* taper off, then draws a slow breath. "Someone is here," she whispers.

"Who?" says Mona.

Mrs. Benjamin's eyes resume wheeling at such a rate that Mona thinks she can hear wet clicks issuing from the lining tissues. "I do not know," she says. "But they are here, on this property. They have announced themselves to me. They do not even try to hide themselves."

"But you do not recognize them?" asks Parson.

"No," says Mrs. Benjamin.

Despite their emotionless, limp faces, the two appear very perturbed by this. Mona supposes that their kind—or the things in their heads—must have a manner of communicating their presence to one another. And whoever is here is being impolite, and refusing to identify themselves.

Mona sees her Glock resting on the bedside table, and reaches out to pick it up.

"No," says Mrs. Benjamin.

"No what?"

"That would do no good."

"A bullet between the eyes would do no fucking good?"

"You presume," says Mrs. Benjamin, "that it has eyes. Which might not necessarily be the case."

Mona pauses to reflect on this.

"Help him," says Mrs. Benjamin. "Help him move. Help him get out. Help him run, very fast. They aren't here for you. They're here for me, I think."

"Well, *fuck*," says Mona, and she grabs Parson by one arm, pulls him to his feet, and partially throws him over her shoulder. She's had a lot of practice at this in her day. "But don't you want help?" she asks.

"Of course I want help," says Mrs. Benjamin. "But help is not something you can give. Not with this. This is—let's say—a family matter, or so I suspect. And you would not hold up well during our squabbles."

She silently flits out of the room and down the hall like a magenta ghost, leaving Mona to limp out the back door and unceremoniously dump Parson over the fence. He groans upon contact with the grass, while Mona hops over, squats, and watches.

Parson grabs her ankle: "No, no. You do not want to even be *near* for this."

She thinks. Then she gathers him up and leaves.

The sun is crawling back under a blanket of black. Swallows skim the dancing grasses in the park, snatching moths out of the air. Two black squirrels in a spruce hear her walk out to her porch, freeze, and swivel to watch, ears perked and pointed. Mrs. Benjamin outwaits them: after three minutes, they snake away. Then the streetlamps come on, with one rusting malcontent taking a full minute to persuade its bulb to shine.

Mrs. Benjamin stands on her porch staring at the street. Once the entity that wore this body before her sat in this spot and watched lightning weave down from the sky like penguins snatching fish. And though this scene is much more quiet, much more calm, it is no less deadly.

Mrs. Benjamin sits.

Waits.

Watches.

And then:

Her eye registers movement, then identifies a white hat in the darkness below the spruce.

"Well, come out then," she says.

The figure does not move.

"Come on then," says Mrs. Benjamin. "Be polite. Don't just stand there."

But he does not move.

"Come out!" she commands.

The white hat tips to the side, just a touch. She imagines its wearer is pleased to see her so frustrated.

"What do you want?" she asks, more softly.

A long pause.

"What?" she asks.

"For you," says a voice, "to stop."

"Stop what?" she asks.

The hat slowly teeters to the right.

"Such a nice house," says the voice. "Such a nice yard. Such pretty flowers. Good porch. Good place to put your heels up, if your hips permit. If I were you—and I am not—I would wish to spend many an evening here."

"Kindly get to your point."

The hat tips back and forth like a ship on turbulent seas. "I wonder," says the voice, "why one would ever want to leave this place. No. No, one shouldn't want to. Better to stay here. Stay here, on your porch, in your town. And do not come out to the wilderness. Leave what is there alone."

Mrs. Benjamin stands. "Who are you?"

Silence.

"Come out."

"But if you *do* come outside," says the voice, "out to the wilderness, it would be tolerated only if you ventured out with purpose."

"What do you mean?"

"I mean," says the voice, "with us. *Help* us. You *are* with us, whether you know it or not."

"Who is *us*?" says Mrs. Benjamin. "Who are you?"

The man steps out of the shadows. He wears a pale blue suit, but his face is decidedly nondescript, clean-shaven and unassuming, the face of a father, criminal, brother, son.

Yet Mrs. Benjamin recognizes him. "Mr. Deirdry?" she says. "From... the doughnut shop? What are you doing here? You aren't... you aren't involved in this. I should know. Who told you to say this to me?"

He smiles wider.

"But, Mr. Deirdry... listen, you've nothing to do with these affairs. Whoever told you to do this or is making you do this, I can help you, I can protect you against—"

"Mr. Deirdry," says the man, "is dead."

This stops her short. He smiles wide enough for her to see his teeth. And as he smiles, there comes a sound like a particularly vicious cicada buzzing from somewhere around the man, like it is hanging on his back.

Mrs. Benjamin's mouth opens in shock. "What? Where did you... did you come from the other side?"

The man just smiles.

"We are all accounted for...everyone who came here is still here. There is no one new. Who are you?"

"All accounted for," says the man, "except two. They have been laid low. Because they forgot."

"What are you talking about?"

He does not answer.

"You?" asks Mrs. Benjamin, shocked. "Do you mean you are behind Weringer and Macey's deaths?"

"They forgot who they were," he says. "Willfully."

"But who are—"

"They chose complacence over truth, comfort over reality. I tried to wake them from their slumber. But still they slept, so I made them sleep deeper, sleep forever." He walks to the front path and stands before her porch. "Do you betray us?"

"I don't know what you're talking about."

"She said to wait," says the man. "To wait for Her. But She never said not to look. None of you old ones have looked for Her. You sat, and waited. You grew soft. *I* had to be the one. *Me.* And She was *here.* Waiting. All around us."

"What do you—"

"All of us younger ones, we knew. We knew we had to look for Her. I went to where they sat or slept in their prisons, be it in the hills or under stones, and they joined me gladly. They were eager. They had been waiting for their chance. They knew that anything would be better than living like this."

"*You* are why the younger ones are missing? What have you done with th—"

"Help me," says the man. He opens his arm like a long-departed relative returning from overseas. "Help us. We cannot go home. But we can bring home here. *She* can bring home here. If only we bring Her back."

"Who are you?" asks Mrs. Benjamin angrily.

"If you do not join us," says the man, "then you must stay here, waiting for Her judgment. And it will come. Do you think you can bear it?"

"You cannot tell me what to do. I do not know who you are, but I am far older than you no matter."

The man moves forward until he stands on the front step of her porch. "Tell me to leave. Make me leave."

"I do not want you to leave," says Mrs. Benjamin. "After what you have said to me? You must answer for everything you've done, if you have really done anything."

"I have done so much," says the man softly. He reaches into his blue coat and takes out a pearl-handled straight razor. He unfolds it with soft, delicate hands. "Make me answer. Make me." He begins to move toward her.

"You cannot hurt me," says Mrs. Benjamin. "It is not allowed for us to hurt one another."

"Hurt me," says the man. "Kill me. Crush me with your hands, O mighty one."

The straight razor flashes out, and Mrs. Benjamin cries in the dark. She grasps her forearm. Red-black blood leaps from between her fingers to spatter on the porch.

She falls back, shocked. "You are not *allowed* to hurt me!"

"And is *this* you?" asks the man. "Is this you, in that dress, in that body? Who are you? Where are you?"

He darts forward again, a bit awkwardly, for he is obviously untrained in physical assault. This strike is less precise, and he winds up nicking her shoulder.

"Stop!" she cries.

He grabs her by the sleeve of her dress. There is a yowl of ripping fabric, and she spins to hit the wall. "I will slough off that skin you wear," he says. "I will, I will—"

There is a flurry of slapping hands. The razor makes cuts and slashes on her fingers until it finally navigates her blows to make a wandering incision on her cheek. Blood wells up from the slash like oil.

"Get away!" she shouts again, and shoves him back. She spins to the side and staggers back into her house.

"I have died so many times," says the man. "But we are not allowed to leave this place. Not now. Not yet. Not until Mother comes." He enters her door.

"Get out!"

"I can show you. Let me show you."

Mrs. Benjamin, ragged, bloody, torn, looks at her hands, which now bear many leaking notches. She remembers that, truthfully, these blue-veined things with skin like paper are not her hands; and she is not really an old woman, defenseless and frail. And though she has not seen violence since arriving at this place, that does not mean she has forgotten it; and simply because she is currently housed within this aging vessel, that does not mean her true nature does not leak into this place.

A deep, low buzz begins emanating from about her person as she begins to rally.

"Go on," says the man. "Do it. Do it!" He raises the razor, intending to make a swooping signature on her shoulder, but Mrs. Benjamin grasps his arm (with a soft series of cracks), plants her feet, and twists.

The man is hurled across the room as if shot out of a cannon. He crashes into a bookcase and collapses in a heap, then looks up at her, head askew as if some stabilizing bone has snapped.

"There it is," he gasps. "There's that"—he coughs—"famous strength."

"Who are you?" asks Mrs. Benjamin, feeling much firmer now.

He uses the cracked bookshelf as a ladder and forces himself to his feet. "Break me," he says. His incisors are smeared with red. "Hurt me. Do it. I will"—he gags, and a blob of blood rolls off his tongue—"show you how *silly* these lives are." He turns, staggering drunkenly, still brandishing the straight razor.

She is ready. Her small, wrinkled fist finds the underside of his ribs. There is a snap like a truck driving over old wood, and he crumples, coughing. When he looks up at her he is grinning, his mouth now brimming with blood.

"It was me," he says to her. "I did it. I killed them. I killed your brothers."

"They were your brothers too!"

"Only by blood. They didn't even know my name. Any of our names." The straight razor flitters up like a red butterfly. Mrs. Benjamin grunts as it finds the inside of her bicep. In response her dainty, patent-leather-bound foot rises up and stomps down on his ankle. His joint is crushed as if made of rubber tubing; seas of blood come roaring out around the exposed shards of bone; when she removes her heel his foot dangles from his shin by a few red and blue harp strings. He exhales, spewing a gnat cloud of red drops into the air, yet the corners of his mouth are still upturned: he is laughing, grinning.

"It all tears away from us," he says, "like paper."

"Tell me," she says, dragging him up, "who you are."

Again the straight razor glimmers through the air, and it buries itself deep in her shoulder. He slaps at it, trying to force it deeper into her, but she snatches his hand out of the air and squeezes. His hand pops like a house settling in the night. Blood begins dribbling through her tiny fingers.

"Kill me," he says. Flags of tissue whip and rattle down in his chest. "Do it."

"We cannot kill one another," she says.

"First it was hurt," he says. "Now it's kill. You don't know for sure, do you? You don't know what She forbade us from. You don't really know what we can do, if we want to."

"Why are you doing this?"

"I'm giving you a choice," he says. "You can't hurt me. Nothing can hurt me, besides being separated from Her. But you...you can either help us, or, when She gets here, learn what hurt really is."

"I am Her daughter," says Mrs. Benjamin.

"Then *act* like it," he snarls.

She reaches out and grabs his shoulder. Her fingers dig into the flesh, pulling it apart as easily as one would cottage cheese, exposing cords and sinews that swell and deflate like concertinas.

Yet he does not react one bit. "When you're all alone, that's when you see who you really are," he says. "And they were alone. But they were weak. I feel no regret. I feel nothing, anymore." His red teeth snap forward and snag a nugget of flesh on her arm. Red drops leap up his cheek like dolphins playing in ocean waves.

She falls on him then, all teeth and fingernails, and the two slash and snap and tear at one another like rabid animals, though the damage she does is by far the greater: her teeth leave flaps of skin missing from his cheek, neck, shoulder. He grabs the razor handle protruding from her shoulder and rips it out. A fan of blood marks her out-of-tune Wurlitzer. He intends to send the razor deep into her belly, but she brings her other palm down and strikes his chin.

A torrential gout of blood begins pouring from his mouth, which is now lopsided, suggesting that the connective tissue of half his jaw has partially snapped, causing a massive hemorrhage in his throat. Yet even though nearly every cavity in his head and chest is now filling with blood, she can still see his teeth open and shut and his tongue thrash about as he mouths, "Do it. Do it. Do it," with a burst of gore gurgling up each time as he tries to force his breath through his ruined mouth.

She drops him. When he hits the ground, he immediately begins crawling toward the pearl-handled razor. Mrs. Benjamin, as if remembering a pie she has in the oven, turns and walks to the kitchen, so she cannot see his labored crawl across the floor, which becomes more and more difficult as each alveolus in his lungs fills with fluid.

The man has grasped the razor and is wheeling around, looking for more flesh to slash, when the front of Mrs. Benjamin's KitchenAid tilt-head stand mixer connects with the crown of his skull. Immediately he goes limp. She brings it down again and again, like an otter crushing a sea urchin. On the third hit, the structural integrity of his skull gives away entirely, the hat (which is now quite red) deflating under the force of the mixer. She keeps smashing the remains of his head against the floor until something ropy and translucent becomes visible among all the shards and viscera, as if there is a jellyfish swimming in the puddle of red. She glimpses tiny, serrated teeth, many writhing tendrils, minuscule suckers...

She keeps striking it. Again and again and again.

Finally there is a reedy cry, like that of a monstrous cricket searching for a mate, and the wriggling translucent thing trembles and turns to white foam whose bubbles coast through the oceans of blood.

It is gone.

Mrs. Benjamin drops the mixer.

She has killed him. She has really killed him.

It could not be done. Mother *said* it could not be done. Yet here he is, this stranger, rapidly cooling at her feet.

What does one do, she thinks, *after committing fratricide?*

Her dress is black and red with blood. She is checking her wounds (something she has not ever had to do before) when the windows flash white, and she sees a bolt of lightning shoot down on the far side of Wink.

She marvels at it, and whispers, "No," though the word has not left her lips when the crash of thunder splits the air.

CHAPTER THIRTY-EIGHT

The world is alive with cheeps and chitters, reels and ribbits. *Are they insects*, she wonders, *or something else? Why have I never noticed them before?* Parson's lame feet scuff the stony ground as she hauls him forward. The moon floods the alleyways with light the shade of Pepto-Bismol; Mona's eyes search the fence-board cracks for movement and listening ears; somewhere a nighthawk twitters and falls abruptly silent. Perhaps even the animals know it is wise to be away.

Mona takes a right, back toward Mrs. Benjamin's house. "What are you doing?" Parson says. "I said we must get away."

"The truck," says Mona, and points. The black monstrosity is still sitting just around the corner from the house. She is glad she didn't park right outside.

As she helps Parson in, a series of huge crashes echo through the street. It sounds like someone busting apart furniture. She looks back at Mrs. Benjamin's house, but sees nothing. Lights blink on in the front rooms of houses all around her. Doors open, casting golden pathways onto yards and sidewalks.

Mona feels for the Glock again. She's not used to inaction, and she especially isn't used to running away. But Parson whispers, "What are you *waiting* for?"

Mona jumps in and starts the truck. She does not peel out, as every muscle in her body wishes her to do, but eases away, eluding any undue attention.

She counts the cars again. They're all still there. No one new, no one missing. She can never say for sure, of course, but she thinks her visit to Mrs. Benjamin's has gone unnoticed.

They drive on in silence, going nowhere except away.

"Is she going to get hurt?" asks Mona.

"I don't know," says Parson. "I would not think so. But now...so much is uncertain. We were told we could not die, and yet we die. We were told not to harm one another, yet clearly some can do so, or at least attempt it."

"Shit. What should happen if they tried?"

He makes a *hmph*, as if the subject embarrasses him.

"What?" she says.

"I have told you this already," he says irritably. "They would break the rules, and be punished. And you have seen the consequences."

"I have? When?"

"Yes. Was I not punished before your eyes?"

"Wait. Wait, your *coma*?"

"Yes. Like I said, I broke a rule. We are not permitted to discuss our nature with any outsiders, with any who do not know. I violated that particular law, a little, but just enough. The same should happen to any who attempt to harm another. Yet some of Her laws now appear malleable. So what do they know—whoever they are—that I do not?"

A bat flits into the stream of headlights, wings gleaming, then darts away.

"There must be some way around them," says Parson. "I do not know. I was not close with Her. She was very hard to relate to. She had many expectations. She was never very...content. I often wonder if She simply had us out of boredom." He pauses, aware he's said a bit too much on an awkward subject. "Anyway, that may be why I know nothing of your own mother. *If* she was somehow...manipulated into bringing us here."

In the sky west of town there is a flash of light, followed by a deep growl of thunder. Parson turns and peers at it, looking through the fluttering clouds like a soothsayer parsing tea leaves.

"Then who was close with Her?" asks Mona. "They'd know, wouldn't they?"

Parson is silent.

"Is there anyone?" she asks.

Parson sniffs, rubs his nose with his knuckle.

"There is," she says.

"Yes."

"Who?"

"He is"—Parson looks out the window for inspiration—"best left alone."

"Best left alone?"

"Yes."

"Mr. Parson...shit, Mr. Parson, are you not aware that this is a goddamn fucking emergency? I honestly don't care what's best done! Tell me who it is, damn it!"

He frowns into his lap. Unbuttons a shirt button, re-buttons it. "He is different," he says.

"Oh, I give a shit."

"You would care. He is *very* different."

"Different how?"

Silence. Then: "Very, very different."

Mona drives on for a bit, not speaking. Finally she says, "He's not...like you, is he?"

"Like me?"

"A person. Or...fuck, I don't know. *Inside* of a person."

"No," says Parson solemnly. "You are right. He is not. He is more like Mother than I am. Than any of us is." He sighs and rubs his brow. Mona can't help but notice how many human mannerisms have seeped into his behavior. "In my family, there were five who were eldest, as I once told you. I am the second eldest. My exact name...well. Many of our names are indecipherable to you. They cannot be translated to anything you would find logical. *His* name, however, is different. His is simple. Its meaning remains the same no matter how it is translated."

"What is his name?" asks Mona.

Parson points out the window, directing her down a dirt road that heads west out of Wink, straggling through pines and under the shad-owy thunderhead of the mesa, until it finally crosses a small, sloping canyon that, Mona eventually notices, has fewer and fewer trees the closer it gets to the mesa.

"His name," says Parson, "means 'first.'"

They park the truck in the trees below the canyon. Parson wants to start ahead immediately, but Mona holds up a hand and has him wait while she surveys the roads behind them. She sees no headlights, and driving without headlights in this country would be suicidal, so she's reasonably sure they weren't followed. *But who knows what else is in these hills*, she thinks.

Mona stops at the edge of the road before the trees begin. Parson walks on a bit before looking back. Again he is reduced to a shadow, indistinct among the pines.

"Are you coming?"

"They said not to go into the woods. And I'm more inclined to lis-ten to them after the crazy shit you just told me."

"They did say so," he says. "But remember that I am one of this *they*. Now I say otherwise. Come."

He walks on. "Shit," Mona says. She grabs the rifle, slings it over her back, and stuffs the pistol into the back of her shorts. Then she hotfoots it to catch up to him, and has to listen for his limping step (for he is still unsteady on his feet) to find him.

The trees overhead shred the moonlight into pieces and cast them at their feet. Mona has been here so long she almost doesn't notice its color—for the moonlight, as always, is pink. The mesa blooms just above them like a vast fungus, lit salmon-pink by the moon; though just above it, in a spindly stretch of clouds, blue lightning plays like otters in a stream. She cannot stop looking around, trying to spy any movement or watching eyes. Will Parson's kin look as he and Mrs. Benjamin looked on the other side? Will she even be able to see them at all? Will they be invisible?

"You appear worried," says Parson.

"How can you tell?" asks Mona, because under the trees it's pitch-black.

He does not answer.

"Mr. Parson...can you see in the dark?" asks Mona.

"Light," says Parson, "is mere radiation. There are other ways of seeing."

She chooses not to follow this line of discussion. "*Should* I be worried?"

"I am not sure. Were you an ordinary citizen of Wink—a person born and bred here, I mean—I would say yes, definitely. There is a reason they do not go into the wilderness. It is not theirs."

"Is it yours?"

"Not precisely," says Parson. "Let us say it is a home to the less adaptable members of my family."

"And you don't think I should be worried about that?" asks Mona. "Because I'm already kind of worried about that."

"Hm," he says, thinking. "No. You are different. I have always believed so. But I am not sure how yet."

"That's not comforting at all," says Mona.

"I did not really intend it to be," he says. Then he stops, and listens.

Mona immediately swivels and brings the rifle to her shoulder. She eyes the trees, looking for a swell of darkness among the tattered moonlight, or the gleam of a rifle barrel parting the branches.

"There is no one there," says Parson. "We are just on the...verge of something. Come along." He stumps ahead, parts a tangle of pine branches with the blade of his hand, and walks into a copse of trees. Mona follows, saying, "If you could let me know why you're stopping ahead of time, it might keep me from popping off a rou—"

As the branches release her she immediately notices the air is different. It's electrical, with that familiar scent of too many copiers running at once. But it is also terribly cold and clammy, and it stinks of stagnation and rot.

As she puzzles over this, she realizes she is now in a place very different from where she was before.

The starlight has turned a dull, jaundiced amber that seeps through the cloudy sky. They stand in an immense, muddy trench, with twisted, cancerous-looking trees clutching the embankment. Sickly white fruit the size of cantaloupes hangs from their branches. The fruit is faintly luminous, like a predator from the ocean deeps.

"Do I want to ask where we are?" she says.

Parson shrugs. "Somewhere else." He continues strolling along as if this otherworldly place is no stranger than your average municipal park.

She gazes up. The sky is thick with mist, but she thinks she can see pink stars peeping through in places.

She runs to catch up. "Are we...on the other side? Because if so, I notice I'm not...well. Almost dying, or whatever it was."

"Correct. We are not quite there, but we are not quite here," says Parson. "Some places are in-between places. Many of them, in fact. Wink itself is riddled with places inside of places inside of places. It extends to many different places, like a continent submerged under many different seas."

"Then time isn't the only thing broken here," says Mona. "Or I guess I should say *bruised*."

"Possibly. Wink is filled with weak spots, where one world—one plane of reality—becomes indistinguishable from another. The town proper is mostly safe. It is—or was—maintained by Weringer, and his followers."

Much as a neighborhood association, thinks Mona, *keeps the medians of its roads carefully weeded*.

They continue into the muddy trench. In the shallower parts she can see over the lip, and she thinks she can glimpse buildings or structures far out in the mist. Is it their city? Do such things have cities? Or is it something they conquered, and took?

"How far does this place go?" she asks.

"It goes," says Parson, "until it doesn't."

She stops. There are markings on the ground, odd, swoopy ones that are strangely tentacular; something has raked the mud here, leaving small, circular patterns in the bottom of the trench, like those of coleoidal suckers...

"Ah, shit. Does something live here?"

"Oh, yes," says Parson. "Or it did, at least."

Again, she brings the rifle up into her hands.

"That won't be necessary," says Parson.

"Why not?"

"Because it is gone, like I said."

"How do you know?"

He points to one side of the trench. There is another set of tracks there: these resemble small, dainty shoes with little heels.

"Because Mrs. Benjamin came here to check," says Parson. "She came to many of the hidden places around Wink. The residents are gone, all gone. To where, we don't know. Just not here." Then he points ahead. "Look."

She sees nothing. "What?"

"Look," he says again.

She looks again. Suddenly there is a line of pinyon pines across the trench. She barely has time to think *What are they doing there?* when things *click*—just as they did at Coburn with the lens—and she is standing in the pine forest below the mesa again.

"See?" says Parson. "Right as rain."

"That is not," says Mona, "my definition of *right as rain*."

"Nearly there." Parson waves her forward once more.

They resume the hike up the slopes to the canyon. Mona notices there are no buzzes and chitterings here, as there were in the town. The woods are totally silent.

"How many of them were out in the woods before?" asks Mona.

Again, Parson shrugs. "My family is like the stars."

Mona suppresses a shiver. "And why did you stick them out here?"

"*I* did not. That was not *my* choice. They were too young to reside within one of . . . well, you, I suppose. They were not wise, not mature. They could not control themselves. So they came to this place much as they are on the other side, only with a slight physical form. But when Weringer and his followers decided to maintain the town, and live as people, and have their fun, they could not allow the young ones to live among them openly. They did not fit in with their image of the town. So they were made to retire to the mountains and the woods and the valleys to conceal themselves by their own machinations."

"That almost sounds"—Mona hops over a gulch—"like they got fucked."

"It sounds that way because they did. We do so many silly things," he says with a sigh, "in service of our vanity. It was then that I ended my support of Weringer, and much of Wink. I am opposed to my brethren. And they have ostracized me. I am alone. Mostly," he adds.

"Mostly?"

"There is Mrs. Benjamin. She vaguely grants her support to them, yet she consults with me frequently, and they do not object—Mrs. Benjamin is much feared within my kin. Mother made her to be a...a weapon, I suppose. And Mother's designs rarely fail." Mona, who remembers the sight of that huge, hulking, many-legged thing on the other side all too well, can completely understand that. "But I am visited also by my brother, whom you are about to meet." He pauses and purses his lips, suddenly awkward. "That is a...secret. No one knows about that. Not even Mrs. Benjamin. Please do not spread it around."

"I'll make sure not to," says Mona, who cannot imagine when she'd ever have the opportunity.

"He comes to me, and we talk, and play games."

"That's charming."

He ignores her. "We are the two eldest. We have always been alone, a little. Now more so than most. But just recently he stopped coming. Right after your arrival, in fact. He walled himself off in his home, and he does not come out, nor can anyone get in. I understand it is a cause of much concern."

"Why the change?"

"Well...I think he is quite happy where he is. He does not want things to change. But things are changing. I think he is preparing for something. He will not share this information with me, but it is...how shall I put this...he has the air of a man filling out his will."

"Ouch," says Mona. "Why doesn't he just stay in hiding?"

"Well," says Parson, and he stops in his tracks, "I do not believe he is hiding. I believe he is waiting. For you."

Mona looks up. They are at the mouth of a small, treeless canyon. Mona realizes how far they've come, for the western side of the mesa surges up just ahead of them. Somewhere in the rock, she thinks, is that mirror, the little glinting hole in everything that started all of this . . .

Mona stares down the canyon. It is gray and barren and winding. The wind makes a soft moan as it drags its invisible bulk over the canyon's lips. She cannot imagine walking down it. She has never seen anything lonelier in her life.

"I have told you," Parson says softly, "that my brother is . . . not like me."

"Yeah. I got that."

"But you must know that . . . I do not know how he will choose to present himself. He has never been . . . orthodox."

"That's if we get in to see him," says Mona, who now finds herself extremely reluctant to proceed down the canyon.

"Oh, that I feel we can do for certain," says Parson. "Mostly because he told me we would."

"He what?"

"He told me I would come here," says Parson. "And he told me I would bring a guest. This was just before your arrival. I had no idea what he meant at the time."

"Well how the fuck did he know that?"

"Did I not tell you that time does not work right in Wink?"

"You kind of glossed over it, yeah."

"For many of my kind, who intrude into many other dimensions besides this one, time performs differently. But for him, it performs very, *very* differently. He has . . . perception. That is the best way to put it. In his hands, time is but a little dog, eager to perform tricks. He does not see time as linear—he sees many branches of it, the things that have happened, the ones that will happen, and even the things that might have or could have happened, if things had gone otherwise."

Mona rotates the rifle so it's back in her hands. "You can understand," she says as she tugs the strap, "that that makes me really fucking nervous."

"I suppose I do," he says, indifferent.

"Because I don't like the idea of someone knowing what I'm going to do before I do. It would be really easy for them to hurt me, or you."

Parson stops walking. He looks down the canyon, and cocks his head.

Mona looks as well. There is someone standing there, waiting for them, revealed by the bursts of lightning just above them.

In an instant the rifle is at her shoulder. But in almost the same space of time, she realizes it's unnecessary. Because this person, who is so skinny-shouldered and frail and anxious, is someone Mona's pretty sure she's met before in this town.

"I do not think," says Parson, "that that is the case."

Gracie nervously raises one hand, waves to them, and says, "Hey."

There are few situations more awkward than when one person has unnecessarily just pulled a gun on another. Mona's rifle, which was originally pointed directly at Gracie's face, now gently wanders south to circle her midsection as Mona considers exactly what the hell to do.

Gracie coughs politely. Mona taps the stock with her fingers, wondering what to say.

She finally decides on, "You're the...girl from the diner, right? Gracie?"

Gracie nods.

"Okay," says Mona. "Well. What the hell are you doing out here, girl?"

"Um. I was waiting," says Gracie. "On you. I'm...supposed to take you inside." She points back down the canyon.

Mona does not lower the gun. She peers at Gracie's eyes, looking for that flutter...

Parson clears his throat. "There is no worry about that. She is quite as human and normal as...you." Though there is something in his tone Mona doesn't like.

Gracie nods, concerned.

Mona does not fully lower the rifle. "Okay, then, again—what the hell is she doing out here?"

"She attends to my brother," says Parson.

"What does that mean?"

"I'm his..." She trails off.

"What? Like, his secretary or handler or something?"

Gracie blushes magnificently.

"What did I say?" asks Mona.

Gracie opens her mouth to speak, rethinks, closes it, then opens it again before wincing and shutting it again. "It's personal."

"What does that mean?"

"I told you my brother was unorthodox," says Parson, "and this is true. His interests are eccentric even for us. And...one of those interests is a common pursuit of yours. Not common to you, personally, I mean—common to your kind."

Gracie is now a bright pink. Mona begins to feel very uncomfortable with the direction this is taking. She lowers the rifle. "Which is what?"

Parson licks his lips, and cringes as he says, "Romance."

"Romance? You mean...wait." Mona almost drops the gun. She looks back and forth between Gracie, who is nervously rubbing her elbow and staring at the ground, and Parson, who appears to now be grimly waiting out this subject.

"Are you fucking serious?" asks Mona. "She's his *girlfriend*?"

Parson reacts as if he has never heard the term. He thinks, bug-eyed, and says, "I...suppose that would be a fair approximation."

Mona incredulously looks to Gracie for corroboration. The young girl says, "It's...complicated."

"I'll fucking bet! He doesn't even look like a, a...person. Right?"

"He looks like many things," says Gracie. "If he wants to. And he keeps me safe." Again: "It's complicated. We have arrangements here."

"Everyone does," says Parson. "My kin have arrangements with the natives of Wink, just as my kin in the town have arrangements with those in the wilderness. It is quite complicated, being civilized.

There are so many rules and restrictions involved in living"—he pauses condescendingly—"a *good life*."

Mona shakes her head. "Okay, whatever," she says. "I am learning *way* too much tonight. Just . . . take us to wherever you need to take us."

"I can take *you*," says Gracie. "But not him."

Mona and Parson exchange a glance.

"Just me?" says Mona.

Gracie nods again. "Sorry."

"Did you know about this?" Mona asks Parson.

Parson, frowning, shakes his head.

"Why not him?" Mona asks Gracie.

"I don't know why," she says. "He just said only you would be coming."

"He being this brother of Parson's," says Mona. "First."

"*Mr.* First," says Gracie.

"Oh, he's big on propriety, then?"

"Titles and hierarchies," says Parson, "are quite important. So am I to just stay here, and wait?"

"I guess you can," says Gracie. "But I think maybe not. He said something about you going somewhere else. That's all." She smiles unhappily. "You know how he is."

"That I do," says Parson. He sighs. "Well. Fine. I shall sit and wait here, I suppose." He groans and begins to sit down.

"You can't be serious," says Mona.

"Why not?"

"You're going to let me walk in there alone?"

"There are *rules*."

"Oh my God," says Mona. "You people and your fucking *rules*."

"You will not be in any danger," says Parson. "I trust him."

Mona looks back down the little canyon. The light within it, she notes, is not pink, as it is everywhere else, but silver-white. Everything in there shines, and it shines more and more the farther it goes . . .

"Is it a different place, in there?" she asks.

He nods. "It is his place."

"What's it like in there?"

"I do not know. I have never been inside."

"Jesus." Mona looks to Gracie. "Do you know?"

"For me, there's only him in there," says Gracie. "But then, he's much more unguarded with me."

There is a soft, fond tone in her voice that makes Mona feel repulsed. What has this thing been doing to this poor girl in there? Do these things desire sex? Do they understand attraction at all?

Shadows ripple at the back of the canyon. She imagines something is coming, and she wonders—*Can it see me?* Then she realizes, no—a cloud is simply passing over the moon. Or is that what this thing, this First, wants her to see?

"Has it hurt anyone before?" asks Mona.

"Oh, yes," says Parson mildly.

Again, she looks to Gracie. "You?"

"Me? No," says Gracie. "He has never hurt me. I don't think he's ever hurt a native."

"Which is what they call humans, I take it? Christ," says Mona. She wipes sweat from her cheeks and takes a deep breath.

"Do not be concerned," says Parson. "You are no concern to him."

"How do you mean?" asks Mona.

"Understand," says Parson, "that to him you are merely a spot of light on a wall, reflected by a bit of metal on the ground. You are the twist of a leaf being blown in a slight wind. You are not even a drop of water to him—you are one ephemeral, fleeting curl of a dribbling stream as it tries to flow downhill. You do not concern him enough to warrant harm. He does not care what you want or need. He does not care what you do, or if you live or die. You should not worry, for he is utterly beyond you. He does not notice. He does not care."

Mona takes two steps forward, then sets the rifle down butt-first and leans on it as if it were a walking stick. She slowly hunches down, the rifle sticking up between her knees. From here she can see the soft glow of the lights of Wink and the dark, rambling countryside. And she knows that what is ahead is not connected to this world in any physical manner. It feels different just being this much closer to the canyon entrance. It is like the room in Coburn, like the scarred bathroom in her mother's home—if she were to take one, maybe two steps forward, she would not be anywhere on Earth anymore. She would be somewhere else. Wherever Mr. First wants her to be, she guesses.

But something else is wrong. That niggling bit of her brain, the cop part that's always cold yet anxious, is trying to tell her something...

Did she not just see a light in the side of her eye?

Yes, she realizes. Yes, she did. Not down the canyon, but from behind her, from where they came. Like a flashlight, but someone turned it off almost immediately...as if that person didn't want her or anyone else to see it.

Mona turns around and scans the trees for movement.

There is nothing, she thinks.

There is something, she thinks.

Someone else is here.

"Parson," she says.

"Yes?"

"Does anyone else know we're out here?"

"I would not believe so."

Mona keeps looking. She lowers herself to the ground and brings the rifle up to her shoulder. She puts the scope to her eye and glasses the tree line. It's almost impossible to see anything at night, but maybe...

"What's wrong?" asks Parson.

She licks her lips, thins her eyes. Something just moved...a head bobbing up, perhaps to see, then down...did she see a finger, white and frail in the moonlight?

"What's wrong?" asks Parson again.

"Parson," says Mona. "Get down."

"What?" he says.

"Both of you. Get down. Get—"

Tree trunks fifty yards away light up with the flash of gunfire. There is a crack, brittle and sharp, then a wet cough.

Something sprays into the air on her left. She looks.

It is Parson's chest. Rivulets of blood are pouring out of his sweater vest.

He looks at her, then down, befuddled. "Is that...me?" he asks. He begins to slump to his knees.

Mona is already moving, leaping over the stones toward Gracie, who is frozen, staring in the direction of their attackers. Mona is aware she is saying "DOWN DOWN DOWN" but Gracie is not moving, so she tackles the girl and brings her crashing to the ground.

Parson is trying to touch his wound but one of his arms is not working, so he touches it with the other hand. He raises his glistening fingertips to his eyes.

"How...silly," he says softly. Then he falls back into a sitting position and wilts, head leaning forward as his spine surrenders, and then he is still.

Lightning splits the air out over Wink. It is brilliant white, a magnesium flare plummeting through the skies. There is a savage crack as air rushes to fill its gap.

Then silence.

Then nothing.

CHAPTER THIRTY-NINE

Neither Mona nor Gracie moves. Nothing moves. Everything is still. No wind, no rustling of leaves or needles. No nothing.

Gracie begins whimpering and trembling. Mona gently places one hand on Gracie's mouth. The girl stops. That gesture alone was too much movement, but Mona could not risk her making more noise, nor could she make any herself by telling her to be quiet.

Mona listens for footfalls, the scrape of branches, the sound of tiny rocks tumbling downhill.

There is none. Whoever attacked them has not yet moved, she thinks.

Slowly, terribly slowly, Mona hauls herself up until she is close to Gracie's ear. There she whispers, "Stay here. Stay down. Do not move."

To her credit, the girl obeys, but she cannot stop herself from trembling. That's bad—even that slight amount of movement will be visible against this barren backdrop. That means Mona will need to work fast to keep Gracie from winding up like Parson, who now lies in a finger lake of red among the rocks. And of course Mona herself could get shot at any time.

They aren't shooting like crazy, though, which would give away their position. That means they aren't stupid. Which is bad.

What to do, what to do.

Okay. So:

The flash came from the right side of the canyon mouth. Which means they are to the southwest of her and the canyon. And if they haven't moved, then that means they can probably see only the eastern inner wall of the canyon.

So the best vantage point would be the top of the western wall.

That sounds great in her head, but she would be outrageously vulnerable up there: she'd essentially be sticking her head up over a wall at them, much like a puppet at a kid's show, an invitation to a bullet.

Mona starts crawling, estimating when she'll be out of their range of vision.

I will figure all this out, she thinks, *when I need to figure all this out.*

When she feels safe, she pops up and silently walks (she does *not* run) to the western wall. The walls of the canyon are fairly shallow here, and aren't hard to climb. She swivels the rifle so it's on her back, and begins climbing.

Halfway up, she stops.

Someone is talking on the other side of the canyon wall. The speaker sounds either mush-mouthed or drunk.

Someone else shushes them. Then it is quiet.

That's interesting. There's more than one of them, that's for sure. And it's hard to gauge where they are by what she's heard, but it sounds like they're in the same area. And if what she heard is correct, someone over there is either sloppy or unpredictable or both.

And Mona is pretty sure none of Parson's brothers or sisters are among their attackers, because she doesn't think they need to use guns. If they wanted her dead, she would be dead.

She keeps climbing until the top of the canyon wall is just above her. *Okay. I'm here. Now what to do.*

Mona thinks. She thinks for a long time.

She doesn't want to poke her head over and look. Just that twitch of motion would be enough to bring attention to this stretch of the wall. And if she's going over it—and she's reasonably sure that's a smart thing to do—then she needs it to be a total surprise. But how to keep that element of surprise while also getting a good long look at what's out there?

There isn't a way, she thinks. *I'm all the way up here and there's no way over the wall. Not a chance, not a way, no sir.*

Then she has an idea.

It is a very dumb idea.

Okay, she admits reluctantly. *There's a way.*

Every muscle in her body is still as she considers it. She is panicking at the very idea of it. Her blood is trying to beat its way out of her veins the more she considers it, as if it knows better and is trying to abandon ship.

Am I really, really, really going to do this?

The rifle swivels around again until it's in her hands. Her legs start to bend, readying to spring up.

I guess that's a yes, she thinks. *Well. It was fun being alive for a while.*

Mona jumps.

Well, she doesn't jump so much as dive up and over, and she completely overestimated the power it would take because she actually does a fucking flip right when she's about to come down on the other side. The stars spin above her, and just before she comes crashing down on the ground a stretch of trees below her lights up with flashes. Hot tunnels of air open up on either side of her. It sounds like there's a chain gang all along the slope cracking open rocks.

Mona thinks: *Fuckfuckfuckfuckfuckfuck*

Yet at the same time, she thinks: *Watch—and remember.*

She sees:

A flashing light beside a large tree trunk.

Large enough, she thinks, for the top of the tree to poke up above the others—remember that.

Someone is crouched there. Two, three feet off the ground.

Still shooting at where she was.

Remember remember remember

Then her tailbone makes a solid connection with the ground, and she starts sliding down, rocks scraping her back and shoulder. They are still shooting, thinking she is hunkered down at the top, trying to hide from their fire.

She extends both feet out, flexes her knees, prays for something to stop her.

That something comes, but it comes only to her right foot, which catches a stone shelf with enough force to make her ankle ache. But her left side keeps moving, and there's an unwelcome *pop!* from the right side of her groin, and she grits her teeth and searches with her left toe for something, anything, please...

Her toe finds a tree root. She stops herself, rolls onto her stomach, brings the rifle swinging up.

They've stopped shooting. She can hear one of them asking something.

She puts her eye to the scope, scans the tree line, finds the tall tree, follows the trunk straight down. It is too dark to see anything clearly. She takes her eye away to watch.

Wait. Wait. Just...wait.

Four seconds.

Do not waste the shot.

Five seconds.

Someone shouts. They are looking for her.

Do not give away your position.

Six seconds.

Time is a knife easing into her rib cage, seeking her heart.

Wait. Wait. Wait...

Then the sky bursts blue with lightning, and the queer electrical light filters through the forest.

She sees a pair of hands floating in the shadows beside the tree trunk.

She puts the scope to her eye, brings the crosshairs in, and thinks, all in one second:

Slight breeze from the north—cold barrel—will dance right if I fire in this wind—wait I'm close enough for that not to matter—forty yards—arc will be negligible—just drop a touch—if this fucking thing is sighted right—is he moving—am I really going to kill him—instinct will be to get low—just—just—will I really—fire already—fire—fire—pull the trigger—fucking do it do it—just

Fire.

Boom.

It is a cannon. A howitzer. It is world-shatteringly loud. At first Mona only thinks: *Fucking tinnitus. I am deaf for the rest of my years.*

Then she dives to the right, away from her attackers. Because now they know exactly where she is.

The world is so silent as she falls. Is she really deaf, or was the shot so loud it has deafened all the world?

But as she slides down away from her roost, she learns she is wrong, because the woods light up with screams.

She has heard screams like this only once before in her life, when she had her vision of the past in the lightning-struck bathroom. Only those screams, screams of such blind terror and agony, can possibly compare to what is echoing across the valley right now, screams so loud and so terrible she cannot understand how a human can make that noise and keep making it, not without breaking his own throat.

Well, she thinks. *I got him.*

A second voice shouts: "Jesus! Jesus Christ!"

As if it has its own agency, the rifle barrel swings back up, nosing out the shouts and screams, hungry to lay the burden of its crosshairs on fresh meat.

Then a third voice, the mush-mouthed voice: "I know that…that's my Mossberg. That's my…my motherfucking Mossberg!"

She recognizes this voice. It's the cowboy from Coburn, the one whose face she caved in.

"You fucking bitch!" howls the cowboy. "You fucking goddamn bitch!"

"Stay down!" shouts the second voice. It's older, and it sounds a lot more clearheaded.

"I'll kill you, you fucking slag!"

He starts shooting. A large pistol, it sounds like—he must have gotten a replacement for his Desert Eagle. She can see flickering lights on a group of tree trunks at the base of a hillock, but she cannot spot more than this.

The cowboy shoots his gun empty.

"Quit your firing, goddamn it!" growls the second voice. "And stay the fuck down!"

The screams persist. Someone rushes to them through the undergrowth, but she sees no movement: it is too dark.

Then the second voice: "Oh...oh fuck."

The third: "Fucking cunt!"

"Dee, are you just gonna sit there and mouth off or are you gonna come help me?"

"Fuck you, Zimmerman! That cunt stole my fucking rifle, my fucking truck!"

"Norris has nearly had his foot blown off, and you have sand in your ass over a *truck*? Kindly shut your fucking yap and stay down, at least!"

Dee, who she guesses is the cowboy, has given up on coherent threats altogether: "Fucking...skull-fuck you! Cut your...fucking bitch!"

The screaming is slowly turning into whimpering. There is the tinkling of what sounds like a belt buckle in the darkness. Then a *thwip* as the belt is pulled tight around what she presumes is her victim's femoral artery.

Two left, she thinks. *But really only one to worry about.*

She does not hear any more movement. Dee, her failed paramour and kidnapper, must still be hunkered down in the same place. She fixes her sights back on that spot.

He keeps talking: "Bitch! I will...I will goddamn fuck you up something good! I will..." Little brass bells tinkling—bullets in the palm of his hand? Reloading? "Can't believe this sort of thing could ever, *ever*...do you hear me? Do you hear me?! Fucking answer! Say something goddamn you!"

Mona does not oblige him.

"Do you know what I will do to you?" he screams. "Do you under-stand what's going to fucking happen?"

Zimmerman, who must be tending to whomever it is she shot, stays silent. She now feels that he is the real threat. She gets the impression that he's had actual training, and he's been quiet for a long while.

Dee is active. She has a feeling he will soon make himself a very good target. But while she could definitely take a shot at him, that would give away her position again for Zimmerman, who she now guesses is the guy who tagged Parson.

There's another cry of pain.

Unless, she thinks, *he's busy with the guy I hit.*

There is a twitch in the branches where Dee is hiding.

She thinks: *Fuck, I hope there aren't any more of them I didn't see.*

"You bitch!" says Dee. "Won't even..."

The big pistol starts going off again. The rounds hammer the slope above her. Some of them are rather close: little shards of rocks rain down on her shoulders and hair. But Mona does not move.

"She's dead, ain't she?" says Dee. "She's dead already. I got you, didn't I! I got you!"

The branches move a little more.

"We got you! We shot your fucking ass!"

And then Dee's head, swollen like a rotting pumpkin, pops up into view. His cheek is clearly defined by the moonlight; she can see exactly where he is and what he's doing.

Right now, he is screaming at her. Mona is so far inside herself that she cannot hear his words. She does not put the crosshairs in the middle of his face, but just above his right eyebrow, at the very edge of his skull; she does this thoughtlessly, as a well-oiled machine would.

She can feel the impulse running down her arm to her finger, tell-ing it to fire.

As it does, she thinks, *You know, I haven't really killed anyone yet.*

But this is followed by, *Well. He's a good one to start with.*

She is so in the moment she does not even register the sound of the gun; she feels it kick, sees the scope spin, and brings it back just in time to see a curious halo swarm up to surround Dee's head, which is not snapping back but is staying perfectly still; the halo dissolves; Dee appears to look down and to the side, as if he sees something in the grass; then he falls from view.

He does not shout again.

Mona starts moving, rolling farther down the hillside. She goes about thirty yards, then finds a new roost.

She expects another salvo. None comes. There is just silence, and sometimes a whimper.

So, just like when she hunted, she waits.

And waits.

And waits.

Which is most of any action, really. Be it hunting or fighting, the most important part is the waiting.

The minutes stretch on.

Killing, thinks Mona, *is such a goddamn boring job.*

Then there's a shout: "Hey, lady!"

Mona's rifle swivels to the north as she tries to guess where it came from.

"Hey, listen, lady." It is the second voice, Zimmerman. "I know now might not be, uh, the best time to try to appeal to your better nature, what with us having shot at you and all, but... this kid here is really hurt, and he's had a bad string of luck for a while and I think it'd be a shame for him to have to die up here. You agree?"

Mona does not answer.

"Okay... well. I am going to come right out and say what my plans are. I plan to pick this kid up and carry him back down the hill to my truck. Then I will drive him out of this fucking town to a hospital, where he will be treated. Please observe that absolutely none of that—*none* of it—includes me taking more shots at you. Okay?"

Mona is silent.

"Okay. Because there might be a lot of reasons worth dying for, but I just don't think this is one of them, and I really just want to go home. So I'm going to pick this kid up, and stand up, and leave my gun behind, and... well. I guess you can shoot me down if you want. I don't have a lot of say in that. But...that's what I'm gonna try and do. I don't *think* you'll shoot me, because I'm pretty sure I've talked enough for you to draw a bead on me"—which is true, Mona notes—"but, well...I don't know. Whatever you gotta do, I guess. Okay?"

Mona says nothing. She hardly moves.

"Yeah," says the man. "Yeah. Okay."

There's a grunt. Then she sees a bulky figure rise up and begin hobbling down to the road.

She follows him with the scope every step of the way. She can see limbs lifelessly swaying in his arms. She feels kind of bad about that. But she just keeps following him. She follows him until she can't anymore.

She waits. Then a horn honks twice from somewhere way down the slope. There's the sound of wheels spinning—*He's spinning them because he wants me to hear him leaving*—and then only silence.

She waits. Again. And she keeps waiting.

She waits for over forty minutes, not moving, hardly breathing.

There might be others he's left behind—any ones who are waiting on her, in turn, to move or speak and tell them where she is. Yet with each blaze of lightning she peers through the dark forest, and she sees nothing.

Finally she begins to crawl down the slope to where they hid.

She sees bent branches, spent rounds twinkling in the grass. She sees footprints and disturbed stones and, eventually, blotches of blood.

Not much else.

That is, until she finds Dee. His ostrich-skin boots, which have been so impeccably shined, gleam brightly from underneath a bush. Mona goes to investigate.

She peers around the bush, and grunts.

She hit him in the mouth. Square in the roof of the mouth.

Jesus.

She looks at him for a long time. She has seen dead bodies many times before but the causality of it—*I did this, I made this happen*—escapes her. She cannot link that desperate, cold moment at the bottom of the hill, when her whole world was reduced to the dark spotlight of her scope, to this dead man lying on the forest floor.

She wonders who told him to be here. Did they come to kill her and Parson? From the way the second one, Zimmerman, acted, he was surprised to find her. Hence why they shot Parson first, and why Zimmerman was so willing to abandon it after she wounded Norris and killed Dee. They must have been here for some other reason.

She sees there is something silver below Dee's body.

She squats to see. It looks ornamental, a clasp to a box—and the rest of the box is underneath him, as if he fell on it.

Wincing, she reaches forward and pulls it out. It is covered in the man's blood, but she can see it is a very nice wooden box with a silver clasp; yet evidently the owner didn't think this was enough security, for it's also fastened with string and tape of all kinds.

She holds it up to one ear: she hears no ticking.

She shakes it: it sounds hollow, but something is rattling around in there. It's not a bomb, then.

She looks back up at the canyon. Were they simply bringing this box here? Why?

Mona unties the string, which is now quite sticky from the blood. Then she flips up the clasp.

She wedges her finger into the crack, and slowly eases it open, certain she is about to be ripped apart by an explosion.

It never comes: the interior of the box is simple red velvet, and resting in its corner is a very strange item that is certainly not a bomb.

It is a skull. A little rabbit skull.

Mona stares, and shivers. Because she is uncomfortably familiar with rabbit skulls, and the mere sight of this one sends old, gray memories howling up the hallways of her mind.

When she was in junior high, Mona, like a lot of kids in her country-ass school, participated in 4-H. While most kids preferred the larger animals, the ones they'd learned about since kindergarten—pigs, cows, etc.—Mona instead opted to raise meat rabbits for a judging competition, mostly because she'd assumed it'd be easier, because what were rabbits besides slightly larger, cuter guinea pigs?

She only did it the one time, for she found the whole process to be one of the most awful experiences of her young life: not only did many of her rabbits die—an experience she was unprepared for, and she is still quite angry at her father for not warning her about—but the first of them was intentionally killed by its mother. There had been something wrong with it—something twisted in its neck and front leg—and in the evening its mother had pushed it out of the nest and allowed it to starve.

Mona knew she should remove it from the rabbits' pen. But when she first found the baby rabbit, with lines of ants marching to it across the barn floor in a gruesome little pilgrimage, and its tiny, rotting eyes swarming with blackflies, she was so horrified she could only bear to kick it into the corner. And she forgot about it until many days and many dead rabbits later, when the whole horrible thing was over and she removed the straw from the pen, scraping it up with a pitchfork, and with one scrape a desiccated, eyeless little rabbit body popped up from the straw, scraps of fur still clinging to its tiny bones, and it stared at her accusingly, as if to say: *You forgot about me. You wished me hidden and so I hid, but I was never gone.*

She had nightmares that night, and for the rest of the week. How she wished she had buried it, respected it, given it the love no one else had—it was as if she had chosen to kill her own child.

It is so strange to find a rabbit skull now, in this bloody red velvet box. Mona almost wonders if they were trying to send a message to her. The mere sight of it fills her with unexpected guilt.

Frowning, she reaches out, and picks it up.

"Where did you come from?" she asks it.

And then the lights go out.

CHAPTER FORTY

There is a certain darkness you can never imagine until you are actually in it. It is a darkness so deep and complete it not only makes you doubt if you have ever seen light, it also makes you doubt if the world is still truly there: *If I stretch out my hands,* you think, *will I feel anything? If I walk in one direction for miles and miles and days and days, will there be only nothing, nothing forever and ever?*

But Mona finds herself lost in a darkness even deeper than that. Her feet do not touch the ground; her lungs pull no air; her nerves report neither heat nor coolness. There is only the dark and the nothing.

Then forms begin to appear. Trees. Rocks. Stars. But it is as if she is seeing them through a dark filter—they are there in only the most muted, superficial sense.

She begins to realize she is still in the same place, still in the pine forest below the mesa, but she is also, like so many places in Wink, somewhere else at the same time.

She begins to see.

She is in a stone chamber, like a crypt. There is no light in the chamber, yet she can see. There are no corners: the chamber is round. The floor is flat and filthy, and in the center of the floor is a pile of bones.

Not just bones. Rabbit skulls.

The double vision slowly fades: she is now within this room only.

Mona swallows. This place, though so much of it escapes her senses, feels trapped, hermetic. Unlike much of Wink, it does not bleed into anything else, does not fade imperceptibly into a park or a backyard or someone's upper room; it is even different from the mirror room at Coburn, which seemed to float in nothing, like a capsule lost below the sea; no, this is a jail cell at the very fringes of existence.

So what is jailed here?

Her eyes struggle to make sense of the space: is this chamber vastly huge, or tiny? When she looks in one direction it feels like a cathedral vault, yet in another it is like a kitchen cupboard.

Maybe it is big to me, she thinks, *but tiny to whatever is trapped here.*

But still the question remains—what is trapped here? The room appears empty, and there are no doors or windows, no hiding places of any kind. Is she alone? She does not think so: she does not *feel* alone. Whatever is here is watching her.

Helpless, Mona keeps slowly turning around, yet on each turn her eye wanders back to the pile of rabbit skulls. Finally she stops turning and walks to them.

She picks one up. Looks at it. Then, very quickly, everything begins to vibrate.

Without any warning, she's suddenly in another part of the rounded chamber, looking in a different direction. It takes her a moment to reorient herself.

She looks in her hand. The rabbit skull is gone.

She returns to the pile and picks up another. For a moment there is nothing, and then everything begins to vibrate again like she's stuck in a paint shaker, and before she can do more she's staring into the stone wall of the chamber. Once more she has been transported to a different part of the room. Her fingers clutch nothing, for again the rabbit skull is gone.

In the inexplicable manner of dream logic, she begins to understand:

The skulls are not skulls. They look like skulls, but they aren't, not really. They're doors. Little tiny doors that, when activated, take you to this place. But when they're activated here, they can't bring you far at all, can they?

Maybe they bring you halfway, thinks Mona, *and allow whatever is in here to venture out halfway as well, and meet you.*

Then she sees it: something is moving over her shoulder, like a portion of the rounded stone wall is rippling liquid. She does not want to look, she does *not*, but she cannot help but see a form begin to emerge, tall and thin, and when she sees what appears to be a face (a face carved of wood?) then everything begins to...

Change.

She first sees a man, standing quite still and wearing a curious blue canvas suit that is covered in tiny wooden rabbit heads. On his face he wears a primitive wooden mask, suggesting the face of a rabbit, but its features are spare and simple, giving it a blank, furious look.

But this is only an image. Behind it, in a deeper way, is something else.

She does not want to look. But she cannot help it.

She sees

(a figure, tall and ropy)
(an arched back and bony shoulders)
(covered in hair)
(arms like needles, stretching for miles)

(how does it stand)
(on such thin legs)

(and its face)
(so, so long)
(and its eyes)
(so terribly)
(huge)

(don't look)
(don't)

Just as with Parson and Mrs. Benjamin, this vision threatens to overwhelm her. But Mona has been figuring out a few things since she's been here in Wink. In Weringer's bedroom she was able to avoid the deep places, the places on the other side. Why couldn't she do the same here?

So she focuses, and breathes, and relaxes...and with a simple push, she picks up this horrible image and packages it away, pushing it in one direction and her own mind in another, until all she can see is the man in the filthy rabbit costume...

Yet as she does so, she understands that whatever this man is—whatever he *really* is—is much, much more powerful than Parson or Mrs. Benjamin. The man in the blue rabbit suit is not a simple vessel, like those used by so many "people" in Wink. Rather, whatever is in this jail cell with her just chooses to manifest as this odd sight, a filthy man in a filthy rabbit suit. She supposes it could manifest as whatever it wished: in this place, the difference between it and a god is too small to matter.

She breathes deeply, and focuses. "Who are you?" she asks.

The man stares at her. She cannot see any eyes through the holes in his mask.

"Am I meant to be here?" asks Mona. "Did I come here by accident?"

The man cocks his head, like a curious dog. Mona finds the sight repulsive. Then the man raises an arm and reaches out to her, but stops, fingers trembling. It is an oddly sentimental gesture, as if he wishes to touch her face and yet adores her too much to bring himself to do so.

Mona withdraws a little. "What do you want?" she asks.

The man slowly drops his arm. He cocks his head one way, then the other. Then he appears to come to some decision, and reaches up to take off his mask.

Mona wonders if she should turn away. The horrors that reside in this town seem to possess many secrets too large for her mind, and whatever lies behind that mask should surely be one of them. But as he removes the wooden mask, she sees something she never expected.

"Oh, my God," she says, surprised.

At first she thinks it is her own face—because those are most certainly her eyes, deep and rounded and charcoal-brown, and her lips, so dark and thin—but it is a male face, with sharp, hard cheekbones, and many lines, as if this face has been exposed to brutal conditions day in and day out for decades. The man looks at her in a manner both wary and full of longing, as if he wishes for her to accept him, even come to love him, but cannot bring himself to believe she ever would.

He looks so much like me, thinks Mona. *He could even be my brother.*

"What is this?" she asks him.

The man slumps forward a little. He looks away as if her response has deeply disappointed him.

"What do you mean by this?" Mona asks him.

He shakes his head. He suddenly looks terribly distraught. He buries his face in his hands.

"Wait," says Mona, "are you trying to say that—"

But then things begin to swim around her, and she hears someone saying her name.

"—ight? Miss Bright?"

It's dark again. Mona realizes she has her eyes shut. She opens them, and sees the lights of Wink just below her. She is back in the forest: in one hand she holds a bloody, empty box, and in the other a rabbit skull. She hears someone crashing through the undergrowth. Then Gracie emerges from the trees at the edge of the clearing.

"What happened?" Mona asks.

Gracie says, "There you are. Are you all right?"

Mona inspects herself. "I think so."

"Where were you? Were you here this whole time?"

The question is simple enough, but Mona is not sure how to answer.

"I've been looking for you for over half an hour!" says Gracie. "I walked by here calling your name, but I swear I didn't see this place. I don't remember it being here at all. So—" She freezes, eye drawn to

the two cowboy boots poking out from underneath the brush. "Wh...
what's that? Is that—is that man...dead?"

"What?" says Mona absently. "Oh. Yeah."

"Did you kill him?" asks Gracie.

"Yes."

"Oh." She stares at the body, not daring to ask more.

Mona's still thinking about what Gracie just said—so this whole
clearing just went missing when she picked up the skull? She turns it
over in her fingers, wondering if it could still pose a threat. She thinks
not: perhaps its batteries have been drained, so to speak. A one-shot
ticket.

She replaces the little skull in the bloody box, kneels, and hides the
box in the weeds. She is not sure what it did to her, but she does not
want to carry it any farther. "They were bringing this here," she says.

Gracie does not answer: she is backing away slowly, her attention
fixed on Dee's body.

"Gracie!" says Mona sharply.

Gracie jumps a little. "Wh-what?"

"They were bringing this box here," says Mona. "They didn't
come here to attack us. Just to bring this. Why would they do that?"

"I don't know. I've never heard of such a thing."

"Has your"—Mona struggles as she wonders how to word this—"*friend*
heard of it?" She nods toward the canyon.

"He's never mentioned it."

Mona turns back to the little bloody box hiding in the weeds. "It
took me someplace. When I opened it, it took me and...I think this
whole clearing someplace. Somewhere not in Wink. I mean, I know a
lot of places in Wink aren't actually *in Wink*, whatever that means,
but...somewhere even farther than that."

"Why would they want to do that to you?"

Mona starts back up the hill to the mouth of the canyon. "I don't
think they wanted to do that to *me*," she says. "Come on. Let's go meet
your boyfriend."

CHAPTER FORTY-ONE

Unlike nearly everyone who works for him at the Roadhouse, Bolan has a vehicle devoid of any overweening masculinity: his chosen chariot is not a neon-colored sports car, or a muscle-y, amped-up truck, but a bland, nondescript Honda Civic whose sole embellishment is satellite radio. Bolan chose to purchase this car the day he drove back to his home in his Camaro with over three-quarters of a million dollars in the trunk, hands jittering all the way as he tried to imagine how he would explain his cargo to any highway patrolman who just happened to pull him over due to a vague dislike for his ride.

No—Bolan does not plan to go out like that. He'd rather drive a nebbishy, emasculated car than get collared that way.

But the Civic has trouble getting to the more remote places here. Bolan never considered that, because he never intended to go into the mountains: he has never wished to go to Wink, never wanted to start down its many winding roads, so he did not choose a car that could handle this terrain. Yet here he is, struggling up an insane incline, wincing as he waits for the road to drop away, when he'll have to start mashing on the brake.

Finally he comes to the highway crossroads. He has seen this destination only on a map: it is a frequent pickup spot for Zimmerman, and he often comes back with several pounds of incredibly pure heroin. It is a bit surreal to finally see it in real life. He can see the sign welcoming everyone to Wink just a few feet down, and beyond that the crystalline spiderweb of the town.

Bolan pulls off the road, throwing up tons of dust, and gets out.

The headlights turn the dust into a swirling khaki-colored mist. It's almost impenetrable to the eye. Bolan remembers what the message on the machine said—*you will have to look down*—and dutifully looks down.

There is just gravel there, of course. But as the dust settles, he sees he's parked on the edge of a small cliff. He never even noticed it. If he hadn't stopped, he would have driven over the edge.

Nervous (for Bolan does not like heights), he walks to the edge of the cliff, and looks down. There's a long ravine at the bottom, which, after the fog of dust recedes, fills with pink moonlight. Just a few yards below Bolan is a small rent in the cliff wall, and there is something uncomfortably organic about it, as if it is the cliff's navel, or (Bolan's mind does not really want to go there but what can you do) some kind of vaginal orifice.

That's the place, of course. It has to be.

Bolan hasn't worked as a legman in decades, but he was still smart enough to bring a flashlight. He takes it out and walks along the roadside, flashing the rocks and the trees, looking for a way down. He finds one path that is incredibly dangerous, almost a sheer drop down to the bottom of the ravine, but it's less sheer than the rest of the cliff wall.

It takes him twenty minutes to climb down. *I am going to get this creepy motherfucker*, he thinks, *to cough up a significant fee for this act.*

But of course Bolan will do no such thing.

He gets to the bottom of the ravine and puts his hands on his knees and puffs for a while. When he finally gains the strength to lift his head, he sees he is not alone.

There is someone standing in front of the hole in the cliff wall. The person is not facing him, but the moon: he stands directly underneath the pale pink orb with one arm up, fingers clawed as if desperate to grasp it.

Bolan can see that the person is wearing a pale blue suit and a white panama hat. He waits for the man to acknowledge him, but he never does: the man just stands there, frozen, reaching for the moon. Bolan gives up and begins to approach, though warily.

When he's about twenty yards away he notices the man in the panama hat is a lot shorter than he remembered. But then, what can he remember about this man? He remembers the briefcase full of heroin, the appearances at the edges of the Roadhouse's parking lot, but not much else. But whatever he remembers, he does not remember this.

Because the person in front of the cave is not a man, but a young girl of about sixteen. She has dirty-blond hair that hangs down from the back of the white panama hat in a crooked sheet—obviously, she does not know how to make long hair work with such a hat.

Bolan stops. He scratches his nose, feeling terribly awkward. Finally the girl drops her arm, stares at her hand for a while, and turns to face Bolan.

Her eyes are wide and mad, but the rest of her face is vacant of any expression at all. Finally she smiles dreamily. "You look surprised."

"That's because I am," he says. "Where's your boss?"

"Boss?"

"Yeah. The man who messaged me."

"I messaged you," she says.

Bolan frowns at her.

"Do you not recognize me?" she asks.

He looks at her for a while. Something flutters in her eyes, far at the back. He says, uncertainly, "No."

She laughs a laugh that's mostly clicks from somewhere in her throat. "That's because I've changed. But it is still me, in here."

There's a sound from the cave entrance, an oddly wet sound like someone emptying a bucket of water. Bolan glances at the cave: it is a surprisingly dark hole in the cliff wall, and he can see no end, so it must continue back for several feet. Or more.

"Okay?" says Bolan.

"You're not comforted."

"No. The guy said he might die tonight. So I have to assume he did."

"Oh, yes. That's right. I forgot I told you that." She smiles wider. "Well. I didn't die. Let's say I wanted to test what my adversaries knew. And I found they don't know much. I feared they might know a way to kill me—after all, they are my elders, and usually know much more—but they didn't. Perhaps they've been trapped here for so long they've forgotten how we fight."

"Okay," says Bolan, who is feeling more uncomfortable with every passing second.

She gazes at him solemnly for a long time. Bolan awkwardly stares at the ground and waits. He has never held such a long in-person conversation with his superior—who might or might not be a teenage girl, he isn't sure. It's like talking to someone from a mental ward, or a prison, like she's been in isolation for so long she's forgotten how to talk with normal people.

"The totem is on its way to the canyon, correct?" she asks.

"Yeah. I sent them up there with the box this evening."

"And you have no reason to expect any issues?"

"No. Should I?"

She stares at him again, that wild, mad gaze of a cultist or a street preacher.

Bolan's impatience eventually outweighs his fear. "So…why am I here, again?"

"You're here because I wanted to show you something." She gestures to the cave. "This way." With stiff, awkward steps, she walks to the cave entrance, and strolls in without looking back.

"Shit," says Bolan, and fumbles with the flashlight as he catches up.

The cave is quite spacious, tall enough to admit him without his having to duck. It is also curiously even, as if it was drilled or carved into the rock. But its sides gleam a little, as if moist, and when he reaches out to touch them the girl in the panama hat says, "I wouldn't," and Bolan does not argue.

"Where are we?" he asks.

"You have your headquarters," says the girl. "I have mine. This is where we've been gathering."

Bolan thinks—*We?* He begins looking backward, trying to see if he can spot any figures following them into the tunnel.

"Have you ever been an outcast, Mr. Bolan?" asks the girl.

"Uh, an outcast?"

"Yes."

"Not really, I guess."

"It is not a pleasant experience. We all wish to belong. We all have our families, our communities, our hierarchies. And we all wish to be thought well of in the eyes of those above us. But to be denied that—to have it withheld, and to be forgotten, when you are so deserving of attention—can you imagine anything worse?"

Bolan decides now is a great time to be diplomatic. "I can't." He is keeping the flashlight trained on the floor, watching the gleaming heels of the girl's two-tone shoes as they pace over the tunnel floor. But at one point the walls recede from his vision, and he realizes they have just entered what must be an immense cavern.

Then the girl isn't there anymore. It's just him and his flashlight, standing at the entrance to this huge cavern. Bolan hears noises in the cavern: that wet, sloshing noise, and what he can only think of as a *sloughing* sound. Something in this chamber is moving, he realizes. Probably because he's just walked in, which makes it—whatever it is—nervous.

A hand snaps out of the dark and snatches the wrist holding the flashlight. He yelps a little, and squirms to see it's the girl in the pan- ama hat.

"I would keep your flashlight trained on me," she says softly, "and what I wish you to view, and nothing else."

"Why?"

"Because there are things in the dark here, Mr. Bolan. Things I do not think you wish to see."

The noises in the cave increase. His ears become hysterical half- wits, telling him he is hearing pits of snakes, octopuses in underground pools, alligators turning over in the churning mud. He stares into the wide, mad eyes of the girl, who is breathing hard, with flushed cheeks. Bolan is uncomfortably reminded of his high school girlfriend, whose cheeks pinkened that exact same way when she was horny, as if she were almost to the point of overheating and had to strip from fear of death.

"Do you know why I engaged your services?" the girl asks.

Bolan thinks of several answers, and knows all of them are wrong. "Not really."

"I contacted you," she says, "because I wished to stage a reunion."

"All right?"

"And some people were very difficult about that. Some people did not wish to reunite with anyone. They claimed they were happy where they were. But no one," she says slowly, with a touch of fear in her eyes, "is ever really happy where they are—are they?"

"I guess you're onto something there."

"No. No, they're not." She looks away into the darkness, as if she can see right into it. She thinks, then looks back at Bolan with a knowing gleam in her eyes. "Look," she says. She forcefully turns his hand over—she's as strong as a goddamn ox, somehow—and shines his light on something lying on the ground at the cave wall.

There is a glistening white deposit of some mineral there, nearly four feet tall and about six feet in diameter. It looks like the ceiling has been dripping down onto this spot for millennia, leaving traces of... whatever that is on the cave floor. The girl drags him over to it, and reaches out and touches the deposit, which crumbles apart like flour.

She holds her fingers up to Bolan's face with the traces of powder still on their tips. "Does that look familiar?"

Bolan looks at it. He slowly begins to understand what the girl is suggesting. "Is that...no. No way."

She smiles. "They're making it now. Can you not hear them?" She cocks her head, and points to the ceiling. Bolan looks up, but can see nothing but darkness above them. Then there's a wet sucking sound, and a soft moan, and a huge dollop of something white plummets out of the darkness to smack into the top of the white pile.

Bolan almost falls back, but the girl holds him up. "It takes a while for it to dry," she says calmly. "And it took us a while to get the formula right. But with the resources I've gathered here, there really isn't much I can't make."

He has never been more repulsed and terrified in his life. Did something up there really excrete or *shit out* a whole fucking kilo of what this girl is suggesting is heroin?

She is clearly enjoying his confusion. "You look surprised."

"Please take me out of here," says Bolan. He cannot stop staring into the shadows, wondering what stands just beyond the penumbra of his flashlight, staring back at him.

"Are you afraid?"

"Yes."

"Why?"

"I don't know. Because I don't think...I don't think we're alone in here."

"You've never been alone. We've always been there at the edges of things, watching. You see us when we wish you to."

"Please. Please get me out of here."

"Not yet," she says. "I have one more thing to show you." She turns the flashlight to the left, where there's something else down along the cave wall.

It's a stack of metal blocks of varying sizes: some are the size of shoeboxes, others the size of nickels. The proportions remain the same, however, each time an absolutely perfect cube, save for the odd notches and scuffs in their edges.

Though the blocks appear rather unremarkable—just bland gray, and six square sides—there is something about them that pulls Bolan's eye to them. He can't stop looking at them—in fact, now that he knows that they're here, he feels that his thoughts will be drawn back to them long after he leaves this place. There is something intensely *heavy* about them: they make his teeth hurt, like the cubes are slowly but inexorably pulling the fillings out of his skull.

He realizes that these are the blocks of metal he's been sending Dee out to get for the past months. He's never actually seen one in person.

Now he knows what Dee is always bitching about: it's as if merely seeing them has left an imprint on his bones.

"What are they?" he asks.

The girl is silent for a long time. He glances sideways at her and sees that tears are streaming down her face. This sight awakens some long-dormant paternal instinct in Bolan, and he briefly experiences the desire to give this crying girl a hug before remembering that the thing holding his hand is probably *not* a girl of any kind.

"Have you ever in your life, Mr. Bolan," asks the girl, "looked on your parents' remains?"

"No," says Bolan, who never knew his father, and whose mother died in prison.

"Then I cannot describe it to you. It hurts to look at them. But it hurts even more to hold them." She releases him, and walks to the stack of blocks. She reaches out to one, stoops, and picks it up.

Immediately her fingers begin smoking. The skin on her palm turns glossy black, like volcanic glass, then crumples and cracks to reveal brilliant red flesh.

"Jesus Christ!" cries Bolan.

The girl stares at her withering hand impassively. "Your kind can't touch Her," she says reverently. "She is too much for you. Only we can touch Her, in our *real* forms. But people tend to take notice of our real forms when we move out in the open."

She looks at Bolan as if she's just remembered he's there. Then she walks to him, smoking, crinkling hand outstretched. He turns his head away, but does not dare step back, for what could be waiting in those shadows?

"Do you see what this does to me?" she says. "Do you see?"

"I see! I fucking see!"

"What I hold in my hand now is more important than your drug, than your money, than the lives of your men. What I hold in my hand is more important than my own life, and the lives of everyone else who's come to gather and work in this cavern with me. I would murder this entire town for what I hold in my hand. Do you understand me?"

"I got you!" Bolan casts an eye back over his shoulder, wondering if he should try running for it.

"Soon I will need you to find the last pieces. I believe I know where one is, one I've asked you about so many times—the largest piece yet. You will find it for me. You must find it for me."

The black has spread to the back of the girl's hand, where the skin is splitting like a shirt several sizes too small. Bolan can see tendons encased in pink tissue, then it all sloughs off and curls away as if the hand is molting.

"I will! Jesus Christ, I will!"

The girl nods. "Good," she says, and—her one hand still sputtering like a dying torch—calmly walks to the stack and replaces the block on the top. She stands there, staring reverently at the block as one would at a gravestone, and nods and walks back to Bolan. "I will take you out now."

She walks to the cavern entrance. Bolan turns to follow her, but as he does his flashlight beam happens to shoot out across the cavern.

And when it does, he sees something.

For one thing, the cave is enormous—bigger than a football field. But though the cavern is vast, almost all of it is occupied: there is something heaped in the center, and the heap is so huge it almost touches the walls on all sides.

As the image fades, he realizes it is not a heap: it is a series of stacks, stacks of blocks like the one he just saw, but there must be thousands— no, *millions* of them. They have been put together almost like a jigsaw, with tiny ones sandwiched between larger ones, and though they are all quite angular, as he considers the sight he realizes they make a shape much like a giant body lying on the cavern floor.

And as he stumbles down the tunnel, he realizes he saw something else.

There were *things* crawling across the stacks of blocks. Dark, shapeless things, dozens of them, hundreds of them, with many arms and legs (or tentacles?), headless, spineless creatures, like enormous jellyfish, all crawling across the sides and roof of the cave...

He is too stunned to think. Then a thought rises through all his numb terror: *What the fuck have I gotten myself into?*

He is still in a stupor when the girl leads him out of the tunnel. She turns and begins speaking to him, but he is too horrified to hear. Then he realizes she has stopped speaking, and is staring at him curiously.

There is an odd sound coming from his pocket: his cell phone is playing its blues-riff ringtone.

"Your body is beeping," says the girl.

"Oh," says Bolan. "Shit. Sorry." He answers it, and, in the manner of cell phone users everywhere, steps a few paces away to take the call. But the girl in the panama hat apparently has no knowledge of phone etiquette, for she follows him step for step, staring at him curiously.

Bolan listens to the call. He says "okay," three times, with various inflections: there's "Okay?" and "Okay..." and, finally, a soft, grim "Okay."

He hangs up. He turns to the girl, wondering how to put this.

"Things at the canyon," he says slowly, "have not gone well. That new girl was there. The girl in the red car? The one you had us investigating?"

She gives no sign of understanding: she just waits for more.

"And I guess she must be a fucking Green Beret or something because, uh...it seems she killed one of my men, and severely wounded another." Ordinarily Bolan would be furious about this—because *what the fuck* was this girl doing there, and *why* weren't they warned about this, and *how* did we not know she could outclass us that way, etc., etc.—but after what he saw in that cave, Bolan is going to try his goddamnedest to stay on the good side of the girl in the panama hat.

She looks away, thinking. She turns 180 degrees and stares in the exact opposite direction as she considers it.

She turns back around. "And the totem?"

"The guy who got killed was the one carrying it."

"And your men did not recover it?"

"He made it sound like he would have gotten shot dead if he tried. This lady is...serious business, it seems."

The girl in the panama hat looks away once more, and again turns 180 degrees as she thinks.

Bolan feels something drip down the side of his face, and realizes he is sweating. No one has made him sweat for over fifteen years, but here he is, being grilled by a teenage girl dressed like a fucking zoot-suiter on vacation in the Caribbean.

Finally she turns back around. If this information is troubling to her, she does not show it. "You brought a car," she says.

"Huh? Yeah. Yeah, I brought a car."

She nods. "I am going to need a ride."

CHAPTER FORTY-TWO

The canyon is narrow but long, a winding, intestinal gouge at the foot of the mesa. Mona and Gracie stump forward for what feels like hours, though Mona cannot tell if they are approaching anything, or even how far they've come. Whenever she asks Gracie if they're going the right way, she always says, with infuriating serenity, "Oh, yes. This is the way."

"How can you possibly know that?"

"There was no alternate path, was there?" says Gracie. "Did the canyon split or fork? Did you see some other way we could have gone?"

Mona cannot help but feel that Gracie is navigating, somehow: though the canyon might appear to be one solid route, Mona suspects Gracie is carefully making choices, picking apart this tangle of a passageway by some invisible method. Though Gracie might not be one of *them*, she knows more than she's letting on.

This would all be a lot more tolerable if it weren't so awkward. It's like they're trapped in an elevator together, forced to make conversation, yet how could they possibly bridge the gap between them, with one a recent killer and the other involved in some repulsive relationship with whatever is waiting at the end of this canyon?

Eventually Mona cannot bear the silence, and tackles the subject head-on: "So how did it happen?"

"How did what happen?" says Gracie.

"You and"—she nods forward—"him."

"Mr. First," corrects Gracie.

"Yeah. Him."

"I don't know. It just...did. He's...always been there."

"What do you mean?"

"I mean he's always been in my life. Ever since I was born."

"Since you were *born*? Like, since you were an infant?"

"Yes. He didn't make himself apparent, not then. It was like having a distant uncle send you gifts, or arranging things at school so you didn't have any problems. Then one day...he approached me directly."

Mona does not speak.

"You think that's disturbing, don't you?" asks Gracie.

"I don't think *disturbing* comes anywhere fucking close."

"You don't understand. It's different here."

"Everything's different here."

"Well, yes."

"But come on. You can't be totally used to it. I mean...it never creeps you out? Not ever?"

Gracie sighs. "Well. Sometimes. I mean...you can't just...never *think* about it."

She is silent for several steps. Mona realizes she has just made Gracie admit something she probably hasn't spoken about to anyone, ever.

"You do what you have to," says Gracie. There's a tremor in her voice. "Things aren't perfect, but they are what they are. My parents live on the very edge of Wink. Do you know what that means? What you're exposed to there?"

Mona does not, but she has a guess.

"We were never safe. But when he came to them, they realized..." She shakes her head. "You have to make arrangements. Everyone has their arrangement. I could have it a lot worse. He takes care of me."

Mona nods, but she's heard this speech before. She's actually heard it a lot, frequently in the wee hours of the morn in the emergency room of some hospital, with machines bleeping and fluorescent lights humming on and on while the skinny young girl seated on the exam table with two blooming black eyes and a busted lip says no, no, I don't want to press charges, no ma'am, I know it ain't perfect but I got what I got.

"He asked about you, you know," says Gracie. "When you first came. Everyone did. Are you *really* here about your mother?"

"Yeah. It's not a cover story. I'm not from the CIA or anything. I'm just here to find stuff out about my mom."

"It's just so strange...I can't imagine how something so normal would bring you *here*."

"Well," says Mona slowly, "I'm not sure how normal it is."

"What do you mean?"

"I think she was mixed up with all this, somehow. I don't know why, or how, but...it's just a feeling I get." She's unable to keep the disappointment out of her voice.

"That's not what you wanted to find, is it?" asks Gracie.

"Fuck no, it isn't. I thought I was just going to inherit a nice house and a little proof that my mom wasn't so crazy after all. Just to get a little peace of mind, you know? To know that things *could* have been normal, or were once...that meant a lot when I came here. I just wanted things to be *quiet* for a minute or two."

"Quiet? What do you mean?"

Mona sighs and rubs her eyes. She feels terribly tired. "Listen—you want some advice, Gracie?"

She shrugs.

Mona says, "Don't get old."

"How do you mean?"

"I mean don't get old. The older you get, the more voices you get in the back of your head." She taps her temple as if to rattle the squatters inhabiting it. "More invisible people telling you what you can and can't do. And I guess I thought coming here would make that go away. Because I figured, if my mom might have been normal, then maybe I could be normal too. And maybe I..." She trails off.

"Maybe you what?" asks Gracie.

"Maybe I could have been a normal mom," says Mona quietly. "The way my momma wasn't for me."

"What do you mean, could have been?" asks Gracie.

Mona doesn't answer. There is a long silence.

"Oh," says Gracie.

They walk on for a moment without speaking.

Gracie says, "I'm sorry."

"You don't need to be sorry. God knows you've got it rough as it is." There's a pause, and she asks: "You can't get out, can you?"

"No," says Gracie. "No one ever comes to Wink, but no one ever leaves it, either. It's protected, he says."

"It is. I've seen the"—Mona wonders what she should call it—"fence."

"Yes. We're here. So we have to make do."

"You must wonder what it's like outside it all the time."

"Outside it?"

"Outside the fence. In the rest of the world. The real world, I guess."

Gracie frowns, confused. "I don't understand."

"Like... outside of Wink. Where I'm from."

Gracie's pace slows. Then she stops, staring at her feet. "I guess I never thought about it," she says in a small voice.

There is something frail and gleaming in her eyes, like her tear glands are just starting up. It takes Mona a while to understand. "You did know that there was something outside of Wink, right?" she asks.

Gracie bows her head. Then, without looking at Mona, she resumes walking ahead.

"You didn't know?" asks Mona. She runs a bit to catch up with her. "You really didn't know?"

"I knew," she says defensively.

"Then why did you seem surprised?"

"Because... I guess I never thought about what it was *like*."

"Are you *serious*?" says Mona, incredulous. "You never thought about it?"

"Stop."

"Does anyone actually know? Or do you all think that Wink is just... it?"

"Stop it. All right? Just stop."

"Christ!" Mona cannot believe it at first. But then she realizes she can, quite easily: the nature of geography, of direction in this place is so mixed up and bizarre that those who have lived in it for too long—or, in the case of Gracie, grown up in it—probably cannot conceive of the world as being another way. Mona's seen their newspaper, which doesn't report beyond the town's boundaries, and their television stations show nothing but sitcom reruns from no later than 1985. These people have no idea what solid ground is like, what the twenty-first century is like, even. In a way, it is a perversion of the insularity of any small town: how many farm boys has Mona met who hadn't ever spent a night away from home? Could they have conceived of metropolises and highways any better than poor Gracie could understand what the world is really like outside this tiny, warped bubble?

"Do you *want* to know about it?" asks Mona.

"*No,*" says Gracie angrily.

Mona is surprised into silence. After a while she hazards, "Why?"

"Because I'm not going to see it!" says Gracie. "I'm not going to get out of here, Mona! For me, for us in this town, this is it! This is what it is and it's not going to change. Nothing in Wink really changes, not ever."

"It's changing now," says Mona. "It's changed since I got here."

"Well, it won't stick. You'll leave too. And then it'll be back to how it was."

Mona wonders how true this is.

"I'm sorry, Gracie," she says.

"Forget it," says Gracie. "Just forget it. It's better that way." She sniffs and wipes her eyes.

Another twist of the canyon. Another precipitous decline. More gray walls and dusty gravel.

"What's he going to do to me?" asks Mona.

"I don't know," says Gracie. "Maybe nothing."

"And you can't tell me what he's going to look like."

"No. I can't really...translate what he looks like, what he *can* look like."

"Is he big?"

"Big, or small. I know he could go into Wink without anyone ever knowing about it, if he was paying enough attention."

"So what *can't* he do?"

"I'm not sure," says Gracie. She thinks about it, and says, "Well, kill, for one."

"What?"

"He can't kill. He told me so. None of them can. They can't kill their own kind, at least. I don't think they're allowed to die at all, but he never came out and said so. The way he talked about it, though— it's like they're *forbidden* from it. From dying, I mean."

"But Parson just died. We just saw it."

Gracie winces awkwardly.

"What is it?" says Mona.

"I can't...I don't think I can tell you."

"Tell me what?"

Gracie scrunches up her mouth. "Well. I guess you're not really from here. So it might not matter. But they're not...people."

"Well, shit, I know *that.*"

"No, I mean—they wear people like you and I do clothing. But if the person they're in dies, then they can just...change them. Change bodies."

"How?"

"I don't know. But though I don't think it's ever happened, that's how he told me it works."

Mona's mind begins to race. She can hardly feel herself walking. They can change *bodies*? Is that what Gracie means? At first the idea seems ludicrous, before Mona remembers how they came to this place originally—the sky opened up, and they were touched with lightning...

And if one of them dies, would there be lightning again?

She remembers the way the sky lit bright right after Parson died, and the roll of thunder...and she remembers the way the same thing happened when the Native American in the white hat blew his brains out.

Is that what he was doing? Just...changing clothes, taking off a ruined shirt and putting on a new one? It would almost make sense, wouldn't it? After all, the body he was in was pretty fucked up. But which bodies do they go to?

Mary Aldren nearly has a heart attack when she hears the thunder. It's the loudest thing she's ever heard in her life, abominably, unbelievably loud. It's so loud it knocks her over where she's standing in her living room. She remembers what it was like thirty years ago, and she thinks—*It's more of them, isn't it? More of them have come here.*

But a second strike never comes. It's just the one.

She stands up. Maybe it was just lightning—*real* lightning. How odd it is that *that's* the good alternative.

Then she smells the smoke, and sees the wisps of white curling out of the hallway.

Her stomach drops. "No, no!" she cries. "Michael? Michael!" She stands and plunges forward into the smoke.

Michael Aldren has not been himself since he fell out of a tree seven months ago. If he had fallen just a little differently—maybe held on to the branch that loosed him just a millisecond more or less—then he would have simply broken an ankle, or an arm, or a collarbone. But Michael fell and hit the very crown of his head, and though he stayed conscious for the next two days, the swelling in his brain eventually became too much, and he lapsed into a coma, which the doctors in Wink—although quite friendly and wholesome—just aren't able to treat.

And God knows Mary isn't willing to approach one of Them about helping her. Their arrangements often come with so many hidden strings.

But it would be so abominably cruel, wouldn't it, she thinks as she coughs and forges forward into the smoking room, for her little boy to have hung on for so long, with no sign of progress, and then to have it all end in a bolt of lightning? Could the world really be this unfeeling?

Yet as the smoke begins to clear, she sees an amazing sight.

Michael's room is completely black—the walls, floor, desk, and picture frames have all been blacked out as if someone has come through and painstakingly given everything three or four layers of black spray paint. Yet Michael is completely untouched: his blanket, mattress, and pillows are fried beyond recognition, but her little boy, still dressed in his rabbit pajamas, is lying there safe and sound.

And more: he is awake, and sitting up.

"Oh my God," mutters Mary. "My God—Michael?"

Michael is looking down at himself, probing his chest. He even unbuttons his shirt, and inspects the skin below it, as if surprised to find it's whole. Then he looks up and stares around himself, and in a voice totally unlike the one he had before—like he's trying to speak in a baritone register—he slowly says, "Well. This is very interesting."

She rushes to him and takes him by the shoulders. "You're all right? You're awake? You're awake!" She feels his limbs and torso, checking for injuries, which he seems to find quite startling. "You're here! You've come back to me! My God, it's a miracle!"

Michael clears his throat, and moves to push a pair of glasses up his nose, but the glasses are not there. "Madam," he says, "I believe there has been a misunderstanding." He gently takes her hands and pushes them away.

"What is it?" she asks. "M-Michael?"

"Not...quite," he says. He looks at his hands, then looks around himself. He sighs. When he looks back at her, there is a fluttering at the edges and backs of his eyes. "It is possible I have landed myself in a very awkward situation," he says to her.

CHAPTER FORTY-THREE

Mona's feet are beginning to hurt when the canyon curls around and she sees something different from more rock walls: the ground slopes down and widens a little until it disappears into a thick, cotton-white mist that is utterly impenetrable to the eye. It is completely unnatural, of course: this place doesn't see enough moisture to make the ground damp, let alone produce a San Francisco–style fog. Its surface seems to catch the moonlight and glow, just slightly.

Mona has never seen anything like it. She remembers what Parson said: *He is more like Mother than I am. Than any of us is.* Her heart begins beating a little faster. She finds it hard to believe that she's here, that she's doing this.

Gracie stops. "This is it."

"Yeah, it sure looks like it," says Mona. She stares into the mist for a while. "So . . . what is it?"

"That's where he is." She nods toward the mist.

"Okay. Lead the way."

Gracie looks at Mona, smiles sadly, and shakes her head.

"Oh, you've got to be kidding me," says Mona. "I've got to go in there *alone*? Why didn't you tell me before?"

"Well, I . . . I didn't want you to be mad at me."

"Well I'm mad now!" says Mona. "Christ! Do I have to leave my gun here?"

"Oh," says Gracie thoughtfully. "Hm. He didn't mention that. I don't think he cares."

Mona rubs her eyes with the heels of her palms. "Jesus Christ."

"I guess you know what it's like now," says Gracie.

"What do you mean?"

"What it's like living here," says Gracie. She turns to stare back into the mist, her pale, sad face lit by the pink glow. "We don't get to choose where to go, what to do. Some think we do—some *want* to think we do. But one way or another, we're told."

Mona looks at her. She suddenly realizes that this pale little slip of a girl, with her moony eyes and skinny wrists, has probably seen and dealt with worse things than she could ever imagine.

"It's not right," she says.

Gracie just shrugs—*What does that have to do with anything?* "I told you not to stay."

"You did?" asks Mona.

"Yeah. On the phone."

"Oh. That *was* you."

"Yeah. Bunch of good that did, huh?" She *tut*s. "I told *him* what I'd done, and he said it wouldn't matter. He said you'd stay. And he was right."

Mona wishes she would stop talking about this kind of thing. "Will you wait for me?" she asks.

"Sure. I don't have anything else to do."

"It might be a while. I don't know how long this will take."

Gracie smiles indulgently. "Do you really think that time in there works the same way as it does out here?"

"Shit," she says. "Stop telling me this stuff." Then she grabs the strap of her rifle to steady it and descends into the mist.

Though the mist looked like a sea of cotton balls on the outside, on the inside it's a soft, chilly veil. Mona knows there are no lights outside the mist except for the stars and the moon, but light is filtering through from somewhere, like there are floodlights up above her or at the end of the mist. And she knows the canyon was tiny—she was just in the damn thing, after all—so it should probably end in a tight little cul-de-sac. Yet she feels like she's walking across a huge field: this place is perfectly flat, with no walls in sight, and she gets the strong impression that it's just going to keep on going.

"Hello?" says Mona.

But, of course, there's nothing.

Then there is a fluting sound in the mist, very soft. Mona thinks, then wanders in its direction. When she sees the lights, she stops.

The lights are small, round, and golden, like little glowing orbs hanging in the mist. It's hard to tell in this fog, but it looks like they're about a hundred yards away. What's odd about them is that the lights form a large, perfect rectangle, hovering about a dozen feet off the ground in four straight strings. She's not approaching the lights head-on, but from the side, so her perspective's a little off, yet she's sure that's what she's seeing.

As she takes another step forward, her toe bumps something. She looks down, and sees she almost stepped on a small cardboard box. On the box is a rather plain red bow with a tag that reads

FOR MONA
—I HOPE YOU ENJOY THE SHOW!

She stoops, picks it up, and hesitates—because after all she's had some bad experiences with boxes in this town—but then throws caution to the wind, and opens it.

Inside it is a single ticket, like the kind you win at an arcade or a raffle. It reads ADMITS ONE, and on the side of it is a number: 00001.

Still looking at the ticket, she keeps walking forward. The rectangle of lights gets closer and closer, and as it does she begins to see letters spelling something out inside the rectangle in big, black capitals.

It's not just a rectangle, but a sign, like a marquee. And it's mounted on the front of a building.

Mona stops. Though there are no roads here, no sidewalks, nor any sign of civilization at all in this mist, she is now standing before a large, red-brick, 1930s-style cinema, with velvet ropes, a box office with old glass windows, and a huge overhanging marquee, whose letters read: AN AMERICAN IN PARIS.

"Um," says Mona.

She looks down at the ticket, then up at the theater.

I do not know how he will choose to present himself, Parson said. *He has never been . . . orthodox.*

She walks to the doors of the theater and tries to open one. It's locked. She looks to the left, and sees a tall ticket box there, but of course there's no usher.

Mona looks back up at the marquee and thinks. Then she walks over to the ticket box and slides her ticket into the slot. As soon as she does, there's an audible *pop* as all the doors unlock.

She shakes her head, opens the doors, and walks in.

The theater lobby is plush and decadent: the walls are carved wood painted red, and the carpet is a rich, floral pattern. It is also totally empty: there is no one at the snack bar or the ticket box, no one before any of the doors. She hears the muted rumblings of a movie already playing somewhere in the building. The air is heavy with the smells of buttered popcorn and cigarette smoke. She walks by the snack bar, which is well stocked: some of the pretzels look particularly appetizing. She has to remind herself that they may not be real, and that if they are real, they are nothing she needs to ingest.

She goes to the theater doors, opens them, and walks in.

An American in Paris is already playing. Gene Kelly is arriving at some fancy penthouse, dressed in a gray suit and dark tie. He looks chipper and endearingly smug in a way that only Gene Kelly can manage.

Mona looks around the theater. It's totally empty, nothing but rows and rows of empty seats bathed in the light of the screen. She looks up at the projection booth, but sees no one there: just the blinking, frigid eye of the projector. There are curtains on both sides of the movie screen, but nothing really behind them: all they conceal is bare brick.

She climbs the stairs and takes a seat in the direct middle of the theater. She sets her rifle in the seat next to her. She keeps looking around, expecting some shadowy figure to sidle in and sit behind her and murmur hushed warnings into her ear, like they do in the movies. But nothing happens. It's just her and *An American in Paris*.

She watches as Gene Kelly charmingly tries to fend off the advances of a handsome, older blond woman. Mona's seen this before, and she recognizes the woman, but she can't remember her name: it's foreign, or something. The woman is wearing an absurd white dress, one that attempts to reveal about as much of her tits as they'd allow back then. Kelly cleverly comments on this, as he should, all gleaming teeth and crinkled eyes, but the woman parries every comment, growing more forward and aggressive each time, which makes Kelly more and more uncomfortable.

Kelly breaks away from his pursuer, and launches into an angsty but charming monologue about love: "It's always elusive, isn't it?" he begins.

"Sometimes everything feels elusive," purrs the older woman.

"You feel like you have it. You feel like you're there. But then you look up and—*poof*—it was all a dream."

"Such a sad dream," says the older woman, maneuvering in her chair so a lot, if not all, of her leg shows.

Mona remembers this now. He's in love with some other woman, but she's married, or something like that, and this older gal is all over him, but he's not into her. She wonders if she's already missed that big ballet scene.

"What we want is just at our fingertips, but we can't grasp it." He stretches his arm out toward the camera, eyes theatrically brimming with anguish.

"*I* could grasp it," says the woman, smiling cunningly.

"No, you can't," says Kelly. "No one can. That's what dreams are, aren't they? It's a sucker's game. They aren't real, but we *feel* they're real. And so we act in very real ways, and often regret it."

The woman produces a cigarette, complete with an ornate black cigarette holder, and lights it in a manner that is positively lewd. "And do *you* regret it?"

"Regret what, specifically?" asks Kelly.

"Leaving."

"Leaving? No," says Kelly. He tilts his head, and smiles a little wistfully. "And yes."

"Really? How can you not regret leaving with every fiber of your being?"

"Were things really better there?" he asks. "Were we all really that much happier?"

"Perhaps," she says. "You were treated as kings."

"Kings," says Kelly. "Queens. Gods."

"Isn't that all anyone would ever want?" asks the woman.

"Maybe," he says, indifferent. "I was told we fled due to danger—everything was falling apart, our world could no longer bear our size, our numbers. The whispers were always vague, always anxious. She wouldn't tell me much more than that. Just that we had to go, go, and never look back. Now, I'm not sure if I care." He sits down on the floor at the woman's feet, chin on his fist, troubled. Delighted, the woman begins running her fingers through his hair. Kelly doesn't even notice.

Mona frowns. She doesn't remember him doing that. Wasn't this a funny scene? And isn't he supposed to be in love with someone else?

"If you care?" asks the older woman.

"If I care if we were ever really in danger. We're here now. That's all that matters."

"But if you weren't in danger, and if you could go back, would you?" she asks him.

"Me?" Kelly's cleverer-than-you grin blooms to occupy half his face. "Oh, no," he says, and leans back, hands behind his head. "I'm happy here. Here, I'm living the dream."

"But I thought you said dreams never came true!"

"No, they don't," admits Kelly. "But sometimes you can trick yourself into thinking they have. Which is almost good enough."

"As good as the way the ruined moon shone on the spires of Tridy-alith?" asks the woman.

Kelly's grin turns both sardonic and a little weary, as if he is hearing an argument he's heard far too often before.

"Is it better than the long lakes of Dam-Uual," she asks, "where the weaker children could not determine where the buildings ended and the skies began, and only the most powerful could perceive the underwater lights glimmering in the courtyard waters? Do you remember? Were those lights not beautiful to you?"

"As beautiful as the red sun filtering through the tunnels in the ice caps at Yzchintre," says Kelly. "It would filter through the blue ice, turning a pale green, and seep down to where we slept in pools underground, listening to the tones and songs of the enslaved."

"A long sleep," says the woman.

"Mmm," Kelly says, "not *too* long."

Mona slowly sits up. Has First altered the movie for her? Is there a message in this? It doesn't seem clear yet...

"Would you say that your dream is better than the diamond rains on the moon of Hyuin Ta'al?" asks the older woman. "Do you remember how they piled in the craters before melting and making silver rivers in the dark?"

"My little sister broke that moon," says Kelly thoughtfully. "She did it as a show of force. Hyuin Ta'al surrendered almost immediately. To think that it will never rain there again..."

"Do you remember the dancers in El-Abyheelth Ai'ain? With their legs like ribbons, their hair like stalks? They burned themselves alive, doing that dance. They did so for you, for you and your family to see."

"We were worshipped there," says Kelly.

"As you were nearly everywhere. So is it better?"

Mona looks back to the projection booth, expecting to see someone there. "What are you trying to say to me?" she asks softly.

"What's the matter, sister?" she hears Kelly asking.

She can't see anyone in the booth. Then she slowly becomes aware that no one on screen has talked for the past fifteen seconds.

She turns around. The camera has pulled in to just Kelly's face. He's just sitting there, grinning hugely at the camera, but when she makes eye contact (or whatever it is when the other person's eyes are a projected image) his eyebrows rise a little, as if he is utterly delighted to be seen.

"Hi!" he says cheerily.

Mona stares at Gene Kelly's face on the screen. "Oh," she says. "Mr. First?"

"Well," says Kelly's face. His eyes shift theatrically, professing innocence in the guiltiest manner possible. "Kind of."

Mona's whole body feels numb with surprise. She has never been addressed by a celebrity *or* a fifteen-foot talking face before, yet here she is having both such things occur at once. She wonders—is this a dream? A vision induced by Mr. First? Or is Mr. First able to physically produce a theater, and cause it to show the things he wishes?

Gene Kelly (her mind refuses to register him as Mr. First) keeps beaming down at her, reveling in her surprise. Finally she manages to speak: "Kind of?"

"Why, sure," he says.

"How are you 'kind of' Mr. First?"

"Is a puppet the puppeteer? Is a painting a facsimile of the artist?"

He actually waits for her to answer. "So…you're not Mr. First?" she asks.

"No, of course not," he says. "No doubt you're wondering why on earth you came all this way if you're not speaking to the real deal. But though a puppet and a painting are definitely *not* their makers, can't they reflect and communicate the wishes and thoughts of their makers? Why, absolutely, yes. Viz, *moi*." He grins and pokes himself in the chest.

Mona remains so shocked her mind can function only in the most literal way possible. "So . . . this is a puppet show?"

"Kind of, sure," says Kelly.

Mona looks down the aisle on either side of her. "Is this theater really here?"

"Doesn't it feel real?" He mimes knocking on the camera glass.

"How?"

Kelly sighs. "Well. Do you really want to know?"

"I'm not sure. Is it something I'd *like* to know?"

Kelly laughs. It's a wonderful sound, a perfectly natural act. She wonders how Mr. First is able to reproduce Gene Kelly here with such astounding detail. "You're catching on! This town abounds in questions best left unasked. Let's just say that things like physical space are perfectly malleable, if you go at it the right way. Density, matter, radiation . . . it's all just construction paper and pipe cleaners and glue, with the proper perspective. If I wanted to, sister, I could have put you in grand old *Italia*, approaching me via the Appian Way, and I'd speak to you through the mouths of those suffering on those ghastly crucifixes." He pauses and cocks an eyebrow. "Would you prefer something like that?"

"No!" says Mona.

"Oh. Good. I much prefer this. It's got so much more"—his eyes dart around the camera frame, taking in the theater—"class."

"So all this was set up just to talk to me?"

"Sure!"

"Okay. But. Why?"

He sighs. "I'll go ahead and give you the usual spiel, if you're so intent on it," he says, a touch wearily. "Talking to lesser beings—no offense—is often a lot harder than you'd think. It'd be like your little self talking to ants—not only are there the obstacles of communication, since ants prefer pheromones to the King's English, but even if you managed to learn how to speak with them, how could you fit the most basic, stripped-down versions of your thoughts and feelings into a form they'd understand?"

Again, he waits for her to answer this ridiculous question. "I guess you can't," says Mona, who is very aware she is the ant in this metaphor.

"Exactly," he says. The camera pulls out a little. Kelly leans up against a bookcase, takes out a nail file, and proceeds to work on his thumbnails. "So this method—though even I admit it's a bit much—is a lot more aesthetically pleasing than most of the alternates."

"Like what?" asks Mona.

"Oh, curious, are you?"

Mona shrugs, but the answer is a definite yes. She wants to know what these things can and can't do, so she's not going to stop him from talking anytime soon.

"In the old days—well, they weren't so much the Old Days as much as the Days on the Other Side, but you get the idea—the only way we could converse with our followers was through a medium." He puffs on his nails: it's like he's discussing the latest news. "Now, this was a person, or something *like* a person, who had given up their whole life to serve as, well, the conduit for our proclamations. The reeds in our instruments. Mediums were hollowed out—sometimes literally—to become chambers in which our voices could echo, and thus be heard by our adoring congregations. Now, me personally, I don't prefer this method. Do you?"

"I wouldn't, no!" says Mona, though she has no experience with such a thing. But a thought strikes her: "Wait. Is that like ... how everyone in Wink has those ... *things* in their heads?"

"Aah," says Kelly coyly. "Aren't you clever? You're kind of on the right track. Ugly little things, aren't they? My brothers and sisters, who use those rather brutal devices to hide so efficiently throughout Wink, do operate similarly to a medium, it's true. Yet the primary purpose of those devices is not communication, but preservation: we are not truly part of your world, so those who are too big to fit—for now, at least—must maintain a physical representation, or link. Though my family are not, in your terms, physical beings, they must have a physical portion of themselves *here*. Otherwise they'd blow away like runaway kites, and remain trapped over there, on the other side of things, which is in kind of a bad state right now."

"But you don't." Mona does not comment on the most concerning part of his explanation: *for now, at least?*

"No. Not me. I'm, I guess you could say, a special case. I don't need a link or representative at all."

Suddenly something clicks in Mona's head—*A person, or something like a person, who had given up their whole life . . .*

Before she can think, she says, "Gracie."

Kelly's face clears of expression, eyes going dead and dark. The camera rapidly wheels in on Kelly's face, as if she now has his full attention. The change is abrupt, disturbing: it's as if First, wherever and whatever he is, just stopped operating all the finer points of the projection. "What?" he says softly.

Mona senses that this is not a subject to be discussed right now. "Nothing."

A trickle of cunning seeps back into Kelly's eyes. "You sure?"

She decides to change the conversation. "Don't you know what I said?"

Kelly screws up his mouth and cocks his head, confused.

"You knew I was going to be here," says Mona. "So you should probably know what I was going to say just now."

"Aah," says Kelly. He smiles and chidingly jabs a finger at her. "You are mighty on the ball, my dear. I take it my temporal nature is a mite troubling to you."

"Yeah. But you should know that."

"Temporal awareness," says Kelly, and he stifles a yawn with the back of his hand, "is not omniscience."

"Predicting the future seems awful close, to me."

"Weathermen don't *predict* the weather," says Kelly. "They don't put on their turbans, touch a corner of an envelope to their foreheads, and pronounce rain or shine. They just have access to things most folks don't. They *perceive* more, lots more. And they can measure it, and watch it. They observe and make assumptions. But ask them where one raindrop is, or what shape this wisp of cloud will take, and they'll be as dumb as any other bum."

"And weathermen are wrong all the time," says Mona.

"Oh, sure," says Kelly. "No one's perfect. In Moscow they fine their weathermen if they predict the wrong thing. Did you know that?"

"Then tell me what's going to happen here," says Mona. "If you know so much, tell me what's going on, what they want to do. Tell me who *they* are, at least, or if there is a *they*."

"Oh, but my dear," says Kelly, comically obsequious, "your interests do not really lie with what's ahead. Or am I sorely mistaken?"

"With what's ahead?"

"You are not interested in the future, not really. Nor are you interested in the present. You want to know about the *past*."

Mona is quiet. For the first time, she takes her eyes off the screen.

Kelly says, "Sister, I know you didn't come all this way—and in the dead of night, too, which is quite brazen for Wink—just to ask me some silly questions about this parlor trick." He gestures to the sides of the screen. "Nor to ask grisly questions about what sleeps behind the eyes of those much-vaunted civic leaders in Wink. Nor to ask me how I see what I see, and know what I know. Did you?"

"No," says Mona. "That's true." She cannot help but feel he is shepherding her, cornering her: now that she remembers what she came here to ask, she cannot help but ask it, so now the conversation cannot go another way. *Am I as much of a puppet*, she wonders, *as that picture on the screen?*

"I wanted to ask you . . . about how you came here," she says.

"Good!" says Kelly. "A gripping story."

"And who brought you here."

"Ah. You've got good taste. That one's a corker."

"And what it all had to do with my mother."

Kelly smiles wide, eyes thin and mysterious. "Mmm," he said. "Yes. That's a very interesting one, too."

"You don't deny it? My mother did have something to do with it?"

"No," says Kelly. "No, I definitely don't deny it."

"And you'll tell me?"

"Oh, yes," he says mildly. "I expect you're used to people being secretive, withholding. That's how things are in Wink, but it's not how I run my show. I'm a perfect bubbling font of knowledge." He taps the side of his head. "It just depends on if you really want to drink from my waters. Go ahead and make yourself comfortable, sister. This might take a bit."

CHAPTER FORTY-FOUR

It calls itself the Ganymede but this is not its name.

Not names, never names. Never ever never names. The names here are chains and shackles, trappings and signifiers of mice and roaches, customs of a culture so inferior as to be unworthy of a mere second of attention, oh how it hates the burden of a name.

But in this place it needs a name, and so it calls itself the Ganymede, by choice.

The Ganymede rides in the car with the Fool driving, zipping along at precipitous, teeter-tottering angles, headlights flashing on the trees; yet all this makes the Ganymede feel trapped, trapped, horribly, claustrophobically trapped, for it is restrained to this *one point* in space, moving in this *one* direction at this *one* speed. I am pressed to the ground, thinks the Ganymede, pressed into this physicality, pressed into this cage of metal, pressed into this flesh, this skull, behind these *eyes* . . .

This is insufferable. Every second is an insult. I am reborn as a flea.

The Ganymede does not talk, but the Ganymede never talks unless it must. It is an affront to talk, to express its thoughts by such a rudimentary, ugly method. Silence is preferable.

But beside it the Fool glances at the Ganymede and uses the dripping hole in his face to say: THIS WAY?

The Ganymede does not deign to answer. The Fool turns back, keeps driving.

Yes, this way, *of course* this way, there is no other way.

Kill you.

The car pierces the trees, passes a truck parked on the side of the road, huge and black and bulky. The Fool glances at it, worried; the Ganymede does not. It knows what is in the back of the truck, and knows that it will need them; but that is for later. These things are details. It can handle details. There are bigger issues at hand.

Because up on the hill, its sibling is waiting. THE FIRST is there.

THE FIRST is always waiting. It always knew, always knows. Always so unconcerned.

And the Ganymede always hated it for that. Always so superior to the rest of us.

Rage curdles deep within the Ganymede, old rage, fermented rage, eons and eons of quiet fury.

It is not fair. It was never fair.

The Fool muddies the Ganymede's thoughts with speech once more: I DON'T KNOW HOW GOOD OF AN IDEA THIS IS. SHE'S STILL UP ON THE MOUNTAIN AND IF MY BOYS WERE RIGHT SHE'S A HELL OF A SHOT. SHE CAN PLUG YOU GOOD IF YOU DON'T WATCH OUT. EVEN IF YOU DO WATCH OUT SHE CAN PLUG YOU.

The Ganymede gives the Fool a withering glance. He shakes his head, keeps driving.

You think I can die? You think I can end? There is no end to me. There is no end to us. We are forever. Time does not touch us. We are beyond time.

We *were* beyond time.

Stop. Enough of that, thinks the Ganymede. Don't think like that.

The Ganymede feels THE FIRST getting closer. It is like drawing near to the eye of a hurricane, feeling the pressure change in the inner chambers of your skull.

It remembers the body, the vessel it is trapped in, this messy assortment of fluid and feelings. It sends its thoughts roving forward, remembering the throat, the jaw, the lips, and it uses them to say: "Not far now."

The Fool says: WELL JUST SAY WHEN I GUESS.

How disgusting it is, to have conversation.

The Ganymede is not to be addressed directly by these worthless beings. They must *work* at it. Their rude meanings and communications must be received indirectly, and indirectly *only*. Really, it prefers to speak in print. Most of its siblings do—there must be some divorce between what is communicated and their thoughts. The Ganymede was so happy to find that printer—the ticker, whatever it was, the Ganymede cannot be bothered to remember—and to understand it functions by simple electric pulses. To harness these, even in this hideously reduced state, was child's play—in fact, the entire matter of the printer could be manipulated (for here reality is confined to a largely physical state, which really is so malleable). But the fun part, the really fun part, was when the Ganymede realized that when it manipulated the printer it could also sense vibrations in its metal and wiring and paper, and could use these vibrations to understand when these things—these *beings*, the Ganymede thinks with limitless contempt—were talking. It could even understand what they were saying.

Thus, it could have a conversation without even looking at them. Which was a relief.

How it hates such . . . intimate contact.

The Fool says: WONDER WHAT THE HELL SHE WAS DOING UP HERE ANYWAY.

The Ganymede sighs inwardly. What it wishes to do right now, more than anything in the world, is turn to the Fool, and say this:

"Do you know how many of you I have killed? How many of you I have left rotting in the mountains? Dozens. Hundreds. Young and old, male and female. They never even knew they died. They were, and then they weren't. My finger touched them, and they were gone."

The look on his face. It would be priceless.

But the Ganymede does not. It needs the Fool. The Fool understands this place, this way of life, a lot more than the Ganymede does.

The Ganymede is not entirely sure, for example, how the car it is in right now works in any way.

But it knows quite a bit in its own right. It knows a big secret. Maybe—and the Ganymede knows this is unlikely, but it hopes it is so—something even THE FIRST doesn't know.

The Ganymede, though it will never admit this, discovered it only by accident. It was long ago, in one of its blackest fits of despair, when it could not help feeling so

so
abandoned.

Even now, remembering it in this car, the Ganymede seeks to control itself. It does not want to see this world—it tells its vessel to shut its eyes.

Mother, Mother. Why did you leave us?

Where did you go? Why do you not come back?

Stop it. Stop it.

Enough.

The Ganymede restrains itself. That feeling is still razor-sharp—it must be handled most delicately.

And one day, it could no longer bear it. It could not bear wearing this flesh, living in this world, trapped in this despicable little plane of reality.

It was not sure how to end it. Death was a subject it was quite unfamiliar with. But it remembered hearing one of them, the awful little people, saying: YOU BETTER WATCH OUT WHEN OUT WALKING IN THE DARK YOU COULD MISS A STEP AND TAKE QUITE A FALL.

A fall.

So the Ganymede found one peak it thought serviceable, and it stared straight ahead and walked forward, and...

Well. It had not quite worked. Its body, its *vessel*, reported pain everywhere, with parts of it from the inside sticking out into the outside, and some parts missing entirely, but the Ganymede just sat there, letting the life trickle out of it, feeling death grasp it tighter, and falling always darkness...

And then... and then...

Then light.

Then *lightning.*

It was in the sky. In the sky between the worlds. For the town lives within a dome, a dome under *their* skies, the Other Side skies, and for a moment it was like the Ganymede had pierced that dome, crawling up the sides, almost out...

But back down, in a burst of crackling light.

Then, before the Ganymede even understood it, it was driving a truck, a big truck. Its steering wheel and seat were black, smoke curling up everywhere, but the rest of the truck appeared fine. The Ganymede looked to its right, and saw there were people in the car, two young ones. It sat there, frozen, and the children said DADDY DADDY WHAT ARE YOU DOING, and the Ganymede, lost, terrified, confused, opened its mouth, and screamed...

A wall. A crash. A splash of blood.

And no more screaming.

Then lightning again. The dome, the wonderful dome, almost out, almost back to where they came from, into their skies with the pink moon, and if it went far enough the Ganymede would glimpse their red stars...

But back down again, again.

It opened its eyes. It was holding something in its hands—the blackened remnants of a rake, it looked like—and dropped it.

The Ganymede looked around. It was standing in someone's yard. The front door opened. A fat woman ran out to him, terrified, and she said MICHAEL MICHAEL ARE YOU ALL RIGHT WHAT HAPPENED.

The Ganymede looked at her, bewildered. Then it looked at its hands.

It did not recognize the watch, the hairy knuckles, the bitten fingernails. Not the same hands.

It was in someone else. In *another vessel.*

It looked at the woman, then shoved her to the ground and kicked her, over and over again until she stopped crying. Then it turned away and ran into the woods.

That was a good day. It was the beginning day.

The Ganymede experimented with this odd phenomenon over several years. It killed itself in a variety of ways: guns, knives, chemicals (ingested and poured onto itself), walking into traffic, driving into traffic, inserting parts of itself into garbage disposals, and so on. At first it did this in the presence of people—often family or friends of the vessel it'd overtaken—before deciding this was unwise: its elders were sure to take notice.

THE FIRST, especially. How it hated THE FIRST.

But what it learned was this:

They could not leave Wink. None of them could—Mother had said so. But they were also not permitted to die. So, if the vessel they were bearing expired, they were simply sent back down into another, apparently randomly.

But though it took the Ganymede a while, it learned how to control it: it could *pick* the vessel it inhabited. So it began to target loners, people alone in their homes or out walking. It toyed with these new hosts for a matter of hours or days before ending its life, rising up, and finding another. In this manner it could operate off radar, and no one could know who or where the Ganymede was.

It could watch its own kind. They did not even know it was there anymore.

Not as smart as they thought, not at all.

But some trappings the Ganymede kept constant. It was not sure why, but it liked certain colors—two of them, specifically: blue and white. The Ganymede, as a rule, despised every single aspect of this world, of this whole grubby plane of reality, but after a while, without ever realizing it, it did find it preferred to be sheathed in those two colors: soft, pale blue, and bright, clean white. They had not really perceived colors well on the other side: light was mere radiation, which was not worth perceiving, for them. But here, using the eyes of its vessel, the Ganymede found itself powerfully drawn to blue and white, and frequently, in the dead of night, it stole blue clothing and white hats from the local stores, just so it could dress itself up and stare at itself in a reflective surface, like a window or a still lake.

Perhaps Mother was blue and white, and he just couldn't remember it. Maybe he hadn't seen Her properly.

Maybe that was it. He wasn't sure.

It wasn't sure.

Don't think like that. *Don't.* You are not one of them. You do not belong here. You *hate* this place.

Yes.

Once it knew this trick, the Ganymede wondered what to do with it. Should it pick off the inhabitants of Wink, one by one? That sounded quite pleasant, but wouldn't one of the elders notice? And besides, what would that accomplish?

Yet when it was up in the dome, wriggling through the sky as a vein of lightning, it realized that if it paid attention it noticed things it had never noticed before. It was like a brief moment of clarity: it just needed to be above it all to see these secrets, to sense them, to be free of its vessel and its trappings of sad little flesh and *look*.

It discovered there were two things in Wink no one knew existed at all.

One was an interloper—there was someone trapped in Wink, someone terrible, someone monstrous. Someone who had been imprisoned (and by accident, it seemed) in Wink from the very beginning.

But the Ganymede forgot about this when it realized something else.

Mother was here.

It was a sense, a feeling, intangible but definitely *there*—and She'd been there from the *very beginning*. She'd never left them at all.

The joy and the pain were so overwhelming. She was here—but *where*? And *how*? And how should the Ganymede go about bringing Her back? Could She even be brought back?

It was troubling. But if there was one thing the Ganymede had, it was time. It just took time, and patience, and hours and hours of watching.

Sitting in the car, the Ganymede holds up a hand. The Fool looks at it, and says: WHAT HERE? YOU WANT OUT HERE?

The Ganymede swallows, and says: "Yes."

The Fool says: JUST PULL OVER ANYWHERE?

The Ganymede nods violently.

WELL OKAY.

The Fool, peering anxiously into the trees—no doubt looking for the girl, and her gun—turns out the headlights and pulls over.

The Ganymede turns to the car door. It is a confusing mess of glass and metal and plastic. "Which piece?" it asks.

The Fool says: HUH?

"Which piece do I pull to make the outside come in?"

The Fool says: WHAT THE FUCK? OH. OH, THE HANDLE. THIS PART.

The Ganymede pulls on the indicated piece. There is a *clunk*, and with a small push out, the door opens.

THE FIRST is so close. The Ganymede can smell it. Its sibling has walked these mountains, over and over again.

The Fool says: YOU WANT ME TO HANG AROUND?

The Ganymede does not even bother to answer. It plows ahead into the woods. After several minutes, it hears the sound of the car pulling away.

Alone, alone. I've always been alone. Alone in the dark with the trees and, worst of all, that memento of home, the pink moon in the skies, so close yet so far.

I will go home. I am going home.

It smells the blood in the air and quickly finds the bodies. One of them, it knows, must have the totem—the secret door to that prison-place, that hidden bubble where the monster (as the Ganymede has come to think of it) stews and paces.

It does not take long to find it. There is a wooden box lying on the rocky ground. It is covered in blood, and the Ganymede is surprised to find it is held closed only by a silver clasp.

Ignorant wretches. Had it not told them the box must be secure? Had it not warned them of what was inside?

The Ganymede, trembling slightly, picks up the box. It refuses to admit this, but at this moment it is deeply terrified, even more terrified than when they left home and came here: for within this box is a door to something *like* the Ganymede and its siblings, even THE FIRST, but also *not* like them.

For the thing in that prison place can do the unthinkable: it can defy Mother's wishes.

This could, if considered properly, upend much of how the Ganymede sees its existence. For at the center of its world, undeniable and immovable, is Mother, forever Mother, beautiful and terrible and vast. None can withstand Her; none can behold Her. She is all and everything.

Yet not to this being in the box. This prisoner, who appears to be somewhere on par with THE FIRST in abilities (or even, the Ganymede thinks with a thrill of pleasure and terror, above him), can do as it likes.

The Ganymede knows it should find this horrifying. To deny Mother is to prove Her fallible, which She cannot be. But it has instead chosen to cherry-pick, and take away one conclusion, and one conclusion only:

If manipulated correctly, the imprisoned thing can get rid of the siblings that stand in the way.

The Ganymede begins walking up the slope to the barren canyon above it.

Maybe, just maybe, it can get rid of another one of them tonight.

Oh, how wonderful that would be. And I will do it personally.

I am not troubled. My mind is clear. She is with me. She has always been with me.

Though I was one of the youngest, one of the weakest, one of the slightest, She made me Her closest servant, Her most trusted confidant, and I was the only one who could make Her happy, I was the only one who could entertain Her, and please Her.

It was me. I am the favorite one. I, the friend, the councillor, the cupbearer.

CHAPTER FORTY-FIVE

"See, you're missing the point," says Bolan, and he pounds the table with a finger, though he is careful to avoid touching any of the blood. This is difficult, because the top of the table is soaked in it. "The point is, I don't give a fuck about our investments anymore."

Dord frowns. "You want to walk away from all this money 'cause Norris got tagged?"

"No!" shouts Bolan. "Because of what I saw inside that goddamn cave! Haven't you been fucking listening?"

"We've all seen our own fair share of spooky shit," Mallory drawls from the corner. She is leaning up against the corner because she's so soused she can't figure out how to lean against just one wall. This is nothing new: ever since going to fetch the last rabbit skull, she's maintained a steady, stumbling drunk. "But what I saw certainly didn't make me want to *stop*. I don't want to go back to them and tell them *no*."

"Yeah," says Dord. "Me neither." He shifts uncomfortably in his chair: he has not yet told them about his own experiences up in the mountains, and what he found in that ravine. But then, none of them have really talked about what they've seen: all three of them have come to the unspoken agreement that, whatever it is they've encountered, it is surely the most horrifying thing to have ever happened in their lives.

"I'm not saying we tell them anything," says Bolan. "I personally never intend to meet one of them again in my life."

"I bet they can make that hard if they want to," says Mallory.

"Well, I can make being found hard too, if I put my mind to it," says Bolan. "My decision's final. The Roadhouse is done. Everything's done. It's over with. I made my buck and I'm out. As of this moment, I am now unemployed, as are all of you."

An uneasy silence fills the room. Mallory and Dord glance at one another.

"It's not the unemployment I'm worried about," mutters Dord.

Bolan sighs. "Me neither."

He wishes Zimmerman were still here. This night has been a nightmare of logistics, never at the right place at the right time. First Bolan had to drive the girl in the white hat up to that canyon below the mesa (and never in his life has he been happier to have someone walk away from him without a glance back), and then on the way down his cell phone lit up.

It was Zimmerman again. He'd returned with Norris to the Roadhouse, but Norris was in quite a state: the entire conversation was overlaid with his screams in the background, plus Mallory and Dord's panicked bickering.

"The kid's bad," said Zimmerman.

"How bad?" Bolan asked.

"The sort of bad we can't take care of," Zimmerman said. Then, lower: "If we don't get him to a hospital, I'm gonna have to send Dord out to start digging a hole somewhere now."

"Shit."

"Yeah," said Zimmerman. "Yeah."

And for the first time Bolan heard something in Zimmerman's voice that he'd been hearing in his own for the past week or so: he was tired. Not just sleep-deprived, but tired of living this way, tired of the paranoia, tired of the dead drops, of the secret messages and invisible warfare and byzantine hierarchies. You can only stay terrified and confused for so long. After a while, it unfolds and flowers into despair.

Bolan bit his lip. Fuck it.

"Then take him to a hospital," he said.

A long pause. "You sure?" Bolan was not surprised to hear

Zimmerman's doubt: since beginning their contract with the man in the panama hat, whoever and whatever he was, none of them had gone more than a hundred miles from the Roadhouse, usually only to towns not much bigger than Wink, and definitely never for anything beyond business. Their agreements bound them to this place.

"Yeah," said Bolan. He thought for a moment. *I guess if I'm going to start having regrets,* he thought, *I'd prefer to have all of them at once.* "And while you're gone, stay gone."

Silence, save for Norris's groaning.

"Do you understand?" Bolan asked. "Go and keep going. Don't come back."

Again: "You sure?"

Bolan turned a corner. The headlights slashed over tree trunks, stones, and then, without warning, a five-year-old boy and an old man, digging a hole by the side of the road with their hands. Though both of them were dressed quite nicely, they were covered in filth, as if they'd been sleeping in a landfill. When his headlights hit them they looked up and stared like raccoons interrupted while rooting through the garbage. The boy even bared his teeth, hissing.

He drove right by them. He didn't wonder what they were doing. He was hardly even fazed by it.

This town starts out strange, then becomes normal, then becomes unbearable, he thought.

"Yeah," says Bolan. "Go on. Get him out of here. You've both done enough."

Zimmerman hung up. And that was it. Bolan's most dependable man, and his longest-lasting business relationship, over with in just a handful of words. Zimmerman was long gone by the time Bolan returned.

He misses Zimmerman now. Here Bolan is, standing before their improvised operating table like a preacher at a lectern, trying to get his last two remaining employees (or at least the ones who aren't just whores) to come over to his side. He cannot believe the two of them are not disturbed enough by what they've seen to *do* something.

"So you're saying we just run?" says Dord.

Mallory brushes a sheet of ginger hair aside to look at Bolan.

He hesitates for a long, long time. Somewhere in Bolan's heart, which has so far sat hidden deep within his chest, scarred, ignored, forgotten, he begins to feel a sinking sensation that he is about to suggest they do something that could be considered selfless.

Because Bolan is not stupid. And he does not think of himself as evil. He is definitely not willing to be complicit in whatever the hell the People from Wink are doing, not anymore.

Crime and sin are one thing, but this...he'd be a damn fool to do what they tell him to, having seen what he's seen.

Why is it now, he sighs mentally, *that I feel like being a fucking hero?*

"No," says Bolan. "We're not going to run. Something is about to happen here. Something...something way, way worse than transporting a little H."

"Or a fuckin' lot of H," says Dord.

"Shut up, Dord," Bolan says absently. "I should have never helped them. I should have never said yes. And I don't think we can stop them. Not now. Not us. But maybe we can make it a little harder for them."

"What the hell are you saying?" Mallory asks.

He thinks back to the last few communications he's had with the man in the panama hat. So often they were about just one curious topic—the newcomer, the girl in the red car Bolan hasn't even had the chance to see yet, the one who is apparently quite proficient with firearms, the one person who seems to occupy so much of the attention of whatever is residing in Wink.

She's important. And, yes, she shot one of his men. Yet still: the spook in the hat wants her.

"We *are* going to run," he says finally. "But we're going to go get someone first."

CHAPTER FORTY-SIX

Gene Kelly leans his head back, staring up into the stage lights (Are there stage lights there? Where is *there*, anyway, Mona thinks?), and sighs. The gesture is meant to be contemplative, Mona thinks, but to her it is alienating: his face is bathed in such bright, cream-white illumination that it appears craggy, carven, a lump of calcite with two twinkling black eyes at the top. "Before we begin," he says, "I think it'd be wise to know what you know, so I don't repeat myself. Time's short. So. You...know where we came from, don't you, Mona?"

"I guess as much as anyone can," says Mona, though she thinks— *Why is time short?*

"Yes. You've seen it, after all. You've been there, and you lived. Very impressive."

"People keep saying that."

Kelly laughs. "That's not quite correct, is it? It's not *people* who keep saying that, but my...closer siblings. You've met all four of them, haven't you? All except one."

"Weringer. Yeah. He died before I got here."

"*Just* before you got here," corrects Kelly. "Very odd, that."

"Why?"

"Never mind. It's just so curious that you've come to know my family so well, and so rapidly, within just several weeks. Though you haven't met *everyone*." He looks at her, and for the first time this picture of a person looks frightened. In fact, it looks more authentically frightened than Gene Kelly himself ever actually did, because then Kelly was *acting* frightened; yet this thing, this contrived image, is genuinely, seriously frightened.

He says, "You know about Mother. Don't you?"

"Yes," says Mona. She realizes this Mother of theirs came into the world only a few hundred feet away, on top of the mesa beside this canyon. It is a little creepy to realize Mona herself stood there just today. And if Parson and Mrs. Benjamin were telling the truth, Mother never got any farther than that.

"Yes... She kept us quite organized, on the other side. *Segregated*, you could even say. There were the five eldest, of which I was the... well. You get the idea. We were the favored ones, the cream of the crop. Then below us were the middle children, who were, let's say, competent but not extraordinary. Limited. Middling. Nothing to talk about. And then below them were the babies, the wee ones who were little more than teeth, gullets, and however many appendages they chose to have. Formidable, sure, but not clever. Now. I bet you wonder why She chose to split us up like that."

His eyes are shining strangely, and there is a bitter edge to his voice.

"To keep a tight hand on the wheel, I'd say," says Mona.

"You are correct, sister," says Kelly acidly. "It's so much easier to control everyone when you have them all divided. A lesson Weringer— to use his colloquial name—learned well, and used in the making of Wink. You have to have everyone reined in if you want to keep what's yours. And on the other side, Mona... we owned *everything*."

It's as he says this that Mona realizes something is bothering her about the screen. Well, not the screen itself, but something *around* the screen: there are the red curtains on the sides, sure, but behind the curtains, in the shadows, there should be just brick wall, right? And there *was* brick wall, just a minute ago. Yet now it looks like there's a gap there: behind the curtains is some kind of backstage area, and something is moving in there, undulating slowly and smoothly, but she can't really see it...

"The other side isn't a where, really," says Kelly. "Nor is it a when. If a world is a machine, with many wheels and belts, ours on that side had millions, even billions more than yours. Compare a pocket watch to a cathedral clock, and you'd be close. It might not have looked like it when you saw it, little sister, but that place was once"—he thins his eyes, and his whole face trembles with passion—"*marvelous*. There was no and *is* no beauty like it, like the places over there. A dark and savage and monstrously wonderful place." He pauses. "Or at least, I think it was. I *think* it was wonderful. Now that I am away from it, it seems far better than when I was actually there. It is so curious." He shrugs, shakes his head. "But never mind. The most important thing about that place, of all the wonderful sights and lands over there, is that they were *ours*.

"Well. Mother's, really. Everything was Mother's. *We* were Mother's. She made us. We belonged to Her. We were Her kin, Her spawn, Her children. With Her, we took these places, conquered them, made them our own. We installed ourselves as gods . . . and we *were* gods to them, of course we were, because what is a god besides a higher intelligence, and was there any intelligence higher than us? No.

"But we weren't . . . unstoppable." The camera pulls back, and Kelly takes a seat on an empty chair—a chair that was occupied by that older woman just a little while ago. Mona wonders where she went. "It started with no warning, totally and completely out of the blue. Everything just began to . . . fall apart."

"How do you mean?" asks Mona.

"Well, you saw what it's like over there, now. Was it particularly pretty to you?"

"I don't know what you all find pretty."

"Touché," says Kelly. "But no, *that* is not pretty to me, to us. Yet let me assure you, what you saw is surely the prettiest part of our world, now."

"What happened? Like . . . a war?"

He purses his lips, and his eyes search offscreen. "You know . . . I don't know."

"You don't?"

"No. I admit it. I really don't. Mother was the only one who knew. She foresaw it. She was the only one who really understood its nature. She told me—and only me, because, well, Miss Mona, I am the favorite son, a bit—that it was because of how huge we were, how powerful, that the mere presence of our family was doing something destructive to the fabric of our world…" He sniffs. "Not very specific, is it?"

"I guess not." Mona wishes he'd stop talking like she knows what the fuck he means.

"No. But I, being the dutiful First, told the rest of the family. And we watched helplessly as, one by one, the worlds and places we had conquered…faded. Burned. And were lost. No. No, gods we were not." He looks at her, his gaze sharp. "What I will tell you now, Miss Mona, is part of some very private conversations I had with Mother. No one, I do really mean *no one*, including—what does he call himself now—oh that's right, *Parson*, knows anything about them."

"If you think I'm going to tell anyone, don't worry," says Mona. "I'm not on friendly terms with much of your family."

"Are you not, now," says Kelly softly.

Mona sees another hint of movement in the backstage space behind the curtains. She tries not to let Kelly see her looking (Is Kelly even the way First looks at things? It's not like his eyes on the screen really work, right?), but Mona finally catches a glimpse of what's back there before it retreats into the dark.

She tenses up. The hairs along Mona's arms slowly stand at attention. She tries very hard not to show that she noticed.

It looked like…tentacles. As if the wall behind the screen, and perhaps the wall on either side of the theater, and maybe even the ceiling and floor and every crawl space in this building, is packed with endless, endless tentacles, some the size of tree trunks, some like the finest, softest hair, all of them writhing and twisting in the dark…

That's you, isn't it? she thinks. *The real you. What you really are, behind this illusion…*

"Mother came to me," continues Kelly, apparently unaware of any problem at all, "and told me She'd found something. *Noticed* something, rather. She said She'd discovered a place in our world…where everything was thin. Not just thin—*bruised.*" Kelly smiles, but it's utterly humorless. "I don't suppose I need to tell you that this occurred just before our own world began to fall apart."

Mona thinks, *Oh, shit.*

Kelly flashes that mirthless smile again. "What Mother had concluded, after examining these bruised portions, was that there were *other worlds* than our own. Realities we never knew about. And here She did not speak in a spatial sense—not merely civilizations on other—what do you call them here—*planets*, but contained, functioning worlds existing within dimensions lower and more rudimentary than our own. There was life there, intelligence, and that intelligence was pushing at the boundaries of its own little world into our own. And Mother thought, just maybe, we could push back. And go *through*.

"It was revolutionary to me. And also ludicrous. Why would we ever want to abandon what we had? I mean, at the time we were totally safe. And were we not happy here? I asked Her. What more could anyone want? But Mother was silent. I could tell She was troubled. Which, naturally, troubled me.

"I did not have much time to dwell on it, though. Because that was when everything began to burn, and fall apart. A holocaust on an unimaginable level. Whole aspects of our reality, shorn away like dead skin. Yet Mother had an answer. One I'd never have expected." The camera slowly starts to pull in on Kelly's face again. "She told me She had *already* made contact with the other side."

"When was this?" asks Mona.

"Mm? Trying to arrange a mental time line?" He laughs. "I wouldn't bother. Time over there is not time over here. It was just at the beginning of the Fall, though. Just when things began to turn. Mother told us we could not stop it. Nothing we could do. There was only one way to survive: we had to escape our world, and find sanctuary in this new one, this primitive, undeveloped place. We asked Her, How? How can we do this? How can we help? And Mother said She had to do this alone. She would go there, to whatever this place was, arrange things for us, and return to take us to safety.

"I, the First, was chosen to assist Her in this task. And what I found was quite surprising. Mother's preparations did not have the look of something rushed, of an emergency solution—it looked like She'd been ready for this for some time." He smiles. "I bet you can guess what Her preparations looked like."

Mona thinks. Then she says, "A mirror?"

"Bingo! Mother had constructed a mirror, or a *lens* of some kind that could look beyond our world and into those bordering it. She told me She had created it when She first learned of the place on the other side, this elsewhere alongside our own. She said this was how She had been communicating with her."

Kelly pauses. He takes a slow breath, in, then out. "This confused me," he says. "I asked—communicating with *who*, exactly?"

For some reason Mona's skin erupts in gooseflesh. Her heart goes cold but it pumps faster and faster and faster.

"She did not answer," says Kelly. "But I helped Her prepare Her exit. And Mother said, all we have to do now is wait, and She turned to look into the mirror. Wait for what? I asked. What is going to happen? Mother said, Wait for her to return to me. And She would say no more, no matter what I asked.

"We waited, and waited. I grew impatient. We did not have time for this, I said. But then, to my surprise, a face appeared in the mirror. It was a very small face, a face unlike any I'd ever seen before. And it stared at us, and when it saw Mother, it said, in a language I did not then understand, 'Oh. There you are.'"

Kelly looks at Mona, smiles ruefully, and scratches the side of his head. "Enter one Laura Alvarez," he says.

"No," says Mona.

"I'm afraid so," says Kelly.

"No. No, that can't be..."

"It's the truth," says Kelly. "You asked for the truth, and here I give it to you."

"You're saying my mother...she...."

"What I am saying," says Kelly, "is that Dr. Laura Alvarez, lauded physicist and dutiful Coburn National Laboratory and Observatory employee, one day looked into the lens she'd spent a decade of her life building, and saw something looking back. This something was so remarkable, so astounding, that Dr. Alvarez stopped and stared. And then that something spoke to her, and whispered to her, and told her many things. And Dr. Alvarez listened."

She remembers Eric Bintly's words—*She would just stare into the lens plates. With her nose about an inch away. Like she was transfixed. I caught her several times.*

And a phrase she now finds even worse: *I think she made a lot of changes to the lens before she left.*

"My mother would never . . ." says Mona, but she cannot even complete the thought.

"Would never what?"

"She'd never help bring you all here," says Mona. "She'd never work with your Mother."

"You haven't let me finish," says Kelly. "My Mother had overcome many things more powerful than a thirty-five-year-old lab scientist. She was quite stronger than me, and I am quite strong in my own right."

"So you're . . . you're saying my mother did this," says Mona hopelessly. "She brought you here, and brought everything down on that little town."

"Miss Mona," says Kelly, "would you *please* let me finish? Allow me to say only this—Laura Alvarez never did anything of her own agency."

"She didn't?"

"No," says Kelly gravely. "But, sister, to be honest . . . I wouldn't take that as any consolation."

"Why?"

Kelly begins to speak, but stops himself, troubled. Then he says, "Well. I told you that getting here is hard for us. It's not easy to navigate across planes of reality. Especially as it was back then, when the boundaries were pretty firm. Wink wasn't like it is now—there were no places that straddled the line, no thin parts. It was all solid.

"But Mother figured out a way. When that woman looked into the mirror, Mother...reached out to her. She could control your lens, the one on your side, if She tried, and She used it to...change her. It was something She did over time, bit by bit, dissolving that mind behind the woman's eyes and...replacing it with something else."

He looks at Mona, anxious, sad, like a doctor bearing terrible news. "I'm afraid Mother replaced it," he says, "with Herself."

CHAPTER FORTY-SEVEN

The ghost on that screen still watches her. Her heart still beats, her mind still flickers in its shell, her muscles tweak and twitch as they should. But she is gone.

She remembers:

It's like there was someone else in there. In her head. Someone who wasn't Laura at all.

And:

To be frank, the behavior of the lens can only lead me to think it was the result of external control.

But most of all Mona remembers how her mother held her on that July day back in 1981, with the sun so terribly bright and her mother's skin so terribly soft, and how the poor woman, naked below her robe, held Mona tight and told her

I love you more than anything, but I can't stay here, I am so sorry. I can't stay because I am not from here, not really, I am from somewhere else, and I have to go back now.

But can I come with you? Can I visit you, Momma?

No, no, it is far, far away, but one day you will join me there, there in that happy place far away, far, far away. I will come for you. I will come and bring you with me. I will bring you with me, my love, I will come for you.

"You're lying," she says softly.

"Why would I lie?" says Kelly. "What would I ever have to gain?"

"Something, anything. Who knows what you fucking things do."

"Oh, please," says Kelly. "I already told you one of our oldest methods of communication—*mediums*, dear. Did you think I told you that for no reason?"

"Then you knew. You knew and you didn't tell me."

"Some things can't just be told. They must be figured out. They must be understood. And you understand, and believe, don't you?"

She wants to reach into her head and gouge out this awful revelation. She does not want to think of her mother as a hollowed-out puppet, a ghastly little doll led about by some inconceivable abomination.

But she cannot erase the image of her mother, standing at a window and staring out at the bleak Texas landscape, faintly confused as if she'd woken up expecting to see something quite different outside her door that day.

And she would have, wouldn't she? Her mother woke up every day expecting to open the curtains and see endless black mountains, and blood-red stars, and a swollen, pink moon...

Her mother had always seemed like a woman out of place. Mona just didn't know how *far* out of place.

Laura Alvarez had never been mad. She'd just had another mind grow within her own, a black, pulsing tumor of intelligence eating away at her very being until there was nothing but an empty shell, echoing with the voice and thoughts of something quite, quite different from far, far away.

Why is it that I am always losing things, Mona thinks, *that were never really mine to begin with?*

Kelly, who has been picking his teeth, looks up and waits. "Then I never...knew my mother," says Mona.

He shrugs. "I would assume not. Not to any significant degree, at least. My Mother never did anything halfway. And Her designs rarely failed."

"And whenever I looked into my mother's eyes...and whenever my mother spoke to me...it was always..."

"Her," says Kelly. "*My* Mother. Yes."

All the slurred, half-intelligible nursery rhymes. All the quiet promises of love and care.

Mona feels herself shutting down. She is not sure if she is angry or
sad or disgusted. Her body and mind, both wiser than she, know that
nothing can be gained by contemplating this and have, essentially,
tabled the issue.

"You seem," says Kelly, with cautious cheer, "to be reconciling
yourself to this."

Mona looks at him. It is the sort of look condemned people give
their executioners.

"Or possibly not," says Kelly. "I do not know if I can help. I assume
you have questions. Many questions."

Mona just shrugs.

"No?" says Kelly. "None?"

She shrugs again.

"Not even about yourself?" he asks.

This rumbles something in Mona. What the hell is he implying?

"Ah, so you do have questions?" says Kelly.

"What...sort of questions should I have?"

"Well...you know now that your own mother was not really your
mother. She was not really a person at all, but an...*extension* of my
own Mother, operating from the other side."

Mona shrugs helplessly. She cannot passively accept such a thing as
true. She can only pick it up, drop it, and leave it alone: it is too heavy.

"If this is true—and I do know that it is—you must wonder, why did
She choose to have a child?" Kelly asks. "Why did She drive east,
straight east, and, as I now assume, find the first willing, fertile man
who would ask no questions about Her history, and proceed to procre-
ate with him?"

Mona understands she should be insulted by his clinical descrip-
tion, but she doesn't have the energy.

"Miss Mona," says Kelly, "have you never felt different from other
people throughout your life? Detached, adrift? Have you never wondered why you appear to age at a much slower rate than anyone you
know? Have you not found the fact that you, and you alone out of the

human race, have visited the other side—even if it was only for a moment—and come back whole and unharmed, to be slightly odd? Do you not find it queer that your arrival in this town—this bizarre, surreal, strange town, where nothing has ever happened for decades—coincides with every terrible event that has happened recently? And do you not somehow feel that you have been to this town before, that you know that it is, in some indefinable, intangible way, a home you never visited, but knew was waiting for you, all along, all throughout your life?"

Mona stares at him. First she wonders how he knows these things about her. But then she begins to understand his meaning.

"My girl," says Kelly in a manner both kind and pitying, "haven't you wondered even once why I've been calling you 'sister' since you came to talk to me?"

MOMMA

CHAPTER FORTY-EIGHT

The municipal park in the center of Wink appears manicured and pristine even in the dead of night. There is never an errant leaf to be found, the sidewalk is cleaner than most dentists' incisors, and the grass puts putting greens to shame.

It is always this way. It never changes, no matter the season.

The residents of Wink do not question this. For though the grass is begging for a blanket or a picnic or a game of catch, these things are strictly forbidden: no one ever goes on the grass, not ever. So they never experience the queer sensation that would wash over them if they did, as if they've passed through the wall of a bubble, moving from the real, vulnerable, changeable world into one that is perfectly preserved, a pleasant summer's afternoon captured and suspended in Lucite.

What is at the center of Wink beyond the sidewalks is not truthfully a park, but a memory, a moment, unspoiled by the passing of time.

The people from Elsewhere have their ideas about how a town should look. Certain scenes must be maintained. You cannot walk there: to do so would be to soil perfection. They just are, forever.

Yet now, in the dead of night, someone approaches.

It is—or would appear to be, if there were a nearby onlooker—a small boy of about nine, wearing slippers and bunny pajamas and smelling just slightly of smoke. He wears a pair of spectacles that are much too large for him that also have no lenses, and he keeps pushing them up his nose. The boy has a knapsack over one shoulder, and the contents clank softly with each step he takes.

The boy stops with a grunt, opens the knapsack, and takes out the contents: two razor-thin, beautifully silvered hand mirrors. He rummages a bit more, produces a large handkerchief, and wraps one of the mirrors in it. Then he replaces them in the knapsack.

He takes a few test steps, and now there is no clanking at all. The boy nods, satisfied.

He walks down the sidewalk to the very edge of the grass, and there he stops and stares in at the park. "Hmm," he says, in a voice almost theatrically deep.

On the left side of him at one end of the park is Wink's white stone courthouse. At the other, on his right, is the pristine white geodesic dome, along with the dark, gleaming memorial tree.

The boy scratches his chin, pushes up his glasses, and takes a step forward. His skin crawls as a tickling warmth passes over him: he has the uncanny feeling of having just passed into an old photograph. But it does not harm him in any way, or at least it does not seem to.

"This appears to have been successful," says the boy, still in the deep voice. He continues looking around at the moonlit park. "Now. Where are you?"

He begins to slowly walk forward, peering around with his head slightly cocked, sometimes with one hand out like a dowser seeking water. "I know you're here," he says softly. "I saw you, when I was up in the sky. When I...died. Everything is so much clearer, outside of these vessels."

He stalks across the park, feeling his way. The streetlights, cutting through the trees, carve strange insignias on the twilit grass. His path winds and bends and loops, until finally one thing in particular swells up before him.

The white, lunar form of the dome, speckled with shadow, blank yet somehow imposing. It is over thirty feet tall, at least.

"Ah," says the boy softly. "There you are."

He steps forward and lifts a hand to the surface of the dome. But he does not touch. He dares not touch.

"How long have you been in there..." whispers the boy.

The dome is silent. Yet somehow, it feels watchful, like the totem of some forgotten god that, perhaps, has left some vestige of itself behind.

The boy turns and marches away, across the street and down the sidewalk and into darkness.

Some places in Wink are more than one place. Some places take you places you never expected. Rooms within rooms, doors within doors, worlds hidden within a thimble or a teacup.

You just have to know where to look.

CHAPTER FORTY-NINE

Mona looks at the screen, but she does not see it: she looks through it, beyond it, ears ringing with the amplified words she's just heard.

She hears herself say: "What?"

Kelly looks back at her, face kindly and anxious. "Oh, my dear. Don't say *what* like that. It can't be *that* much of a surprise to you. You knew. You felt it in your bones when you came here. Something resonated inside of you—something woke up, poked its head out of its dark hole, and recognized what it saw. You *knew* you'd come home. Didn't you?"

"What are you... What are you saying that I..."

"Oh, I'm sure you passed all your physicals," says Kelly. "Blood pressure, check. Cholesterol, check. Proper reflexes. Good eyesight. You are, no doubt, a person. Or at least you register as a person here, in this little place, and don't set off any alarms. And I'm sure that, if someone were to take your blood, you'd register as Laura Alvarez's progeny with absolutely no doubt.

"But Laura Alvarez wasn't your real mother, Mona. She wasn't what bore you, shaped you, made you. And you aren't *just* a person. There's more to you. Parts you didn't know were there, and never used. But they've always been there, Mona."

"You're crazy," says Mona. "That's fucking crazy."

"Please think, Miss Bright," says Kelly. "When you came to Wink, you sometimes looked at a thing and saw *two* things, two different objects or places somehow occupying the same physical space. Did you not?"

"That's because of that fucking mirror trick Mrs. Benjamin showed me."

"No. If anything, that mirror trick *activated* something in you. How did you think you were able to do the trick itself? You made something in her house suddenly appear in two places at once, didn't you? Isn't that, well...quite an unusual talent?"

"That was *her*. She did that to me!"

"No," says Kelly calmly. "It was a test. She realized there was something different about you. And she was right.

"The things that make us *us*, Mona—the characteristics that make my family so esteemed, so privileged—they don't show up on any CAT scan, or any blood test. They have nothing to do with this shoddy, muddy, physical world. They *transcend* them. *You* transcend them. Less than most of my family—much less than me, of course—but it's there. What's that word Parson tried so hard to tell you? Ah, I remember it now—*pandimensional*." He says it with relish, like an exotic, foreign term. "Miss Mona, you are, to a very slight degree, pandimensional. Not all of you is *here*. Some of you, some functioning part of your being, is *elsewhere*. Because you are Mother's. Because you are my sister, my kin. And isn't it so good, to finally find a place where you belong?"

Mona feels nothing—there is nothing she can feel, not anymore, especially at this insane suggestion. Is this thing really suggesting she is like the vague, shadowy monsters lurking in the mountains of this town? That she is connected to those horrific, fleshy, wheedling beasts occupying the skulls of Parson, and Mrs. Benjamin, and whoever else besides? Or, worse, the things that *operate* them, those beings and shapes she glimpsed in that place with the red stars and the barren earth?

It's impossible. That can't be right. It *can't*. She's just an unemployed drifter, for Christ's sakes. She's not a...a...

Then Mona remembers the dream she had the last night in her mother's house: walking down the hallway and seeing the mirror-version of herself pluck the light from the bulb in the ceiling and shove it down her throat, its radiance filtering through all her tissues and membranes in a soft pink glow...

And she understands now: that dream made sense. It was a sense Mona could not articulate, could not even name, but the dream acknowledged a deep, sad feeling that has, over time, pervaded every part of her life:

She is empty. And that emptiness makes her monstrous.

She thought she felt this way because of her lost daughter, all the promise and hope of a new life and new love wiped away in a burst of chrome and glass. But perhaps not. Perhaps she had always been this way, always monstrous, always alien, always hollow, always gutted.

Kelly's words feed a fear of Mona's she has tried to ignore for so long: that she, in some sick, twisted way, was *relieved* to lose her child, because how could she, a cold, angry tomboy, whose own mother had been (as she once thought) suicidally schizophrenic, ever make a good mother in her own right? Was it not better that her child died, rather than living and being so thoroughly failed by her parent? She is a creature poorly made, half-made, a distorted, deformed thing created by distorted, deformed things. It is not too far a step to go from thinking of her mother as a maddened, sad schizophrenic to thinking of her as something very much...else.

"Then why am I here?" she asks softly.

"Here in what manner?" asks Kelly. "Here in existence? Or here in Wink?"

Mona doesn't answer, not just because she finds the question stupid: she just can't find the will to speak.

"Well, I think I know one answer for sure," says Kelly. "Let me ask you something, Mona—how did your mother die?"

Mona has no desire to slip down the slope into this topic any further. But she says, "She killed herself."

"I see," says Kelly. "And I'm willing to bet that her death coincided with a certain date—the day my family arrived here. Didn't it?"

Mona blinks slowly. She is too tired, too worn out to process this.

"Yes," says Kelly. "Mother, of course, had to return back to our world when She deemed it time to get things started. And there's really only a couple of ways to do that, the death of the medium being the easiest, I'd imagine." He rubs his chin, thinking. "I remember... when She projected herself into this world—into Dr. Alvarez—it was as if She fell into a deep, deep sleep. It seemed like She slept forever, dead to the world as it fell apart around us. But then, one day, without warning, when I had almost given up all hope, She awoke. She did not explain anything—which was typical—but made us promise two things: one was to wait for Her there, in the place we were going, because She would be gone for a bit—just a bit. And the second was to always obey the next eldest, and never hurt one another. We, terrified, confused, quickly agreed, and then there was lightning in our skies...

"Well, of course, the next thing we knew, we were here. Yet She destroyed herself in the effort. I had never seen a member of my family die before—we are, in so many ways, beyond death—but then, none of our family had ever done what Mother did. But perhaps She knew something more...perhaps She knew that, if She were to perish, it would release enough destructive energy to bridge the gap between our worlds. Like punching a hole in a wall, I suppose. Perhaps we would have never gotten here, if She had not died.

"She was gone far more than 'a bit.' I thought She was gone. Truly gone. Yet not too long ago I heard of three events that seemed highly coincidental. First, Weringer died, which did get everyone in a fluffle, but to me it seemed much less impossible, after Mother and all. But then I began to see lights on the mesa again...as if the laboratory—the one with the mirror that had, in essence, brought us here—was up and running once more.

"And then, finally, you came, Mona. Doesn't that all seem quite odd to you?"

"I'm just here because my father died, and I inherited a goddamn house here."

"Yes, yes. But it's almost like—what is that quaint expression—the stars aligned to bring you here. Isn't it?"

What now? thinks Mona. *What else could there possibly be?*

"I don't contest the idea that the death of your father brought you here," says Kelly. "But I do wonder if his death—like the death of your own mother—coincides with something that happened in Wink. In this case, Weringer's death."

"Are you really telling me," says Mona, "that someone from Wink traveled all the way to a shithole in Texas just to give my father a stroke, which would get me to inherit the house, which would get me to Wink?"

"No," says Kelly. "But what I am suggesting is that the death of one of my family members seems to release a terrible amount of energy, causing ripples in existence. Mother might have even used Her own death to bring us here. If Weringer were to die near a—a *focal point* for this sort of energy..."

"The lens," says Mona.

"Yes. Then someone could have used it. It could change the very nature of reality, like the finger of a god. A death, an inheritance, an impetus to return...that would be easy. Probability itself could realign to ensure that what the focal point wanted to happen happened. I can see the way fortunes and potential futures fade, merge, emerge, broaden. It is much more shapable than you imagine, Miss Bright. The possibilities of such a focal point—and such an energy—are limitless." Kelly stands, stiff and erect, hands clasped behind his back. "Personally, I think it was used as a beacon."

"A beacon for what?" asks Mona.

"For all the pieces of Mother that were missing," says Kelly. "To pull in all the missing bits beyond Wink. Or the *one*, really. You, of course."

"What the fuck do you mean?" asks Mona.

"Most everyone here of note has an anchor, don't they, Mona?" says Kelly. "My kin in the town operate from afar, anchored to this place by those awful little creatures buzzing in people's heads. Some physical part of ourselves must remain on this side, holding us down, acting as a window into this world, while their true selves remain sealed up in not-quite-heres and inaccessible facets of reality and...what have you. It's all very complex, but the more I realized exactly *how* Mother had set up our existence in this world—and She *had* set it up, micromanaged it to the tiniest possible degree—I began to wonder why She hadn't thought to do something similar for herself before She died.

"But when you showed up, I realized She had, of course. I mean, why else have a relationship with a man? Why else have a child? She had to leave some piece of Herself behind, some tiny, living part of Herself to anchor Her being to this world. Having a child, of course, would be the easiest possible way to do that."

"What the fuck are you saying?"

"It's easy enough," says Kelly. "You've seen those fleshy, reedy little creatures swimming in the backs of peoples' eyes."

"So?"

"Well, what do you think *you* are?"

"What? I'm me. Just me."

"No. You know you're much more than that. The question you asked remains quite valid, Miss Mona—why are you here? The answer, I think, is because Mother is bringing Herself back. Before She died, She designed a way for Her to reenter this world, to return from death. For though some of us—like Weringer, like Macey—are not quite as beyond death as we'd assumed, Mother, well…Mother remains a very different sto—"

Kelly stops. The screen flutters, like the film has just run off its track. Yet what lies behind the film is not a bright, white space, but what looks like a dark, shifting abyss…

It's only for a moment, for Gene Kelly's handsome, smiling face quickly returns, but Mona realizes she didn't see an abyss, not really: she saw a face, long and dark and bereft of most conventional features—mouth, nose, ears, etc.—but one surrounded by coils and coils of writhing arms and feelers, as if the face of that thing in the screen was at the center of a monstrous tangle of tentacles…yet at the top of that long, narrow face had been two black, bulging eyes, like the eyes of a shark, facing outward.

Yet now there is only Kelly, who says, "Whoop! Looks like we had even less time than I thought."

Mona, who is still shocked by what she glimpsed, tries to focus. "What? What do you mean?"

"We're going to have to cut this short. Someone is about to try to kill me," says Kelly cheerfully.

"What?"

"Oh, don't worry about it," says Kelly. "I'll be fine. You already saved my life. And thank you, by the way."

"I . . . I what?"

"I do wish we could have talked longer, little sister," says Kelly sadly. "I am sure we have so much to discuss. And I wish I could prepare you for what's about to happen. But don't fret. It's my experience that it's best to sit back and allow the tides of fortune and fairness to take you where they wish. Though it can be a little confusing, sometimes." He winces a little. "You may especially want to relax *now*, considering what I'm about to do to you."

"Wait. Stop. You're going to do what now? To me?"

"You do love the word *what*, don't you?" asks Kelly. "It is a good word. It can mean so many things. You remember when I said that, to beings such as myself, physical existence is mere construction paper and pipe cleaners?"

"Yeah?"

"Well," says Kelly, "I am about to break you down into paper and glue, and put you back together again somewhere much safer. So hold on."

"Wait. Wait!" says Mona. "You're going to do *what* to me?"

"There's that word again!" says Kelly. "Relax, Miss Mona. Back in the old days, some found this experience very enlightening. It's just a matter of . . ."

Things slow down. Then they stop.

Then Mona's body begins to report many disparate sensations.

First her eyes freeze in her skull, which makes it impossible to confirm any of the other sensations: her skin begins to crackle, as if waves of static electricity are crawling along her arms and legs; her hair curls like slashed harp strings; her fingernails, like switchblades, recede into her flesh; some bones lengthen, others twirl into corkscrews, while still others dissolve into powder; her brain turns to water, which washes down the back of her throat, drips down her spine, and puddles on the floor; her teeth turn to fire in her head, and wither into ash; and so on, and so on, and so on, and she cannot even find the voice to scream.

But one thing stays constant: that wry, smug grin on the shimmering screen, and those dark, crinkled eyes...

Somewhere a voice says: "...*place*."

Then everything is lost.

CHAPTER FIFTY

Mona's only been gone for what feels like five minutes when Gracie hears the footsteps from the canyon behind her. This should surprise her: since the beginning of their relationship (which was so long ago Gracie can't even remember it now), this canyon was utterly secluded, unreachable for everyone except her and Mr. First. But then came Joseph, and Mr. Macey, and then Mona, until finally it started to seem as if this place were some kind of bizarre town square, with everyone showing up and bumping into one another and sharing the price of vegetables.

But what Gracie does find troubling is that Mr. First never mentioned anything about a second visitor *tonight*. So Gracie, remembering the flashes of gunfire and old Parson on his knees, drops to the ground and crawls away to find cover behind a long, flat rock. She is not sure what is coming, but she knows it could be dangerous.

What comes strolling down the canyon completely flummoxes her: it is Velma Rancy, a sophomore at Gracie's school. Gracie has no idea what she could possibly be doing here, especially dressed so strangely in a powder-blue suit and a white panama hat. And she appears to be bearing a blood-covered cigar box like a holy relic, and her hand is *horribly* injured...

As Velma approaches the thick white fog at the end of the canyon, there's a sound like a whip crack; then the fog begins to swirl around one point, and then it begins to draw back, like dirty water circling down the sink drain, until it reveals...

Nothing. No Mona, no figures, no nothing. Just the empty end of the canyon, which is about sixty feet across in all directions... but there is, just maybe, the soft sound of fluting.

This does not dissuade Velma, who just keeps walking straight ahead with the bloody cigar box held out. Finally, at a point that seems fairly random to the naked eye, she stops.

There is a silence. Then the canyon fills with a low, soft hum, a hum that is so deep Gracie's ears can hardly register it: it is like thousands of yogis softly murmuring the *om* mantra, building and leveling off until the tissues just behind her eyes begin to vibrate.

Gracie knows this sound: it is the sound Mr. First makes when he wishes to communicate. It is not, she knows, the sound *of* him communicating: it is simply a noise that is produced, perhaps by accident, when First speaks.

"Stop that," says Velma in a voice totally unlike hers: the words are mealy-mouthed and ill-formed, like a deaf person's. "If I am stuck in this vessel and I speak this way, you should have to do the same."

The bass hum swells slightly. Tears well up in Gracie's eyes.

"No," says Velma. "I won't listen. Speak. Speak like I do. It's only fair."

The hum tapers off. Something invisible moves in the canyon: the gravel on the ground shifts in huge piles, as if, perhaps, two enormous, invisible feet have risen slightly, and fallen.

Then there is a voice like enormous stones being ground against one another:

HMM.

Gracie is shocked. She never knew he could *talk*, if he wanted to...

"It's not so pleasant," says Velma, "having to talk in such a manner."

The gravel shifts again. *I DO NOT HAVE MUCH EXPERIENCE WITH IT,* says the huge voice contemplatively, *BUT I HAVE NOT YET FOUND ANYTHING TERRIBLY OBJECTIONABLE ABOUT IT.*

"And you wouldn't, would you," says Velma. "You never find anything to be terrible. You've never had to struggle."

There is a silence.

"Do you know who I am?" asks Velma.

I KNOW, says the voice, *THAT YOU ARE MY KIN.*

"Then what's my name?"

Silence.

"You don't know," says Velma. "There are so few things that are unknown to you. Yet I am one of them."

I AM SURE YOU KNOW MANY THINGS THAT I DO NOT, says the voice.

"Stop it!" says Velma. "Stop being so…"

REASONABLE?

"Be quiet! Don't…don't you understand how shameful this is for you?"

WHY SHOULD IT BE SHAMEFUL?

"Because you're going to die here today. And you won't even die knowing the name of the person who killed you. None of them did. They never even knew I was there."

THEY?

"Yes. I killed Weringer. I killed Macey. I figured out how." Her words are gleefully, hatefully mad. "Because Mother wanted me to. That's what She wanted me to do. There was another way. One you didn't know about, one you ignored. You aren't so perfect. I don't know why She loved you so much."

The voice sighs. *I AM AFRAID I MUST TELL YOU THAT YOU DON'T KNOW WHAT YOU'RE TALKING ABOUT THERE.*

"Shut up!" snarls Velma. "You always pulled Her away from me! She was always leaving me! Any time we were together, when I brought Her beauties and delicacies and wonders for Her amusement, you always came in and ruined it! You never let Her love me!"

DELICACIES? the voice says. *AH…I THINK I REMEMBER YOU. YOU WERE THE LITTLE ONE…HER SERVANT?*

"I was more than just a servant!" screams Velma. "She loved me! She would have loved me more if you hadn't been there! And you don't deserve Her love! You're not even...not even First! Do you know that? She didn't make you first at all! There was one before you, one that went wrong, one bigger and stronger and meaner than you! Did you know that?"

The voice sighs. *YES, I KNOW THAT.*

Velma appears taken aback. "You...you do?"

YES. I FOUND THAT OUT LONG AGO. AND I MADE MY PEACE WITH IT.

"How...how can you...how can you know and not care!" cries Velma.

THEY HAVE A VERY GOOD SAYING HERE, says the voice. *IT GOES—FAMILIARITY BREEDS CONTEMPT.*

"What does that have to do with anything!" says Velma. Her voice is almost a screech.

IT MEANS, ONCE YOU COME TO KNOW A THING—ANY THING—YOU TEND TO DESIRE IT LESS. AND IF YOU WANTED MOTHER'S LOVE, BROTHER, I WOULD HAVE FREELY PASSED IT ON TO YOU. BECAUSE, TO BE FRANK, I HAD HAD ENOUGH OF IT.

"What!" says Velma. She almost chokes. "How...how *dare* you! How dare you say such a...a *blasphemous* thing! How could you be willing to throw such a blessing away!" Velma sputters for a moment, incensed beyond words. "You don't deserve to live! And it gets to be me who does it, me who kills you! It's *here*, did you know that? The wildling's in Wink! Why don't...why don't I just show it to you?"

Velma flips the top of the cigar box open, then swoops the box up.

Something small, round, and white flies toward the center of the canyon.

Then it stops, frozen, hanging in space as if it's been grasped by an invisible hand.

Everyone is still. Velma leans forward a little, greedily waiting for...something.

Yet nothing happens. The little round thing—which appears to be a skull—slowly rises up as if it is being brought closer to a set of invisible eyes.

THE TRICKY THING ABOUT THESE TOTEMS, says the voice, *IS THAT THEY CAN REALLY ONLY BE USED ONCE.*

"W-what?" says Velma.

ONCE THEY'VE TAKEN SOMEONE WHEREVER THEY'RE SUPPOSED TO—IN THIS CASE, TO THE WILDLING, I PRESUME—NO ONE ELSE CAN USE IT AGAIN. IT'S A BIT LIKE A ONE-WAY TICKET. BUT YOU WOULDN'T KNOW WHAT THOSE ARE.

"No," says Velma. "No! I . . . I can't believe it! Who could have used it already?"

THE GIRL, says the voice. *WHO ELSE?*

"So . . . it killed her instead of you?" asks Velma, perplexed.

OH NO. IT LET HER LIVE. SHE IS QUITE SPECIAL.

Velma drops the box. "It's not fair. It's not *fair*. Why do you always get away with everything?"

I AM SORRY. I DID NOT KNOW IT HURT YOU SO MUCH.

"You did. Don't say that. You did." There is something brittle and pained in Velma's face: there is nothing worse than an opponent who is suddenly revealed to be understanding and compassionate.

YOU KNOW SHE WILL NEVER WORK AS A HOST. YOU CANNOT USE HER TO BRING BACK MOTHER.

Velma grows eerily calm. "You think so, do you," she says softly.

I KNOW.

"That's nothing special. I found that out long ago. I tried to show her Mother—tried to open her eyes to where She lay sleeping. But she resisted. She is quite strong. But there are other ways." She turns and starts to walk back down the canyon.

WHAT WILL YOU DO? asks the voice. *I TOLD YOU SHE WOULD NEVER WORK FOR YOU.*

"*She* won't," says Velma. "But she was once a mother in her own right. Or she *could* have been. I know. I saw it, when I touched her."

EVEN IF YOU WERE TO TRY . . . I WOULD STOP YOU. SHE CANNOT COME BACK. SHE CANNOT.

"You would fight? They think you a monster here, you know. And what you have done here is pathetic and wrong."

*I KNOW. BUT DO YOU NOT SEE... THAT IS WHY I AM WILL-
ING TO FIGHT?*

"No."

I HAVE DONE WRONG, SIBLING. I WILL NOT DO MORE.

"How sad you've become. Maybe, when She comes, She'll spare you out of pity." Velma reaches into her coat pocket and takes out something dark. As she maneuvers it in her hands, Gracie sees it is a snub-nosed .38. Velma looks toward the end of the canyon, and attempts a smile—a crooked, awkward, mangled version of a smile—and, with a, "See you around, Brother," she holds the pistol to her head.

Oh my God, thinks Gracie, but before she can move there is a small (really just *amazingly* small) pop.

Something dark burbles up from Velma's head. It pools in the brim of her white hat for a moment. Then she tips forward, toward the end of the canyon, and blood begins to course out of her skull to soak into the gravel. Then she is still.

Gracie covers her eyes with her hands. The air fills with that low, low hum, and she hears a quiet, soft voice in her ear:

I'm sorry you had to see that.

Gracie lowers her hands, but keeps her eyes shut. She thinks, *You never told me you could talk out loud.*

It's very uncomfortable for me. And this is more intimate. More private.

Where's Mona? Is she safe?

She is... away, says the voice in her ear. *But I do not think she is safe, no. Not... after that. I tried to protect her, but it seems I underestimated the resolve of my opponents.*

How could Velma... do something like that? Why?

It wasn't the girl you knew. Not inside. I think whatever was inside her has found a loophole in the way things work here. Probably a lot of loopholes. Perhaps ones that were intentionally put there.

What was it trying to do to you? thinks Gracie. *What's the wildling?*

Another one of the loopholes. The wildling is . . . my big brother.

Gracie sits in shock for a moment. *I thought you didn't have anyone older than you?*

I do. I thought it was lost, or dead. Mother abandoned it when it was very young. But it appears it has survived, and even followed us here. But because Mother did not help it come here, did not deliver it as She did all of us, its transport was . . . marred. It is here, but it is trapped. Yet it seems someone has figured out how to give it entry to our lives. And since it never promised Her anything . . .

It can do what it likes, thinks Gracie.

Yes. And it is . . . incredibly powerful. The older we are, the more we're like Her. So what will you do?

A pause.

Gracie says, out loud, "Anything?"

The quiet voice says, *I will do what I must. I never raised a hand to Her. No one did. But maybe I should have.*

Gracie thinks, *What do you mean?*

Come here. Down the canyon. To me. Do you see me?

No, thinks Gracie. There is a fluting sound again, like a pipe organ, and something appears to form in the air. *Yes. Now I do.*

Come to me. I will make you ready.

Gracie stands and makes her way down the canyon, stepping around the reddened spots of gravel. *For what?*

Your departure. I just have one last question.

Yes?

Do you know how to drive a car?

CHAPTER FIFTY-ONE

People tend to assume consciousness is a single, unified act. You just *are*: there's you, being alive, and you knowing you're being alive, and that's really all there is to it.

But that's not really all there is to it.

Consciousness (like, some would eagerly point out, pandimensional space) has levels: your mind is not one whole, but a wild variety of systems layered on top of one another and, in some key places, blended together. A person, a consciousness, is many, many moving parts, all clamoring to eat up information or transport information, or, in some cases (such as Mona's for the years before her arrival in Wink), angrily trying to block any information altogether.

And though Mona—or at least the overarching consciousness referred to as "Mona"—sees and experiences nothing but darkness as she is instantaneously transported through physical space (with mountain walls becoming permeable, like great walls of soft, rippling water), there are parts of her that are not only aware of themselves, but are also aware of their distant, separated parts, which are being transported alongside one another.

It is in this moment (which really isn't a moment, of course, because all this is happening instantaneously) that Mona could, if she wished, experience blissful and total self-examination. For there is no better time to examine and understand one's selfhood than when it is dissected and hurtling through darkness.

But Mona does not do this. Because there is one part of her that cannot be broken down into any smaller parts, and it occupies the whole of whatever attention she has left.

Mostly because it is a part of her she never knew was there.

It is a piece of awareness, a piece of perception, a piece of her that can observe and see and know; yet it is independent of all her normal faculties, independent of her eyes and conventional sight, capable of looking into and perceiving a world (or even worlds) unapproachable to her physical self.

She remembers, as Parson said, that light is mere radiation—there are other ways of seeing. It is as if she has a tiny lens of her own inside her.

Though Mona is in no way fully conscious, or even self-aware, she immediately imagines this ability as a black, cold, bead-like eye planted on the surface of her beating heart, buried deep within her but by no means limited or blind: this thing, this part of her, can peer through her ribs and sternum and flesh, past solid walls and the very earth to glimpse...

Elsewhere.

Home.

Where it—and she—belongs.

Her systems all begin crashing back together, reassembling themselves somewhere quite far away from where she started. Yet as her nervous system blends back into her musculature, and her self-awareness melds with her instincts, she wonders about that black eye, like the eye of a squid or some undersea horror, and wonders what it has seen inside her. Then she sleeps.

"No offense to anyone in the car," says Dord, "but this is maybe the dumbest fucking thing I've ever done, and I've done some pretty dumb shit in my day."

"Shut the fuck up, Dord," says Bolan.

But he silently agrees. Bolan has the distinction of never having done a dumb thing in his life, up until a few years ago, when he bought in with the spook in the hat. But at the time it didn't seem that dumb. Yet *this* seems dumb, so very, very dumb: they are all piled into Bolan's shit-ass Honda Civic, which is straining to carry their weight (especially Dord's, which is ample) up the incline of one of Wink's Picturesque New Mexican Mountains. They are here, as Bolan heroically phrased it, to complete a rescue mission: they are going to get this bitch with the rifle out of town, because, for whatever reason, the spook in the hat needs her to do something pretty fucking bad, and they don't want him to do that.

Bolan had to keep asking them that on the way up here. Did they want the spook to do something pretty fucking bad? And Mallory and Dord would mumble no, of course not, of course we don't want that. And Bolan would say, each time, "Well, all fucking right, then," and they'd all drive on for several minutes in silence before Mallory or Dord would voice some reservations again.

Bolan isn't sure where she'll be. Just somewhere around that barren canyon next to the mesa (which seems to be the source of a hell of a lot of traffic tonight). His plan is 100 percent improvisation: if he'd actually sat down and planned this out, he would've realized how impossible it all was, and given up.

So he is totally and utterly astonished when the ghostly form of a woman lying on the ground with a rifle in her arms comes sliding out of the predawn darkness, as if she is being carried to him on the reflective paint on the asphalt.

Everyone in the car goes dead silent. Bolan slowly, slowly brings it to a halt about ten feet from the unconscious woman.

"Holy shit," says Dord. "Is that her?"

Bolan is about to say yes, but he really has no idea what this woman looks like: he only knows she has a red car, which she has inconveniently chosen not to bring along for identification.

"It's got to be," says Bolan.

"Maybe it's a trick," says Mallory.

At first Bolan scoffs, but then he realizes Mal could be right. Who could possibly guess at the minds of these people, these things?

"Let's just get her into the car," says Bolan.

They pile out and slowly circle the unconscious woman.

"She's pretty," says Dord appreciatively.

"Jesus," says Bolan. "Get her legs, for God's sake."

They pick her up and start hauling her toward the Civic. Bolan points her at the back door, but Dord keeps walking, tugging her ankles right by.

"Where the hell are you going?" says Bolan.

"The trunk. Are we . . . not putting her in the trunk?"

"Why the fuck would we put her in the trunk?" says Mallory.

"Well, that's usually where I put unconscious people," says Dord.

Mal and Bolan glance at one another. Mal shrugs.

"Let's put her in the fucking trunk," says Bolan.

The trunk of a Honda Civic is not made to accommodate the supine form of an unconscious human comfortably, but Bolan and company do their best (mostly by removing the tire iron and putting a blanket over the spare). "What about the gun?" asks Dord.

Bolan looks back. He is surprised to see that the gun is none other than the goddamn cannon Dee sometimes brought into the Roadhouse. "How the fuck did she . . ." says Bolan, before shaking his head. "Never mind. Get that too. But *don't* put it in the trunk with her! Throw it in the backseat, or something."

Then they pile back into the car, throw it in reverse, and haul ass back down the mountain.

That, thinks Bolan, *was a little too easy.*

His suspicion does not abate when Dord chipperly says, "Well, that was easy!"

"Did you know she'd be there, Tom?" asks Mal.

"No."

"So do you think it's a trap?" she asks.

Bolan is silent.

"Do you think so, Tom?"

"I guess we'll find out if we get down this fucking mountain, okay?" he says.

Which, to everyone's relief, they do: their trip down is entirely uneventful, save for a deer who peers at them from the side of the road, eyes flashing a fluorescent orange, before withdrawing into the dark.

"Are we out?" asks Dord. "Are we done?"

"Quiet," snaps Bolan, as if they are a submarine crew trying to slip past sonar.

The street blocks of Wink swell up on their left, then gradually float away. There is a gray-pink hue in the east: dawn is coming, and this long, long night is finally done.

Done. They are Going. They are Out. They are almost Gone. This strange town, with its strange inhabitants and their catatonic stares, will hopefully become just an unpleasant memory, just a "can you fucking believe that happened" story they will all share one day.

Which is when they hear a crackle up in the skies.

"Is that thunder?" asks Dord. He presses his head up against the window glass to see up.

"It can't be," says Mallory. "There's not a cloud in the—"

Then everything goes blue-white.

Bolan's ears don't register an explosion so much as they do a huge, rather fartish flapping sound, like someone has just crushed a massive, inflated ziplock bag right beside his head. It throws him toward the side of the car, his head cracking up against the window while his foot, over which he still retains some amount of control, stabs out at the brake. The car immediately fills with smoke, and not wood smoke or anything so pleasant, but a smoke that is acrid and fumy and somehow *electric*.

He can't see out, but Bolan is pretty sure he's stopped the car. "What the fuck was that!" he shouts.

He hears Dord coughing in the passenger seat to his right. Mallory, however, is silent, so he turns to look, not quite sure what he'll see but expecting carnage of a most horrific sort.

The entire backseat has been burned black. He can see bits of the wire frame showing through the charred fabric, like ribs. The back and right side windows have both melted, leaving viscous, drooping holes in the frames.

But Mallory…Mallory seems completely fine. There's not a mark on her.

She looks at Bolan as if just slightly surprised. Then she glances around the smoke-filled car.

She opens her mouth and says, in a curiously nasal voice, "Ah. I've been here before. Haven't I?"

"What?" says Bolan. His voice is a little hoarse from the smoke. "Mal, are you all right?"

Mallory looks down. There's something at her feet: the huge rifle the girl had with her.

Mallory picks it up and turns it over in her hands, as if she's a little unsure of it. "This is big," she says.

Dord continues groaning and coughing in the passenger seat. "Fuck," he says. "*Fuck*, man. It burned the hair off the back of my head."

Mal looks at Dord, who is turned away. Then she points the rifle at the back of the seat and turns off the safety.

"Mal?" says Bolan. "Mal, what the—"

She pulls the trigger.

The shot punches through the seat, as well as most of Dord and what's left of the windshield. The top of his belly bursts open, and the smoke whips around the bullet's now-vacant trajectory.

Dord chokes and struggles against his seat belt. The gaping hole in his chest brims with blood, then overflows, dribbling down his white-shirted belly. Bolan is trying to shout, "Mallory, what the fuck!" when she cocks the rifle with a harsh *click-clack*, raises it a little higher, and fires again.

This time the bullet goes through Dord's upper chest, and part of his neck. He slumps forward, blood running down the gray, slick seat belt, and goes still.

Mallory looks at Bolan. There's something wrong with her eyes: something fluttering or flickering, as if her eyes were lamps filled with moths.

"Mal?" says Bolan.

She cocks the rife, then raises it toward him.

And that's the last thing he sees: just the dark eye of the rifle, and her hand, and the curl of the smoke.

*   *   *

Mona wakes up when she hears the blast. She thinks it might be part of whatever the hell it is that First did to her when she hears people screaming and coughing. Whatever just happened to her, or whatever First meant to happen to her, something's gone wrong.

She wonders where the hell she is. It's dark, wherever it is. She feels around, finds something hard and circular hidden under a blanket below her. She knows what it is almost immediately.

All right, she thinks. *I'm in the trunk of a car. This is . . . not good.*

Everything gets spectacularly less good when she hears the gun start going off. And there's no mistaking that sound: it's a .30-06 rifle, probably hers, she's guessing, since it's nowhere in the trunk. Someone starts screaming at a much higher register, which means he got tagged. Then the gun goes off again, and the screaming stops, which is really, really quite bad.

Someone asks a question. And the gun goes off one final time.

Silence. Mona waits for a good noise. Maybe—praise God—a siren.

But this is Wink. She can't remember the last time she heard a siren, or even *saw* a cruiser.

The car's shocks creak very slightly as someone shifts from one end of the car to the other. Seat springs cluck like chickens; the nasal *thunk* of a car handle; then feet on asphalt, coming her way.

Mona has no idea how it could help, but she feigns unconsciousness.

A vein of light erupts above her. She cracks an eye, just barely, and sees a rather pretty but questionably dressed woman looking down on her. Mona's never seen her before, but she knows that fluttering in the woman's eye, the suggestion of movement where there should be none.

"Hm," says the woman, and she slams the trunk shut.

Mona hears footsteps, definitely going away. They keep going until she can't hear them anymore.

Then silence.

Silence for a very, very long time.

Mona says, "Well, fuck."

CHAPTER FIFTY-TWO

Mrs. Benjamin does not precisely understand first aid, but she thinks she gets the general principles: things that are within the body must stay within at all times. If they do not stay in, they must be forced in, and kept there via things like gauze and sticky tape.

It seems simple, but it proves both complicated and painful. She would have preferred more help from Morty Kaufman, who runs the neighborhood drugstore, but when he arrived at seven thirty a.m. and found that not only had his shop been broken into but Mrs. Benjamin was sitting on the floor bleeding from over a dozen wounds and covered in copper-stained gauze, he chose instead to back away silently and sprint down the street without another word.

Really, Mrs. Benjamin can't blame him. She is not at her most presentable. And she hates not being presentable.

So when she hears the footsteps on the walk out front, she feels both resigned and a little anxious about what the reaction will be. To her surprise, her visitor, who is a thin woman in a dress so short the original Mrs. Benjamin (the "real" one) would have positively *died*, simply looks at her with a curious, blank smile, and says, "Still alive, I see."

"What?" says Mrs. Benjamin. "Yes, I'm still alive. I'm trying my very hardest to stay that way, too. Who are you?"

"Don't you recognize me?"

"No. No, I do not."

"Well, I recognize you," says the woman. She walks inside the store. There is something self-satisfied and smug in the way she moves: she's like a cat who's cornered a mouse, and is taking the time to enjoy it. "And I recognize all those wounds. I should. I did them to you."

Mrs. Benjamin peers closely at the woman. "No..."

"I told you I'd died before," says the woman. "You should have listened. You can't kill me. No one can. It's not allowed."

"Who are you?"

"Just a sibling. A concerned sibling who is willing to take up the matters of the family when its elders have fallen into lethargy." She smiles coldly at Mrs. Benjamin. "And you're going to help me."

"I certainly will not," says Mrs. Benjamin. She wants to stand and thrash this stranger, except one of her arms isn't working too well and she feels quite faint. How fragile these vessels are...perhaps that's for the best since, if this stranger is to be believed, physical violence wouldn't actually hurt the occupant of that body.

Well, that's not right—Mrs. Benjamin knows it would certainly *hurt.* It just wouldn't accomplish anything.

"You are," says the woman. "I'm going to bring Mother back. And you're going to help me. Did you know that?"

"That's...that's ridiculous," says Mrs. Benjamin. She coughs: one of her lungs is not working so well. "If Mother comes back—and She's quite late to do so, if you ask me—it'll be of Her own accord. Such a thing cannot be forced, especially not by us."

"I am doing Mother's wishes," says the woman softly. "I am part of Her great plan. And you will help me."

"I will not."

"You will. Because I have the woman."

Mrs. Benjamin's steely glare softens. "You what? Which woman?"

"The one you and Parson groomed and escorted and tested so thoroughly. She is safe, to a certain extent—she is trapped in the trunk of a car out in the wilderness. It is quite dry there, and it will get cold at night. Her situation will quickly become uncomfortable. So unless you wish her to perish—and I don't think you do—you will help me."

"You wouldn't kill her," says Mrs. Benjamin. "You need her."

The woman stares back, smiling serenely. "Do you know," she says, "how much I hate this flesh? How much I hate wearing this awful skin? Breathing this air? *Needing* to breathe this air? It is…incredibly frustrating, like itching, all over your body. I despise it. And I despise these people. Including her. I wouldn't kill her, no, but I would have no qualms about relieving some of my frustrations on her. Do you understand?"

If Mrs. Benjamin were not sitting here, her body reporting terrible pain in nearly every limb, she probably would not have had much of a reaction to the idea of the woman's being tortured. Yet now that she knows what physical pain is, she finds herself holding the curious belief that it should never be willfully visited upon anybody.

Mrs. Benjamin nods glumly.

"Yes, you do," says the strange woman. "Isn't it sad? How pathetic you've become. You care about her, just enough to spare her that misery. Imagine that, a little thing like her."

"I do not find it particularly pathetic," says Mrs. Benjamin. "But you wouldn't understand."

"Nor do I wish to. You're going to help me now, aren't you?"

"What is it you need me to do?"

"I need your strength."

Mrs. Benjamin spreads her arms. They crackle slightly: she is covered in dried blood. "I am in no condition to use it."

"Come now, Sister," says the woman, "you wouldn't be one of my elders if you were so easily defeated. Get up. Now."

She prods at Mrs. Benjamin with her toe, first gently, then harder. Mrs. Benjamin has half a mind to take her foot and tear it off at the ankle. But she sighs, grunts, and forces herself to her feet.

"Where are we going?" she asks wearily.

"To a motel," says the woman.

Mrs. Benjamin is not at all surprised to see the motel is Parson's deserted Ponderosa Acres: it is not like there are many motels in Wink. The walk there is not half as torturous as the walk down the wooden staircase in the back, which was hidden behind a small, secret door. The existence of the door is news to Mrs. Benjamin: she would wonder why Parson hid it from her, and how this stranger managed to discover it, if she weren't wearied and pained beyond articulation.

At the bottom is a wide, large basement with a concrete floor. There is no light in the basement, and if the two of them saw the world with just their eyes, they would be blind; but as this is not the case, Mrs. Benjamin peers out and sees there is a large block of metal sitting in the center of the floor.

And there is something both intangibly heavy, and also *familiar*, about that object...

The stranger prods Mrs. Benjamin down the stairs. "Go on."

"Is that what I'm here to collect?"

"It is."

"What is it?"

A queer smile. "You will know it when you touch it."

Mrs. Benjamin descends to approach the block while the strange woman stands on the bottommost landing of the staircase, watching. With each step toward the object, which seems bigger and heavier the closer she gets to it, the more Mrs. Benjamin remembers...

(broken worlds)
(a shattered moon)

(a figure standing)
(over)
(a dying city)

Mrs. Benjamin stops. "Mother," she says softly. "It's...this is *Mother*, isn't it?"

"In a way," says the woman from behind her.

Mrs. Benjamin holds her hands out to the cube: the air around it is nothing short of frigid. She screws up her mouth, squats, and puts her hands on it, preparing to lift it....

There is a hiss, and her hands scream with pain. She grunts and snaps them back.

"I can't touch it!" she says, and she turns back to the woman on the staircase.

"No," she says. "Only our kin can touch Her. And your hands do not truly belong to our family. But you will simply have to bear the pain. You can do that, can't you? Are you not my mighty big sister?"

If Mrs. Benjamin paid much attention to the woman, she would feel insulted; but her attention is not directed to the woman standing on the staircase landing, but to the person hiding just below it: a small boy of about ten, wearing rabbit pajamas and ugly glasses far too large for him. He appears to have been waiting for her to notice him, for the moment she does he raises a finger to his lips. Then he holds something out to her: a slim bag. With slow, obvious movements, he slips the bag onto one of the stairs below the woman standing on the landing, so she cannot see it. Then he stands perfectly still.

"Well?" says the woman. "Are you so intimidated? Hurry up."

Mrs. Benjamin looks at him for one moment longer: there is something irritatingly familiar about the boy...

She says, "Fine," then turns back to the block, grasps it on either side, and lifts it.

Her hands howl with pain again, as does the rest of her body: not only does its very touch harm her, but the block must weigh tons, as if its metal is impossibly dense. Yet Mrs. Benjamin does not scream or cry as she carries the block to the stairs; nor does she grunt or whimper when she dips down just a little with one free hand feeling along the stairs for the bag; and she definitely does not hiss when the cube brushes up against her cheek during the juggling act to tuck the bag within her dress, unbeknownst to the strange woman, who is already walking back up the stairs.

For all Mrs. Benjamin can think throughout the beginning of this painful ordeal is, *What is that old bastard up to?*

They walk.

They walk for what feels like hours or days; Mrs. Benjamin,

trapped in her leaking, broken body, staggers along with the enormous weight of the metal cube in her arms; and though her true nature has no small effect on the physical world, it fades as her body grows weaker and weaker.

They walk south, straight south, to the side of Wink opposite the mesa. No one witnesses them. It is still far too early to be outdoors in Wink.

Mrs. Benjamin is sure she can bear it no more when they come upon a small hole in the side of a cliff. And when they enter the tunnel, she immediately feels that she is being brought to something...

Big.

The walls of the tunnel fall away as they enter a vast space. Mrs. Benjamin can hear noises from the sides and the ceiling, chitterings and chirps, and she looks up and sees...

"The children," she says softly. "The young ones. They're all here."

"Yes," says the woman.

"You brought them here? Why?"

"For that," says the woman, and she points ahead.

Something takes form in the darkness—something colossal and primitive, as if the pieces of Stonehenge had been disassembled and piled together into some sort of organic shape...

Like a person, Mrs. Benjamin thinks. Like a huge person lying there in the darkness, each curve and bulge composed in increments of sharp, ninety-degree angles. And as Mrs. Benjamin comes closer, she sees that the massive stones are actually made of small metal blocks of varying sizes, but all in the same proportions as the one she now holds in her arms...

Yet she sees none as big as the one she holds. The rest are all tiny, tiny things...

"It must have taken years," she murmurs.

"More," says the woman. "Decades. Once I knew the pieces of Her were here, in Wink, it was just a matter of finding them. It ruined the bodies I used—the hosts. Burned their hands, burned right through their bones. So I had to talk a few of the young ones into helping me—the ones small enough to have come here in their original forms. The pieces did not burn them.

"The young ones gladly helped me. They hate it here as much as I do, did you know that? They hate being told they have to hide in the woods. They aren't allowed to playact like you and Weringer and Macey and all the rest. So we all labored, in the dark, at the fringes of the town, building the thing you all had given up on so long ago."

The shapes of the children stream down from the walls and the ceiling. They crawl across the cavern floor to her, and in one mass reach forward with claws and limbs unlike any on Earth, take her monstrous burden, and carry it to the giant lying in the dark. Mrs. Benjamin, relieved of the weight, falls to her knees. She watches as her youngest siblings hoist the huge block of metal up, over the giant's shoulder, towards its chest.

"I'd been looking for that piece for so long," says the woman. "I knew it had to be somewhere. I could *feel* it. But it was hidden from me. By Parson, of course—the reluctant bastard. I don't know how he found it, and I don't know how he managed to move it, but he must have known what he'd found. Otherwise, why hide it at all? He must have known it was Mother's heart. Yet when he 'died,' it was an easy thing to find it."

The children lower the huge block down, and slide it into some shaft in the giant's chest. There is the hiss of escaping air as the block glides down, and finally a soft *thunk* as it falls into place. And then things...change.

Just slightly. The giant does not come to life. But it seems to soften, its edges and curves becoming distinctly more organic. It is, Mrs. Benjamin understands, almost whole.

"Now what will you do?" she asks, panting.

"Oh, now you are a willing helper? After all these years?"

Mrs. Benjamin lifts and drops her arms—*What else is there for me to do?* "Wasn't it the last piece?"

The woman stares off into the darkness. Her face is hidden in shadow. She says, "No. Second."

"What?"

"The second-to-last," she says softly. "It's looking for the last piece now. Mother is. She's alive now, blindly seeking Her host. It will just take one more thing." She walks back toward the entrance to the cave. "Come," she says. "I will show you."

Mrs. Benjamin limps after. But now she can feel it. Something is happening. Not here, but

(otherside)
(elsewhere)
(the betweenplace)

(where a single eye)
(great and dark and gleaming)

(slowly opens)
(for the first time after)
(a long sleep)

(and begins roving, whirling)
(spinning blindly)

(feverishly seeking)
(a way in)

CHAPTER FIFTY-THREE

Time stretches on in the dark. On and on and on.

More than once Mona goes into a fit of rage, kicking at everything in the car, breaking the wiring to the taillights, grinding the balls of her feet into the roof of the trunk, anything…

Nothing gives. She is stuck here. And the trunk is getting fucking hot with the sun beating down right on it.

She gives up. She decides conserving her energy is the wisest thing possible. Because she is going to go fucking wild when she gets out.

If she ever gets out.

So she waits. And there, in the dark, with all the world hot and close and still, the truth of what Mr. First told her becomes inescapable.

Mother.

Mother, Mother, what am I?

And as she wonders this, she remembers something.

All her life, Mona's family was moving. Her father's job required it: he had to keep up with the drills, with the oil, and move from place to place, always new homes and apartments, almost always rentals.

And though Mona's mother was never really happy in her life, she was always happiest when they moved. "It's a fresh start," she would say each time. "A new chance. We can do it right this time." And Earl, being Earl, would simply grunt.

Mona was never quite sure what her mother meant by this. What had they been doing wrong before? And what was it they had to do right?

She had only asked her mother this once. The answer was simple: "Every-thing."

Yet these dizzying, anticipatory highs never lasted. When they would arrive at the new house, and actually walk through it—seeing, in almost every case, the awful carpet, the Pergo walls, the dim, dreary living room—her mother would go silent, and fall into a deep depression that would last for days.

Mona was never sure why this was, but it troubled her. She did not want her mother to feel so hurt, so injured, by something as simple as a house. Which, of course, would change eventually, when they moved again.

She tried to cheer her mother up, but it never worked. Her mother would simply say, "It's not worth it. Not worth doing anything to it."

And Mona would say—"Why not?"

"It's supposed to be perfect. Everything's supposed to be perfect. It can be, so it should be. But I can't make this perfect. Not this house. It's not even worth trying."

Mona asked her mother to please forget that, to please try to be happy anyway.

"I can't. Things must be arranged a certain way. Things must be beautiful, my dear."

When they moved once more, just days before that afternoon with the shot-gun and the bathtub, it seemed the same as all the other times: there was the ecstatic joy leading up to their arrival, a million plans dreamed up, a million possibil-ities; and, upon arriving, the crushing, complete disappointment, thorough and abysmal.

But this time it was a little different. Her mother, weeping, said, "I can't stay here. Things can't be perfect here, not like this. I have to go back. I have to go back and get everyone else. And then we'll come and make a place where everyone can be perfect and happy, forever." She looked up at Mona then, and there was something alien in the way her eyes looked out at the world: they seemed strangely glassy and shallow, like the eyes of a doll.

Her mother said, "And I will come back for you. I promise."

*   *   *

And now Mona understands. Whoever said those words was not Laura Alvarez. And possibly that desire for newness, and perfection...perhaps that had no earthly origin, either.

Give up, says a voice. *Just give up.*

And she does. She is all too happy to give up.

But as she gives up something awakens inside her, unfolding with the gruesome delicacy of a butterfly emerging from its chrysalis: it's as if the release of all that energy has prodded open the third eye in her mind, that black, merciless shark eye she just discovered. And now that she knows that it's there, it seems so much easier to use it.

She sees...

So much. Too much. Far, far too much.

"No," she whispers. "No. No, *God...*"

But one thing she's learned during her time here in Wink is how to control what she sees, and how she sees it. She must have been using this undiscovered eye of hers all along. So though her body is limp and her eyes stare blindly into the roof of the trunk, she focuses, and sees...

Something. A light in the dark.

A room.

A rounded stone chamber, a bit like a crypt. There is a pile of tiny skulls in the center. And beside it, sitting Indian-style on the floor and staring into the ground, is a man in a filthy blue rabbit suit.

Oh no, she thinks.

He seems to feel her watching him: he sits up, and turns to look. His face is once again concealed by the wooden mask. This time he does not take it off. Yet she gets the impression that he is very surprised to see her watching him.

He raises a hand to her. Then drops it.

She is a bit confused by this. Mona says: *Hello.*

The man nods slightly toward her. He stares at her a moment

longer. (Where is she, anyway? How can he see her? It seems very hard, all of a sudden, to keep herself in one place.) Then he looks around at his chamber. The light is dull and dusky; here all things are yellow and crumbling, a world rendered in musty stone and fading parchment and rusting chains.

He points at her. Then he points at the walls. Then back at her. Then he cocks his head a little.

Mona is not sure what he means. Then she understands: *You are imprisoned? Like me?*

Mona says to him: *Yes. Like you.*

And immediately she understands that this is how she can see and speak to him, that this might be why he chose not to harm her when they first met: the two of them are alike. Not just in circumstances; not just because the two of them are currently captured. That's just the start of it. The real reason is that Mona, like this ragged, filthy man, is a child left behind, neglected, and eventually forgotten, a sibling of a family she never got to know. They share the same story, the same nature: though he is much older than she, and she is the youngest, the two of them are connected. She understands this immediately, without words, without gestures: she understands this more than she has understood anything in her life.

She says: *You are my brother.*

He nods.

She says: *Can you help me? I am trapped.*

He looks at her. Then he shakes his head slowly.

What can I do? How can I free myself?

He lifts a hand and pats his chest, where his heart should be. Then he holds his hand out, and makes a fist. He clenches the fist so hard that his knuckles quiver, and trickles of blood begin to ooze down his palm. Then he relaxes it, reassuming his Indian-style position. His hand smears the canvas on his knee with dark blood. Then he hunches over, and resumes staring into the ground.

The connection fades. The vision falls away from her. And she is back in the trunk again.

She realizes she hasn't breathed in quite a while, and takes a deep gasp that quickly turns to coughs. Apparently this astral-projection thing—or, rather, pandimensional thing—takes some getting used to.

But though he did not speak, there was no mistaking his message:

Rage makes your heart free.

CHAPTER FIFTY-FOUR

At some point in time she sleeps, because when the car starts she finds herself waking up. Then, to her concern, the car starts moving, cutting what feels like a very sharp U-turn before continuing in a direction that definitely feels upward.

If she had to guess, it would be upward as in away from Wink, and away from civilization.

Though it's dark, Mona's inner ear tells her the incline keeps getting sharper and sharper. They're definitely going up somewhere high.

There's only one place Mona's been to in Wink yet that was this high: the road to the mesa, when she first went to Coburn.

"Shit," she whispers.

The ride gets incredibly bumpy, which confirms her theory. She feels around for a weapon, anything, but all she finds are frayed wires from the taillights. How did things get so incredibly fucked so fast?

They drive for over an hour before the car slows to a stop. She hears footsteps around the trunk.

Now, Mona decides, would be the time to think up a plan.

She decides the plan is to jump out and punch someone somewhere soft, and she won't be picky about who or where. She readies herself.

There is whispering outside the trunk. Then a soft pop, and light pours in, blinding her. She tries to spring out, but her body is so cramped and weak that she only manages to roll forward, falling onto very hard, hot stones as she blinks and waves her arms about.

When her sight comes back to her, she sees someone is standing over her: a very pale, very bloody, very defeated-looking Mrs. Benjamin.

Mona shields her eyes and squints at her. "Hey?" she says.

Then there is a sharp pain in her shoulder. She barely has time to look and see the hand holding the syringe that's buried in her flesh before things go—

"Motherfu—"

—dark.

Mona sees light. It is a dull, flat, soulless light. Her eyes don't work immediately—the general feeling she has is akin to what it was like directly after she had dental surgery in high school. Her body's so numb it's hard to tell, but it feels as if she's sitting upright in a chair with her hands behind her. Then she feels someone massaging her left upper arm.

"So she *has* to be alive for this?" says a voice.

"Well…I can't say."

"Then what *can* you say?"

"I can say that there is no added risk to her being alive."

"And you feel there is added risk if she isn't?"

"I would say so. But I am just a doctor. I do not specialize in these matters. Please remember, this is your idea. But if this should fail, then we will need to attempt…with more material. Provided she's secured…"

Someone shakes her hands. There's the dry gasp of rope, and she feels something around her wrists.

"She's secure," says a man's voice.

"Then I do not see a problem."

"Go ahead, then."

So she's tied to a chair, and since they didn't check any other bonds, it must just be her hands. Before she can think more on this, something sharp bites at the inside of her elbow. She sits up sharply and shouts, "*Fuck!*"

She blinks, and sees the blurry forms of many people standing around her in a dark room, but her eyes still aren't working that well.

"See?" says a voice. "I told you she was strong."

"Will it matter if her blood has sedatives in it?"

"I do not believe so. We only need an amount of her matter to form a connection to one of the alternates. Same to same, if that makes sense."

"Like red to red and black to black when you're jumping a car?" asks a voice. Mona recognizes this one: it's Mrs. Benjamin, and she sounds like utter shit.

"*Shut up*, you. I didn't bring you here to talk."

Mona's eyes manage to focus further. She's surrounded by a dozen or so people, men and women: the men wear sweaters with collared shirts and ties, and several of them are either holding pipes or are actively smoking them; the women wear poofy-sleeved dresses and high-heeled shoes, and some of them even have aprons on. Their faces are white and bloodless below the overhead lights.

"The fuck is this?" Mona asks in a slow, slurred voice. "Fucking... *Leave It to Beaver* casting call?"

"What does she mean?" asks one of the men softly. His eyes flutter. Mona grows a little more alert, and realizes all their eyes are fluttering, of course. But there's something huge and shining behind them, something hard to see...

"She means nothing," says a voice beside her. "She's drugged."

Mona successfully makes her head loll to her left. She sees a man attaching a tube to a catheter in her arm, right on the cubital vein. He's definitely a doctor: not only is he wearing old-fashioned OR scrubs, but he also has a moustache, small glasses, and a black pipe. Every part of his appearance is meant to suggest *I am a doctor!* Yet when he looks up at her, just the briefest of glances, she sees his eyes fluttering too.

"Motherfucker," says Mona, "I hope you know something about human anatomy."

He averts his eyes. Standing behind him is the woman who looked in on her in the trunk of the car, but now she looks queerly androgynous in a powder-blue suit and a white panama hat.

Something in Mona's drugged brain sputters. *Remove their bodies like clothes . . .*

"You're that asshole I shot on the highway, aren't you," she slurs.

The woman in the panama hat looks at her dispassionately, then turns to look down the room. "Is it ready?"

"Ready enough," says one man, who looks a lot like a Hardy Boy all grown up. He's standing in front of that shining thing Mona had trouble making out . . . but now it's a lot easier to see.

It's the lens. She's in the lens room at Coburn. She can see their reflections in the lens's surface, somehow cleaner and purer than they are in reality.

"Oh, shit," says Mona. "What the hell are you going to do with th—" Mona's arm goes cold. She hears fluid falling nearby, almost exactly the sound of someone pissing in a bucket. She lolls her head back, and sees that the tube snaking out of her arm is pouring her blood into what appears to be a gallon-size glass tub.

"What the hell are you doing?" she says. "You're taking my *blood*? What are you going to do with *that*?"

The people in the circle do not move or speak. They just stare at her, pale and impassive.

"If you're going to bleed me to death, at least do me the favor of shooting me first," says Mona. "Or, hell, cut my throat or something. There are better ways of killing someone than this."

"I don't think talking with them will work, dear," says Mrs. Benjamin's voice. Mona lolls her head the other way, and sees Mrs. Benjamin slumped in a corner, bloody and ragged. "If I were you, I'd stay quiet."

"What happened to you?" asks Mona.

But Mrs. Benjamin looks away, as if to avoid more punishment.

Mona turns back to the woman in the panama hat. "You're the

bitch who shut me in the trunk, aren't you? And the same one I shot in the road...I'm willing to bet you're behind all this stupid shit, ain't you? What are you trying to do? What's the point of all this?"

The woman does not answer. She just watches as more of Mona's blood pours into the glass tub.

More and more. A *lot* of blood. Mona strains at her bonds, but she's growing weak, and when two men come and put their hands on her shoulders to hold her still she can hardly resist. She starts to grow faint. "Hey, now..." she says. "How much...how much are guys going to...take?"

"You're sure this will work?" asks the doctor.

"Fairly," says the woman in the panama hat. "Time for them is strictly linear. They don't see all the alternates. All the way things could have gone, and are still going, moving away from them..."

"We can't see that, either, now that we're here," says one of the aproned women. "We're limited. Blinkered. Blind."

"We are," says the woman in the panama hat. She points toward the lens. "*That* isn't."

"How?"

"Because *that* was made by Mother."

They all glance sideways at one another. One of the women wrings her hands in her apron. "Perhaps we should ask First," she says. "He has always been better with the nature of time...he always saw alternates so much clearer than we."

"*No*," snarls the woman in the panama hat. "I will *not* have him involved in this. This is not his. This is *mine*."

Mona starts breathing hard. Everything begins to feel very woozy, yet the flow of blood continues. "Jesus," she murmurs. "Jesus Christ, *stop*." She knows a little bit about blood loss, from her cop days—more than 40 percent and it's a Class IV hemorrhage. How much would that be for her? A liter? More? How much is a liter when you actually look at it, anyway?

It's awful. She starts to *feel* the blood flowing out of her, all the fuel leaving the necessary systems and running out the now-dark rubber tube and into the glass tub. Her head pounds, and she wants to sleep...

Finally the doctor says, "I think that should be enough."

"You're sure?" asks the woman in the panama hat.

"Yes. I've read the statistics on children of that age—this should be sufficient for submersion. The tricky part will be getting it out before it drowns."

"Leave that to me."

"You're sure? I believe that for your purposes, the child would have to be most definitely alive."

"I said, leave it to me."

Two men reach down and help lift the giant tub of blood and carry it to a small steel table before the lens. *If those fuckers drop that thing*, thinks Mona, *I am going to shit a brick*. She wants to say so, but her arms and head and legs are leaden. She cannot even summon the energy to move. Breathing alone is hard.

"If this fails, we can always recreate the pregnancy," says the woman in the panama hat.

"I doubt it," says the doctor. "I believe the child would die in the transfer. There are a lot of...systems involved in pregnancy." He says this with the vagueness of someone who has scanned a lot of literature on the subject. "One would die, and then probably the other."

The woman in the panama hat pulls a face—*Enough of this bullshit*. "Fine."

Once the tub is before the lens, the men back away. All of them, except for Mona and Mrs. Benjamin, of course, form a circle around the blood and the silvery surface before it.

"I can still feel Mother on it," says one softly. "In it. Around it."

"I *told* you so," says the woman in the panama hat. "She made this for us. She is here. She never left us. She is coming back."

"We must concentrate," says one man.

"Yes," says the woman in the panama hat.

They stare at the lens. Their eyes grow wide. Then a soft sound begins to seep through the room. It is not quite a whine, and not quite a hum, but it is of a frequency so strange, and so intense, that it makes Mona's eyes water even though she can hardly lift her head. Though they are facing away, she is sure their eyes are fluttering like mad...

The surface of the lens ripples, as if it's bending inward.

They're singing to it, she thinks. *Open sesame*...

The humming intensifies. The tub of her blood appears to grow a little faint—as if it's about to flicker, like the croquet ball in the film. But where could they be sending it?

Or, she thinks, *are they bringing something here?*

The lens continues to shift. Then it seems to grow transparent, and Mona thinks she can see bright, clean daylight filtering through its top...

"It's working," says one man.

"I know it's working," says the woman in the panama hat, irritated. "Quit talking and concentrate."

Mona tries to watch as the lens seems to bring the image into focus, but something bumps into her from behind. "Hold on to these," whispers Mrs. Benjamin's voice. Something is shoved in between her buttocks and the chair, something flat and thin. With her tied hands, she feels something metallic and cold...

Mirrors? Maybe hand mirrors?

The people around the lens do not notice. Mona can see why—the mirror is changing, changing, until it's as if there's half of another room sitting at the end of the lens chamber.

Mona, whose breath feels very faint right now, squints as she tries to decipher what she's seeing.

It's a nursery. Bright morning sunlight pours through a floor-to-ceiling window. The walls are a faint yellow, the curtains have orange polka-dots, and there is a white crib just beside the window with a mobile hanging above it. Horses of many shapes and colors dangle from the mobile; it looks quite old, actually, which is strange because the rest of the nursery looks terribly new.

She's seen that mobile before. She knows she has.

Actually, Mona thinks, the rest of the items in the nursery also look familiar. She bought things just like them, once. She's positive that years ago she bought almost the exact same tree decal to stick in the corner of the room—though she never took it out of the packaging. She never got the chance. Mona's also sure she picked out a shade of yellow paint so similar to the color of the nursery in the lens that you almost couldn't tell them apart, though her paint job wound up only half finished. And she ordered that same model of diaper pail on the internet, one of those space-age ones with expensive technology to keep the fecal reek contained (because during her pregnancy Mona became hypersensitive to the scent of shit), though Dale wound up returning it for a refund.

After everything. After the funeral.

And now she realizes where she's seen that mobile. It was hers, once—more than thirty years ago, when she was a baby. One her own mother used for her crib—though now the idea makes her stomach squirm. But just a few years ago she looked at it with Dale, and said— *Maybe we don't need a mobile for our nursery. Maybe we have a perfectly good one right here.* And Dale, who wasn't an idiot, knew what Mona meant, and agreed, and kissed her on the forehead.

Something begins to contract inside Mona. Are they torturing her? Is this some form of psychological warfare? Why would they ever want to see this place, this place that should have been but never was?

Then something shifts in the crib ahead of them.

There is a grunt, tiny and irritated.

It looks like a lump of fabric is at the bottom of the crib. It shifts again, rising up.

Mona recognizes the pattern on the fabric. It's a pair of baby pants she bought when she first became pregnant. She remembers the pattern, because she thought, *I wonder how well spit-up will come out of this...*

She is seeing a child lying on its stomach in the crib, scrunching its knees and shoulders together so its tiny butt rises higher. It is waking up, slowly scrunching and unfolding and remembering its muscles, shifting in discomfort...

No, she wants to say. *Don't show me this. Don't you show me this.*

The child in the crib moans. It lifts its head. There is the gleam of a tiny blue eye peering through the crib bars, and a mass of dark, moist hair.

No, no, no.

The child blinks in the sunlight, and wrinkles its nose.

"Is that it?" asks one of the men in sweaters.

"Yes," snaps the woman in the panama hat. "Keep concentrating!"

A tiny, frowning mouth opens, and allows out a reedy mewl.

Then the child flickers, like an error in a filmstrip—the child is there, then it isn't.

A voice sings from somewhere: "Coming! Coming!" But it didn't come from inside the lens chamber. It was in the room in the lens, the nursery on the other side...

And Mona knows that voice. She's heard it before.

What is this? What is happening?

"Concentrate," says the woman in the panama hat.

The humming in the room grows louder. The child in the crib briefly grows faint, and when it does...

Did Mona just see movement in the glass tub? Did the lake of blood there twitch?

"Keep going," whispers the woman in the panama hat. She speaks in the voice of someone on the verge of orgasm.

The child in the crib flickers once more. It begins bawling loudly.

"Coming! Almost done, little one! Just one more second!" shouts the voice in the lens.

The child slips out of the world in the lens... and very briefly, Mona sees a tiny hand in the glass tub, floating up out of the sea of blood to paw at the walls...

Oh, my God, no.

"Almost there," whispers the woman in the panama hat.

The child in the lens, now crying hysterically, blinks out of existence once more...

Mona remembers what Mr. First said: *It could change the very nature of reality, like the finger of a god.*

And Coburn's words: *And in that moment, the thing it is examining is shoved—partially—into all those various other realities as well. So it could exist in a variety of states, places, et cetera. Even* times, *possibly, though of course that is quite hard to quantify . . .*

No, no, thinks Mona.

The surface of the blood begins sloshing back and forth. Something in the tub is struggling, flailing . . .

It's like lubricant, thinks Mona. *Easing transition from one place to another . . .*

Then someone steps into view in the lens. Though Mona is barely conscious, her eyes spring wide at the sight of this new person. At first she thinks it is her mother, for it looks so much like Laura Alvarez . . . even though this person is shorter and her skin is so much browner . . .

This new woman looks in the crib, and sees the child is missing. She freezes.

At the exact same time, the woman in the panama hat darts forward, reaches into the tub of blood, and pulls out something red and dripping and coughing . . .

A child. A naked human child, which is hacking and coughing horribly.

The woman in the lens turns around. Mona sees her face.

"Is it alive?" asks one of the men.

Mona barely hears them. She is staring into the mirror. Because this new person is not Laura Alvarez. It is *her*—Mona Bright herself. Slightly fatter, with slightly fewer wrinkles, and slightly longer hair. But it is most certainly Mona Bright, staring around the room, anxious, worried, wondering where her child could be . . .

The bloody, dripping baby coughs again, then begins shrieking in fear.

"It's alive," says the woman in the panama hat. Her hands and sleeves are soaked in blood, but she grins in manic triumph. "It's alive. It's a baby girl. It's alive."

The humming in the room stops. And the other Mona—the mother Mona, in her nursery, staring about in fear—fades from view, swallowed in a sea of shining silver as the lens reverts to its reflective state.

The woman in the panama hat begins laughing. "It's here. She's finally here. She's coming!"

CHAPTER FIFTY-FIVE

In the south of Wink, just below the skin of the earth under the highway crossroads, many eyes open in the dark.

The dark does not bother them. They were born in the dark. They have lived their whole lives in the dark. They were made for the dark and their hearts will always belong in the dark. So they open their eyes, and see:

Movement. Their creation is hissing. Melting. The blocks of metal (of *Her*) bubble at all the seams and edges, swirling together like boiling lead.

At first they are concerned: they chirp and tweet and grumble in the darkness, shifting in their roosts and rolling over one another in their shallow pools. They spent so much time on it, so many hours hunting through the ravines and empty homes of this place...they spent days bearing the stupendous, horrible weight of those blocks up and down mountainsides...and now, without warning, it is to melt?

But then they feel it: the world here grows soft. The barrier, which is already quite permeable in Wink, begins to disappear entirely. All places—those distant and disparate, those Here and There, Elsewhere and Nowhere—converge into one.

Their tone changes. They begin to flute and cry and sing in the darkness. This is not an ending, not a death in the dark. This is a new day, this is a beginning, a new world.

She is coming.

CHAPTER FIFTY-SIX

The child screams, and screams, and screams. She looks horrific, a tiny, shriveled person soaked in red with its face contorted and eyes streaming tears. The woman in the panama hat surveys the baby coldly. "Should it be so small?" she asks.

The doctor looks at the baby as if he's never seen one before. Which, Mona realizes, he probably hasn't. "It appears to be the acceptable size..."

"Well," says the woman in the panama hat, "it won't matter when Mother gets here."

"Is this as you expected?" asks the doctor. "We need it to be the woman's progeny, to be *Mother's* progeny. Like us, but of this place. Is this Her child?"

The woman in the panama hat shuts her eyes, as if to think. Then her eyes snap open. "Yes," she says. "It will work. Mother is coming already. I can feel it." She sighs deeply, as if she has just smelled a particularly alluring fragrance. "It is Her progeny, indirectly. It will work. It *is* working."

Mona stares at the bloody child. It's difficult to really study its features, since it is so slick with blood... but she thinks she sees her brow line, and maybe Dale's eyes, and could that be her mouth?

This can't be. I don't believe it.

The woman in the panama hat holds the child out to the doctor. "Take it. Take it to the highway crossroads just south of town."

He hesitates. "Do you not wish to do it?"

"No. I have matters to attend to here. She should be there. You must meet Her when She arrives. And when She comes to see me, it will be me...and only me. No"—she glances sideways at Mrs. Benjamin—"distractions."

"We have not broken any of Mother's edicts in bringing Her here, have we? We have kept to Her rules?"

The woman in the panama hat gives him a flat stare. "Are you suggesting," she asks, "that it is possible to defy Mother?"

He bows his head, and takes the child. "Will I need protection?"

"One of the children will assist you."

"But it's daylight."

She rolls her eyes, exasperated. "And *why* do we need to keep to this town's rules?"

"You make a fair point." He and about half of the men and women file out of the room with the screaming child. Mona can still see tiny feet with flexed toes, and struggling arms trying to pull out of his grasp...

"No," whispers Mona. "No, please..."

One of the men in sweaters—this one a soft brown—turns and looks at her. His gaze is discomfortingly alien. "What do we do with her?" he asks in a quiet monotone.

"Do you know how to use a knife?" asks the woman in the panama hat.

He frowns, nods.

"Do you know how to use one *well*?"

"I understand the concept."

"Beside the door is a box. Within it are several knives. Cut her here"—she points to a specific point on her throat—"cut her deep, and make sure she dies."

"She can die like *that*?" asks the man, as if this is a foreign concept.

"Oh, yes. Her kind die quite easily. They all do it, eventually."

"And that's all it takes?"

"That's all."

He nods again, impressed.

"You, and you." The woman in the panama hat gestures to the remaining men. "Take *her*"—she points to Mrs. Benjamin—"and come with me. I want to have a discussion with her."

"Oh, goody," says Mrs. Benjamin, as the two men grab her by the shoulders. "Am I to get another lecture?"

The woman in the panama hat does not answer as she leads the men dragging Mrs. Benjamin from the room, leaving Mona with the man in the soft brown sweater, who is staring at her with a look of some anticipation, as if about to start a new and exciting experiment.

First he practices the motion: he holds an imaginary knife, and swoops it down in a slash. But he shakes his head, dissatisfied. "Are we too near the wall?" he asks.

Mona is too fatigued by the blood loss to answer, but of course even if she had the strength, she wouldn't.

"I think we are too near the wall," says the man thoughtfully, "for the full range of motion." He pushes her chair over to the center of the room. Mona's eye registers movement to her right, but it's only their reflection in the lens. In it, she sees her wrists are bound to the back of the chair by thick ropes. She can also see the doorway out to her left, and beside it there is indeed a small black box. Beside this box, she sees, are her rifle and her Glock.

The man in the soft brown sweater walks to the box, opens it, and says, "Ah." He scratches his head pensively. Then he takes out three different knives, examines them carefully, and selects the largest one. The other two he places on the ground beside the box.

As he goes through this scrupulous procedure, Mona flexes her fingers. To her surprise, they can move, though she feels very weak. She paws at the seat of the chair, where Mrs. Benjamin wedged the mirrors. She can manage to grasp and retrieve only one, in her right hand; her left remains disturbingly dead, but then it was the one that got tapped.

The man in the soft brown sweater holds up the big knife, and slashes it through the air. "Cut," he says. "Cut! Or—perhaps like a surgeon?" He makes a small, dainty slice in the air, and says, with great delicacy: "*Cut.*"

Jesus, thinks Mona. *He must be one of the really young ones . . .*

But what is she going to do with just one lens? She's only done this once before, and then she had to have two lenses to get anything to move . . .

She realizes she's staring at her reflection in the big lens.

Oh, she thinks.

"Cut," says the man in the soft brown sweater. He wheels to look at her. "Cut!" he says, and swipes the blade through the air. "I've never killed one of you before. Is it messy?"

Mona ignores him. She tries to concentrate on wriggling her right wrist around to rotate her little lens toward the big one . . .

"I bet it is," he says. "You're all full of . . . fluid. Matter. Hm." He looks down at his sweater. He plucks the front and stretches it out. "Hm," he says again.

Is it pointed in the right direction? She can see part of the face of the hand mirror (or hand lens) in the reflection of the big lens. Two little bubbles of space, floating free and unattached in the air . . .

She remembers the nursery. The face of the woman who looked so much like her.

Because it was you, she thinks.

Stop. Don't think about that.

She thinks she has the angles right, so she tries to concentrate. But this time it's not hard at all: she senses immediately that the big lens is a different animal altogether. Using the hand mirrors in Mrs. Benjamin's house was like using tweezers to pick up pebbles, but this thing is a fucking bulldozer on and rumbling and ready to go, leaping at the slightest touch of the pedal. The challenge won't be getting it to work, but controlling it.

The man in the brown sweater is now carefully removing his sweater, but he hasn't thought to put down the knife, which makes it pretty tough on him.

Mona focuses on one of the little knives next to the black box. For a long time, nothing happens. But then it appears to grow just slightly, slightly transparent…

She opens her left hand wide. *I hope I get the right part in my fucking hand*, she thinks, *otherwise I'm going to cut my palm wide open.*

"Ah!" says the man. He's finally gotten one arm and his head out of his sweater. "There we go!"

Come on, come on.

The knife flickers. Then she feels something hard and cold in her left hand. She begins to close her fingers around it…

…but just as she does, she sees something in the big lens. The lens, she thinks, is a bit like a door, and this one's been left slightly ajar, opening onto wherever it opened onto last. It's like looking at something down a long, dark hallway (and Mona isn't really looking at all, except possibly with the little dark eye inside of her), but she thinks she's starting to understand.

The lens opened onto a place ghostly and distant, something ephemeral and far away… something that didn't happen, or at least it didn't happen *here*.

Was that me I saw? Or another version of me?

She remembers her current situation when she hears a voice say, "Cut."

She releases the big lens. She's still sitting in the chair with her wrists bound behind her, the hand lens in her right hand and the knife in her left. She begins sawing at the rope as fast as she can, trying to summon all her remaining strength. Her left hand and arm are so numb that it's difficult to tell how far she's getting.

The man, now sweaterless, takes a breath. "All right," he says softly. "All right."

He takes a step forward, still staring at her with that detached, blank gaze. Whatever swims in his eyes is wriggling madly.

Mona feels the rope begin to give way. She frees the pinky and ring finger of her right hand and twists the rope, trying to stretch the fibers against the blade.

"Just a cut," whispers the man.

He takes another step.

The rope frays. Pops.

Mona strains her left shoulder. More pops sound from the rope.

"Hm?" says the man. He leans in, confused.

The rope snaps.

Mona clenches her teeth, and swings her left hand around.

There is a soft thud. It is so soft that it is surprising, really. But then, the knife does bite into a very soft place, just behind the esophagus of the man in the brown sweater, piercing God knows how many tendons and muscles and veins.

Blood sprays from the corners of the knife in tiny, furious geysers, like pinholes in a dike. The man stares at Mona, mouth open. She can already see blood welling up in his mouth. Mona, in disbelief, stares back.

Then rage begins to bubble inside her. *My fucking daughter*, she thinks.

She drops the hand lens, brings her right hand around, grasps the top of the man's head with it, and rips the knife forward with her left.

She is totally and utterly showered in a hot wave of blood, which shocks her, but she really should have expected that since she's just partially decapitated this man. As he tumbles to the ground, all she can think is *Man oh man am I happy I kept my mouth closed.*

He twitches for a moment, still just spewing blood (this does not surprise Mona—she's seen a few murder scenes, which is when you realize the shocking amount of blood in the human body), and then he goes still.

There is the soft sound of thunder from somewhere.

"Shit," she says. She hopes she didn't just send this stupid bastard into someone else's body. But that seems highly plausible right now.

She looks at herself in the lens. She's bloody from head to toe. But she's alive. And she's not quite as weak as she thought. Which doesn't make a whole lot of sense, since she's just lost a shitload of blood.

But maybe, she thinks as she stares at herself in the lens, *it's because you're not completely human.*

She looks at the vat of blood before the lens. She almost wishes to touch it. She cannot conceive that a child was just there, and that that child might have been her daughter . . .

Mona decides she doesn't understand a goddamn bit of this. But she knows someone who does.

She takes off her shoes before venturing out into the hall, and she moves silently and swiftly over the cracked concrete floor. She has her Glock, but she doesn't want to use it (because fuck knows what that bitch in the blue suit would do if she heard her coming), so she's got two of the knives stuffed into the belt loops of her shorts as backup.

It isn't very long until she hears voices echoing down the hall.

"—if She'll be happy to see us," says a man's voice.

"Of course She'll be happy to see us," says another's. "We're Her children."

"But She's been gone so long. Will She remember us?"

Silence for a moment. "I had not thought about that. I had not thought that She could forget."

Mona creeps toward the voices. She comes to a hallway entrance on her left, and listens.

"Do you forget Her?" asks the first voice. "I do, sometimes...it seems awfully hard to remember Her. I remember being happy. I think I remember being happy. But it seems very long ago."

"We were meant to be happy here. That was what we decided."

"I know."

"But I...I will admit that I found it...hard. It was not as easy as I had expected. Maybe Weringer was wrong."

There is a long pause. "I don't know. Maybe we were all wrong. Maybe She will know."

Mona uses one of the hand lenses to look around the corner. She sees two men before one of the lab doors, sitting on the concrete floor cross-legged like children. She wonders what to do before remembering the extreme incompetence of her last captor. The bitch in the blue suit, she decides, must have really scraped the bottom of the barrel for help, but that makes sense—the older and smarter ones would have been too dangerous to approach.

She feels her pockets, and finds a spent round casing from the fight in the canyon the night before. She weighs it carefully, then throws it across the hallway entrance where it tinkles loudly as it rolls away.

"What was that?" asks one man.

Mona shrinks up against the wall. She hears footsteps growing louder. The two men emerge from the hallway entrance, and sure enough they turn immediately in the direction of the sound: they don't even *think* to check the other end of the hallway.

So the one on the left is incredibly surprised when Mona stabs him in the back of the leg, just behind his knee, and the other is too stunned to even look at her before she brings the butt of the Glock down, cracking him on the side of his head.

Both of them collapse. "My leg," says the stabbed one, with an air of wonderment. "What's happened to my leg?"

There were people in those bodies, once, thinks Mona. *I wonder where they went...*

Still, she can't risk these two causing any more trouble, and she doesn't want either of them hopping into another poor soul's body. So she stoops down and stabs them in the knees, just next to the knee-caps, severing the iliotibial band.

"My other leg!" cries the stabbed one. "Oh, my other leg!"

"Shut up," says Mona softly. "There are worse ways to incapacitate you. You want me to try one?"

He doesn't answer. Mona wonders if he even knows what the word *incapacitate* means.

Forget it. She leaves them both behind and heads for the door they were guarding.

Mona eases the door open just slightly. The room is the typical Coburn lab (excepting the lens chamber, of course): bare, concrete, wreathed in stains and shadows from equipment long gone. Mrs. Benjamin sits in a heap in the corner, and in the center stands the woman in the blue suit. The two seem to be in the middle of a discussion.

The woman in the panama hat is saying, "—d you know I've been farther than you, big sister?"

"Oh?" says Mrs. Benjamin. She looks quite weak, and not very interested.

"You were trapped here in Wink like all the others. But I went to its very limits. When I died, I turned to lightning, and rode the curves of the skies above us...and I've been to the fringes. I went there all the time. Maybe past them, just a bit. You can't claim the same, can you?"

Mrs. Benjamin does not answer.

"No. I even went to that Roadhouse of theirs. That's where I met them. The *natives* who helped me. Everyone here thought it was outside the limits. And no one ever tried, because you were lazy, and afraid. But I did. I went there. Imagine how silly it is: a bunch of men, drunk and drugged and stupid, bringing down our five eldest family members. Do you want to find out how?" She reaches down again, and lifts up something: a small, lacquered box.

"I wanted to kill First," says the woman. "But I wasn't sure what it would take. So on the last trip, I sent them to get *two* totems. Just in case. So convenient to have a spare on hand now, isn't it? I had to go back to their Roadhouse just this morning to get it. You've caused me a lot of traveling, Sister."

"Totems?" asks Mrs. Benjamin, confused.

"Oh, you don't know? No, you wouldn't. Listen—do you remember the stories we used to tell one another about the wildling?"

Mrs. Benjamin looks up a little, but does not answer.

"Yes, you do. About the real first, the first child Mother ever had. But it displeased Her, and She abandoned it. But we always used to tell one another that it was following us, following everything we did, trying to catch up." The woman opens up the box. "Well. It did, Sister. It came with us to Wink."

Inside is, as Mona expected, a small white skull. Mrs. Benjamin and the woman stare at it, though one does so with a look of reverence and the other with a look of profound dread.

"You *do* remember," says Mrs. Benjamin, "that I did just help you."

"Yes. And I don't care. Do you feel afraid, Sister?"

"Yes, I feel afraid."

"Do you feel weak?"

"I suppose I do."

"That's how I felt. How I've always felt. Weak and scared. It isn't fair, that I was weak. It wasn't fair that all I could be was Mother's Ganymede. I could have been stronger. I could have been better. If you had given me the chance."

"Ganymede?" says Mrs. Benjamin. "I don't understand."

"All I got to be was Her servant. I carried Her cup, I brought Her entertainment. Yet She never thanked me. Because all She ever thought about was you. You five, my elders, always off rushing about, doing *important* things. She never cared about anyone else. And she *should* have cared. She *would* have, if She'd had the chance. You all fought for Her, made sure no one else could ever have Her favor! You manipulated Her!"

"*We* manipulated *Her*?" asks Mrs. Benjamin sniffily. "That is a stunning revision of history."

"Shut up!" snarls the woman. "Don't act like you didn't! I...I *know* what She would have done if you hadn't made sure you were the favorites! She would have...She would have *loved* us. She would have loved *me*. You don't know what it's like, being so forgotten. You don't know what it's like, to be cast aside. She never even knew us. Never even cared about us. You don't know what that's like. None of you do!

"But all that will change." She thumps herself on the chest. "I am the weapon in Mother's hand! I am the tool of Her mind! I am Her device, Her emissary, Her herald! I am first in Her eyes! And when She comes I will be rewarded, and I shall be loved! She will come back, and She will love me! Do you hear me? Do you hear my words?"

"I do," says Mrs. Benjamin warily. "But I wonder if it is really worth it."

"It is!" says the woman. "It must be! It has to be!"

"Are you sure Mother is even coming? You showed me Her body in the cavern, but..."

"She is! Mother will wake when Her host comes near! That last piece of Her!"

"A child. A human child."

"Not for long. Soon Mother will wake and take Her rightful place at the center of this world."

"And then what? You will replace First, replace the rest of us?"

"Yes!" shouts the woman. She is on the verge of sobbing now. "I found Her! I'm the one bringing Her here! I brought down those who would stand in Her way! I brought the woman here! It was me, me, I did it all, it was me! Not you, never you! You never helped! Never helped me, not once!"

"We never knew…"

"You did know! You had to know! Stop…stop saying that!" The woman begins to thrust the open box forward, preparing to send the little skull tumbling onto Mrs. Benjamin…

…which is when Mona's hand darts forward, and shuts the box with a snap. Before the woman can react, Mona shoves the barrel of the Glock up against her back, right at the base of her spine, and pulls the trigger.

Immediately the woman's legs give out underneath her: the round has just cleanly severed her spine. She flops awkwardly on the floor, rolls over, and stares at her belly, from which the round has rather messily exited; blood is pouring out at a fairly alarming rate.

Mona stands over her, breathing hard, and looks between her and Mrs. Benjamin. "Right," she says.

The woman stares up at Mona, then at the wooden box in her hand. "You, you…"

"Yeah," says Mona. "I shot you. But don't worry, you're not dying, at least not fast. I'm smart enough to know that shooting you would just shift you around." She points her gun at the woman's chest. "I can make you hurt, though. Real bad. I'm learning to be pretty good at that. Now I want you to tell me what happened in that room back there."

The woman looks at her blankly, then examines her wound again. She does not seem all that pained or concerned by it.

"Tell me," says Mona again.

The woman remains still, unresponsive.

"I don't think physical threats will work, dear," says Mrs. Benjamin. "It's my understanding that it has died or hurt or maimed itself numerous times before."

"It?"

"The Ganymede. That's what it calls itself."

"Huh. Well." Mona sticks her Glock in her shorts (the barrel is hot, but she doesn't care) and opens the wooden box. The pearly little rabbit skull roars at her silently from its pillow of blue satin.

She looks down at the woman in the panama hat. Her eyes have gone wide. It's clear she realizes what Mona's thinking.

"Dying," says Mona. "It's a weird idea to you all, isn't it? I'm pretty sure it's why your buddy in the brown sweater did such a shit job of trying to kill me. But you—you've killed before. I think you've killed plenty of times. You get it."

"I never killed anyone," says the woman. "It's against the rules."

"Mm, I'm willing to bet you killed plenty of *people* just by body-hopping. Which is a pretty fucked-up thing to do." Mona takes a step forward and puts her foot on the wound in the woman's belly. The woman grunts and tenses up, obviously pained. "You're not as tough as you think. Now. What the hell happened back there? Whose baby was that?"

"Yours," groans the woman.

"That can't be. My baby died. We buried it. It was the worst thing that happened to me in my fucking life, and I can't forget it. So whose was it?"

"Yours!" says the woman again.

Mona leans on the wound harder and lowers the box threateningly.

"It's yours, I swear it is!" the woman shouts.

Mona eases up on the wound. "How?"

She swallows. Her lips are lined with red. "Time…is broken here…"

"Oh, God, not this speech again. I've heard it a million fucking times."

"Time is *broken* here," says the woman angrily, "so here you can see the *alternates*."

"The alternates to what?" Mona asks.

"To everything!" shouts the woman.

Mona eases up more on the wound. She thinks, and asks, "What the hell does that mean?"

Mrs. Benjamin clears her throat. "I believe I can help with this. Time is not linear, dear—you and your kind experience it as linear, but it isn't, not really. It branches off, spins into different directions. Some of these offshoots fade and die, some keep going. And, occasionally, these can be accessed."

"Yes," gasps the woman. "If the...the difference is very slight, the alternate can be breached."

"And that's what you did back there? Accessed an alternate... *time*?"

The woman nods.

"It's not something that would occur to us on our side, since when we're in our element we do *not* experience time the same way you do," says Mrs. Benjamin. "But here it's...different."

Mona realizes her hands are shaking. She flexes them to try to make them stop. "So what we saw was an alternate time. Another way things could have gone."

"Yes," says the woman. She is white and panting now.

"And what was the difference between where we are here...and what I saw in the lens?"

"We had to have a piece of Mother that was...willing to cooperate," says the woman. She coughs, turns her head, and burps up a significant quantity of blood.

"Yeah?"

"We had to have a piece of Her that was from both here and the other side. *Our* side. To anchor Her here, to pull Her in. I had...I had intended this to be you. That's why I...called you here."

"That's what you tried to do to me on the highway, isn't it? Make me Her...conduit."

"Yes," says the woman savagely. "But you rejected me, rejected

Her. You were too old, too...resistant. So we had to find another way. You had had a child, but...it had died in this time."

Mona's whole body is trembling, and she knows it is not from blood loss. "So you just found a different time," she says. "You found a time where...where my baby didn't die. Where I had her, and she was alive."

"Yes."

She's alive, Mona thinks. *My God. She's alive, and she's real.*

She remembers the look on the face of the Mona in the lens: the complete terror and disbelief when she walked into the nursery and saw the crib was empty...

The woman continues: "We had to have your blood, because... alternates are so difficult to access. The child is a part of you—she is your progeny. We had to...bridge the gap."

"Like you're doing with Mother now? Now that you've got her, she'll bring Mother here?"

"She already is here!" snarls the woman. "It's already happening! The breach has occurred, and the wound is only widening! You can't stop it! She's coming!"

She looks to Mrs. Benjamin. "Is this possible?"

"It seems so," says Mrs. Benjamin gravely. "I cannot pretend to understand all of it...but it seems so."

The woman's breath is now shallow. "I'll see Her," she whispers. "I'll see Her and She'll see me and we'll be happy again...it'll be like the past...never happened."

Mona studies the dying woman. "Think you're just going to jump ship out of that body?"

The woman's face is still, but her eyes twitch to look at Mona.

"If you'd just killed a few of your kin, I wouldn't have cared," says Mona. "I don't give a shit about your family squabbles. But you had to drag me into this. Me and my—my dead little *girl*..."

The woman tries to mouth something. It looks like she's saying, *Mother's wishes.*

"I don't give a shit what Mother wanted. You're pathetic. You're all...you're all so goddamn pathetic."

And she turns the box over.

The pale little skull falls through the air.

The woman's eyes go wide and track it.

And the second it touches her chest...

All three of them become aware of a fourth person in the room with them, who has apparently appeared without any of them knowing it: it is as if this person, who strikes such a strange figure in his ragged, mud-smeared blue canvas suit, and his wooden rabbit mask, has been here all along, and someone has merely turned on a light behind him, outlining his figure and alerting them to his presence.

The room is now two rooms. First the light changes, very subtly: it turns a faint yellow, the color of old parchment. And if she really looks, Mona thinks she can see old, worn stone in the shadows, and somewhere above them is a high, vaulted ceiling...

The woman mouths, *No! No!*

And then things go

dark

The other side.

Mona opens her eyes, and looks.

A tiny blue-and-white form stands on a black plain.
It is a measly little gangrel, a capering little clown.
It cowers and covers its head, whimpering.

The pink moon hangs above it, fat and swollen.
Yet something dark and spindly rises up, crossing the face of the moon...

Something is standing on the horizon.

Mona can see a long, thin skull, a skull like a needle, and two long ears.
It is huge. The size of skyscrapers. Miles of brambly, dark hide.

And its eyes... so huge and yellow, yet so human, and so angry.

The tiny blue-and-white figure waves its arms. There is a tinny scream:
"No! No! Please, no! Momma! Momma, please!"

The immense, dark thing cocks its head. Its yellow eyes roll.
Hands appear in the darkness, thin and clawed.

"Momma," whimpers the little figure.

The hands clench. Quiver with rage.
The huge thing dives forward.

A spray of gore, a shriek. Something dark pools on the rocky field.
Whimpers in the dark.

Then...

There is a gasping sound. The air shudders. They are back in the little room at Coburn.

Mona and Mrs. Benjamin look down. The skull is still on the woman's chest, but she is utterly still. The man in the rabbit mask is gone.

"I've never seen any of my family members die before..." says Mrs. Benjamin. "That was..."

"Fast. *Real* fast. Are you all right?"

"I have been stabbed several times, so—no."

Mona starts to help her up. "Why the hell did you help me?"

Mrs. Benjamin appears to pout just slightly. "Well. Perhaps I've assumed the role of a cranky old woman a little too thoroughly. Sabotage comes to me very naturally, it seems. Or perhaps I don't like to see people causing havoc."

"Whatever the reason, I'm grateful. Let's get the hell out of here."

They return to the lens chamber to grab Mona's rifle and some rounds. Then they make their way out. Mrs. Benjamin has to lean on her as they move. "So what happens now?" asks Mona.

"Well…if that Ganymede person was correct, it is possible for Mother to manifest here in some form, but She would be bound to this place, to Wink. Because Wink is not quite here and not quite there. She would need to meld or merge with some element of *this* side. Only then can she make the full transition."

"Meld or merge with my—my daughter." She says these words, though she cannot believe them.

"That is correct," says Mrs. Benjamin dourly. "The child is young, and weak—Mother can force Her entry."

"If that were to work, would she…what would happen to the baby?"

Mrs. Benjamin's eyebrows rise as she considers it. "Well, for one thing, I would not imagine she would look much like a baby at all, after that."

Getting up the ladder to the roof of the mesa proves quite hard: Mrs. Benjamin has to use Mona's head or shoulders as a stepping-stone, until finally the blazing, merciless New Mexico sun greets them in a triumphant blast.

"What sort of car was that fucking doctor driving?" Mona asks in a rasp.

"Erm," says Mrs. Benjamin. "A black Lincoln, I think?"

"Good," says Mona. She stands. "The way down is over here."

"Do you intend to catch up with them?"

"Yeah."

"I am not an expert in automotive matters, but I believe you'd need a car of your own to do so."

"I know."

A grunt as Mrs. Benjamin extends one wobbling, swollen foot toward a rocky purchase. "Do you have a car of your own?"

"No. We'll just have to…I don't know, figure it out."

"I can't imagine that there is anything nearby. You will have to do some very good figuring."

Mona stops. "No, I won't."

"Why not?"

She points. "I just have to ask her."

Waiting at the start of the road, just before the broken, locked doors of Coburn, is Mona's 1969 cherry-red Dodge Charger. A skinny teenage girl is standing beside the passenger door, looking very awkward, which, after all, is a very easy thing for a skinny teenage girl to do.

Gracie clears her throat and waves to them. "Hello," she says.

CHAPTER FIFTY-SEVEN

Mona drives.

She drives unwisely, stupidly, recklessly; she chooses to ignore fenceless bluffs and sharp turns and loose gravel roads; her foot knows only the most extreme angle the gas pedal can occupy, and refuses to release it any. On the whole, she cares not a fucking jot for physics, friction, or the limits of air bags or seat belts: all she cares about, all her weary, brutalized, angry mind can think about, is speed, speed, speed.

That, and the sight of that mottled, bloody little face as it wrinkled up and squawked, its tiny cry almost dead in that lead-walled room.

I have a daughter. I have a little girl.

She's real.

I think she's real...

Behind her, Gracie is trying breathlessly to explain how Mr. First directed her to where the Charger was hidden, and how he produced (she keeps stressing that he "produced") the keys; and Mrs. Benjamin just keeps saying, "That's good, dear," and, "Why, how nice of him," and so on. Mona asks how in the hell the doughnut got replaced with a real tire, and Gracie professes ignorance; though she does say that First is fond of fixing things for her and other people, when no one is looking.

Mona can hardly listen. She feels horribly confused. Her daughter is alive, and real, and though she feels a huge swelling of hope, it does not feel...honest.

I wonder what her name is. What I named her.

And again, she remembers the sight of her own face, shorn of all the years of drunken wandering, staring about the nursery as she wondered where her little girl was...

My head hurts.

Mona thanks fucking Christ that Wink is so small, because there's only one street that cuts all the way through town, all the way across to the other side. So there's only one way the doctor and her baby could have gone.

But as they come plummeting down from the mesa, the Charger's wheels shrieking and the engine sometimes threatening to leap out of the hood, she notices something is different now.

The color seems to be leaching out of the sky: it is no longer the bright, electric blue that Mona first found so striking about New Mexico, but a hazy yellowish red, like the color of bloody pus. There is something wrong about the light, too: it feels like a thin gray wash, too weak to project any real shadows.

The yards and streets of Wink are just ahead. But the town appears to be crawling with activity.

The doors of the houses and buildings—nearly all of them—are open. And people are either walking out to stand in their yards, or they are already there.

It is as if everyone has come outside to wait for something. And there is a sound that is audible even over the roar of the Charger's engine—a low, loud buzz, like a dozen propeller planes starting up.

"Something's wrong," says Mona.

"Yes," says Mrs. Benjamin softly. "Something is wrong."

Mrs. Benjamin knows this sound. She knows it better than almost any sound. Was this not the tremulous, terrifying note that always rang through the skies when they approached? And always she was in the vanguard, the most dangerous, the most frightening, the most intimidating of all of Mother's children...

It was a way of saying to new worlds: *We are coming. We are here.*

And now she hears it echoing down these quaint suburban streets, across the green parks and verdant lawns, filtering through the tall pines and rebounding along the mountain peaks. She sees all the familiar faces: the estimable Mrs. Greer, the Elms, odd Mr. Crayes and old Mr. Trimley, Mrs. Huwell, the Dawes children. And all of them stand there, faces blank and eyes unseeing, a faint buzz rattling from their skulls and adding to the ocean of sound...

Mrs. Benjamin can feel the pull herself. It was one that always arrived right when they were about to depart for a new place, a tickling in the back of the head as if to say—*Wake up! It's time.*

It's time now.

Mother is here. She is coming back.

"Oh, my," says Mrs. Benjamin. She reddens as if having a hot flash. "I have a feeling that we will need to hurry."

As the buzz floods through the barren canyon beside the mesa, Mr. First sighs.

He has been waiting for this sound all day. He knew it would come. It was just a matter of when. To be honest, he expected it earlier.

It is a difficult thing, crossing the worlds. It takes incredible preparation, much like building a mousetrap from scratch; and in one moment, one cautious, creeping moment, it must all be executed cleanly, perfectly, accurately.

And in the past few days, he's finally come to understand what's been staring him in the face for so long.

Establishing the town of Wink was never Mother's intended goal, any more than ushering Her children to safety was: those goals, while selfless and admirable, were all pretense. The point of all Her efforts, of all Her planning and scheming, was to pull Her intelligence, Her being, from one world to another.

It would be so hard for Mother to cross in totality, he thinks. Much harder than for him or any of their other family members. It would take an amazing amount of work to build that mousetrap...

And he now knows that Mother's mousetrap—the whole of Wink,

its place and its history—is about to spring. That buzz, that war song like so many trumpets and bagpipes, announces Her arrival. Somewhere down in Wink, the Ganymede has made the keyhole through which Mother's essence will soon flood.

Mr. First pulls himself to his feet. This takes some time, as there is a lot of Mr. First to pull. Then he looks to the town, sighs again, and starts off.

It's not all hopeless. He's laid a few of his own mousetraps. He only hopes they'll spring correctly.

Once Mona hits level(ish) ground she starts using driving techniques she learned in her training as a police officer, and has never used: a bunch of really reckless shit involving the emergency brake, downshifting, and manipulating the clutch in a fashion that would give any nearby mechanic a stroke.

Then she spots it: a low, long rectangle of brightly polished black taking up the whole lane a few hundred yards ahead.

A Lincoln. Definitely a Lincoln.

"I see it!" she says.

But as she closes in on the Lincoln, she sees something else odd. Ahead of them, past the Lincoln and past the town, is a somewhat tall, sloping mountain: the very mountain Mona had to drive down when she first came to Wink. Normally Mona would not glance twice at the mountain, but something is very visibly wrong with it: it looks like something is flooding out of a very small aperture in the mountain's side, something dark and ethereal, like the mountain is bleeding oil. Yet the more Mona looks at it, the more she realizes that it is not liquid, but a crowd of somethings that are distinctly liquidy...

Bodies. Forms. Slouching, staggering shapes, rushing down the mountainside in a long, sluggish river. And in that river she sees twisting necks, and writhing hands and limbs, black or silvery or chitinous... .

"What the fuck is *that*?" asks Mona.

Mrs. Benjamin sits forward and shields her eyes. "Oh, dear," she says. "I believe that would be the children."

"The *what*?"

"You are aware of the members of my family who had been hiding in the woods and the mountains? It seems as if in recent days they have all been hiding in a cavern. It looks like they are all exiting... quite rapidly. And headed for town."

"What does that mean?" asks Mona.

Mrs. Benjamin rubs her temple. "If I were to hazard a guess," she says, "I would take it to mean that Mother is imminent."

"Imminent? As in, coming here? Right *now*?"

"Yes."

Mona looks at the mesa in her rearview mirror, as if expecting to see that vast, swollen form straddling the top. "Where is she? How far away?"

"How thick is a candle flame?"

"Jesus," whispers Mona.

Places layered on places layered on places... and somewhere Mother is rising up, like a sea creature bursting through sheets of ocean ice...

"Mona, what are you going to do?" asks Gracie.

They close the distance between the Charger and the Lincoln. Mona can see numerous shadows in the car's windows. And someone in there has the child, possibly *her* child...

Mona thinks. There are about twelve .30-06 shells in her pocket, and about fifty more in her bag. "Are you buckled?" she asks.

"No," say Gracie and Mrs. Benjamin.

"Then hold on to something," says Mona. "And if something happens, go limp."

"Wh—" says Gracie, but it's a bit too late.

Mona noses the car into the oncoming lane, which is empty.

She drops the stick from fourth to third.

The engine screams. The Charger pounces forward like a very large cat.

They fly by the Lincoln. Mona catches a flash of the face of the doctor peering out the window, looking slightly incensed to see this display of automotive engineering.

Mona waits for the right distance. Then she stomps the brake, pulls the emergency brake, and cuts the wheel.

Everything in the Charger shrieks: the wheels, the engine, Mrs. Benjamin and Gracie. All except Mona, who has gauged this pretty damn well, she thinks.

When the car slides to a stop, it's blocking the road far enough ahead of the Lincoln to give it time to brake, but not far enough ahead for it to do something evasive or drastic.

Mona throws open the car door, hops out with the rifle, takes a knee, and puts the optic square on the driver's side door of the Lincoln. She hears Mrs. Benjamin and Gracie piling out of the passenger side behind her. (Ordinarily Mona would have maneuvered it so that the driver's side was away from the Lincoln, allowing her cover behind the Charger, but since she was driving with a wounded old lady and a teenage girl she decided to be charitable.)

The doctor looks quite perturbed at Mona's driving techniques. He does not slam on the brakes, or try to cut across the park at the center of town: he just slows to a stop and gets out with a "Well now, what is all this?" look on his face.

"Good gracious!" he shouts at Mona. "What could possibly be the meaning of your driv—"

But he doesn't finish, because then Mona shoots him in the calf.

For a doctor he seems totally unaware of the nature of physical injury: he stares quixotically at his leg, which pumps blood for a while before collapsing underneath him. He's so confused he doesn't even shout. Somewhere behind Mona, Gracie screams.

Mona finds herself thinking, *That girl really should be used to this by now.*

She doesn't waste a second more: she reloads and advances on the Lincoln. She knows she saw more people in there. It's just a matter of time until...

A short, plump, dark-haired woman jumps out of the back of the car and runs at her, seriously runs at her, head-on. Mona has no idea who she is but she tags her anyway, putting a round in her right hip that sends her tumbling to the ground.

Mona keeps advancing. She wants to put a round through the windshield to try to flush out anyone else, but she's not willing to send broken glass flying throughout the car, not with the child in there.

"Get out of the car!" she shouts.

She feverishly hopes they won't hurt her daughter. But she knows they won't—they *need* her.

"Get out of the fucking car!" shouts Mona.

The other back door of the car opens up.

Mona puts the optic on it.

But when she sees what emerges from the car, her pose relaxes, and the scope falls away.

"Oh my *God*," she says softly.

What steps out of the other door of the Lincoln is not a person. It is not even vaguely shaped like a person. Rather, it looks like the curled back of a lobster: segmented plates of black, chitinous armor bow away from her to form a twitching half-ball. Mona can see dozens, perhaps hundreds, of tiny, hairlike legs or swimmerets squiggling underneath the armor, each one thrashing as if it has a mind of its own.

That, she guesses, is probably the bodyguard sent along with the convoy. *So that's what the children look like*, thinks Mona. *Or one of them, at least.*

The balled-up, arthropodan thing stands in the street with its back to her, shuddering. Then, with a sound like someone crinkling wax paper, it begins to unfold.

Mona sees a head that is far less rigid than its body: though it is not facing her, she sees something pendulous and flabby, with scarab-like pincers protruding from the trembling flesh. Four spindly legs tipped with tarsal claws hesitantly reach out and begin tapping the asphalt. But the most horrifying feature of this thing is what emerges from either side of its midsection: two quivering appendages that very distinctly resemble human arms and hands, each one with seven fingers, the first two fingers bearing flagella or antennae that are over a foot long.

Mona doesn't wait for it to turn around: she puts a round just below the thing's head, where she thinks its neck should be. There's a dull thud, like a hammer striking wood, and a spot on its plated back turns a somewhat lighter color. But the shot does not penetrate.

She reloads, fires again. Another *thunk*, another divot in the thing's back. It does not seem to notice or care at all: it just keeps unfolding, until it is well over seven feet tall, a shuddering, hunched thing that slowly begins whipping its antennaed fingers about, as if it's using them to smell the air…

It starts buzzing, making the same nauseating whine that seems to be echoing throughout all of Wink right now. Then it turns around.

It is like nothing Mona has ever seen before: the bottom half is four spider legs, the top half two distended arms with feathery fingers, and there's an eyeless lump of a head. Its mouth is a gash, a rent, dripping something quite runny that hisses on the asphalt. Swimmerets and feelers and all sorts of tiny appendages line the edges of its underbelly, each squirming like mad.

Mona dimly realizes she is somehow related to this thing, and feels sick.

The thing makes no noise, no hisses or screeches: it simply scutters toward her, its four clawed legs daintily picking their way around the car and over the road. It is such a queerly delicate, teetering thing, like a dancer.

Mona picks what she thinks is a weak spot in its armor—right where its shoulder merges with its underbelly—and fires again. It nicks the creature a little more deeply, but it still does not penetrate. The thing hardly twitches at the shot. It waves its feathered fingers toward her, as if trying to see her.

Mona starts backing away. She tries to draw a bead on its legs, but they move shockingly fast. Does she run? Draw it away from the car, then circle back for her child?

"Oh, goodness," says Mrs. Benjamin's voice. "Must I handle this myself?"

The old woman stumps around the hood of the car and toward the scuttering black creature.

"No!" shouts Mona. "Get back, goddamn it!"

"You are mistaken," says Mrs. Benjamin. "*I* am not the one in over my head here."

She walks to stand directly in the creature's path. Its feathered fingers swish in her direction.

The thing pauses. Then, in a move that is blindingly, blindingly fast, it *gallops* toward her, and when it's mere feet away it rises up on its back two legs, the top two legs shooting forward like giant pincers, and leaps.

Mona ducks down. Yet Mrs. Benjamin is ready: she dodges to the side, grabs one of the pincer-legs, and yanks the thing to the ground. Then she grasps the top of its armor, plants her foot in the small of its back, and pulls.

The thing shrieks, and it is a terribly human sound, like that of many children. There are pops, like stitching popping in a pair of jeans; its many arms and feelers wave wildly, trying to find flesh to tear; one of the segments begins to separate; and then, with a sound like a sewer line breaking, white, creamy intestines spill out of its body to flop onto the ground, where they begin sizzling on the asphalt.

Mrs. Benjamin—and though Mona knows what she is, she can't help but think of her as "old" and "doddering"—has just torn this horrific monstrosity in half. She holds its top half aloft, as one would a severed head, though this is about the size of a municipal garbage can and God knows how heavy.

The thing is still somewhat alive, however, its arms wheeling back and forth and its dollop of a head thrashing about in its carapace, and one of its feathered index fingers just happens to whip around and catch the slightest bit of Mrs. Benjamin's neck...

The spray of blood is obscene, spurting nearly seven feet. Mrs. Benjamin angrily shouts, "Oh!" as if she's just stubbed her toe. She drops the top half of the creature, which curls up on the ground like a wood louse. Then she staggers back a few feet and falls on her ass, blood spurting arrhythmically from just under her jawline. She holds her hand to the tiny nick—which must be just on her jugular, or something just as important—before taking it away and looking at it: her hand is coated in blood.

Mona, keeping a safe distance from the twitching thing on the ground (which does not appear to be mortally wounded as much as disabled; but then, Mona remembers, killing in Wink is not allowed), circles around to her. Mrs. Benjamin looks up—she is already paler—and hoarsely says, "Tell me—is this fixable?"

Mona looks at the flow of blood, which is extreme. She shakes her head. "I doubt it."

"Really?"

"Really."

"Damn," says Mrs. Benjamin. "I...I quite liked being an old woman. No one asked you...to do much. Left you alone."

"You can...come back, right? As someone else?"

She shrugs. "Though that does mean...killing another person in Wink, and taking their place. But I suppose...that's the way things are."

"Will I see you again?" Mona asks.

"Oh, probably," she says wearily. "I expect everyone...will be seeing...quite a lot of you, dear."

"What do you mean?"

Mrs. Benjamin coughs and sits forward a little. One hand plays with the string of pearls around her neck, smearing them with red. She says, "Oh...how I wish it were...night."

"Night?"

"Yes. Liked the look...of the stars."

She sits forward a little more, then a little more.

"Oh," she says. "Oh, goodness."

The flow of blood trickles away, and she is still. And somewhere in the distance, there is thunder.

"Is she dead?" asks Gracie, emerging from behind the Charger.

"Yeah," says Mona. "As dead as her kind can get, I guess." *My kind,* she thinks. *I wonder if I'll be loaded into someone's body if I snuff it...probably not.* "You okay, Gracie?"

"I think so."

"Didn't hit your head or anything? You can move your arms and legs okay?"

"Yes, I—"

She stops. There is a sound over the buzzing: a tiny, croaky sound, like someone working the rusted hinges of a door.

Crying. A baby, crying.

"Oh my God," says Mona. She stands and runs to the Lincoln.

She can see there is something in the center of the backseat, wrapped in sheets and twitching.

She dives in and pulls the sheets aside. She expects it to be wounded, because Mona's never done these things right and it can't have gone right can it, it just can't have, but then...

The little girl pulls the sheets aside herself. She is not, Mona sees with some surprise, a newborn. She looks about six or seven months old. And when she sees Mona she reacts with obvious relief, and throws her arms out to her and cries.

Mona slides her fingers underneath the baby (and Jesus *Christ* she is *small*) and picks her up. The baby is not at all weak or limp, and she sits forward in Mona's grasp and haltingly puts her arms around Mona's neck for (Mona cannot believe this) an embrace.

She is hugging her. Her baby is hugging her.

She thinks I'm her mom.

I am *her mom.*

Mona tells the voices in her head to shut up, but she cannot stop laughing and crying at the same time.

Gracie tentatively approaches the car. "What's that?" she asks in a hushed voice.

"It's my baby," says Mona. And as she says it, it finally seems to become real. "It's my little girl. My own little girl."

"How?" asks Gracie, positively flummoxed.

And Mona can hardly answer.

"Is she hurt?" asks Gracie.

"No, I think she's just scared. It's not her blood."

Gracie looks at the whimpering baby, concerned. "I thought you said you lost your baby, or...something like that."

"I did."

"Then how can she be your baby?"

"I don't know. I don't know how to explain it. She just...is."

The baby warily peers around Mona's head at Gracie. "She definitely seems to think you're her mom," says Gracie. "Listen, I don't think this is the issue right now. Those...those *things* are getting closer."

Mona peers out the car door: the rivers of those horrors are about halfway down the mountain now. She has no idea what they plan to do when they get to Wink, but she does not want to be here for it.

"We got to go," says Mona. "That's what we have to do."

"Leave Wink?"

"Yep."

"But we can't! No one ever gets out of Wink!"

"I did, once. When I went to Coburn through the back way. I had to walk out of town, then back into it." She leverages herself up and out of the car, clutching the baby to her chest. "Get back in the Charger. We'll just head to—"

A new sound joins the buzzing reverberating through Wink. It is incredibly, *incredibly* loud, so loud it feels like it reaches past her eardrums and vibrates her brain directly. It sounds like someone is slapping a bass string miles long, or maybe as if some vast engine is trying to turn over, gears guttering and cranking...

It sounds, Mona thinks, a little like the buzzing coming from the necks of all the people in Wink, only much, much larger.

"What is that?" asks Gracie.

"I don't know."

Then Mona sees something in the landscape. It is so vague it is hard to pinpoint it, but she finds herself looking to the south, where she first entered the valley and passed the sign with the antenna on the mesa. She stares at one of the mountaintops there, and then she sees it.

No way, she thinks.

"What?" asks Gracie.

"Shh," says Mona. She raises a hand.

Gracie comes to stand beside her. "What?" she asks, more softly.

The river of children is thinning out. Mona guesses that must be all of them. But did she see...

It happens again. Gracie sees it too, and gasps.

"Did that just...did the mountain just *move*?" she asks.

"Yes," says Mona slowly. "Yes, it did."

The movement is so large it dupes the eye into thinking it impossible, but it is really happening: they watch as the entire top half of the mountain rises just a little bit, then falls back down again. The motion is uneven, lopsided: the left side of the mountaintop teeters and slides away more than the right. Trees are uprooted and go tumbling down the mountain like sticks. Huge clouds of dust go roiling up, filling the sky.

"Is it an earthquake?" asks Gracie.

"No," says Mona. "No, I don't think so."

It happens again, harder. Mona is reminded of someone kicking blindly at a door, trying to break through any way they can, and then...

The mountain does not burst, as Mona expects: there is no eruption, no explosion. At one point the mountain lifts up again, but it just keeps lifting; or actually it *pivots*, like the peak is the top to a hinged box that is slowly being opened; yet as it pivots more and more, the entire mountain is sloughed away, tons and tons of rock and earth sliding off. Dust fills the air, rushes down to the town in a tidal wave. It is as if all the topography was resting on a carpet someone has just started ripping up.

No. No, that's not right—it's not ripped up. It's being *pushed* up. There's something underneath the mountain, as if the whole of it is resting on something's back...

Mona can see it now, just barely: a dark, bent form lost in the mushroom cloud of dust. It is not *just* big: the mere glimpse of it forces her to redefine all her preconceptions about the concept of "big."

It stands. There is so much of it, it seems to take forever. And the buzzing sounds around them increase, as if an audience applauding.

"Oh, my *God*," says Gracie.

It takes up the whole sky, the whole horizon. It keeps standing until it blocks out the sun, its shadow stabbing forward to swallow the entire town, and then it lifts its arms from the cloud of dust and stretches them out, buzzing horribly, a deep, abysmal voice that makes the very skies shake as it glories in its newfound freedom...

"Yeah," says Mona.

Mona has seen this thing only once before, in a vision of the mesa north of Wink, long ago. On that occasion she did not get a very good look at it, but now she has a chance to review.

It looks somewhat like a person: it has legs and arms and a torso, but it is far too huge, far too bulky, a massive, cyclopean person easily over six hundred feet tall. Its skin is dark and pockmarked like that of a humpback whale, something used to lightless submersion. It is covered in veins and black, sinewy muscle. Its shoulders and arms and deltoids are huge and swollen, its thigh muscles are mammoth, rippled tumors. Its belly sags down over its groin in a spill of collops and rolls that quiver with each motion.

And its head...the head is tiny in comparison to the body. It is a grayish, gleaming little pearl atop the vast mountain of shoulders and biceps and belly. It has no mouth: just a section at its neck where it becomes a dripping patch of baleen and pinkish flesh.

But its eyes are the worst part. They are so huge and round, and they glow like lighthouses, the golden light blooming through the dust...

But though Mona registers this form as an abomination, a total violation of every concept of beauty and symmetry and biology she possesses, it also *registers* with her, somehow. This image, this form is imprinted in her, as if etched into the space right between her eyes. This thing has been with Mona her entire life, casting its immense shadow over every second, every moment of her consciousness.

She knows it. She knows it as well as she knows herself.

"Hello, Momma," she says softly.

CHAPTER FIFTY-EIGHT

The natives of Wink—the real, human natives—have up until this point stayed inside their houses, eyes obediently averted from all windows. Because when Things Happen in Wink, you stay indoors, and you stay quiet. That's the way it's always been, and if they keep to this, they think, then they'll be fine, just like always—though some do mutter that really, this is ridiculous, don't they have their time at night for these sorts of goings-on?

But then the natives feel the earth shake, and the air turns beige with the crush of dust, and when they look out the window they notice the queerly pale red skies, and the thin shadows...

This is different. This is not supposed to be happening. This is not normal.

And then, one by one, they begin to See.

It starts happening at the southern end of Wink first. They, of course, are closest to the Arrival: they cannot avoid seeing the form rising up from the mountaintop, arms extended as if seeking to embrace the valley. Mark Huey of 124 Littleridge Lane is given the inauspicious honor of being first: he runs a fairly decent lawn mower repair shop, and when the earth begins to shake he looks up from his work. His wife bursts in and frantically asks what is going on, and Mark, being the man and all, takes the responsibility of peeping out his blinds.

And he Sees.

He looks for ten seconds. Then, without a word, without answering a single question from his wife, he walks to his workbench, opens a drawer, takes out a lawn mower blade he's been working on, and jams it into his throat.

He dies almost instantly: all the blood in his skull simply falls out in a rush. His wife, shrieking in terror, runs out of the shop. When she hits the street, she looks back. And she Sees.

She stops screaming. Instead she walks back to the shop, rummages in its front flower bed, finds a good-sized rock, and begins to pound it against her temple with a very singular concentration. This proves less efficient than her husband's method: it takes nearly a minute before her right eye socket caves in, followed by the coronal suture of her skull, which causes her brain to begin madly swelling. She drops to the ground, shivering and dying, but thankfully blind.

Slightly more effective is Angela Clurry's approach: she walks out to her back patio to try to see the source of the dust; and when she does, she walks back in, goes to her sink, turns on the Dispose-All, and, with calm, Buddhist-like focus, slowly inserts one arm all the way up to the elbow, and then the other.

It takes her a little over three minutes to bleed out. But this, of course, is better than Seeing.

Ashley and David Crompton, married for three years, happen to See together. Without any discussion they walk upstairs, wake their children from their naps, and usher them into the garage. The two parents buckle them into their seat belts, give them their preferred comfort toys (for Michael, a blanket; for Dana, a bear), turn on both cars, and patiently sit back and wait for the fumes to do their work.

It takes a lot less time for the children, small as they are. But this is so much better than allowing their children to See.

Seven-year-old Megan Twohey is quite fortunate: she has chosen to stay hidden down in Lady Fish's home. She does not want to come out—she *never* wants to come out, ever again—but when she hears the rumbling and feels the earth shaking around her, she tries to burrow ever deeper (for Lady Fish's home is quite extensive). Though she does not know it, her father has drunk a pint of bleach upon Seeing, and collapsed on the kitchen floor in spasms; and her mother does not See at all, having drunk herself to death in the night.

As the Arrival becomes harder and harder to ignore, the natives of Wink all take the same action: some choose blades, others poisons, the calmer ones choose automobiles, and those who have access to firearms use them both clinically and carefully: if you could listen over the buzz, you would hear a series of little pops all throughout town, as if someone's wine cellar were overheating. Of course, there is the odd boom of a shotgun: for example, Julie Hutchins uses her shotgun on her husband, who has not yet Seen, but she finds him in an odd state: he is standing in the garage, but the floor and walls are black and smoking, as if the garage has just been struck by lightning. Her husband is staring at his hands with a very confused look on his face, and when she enters he looks up and says, "Who are you? Ah. I know...I seem to be a man this time. Tell me, where is the center of town from—Is that a gun? Wait, *no!*"

The shot catches him in the belly. He falls to the floor with a disappointed look on his face, and just before Julie puts the gun against her jaw, she hears him say, "Oh, *bother.*"

Joseph Gradling, hopeful paramour to Gracie Zuela, is called into the living room by his father. Joseph expects his father to explain what's happening—his father always understands these things—but as he enters the living room his father, who is standing just beside the entryway, lifts his .22 revolver and shoots his son twice in the head. Joseph dies immediately, which is actually quite good, for he never quite sees the sight waiting for him: his mother and baby sister lying on the couch with pillows stuffed over their faces, each pillow smoking and bloody from muffled gunfire.

Unhappy Margaret Baugh is one of the few who manages to resist for some time (her husband, on the other hand, did not: he lies dead on their porch with a nail gun in his hand and a clutch of nails in his right temple), and she staggers out the front door and over to the neighbors' house, seeking Helena. When she enters the house, it is silent and seemingly empty. She stalks through the rooms, wondering if (and maybe hoping) they have left; but then she sees Helena's husband, Frank, or at least what's left of him, sitting on the floor and propped up against the pump-action shotgun.

Margaret sees the back door is open. She slowly, slowly walks out.

Helena is there, as if she was waiting for her. She lies facedown in the grass, her body pointing in the direction of the fence. Her back and neck are perforated with buckshot—and Margaret wonders if Frank thought he was putting her out of her misery, or if desperation drove Helena to reveal her relationship with Margaret, and he retaliated...

It doesn't matter. It's over now. And Margaret knows where Helena—*her* Helena—was going.

She sits down beside the body in the grass, and picks her up so her head is in her lap. She strokes Helena's hand, and carefully coils her index finger around Helena's. Then she looks up at the hole in the fence before them, and remembers what they had, which was always enough.

"It's okay," Margaret says. "I'm here. I'm here with you. We'll see it together."

And they do.

One by one, all the natives of the town, who have bartered so carefully for their little piece of property, who have agreed to willfully ignore what is outside their doorsteps so they can live in peace and harmony, begin to wink out like candle flames in the wind, starting at the southernmost tip and moving northward in a wave.

Because it is possible for something to enter your world that is so vast, so terrible, so foreign, that you cannot coexist with it: you must, in some way or another, vacate the premises, give up your seat. Merely knowing that this thing exists pulls the supports out from everything you know and trust: the established world falls around you like a circus tent whose center pole is cut.

And you must go with it. You must get out. You *have* to get out.

CHAPTER FIFTY-NINE

Mona and Gracie stare at the giant standing on the mountain. Mona is still struggling under the realization that this—this *thing* was what looked at her from behind her mother's eyes all her life. This thing orchestrated the conception of this entire town, and Mona's return to it; this abomination constructed and planned her entire life, from her inception to her childhood to now; and it was all for this moment, all for this chance for complete and total breach...

They watch as the yellow eyes swing back and forth, flashing through the dust clouds.

The baby coughs in Mona's arms. Then she realizes—*It's looking for her. It's looking for my daughter.*

The giant pulls one mammoth foot free of the pile of earth that the mountain has become, swinging its leg out and forward, and finds purchase on the slope down. It is so huge that watching this small step is like seeing a cruise liner dock, and it completely outpaces the rivers of children rushing down to the town.

"It's coming," says Mona. "Jesus Christ, it's coming for her!"

"For the *baby*?" asks Gracie, incredulous.

Mona doesn't stop to explain. She runs for the Charger, intending to jump in and...hell, she doesn't know. Go somewhere. Anywhere.

But as she approaches, a small figure comes running down the street to her. Mona stops: though she has the baby in her arms, the rifle is still slung around her shoulder. She wonders how to bring it up and use it safely when the figure cries: "No! Miss Bright! Stop!"

Mona grabs her rifle with one hand, but does not bring it up. That voice is somehow familiar, but she cannot understand why: as the person gets closer and Mona sees him better, she is positive she has never seen this young boy in the bunny pajamas and the huge glasses before in her life.

"You do not recognize me," says the young boy as he stops in front of her, panting.

"No..." says Mona. But as he looks up and pushes his glasses up his nose, an absurd thought comes to her. "Wait a minute... *Parson?*"

"Yes."

"You're in that... in that little boy?"

"Yes. I have been since last night. Though you are not aware of it, I have been attempting to assist you since my, well, death." He looks her up and down. She realizes she is still covered in blood. "Though it may not have been particularly effective..."

The dark giant pulls its other leg free of the earth. Mona gauges the distance: it can cross the valley to Wink in only about three or four more steps.

"What the hell do you want, Parson?" asks Mona. "We don't have fucking time to sit here and talk!"

"We do," says the little boy (who Mona tries to remember is Parson). "She is about to be delayed. I assume you wish to run?"

"Well shit yes, we do," says Mona.

The giant's next step is slowed very slightly by the uneven terrain, but it is not much of a delay, if that's what Parson was talking about.

"You cannot," says Parson. "The child is linked to Her. She can see it—She will always know where it is. And She will not permit it to leave Wink. You cannot run from Her."

The giant's next step toward town is totally unhindered, and its massive leg moves so quickly they can hear the air being split from here. It is like low thunder, a crackling in the air.

"Then what the fuck do we do?" cries Mona.

"There is another way," says Parson. "You must wait for Her. And meet Her."

Both Mona and Gracie are stupefied by this. In unison, both shout, "What?"

"She does not control everything in Wink," says Parson. "Not everything here has happened as She intended. There are flaws. One, in particular."

The giant's foot crashes down on the highway out of town. Chunks of asphalt go flying up. Its yellow eyes are fixed on where the three of them stand before the Charger.

The baby shrieks in her arms. Mona is so anxious she thinks she might faint. "Will you kindly get to the fucking point!" she says. "We are about to die here!"

Parson says, with infuriating calm, "No. We are not."

Mona screams, "What the fuck do you mean b—"

The giant is taking another step forward when it is suddenly thrown off balance: it is like it has been pushed by some invisible force, staggering backward and falling (with the astonishing enormity of the *Titanic* falling out of the sky) onto the ruined mountain behind it, accidentally crushing a sizable number of the children. A squeal rises up from the mountain as all the tiny horrors try to get clear of their progenitor.

The giant itself seems no less surprised by this than Mona or anyone else: it stares around, bewildered, before looking up at something on the outskirts of town.

There is a shimmering there, like a crinkle in the air. If Mona looks at it just right, it looks like a huge . . . well, a huge *something* standing on the edge of town, something extremely tall, but not half as tall as the giant: in comparison to the behemoth lying on the mountain, it is about the size of a toddler. Mona thinks she can discern long, thin arms, and many wriggling *somethings*, as if the top half of this creature is wreathed in tentacles . . .

Then she hears the fluting. It is hauntingly beautiful, yet also alien. Beside her, Gracie gasps. "What?" she says softly. "No. *No!*"

The buzzing in Wink tapers off. The children, who are trying so desperately to get free of their Mother (who, in turn, seems to hardly notice them), stop struggling and stare.

A second noise begins echoing through the valley: a deep, resonant *om*, like thousands of monks beginning to meditate.

The giant cocks its head, and slowly starts to rise to its feet.

Gracie bursts into tears. She tries to run forward, but Parson grabs her by the hand and holds on. "We cannot let her go!" he shouts.

Mona, who is juggling just a hell of a lot of shit right now, manages to free a hand and grab Gracie's other arm. "Stop, Gracie!" she shouts. "Just stop!" Gracie fights for a bit before giving up and crumpling to the ground, sobbing in terror.

Mona looks down on her for a moment before glancing back up at the shimmering thing on the edge of town. "What the hell is *that*?"

"That," says Parson, "would be the rebellion of the obedient son."

CHAPTER SIXTY

The fight begins.

It is a fight beyond nearly everyone and everything in the valley, save for the two fighting: it is a fight that takes place on many invisible fronts, using methods and modes undetectable to nearly everyone's senses; and it is a fight that only rarely intrudes into the physical realm and its rudimentary dimensions. To nearly all onlookers, each blow and each small victory has completely random results throughout Wink, while First and his Mother stand almost utterly still, staring at each other across the ruined southern end of the valley.

The first effect of the fight—a warning shot, a glancing blow, perhaps—is the sudden appearance of a river in the sky, stretching from north to south along Wink. It is an immense rope of water, suspended about seven hundred feet above them all, and were it to fall it would surely drown them.

Thrust.

First shifts his feet. The river in the sky dissolves, and there is a sudden deluge, a blitzkrieg of a torrent that comes howling down, even though the sky is completely cloudless. It rains for six seconds before it halts as suddenly as it started.

When the rain stops, it is, without warning or reason, night: stars twinkle above them, and the pink moon is there as always.

Parry.

On Grimmson Street seven homes abruptly burst into flames, which turn bright green before going out, with no structure showing any aftereffects of a fire. As the fire dies out, the sun returns, and it is day again.

A riposte, perhaps.

In eastern Wink, buildings and roads and the ground shatter in a straight line across a city block, as if an enormous blade has swung down out of the sky. Several family members who gathered there to watch the fight are crushed, obliterated: as there are no more human hosts available, they are gone from Wink forever.

A lunge—most certainly.

A pinhole appears in the space behind the giant, which grows and grows, sucking all nearby matter into it: earth, broken trees, chunks of asphalt, and several dozen of the children, who tumble into its nothingness with tinny screeches.

A definite *coup d'arrêt*.

The giant cocks its head, and the hole slowly shrinks and disappears, sending a bolt of pink lightning arching across the skies. First shifts his feet again, and the lightning bolt disappears, though another massive, invisible blade goes slashing across the city, vivisecting homes, trees, and several people: it is as if an enormous, imperceptible force has been captured and diverted into purely physical energy, which is far less dangerous than its original state.

Perhaps—a *croisé*?

And does it succeed, and throw someone off their stance?

The skies quiver. Suddenly there are two suns above the town, one large and pink, the other small and blood-red, like an infected eye.

Thrust.

The skies quiver again: now it is night again, and the skies are filled with eight moons of many sizes and many colors. Some have rings; others have tiny moons of their own.

Again, a thrust.

The skies quiver again: they are now filled with a cold, frigid mist, and there are no mountains on either side of the town—only huge blue ice shelves, as if the town lay in a valley in the Antarctic. But there are buildings or colonies among the icy peaks, blocky, gray, ancient-looking structures that do not align to any building principle on earth.

A riposte, but a desperate one...

The skies quiver again: the ice is gone, the mist is gone; above the town is nothing but black, solid black: no moon, no stars, no suns or clouds, just...nothing. Just abyss.

A lunge, and—perhaps—a touch?

Slowly the streetlights of Wink flicker on, as if someone somewhere has flipped a switch. The streets fill with white, fluttering incandescence. The many figures standing in their front yards cast stretching shadows like a line of fence posts.

An attempt, possibly, to disengage?

Then there is a series of bursting lights at the south end of Wink, like soundless fireworks; with them, the streetlights die, and the world is bathed in darkness.

A touch. A touch.

(In the dark, Mona feels a small hand grip her wrist. It pulls her down, and there is a voice in her ear: "You know that the wildling is in Wink?"

"Yes," whispers Mona. "I know."

Parson asks, "But do you know *where*?" And Mona listens very carefully as he continues speaking.)

Blue pinpricks appear in the darkness above Wink. They flare like magnesium, and light slowly returns to the sky.

What they illuminate indicates that though things went queerly dark and silent, the fight continued: for example, huge, twisted, oddly fleshy trees have sprung up through the streets and even through a few homes, crinkling the asphalt and foundations like paper; stretches of the lawns and parks have become flats of black volcanic glass; the western end of Wink now features a mammoth, leaning tower of five-sided basalt columns; and the ground between the two combatants—the giant at the southernmost end of the valley, and First at the southern edge of the town—is now a reeking, bubbling, black marsh.

First, though mostly invisible, appears tired: though he stood stock-still before, now he sways like a willow in a storm. The giant, though it has been barred from entering Wink, does not appear winded by any of this exertion, nor is it irritated or angered at all: it is as if this has been an interesting, diverting little game, but no more.

The giant studies First coolly, then cocks its head again. Immediately a fierce buzzing rings out over the whole town, as if a hive of hornets a billion strong has just been punctured with a rock.

The people standing in their yards and in the street turn all at once, and begin marching toward First.

The giant cocks its head in the other direction. First becomes a little more corporeal: the crinkle in the air becomes slightly gray and filmy, though still translucent. He turns to see his brothers and sisters approach him.

The giant cocks its head once more. The crowds of people begin to sprint.

First waves a shimmering hand at them: *No, no. Do not do this.* But they pay no attention.

First flickers, and seems to melt off in one direction, as if he is sliding through the air, attempting to get away. But the giant's fingers twitch, and it is as if First strikes a glass wall.

He attempts to transport himself away again, but meets the same obstacle: Mother has trapped him.

The crowds of people—and, now, many of the children—swarm down to surround First. They ring him in completely, staggering across the black marshes to contain him.

Then, without a word, they charge.

Mr. First, of course, cannot kill any of his brothers or sisters in Wink, nor can they kill him: this is the agreement all of them made before making their home here, and it binds them like a law of physics. But his brothers and sisters do not seem intent on killing him as much as holding him down, grasping one of his many invisible limbs and pinning it to the ground. Though First is quite strong, and is capable of resisting for a time, their numbers grow too great, and he, shrieking, bellowing, is brought to his knees.

They pile onto his shoulders. He tips forward, and falls onto the ground.

The giant approaches. It bends over the prostate First with a vaguely self-satisfied air, as if to say—*Now do you see what that sort of behavior gets you?*

First bellows and tries to stand. The pile of people—there must be several hundred on him—billows up, then falls back down. First moans, weeps, screams.

The giant bends its knees, and begins to reach down to him.

As its fingers near him, a shout rings out across Wink:

NO! NO! I WAS HAPPY! WHY CAN'T YOU LET ME BE HAPPY? WHY CAN'T YOU EVER LET ME BE HAPPY?

CHAPTER SIXTY-ONE

Throughout all this, Parson speaks.

Mona tries to listen. It is almost impossible, as the geography of the town keeps changing so wildly and abruptly (at certain points Mona is not even sure she has ears, feeling as if her physical being has, again, been disassembled and reassembled), but the words start sinking in, as if she is listening without knowing she is listening.

When everything comes roaring back, Mona is sitting on the ground with her baby sleeping in her arms. Gracie has her head on Mona's shoulder, and is weeping silently, shoulders trembling. The rifle is on the ground beside them. Mona has no idea how they got into these positions. She especially has no idea how her daughter managed to fall asleep during all that.

"I'm sorry, Gracie," says Mona, though she is hardly aware of what's going on.

Gracie only sobs, despondent, and buries her face farther in Mona's shoulder. Soon she's infringing on the baby's space, much to the baby's dislike.

"It'll be okay," Mona says. "I promise, we'll figure out—"

Then the intense buzz fills the air, many times louder as it was before. Even Parson looks up, disturbed, and Mona's daughter wakes and begins crying again.

They watch as all the people of Wink—if they could be called such—turn and begin encircling Mr. First.

"No!" cries Gracie. She stands. "They're going to trap him! We—we can't let them do this!"

"I am afraid we can," says Parson.

"We can't! We have to do something!"

"There is nothing to do," says Parson. "He knew this would happen."

"How do you know that?" Mona asks.

"Because he discussed it with me."

Gracie turns on him. "He *what*?"

"When you left him to go fetch Miss Bright's car," says Parson, "I returned to him in his canyon. We knew what was happening, and tried to think of something to do. This was our solution."

"You…you *planned* this? You're *letting* him do this? Letting him *die*?"

"It was the only way," says Parson.

"The only way *what*? The only way you could get what you wanted? The only way to win another one of your f—your *fucking* family tiffs?" It seems to take some effort for Gracie to swear.

"No," says Parson. "The only way that you would live."

Gracie blinks. Mona can see her reviewing the statement in her head. "What?"

"First has known something was coming for some time. Not *this*, precisely, but something. He has taken steps to prepare." Parson's small, boyish face grows queerly intense. "You understand this. You know what steps he has taken."

Gracie shrinks a little, as if some inner part of herself is collapsing. Whatever steps First has taken, she is clearly not keen to discuss them.

"Yes," says Parson. "These steps, these choices, limited his options later on. And he was most specific that you should be spared."

Gracie is so shaken by this that she cannot answer. Mona says, "So you're saying that we're going to live?"

"No," says Parson. "First is never quite sure of anything, temporally speaking. He does not predict, he estimates. But this provides the greatest chance for succe—"

A deafening scream echoes through Wink: *NO! NO! I WAS HAPPY!*

*WHY CAN'T YOU LET ME BE HAPPY? WHY CAN'T YOU EVER
LET ME BE HAPPY?*

Gracie wheels around. She sees the giant bending down to something trapped on the ground. She clasps either side of her head, falls
to her knees, and screams.

None of them quite sees what the giant does to First. It looks like
nothing at all: there is no light, no noise, no gore or blood of any kind.
They can just see First's translucent form struggling under the masses
of people, and the giant seems to brush something with its fingertips,
and then...

The mound of people collapse as if they had all been piled on top of
a balloon that's just popped. It's as if First was there...and then he
wasn't. As if the giant has simply wished him out of all realities
altogether.

For the first time, Mona begins to understand exactly how powerful her Mother really is.

Yet the moment First is gone, Gracie begins to change. She doesn't
notice it initially: she is bent over on the ground, sobbing...yet then
her hair begins to rise, as if she is holding on to a Van de Graaff generator. Her sobs taper off, and she looks up, confused.

Mona jumps slightly: Gracie's eyes are now coal-black.

"What's happening to me?" Gracie asks. "What...what's going
on? Mona?"

Mona, in turn, says, "Parson?"

"A transfer of power," says Parson.

Gracie starts breathing very quickly. Then, as if suddenly, terribly
pained, she begins screaming. She stands up, but there's something
unnatural about it—something in the way her arms appear limp, and
her torso is slumped forward—that makes Mona think she's not standing, but being *pulled*...

Could it be, thinks Mona, *another of Mr. First's puppet tricks?*

Gracie flings out her arms to point to the sky. She stops screaming;
then, slowly, she begins to levitate, rising about nine feet into the air

and turning to face the giant. The air grows shimmery around her, as if her body is radiating immense heat, and her skin loses color until it's as white as paper...

"I always wondered," says Parson beside her as this horrific change takes place, "why he made her more like him—more like *us*. He didn't need to, not for his little dalliances. But eventually I understood—he was getting her ready. He wanted to leave her a way out. He wanted to give her the abilities to punch through the fence encircling Wink, evade capture, and go free. Naturally, in all of Wink, only Mr. First himself had that sort of power. And the only way to give it to her..."

"Was for him to die," says Mona quietly.

"Yes."

Gracie's body slowly relaxes. The hairs on her head begin to lie back down again. Then, slowly and gracefully, she descends to stand on the street again. But there is something about the way she stands that causes Mona to wonder if she's still floating: it's as if, should she want, she could go flying up into the atmosphere, shrieking like a fighter jet, and never return.

"Gracie," says Parson (and Mona is pleased to hear that he is a bit wary), "are you all right?"

Gracie does not answer.

"Can you hear me, Gracie?" asks Parson.

Gracie nods.

"Do you understand what has happened, Gracie?" Parson asks.

"Some of it," says Gracie softly. There is something hollow and resonant to her voice, as if it is echoing down many invisible passageways.

"Then you know this change will not last forever," says Parson.

Gracie nods again.

"How long do we have?" asks Mona.

"An hour, perhaps less," says Parson.

"That's *it*?"

"Yes. I believe this change was only intended to get Gracie out of Wink." He looks back at the giant, which is quickly approaching the town proper. "Along with us, if things had gone accordingly..."

"What the hell do you mean, *if*?"

Parson's tiny child-face begins sweating. "Unless I am mistaken... First's skirmish with Mother did not quite go as he foretold. It was meant to take longer, give us a chance to prepare. He must have forgotten Mother's strength."

"Prepare for what?" asks Mona.

"I told you where the wildling is," he says. "But with Mother approaching so quickly, I do not know what to do with it. This is *not* what was predicted, Miss Bright. I was supposed to have more time."

"So... you don't know what to do?"

He shakes his head. "I did not plan for this. I could try what I'd originally planned, but we have only minutes to spare... I am sure it would not work. I'm sorry."

Mona looks at Gracie. "You got any ideas?"

Gracie stares off into space with her black eyes, head cocked. It's like she's on some wonderful drug. Mona envies her, a little.

"Well, fuck." Mona sighs, and looks at her rifle.

Gears start engaging one another in her head.

After all, deep in every Texan's heart, there remains the steadfast belief that any problem can be solved with a big enough gun.

"I think I have an idea," says Mona quietly. "But it's a desperate one."

Parson watches the giant run toward them. "Well, I, personally, am quite desperate."

The idea keeps dripping into Mona's head, taking shape, turning color.

This is such a dumb thing to do, she thinks. And it is. Because it would take innumerable things happening in the right ways at the right times, and Mona has become intimately aware that the rules in Wink are, at best, whimsical. But it's this, or they all just sit here and wait.

"Parson," she says, "you're going to take my... the baby."

"Me?"

"Yeah, you. And Gracie... I think you'd be a lot better with these than I am." She holds out the two hand lenses to her. Parson has to poke Gracie to make her notice. She looks at the mirrors, then takes one in each hand. Immediately they gain a shimmering, pearly sheen.

"I'll take that as a yes," says Mona. She stands, and looks at her daughter, who is watching the giant approach with marvelously alert eyes.

It hurts to look at her, just to see her. A tiny, independent creature, sitting up straight in the crook of Mona's arm and toying with her left ear. It is so astounding to see *thought* in those eyes.

If I were to die today, thinks Mona, *I would die so happy. Because any world with you in it is a good one.*

But she's not going to die today.

"I'm gonna give you away for a bit," whispers Mona to her daughter, "but don't worry. I'll be back. It'll just be a minute." She holds her out to Parson. The child starts protesting almost immediately.

"What are you planning to do?" asks Parson as he takes her.

Mona tells him.

"Oh," says Parson. "Oh, my goodness."

"No shit. You hotfoot to the town square, okay? And you," she says to Gracie, "you head to the mesa. Can you do that qui—"

Gracie smiles at Mona, her dark eyes shining, and then it's as if she steps behind an invisible wall, and she's gone.

The two of them stare at the empty space where she was.

"It appears she can do that quite quickly," says Parson.

Mona looks to the mesa as if expecting to see Gracie standing on the top. "I hope she's in place."

"We must assume so. Are you sure you wish to do this?"

"I can't think of a better idea. But you listen—if things don't go to plan, you grab that little girl and you run. I don't care about any of this 'can't leave Wink' shit, you figure out something. And don't you come back for me. Just get her out of here. You understand?"

Parson nods.

"Good," says Mona. "Then get moving." And she turns and sprints across the street.

CHAPTER SIXTY-TWO

Mona has to break in to enter the store of her choice—a picture frame shop—and she heads straight to the back. With each boom the pictures rattle on the walls and resettle at new angles. She knows she should feel terrified, but after giving up her daughter, everything's on mute.

She grabs a mirror off the wall as well as a thin drape, one that's see-through. She takes the stairs in the back to the roof, and though she stays low she can see the hulking form of the giant kicking its way through Wink. Pipes and bricks and streetlamps fly around its feet like shrapnel.

"Fuck," says Mona. It will be here even sooner than she imagined.

She can see Parson standing in the park in the center of town, and in his arms... "Oh, Jesus," says Mona. Her daughter is hysterical, screaming at the top of her lungs. *It'll just be a little bit, baby. Just a little bit. Just hold on.*

She takes the mirror and wraps the drape around it so it will not cause any noticeable glare, though she can still see its reflection. Then she props it up against an air-conditioning unit on the eastern side of the building, so the mirror faces the town square, where the courthouse and the park are.

Once she has it situated, she lies down perpendicular to the edge of the building, hidden from the street behind a short wall about two feet high. If she looks straight down along her body she can see the mirror, and in its reflection what is just over the wall behind her: right now there is nothing but more shop fronts, trees, and the pink water tower that just says WINK.

Good. This works. Now she sits up to see if the rest of this stupid idea of hers is going to.

Parson and her daughter are still standing in the park. Her daughter's face is flaming red, just utterly beet-red.

The earth shakes. The giant is eight blocks away now.

It is huge. Tremendous. So big Mona cannot even understand what she's seeing. With another step, it's six blocks away.

The streets below begin to crack, like fibers of a net unable to contain their catch.

Mona looks to the mesa. She hopes Gracie is ready, because it needs to be...

"Now," whispers Mona. "Now. *Now.*"

Does she imagine a glimmer of light on the mountain? Maybe reflected from a tiny surface...

Parson and her daughter grow slightly translucent. Then with no warning, they vanish.

The giant stops in its tracks.

Mona drops to lie flat on the roof of the building.

There is no sound but the buzzing that echoes across Wink. Mona imagines the giant standing there, wondering exactly what the hell happened. Because after all, She'd imagine that with First gone, so went all the real threats in Wink...

The earth shakes, but much more softly, much more slowly—a hesitant step. Mona can hear roads and buildings cracking behind her like icebergs in the Arctic.

Mona quietly eases the bolt of the rifle up and checks the chamber: a glint of gold winks back at her. She reaches into her pocket and sets the five or so shells still there on the ground beside her. Ideally she won't need them: if Parson was right, this will take only one shot.

Then two incredibly loud steps, very fast and very close. Mother must have realized the baby is on the mesa, near Coburn and the lens. Mona imagines Her terror as She wonders if someone in Wink knows something She doesn't, and if there is some secret to the lens that might reverse all this. Could they know? Could they possibly know?

The roof of the building starts going dark, as if in an eclipse. But Mona knows better. It's Her shadow.

The trees quiver madly. The glass in a nearby building quakes, buckles, shatters. Shards make a twinkling rain on the sidewalk below. The giant must be so close...

Then the mirror goes dark with a sea of black, pockmarked flesh. Right outside the park.

Now.

Mona springs up, wheels around, and brings the rifle up, the jittering optic bewildered by the sight of such huge, sprinting legs, and then...

The booms stop.

Mona puts the optic square on her target. She considers the distance, the wind...yet it doesn't really matter, because it's such a *huge* target...

But the giant has stopped. It is turning around.

Mona becomes aware of two huge lamplight eyes looking down on her.

She begins tightening her trigger finger.

Time seems to slow down, and the next few events take place in what must be a millisecond:

Mona thinks: *It can't have seen me. It can't.*

(But is Mona not that creature's daughter? Perhaps the giant can sense her just as it can Mona's own daughter. Maybe it always knew she was there, waiting. And now it begins to suspect...)

The giant's hand twitches.

There is a crackle in the air.

A scent of ozone. A burst of white.

And, somewhere, the echoing sounds of distant thunder.

*   *   *

Parson sees the lightning bolt come shooting down to strike the building's roof. A dull *boom* echoes across the valley to where they stand on the mesa.

"Oh, no," Parson whispers.

Behind him the baby grunts disconsolately as Gracie rocks her. She is placated chiefly by Gracie's dress, whose stripes the child finds very interesting. Gracie is slowly becoming less... *whatever* it is she became, and more human, and more catatonic. She stares off into space, eyes vacant, as if she is too bruised and wounded to cry.

Parson ignores them, and peers at the town. The roof is now black and covered in smoke. He assumes Mona is dead, which means he will have to try to do this himself somehow... yet then he sees a figure standing in the smoke, completely still, with a rifle saddling her hip, staring ahead.

He keeps watching. Neither she nor the giant moves.

"What is she *doing*?" he asks.

CHAPTER SIXTY-THREE

Mona does not immediately become conscious. Rather, the first of her senses to revive itself is olfactory: she smells laundered sheets, a freshly vacuumed carpet, and, perhaps, the smell of something baking.

Then a thought cracks across her mind, waking the rest of her up: *This is . . . not right.*

She opens her eyes.

She sees there is a ceiling above her. Not just any ceiling—the ceiling from her childhood home in West Texas, the one she lived in for the fourth and fifth grade. She knows it exactly. How many times did she stare at it as she tried to fall asleep? She can see the remnants of her Glen Campbell poster, which she pinned up there before her father told her to take that shit down, and the few glow-in-the-dark stars she never bothered to peel off.

She sits up. She swings around and puts her feet on the ground. Her multicolored carpet still bears some old stains (she can see where she tried to melt crayons in the second grade), but overall is clean; her shelves are stocked with books, and bedecked with little plastic horse figurines; standing in the corner is her battered old BB gun, which she has cleaned as though it were a rifle. And someone, somewhere, is baking bread.

Mona opens the door and walks down the hallway, rubbing her eyes. As she enters the den, she sees a dull orange blaze as the afternoon sun filters through the glass pendant lamps, and in the corner a stringy pothos that's in need of some severe trimming, and a fresh bowl of potpourri on the entryway table. And there, in the battered old chair across from the television, is Laura Bright, née Alvarez.

She is in a state Mona has seen her in only once before: she wears the red dress from the can of film Mona found in the attic, and she is immaculate, incredibly perfect, hair curled and lipstick so clean it could have been applied by a surgeon. She is flipping through an issue of *Southern Living* with a look of slight disinterest. As she licks her fingers, Mona sees her nails are beautifully done in bright red; she cannot *ever* remember her mother having such excellent nails.

This is wrong. She knows this is wrong. But the dreamy nature of this place makes it very hard for her to really understand why...

"It'll still be a minute before it's ready, hon," her mother says absently as Mona walks in.

Mona stares at her. She takes a few steps forward, and asks, "What will?"

"The bread, silly." She licks a finger, and turns down a page, perhaps marking a recipe for further study. "The cinnamon bread."

Mona looks into the kitchen. The light in the oven is on, and something is definitely baking there.

She walks toward her mother. "What's... what's happening?" she asks.

Her mother looks up. "What's happening? What do you mean, what's happening?"

"This... wasn't happening just now. I was somewhere else. And you were... you weren't there at all. I don't *think*."

Her mother smiles. It is such a warm smile. Her eyes are the color of rich toffee. Mexican eyes, like Mona's. "Well. I did think we needed to have a talk. Why don't you sit down?" She pats the couch beside her chair.

Mona slowly, reluctantly sits. Something bothers her about the kitchen: the ceiling fan. She remembers when her father installed it, and how he cussed up a storm as he tried to figure out the circuitry, because after that the lights in the den stopped working, and it was because—

"This was a new house," says Mona.

"What was that, hon?" asks her mother.

A new house. The house they moved into years after Mona's mother killed herself.

A memory swims up to her: Gene Kelly's face smiling down at her from the silver screen...

"This never happened, did it," she says.

"What didn't?"

"This. This moment."

"It's happening now," says her mother, amused.

"Yeah. But when I lived here...you were already dead."

"I wasn't dead then, my dearest. I just wasn't *there*, with you."

"Then this isn't real. None of it is. And you're not my momma."

"Of course I am," she says, slightly hurt, yet still forgiving. "I've always been your mother, Mona. And I know you must feel a little scared right now. You haven't seen me in so long. And you don't really know me. But I'm *back* now. And I want to be here to stay. Are you fighting that? Do you not want me to stay?"

Mona furrows her brow. Something about this place—perhaps something about this *time*—makes it very hard to think, and remember.

There was a fight. A baby. And she lay in the sun on the roof of a building, watching a mirror...

The mirror.

She opens her eyes.

Things tremble. There is a world behind this world, full of sun and mountains...

Then back. Back to this orange-colored den, and the smiling woman in the chair.

She begins thinking. "Why have you brought me here?"

"Because I want you on my side, dear. That's where daughters belong, on their mother's side. I want you to be a good daughter. I want you to be what you are supposed to be."

"What you wanted me to be."

"Yes, I suppose," she says. Her voice is incredibly soft and soothing. "I want you to be here, with me."

"Why?"

"Because you would be happy here. Happy's a very hard thing for you to be—isn't it, Mona?"

"How...how could you ever know what makes me happy?"

"I know a lot, dear," says her mother. "Mothers always know more than people think."

"You don't know me."

She smiles. "Yes. Yes, I do." She raises her finger, and *taps* the air...

...and ripples radiate outward, as if she's tapped the surface of a pond, and as things ripple they change...

Mona becomes aware of a change in height. She looks down, and sees she is, without a doubt, a little girl of about nine, sitting on the couch beside her mother. But now it's her mother's house in Wink, the rambling adobe ranch house. It's the perfect image of how it looked in the film Mona found, shining with Mid-Century chic and little New Mexican additions. It's mid-afternoon, and the sunlight through the windows is purer than snow.

Her mother remains the same: red, smiling, perfect. "You wanted this," she says. "And I can give it to you. You can grow up here, with me. And we can do it right this time. We'll have Christmases, and Thanksgivings, and I'll help you with your homework, every night..."

Mona is silent. It hurts to hear this, for this is exactly what she has wanted all her life. But it does not feel *right*.

"What's wrong?" asks her mother.

"This isn't what I want," says Mona. "Or at least what I want *now*. I'm not a little girl anymore, Momma. This all...and this all happened so long ago."

"But it could happen now. It could happen the right way."

Mona doesn't answer.

"Do you want more?" asks her mother. She reaches up again and taps the air, and it ripples, and then...

Mona is sitting on a front porch. It's unmistakably Wink, the sky bursting with a magnificent sunset, and though the house isn't familiar there's a cup of tea on a coffee table before her. She somehow knows immediately it's made just the way she likes it—half-and-half and Splenda.

She looks around, and in the same way she knows this house is her own. She must live here. She has lived here for years.

She looks down, and sees she is no longer the nine-year-old Mona: she is twenty-five, maybe thirty. She hears a door open down the street, and turns. It's her mother. They live on the same street, apparently. Her mother walks out the front door, smiling, her hair slightly gray, eyes bearing a few more wrinkles, though she is still clad in the dazzling red dress. "It could be like this," she says as she walks down the sidewalk to her. "We'd spend years together. You'd become your own person, but I'd never be far." She walks up and rests her arms on the top of Mona's porch rail. "We'd have tea in the afternoon, and bake pies, and gossip, becoming friends. We'd play cards, I'd tell you tales, and we'd read the paper together on weekend mornings. And I'd always be on hand if it got difficult."

"If what?"

Mona's mother, smiling like a magician with a particularly good trick, nods toward the front yard.

Mona looks up.

There is a tree in her front yard. And, hanging from the lowest branch, there is a tiny pink swing.

Mona shuts her eyes, and looks away.

"I'd help you when she cries all night," says her mother's voice. "I'd watch her while you nap in the bedroom. I'd show you how to deal with a blowout—which is what we'd call it when diapers overflow." She laughs a little ruefully, as if she's dealt with plenty of those in her time, and Mona has to remember—*She hasn't. She's making this all up. All of this is made up.* "I'd always be on hand to tell you what she can and can't eat, and tricks about storing bottles, and teething. I'd always be there for you. For her."

Mona shakes her head, and says, "No. *No.*"

"No what? Why no?"

"I *lost* my baby, Momma." Mona feels her cheeks are wet. "I did. It's hard, and I wish to Christ it hadn't happened, but it did."

"But you could have her back. You have her back now."

"But is she really mine? You want her for your own reasons, I know that. Would I get her back after you do what you need?"

Her mother does not answer.

"So what would you give me when this is all over? A real girl? My real daughter? Or another version of her, stolen from God knows where?"

Mona's mother does not react to this, nor does she really answer her. She just keeps smiling, and says, "You would be *happy*."

"No, I wouldn't. These are just—just *pictures*, Momma. They're not real things. They aren't."

Mona blinks back more tears. When she opens her eyes, they're back in the 1980s West Texas house.

"Are you sure?" asks her mother. "Maybe you don't know all I can do..."

Mona fights to remember where they are, what's happened, and who her mother really is, and a question comes bursting out of her: "What do you want with my daughter? Do you want to hurt her?"

"Hurt your daughter? Why, no, my love. I would never do such a thing."

"You want something with her. What?"

"I want to take care of your little girl. I want to keep her safe—finally, really safe." Mona has never heard someone sound so painfully earnest before. "I don't want to be cruel to you, Mona my love, and I don't want to say that you *didn't* take care of her, originally... but she did die, Mona. She died. You weren't able to protect her, and she died."

Mona bows her head. "That wasn't my fault."

"Maybe not, but you weren't able to do anything about it. *I* can, my love. Let me help you. I want to take care of you all. I want to save you from danger. I want to help."

And as she says this, something slides into place in Mona's mind, like tumblers in a lock. There was something Mr. First said...

"To save us all from danger," Mona says quietly.

"Yes."

Mona starts thinking. She tries to disguise how fast she's breathing.

"What's wrong, dear?" asks her mother.

"You've said that before, haven't you?" she asks.

"Did I? When?"

"When you first brought the rest of your family here. The rest of the children. You brought them here when you wanted to save them all from danger."

Something in her mother's eyes flickers. "They told you about that?"

"Yes."

"Yes, but I was *right* then," says her mother. "Our world on that side . . . it was falling apart."

"But why? No one's ever been able to tell me why."

"It just . . . was. We were too great. There were too many of us. That world, that plane of reality, it could no longer support us."

Mona opens her eyes again. And, as she has so many times before, she sees two things: she sees this quaint, homey living room, a pleasant mishmash of Mid-Century furniture, perfumed with the aroma of baking bread; and she also sees, just behind it, a broken, smoking town, and an enormous, dark form standing over her . . .

"When you made me," Mona says, "you put a piece of yourself in me. You made me like you. Didn't you?"

"Yes, in a way. I helped you. I made you stronger, smarter. Bigger and greater than you could ever be."

"But you made a mistake," says Mona.

For the first time, her mother's smile retracts, but just very, very slightly. "W-what? A mistake?"

"Yes."

"I . . . I couldn't have. I don't make mistakes, love. I don't."

"You did. The part of yourself you put in me was one that could see. One that could see farther and clearer than anyone else. And now I see you, Mother. I see you so clearly. You're still the woman I knew in West Texas. I knew you then and I know you now. You always liked fresh starts." Mona takes a deep breath in, then lets it out. "*You* were the one who ruined your world over there, weren't you?"

Mona's mother is silent.

"You did it because otherwise, you'd never get your family to move," says Mona. "And that was what you really wanted. Wasn't it? You wanted a new beginning."

Her mother's smile slides away.

"That's why you took so many places, there on the other side. But one day you ran out of things to take. And you almost despaired. Because you still didn't feel happy, did you, Momma? No matter how many children you had, or how beautiful and powerful they were, or how grand your homes were, you never felt good about it. Not once."

"That's enough," she says softly.

"And then you found out about another place," says Mona. "Several planes of reality lower, or... whatever. And you thought—Why don't we try there? But the only way to get your family to make that move was to convince them their own world was falling apart."

"Be quiet," whispers Mona's mother.

"And now you're here," says Mona. "You're finally here. You're ready to start your simpler, easier life. Even if you've killed many of your own children, or made them so... so awfully *wrong*."

"That's not my fault," her mother says. "*I* didn't make them that way. If they're unhappy, it's their own fault. They should have listened to *me*."

"God. You can't admit it," says Mona. "You can't admit that... Jesus, that *everything* you've done has been a mistake. That's why you can't leave them alone, can you? If you did, it'd mean you were wrong."

Mona's mother does not answer.

"You can't find happiness this way, Momma," says Mona. "You can't. You can't just set it up and move in."

"No one *ever* finds happiness," snarls Mona's mother, suddenly bitter. She takes a little breath. Then, serene once more, "No one does. No one really knows how to be happy. You just get close, sometimes. That's all I want—just to get close."

"No," says Mona. "There is happiness. Real happiness."

"That's a lie."

"No. It's true."

"And what do you know about it?"

Mona looks down at her hands. She suddenly remembers dark hotel rooms, the neon lights of bars, the dull yellow strobe of passing highway stripes; she remembers her father, eyes flat, face averted, as he tore the skin from the shank of a doe, blood pooling on the driveway; and she remembers a tiny black casket, unadorned and shining in the sunlight, fading from view as it descended into a small, careful cubbyhole carved into the earth. "I know...I know what it's like *not* to have it," she whispers. But then she remembers the child she just held in her arms, tiny and squashed and luminous and perfect, and how looking at her made her feel that she'd never want anything again in the world. "I don't know," she says. "I don't know, Momma. Sometimes you find something that makes you feel like you could have nothing or everything and it wouldn't matter to you at all. Nothing in the world could be better than that thing. And you've never had that."

Her mother is silent for a long, long time. Then she takes a breath. "It doesn't matter," she says again, slowly. "I'll do it anyway. I'll still try again."

"Why can't you just leave us all alone?"

"Because that moment," says her mother, "that moment of pure, perfect anticipation...that is such a good feeling. You don't know what I would do to get that feeling again, my love. I have been alive for so long...I have seen so many things...I had children just because I'd never had any before. It was just something *new* to do. That newness is...indescribable. Even if it only lasts for a little while. But there are so many new places in this plane of reality. I can come close to that happiness again, and again, and again...it will be like heaven, for me. For a little while." She grows terribly still, dark eyes shining. "Now tell me. Tell me what you're doing with the child. Tell me what is up there on the mountain."

Mona swallows. She hopes she can do this.

"I'll tell you," she says softly. She shuts her eyes again. "As a matter of fact, I'll show you."

Mona sets her arms at her hips, miming holding something:

perhaps something long and thin, like a rifle. Then, slowly, she pretends to lift the invisible thing and hold it to her shoulder.

Parson squints through the smoke and the dust at Mona. Were he looking normally, he wouldn't be able to see anything—but as he himself has said before, there are other ways of seeing than through mere radiation.

She moves. Just a bit—then more. For so long she was still, but now, even though her eyes are closed, she is lifting the rifle to her shoulder and appears to be aiming.

"Hm," says Parson.

"Watch, Momma," says Mona.

"What?" asks her mother. "What are you doing?"

"It's a trick I learned. Watch."

Then she sets her cheek along the invisible barrel, takes a slight breath, and says:

Boom.

Boom.

The round flies through the giant's legs, zipping through the tiny gap between its knees and hurtling toward the park.

It whines through the three tall pines that stand in a row beside the courthouse, narrowly dodging several branches.

It slashes through a single pinecone, turning it to fluttering shrapnel. Then it falls, falls, falls...

And punches a hole in the side of the fat white geodesic dome.

For a moment, nothing happens.

Then something moves inside the dome. Something long, and dark, and ancient.

And one large, furious eye appears in the hole in the dome, staring out.

*   *   *

When the storm first came, everyone knew the dome had been struck by lightning. But, the dome being the dome, no damage was done. After all, the outside had showed no change, no damage.

But the inside ... that was another matter. No one had thought that, perhaps, the inside of the dome had changed and become, like so many places in this valley, another place.

Perhaps a prison. A prison chamber for something very old, and something very angry.

CHAPTER SIXTY-FOUR

It is then that, as is so often the case in Wink, things begin to happen in two places at once.

On one plane, Mona Bright sits on her mother's couch, with her mother across from her in her chair. But as Mona whispers *Boom*, her mother looks up, as if she can hear something happening outside this dream house.

"What was that?" she asks softly. "What have you done?"

On the other plane, back in the smoking city, with the bloody woman on the rooftop and the giant standing in the park, something begins to poke its way out of the tiny hole in the skin of the dome: a long, black, gleaming claw. It makes the hole bigger and bigger, then slashes down, straight down, nearly splitting the dome in half...

Mona's mother sits up. "What have you done, girl?" she asks.

"I let him out," says Mona.

"Who?"

Mona does not answer.

"Who?"

Something changes in the air of the house. It is as if another room has just appeared, connected to their pleasant living room; a room small, dusty, yet invisible; but they can *feel* it, a hall or a chamber just nearby, always glimpsed out of the corners of their eyes.

Then Mona sees him.

He stands in the dining room, watching them. A still figure wearing a filthy blue rabbit suit, and a strange wooden mask.

Mona's mother sees her looking, and turns to see. When she sees this strange man standing in the dining room, she seems to deflate a little.

With quaking legs, she gets to her feet. "Oh," she says in a crushed voice. She begins taking shuddering breaths. "It's you."

The man does not move. Mona becomes aware that whatever relationship she has with her mother, there is so much more—both in quantity, and in tortured complexity—between her mother and this new figure.

"You've... you've quite outgrown me, my boy," whispers Mona's mother. She stares at him, then slowly looks back at Mona. "Please, don't."

Mona is quiet.

"Please... please don't let him hurt me."

"I can't tell him what to do," says Mona.

"I didn't do anything wrong. I didn't."

There is a flicker. The man in the filthy rabbit suit is now standing just behind Mona's mother.

"Please don't," her mother says to her. "Please... I just wanted things to be *right*. I just wanted things to be as they *should* have been..."

But the man in the rabbit suit reaches out...

In Wink, something long and skeletal begins to emerge from the broken dome. It is impossible to truly see it—it is somehow even bigger than the colossal giant standing in the park—but it only partially emerges, as if just poking out its hand, and its head...

And though no one in Wink, even the People from Elsewhere, can really understand what they're looking at, those that see think they see a long, thin skull, and two tattered, pointed ears, and a bony, clawed hand reaching for the backs of the giant's ankles, as if to slash at them...

Tears fall and strike the living room carpet, a soft *pat pat.*

Mona's mother, quivering, makes a fist and holds it to her lips.

The man in the rabbit suit touches her shoulder...

The claws strike home.

The giant begins toppling backward, moaning in dismay...

Mona's mother, beautiful and perfectly arranged, falls backward, her red dress rippling like a flag as she tumbles...

The giant is so vast, it takes nearly twenty seconds to fall.

It falls in such a manner that it practically eclipses the park, smashing the courthouse, barely missing the dome, its broad back hurtling toward the dark, lacquered splinter of a tree on the north end of the park...

The tree stabs up, piercing the giant's breast, poking through its chest just where its heart would be...

Mona's mother gasps. "Oh," she says, and touches her chest.

There is a spreading stain of bright red blood there, seeping through her dress.

"Oh, no," she whispers. "Not like this. Not like this."

Mona and the wildling both stand over her, watching. She looks up at them, eyes brimming with tears, but she cannot see either of them anymore.

"I just...wanted things to be perfect," she whispers. "Just the way I wanted them...is there anything...wrong with that?"

She moans a little. Then she is still.

*   *   *

In Wink, the people from elsewhere stare, horrified, astonished.

"No," says one. "No. No!"

On the mesa, Parson lets out a huge breath, and says, "Yes."

Mona and the wildling stare down at their dead mother. Then, slowly, the wildling kneels and reaches out with trembling hands to caress her still, pale face.

Mona understands. She still feels the same, despite everything: she wishes her mother were here, alive, healthy, and that her mother loved her daughter with all her heart. Such desires can never really go away, no matter what you learn about your parent.

The wildling looks up at her, and though his wooden face is as inscrutable as ever, Mona thinks she understands him. He is asking— *What now?*

"I don't know," says Mona. "I don't know. I'm sorry."

Crushed, the wildling looks back down at his mother. Then, slowly, he gathers her body in his arms, stands, and carries her away, away from this perfect living room, down the hallway, and out of sight.

CHAPTER SIXTY-FIVE

As he carries Her he cannot help but think about how small She is. He did not know he had grown so great. Or perhaps, underneath it all, She had been this small all along.

The wildling carries his Mother down a long, dark tunnel. It stretches on and on, dipping through planes of reality, over and under and around Wink.

Finally it ends in a small stone chamber. In the center of the floor is a pile of rabbit skulls. The wildling kicks these away, clearing a space, and gently, gently lays his Mother down in its center.

He has Her now. They are reunited. At last.

He has dreamed of this moment. During his long, dark days chasing his family, and all throughout his long imprisonment, this is what he dreamed of, what he hoped for, what he needed.

He hates Her and loves Her. He wanted Her to love him, and hated Her because he knew She never would. But now he has Her.

He sits down across Her. She is terrible and beautiful, all at once. Even in death.

And he waits. For death can only last so long. Things like Mother can never truly die.

And when She reawakes... She will be here. She will be trapped here, with him, with nothing to see but these stone walls, and no one to speak to but Her son. Her beautiful son.

And he will make Her love him. Forever and ever and ever. And ever and ever and ever.

CHAPTER SIXTY-SIX

Mona opens her eyes to a scene of total devastation.

The giant, strangely, is gone, yet she can see where it fell, leaving a huge indentation like a drained lake. It looks like it broke a gas main when it fell, and the shops on the northwest of the town square are ablaze.

All the children and the people from elsewhere are gathering at the square, staring at where their Mother once was. None of them move or speak. They don't even notice the flames beginning to encircle them.

Mona walks down the stairs and out to the street.

The fire has reached the residential neighborhoods now. It is dancing up the walls and crawling across the roofs and leaping from structure to structure. The people (and the not-at-all people) watch the fire helplessly. Some do not even move or struggle as it consumes them.

One person asks her, "What do we do now? What do we do now that Mother is gone?"

But Mona has nothing to say. She climbs into the Charger, wheels it around, and points it back at the mesa again.

CHAPTER SIXTY-SEVEN

The People from Elsewhere look around themselves helplessly. They have waited so long for Her to return, and now She is lost again. What is there to do?

It is Mr. Elm who speaks first, whispering in his wife's ear.

"The car?" Mrs. Elm asks. "What about the car?"

He mumbles something.

"Oh," she says. "Oh, you are right, aren't you. The car does need work. It's not quite right, is it?"

He shakes his head.

"No, it isn't. I think you're right. We do need to go home. We have some things to take care of. What if I make a nice pitcher of lemonade, just for you?"

But Mr. Elm is not listening—he turns and walks away, back to the house, back to do what he did the day before, and the day before that, and several hundred days before that.

One by one, they all agree—they have work to do. The Dawes children had planned to build a pirate ship out of sand in their sandbox, Mr. Trimley had intended to put up a new train, and Mrs. Greer must arrange for the next dinner party (which will be very nice indeed). Some of them even invite the children home, for despite their unusual appearance, the people of Wink have not seen their little siblings in so long, and taking care of one's guests is what a proper host should do.

So, one by one, they return to their homes, and they go about their business. Even when the fire begins licking at the sides of the houses, even when it bursts through the kitchen windows and crawls across the kitchen cabinets, even when it dances in their beds and across their carpets, they do what they did yesterday, and the day before that, and the day before that.

There is a way things should be. This is what we are. This should save us, shouldn't it? Shouldn't it? Now that we are these things, shouldn't everything be fine?

CHAPTER SIXTY-EIGHT

The midday sun bakes everything, anything. It is so bright it has baked the blue out of the sky, the red out of the earth. The very air shimmers as if to get out of its way.

Mona sympathizes as she drives. She feels blackened, burned, both inside and out. She has walked through fire, now she is filled only with ash.

When she arrives at the mesa she sees things are much as she expected: Gracie, Parson, and her daughter sit on the shady side, under a shelf of rock. Gracie's eyes are bright, bright red, veined and wet like peeled pomegranates. Her daughter sleeps in Gracie's arms. The child's fat cheeks make her lower lip jut out as though she is pouting over some recent slight.

Parson is waiting for her, as is someone else: a young girl of about ten, with mousy brown hair and yellow tennis shoes. She looks up at Mona with a piercing gaze, and she slowly stands as if this action normally causes her great pain.

"Mrs. Benjamin," says Mona.

"Hello, dear," says the little girl. "You've done quite wonderfully."

"So that is you in there?"

"Yes. It is a bit unwieldy being so . . . short. But I manage."

"It all worked?" Mona asks Parson. "You all got here safely?"

"We did," says Parson. "Though some of us are the worse for wear." He looks back at Gracie. "She has lost everything."

Mona walks to Gracie, stoops, and holds her hands out. Gracie takes a moment to register this, then looks up at Mona and slowly holds out the sleeping child. Mona takes her and says, "You did a good job taking care of her, Gracie."

Gracie stares into the stone. Her cheeks are so lacquered with tears it's hard to see if she's still crying. Any new ones simply dissolve and run down her face in a sheet.

"Thank you," says Mona. "I really do thank you, Gracie."

She sits down and holds her child in her arms. She stares at her daughter, and, without even knowing it, bends over to shelter her from the heat.

"What happened to Mother?" asks Mona.

"The wildling," says Mrs. Benjamin. "He took her body, back to . . . wherever he resides. I do not know why, but I do not really wish to find out. I feel the answer would be unpleasant."

"Then it's over?" asks Mona. "It's really all over?"

"Nothing is ever truly over," says Parson. "At least, in my experience. But Mother's efforts here do seem at an end."

The little girl wakes and looks at Mona, then spies Mona's watch and begins picking at it with her thumb and forefinger. "You want that? Here. Here." Mona unclasps it and hands it to the girl. She holds it out as a fisherman would his prize, and smiles in glee and disbelief. "My goodness," whispers Mona. "Isn't that something."

She revels in this maternal moment for a while, basking in the presence of her child like the warmth of a fire.

"What will you do with her?" asks Parson. "Keep her? Raise her?"

"Could I?" asks Mona.

"There is nothing stopping you."

Her daughter's interest in the watch wanes. She flops over, rests her head on Mona's chest, and heaves a great sigh. "She's tired. She's had a long day."

She thinks, *I don't have anywhere to put her to sleep.* Then, with a shrill of fear: *I don't even know what name to say when she wakes up.*

Once more she remembers the look on the face of the Mona in the lens.

"But she's so beautiful," says Mona softly, as if arguing with someone. "She's even more beautiful than I thought she would be..."

"She is quite terribly pretty, yes," says Mrs. Benjamin.

Mona sniffs. She wants to walk away and to walk away now, because if she did she'd never revisit this decision and wouldn't she be better for it? But she can't help herself, and she says, "Parson—those alternates...the way things could have been..."

"Yes?"

"Are they...real?"

"Real in what sense?"

"I don't know. In any sense. Or are they, like, ghosts? Echoes?"

"Well, the people in those alternates think themselves as real as the people here do. They have no reason to think otherwise. To themselves, they are real. After all—how real is the child you hold in your hands?"

Mona shakes her head. "God. God, damn it all."

She has wanted this so much. For so long, this was all she wanted. And now she has it, with what amounts to the waving of a magic wand...

She wonders what she would be giving up were she to raise the child as her own. Would this be, in some distorted way, as if she were buying something? So many people in Wink did the same—they got to live their dream just by giving up one little thing, like an exchange. Mona looks at Gracie, and wonders if she ever saw a creature so violated and so abused in her life, a child whose parents traded away her health and sanity and dignity so they could live in peace and quiet...

The child's tiny fingers probe the collar of Mona's shirt with incredibly delicate movements as she drifts back to sleep.

How broken she felt when she lost her daughter. Is it possible that somewhere, in one of the strange sisters of her own time, the same thing is happening again? A grieving mother, wondering where her child is, and left feeling incomplete, as if suffering a monstrous amputation?

But she's mine, thinks Mona. *I love her. I would be good to her. I would be so good, maybe even better because I lost her once before...*

It feels as if something is gripping her intestines, twisting and twirling them into one big knot.

"I don't want to lose you again," she whispers to the little girl. The child takes a deep breath in, and sighs it out. Tiny lungs, functioning perfectly. Her lips mime suckling. "But it wouldn't be right, would it. You ... you have a momma. They took you from her. And if I keep you I'd be part of that, and I can't do that to her. I can't do to her what happened to me. And I would know. I would know I'd done it. It would be inside me every day, every time I looked at you, and it would poison me. It'd poison me and it'd poison you and it would all just wind up wrong. I just ... I mean, *damn* it, sweetheart. I just wanted to give you all the love I never got. Just a chance to put things right. I was gonna spoil you rotten, girl. I was gonna work my fingers to the bone for you. But that's different from ... from just *having* you. Having you is different from loving you. And I love you. I do. So I don't think I can keep you, honey. I just don't think I can. I want to. More than anything in the world, I want to. But I love you, so I *can't*."

She imagines desperate protestations—*No, Momma, don't send me away again*... "I'm sorry. I'm so sorry. You won't ever know how sorry I am. You won't ... hell, you won't even *know* me, you'll never even know that this happened. But you can't do that to someone. You can't make them something they're not. Because then they're just ... window dressing. Just a face in a picture. And you mean so much more to me. So, so, so much more to me." She kisses the child on the cheek. "But I want you to know that I love you. Someone out there loves you. I don't know what life will hold for you, if it'll be a good one or a bad one. But you are loved. Loved beyond words. Loved here, and ... and I'm sure the momma over there loves you, too. I'm sure she does. I do, so she must. She must. How could she not?" Then, more quietly: "How could she not."

Mona bows her head to touch her brow to her child's. She listens to the tiny breaths for a moment. "Now come on." She sniffs, and stands, though her legs wobble. "Let's go home and see her."

The lens is blank. Again, when Mona nears it she can feel it is like a door still slightly ajar.

"Are you quite sure about this?" asks Parson.

"Do it," says Mona. Her daughter bows her back, tired of being held for so long. "Just do it."

"We'll need your help," says Mrs. Benjamin. "You will need to give a *push*. But I think I've given you enough training on this, yes?"

Mona nods. The two of them start to hum, or the things inside them do. Mona faces the mirror. Her eyes search its depths. It suddenly does not seem flat, but concave, like she's staring into half of a bubble, or maybe a tunnel...

Mona feels something give way in the mirror. And an image begins to solidify in the glass.

A yellow nursery, with polka-dotted curtains.

How she wanted that life in the mirror. How she dreamed of it.

"You can cross, if you want," says Parson. "This is, after all, your own time, just slightly different."

Mona looks at him, and he nods toward the silvery image. She takes a breath, and walks toward it.

She expects to feel something, as if she's jumped into a lake or parted a veil, but there is nothing. It's as if there's just a hole in the world, and this pleasant nursery lies on the other side.

There is the fragrance of laundry sheets and diapers and Lysol and fresh bedding. Everything is neat and tidy; all the tiny little clothes have been properly put away; and unless she's mistaken, there are lines in the carpet from a recent, vigorous vacuuming. Something inside her swells to see all this.

Mona wishes she knew what time it is over here; she thinks it's just minutes after the child was originally stolen, but she isn't sure.

She walks to the crib. The baby begins squirming, already anticipating being forced to sleep.

Do it now, or you'll never bring yourself to do it again.

She lays her child in the crib and kisses her on the head. "Thank you for showing me that I would have been a good momma," she whispers. "Your own momma might be kind of scared for a while. But don't worry. She'll get over it. It might take her a while, but...but I know she always gets over it."

Mona begins to back away.

She knows this is the right decision, so why is she crying so much? Why does it hurt so much to accept how things are?

The child sits up and squawks a tiny protest.

Mona begins to walk back through the mirror. As she does, she hears a voice in the hall—*her* voice—say, "*Wendy?* Wendy, is that you?"

And she thinks: *Wendy. Her name is Wendy. What a good name.*

CHAPTER SIXTY-NINE

Through the chamber, through the door, down the dusky hall. She parts the dying memories with the blade of her hand, sends echoes scuttering over dusty stone. The spying eye of the past clapped to cracks in the air, watching, listening, snickering.

What more is there to this dark earth than halls and halls of empty rooms?

Up the ladder (her hands shake on each rung), up up and up, until the screaming red supernova erupts over her, sunlight howling and blistering and blank, pouring down the shaft to swallow her and fill her ears with silence, blissful silence.

The stone so hot her hands should sizzle. A sky shorn of clouds, all moisture scraped away. This land is so empty. And in the distance, the ribbon of black smoke, and the streak of gray where a town once stood.

I have lost her again.

She walks to the edge of the mesa. Gracie sits below, staring into the valley. She asks a question, but Mona cannot hear—she walks down and sits beside her and looks out.

In the shade the stone is cool. The air is redolent with pine sap. The wind blows southward, so each breath is free of smoke. Below her, among the trees, there is the flit of birds' wings, and the buzzing, aimless twirl of grasshoppers.

Gracie says something. Her words have a dull ring on the shelf of stone.

"What?" Mona whispers.

"I'm sorry," she says.

Mona sits there, frozen, broken, empty.

Gracie says, "I think you did the right thing."

She holds a hand out to Mona. Mona bows her head, reaches out, and takes it and squeezes and holds on as hard as she can, just as hard as she possibly can.

CHAPTER SEVENTY

They sit in silence for what feels like lifetimes. After a while Mona realizes Mrs. Benjamin and Parson are watching them from down the path. She feels a wave of irrational rage, for *they* did this to her, they or their kind, but she swallows it to ask, "What do you want?"

"To ask something of you," says Mrs. Benjamin.

"What the hell do you mean?"

"We have discussed it in detail," says Parson, "and we have decided that, though there are many things to endear us to this way of life"— he exchanges a glance with Mrs. Benjamin, who nods—"it would be best for us to go home."

"Home? You mean to—"

"To the other side, yes," says Mrs. Benjamin.

"You can do that?"

"There is no one now to say that we cannot," says Parson. "And with the lens, we have concluded it is perfectly possible. It should be just a short step away. I do not know what state it's in—Mother's machinations likely left our home quite in ruins. But that does not mean it cannot be rebuilt. With Her gone, perhaps there is some hope."

"What about the rest of you?"

"I believe most of them perished in the fire," says Mrs. Benjamin. "They, or their vessels, or their physical forms. They are no longer bound to this world. They are, most likely, on the other side already, in some fashion or another. Lost, drifting, helpless…it would simply be a matter of reuniting them, and giving them a little leadership."

"Then you could do all this again," says Gracie. "You could come back, and try all over again…"

"No," says Mrs. Benjamin. "For one, Mother is no longer with us, so I doubt if we would have any motivation to return. And for another, we will not have the lens."

"Why not?" asks Mona.

"Because we want you to close it after us," says Parson.

"Close it, and *lock* it," says Mrs. Benjamin.

"Why?" asks Mona.

"What was done here was foolish, and vain, and proud," says Parson. "I wish to forget it ever happened."

"Or, failing that, at least to learn from it," says Mrs. Benjamin.

Mona turns away.

"Will you help us with this?" Parson asks. "Will you help us close the door?"

"We have asked much of you, we know," says Mrs. Benjamin. "But there must be someone behind to close it. Just one more thing, Miss Bright. Just this one thing."

Mona looks at Gracie. She sighs—for there is no place she'd more prefer to avoid than the innards of Coburn—but says, "Wait here for me. This should only take a little while."

They wend their way back, through the empty, whispering hallways. But the halls do not feel quite as frightening to Mona as they did before. Now they are hollow, broken. She asks, "Will this be dangerous for you?"

"Oh, yes," says Parson. "I expect so. Our world is in quite a bit of turmoil. Mother meant it to frighten us into leaving. Her threats were rarely hollow."

"Then why would you choose to leave?"

"You'd want us here? The people who did all this to you?"

"Well…they're all gone. And that wasn't *you*, really."

Parson thinks on it. "You talked to Mother, didn't you?"

"What?"

"When you were struck with lightning. I know her devices. She spoke to you, didn't she?"

"Yeah. She did."

"And did she offer you something?"

"How did you know that?"

"Mother *always* offers something, Miss Bright," says Mrs. Benjamin.

"Well, yeah. She did," says Mona.

"And you turned it down," says Parson.

"Yes."

"Why did you do that?"

"I don't know. What she offered me just wouldn't feel...honest. It would have been as made up as the rest of the things in Wink."

He nods. "That was a very wise choice, then. We make the same choice now—we have the option of living there as we are, as we *really* are, with all its misfortunes and difficulties, or living here as we are *not*—without pain, without hardship, and without value." They arrive at the lens chamber again, which has lost none of its unearthly quality. "What lies on the other side of the lens may be dangerous. But I would rather have it than the alternative." He looks back to Mrs. Benjamin, extends a hand, and helps her over the threshold to the chamber.

"You know, Miss Bright," says Mrs. Benjamin, "you could come with us."

"Why would I do that?"

"Well, you are one of us, to a certain extent. Where we are going is, I guess you could say, our ancestral home. I do not know if you have ever felt at home in this place...but perhaps you may have better luck with us. Though it would leave the door open, since there would be no one to close it." Parson gives Mrs. Benjamin a disapproving look. "I only wish to give her the option," she says mildly.

Mona thinks about it. She stares into the mirror, and wonders what she would see if she accepted. But she shakes her head.

"I am happy to hear that," says Parson. "I believe your chances are better here."

"What makes you say that?"

"I find it difficult to say. I suppose I think you to be a caring person, Miss Bright. You are not Mother—you have much to give others. I cannot tell you what to do, but I suggest you leave this place, find someone to care for, and live as honestly as the world allows."

A hum fills the lens chamber once more. Their eyes shudder like candle flames. "Remember," says Mrs. Benjamin, "you must shut it behind us."

"But I don't know how," says Mona.

"It is simple," says Parson. "A mirror that looks in on itself is not a mirror at all."

The surface of the lens ripples. Mona sees red stars, and many peaks, and a far, strange country of leaning gray towers…

"Goodbye, Miss Bright," says Parson.

"Goodbye, dear," says Mrs. Benjamin.

Two childlike figures stand in the center of the chamber, watching her with old eyes and youthful smiles.

They blink out, once, twice, three times—and are gone.

Mona stands still and reaches out to the lens, feeling its boundaries as she did mere minutes ago. *It could go to so many places, so many times, if I wanted it to.* But she remembers what Parson said, and bends it, pushes it, slowly and carefully, until the only thing the lens opens on is this chamber, and the lens itself, until…

There is a sound like freezing ice. Mona looks and sees the lens no longer reflects anything: it is solid, like a plate of lead.

She reaches out and touches it. It is slightly warm, but solid. "Gone," she says.

Gracie is waiting for her on the edge of the mesa when Mona returns. She says, "I've been thinking—should we go down?" She nods toward the flaming ruin miles below.

"To Wink?" asks Mona.

"Yes. There could be people that need our help, or things we need, or…I don't know. Anything."

Mona thinks about it. "No," she says.

"Why not?"

"I think that's all gone now, Gracie. I think it all burned, or... worse. I think we need to leave it alone."

"But we should at least see," says Gracie. "We should at least go down and look for..."

"For what?"

"I don't know, but... but it can't *all* be gone. I... I had a boyfriend. He was *good* to me. I just..." She trails off.

"I'm sorry, hon," says Mona. "But from what Parson and Mrs. Benjamin said, I think it's all gone, or close enough to count. I think... I think we need to let it go."

Gracie stares out at the valley. "Then what do we do?" she asks helplessly. "What do I do now?"

"You've never been outside Wink before, right?"

Gracie shakes her head.

"Well, would you like to go?" asks Mona.

"To... go outside?"

"Yeah. To go outside and see."

"What is there to see?"

"Everything. Everything that's out there."

Gracie stands up and looks north, as if imagining the horizon extending and extending, past the mesa and past the borders of Wink. "So it all keeps going?" she asks.

"Yeah," says Mona.

"It just doesn't stop?"

"It just goes," says Mona, and she extends her hand to the young girl, "until it doesn't."

Gracie takes her hand and pulls herself up. She looks both excited and a little frightened by the idea. "We can just go? Right now?"

"Right now. We don't need anyone's say-so. We don't have to wait. We can just go."

Gracie reflects on this. Finally she nods and says, "All right, then."

CHAPTER SEVENTY-ONE

They drive.

They drive far and fast, the great red machine singing joyously as it eats up the miles. They cruise over mountains, over drifting peaks drizzled with wildflowers, over waterfalls cheerily spewing white-water diamonds onto the rocks. Thousands of curves, thousands of bridges, thousands of slopes and twists and turns. Enough pines and grasping trees to outnumber the stars.

They pass cars. They pass motorcycles. They pass great rattling trucks. They pass vegetable vendors and crafts stores and highway patrolmen parked on the side of the road. They pass parking lots and highway junctions and stoplights and ghost towns. Strangers and strangers and strangers.

A man sits on his porch, smoking and playing solitaire, and as they pass he raises a hand in a lazy wave. "Who was that?" asks Gracie.

"I don't know," says Mona.

"You don't?" says Gracie.

"No. I don't."

Gracie stares back at him, amazed, perplexed.

They drive and drive and drive until evening. The sky changes from the great, trumpeting blue they have seen since dawn into a regal, courtly purple that comes blooming up from the horizon. Every crevice and pothole is filled with deep violet hues: it is as if some painter has spent so much time working on the sky they did not notice the colors dripping to pool on the earth.

Then, slowly, the stars come out.

"Slow down," says Gracie.

"There's a speed limit," says Mona.

"Just for a bit."

Mona *tsk*s. "Okay."

Mona slows down. Gracie sticks her head out her window and looks up. "Wow," she says. "There are so many. I never saw them all, not all of them. Because of the lightning."

"I guess you wouldn't have."

Gracie's awe is infectious. Mona waits for a straightaway and leans out her own window.

Thousands of them. As if someone smashed a jewel on the fundament of sky.

It is all like a dream. Like a dream she had long ago and forgot, of a dark road through the mountains, and a million lights ahead and all that lay beyond them, waiting for her, waiting for them, waiting for everyone to see.

"What will we do tomorrow?" asks Gracie.

"I don't know," says Mona. "Something."

And they drive.

extras

orbit

meet the author

Josh Brewster Photography

ROBERT JACKSON BENNETT was born in Baton Rouge, Louisiana. Winner of a Shirley Jackson Award, the Sydney J. Bounds Award, and an Edgar Award, he is the author of the novels *Mr. Shivers*, *The Company Man*, *The Troupe*, and *American Elsewhere*. Find out more about the author at www.robertjacksonbennett .wordpress.com.

introducing

If you enjoyed
AMERICAN ELSEWHERE,
look out for

THE TROUPE

by Robert Jackson Bennett

*Vaudeville: mad, mercenary, dreamy, and absurd, a world of
clashing cultures and ferocious showmanship and wickedly
delightful deceptions.*

*But sixteen-year-old pianist George Carole has joined
vaudeville for one reason only: to find the man he suspects
to be his father, the great Heironomo Silenus. Yet as he chases
down his father's troupe, he begins to understand that their
performances are strange even for vaudeville: for wherever
they happen to tour, the very nature of the world seems
to change.*

*Because there is a secret within Silenus's show so ancient and
dangerous that it has won him many powerful enemies. And it's*

*not until after he joins them that George realizes the troupe is
not simply touring: they are running for their lives.*

And soon... he is as well.

Friday mornings at Otterman's Vaudeville Theater generally had
a very relaxed pace to them, and so far this one was no exception.
Four acts in the bill would be moving on to other theaters over
the weekend, and four more would be coming in to take their
place, among them Gretta Mayfield, minor star of the Chicago
opera. The general atmosphere among the musicians was one of
carefree satisfaction, as all of the acts had gone well and the next
serious rehearsals were an entire weekend away. Which, to the
overworked musicians, might as well have been an eternity.

But then Tofty Thresinger, first chair house violinist and
unofficial gossip maven of the theater, came sprinting into the
orchestra pit with terror in his eyes. He stood there panting for
a moment, hands on his knees, and picked his head up to make
a ghastly announcement: "George has quit!"

"What?" said Victor, the second chair cellist. "George? *Our*
George?"

"George the *pianist*?" asked Catherine, their flautist.

"The very same," said Tofty.

"What kind of quit?" asked Victor. "As in quitting the
theater?"

"Yes, of course quitting the theater!" said Tofty. "What other
kind of quit is there?"

"There must be some mistake," said Catherine. "Who did
you hear it from?"

"From George himself!" said Tofty.

"Well, how did he phrase it?" asked Victor.

"He looked at me," said Tofty, "and he said, 'I quit.' "

Everyone stopped to consider this. There was little room for alternate interpretation in that.

"But why would he quit?" asked Catherine.

"I don't know!" cried Tofty, and he collapsed into his chair, accidentally crushing his rosin and leaving a large white stain on the seat of his pants.

The news spread quickly throughout the theater: George Carole, their most dependable house pianist and veritable wunderkind (or *enfant terrible*, depending on who you asked), was throwing in the towel without even a by-your-leave. Stagehands shook their heads in dismay. Performers immediately launched into complaints. Even the coat-check girls, usually exiled to the very periphery of theater gossip, were made aware of this ominous development.

But not everyone was shaken by this news. "Good riddance," said Chet, their bassist. "I'm tired of tolerating that little lordling, always acting as if he was better than us." But several muttered he *was* better than them. It had been seven months since the sixteen-year-old had walked through their doors on audition day and positively dumbfounded the staff with his playing. Everyone had been astonished to hear that he was not auditioning for an act, but for *house pianist*, a lowly job if ever there was one. Van Hoever, the manager of Otterman's, had questioned him extensively on this point, but George had stood firm: he was there to be house pianist at their little Ohio theater, and nothing more.

"What are we going to do now?" said Archie, their trombonist. "Like it or not, it was George who put us on the map." Which was more or less true. It was the general rule that in vaudeville, a trade filled with indignities of all kinds, no one was shat upon more than the house pianist. He accompanied nearly every act, and every ego that crossed the stage got thoroughly massaged by abusing him. If a joke went sour, it was because the pianist was too late and spoiled the delivery. If a dramatic bit was flat, it was because the pianist was too lively. If an acrobat stumbled, it was because the pianist distracted him.

But in his time at Otterman's George had accomplished the impossible: he'd given them no room for complaints. After playing through the first rehearsal he would know the act better than the actors did, which was saying something as every actor had fine-tuned their performance with almost lapidary attention. He hit every beat, wrung every laugh out of every delivery, and knew when to speed things up or slow them down. He seemed to have the uncanny ability to augment every performance he accompanied. Word spread, and many acts became more amenable to performing at Otterman's, which occupied a rather obscure spot on the Keith-Albee circuit.

Yet now he was leaving, almost as abruptly as he'd arrived. It put them in a pretty tight spot: Gretta Mayfield was coming specifically because she had agreed to have George accompany her, but that was just the start; after a moment's review, the orchestra came to the horrifying conclusion that at least a quarter of the acts of the next week had agreed to visit Otterman's only because George met their high standards.

After Tofty frantically spread the word, wild speculation followed. Did anyone know the reason behind the departure? Could anyone guess? Perhaps, Victor suggested, he was finally going to tour with an act of his own, or maybe he was heading straight to the legitimate (meaning well-respected orchestras and symphonies, rather than lowly vaudeville). But Tofty said he'd heard nothing about George making those sorts of movements, and he would know, wouldn't he?

Maybe he'd been lured away by another theater, someone said. But Van Hoever would definitely ante up to keep George,

Catherine pointed out, and the only theaters that could outbid him were very far away, and would never send scouts out here. What could the boy possibly be thinking? They wasted the whole morning debating the subject, yet they never reached an answer.

George did his best to ignore the flurry of gossip as he gathered his belongings, but it was difficult; as he'd not yet made a formal resignation to Van Hoever, everyone tried to find the reason behind his desertion in hopes that they could fix it.

"Is it the money, George?" Tofty asked. "Did Van Hoever turn you down for a raise?"

No, answered George. No, it was not the money.

"Is it the acts, George?" asked Archie. "Did one of the acts insult you? You've got to ignore those bastards, Georgie, they can be so ornery sometimes!"

But George scoffed haughtily, and said that no, it was certainly not any of the acts. The other musicians cursed Archie for such a silly question; of *course* it wasn't any of the performers, as George never gave them reason for objection.

"Is it a girl, George?" asked Victor. "You can tell me. I can keep a secret. It's a girl, isn't it?"

At this George turned a brilliant red, and sputtered angrily for a moment. No, he eventually said. No, thank you very much, it was not a girl.

"Then was it something Tofty said?" asked Catherine. "After all, he was who you were talking to just before you said you quit."

"What!" cried Tofty. "What a horrendous accusation! We were only talking theater hearsay, I tell you! I simply mentioned how Van Hoever was angry that an act had skipped us on the circuit!"

At that, George's face became strangely still. He stopped gathering up his sheet music and looked away for a minute. But finally he said no, Tofty had nothing to do with it. "And would you all please leave me alone?" he asked. "This decision has nothing to do with you, and furthermore there's nothing that will change it."

The other musicians, seeing how serious he was, grumbled and shuffled away. Once they were gone George scratched his head and tried not to smile. Despite his solemn demeanor, he had enjoyed watching them clamor to please him.

The smile vanished as he returned to his packing and the decision he'd made. The orchestra did not matter, he told himself. Otterman's did not matter anymore. The only thing that mattered now was getting out the door and on the road as soon as possible.

After he'd collected the last of his belongings he headed for his final stop: Van Hoever's office. The theater manager had surely heard the news and was in the midst of composing a fine tirade, but if George left now he'd be denied payment for this week's worth of performances. And though he could not predict the consequences of what he was about to do, he thought it wise to have every penny possible.

But when George arrived at the office hall there was someone seated in the row of chairs before Van Hoever's door: a short, elderly woman who watched him with a sharp eye as if she'd been expecting him. Her wrists and hands were wrapped tight in cloth, and a poorly rolled cigarette was bleeding smoke from between two of her fingers. "Leaving without a goodbye?" she asked him.

George smiled a little. "Ah," he said. "Hello, Irina."

The old woman did not answer, but patted the empty chair next to her. George walked over, but did not sit. The old woman raised her eyebrows at him. "Too good to give me company?"

"This is an ambush, isn't it?" he asked. "You've been waiting for me."

"You assume the whole world waits on you. Come. Sit."

"I'll give you company," he said. "But I won't sit. I know you're looking to delay me, Irina."

"So impatient, child," she said. "I'm just an old woman who wishes to talk."

"To talk about why I'm leaving."

"No. To give you advice."

"I don't need advice. And I'm not changing my mind."

"I'm not telling you to. I just wish to make a suggestion before you go."

George gave her the sort of impatient look that can only be given by the very young to the very old, and raised a fist to knock at Van Hoever's door. But before his knuckles ever made contact, the old woman's cloth-bound hand snatched his fist out of the air. "You will want to listen to me, George," she said. "Because I know *exactly* why you're leaving."

George looked her over. If it had been anyone else, he would not have given them another minute, but Irina was one of the few people at Otterman's who could command George's attention. She was the orchestra's only violist, and like most violists (who after all devoted their lives to an ignored or much-ridiculed instrument) she had acquired a very sour sort of wisdom. It was also rumored she'd witnessed terrible hardships in her home in Russia before fleeing to America, and this, combined with her great age, gave her a mysterious esteem at Otterman's.

"Do you think so?" asked George.

"I do," she said. "And aren't you interested to hear my guess?" She released him and patted the seat next to her once more. George sighed, but reluctantly sat.

"What is it?" he asked.

"Why such a hurry, child?" Irina said. "It seems like it was only yesterday that you arrived."

"It wasn't," said George. "I've spent over half a year here, which is far too long."

"Too long for what?" asked Irina.

George did not answer. Irina smiled, amused by this terribly serious boy in his too-large suit. "Time moves so much slower for the young. To me, it is as a day. I can still remember when you walked through that door, child, and three things struck me about you." She held up three spindly fingers. "First was that you were talented. *Very* talented. But you knew that, didn't you? You probably knew it too well, for such a little boy."

"A *little* boy?" asked George.

"Oh, yes. A naïve little lamb, really."

"Maybe then," said George, his nose high in the air. He reached into his pocket, took out a pouch of tobacco, and began rolling his own cigarette. He made sure to appear as nonchalant as possible, having practiced the motions at home in the mirror.

"If you say so," said Irina. One finger curled down, leaving two standing. "Second was that you were proud, and reckless. This did not surprise me. I've seen it in many young performers. And I've seen many throw careers away as a result. Much like you're probably doing now."

George cocked an eyebrow, and lit his cigarette and puffed at it. His stomach spasmed as he tried to suppress a cough.

Irina wrinkled her nose. "What is that you're smoking?"

"Some of Virginia's finest, of course," he said, though he wheezed a bit.

"That doesn't smell like anything fine at all." She took his pouch and peered into it. "I don't know what that is, but it isn't Virginia's finest."

George looked crestfallen. "It...it isn't?" he asked.

"No. What did you do, buy this from someone in the orchestra?"

"Well, yes, but they seemed very trustworthy!"

She shook her head. "You've been snookered, my child. This is trash. Next time go to a tobacconist, like a normal person."

George grumbled something about how it had to be a mistake, but he hurriedly put out his cigarette and began to stow the pouch away.

"Anyway," she said, "I remember one final third thing about you when you first came here." Another trembling blue finger curled down. She used the remaining one to poke him in the arm. "You did not seem all that interested in what you were playing, which was peculiar. No—what you were mostly interested in was a certain act that was traveling the circuit."

George froze where he was, slightly bent as he stuffed the tobacco pouch into his pocket. He slowly turned to look at the old woman.

"Still in a hurry, child?" asked Irina. "Or have I hit upon it?"

He did not answer.

"I see," she said. "Well, I recall you asked about this one act all the time, nearly every day. Did anyone know when this act would play here? It had played here once, hadn't it? Did they think this act would play nearby, at least? I think I can still remember the name of it…Ah, yes. It was the Silenus Troupe, wasn't it?"

George's face had gone very closed now. He nodded, very slightly.

"Yes," said the old woman. She began rubbing at her wrists, trying to ease her arthritis. "That was it. You wanted to know nothing but news about Silenus, asking all the time. But we would always say no, no, we don't know nothing about this act. And we didn't. He'd played here once, this Silenus, many, many months ago. The man had terribly angered Van Hoever then with his many demands, but we had not seen him since, and no one knew where he was playing next. Does any of that sound familiar to you, boy?"

George did not nod this time, but he did not need to.

"Yes," said Irina. "I think it does. And then this morning, you know, I hear news that Van Hoever is very angry. He's angry because an act has skipped us on the circuit, and is playing Parma, west of here. And the minute I hear this news about Van Hoever today, I get a second piece of news, but this one is about our young, marvelous pianist. He's *leaving*. Just suddenly decided to go. Isn't that strange? How one piece of news follows the other?"

George was silent. Irina nodded and took a long drag from her cigarette. "I wasn't terribly surprised to find that the act that's skipped us is Silenus," she said. "And unless I'm mistaken, you're going to go chasing him. Am I right?"

George cleared his throat. "Yes," he said hoarsely.

"Yes. In fact, now that I think about it, that act might be the only reason you signed on to be house pianist here. After all, you could've found somewhere better. But Silenus played here once, so perhaps he might do so again, and when he did you wished to be here to see it, no?"

George nodded.

Irina smiled, satisfied with her deductions. "The famous Silenus," she said. "I've heard many rumors about him in my day. I've heard his troupe is full of gypsies, traveled here from abroad. I've heard he tours the circuit at his choosing. That he was touring vaudeville before it was vaudeville."

"Have you heard that every hotel saves a private room for him?" asked George. "That's a popular one."

"No, I'd not heard that one. Why are you so interested in this man, I wonder?"

George thought about it. Then he slowly reached into his front pocket and pulled out a piece of paper. Though its corners were soft and blunt with age, it was very well cared for: it had been cleanly folded into quarters and tied up with string, like a precious message. George plucked at the bow and untied the string, and then, with the gravity of a priest unscrolling a holy document, he unfolded the paper.

It was—or had once been—a theater bill. Judging by the few acts printed on it and the simple, sloppy printing job, it was from a very small-time theater, one even smaller than Otterman's. But half of one page was taken up by a large, impressive illustration: though the ink had cracked and faded in parts, one could see that it depicted a short, stout man in a top hat standing in the middle of a stage, bathed in the clean illumination of the spotlight. His hands were outstretched to the audience in a pose of extreme theatricality, as if he was in the middle of telling them the most enthralling story in the world. Written across the bottom of the illustration, in a curling font that must have passed for fancy for that little theater, were three words: THE SILENUS TROUPE.

George reverently touched the illustration, as if he wished to fall inside it and hear the tale the man was telling. "I got this in my hometown," he said. "He visited there, once. But I didn't get to see." Then he looked at Irina with a strange shine in his eyes, and asked, "What do you remember from when he was here?"

"What do I remember?"

"Yes. You had to have rehearsed with him when he played here, didn't you? You must have seen his show. So what do you remember?"

"Don't you know the act yourself? Why ask me?"

But George did not answer, but only watched her closely.

She grunted. "Well. Let me think. It seems so long ago..." She took a contemplative puff from her cigarette. "There were four acts, I remember that. It was odd, no one travels with more than one act these days. That was what angered Van Hoever so much."

George leaned forward. "What else?"

"I remember...I remember there was a man with puppets, at the start. But they weren't very funny, these puppets. And then there was a dancer, and a...a strongwoman. Wait, no. She was another puppet, wasn't she? I think she might have been. And then there was a fourth act, and it...it..." She trailed off, confused, and she was not at all used to being confused.

"You don't remember," said George.

"I do!" said Irina. "At least, I *think* I do...I can remember every act I've played for, I promise, but this one...Maybe I'm wrong. I could've *sworn* I played for this one. But did I?"

"You did," said George.

"Oh? How are you so certain?"

"I've found other people who've seen his show, Irina," he said. "Dozens of them. And they always say the same thing. They remember a bit about the first three acts—the puppets, the dancing girl in white, and the strongwoman—but nothing about the fourth. And when they try and remember it, they always wonder if they ever saw the show at all. It's so strange. Everyone's heard of the show, and many have seen it, but no one can remember what they saw."

Irina rubbed the side of her head as if trying to massage the memory out of some crevice in her skull, but it would not come. "What are you saying?"

"I'm saying that when people go to see Silenus's show... something happens. I'm not sure what. But they can never remember it. They can hardly describe what they've seen. It's like it happened in a dream."

"That can't be," said Irina. "It seems unlikely that a performance could do that to a person."

"And yet you can't remember it at all," said George. "No one else here can remember, either. They just know Silenus was here, but what he did up on that stage is a mystery to them, even though they played alongside it."

"And you want to witness this for yourself? Is that it?"

George hesitated. "Well. There's a bit more to it than that, of course. But yes. I want to see him."

"But why, child? What you're telling me is very curious, that I admit, but you have a very good thing going on here. You're making money. You are living by yourself, dressing yourself"— she cast a leery eye over his cream-colored suit—"with some success. It is a lot to risk."

"Why do you care? Why are you interested in me at all?"

Irina sighed. "Well. Let me just say that once, I was your age. And I was just about as talented as you were, boy. And some decisions I made were…unwise. I paid many prices for those decisions. I am still paying them." She trailed off, rubbing the side of her neck. George did not speak; Irina very rarely spoke about her past. Finally she coughed, and said, "I would hate to see the same happen to you. You have been lucky so far, George. To abandon what you have to go chasing Silenus will test what luck you have."

"I don't need luck," said George. "As you said, I can find better places to play. Everyone says so."

"You've been coddled here," she said sternly. "You have lived with constant praise, and it's made you foolish."

George sat up straight, affronted, and carefully refolded the theater bill and put it in his pocket. "Maybe. But I'd risk everything in the world to see him, Irina. You've no idea how far I've come just to get this chance."

"And what do you expect will happen when you see this Silenus?" she asked.

George was quiet as he thought about his answer. But before he could speak, the office door was flung open and Van Hoever came stalking out.

Van Hoever came to a halt when he saw George sitting there. A cold glint came into his eye, and he said, "You."

"Me," said George mildly.

Van Hoever pointed into his office. "Inside. Now."

George stood up, gathered all of his belongings, and walked into Van Hoever's office with one last look back at Irina. She watched him go, and shook her head and said, "Still a boy. Remember that." Then the door closed behind him and she was gone.

Less than a half an hour later George walked out the theater doors and into the hostile February weather. Van Hoever's tirade had been surprisingly short; the man had been desperate to keep George on until they could find a decent replacement, and he'd been willing to pay accordingly, but George would not budge. He'd only just gotten news about Silenus's performance today, on Friday, and the man and his troupe would be leaving Parma tomorrow. This would be his only chance, and it'd be very close, as the train ride to Parma would take nearly all day.

Once he'd been paid for his final week, he returned to his lodgings, packed (which took some time, as George was quite the clotheshorse), paid the remainder of his rent, and took a streetcar to the train station. There he waited for the train, trying not to shiver in the winter air and checking the time every minute. It had been a great while since he'd felt this vulnerable. For too long he'd kept to the cloistered world of the orchestra pit, crouched in the dark before the row of footlights. But now all that was gone, and if anything happened before he made it to Parma, the months at Otterman's would have been in vain.

extras

It wasn't until George was aboard the train and it began pulling away that he started to breathe easy. Then he began to grin in disbelief. It was really happening: after scrounging for news for over half a year, he was finally going to see the legendary Heironomo Silenus, leader of wondrous players, legendary impresario, and the most elusive and mysterious performer to ever tour the circuits. And also, perhaps most unbelievably, the man George Carole suspected to be his father.